Tal Diamond is an Outs... trade stop. He's a produ... mating, an illegal bei... Under sentence of deat... discover him—you can... ies more comfortable."

Iolanthe blinked, but she was taking it in. "I don't understand why he's under sentence of death from the Outside."

Quince said patiently, "Because Elaphite/Human mating is forbidden."

"Why?"

"Because it produces demons. They don't call them demons, they call them sociopaths, but it comes to the same thing. 'Children who never learn to socialize properly.'"

She swallowed, hoping she didn't look pale, and tried to rally. "He's not a child, though. How old is he?"

"Ah, there you have me. There are four things all Apheans—that's what they call these Elaphite/Human products, by the way—have in common. Genius IQs, the inability to socialize normally, and a theoretical lifespan that goes on for miles. This one seems about your age; but who knows?"

Iolanthe looked at him with forced coolness. "That's three things. You said four."

"So I did. The fourth thing is that none of them ever manages to turn theory into practice in the lifespan department. Every one of the little criminals listed in my research managed to get executed by the state or just plain killed by some outraged person before their fortieth birthday—a fair number while still in adolescence, in fact. Makes you wonder what they were like as toddlers, doesn't it? Talk about hiding the kitchen knives."

Io had a sudden, horrifying thought. "You're not making all this up, are you? You don't seem very . . . *serious* about this. You're telling me about a creature of hell."

"Oh, a bit of hell here, a bit of hell there." He shrugged cheerfully. "One gets used to it."

CITY OF DIAMOND

JANE EMERSON

DONALD A. WOLLHEIM, FOUNDER
375 Hudson Street. New York, NY 10014

**ELIZABETH R. WOLLHEIM
SHEILA E. GILBERT
PUBLISHERS**

Dedicated to
Bennett Claire Ponsford,
who knows why

Prologue

City Year 542

Everyone knew he was dying. By rights, he thought irritably, the bedchamber ought to be filled with hangers-on and low-voiced mourners waiting to catch his final words and pass them on to the packed waiting rooms outside.

Except the waiting rooms weren't packed and all he had was one fifteen-year-old valet for company. What a comedown for the leader of four million people. "It's not as if it were a bloody secret," Saul Veritie muttered.

"I beg your pardon, sir?" asked Lucius, as he stopped clearing the table of the smokeless cigarettes the councillors had left behind in their hasty departure. His whisk broom paused and he turned an inquiring expression toward the Protector.

"Where's Adrian?" Saul demanded querulously. "Doesn't he know I'm ill?"

"He was here this morning, sir. He brought you the picture." Lucius nodded toward the portrait that hung opposite the sickbed. "You spoke for an hour."

"Oh." Saul gazed at the portrait, a blamelessly correct version of a younger Saul Veritie at the head of a council meeting. "Bet Brandon picked it out for him. The boy's got more taste than to get me something so dull."

"Yes, sir." Lucius saw the pain come over Saul's face. He put down his whisk broom, walked over to the bed, and moved the pillows so that Saul could lie back. The Protector was only fifty-six, but he looked eighty. Two weeks ago the trade team had brought back a fever from their last days planetside, a bug that had gotten past the medical screening. It happened sometimes, and as usual, this one was no worse than a bad cold for most people. It was unfortunate that one of the rare exceptions to the rule happened to be the Diamond Protector. It had made the last few days very ... eventful, Lucius thought, for everybody else.

Saul lay back and muttered to himself some more. Then he said—very loudly for a dying man, Lucius thought, "Well, where *is* Adrian?"

"I'm sure he'll be back as soon as he can, sir."

"I named him my successor. You'd think the least the boy could do would be to show up and fake some tears!"

Lucius didn't respond. He was aware of Saul's genuine fondness for Adrian. Instead he poured a few swallows of medicine into a shot glass and held it to Saul's lips. Saul pursed them like a three-year-old. "It's time," said Lucius. "The doctors said every four hours—"

"I'm dying, dammit. I don't have to drink that stuff if I don't want to."

Lucius sighed and set the glass on the bedtable. He helped Saul to lie down again. After a moment the Protector said weakly, "Lucius? Where's Adrian, isn't he coming today?"

"He was here this morning, sir." Lucius knew very well where Adrian was, but there was no need to burden a dying man with that knowledge.

"He was? I need to talk to him, you know. There's something I have to tell him."

"You told him, sir."

"Well, how the hell do you know?" asked Saul, in a sudden return of spirit. "You don't know what I want to tell him."

"No, sir, but when he left, you led me to believe you'd given him some information."

A slow smile came over Saul's pallid face. "Did I?" He relaxed, seeming to lose interest in the conversation. Lucius took advantage of the moment to try the shot glass again; this time Saul downed it obediently.

While Saul was quiet, Lucius returned to sweeping up the remains of the deathwatch. He started into the next room to fetch a trash bag. "Lucius!" came the cry from the bed.

"Yes, sir?"

"I wanted to tell Adrian something, but the boy's not here. I'll have to tell you instead."

"No, you don't, sir," said Lucius, in a reasonable tone,

as he continued his efficient circuit toward the outer rooms. Lucius was fifteen, but he'd been born in service and had every intention of living a long and happy life in it. He had no desire to hear anything that had to be passed to the next Protector from a deathbed.

"Baret Two," said Saul hoarsely, as Lucius closed the green baize doors behind himself. "Baret Two." He stared blindly toward Adrian's gift on the wall and the young version of himself who stood there in immortality. "Tell him, Baret Two. But tell him . . . not to be obvious about it."

Adrian Mercati jumped as the streetlamp beside him exploded. He rolled behind a transport cart and came up with his weapon in hand, peering carefully through the openings in the top of the cart. The two knights with him, Roger Breem and Streph Wolansky, had ducked as quickly as he had. Given everyone's state of nerves, it wasn't surprising. Roger was standing in the front doorway of a clothing store and Streph was behind a garbage cart. The third knight was nowhere to be seen.

The third knight, Gil Veritie, the final member of Adrian's protective squad, was the person who'd shot the streetlamp.

"Gil, you missed!" called Adrian, in the exact tone of sympathy he'd have used at a tournament.

Gil had been stupid enough to fire just as Adrian had moved, but he wasn't stupid enough to answer him now. Pity.

Fortunately there had been enough rumors of trouble coming somewhere that Mercati Boulevard was almost deserted tonight. The dimmed lamps of the *City of Diamond* lined rows of dark shops: tailors, jewelers, carpet merchants, linkhouses. The dozen levels of walkways high above them couldn't have held more than a hundred people—nothing at all for the Boulevard on a Friday night. At least innocent pedestrians were unlikely to get shot, Adrian thought, then dismissed said innocent pedestrians from his mind.

There was no further fire from Gil Veritie, who was apparently reviewing his options. "Care to throw yourself on our mercy?" suggested Adrian. He saw Streph give him a pained look from behind the garbage cart and smiled. It was a reasonable question. If Gil's group—now that they knew which group he belonged to—won tonight, he'd be safe enough. If not, it was no time to be above a little groveling. After all, Gil may have taken a potshot at Saul's lawful successor, but he'd had no opportunity to call his fellow rebels and tell them where Adrian was, which was more to the point.

In about fifteen minutes, the rebels were due to storm court level. It was important they believe Adrian to be there, rather than huddling behind a transport cart on the Boulevard with a small and inconspicuous escort of friends. Brandon Fischer, Saul's First Adviser, had made this very clear to Adrian before he sent him off to hide.

"Is hiding the way to begin my duties as Protector?" Adrian had said. But he trusted Fischer, and made his complaints while packing.

"A few days only." Fischer stroked his beard, still red-gold despite his age, and frowned thoughtfully. Then he picked up a shirt Adrian had rolled into a ball, and shook it out before handing it back, for all the world like somebody's distracted mother. Adrian smiled with real affection, then tried to hide the smile. "We'll move you around a bit so they can't find out where you are. Then we'll plant a few rumors that you'll be addressing the City from the Cavern of Audience. If I know Saul's cousins, they'll be out in force—swords, pistols, and protest signs."

"And around the Cavern—"

"Five companies of the City Guard."

"Five?" Adrian paused in his chore. "Isn't that over-kill?"

"The operative word," said Fischer grimly, "is kill."

Adrian stared into the distance, a pair of blue silk pants dangling from one hand. "I see," he said finally.

"You want to live," said Fischer.

"I know."

"Saul made me responsible for you—"

"I said I know."

He finished packing. Five minutes later he met his three escorts, all young men of good class and background, who could easily be walking together on any street in the City without causing comment. None of them had ever been part of the anti-Adrian clique. One of them, though a Veritie by birth, had been a friend of Adrian's since they were thirteen.

Good old Gil, thought Adrian. They'd gotten drunk together a good dozen times. They'd visited the girls on Requiem Row more than a dozen times—in fact, it was Gil who'd introduced him to the Row, he remembered. Good old backstabber Gil.

Fischer had warned him about court friendships, but Adrian had believed himself capable of telling a false heart, certainly over the course of eight long years. And Gil was an outcast among the Verities; he'd proven his loyalty a thousand times—

The broken glass of the streetlamp crunched under Adrian's boots as he changed position. He looked down, and in a slow, dreamlike movement he picked up a small piece of the glass. He wrapped it in a white handkerchief and put it in his pocket.

"Gil, give up!" Adrian called. "Your friends will be out of the picture in half an hour. I know you didn't warn them, you didn't have a chance." He paused. "Surrender now, and I promise you won't be executed. I'll have you exiled from the City at our next port of call. You can bring what you want with you. Gil!"

Damn. He was due to be in his next hiding place, an office on the admin levels, in fifteen minutes. Fischer would be calling him there.

Assuming Fischer was still alive. There'd been no message from him in a day, and the communication links had gone down four hours ago, city-wide. Adrian's fist hit the back of the cart in frustration.

And in a matching burst of frustration, the outer edge of the cart began to sizzle, hit by a pistol burst coming from . . . that butcher shop next door? A sign proclaimed the Well-Fed Pig, a gourmet food and fresh meat store, whose deep doorway would be an excellent place for an assassin to hide.

He met Streph's eyes and looked toward the shop. Streph nodded. Roger, at the clothing store, was just out of his line of sight. Adrian's inner motor started to turn over, as it always did at tournaments, at trials of strength, at anything from a swordfight to a spelling contest. He felt his body warming up, as though it had come out of a long hibernation into pure morning sunlight. . . .

If Streph kept firing toward the doorway, Adrian could get to the side of the store—

A cry of pain came from the doorway. Roger's head popped cautiously from the shop next door, and the three of them looked at each other.

From the butcher's, there was only a mysterious silence. Adrian half rose, to be met by Roger's fierce, "Don't you *dare!*" It was hardly the way to address one's nearly liege lord, but Adrian decided this was not the time to go into that. Slowly, Roger advanced toward the shadows of the doorway.

He leaped around the corner, pistol extended in both hands, and only pulled off his aim at the last millisecond. The shot hit the pig sign, charring it to ashes at once. Roger's arms went down, and he started to laugh. Hysterically.

Streph and Adrian exchanged glances. Hitherto, Roger had given no evidence of mental illness. They rose slowly, and walked over to join him.

A body lay on the threshold of the open doorway of the Well-Fed Pig. Gil Veritie's hand was flung out behind him, and a small pool of blood was gathering on the floor beneath his skull. Above him stood a portly, middle-aged man in a white apron with red-brown stains, holding a bat. The man was red-faced and half-bald, with dark eyes that turned now to the three in his doorway. He looked thrilled and appalled.

"I saw you from the window," he said. His eyes went wildly to Adrian. "I saw your picture last week, when Saul announced you."

"Thank you," said Adrian quietly.

The butcher relaxed suddenly. "We always liked the Mercatis around here, sir. And if you're good enough for Saul, you're good enough for me. It's his right to pick who he wants to go after him."

Adrian grinned then. "I thought so, too."

It was the Mercati family smile, the same one that his grandfather had used to become the unofficial lover of the Protector's wife. The same one his father had turned on Saul with a joyful sincerity that was almost indecent in a

public person. The butcher's face turned into a mirror of
Adrian's.

Roger glanced over and saw that, beneath the smudges
and grime, the boy had started to glow. *The boy, indeed.*
He'd have to stop thinking about him the way Fischer and
Saul had always referred to him: Adrian was twenty now.
But he'd thought the boy—Adrian, dammit—would be
shaky from this encounter, not so . . . well . . . *happy*.

Roger looked into Adrian's eyes and realized with a
start of horror that Adrian *loved* being shot at. By god, it
fit with his reaction to tournament competitions. He loved
being shot at, he loved having a situation come out his
way, and he loved being loved; put it all together, and
Adrian Mercati was glowing at this moment with enough
candlepower to light the Boulevard. No wonder the shopkeeper looked ready to offer his firstborn child.

"We must do something for this fine gentleman," said
Adrian, still looking at the shopkeeper. "I think I'll make
him a knight. Roger, Streph, be my witnesses, would
you? Mr.—I'm sorry, what *is* your name, sir?"

"Leapham," said the shopkeeper, who found he
couldn't stop matching Adrian's grin.

"Mr. Leapham, my dear Mr. Leapham, would you mind
kneeling for a moment?"

Clearly Mr. Leapham would have stretched himself out
in the gutter and acted as a bridge if he'd been asked. He
knelt immediately. Roger, aware of what Fisher's reaction
to this piece of work would be, tried to take action.

"Adrian, you can't just make somebody a knight. He
hasn't passed the tests. He's never piloted a drop. His
family—"

Still gazing happily on his first Diamond subject,
Adrian said, "Isn't that how they made knights in the old
days on Earth? For valiant action in the field?"

"But this isn't the old days on Earth, and people
will—I mean, just think of what Fischer will say." Ac-
knowledging his cowardice, Roger added, "He'll hold me
responsible if I agree to witness."

Turning that same look of happiness onto his friend
like a knockout blow, Adrian said simply, "But this is for
me, Roger."

Roger sighed. Not that he didn't curse himself for a

fool, not that he didn't anticipate Fisher's set down, not that he didn't find the whole situation ridiculous; but denying Adrian the right to give Mr. Leapham a knighthood seemed at that moment almost like a cruelty.

And after all, if they didn't live through the night, it would be a shame not to have let Adrian have his way. If they did live through the night, this Mercati boy would be new Diamond Protector. And it would be a toss-up whether it would be worse to have Fisher or the Protector annoyed with him.

It took less than a minute to ask Mr. Leapham if he would defend the City of Diamond with his life and obey all lawful commands, and then Sir Tom Leapham was getting up, with Streph's help, looking a bit shaky.

Streph met Roger's eyes. "Can't wait till he brings his family to the next tournament." The comment was barely audible.

"Don't be a snob," began Roger, when they all froze.

Up and down Mercati Boulevard, from speakers over the shops, came the sound of bells from a recording made five centuries ago. They looked at each other, the fey glow ebbing from Adrian's face.

"He's dead," said Streph.

"I can't believe it," said Roger. He suddenly looked faintly sick. "He was there all my life." He turned blindly toward Leapham. "I thought I was prepared. . . ."

Adrian touched his arm. "Come on. We've got a lot to do."

The voice was businesslike. Roger turned and followed him. Behind him, he heard the new knight starting to cry.

Three hours later First Adviser Brandon Fischer reactivated the commlinks and called Adrian at his secret office on the admin level. "The conspirators have all been captured."

"Conspirators'?"

"It sounds better than calling them rebels, Adrian. And it suggests smaller numbers than there actually were."

"And how many actually were they?" he inquired bleakly.

"Thirty-eight of the knights. Two hundred plus in all, including their paid employees. Just about all the Verities,

I'm afraid, but that comes as no surprise. I'm glad for
Saul's line that Gil wasn't such a fool."

"He was," said Adrian briefly.

"Oh. I'm sorry." Fischer cleared his throat. "I'll send
an escort down to pick you up. You ought to address the
court and security forces as soon as possible. Particularly
the security forces, they did a good job for you tonight.
If you'd been here instead of six companies of the City
Guard, the rebels would be the ones addressing the
court."

"And Saul? He's really dead?"

"He's gone." They were both silent. Fischer had been
Saul's First Adviser for thirty years now, until Saul had
bequeathed him to Adrian in an effort to protect his chosen successor. Fischer had not gone willingly at first.

"Was he alone when he died?"

"Well, his valet was with him."

Adrian made a sound that would have been a laugh if
it weren't so unhappy. He said, "Tell them I'll be speaking in an hour."

"All right. Sir." Fischer cut the connection. It was the
first time he'd ever called Adrian "sir."

Five hours later, Fischer helped Adrian to his bed in
the suite near Saul Veritie's. A corpse was laid out in
there now.

"I heard about that stunt of yours with the knighthood,"
said Fischer.

Adrian chuckled. He pulled back the covers and let
himself down, nearly groaning with the sudden relaxation
of muscles. He'd been awake for the better part of three
days. "Roger said you'd be upset."

"I was. I'd still be, except the commons seem delighted
with it. They're putting banners out up and down the
Boulevard to celebrate your elevation to the Protectorship."

Adrian smiled, luxuriating in the clean sheets.

Fisher said, "I understand this fellow you raised already has a sign outside his shop with his new title on it."

The smile widened.

"Don't you think the nobles might be a little upset?"

"They never go to that kind of shop. They'll forget

eventually. But the neighborhood people will pass by every day, and they'll be happy."

Fischer watched as Adrian turned his head into the pillow. On the bureau beside him was a white handkerchief and a piece of glass, where Adrian had placed them when he pulled them from his pocket before climbing into bed. "And Saul always said it was important to have their support."

"He did."

"Is that why you let him give you the Protectorship?"

"Had to take it to live, Brandon. You know that."

"I was just wondering if there were any other reason."

"Outside."

"I beg your pardon?"

"See the Outside. No one can stop me, if I'm Protector."

Fischer blinked. This was the first time he'd heard of this. "Adrian, do you—"

"Go away, Brandon, let me sleep. Talk to you tomorrow."

Brandon Fischer sighed and walked to the door. On the other side were City Guards, councillors from Saul's reign, and ten thousand duties. He turned at the door and looked back at Adrian's sleeping form. "Poor boy," he said under his breath. "It's damned little of the Outside you'll ever see."

SECTION ONE:
Enter Two Ladies

Chapter 1

I know the tune that I am piping is a mild one (although there are some terrific chapters coming presently).

WILLIAM MAKEPEACE THACKERAY

City Year 545

It was Thursday, and on Thursdays Stratton Hastings Diamond always visited his mother.

He checked to make sure that the small Keith pistol was strapped securely on his forearm, and tapped the knife bulge in his soft boots from time to time as he walked down Mercati Boulevard toward the lower decks. After the third level lock, gaily decorated with its long blue banners, brought him to E deck, he began glancing over his shoulder; by the time he entered G he was scanning the balconies of the tenements on each side and watching the crowds of beggars, streetsellers, and troublemakers with a practiced eye. There was no reason to believe that his past associates were aware of his visiting pattern, or even his mother's address, but Stratton Hastings (known as Spider to friends and enemies) was a careful soul. The forty-three years of his existence had been crammed with more incident than he cared to remember, for Spider prized the quiet life. As it was, he made do with the quiet moment.

He climbed the stairs to Reynardine Street and tipped his hat at the crosswalk to a man in black. "Hello, Father Brady."

"I've just come from your mother, Spider. You cause her a lot of pain."

"I know, Father."

The young priest sighed. "Were you not damned, I'd bless you, Spider."

"Many thanks for the thought." Even as they were speaking, he glanced up and down the street, gauging how close the other pedestrians came, noting where weapons might be hidden. "Is Mother all right?"

"Nervous palpitations, as usual. And concern over you."

"Ah. I'll be seeing you, then, Father." Spider respected the religious orders but avoided them when possible; not that Brady wasn't less abrasive than most. He produced a shameless smile for the priest, who hesitated at the Boulevard stairs as though wondering whether to spread another net for Spider's soul. "Don't want to keep Ma waiting, now, especially if she's feeling delicate."

"No, of course not." Brady buttoned the top of his black cape. "Good-bye, Spider."

"Father."

Spider passed on along the narrow metal walkway, avoiding the wet laundry hung over the rails and piled on dirty gratings. His mother's compartment was third from the left. He touched the bell.

The door was flung open. "Stratton, my own." Mrs. Hastings enveloped her son in a hug. She was taller and more substantial than he and her bosom was more than ample for maternal comfort. Spider nearly disappeared in the folds of her blue housedress. "Come in, my sweet. Father Brady was just here."

"I passed him."

"He's greatly disappointed in you."

"Ma, wait till I get in before you start on me."

Mrs. Hasting grinned and took him inside. It was like being taken into the heart of an old and much-repaired doll house: A snug compartment, two rooms of soft plush chairs, a pull-out bed with a quilt, and a one-legged table with a lace cloth where a teapot and cookies were presently resting.

"Iced shortbread, sweetheart—have some. It's the same as I gave Mrs. Cathcart and Jenny Pierce when they came by yesterday." Spider smiled and grabbed a couple of cookies as he fell back into the old armchair. His mother loved to have her cronies by to see the style in which she now lived; and he was pleased at her pride, since it was all produced from his own illegal funds. "I didn't quite know what to tell them when they asked about you, my heart."

"Tell them I'm a corporal in Inventory, respectable as anyone."

"That doesn't explain why you can't attend church."

"How should they know I don't attend church unless you tell them, Ma? Maybe I go to Saint Tom's up on court level."

His mother poured tea into a cracked china cup. "You haven't escorted me to Christmas service in two years. You're not a ghost anymore, what can I tell people?"

He stretched out his legs and examined his boots broodingly. Damned souls aren't allowed to attend church, as his mother very well knew. Mrs. Hastings said, "It's unnatural, Stratton, consorting with demons the way you do. It tears the meat from my heart whenever I think about it."

Spider did not reply to this. It was his demonic connections that made possible this snug compartment on the very border of middle-class territory, far from the level where he'd been born as the son of an unknown father and a mother on the Sin List—for the one and only time, to hear her tell it. Ma knew as well as he that her present comforts depended on his ultimate damnation, which was why she pricked him about it, but never too hard. Ma was a practical woman.

"Heard anything from the old neighborhood?" he asked.

"Your friend Rat's been taken in the lottery."

Spider whistled between his teeth. "When?"

"Last Thursday—probably when we were having tea, now that I think on it. Well, you can't say you're surprised, Stratton. Rat was in trouble since the day he was born; if he wasn't drunk on the church steps, he was sassing somebody who oughtn't to be sassed. With all the times his name went in, it was bound to come up one day."

The cookie was dust in his mouth. Rat had never been a real friend, but he was the last of the childhood gang still living; the rest had gone to the lottery, the recycler, labor on the radiation levels, or the ghosts.

The ghosts . . . "Did he get away?"

"Stratton!"

"Just asking, Ma. Be fair—if I hadn't got away to the ghosts when my name came up, we wouldn't be having tea here now, would we?"

"I heard," she said, lowering her voice, and jettisoning any pretension to moral outrage, "that he approached a runner on K level who said he'd put him in touch with some ghosts down there; but the nathy just turned him in for the reward."

"No surprise there." The shock was wearing off; Spider took another cookie. There were always people who claimed they could reach a ghost or two, but they were generally liars. Ghosts chose their contacts carefully, and not for their talkativeness. He should know; he'd lived with a ghostband for a year and a half, dodging the priests and police, stealing food and clothing, sleeping in places respectable folk never knew about. He could still recall the day they came to tell him he'd come up black in the lottery—his own damn fault for not getting that jail stint wiped off his records fast enough. Shit. What a day that had been, with Ma hysterical and himself under house arrest. Good thing Pete was right about the ghost trail he'd found, good thing he could run faster than the bored escort he'd dumped out in Reynardine Street South. Of course, he'd hadn't had these one or two extra pounds then. . . .

"Best hold back on the sugar, love," said his mother disconcertingly. "You're getting a bit of a paunch."

He glared at her in mild outrage. She should talk! Ma weighed two hundred and fifty, if she weighed an ounce. "Maybe I should join the ghosts again, hey? I was skinny enough then."

"Don't be difficult, Stratton. What's the news from court deck?" She settled into her chair, leaning forward just a bit to hear better.

"Busy as fleas up there, the admin decks, too. Tal says we haven't officially approached Baret Two about trading yet. He says we'll make first overtures at Baret Station so we can feel the situation out."

"Never mind what your demon says, Stratton, I want to hear about the *wedding!*" She bounced impatiently on the cushions, and the ancient chair gave an alarming groan.

"Oh." Of course. "Adrian's having a welcoming cere-mony for the lady's representatives this afternoon—right now, in fact. Tal's there, that's why he could spare me for a while."

"They let a demon go to the ceremony?" For the first time Mrs. Hastings sounded impressed with the person responsible for leading her Stratton into a life of sin.

"Ma, he's a Special Officer of the Diamond. I wouldn't be surprised if Adrian made him best man."

"No!" Clearly the scandal thrilled her. She reached into a bowl of walnuts without looking.

"Well, he'd get the ten thousand other people who think they're going to be in the wedding off his back. And he could avoid having to single out any of the fam-ilies on court deck as a mark of favor. They're ripping each other's throats out over it now, I hear." Spider took another cookie without opposition, pleased he could speak so intimately about social jockeying on court level.

"And dear Adrian still hasn't seen the lady?"

"Not yet. She'll be presented in a few days."

Mrs. Hastings sighed happily, forgetting the wonders of baked goods she'd set out for her son. "You'll let me know, won't you, my own? So I can mention it, in pass-ing, to Mrs. Cathcart."

"Sure, Ma."

She leaned even farther forward, placing the small china plate on her knees in danger. "Is there any chance we'd be invited to the wedding?" she whispered. "There's lots of room in St. Tom's, and your demon seems to have influence with Adrian. . . ."

"I wouldn't set my heart on it."

She pouted and leaned back in her chair. "Ah, well," she said philosophically.

There was a knock at the door. She hauled herself up from the armchair with difficulty, walked over, and slid the door open a crack.

"It's Timmy," said a young voice outside. She looked down on a small blond head and scuffed shoes.

"Only the link-boy," she called, as she turned back in-side for a second and blinked. "Stratton?" Her son had disappeared from the front room. She looked down again at the boy. "You have a message for me, Timmy?"

He nodded, producing a blue envelope from his shirt. "Came over the corner link for you just five minutes ago."

"And weren't you fast!" She pulled a coin from her dress pocket and put it in Timmy's. "Many thanks, sweetheart."

She closed the door and began opening the envelope. Spider reappeared beside the tea tray with a questioning expression. His mother glanced at the contents, looked disgusted, and handed it to him. A smaller envelope was inside the larger, marked "Stratton Hastings."

Spider ripped it open. A short printout was there: "Meet me under St. Kit's Bridge at six o'clock. If I'm late, wait for me." No signature. He checked his timepiece—it was only three-thirty, plenty of time for a rest and a snack.

"Nothing important," he told his mother, falling back into the armchair again.

"I suppose your demon knows where I live," she said disapprovingly.

"He just knows where to reach me. It's no big deal, really." She set her mouth firmly, and Spider said, "Come on, Ma. If Tal hadn't pulled me out of the recycler line, where would your only son be?"

"Father Brady says—"

Spider was not the sort of son who interrupted his mother, but he said suddenly, "Is Father Brady your only confessor?"

"Dear heart, I don't think that's any of your bus—"

"I'm only wondering how many people know I'm on Tal's payroll."

"No one breaks the seal of the confessional, Stratton."

"I don't think Brady would. But it never hurts to know where you stand."

She sniffed. "As it happens, he kept after me about why he never saw you in church. I had to tell him in confession just to shut him up." She paused, seeming to hear how that sounded, and said, "Well, it was his duty."

They were both silent a moment, considering the problem. There was an automatic excommunication order, based on very old church law, on anyone who went out of his way to abet demons. Of course, no one knew of his moonlighting for Tal, so no one knew he was excommunicate. And technically, since he was damned anyway, he might as well pile sin on sin and go to church alongside the righteous. Neither Spider nor his mother thought it illogical that he would not.

Spider sighed. All right, it was true Tal was a demon—nobody knew better than he—but it was Tal who'd gotten him out of the execution line and given him a new chance and a new roll of cash, where the best City society could come up with was ghosthood or death. Poor Rat, the stupid bastard. One did what one could. Spider, too, was practical.

"Ma ..." he said, wondering how to broach the subject. "Uh, does Father Brady know where the money comes from?"

"Are you crazy?" She looked around the cozy little room at all her dear things. "It would be 'tainted fruit.' He'd want me to have it confiscated."

Spider leaned back with his cup and grinned. Good old Ma.

Chapter 2

Exporting a religion across cultures can lead to unfortunate consequences. Exporting a religion across species would seem disastrous.
WANG CHANG'AN,
"The False Promise of Redemptionism"

Brandon Fischer watched in horror as Adrian rolled up his dress shirt into a ball and threw it across his bedchamber.

"Adrian, that suit has been approved—"

"You approved it, Brandon." The Protector of the City of Diamond grinned, pleased with the effect he was having. He'd been far too cooperative this last week; it gave Brandon a false sense of security, of which he needed to be disabused. "You approved it, the tailor made it, and Lucius got me into it; have you ever heard about 'leading a horse to water'?"

"But—" Fisher groped for words. "You've never complained before about my choice of costume for official affairs."

"I was never engaged to be married before." The young man and the old one looked at each other, while Adrian's valet, unimpressed, walked over to the discarded shirt, picked it up, and brushed it off. "The shirt is brown, the breeches are brown, the boots are brown. My hair is brown. My skin is brown. I look like something thrown out of the recycler."

Fischer said patiently, "It's a very inoffensive color. No symbolic values attached to it at all. Green would have been too religious, yellow would have suggested the Veritie family colors, white—"

"Brandon, I have as much respect for the political values as anyone, but was there some reason my personal appearance couldn't have been taken into account in this equation?"

Fischer pursed his lips. The Mercatis were known for a streak of vanity a mile wide, but the boy had never given him trouble in this area before. Finally he said, as though explaining to a student, "This is a historic meeting. I know we've been messaging back and forth incessantly, but from an official point of view—"

"—*official* being the only point of view that matters—"

"It's the first reception of anyone from the City of Opal since the end of the Civil War. This will be their first impression of you. You will be greeting them as the Diamond Protector, Adrian, not as a fashion plate."

His boy, his protégé, his pride, turned and slashed a look toward Fischer that made him reevaluate his tone. It was a look that suggested the Diamond Chief Adviser had taken leave of his senses. "Brandon," said Adrian slowly, "I am officially betrothed. *They will be reporting back on what I look like to the lady in question.*"

Ah. Fischer controlled the smile that rose to his lips. *Of course* that aspect of things would be on Adrian's mind. "Believe me, they'll say only good things," he assured him. "They'd say only good things if you were a hunch-back with one leg; they want the marriage to go through."

Adrian sighed, a meaningful sound that suggested it had been a long time since Fischer was twenty-three. He said, "Already one of the hangers-on in the Opal delegation told one of the Diamond hangers-on that Iolanthe's well-known for being a shrew that nobody on Opal would go near, regardless of the wedding portion." He shrugged. "It might be true. Or he could have made it up on the spot. It's remarkable how many things people come out with just to have something to say."

Fischer looked faintly shocked. "They're not supposed to be speaking to anybody before the reception! And what hangers-on?"

"Oh, some clothes-peg who came along to make the Opal delegation look a little grander. He mentioned it in passing to one of the folk we have assigned to look after them."

"How did you hear about it?"

Adrian inspected himself in his full-length mirror, a dissatisfied expression on his face. "That's not the point. The point is, what are they saying about *me?* The girl's only seventeen, Brandon. We don't want to scare her." He glared at the image in the mirror as though that would somehow alter it for the better. "I cannot wear this suit in public. Lucius! Don't we have another shirt *somewhere?*"

Lucius Stringfellow was now an eighteen-year-old who moved with the careful dignity a mountain peak might possess if it suddenly became mobile. He met Adrian's gaze in the mirror. "Sir, you threw your blue silk cape and shirt at me last night and told me to put it with the pile I sent for cleaning. And they were very in need of it, too. Your white shirt of Tuesday has still not been located, but assuming it was lost here, and not . . . elsewhere . . ." Adrian seemed oblivious to this reference, but Fischer's complexion, naturally ruddy, took on a slightly pinker cast. ". . . it will no doubt appear when one of the maids does the room this afternoon."

"Damn! I wish Tal were here. He always has ideas."

"He's in the outer rooms, sir," said Lucius, before Fischer could speak. "Shall I fetch him?"

"We don't need him for this, do we?" Fischer inquired.

"Call him in," said Adrian, and Lucius went away.

Fischer seated himself on the edge of a table. He did so awkwardly, with the movements of a man whose bones were aching, though he'd seemed healthy enough a moment ago. "Adrian," he began.

"Oh, that earnest tone." Adrian smiled with genuine affection. "How well I know it. Can't you leave Tal be for a while? You've been peering at him for two years, and he's done nothing to justify this constant suspicion."

"He is what he is."

"On the Diamond he is what I make him, and I've given him sixteenth rank."

Fischer shook his head. How could the boy be so blind? You'd think after that business with Gil Veritie during the rebellion, he'd be more careful with his companions. But Adrian had never mentioned Gil's betrayal again, never seemed to give it a second thought. *"Tal,"* Fischer said, rolling it around in his throat, *"Tal!* He doesn't even have a last name. He's an Outsider. He's an acknowledged demon. And you spend far too much time in his company, Adrian."

The Protector smiled, his eyes distant. "Really, how can you be so conventional, Brandon? When I think of all the years you warned me against court friendships, you should be glad I've found an intimate with no pretensions to power."

Fischer followed his glance to the rather eccentric objet d'art that sat on Adrian's dressertop: a tall block of clear crystalline material with a shard of glass embedded in it. "Power comes in different forms," he snapped irritably. "Look, what is that thing anyway? It's the only abstract piece you own. When you tossed out Saul's old pictures, I thought you said you didn't want 'art' following you into your bedchamber at night."

"Just a memento of the rebellion." Adrian's gaze cleared. "Tal! Come in, I need your advice."

A figure in pearl-gray detached itself from where it lounged against the door, and came in. A visual recording would have shown the new entrant as the youngest person in the room, younger even than Lucius Stringfellow, who accompanied him; perhaps seventeen years old, on the slender side, with dark hair and gray eyes. But the other

three people in the room did not see him that way. Nobody who came to know Tal for more than half an hour
ever thought of him as seventeen, ever again. As for his
chronological age, for all they knew, he might have been
the oldest there; that information, along with his surname
and place of origin, was kept to himself. It was simple
prudence, in a demon.

Without a word, Adrian picked up the chocolate-
colored shirt that Lucius had rescued from the floor and
held it against himself.

Tal said, "You look like something tossed out of a
recycler."

Brandon Fischer threw up his hands and turned away.

"But what to do about it?" asked Adrian. "If we were
closer in size, I could change shirts with you, but—"

Tal's glance was ranging the room. He stopped.
"What's this?" He walked to Adrian's bed and tugged on
a scrap of white that hung from the snowy bedclothes. It
turned into a sleeve. He tossed the shirt to Adrian and
said, "It's fortunate you're unacquainted with neatness."

Adrian said happily, "I knew you'd come up with
something. Lucius! How fast can we press this?"

"It should be washed, sir."

Tal took a chair, lounging back comfortably. "They
won't be close enough to smell anything. You humans
have underdeveloped olfactory senses anyway."

"Press it, Lucius," said Adrian.

Fischer said, "White suggests—"

"It suggests a chaste and proper bridegroom," cut in
Tal, whose patience with Diamond symbolism had clearly
defined limits. His gray eyes rested coldly on Brandon
Fischer's figure, where the old man sat tiredly on the
edge of the walnut table, his weight eased back to take
the burden from his legs. The boy, or man, known as
Adrian's demon did not suffer gladly those he considered
fools. More than once, he'd suggested to the Protector
than an early retirement for the Chief Adviser would be
in everyone's best interest; but Adrian seemed to have a
sentimental attachment to the old dodderer. As if loyalty
to past bonds ever got anyone anywhere. Humans lived in
constant illusion; he, Tal, did not live in illusion. "What's

the arrangement today?" he asked. "Any taboos I should be observing?"

"The reception is purely for show," said Adrian. "No business or policy discussion. I'll be introducing myself as a Mercati—as though they hadn't already heard—and we'll all accept each other as one big family."

"I do hope the family's been checked for weapons."

"It's a public reception, Tal. Ambassadors and other boring folk. I doubt if anyone's going to pull out a pen-knife and strike a blow for their City."

Fischer said to Tal, "We don't all have your keen grasp of how to remove obstacles."

Tal smiled. It was a different smile from Adrian's.

Adrian knelt beside his dresser and pulled a wine-colored sash from a drawer. Fischer said nothing; he was past commenting on the clothes. With his usual regard for household order, Adrian tossed the wine sash over his shoulder to the floor and unrolled one of white. As he tied it around his waist, he asked, "What are the lower decks saying about the wedding?"

Fischer hadn't a clue what the lower decks were saying. He opened his mouth to report this, when Tal said, "The idea seems to have a lot of appeal. They're a sentimental bunch, particularly below G deck."

Tal met Fischer's startled glance blandly.

"I was not aware," said Fischer, "that your demon had some sort of information-gathering imperative."

Tal said, "I wasn't aware the Chief Adviser was required to be informed of every step the Protector takes."

Adrian looked up from the mess he was making of the sash's knot—he knew he should leave these things to Lucius, but he was impatient to get out. "If you two are going to start referring to each other in the third person again, you can damn well leave. I've got enough on my mind today as it is."

"Nor was I aware," said Fischer, turning to face Tal, "that you possess contacts outside of court. I know you have few enough *there*—"

"Maybe your focus has been too narrow."

"Maybe it should be widened."

Adrian cleared his throat, and Fischer fell silent, at least for a moment. Then he turned back to Adrian.

"You've always cared too much what the lower decks think. Regardless of what Saul used to say, their approval can only go so far. The knights are the group that matters; they're the ones with weapons. Them and the bankers."

"He's probably right," said Tal.

Fischer, who had been about to continue the argument, paused, looked uncomfortable, and switched directions. "Of course, it doesn't hurt to sound their opinion," he admitted, grudgingly.

"And what about the girl?" asked Adrian. "How do they feel about Iolanthe?"

Tal said, "Oh, they're ready to accept her as a pure, untrammeled flower, a funnel of all virtues. They have every expectation that you two will fall in love at first sight, or at least do them the courtesy of faking it for their benefit. I hope you're not going to disillusion them?"

"I'll try not to," said Adrian, "but someone may have to cue the lady." He looked up, surrendering his struggle with the sash, and met Tal's eyes in the mirror. Adrian said, "You're wearing your gray lenses!"

"You asked me to."

Fischer peered into Tal's face, and stirred uneasily. "Adrian, if they've heard he's a demon . . . do we want to offend them? Everybody knows demons have gray eyes when they fully incarnate. Couldn't he have worn the green or brown lenses?"

For the first time Tal looked less confident. "I took your request at face value. If it was one of those aspects of humor you say escape me—"

"No, no!" said Adrian. "That is, it was, but I meant what I said. It appealed to my own humor to have you attend with gray eyes. Come on, Brandon, take it in context. He might have attended without any lenses at all. *That* would get their attention."

"Adrian, I wish you would consult me before—"

Lucius returned with the shirt, and Adrian seized it gratefully, saying, "We really *must* hurry, you know." There was a slight note of accusation in his voice as he looked at Tal and Fischer. One would think he'd been delayed unreasonably for hours. He tucked in the shirt hastily, while Lucius made disapproving sounds over the sash, and the demon and the Chief Adviser exchanged a rare glance of accord.

The upper corridor to the Cavern of Audience was a long one, and Adrian took the opportunity to drop back a few paces and address his demon.

"Do try not to provoke him."

"I beg your pardon?" Tal inquired.

"Brandon." Adrian nodded to where Fischer strode ahead with the three lead members of the Protector's Squad. "It's not that he's stupid, you know, it's just that he's conventional. You pluck at all his nerves."

"I pluck at his nerves just by being."

"That's my point. You could try not to rub his nose in it by always giving him the benefit of your—unique viewpoint."

"I thought you asked me to stay *because* of my unique viewpoint."

Adrian smiled. "My dear demon, let me put it this way: I don't ask you to change your nature. Don't expect Brandon to change his. He *is* conventional. That which is outside the bounds offends him. But he knows everybody on court level, and I owe him a great deal."

Tal grunted. Adrian knew enough not to take this for assent. He said, "Three years ago—before we had the honor of your company—this corridor was full of rebels. Nine-tenths of Saul Veritie's inbred relatives tried to storm the Cavern. If Brandon hadn't handled the situation for me, I'd be dead." He smiled. "And by extension, so would you."

"I find it difficult to believe that one clear thought ever made it through that man's brain in his entire life."

"He finds it difficult to believe one moral thought ever made it through yours."

"We know each other so well."

Adrian laughed. One of the advantages of Tal's company was the privilege of saying anything you were thinking to him. He didn't judge anything, and nothing offended him. Meeting a demon had been one of the greatest *reliefs* of Adrian's life.

At the end of the corridor, the group passed through the double doors that opened onto the upper landing of the Grand Staircase. The entire Cavern was before them, a huge expanse of onyx floor, walls, and ceiling; gleaming black surfaces that curved into each other, reflecting the colors of the parties assembled below. The three-story staircase unwound beneath them, cut out of the ebony rock six centuries ago by nonhuman engineers for whom aesthetics had been at least as important as function. Adrian, Tal, and Fischer gazed out at Diamond courtiers, admins, knights, ladies of the court, and Opal delegates, all dressed as flamboyantly as the occasion would allow. The two security guards flanking the landing were in full dress colors and ruffles.

Adrian took a step down. Tal touched his shoulder. "Wait."

Fischer watched as Adrian stopped. *Certainly,* he thought, *for his demon he's all cooperation!*

"What is it?"

"There are more Opal delegates than there should be."

Adrian murmured, "My, don't you count quickly." He looked down at the court, as more and more faces turned up to see them. "How many?"

"Thirty-one."

Fischer peered at the folk below. He could barely make out gowns or breeches from here. Of course, his eyes weren't as good as they used to be—

Adrian said, "They've only been approved to bring eleven."

Fischer opened his mouth to give the order, but Tal was already striding just outside the double doors, where a link-station was active. Fischer heard his voice, "—by order of the Protector. This is Tal Diamond, officer of the Sixteenth Rank. . . . Of course we mean *now,* you feeble-minded idiot. Were you assuming—" Tal delivered his invective without anger, but with a razorlike simplicity that carried its own logic. Fischer winced, grateful that he was not the object of it at the moment.

A few seconds later Tal returned.

Adrian quirked an eyebrow. "May we continue?"

"Not yet."

Nobody else, thought Fischer, would address the boy in quite that tone and get away with it. Adrian waited patiently.

Still looking at the crowd, Tal said, "The security officer told me that they'd had to admit the extra Opallines rather than offend the Lord Cardinal. He said that they had it under control. I asked if this meant he'd brought in extra security. He said no." As they watched, about a dozen nonuniformed men entered the great bronze doors below and fanned out into the crowd. "All right. Go ahead."

"Thank you so much." Adrian took a step. "You know, Tal," he said conversationally, "the Lord Cardinal was only trying to throw a little territorial weight around. This is just a reception. Bad canapés are the worst we can look forward to."

"No harm in being careful." He and Fischer followed Adrian, two paces behind.

"Fortunately the pause added a little drama to our entrance. Knowing the boredom that lies ahead for these fine people, I couldn't begrudge them any extra excitement."

"Adrian," said Fischer reprovingly, in the same tone he'd used when the Protector was fourteen and unranked.

"Come now, Chief Adviser," said Adrian, "you know very well that if anybody says a thing today that falls outside the welcome ritual, I'll eat that disgusting sash you wanted me to wear."

They'd reached the final third of the staircase, and Adrian stopped talking so he could enter the court with the proper attitude of dignity. He didn't want Fischer to lecture him later. They descended into a lake of crimson and blue ball gowns, formally attired knights in the sigils of their squadrons, and court hangers-on of both Cities decked out in their most impressive silk and brocade. Primary colors were fashionable this year; the Cavern was a giant jewelbox of human artifice. At the final step, Tal and Fischer halted, leaving Adrian to step forward and accept the embrace of Lord Cardinal Theodore Richard Arno, chief envoy and head of the Ecclesiastical Council of the City of Opal.

Arno was a big man, tall and stocky, who looked as though he'd been hauling crates all his life instead of looking after spiritual interests. Adrian hadn't expected the embrace, but he joined it, he thought, without obvious awkwardness. He felt Arno make a sketchy blessing motion as the cardinal released him, and his gaze went to Bishop Aldgate, who looked like a man gnashing his teeth. As chief bishop of the Diamond, and Adrian's *official* spiritual adviser, Aldgate ought to be doing any blessing that was going to be done here. *More feathers to be soothed later,* Adrian thought. *Everybody wants to be loved.* He stepped back from Arno's embrace and threw a smile toward Aldgate that shared just the right amount of pained politeness: *What could one do?*

"My son," intoned the Lord Cardinal, choosing a politically unfortunate term of address.

Throwing that territorial weight around again. "My dear Lord Cardinal," said Adrian. "Our beloved *brother* of Opal. The Diamond rejoices to see you well. Families should not be divided."

"Opal is overjoyed to hear you say so. The Separation has been far too long; though your father's wisdom in suggesting it was deep. Tensions were too high. But that was twenty-five years ago; on Opal, we all hope that *unpleasantness* can be forgotten, and our two Cities can live in harmony and prosperity once again."

It rolled off his tongue as any good speech should, with a practiced flair; but then, why the "father" when he spoke of Saul? The man must have been warned that this last succession had not gone to a member of the Veritie family.

Adrian kept his smile firmly in place. If Arno thought he could outdo him in hypocrisy, he was wrong; three years as Diamond Protector had not gone for nothing. "Your kindness in forgiving the past is too much," he said modestly. "My *guardian,* the great Saul Veritie, often wondered if he'd been too stringent in insisting on the full twenty-five years of Separation. But I gather that, at the time, the Civil War—"

" 'War' seems too harsh a term," said Arno, smiling.

"It does," Adrian agreed at once. " 'Misunderstanding,' perhaps, would be better."

Arno nodded.

"At that time, as I say, tempers were strained." *And strained tempers and highly explosive weapons do not go together. Maybe we should call it "The Civil Slight Disa-*

*greement In Which Eight Thousand People Were Killed in
Twenty Minutes.*" "Tempers always seem worse among
those who truly love one another, do they not?"

"You have such wisdom. For one of your age."

"My thanks. May I present my Chief Adviser, Lord
Brandon Fischer—"

Fischer gave a scrupulously correct bow—about one
inch deeper than the one Arno returned. The cardinal said
to Adrian, "We met before, briefly—in your father's
time."

Adrian's teeth showed in his return smile; more *bared*
than showed, Fischer thought, as he glanced over to see
how the boy was taking it. Arno was really pushing the
father thing. Already he longed to hear what Adrian
would have to say about the cardinal later.

"And Special Officer Tal Diamond," Adrian continued,
unscripted, motioning for Tal to step down and join them.
Fischer's eyes widened slightly. Tal was there to observe,
not to be officially presented to Opal notice; this was
Adrian's way of annoying where annoyance had been
given.

What had Arno heard? Would he make formal recognition of a creature of hell? Fischer was appalled, but not as
much as he was fascinated. He leaned forward, noting
as he did that a great many of the court were doing so as
well.

For a moment the Lord Cardinal seemed actually taken
aback. He wet his lips. Then he said, "An honor." Tal, at
least, had been coached in giving the bow of a sixteenth
rank, and he gave it, his eyes flicking toward Adrian as
he came up. Arno gazed at him. " 'Special Officer?' " He
let the sentence hang.

"My personal bodyguard," said Adrian blandly.

Tal's eyes went again to Adrian, but he said nothing.

"A post of honor," said the cardinal politely. He turned
back to Adrian, dropping Tal from his notice. "I hope that
in the days to come, as we renew old friendships, you'll
come to know all the gentlemen in my delegation; but
meanwhile, will you allow me to bring our First Secretary
to your notice? Officer Hartley Quince, Twelfth Rank."

A young man detached himself from the party of
Opallines and stepped forward, bowing deeply. He had

light gold-brown hair and even lighter brows, and a fine-boned, sensitive face, good-looking enough to border on pretty. He bowed with the gracefulness of childhood training and met Adrian's gaze just as gracefully when he came up.

"The Diamond will always be glad to welcome anyone the Lord Cardinal recommends as our friend," said Adrian, but he said it uneasily. There was something familiar about Quince, and that was impossible. He couldn't be more than twenty-two or twenty-three; and even if he were a little older, he couldn't have been more than a baby when the Separation took place. The Cities had not only been parsecs apart, there had been a complete communications blackout since the war. On different drive-times, they couldn't have communicated if they'd wanted to. Certainly pictures couldn't have been transmitted. So how could his face strike with such recognition?

Quince was smiling and saying something polite and forgettable; Adrian responded automatically in kind. Then Arno was speaking again.

"—before your time, of course, but we who remember your father will always cherish his wisdom in setting forth the treaty."

Adrian blinked, then his lips curved. One problem at a time. "I see, my dear friend, that I have need to present myself to your notice properly. You must forgive me for being derelict. I know that my surname hasn't always been popular in your City, but as you've said, all that past unpleasantness can be forgotten. Saul was my guardian, not my father, and my name is *Mercati*."

Arno looked as courteously surprised as if he'd never known. "Unusual for a Protector to pass his position to someone outside his own family, is it not? Of course, the City of Opal has no hereditary posts, so perhaps I'm simply showing my ignorance."

"Oh, it's been done often enough in the past." *Though not in the last hundred years.* "It's only custom, not law, to pass it through the family; the Protector has every right to give the responsibility to the person of his choice."

"I do hope everyone saw it that way. No hard feelings, I mean, among the Verities."

Adrian's face went blank. "None at all."

"And I must say, your advisers have misled you if they've given you to believe the Mercati name isn't honored on the Opal."

"Oh? We have a reputation, you'll admit, for being progressive."

"Opal is a very progressive city," said Arno, in such a flat-out lie that Adrian could only admire it.

He coughed. "I trust the Lady Iolanthe is enjoying good health."

"Excellent. She looks forward to her new life with you."

I'll bet she does. "Please send her my love, and give her this, if you would." He reached out a hand without looking around and Tal set something gleaming and golden into it. Adrian passed it to Arno.

It was a fine gold chain with two hearts, each heart intricately engraven with their names, repeated over and over in miniature script.

"Beautiful workmanship," said the cardinal, peering at the tiny letters. "I know this will please her."

"I hope so." *Whoever the hell she is.* For a moment a succession of cronelike images flashed through his mind. He dearly wished that City etiquette allowed him to ask for her picture. It might amuse the old men on the Opal Ecclesiastical Council to tie him to a humiliating marriage, though that was unlikely. Still, he did seem to dwell on the fringe possibilities lately. When it wasn't a kinetescope of crones moving through his mind's eye, it was a slower stream of dreamlike beauties that seemed to trickle in whenever he let himself wonder about Iolanthe Pelagia. Odds were far more likely that she was some skinny, plain young lady somewhere firmly between the two extremes; and why shouldn't she be? She was just a seventeen-year-old girl. If she could stumble her way through City functions, that was the most he could reasonably ask.

Adrian said, "And now, if you'll allow me, I'll have you shown back to your suite so you can start becoming settled."

Arno planted himself firmly. "I'm sure the Protector hasn't forgotten his role in the full welcoming ritual," he said. He reached into his robe and came out with a turquoise-handled dagger. "Duty sometimes slips the mind of youth, but maturity is ever a leader."

It was a fully inscribed sacrificial knife. *Oh, lord,* thought Adrian, *he's not actually going to insist—*

He was. Adrian sighed and made sure his white satin cuff was far enough from his palm that it wouldn't get bloody. Lucius would have a fit if he ruined another shirt, and besides, this was Adrian's favorite. With an air of martyrdom, he held out his palm, saying, "Three Cities, one blood. Redemptionist knows Redemptionist wherever they may meet."

Arno was not a man with qualms about cutting through skin. He slashed quite competently along Adrian's life-line, then his own. "One truth, one family, never can be parted." He laid his palm on Adrian's.

Their eyes met. Mindless Opalline adherence to ritual the words might be, but Adrian was terribly afraid they were true.

"No hard feelings among the goddamn Verities," muttered Adrian as Tal pressed a clean cloth into his palm.

"It could have just been a shot in the dark, to irritate you," said Fischer. "It would make sense that the Verities might have been unhappy."

"The man *knew*," said Adrian. "I was standing next to him, I could see his face. How did he get up to date so quickly?"

Tal removed the cloth, checked to see the bleeding had stopped, and began cutting a bandage. "I'm sure Opal has plenty of spies on the Diamond." He wrapped the adhesive efficiently around Adrian's hand.

"Of course, but they haven't spoken to them in twenty-five years. Arno's been on board for three hours and he hasn't seen anybody but the people we assigned to settle them into their quarters." He looked down at the bandage. "Thank you. Under the circumstances, you can't blame me for finding the whole situation rather depressing."

Tal tossed the gauze back to the boy who'd brought it from the medical closet. "If it starts to ache, I have aspirin in my quarters."

Fischer opened his mouth, closed it, looked up and

down the corridor, and turned away. "Adrian, please tell him not to say things like that in public."

He was genuinely perturbed. Adrian said, "Tal, you will not refer to interdicted drugs in public."

"All right." The demon shrugged. "I thought you should know."

Adrian sighed. "I suppose the polite thing would be to warn the delegation that I'll be asking for an official Oracle at dinner tonight."

"Surely they're expecting that," said Fischer.

"But it would be polite to warn them. In case the Oracle comes out with some bizarre statement they feel bound to respond to."

They emerged from the corridor at a high walkway overlooking the court level grounds. Below them, early spring had been enforced on the greenery at a temperature of 55 degrees Fahrenheit and a daily light-dose equivalent to Old Earth temperate latitudes in the month of March. Under this iron hand, pink and yellow buds would shortly be growing in profusion. The skinny silver band of the Katherine River wound past them. A canoe was out already, a court lady perched precariously in the rear; as they descended the stairs toward St. Kit's Walk, the aristo in the front of the canoe put down his paddle and leaned toward the lady.

Fischer leaned forward as well, with interest. He was conventional, but no prude; spring was made for breaking the Purity Laws. Then he saw Tal follow his gaze, and made himself turn back toward the stairs.

Tal said to Adrian, "We can safely assume the Oracle won't say anything specific enough to warrant attention."

"You can't predict an Oracle," said Fischer severely. He risked a glance over his shoulder; alas, the lady was simply handing her companion a sandwich. The clichés were true: Youth was wasted on the young.

"Not word for word. I can predict a certain amount of vague generalization in whatever it says."

"You're an Outsider," snapped Fischer. "If you'd ever read the Book of Prophecies—"

"I have read it, and a more irrational mishmosh of phrases would be hard to find."

Adrian increased his speed down the steps, causing the four members of the security squad to speed up as well.

Fischer said, "It predicted Olin's execution in 392."

"It's predicted somebody's premature death at some time. A relatively safe bet. And a few good hits among six hundred prophecies fail to impress me. Random chance alone would dictate—"

Fischer was starting to hiss between his teeth.

"As for the writing style," Tal continued, "verbs with only a spurious attachment to nearby nouns, an inability to get to the point, a lack of clarity that can only reflect a lack of cognitive function—"

"I don't need to hear literary criticism from a product of hell!" said Fischer.

"Take good criticism where you can find it," replied Tal calmly.

Fischer was starting to change color again. Adrian reached the landing just above St. Kit's, slowed down, and managed to tread on Tal's boot as he crossed. Tal looked into his face and met clear brown eyes focused on his own. Human expressions were not always fully decipherable to Tal, but apparently he decided it was time to drop this topic with Brandon Fischer. He looked down at his timepiece and back to Adrian. "It's quarter to six."

"You see, Brandon, just another example of how well-informed he keeps me."

"I meant that I have to take my leave. I've an appointment at six."

Adrian nodded. "Someday you must tell me how you spend your spare time." He made a dismissive gesture, and Tal turned and started down the last vertical walkway, toward the greenery this side of the river. "I'll expect you at the reception dinner tonight," Adrian called, knowing Tal would hear.

Adrian moved down the walkway, but Fischer put out a hand. "I think we should talk. In private, for once."

Neither of them seemed to feel their privacy would be intruded on by the four squad members standing just on the edge of earshot. They faced the railing, backs to the security guards.

Fischer said, "Was it wise to introduce him to Arno?"

Adrian seemed faintly surprised. "They know he's

here. And if they didn't, they'd find out soon enough. We might as well get the socially awkward part of it over."

"I was thinking of the Book of Prophecies, which your nonhuman friend thinks so little of."

"Oh?"

" 'After darkness and silence, when demons will walk in the City'? 'Tribulation, death, sorrow'? Any of these sound familiar?"

"I do know that one." Adrian grinned. "It ends, 'The triumvirate shall find the Crown.' "

"Precious helpful that is. We don't have a triumvirate, and neither does Opal, and the Sawyer Crown's been gone for centuries. I'm talking about the tribulation and death part of it."

"You've never been an optimistic man, Brandon."

" 'Darkness and silence'—the communications black-out with Opal, that ends today. 'Demons walking the city.' " He pointed to Tal's figure down below, heading toward the arched bridge of St. Kit's. "Mark my words, something bad is coming. And I'll bet the Lord Cardinal knows the Book better than you or I."

Adrian hesitated. "Have you heard any speculation from the Opal delegates as to why we named Baret System as our rendezvous?"

Fischer was taken aback. "What does that have to do with the subject? Is there any reason to believe we won't be welcome at Baret Two? I thought it was a fairly peaceable planet."

"Of course. I was just wondering if you'd heard anything."

Fischer looked at what he still saw as a face too young and vulnerable. The older he got, the more Adrian appeared to be a twelve-year-old decked out in grownup's clothing. Adrian returned the gaze with one of open innocence.

"You look the way you looked when you convinced Bryan Veritie to give you his place in the 540 tournament."

Adrian burst out laughing, one of his rare all-the-way-through laughs that transformed his face like a halo. Below them, near the stairs, two young women of the court walked with two highly dressed spaniels whose fur appeared to be dyed green. The young lady in front wore a spangled headdress and sheer veil that swayed with her body; the young lady behind kept trying to gather her patterned skirt away from her spaniel's footsteps. She tripped and looked around quickly to see if anyone had seen her.

She did not look up toward Adrian, who was watching with deep appreciation. He sighed happily. "You know, Brandon, when I'm married, I'm going to give up this dallying with other women. Give it up totally, I mean—a firm break. After all, I owe a certain responsibility to my wife. She'll be leaving all her friends behind, and we wouldn't want her to feel unwelcome." He spoke with every evidence of sincerity.

"Of course," Fischer agreed.

"I mean it! Never, ever again." The light voices of the two women fluted up from below as they argued, without rancor, in the kind of practiced rhythm that belongs to old friends. Gold hair showed beneath the hat of the girl who'd tripped. "Or certainly not for a very long time," Adrian amended.

The ladies vanished around a curve of trees. "And I'll be very discreet if I do," he added softly.

Busy watching the two young ladies, neither Adrian nor Fisher noticed Tal's figure in the distance, as it veered off the pathway to disappear under St. Kit's bridge.

"God, I'm glad it's you," said Spider, his shadow separating abruptly from the darkness of the archway. "I'm not dressed for court level. I keep thinking people are staring at me.

Tal shrugged. "If anybody stops you, just show the pass."

"Some of these guardpost types aren't above taking your pass and beating you up to kill time," said Spider, "especially if you're just a corporal in Inventory hanging around where you shouldn't be."

"Even now? Adrian will be interested in that. He's been trying to clean up the City Guard for two years now." Tal leaned against a damp wall. "Could we speed this along, Spider? We're partially visible from that look-out over the river."

Spider drew back into the shadow again. "There are two citycops on beat up there somewhere. What'll they think if they see us?"

"I imagine they'll think we're having sex."

"Are you out of your mind?" Spider disappeared farther into the darkness. "Sodomy's a death offense!"

"They aren't as picky about these tribal taboos on court level, Spider. I suspect they have an entirely different set of taboos. Relax. . . . How's your mother?"

"Fine." Spider did not reemerge.

"And how are my private messages to Baret Station?"

Spider sighed and reached into his breeches pocket. "One positive response." He handed over the link replies. "In case anything comes of it, you should know I had to forge the duty officer's com-signature. A sweet job, he'll never even realize it himself, but if they ever verify these . . . I mean, you said you'd take care of any problems that arose if I used my initiative. . . . Are you listening to me?"

Tal was shuffling rapidly through the messages. "Was the response from a station source, or one of the planet-side reps?"

"It was from the *Kestrel*. A visiting Republic ship in dock at Baret Station."

Tal looked up. "You didn't say it was a Republic ship."

"Well, I didn't know it was important to you. If you'd keep me better informed—"

"It will make things complicated."

"I don't see why. Adrian lets you in and out of the City whenever you want. You can slip over to Baret Station, meet this person," he pulled one corner of Tal's papers back and consulted the message, "this Cyr Vesant, and be back here in just a few hours."

Tal looked around and sat down on a boulder. His expression was distant. Spider went on, "Look, I know the Republic police want you, but you don't have to set foot on their territory. 'Cyr' is an Empire title, right? So this Vesant person's no Republican. I mean, technically, the ship's owners might be Republican, but they're a long way from home."

"Not that long."

"Sure they are. Hell, probably the ship's passengers are all Empire, and the Empire's never even heard of you." He paused uncertainly. "So you've always said."

"Spider, Adrian's intelligence was out of date. Baret System's a half-and-half."

Looking taken aback, Spider sat down, too. "That can't last."

"No. Baret One went over to the Republic twenty years ago. They probably have provocateurs on Baret Two now, trying to get it to secede from the Empire."

Spider's boulder was wet, and his pants started to transmit the dampness to his skin. He'd never imagined himself hanging around under a bridge like a damned troll, talking interstellar politics. Maybe his mother was right about bad companions. "Won't that piss the Empire off? We're not getting into a war, are we?" Shifting uncomfortably on his rock, he noted that moss was growing on the underside of the stone bridgework; typical of the nasty, messy places Tal liked to go to.

"This far from the action, the Imperial Senate doesn't care all that much. They have other things on their minds." The footsteps of two pedestrians clattered overhead. They waited till the sounds passed. "Try to grasp this, Spider: The reason the *Kestrel* is a Republic ship is because it's registered out of Baret One, a Republic planet. They have friends within hailing distance, armed friends."

"Well, I mean, still . . . what difference does it make to us? Since when do we care about politics?"

"Since I'll be alone on the *Kestrel,* we care."

Spider stared. "You're going to board the bloody ship? In the name of God, why?"

"It's a half-and-half system, Spider. The Republic will want to keep all its little chicks in one basket. That means they won't let passengers off at the station unless the station is their official destination—which it isn't for Vesant. I'll have to board the ship for a meeting."

"Forget Vesant! How important can this information be? It's not worth risking your life, is it?" When Tal didn't answer, he said, "For God's sake, you're perfectly safe on the Diamond! Isn't walking around on a Republic ship just asking for trouble?"

"I'll be wearing my lenses, Spider. But thank you for your concern."

"You're an illegal person in the Republic! Anybody can do anything to you! And they know you, Tal—"

"Not individually. I doubt if the twelve billion Republicans in this system have even heard of me . . . beyond a few in the police net, anyhow."

Spider hit the side of the bridge in frustration. "It's not fair! My safety depends on yours, you know."

"Does it?" Tal smiled.

"The City Guards are just waiting to pounce. I'd have to run for the ghosts again, and the ghosts don't want me."

"From what I hear, that's putting it mildly. Cheer up, Spider, I won't be taking any chances. Believe me, my safety is even more important to me than it is to you." He folded up the messages and slipped them into an inside pocket. Then he turned, left the darkness beneath the bridge, and began making his way up the side of the hill, leaving Spider to follow at a discreet interval.

Tal started over the bridge. It was an early spring day, designed to please, with a carefully generated series of breezes that brought the scent of wildflowers over the river. He could appreciate the aesthetics, intellectually, as well as the intricacy of planning on the part of the ancient engineers. But the lifting of the heart it was claimed to engender was beyond him, or possibly he was beyond it; biological slavery to their roots, he thought, not without contempt, glancing at the crocuses on the bank across the way.

A group of young gentlemen, well-dressed, laughing, emerged from the trees and started across the bridge from the other side. One of them had a guitar strapped to his back. Tal focused on the edge of the riverbank, a piece of body motion he had learned was useful in not provoking human males; there had been several unfortunate experiences in his past.

They met in the middle. There were five of them, and two moved to block Tal's way.

"What have we here?" called one merrily to his companions. "A Diamond in the rough, it looks like."

"Demon in the rough, I think," replied the young man with the guitar. "Don't you recognize him? It's Adrian's Outsider."

"Is that true?" asked the first speaker, a large, light-haired boy, twenty at the most. The butt-end of a pistol showed beneath his cape. "Are you a demon? They're sending them out of Hell young, aren't they?"

Tal knew this dance, the display dance of young human males as they worked themselves up to acts of violence. Tal himself did not require working up, and he always carried a Keith pistol where he could easily reach it. However, he was not supposed to be armed, and no doubt it would cause talk if he killed these five people, though his reflexes were quite capable of it. More importantly, Adrian would be bound to hear about the incident, and it would upset him.

"You hear me, demon?" said the blond-haired man.

On the other hand, the high walls of the bridge meant they were out of line-of-sight of nearly everybody. If he killed them, who would ever know?

"I believe you're mistaken," he said politely. He tried to brush past, but the aristo stood his ground. Tal heard footsteps behind him.

"I'm mistaken, am I? Who are you, then? What's your name and rank?"

The owner of the footsteps came into his peripheral vision; Spider, the idiot, no doubt feeling that a witness might keep violence to a minimum. And probably thinking, much as Tal did about Adrian, that his meal ticket was in need of protection.

"Special Officer Diamond," said Tal, "of the Sixteenth Rank, which would seem to put me ahead of anybody here. So stand aside."

"I don't want your ship-name—how stupid do you think I am? I want your family name."

"You want?" repeated Spider. "Who are you, the bloody Inboard Revenue?"

"I didn't ask you, Corporal—"

A voice rang out. "Can I assist you gentlemen?"

Adrian stood at the back end of the bridge. Tal's identity might be in doubt, but Adrian's face had been plastered up and down Mercati Boulevard ever since the wedding was announced. The five aristos stared at him, then at each other.

"No, thank you, sir," said the blond. "We were just crossing."

Tal positioned his hand beside his holster, nudging the Diamond Protector with his elbow. "They're armed!" he said under his breath. He didn't want them strolling past Adrian.

"I know. It'll be all right."

Tal, adrift, searched for some other verbal fact to offer, but there was nothing beyond the unanswerable logic he'd already given. Adrian's lips curved. "It'll be all right," he repeated gently. "It'll be all right."

Neither of them realized, but it was the very tone Adrian had heard the Diamond kennelmaster use with his beloved dogs for all of his court life. Tal slowly let his hand drift away from the pistol bulge near his thigh, but the shifting of his eyes showed he was far from reassured. At least, it showed it to Adrian. Not being Tal-scholars, the others would only see a brief movement in an impassive face.

Adrian turned his attention to them now, favoring them with one of his best smiles, and forcing himself with the discipline of habit to ignore the rush of pure, chemical pleasure this sudden drop into danger brought. Brandon Fischer had long ago impressed on him that discipline in that area was necessary if he was going to be the Protector; and that if he ever stopped being the Protector, he'd be dead.

Warily, the aristos filed past. Adrian told himself to stop enjoying the situation. As the blond brought up the rear, Adrian addressed him: "In future, you'd be wise not to wander around a strange place without an escort. Just some friendly advice; I hope you don't take offense."

"No, sir," said the blond unhappily.

They left the bridge. Tal said, " 'A strange place?' "

"They were Opalline," said Adrian. "Didn't you recognize their accents?"

"As far as I'm concerned, you all have accents."

Adrian grinned. "It would've been a major political blow if you'd killed them."

"Where do you get these ideas about me?"

The grin widened. "I could see you from the walkway, and I ordered the squad to wait down by the river path; I said I wanted to be alone for a minute, and I'd yell if anybody came. It would've considerably complicated things, you know, if they'd been witnesses."

"I wasn't going to kill anybody." Adrian continued to look at him. "At least, I was working to avoid it."

Adrian's grin faded. He said seriously, "I can't refuse to give them the run of the city. We need the same privilege on Opal."

"You're telling me to watch my back."

"Good advice at any time." Adrian turned toward Spider, who'd been trying to blend magically in with the stonework, and said heartily, "Corporal Hastings, isn't it?"

Spider started. "Yes—yes, sir." How in the name of all the powers of heaven did Adrian know his name? The main purpose of Spider's life was the avoidance of notice, particularly by people with power. A demon was bad enough—

"I've heard fine things about you."

"Thank you, sir." *Oh, God. I want to go home now. I want to go home now. I want to—*

Adrian turned to Tal. "I'll have to get back, or in three minutes the squad will be all over the bridge. Don't be late for the reception tonight—"

"Adrian, I need a station pass."

The Protector looked at Tal, who was expressionless. Adrian said, "There's a Republic ship in port there, my friend."

"Yes, I know."

Adrian studied his boots for a moment. "You wouldn't care to give me your reasons?"

"Private."

"As usual." He sighed. "As usual, I'm going to tell you to be very careful."

"I'm always careful," Tal said, in a faintly injured tone. "It's just that sometimes my priorities are somewhat exigent."

Adrian's eyes sparkled as he controlled a grin. "I'll look that word up when I get home. All right, pick up your pass in Transport. I'll tell them to have it ready for you. How long will you need?"

"Probably a few hours. But give me a full-day one, just in case."

Adrian spread his hands as though to disassociate himself from the whole risky enterprise. Personal physical danger was one thing, but this was chancy on quite a different level, and he took no pleasure from it. "If you're arrested, *please* tell them we had no idea who you were."

Tal's lips quirked. "Of course, Adrian."

"And don't leave till after the reception dinner."

"Whatever you say, Adrian."

Adrian rolled his eyes, turned, and strode off the bridge. Spider's heartrate started to return to normal. "Oh, lord," he said. "The fucking Protector." He turned at once to Tal. "What did you *tell* him about me?"

"Absolutely nothing."

"He *said*—"

"He was just showing off his private news sources. A symptom of youth. I'm sure it will pass."

They were off the bridge now, and making their way along the river path. A row of ducks sailed past. "And what about the other one? The delight from Opal. He called me 'Corporal.' "

"They saw your insignia. Let's not be any more paranoid than the situation warrants."

"But my collar was folded over it. Are you listening to me? Tal!"

Another row of ducks, this time waddling out from the trees, was aiming for the water's edge. Their direction crossed the pathway. "Hold on a minute," said Spider, but Tal ignored him. Ducklings scattered as he strode ahead. Spider clicked his tongue. "Now look, you've scared them."

They walked a moment in silence, and Spider pondered the way his life seemed to get more complicated each time his salary went up. Finally he said, subdued, "A Republic ship. Jesus, Tal, sometimes I think you do these things just to make me nervous."

"Don't flatter yourself."

Chapter 3

*There is nothing like the education of a woman of
quality as that of a prince. They are taught to dance
and the exterior part of what is called good breeding, which if they attain they are extraordinary
creatures of their kind, and have all the accomplishments required by their directors. The same
characters are formed by the same lessons, which
inclines me to think (if I dare say it) that nature has
not placed us in an inferior rank to men, no more
than the females of other animals, where we see no
distinction of capacity, though I am persuaded if
there was a commonwealth of rational horses (as
Doctor Swift has supposed) it would be an established maxim amongst them that a mare could not
be taught to pace.*

LADY MARY WORTLEY MONTAGU

Women, like princes, find few real friends.

GEORGE, LORD LYTTELTON

Pain. The universe of pain has a very small diameter. Its
population is one and its limits extend about a meter beyond one's body; outside that boundary is gray space, incomprehensible not through lack of knowledge but
through lack of caring.

Iolanthe knew this universe so well, was so familiar
with its depth and texture, so intimate a dweller in it, that
she never gave it a questioning thought. Her first migraine, at the age of ten, had come without warning. "The
light has a halo," she'd said, pointing to the chief candle
on the chandelier in the dining room.

Her older cousin James had cocked a head at her, not
kindly, but not mocking either. "You'll have to get your

eyes checked, cousin. Maybe you need spectacles. Big, thick, black ones with two-inch glass in 'em—"

"They'll never give me glasses," the ten-year-old Io answered primly, satisfied with her beauty, of which she'd heard so much, and aware of its market value, of which she'd heard even more. She'd go blind before her parents would fit her out with spectacles.

"The candles aren't lit," James had said gently.

She blinked toward the beautiful starburst halo, startled. Even with her eyes shut, the image remained steady. She felt a thrill of alarm. "Maybe it's a vision from heaven," she'd said uncertainly, for they were doing the lives of the saints in the Pelagia schoolroom that year. "They're sent as gifts to very holy people, you know."

"With your temper?" James inquired dryly. "I wouldn't count on it."

Two hours later she'd been stretched on her bed, moaning. "Make it go away," she told her father, who could make plush puppies and silk hats and drawing boards with pastel chalk appear. He could bring in tutors and send them away with a wave of his hand. Surely he could make a doctor appear who would take away this world-filling pain.

And he did make doctors appear, but their foul potions only made her feel worse. She threw up twice, and her father sent the doctors home. As the hours went by, she still railed at him: "Make it go away!" Baby," he said, smoothing her long dark hair, "I'm sorry." Why are you being mean to me," she cried, her eyes wet, her voice bewildered. It was not that she'd never be denied before; but it had always been understood that, if her parents had decreed it, she *could* have had anything.

That migraine lasted two days, and years later Io still considered those days the core of her education, not only in pain but in the limits of reality.

Now, at the age of seventeen, Iolanthe knew her migraines as she would know a twin sister. When the first warnings came, she notified her friends and tutors she would be unavailable for two or three days, and retired to her darkened bedchamber to ride out the pain. Her parents made no objection, seemingly aware that exposing potential suitors to an ill, frowning, pale daughter with no charm or conversation would not be in their best interests. The illness only came on her five or six times a year, and the rest of the time she was all they could hope for, and all that luck, instruction, and fine clothes could make her: A beauty just reaching her bloom; midnight hair, fair skin, improbable violet eyes. Bravos from the best families in the *City of Opal* sought out every excuse possible to visit the Pelagia apartments. Io's male cousins found themselves very popular among their agemates. Io's parents discovered dinner invitations raining down on them. And Io herself, though she would have preferred a dark knight with an air of mystery to present himself at a ball and ask—no, *insist*—on her hand—Io knew her duty. The most boring and unattractive of Opal's aristos could appear at the Pelagia home and receive a smile from Iolanthe that was proper to the millimeter. So long as she wasn't ill.

But stress could bring on her twin sister. Iolanthe lay in the darkness of her room now, thinking that, regardless of her parents' stated opinion, a betrothal was a stressful situation. An arranged marriage with a man one has never seen was a nerveracking situation. And an engagement that entailed leaving the *City of Opal* forever and marrying the leader of the rival, much-disapproved *City of Diamond,* was a situation that would send even a girl of normal health to her bed.

And when the lights in the dining room had begun to show halos, that's where Iolanthe had gone.

From outside she could hear the sounds of celebration, the cheerful talk and laughter from the women her mother had invited to rejoice with the Pelagia women this fine afternoon. The sounds were outside her universe, however. They emanated from the gray space beyond the pain, and as such, they were irrelevant to her life.

Io changed position on her bed, moving carefully to avoid any increase in the size of the monster that fed on her head. A crack of light appeared in the doorway to her room. She blinked at the silhouetted shape there: her Aunt Bella.

"Iolanthy, darling," said her aunt, her stocky shape peering in uncertainly. "My, it's dark in here." She opened the door wider and stepped inside. "No wonder you've got a headache, lying in the dark when everybody else is having a good time. You should go out and join the party."

Io was in too much agony to answer, but if she'd possessed a gun and the strength to raise it, Aunt Bella would have died then and there. Unaware of the effect she was having on the victim of her charitable advice, Aunt Bella waited a moment for a reply, then sighed. "Some people are too stubborn for their own good," she intoned, and shut the door.

It had been a bad week for Io, and she would have cherished her anger at this sanctimonious advice if she'd had the capacity for actual thought or feeling, but already Aunt Bella's image was receding into the gray space. Iolanthe could only file her remarks away for later resentment. Filed away with her mother, who didn't care whom her daughter married, and her father, who she always thought *would* have cared, and the unknown Protector of the *City of Diamond,* whoever was holding that post this year. Her future husband. Whatever his cursed name might be.

But that was for later. When it was over and she was reborn into real life. For now, it was all gray space. And pain.

"Who the hell is Iolanthe Pelagia?" William Stockton inquired. He pushed his dark hair off his forehead and adjusted his uniform jacket, trying to look as dignified as possible, which was difficult under the circumstances.

The duty sergeant gave him a look of bored patience. "Do I know? Do I care? Some aristo brat, by the name. Needs her hand held till they palm her off on some sucker of her own class. Congratulations." He spat, clearly not for the first time, into a small transparent cup on his desk.

Will averted his eyes from the cup and looked down at the official duty sheet. "You will report to Residence A79 at 12:00, and present yourself as chief bodyguard to the Lady Iolanthe Pelagia. Further orders will be given to you there." Nothing like being terse. You'd think after four years in the City Guard with a record nobody his age could match—nobody from Sangaree Section, anyway—they'd give him something with a little responsibility, a little status. You'd think they'd throw him a fucking crumb—

He turned over the sheet and froze. He looked up at the duty sergeant. "It's got the Ecclesiastical Council imprimatur on it."

"So?"

"I'm not in the EPs. I'm just a City Guard." He swallowed. Responsibility and status were overrated. "Why would they send me on a council assignment?"

"I told you everything I heard, sweetheart. It's got your name on it, right? Somebody asked for you."

Will's dark eyes were wary. "Who would ask for me?"

"The Lord Cardinal asked for you, asshole. It came to him in a vision while he was taking a dump. I keep telling you, I don't know. Are we speaking the same language?"

Will refolded the page and slipped it into his outer jacket pocket. His fingers felt cold. He turned and stepped down from the platform beside the duty sergeant's desk.

"Congrats," said the sergeant.

"Yeah, thanks a whole lot."

"Not for this," said the sergeant. "Turn around."

Will turned.

"For *this*," the sergeant said, and he tossed something flat and shiny through the air. Will raised a hand and caught it.

It was a gold First Sergeant's bar. He blinked down at it, not understanding. Nobody from Sangaree was ever promoted past Third, and not many got that far. He met the duty sergeant's eyes.

The man grinned. "You impressed hell out of *somebody,* sweetie."

Will stood there a minute. His thoughts seemed to be extraordinarily slow. "It's a mistake," he said finally. "They'll straighten it out in time."

"Right," the duty sergeant agreed. "Better haul, Stockton. You have to be on A deck by twelve hundred."

Will's hand went involuntarily to his jacket pocket and he heard the faint crackle of paper. He turned and left.

* * *

Instead of taking the train straight to A level, he boarded one at Seacum Street Station going in the opposite direction. Street after street, level upon level flashed by; he sat with his long legs stretched out in the aisle, watching. Outside the windows, the clean lines of middle-class shops began to look less well-maintained. Women appeared, walking freely, working in dirty shop windows beside the men, and the closed chairs of the upper decks vanished. At Tanamonde Street he stepped out, checking the time as he did.

Here the buying and selling spilled over into the streets and walkways, where bins of used clothing and wrapped leaves of home-cured smokeless blocked the way for pedestrians. Will stripped off his red uniform jacket and rolled it under one arm. At the foot of the third Tanamonde walkway he turned into an entrance beside a shop-window so unaccustomed to cleaning it was impossible to see inside. A tattered sign taped to the window could just be made out: "Stretch's Chicken Savoy."

Willie stepped into the dark. The place was empty. He walked over to the ruddy, balding man wiping the counter and waited. The man looked up.

"Willie!" He grinned, showing a handful of rotting teeth. "Been a while, now." The balding man spoke in pure Sangaree dialect, a combination of traditional accent and phrasing and a half-deliberate slurring of words that non-Sangaree dwellers claimed to find too hard to follow.

"Too long, Sam." He took one of the stools. "You seen my gorgeous, intelligent kid sister?"

"Nah, but I seen Bernie. She went to Rafael's to order me some supplies."

"Shit. She gonna be long? I'm workin' to a schedule."

"You were workin' to a schedule when you were five. Want me to tell her you were here?"

Willie considered. "Your link-station still up?"

"What else've I got that sets me apart from every other four-star restaurant?"

Willie grinned and went into the back, walking past the crates that hid the restrooms and the link. The compartment he'd grown up in with his sister had no link, and he knew it would please Bernie to have somebody deliver a message to her, as though she were some fine lady on the letterdecks. It'd cost him a good percent, but he wanted to minimize her anger when she found out what he had to say.

"This is for Bernadette Stockton, Eight Below Z, Compartment 32981." He dropped the Sangaree speech and spoke in the clear, letterdeck accents he and Bernie had forced themselves to use at home. "Uh, Bern, this is Willie. I just got an assignment that's going to keep me away from the neighborhood for a while. Nothing dangerous, but I'm going to have to miss some wedding rehearsals." He winced, imagining her reaction when she heard *that.* "Uh, I don't know when I'll be able to get away from this thing. Please tell Jack I'm sorry, too. Take care of yourself and, I guess, good-bye ... Uh, from your loving brother, who wouldn't miss any rehearsals unless he had to. End of message." He felt around in his pockets for some dollar coins. "Link, how much was that? Write it out in nice script."

"Twelve-fifty," said the link-station.

This was more than twice what he'd anticipated. He had enough to cover it, barely, but— "Piracy," he muttered.

"It's justified by maintenance costs," said the link primly. "And considering that most of the link-stations in this neighborhood are too damaged to be fully operational—"

"Fine," said Will, as he dropped in another handful of coins. You didn't find links extending credit in this neighborhood either.

He walked out past the crates and back to the counter. "Your link's a little mouthy," he said.

"Ain't mine, I just rent it." Sam looked at Will speculatively. "Carter was in, this morning."

"In here?"

Sam nodded. "Bernie was in the back. He wanted to talk to her. I had to call the guys to get him out."

"He's got nothing to say to her. She's engaged to somebody else."

"I told 'im. He didn't wanna hear it. Figured I mention it to you, Willie. Bern might not."

"Damn, I don't have time to visit him, Sam; I got to be out of here in fifteen minutes. Look, you'll keep an eye on her, won't you? I'll give you a number you can call to reach me, if you have to." He ripped a strip off the bottom of his order and wrote the number of the City Guard Station at Seacum Street. "They can find me here, but you have to tell them it's an emergency."

Sam nodded. He accepted the paper with a solemn expression. Everybody knew Willie was in the Guard these days, but this was the first time he'd officially acknowledged it. Sam hesitated, then met Willie's eyes. "No disgrace bein' in the red jackets, son," and then he stopped short, sensing at once that Willie didn't want to hear it. Sam said, "I wish Carter'd join up, or do *something*. He's a waste of space; it's a shame that good people go off to work the radiation levels while that asshole keeps gettin' missed. It's the grace of God that Bernie finally sees through him, weasel that he is."

Willie agreed that this was so. He said, "You'll watch her good for me, Sam, won't you?"

"I swear." Sam folded the paper with exaggerated care and put it in his apron pocket. Willie smiled, a little sadly; they clasped hands for a minute, then he turned and wandered out into the day lights of Sangaree. When he reached the train, he pulled the red jacket back over his long arms, and went to go where nobody ever called him Willie.

"A disgraceful affair, but no more than what we expected." Lord Cardinal Arno handed his leather case to his assistant, Hartley Quince, who accepted it without comment. "Men and women dining together, a liberal use of liquor—" He waved aside the functionary who would have guided him toward a covered chair. "Thank you, Luke, we'll walk."

Hartley Quince fell in beside him, still carrying the case. "Actually, sir, I must admit that the liquor consumed at the average gatherings of Opal males far exceeds that of Adrian's table."

"Really? Another reason to give thanks that I never attend those affairs."

Quince smiled. "Opal bravos are not at their best when intoxicated."

"They're not at their best when sober. You know, I'm

sorry I keep sending you off to these tedious functions in my place, Hartley. You've been a saint about it."

"Oh, I don't mind, sir."

Arno's mind drifted back to the complaints at hand. "Not that one enjoys sharing a table with a murderer and a demon, but you'll find, Hartley, that I always go the extra distance for the sake of peace."

"I know that, sir," said Hartley, without a trace of irony. "I recollect the demon, but who was the murderer?"

"My boy! You don't expect that Saul Veritie died of natural causes, do you?"

Hartley said slowly, "I understood it was a sickness that came in through a trade stop."

"And the Diamond Protector just happened to be extravulnerable? Really, now. And I suppose his cousins and nephews all died of bad colds at the same time."

"They seem fairly open about there being an uprising after Saul's death. My information—"

"I know you always seem to acquire these remarkable sources, Hartley, but in this case you've only got to use your head to see what happened. The Mercati boy wormed his way into Saul's affections—bearing in mind that the Mercatis have always started to rot, morally, at a young age—and then, as soon as he felt old enough to get away with it ..."

"I see. Of course, sir, that must be what happened." Hartley's voice was toneless. He pressed for the lift that would take them off the admin decks and down to Residential. "I trust the lady Iolanthe hasn't heard any rumors regarding her husband's character. It would explain her unhappy humor."

"I can't imagine anyone would be fool enough to tell her." Arno frowned. "I'm sure it's just a bout of nerves. Her mother's a fine woman in her way, but she tends to the dramatic. Iolanthe will be all right."

"I'm glad to hear it, sir. Seventeen-year-old girls are generally ... unreliable in their duties." They entered the lift.

"Oh, she's not unintelligent, for a female, and she's a good, obedient girl. A bit high-spirited at times, but that's all to the good for what we're asking her to do. Believe me, Hartley. I was her confessor for eight months."

"A touch of spiritual pressure?"

Arno glanced sharply at his assistant, and met clear, open brown eyes. He relaxed, smiling. "Nothing one would object to."

"Of course not, sir."

"And we do need her help very much."

"Yes, sir."

"Those remarkable sources you have are forthcoming enough with information, but not with the strategy behind the information."

Hartley made a sound that might be taken for assent.

"It's all very well to learn that Adrian pressured the Diamond council to change the trading schedule. It's all very well to know he moved the rendezvous to Baret System. But in God's name, why? What's in Baret System but two fairly forgettable planets? Why go to all that trouble?"

Hartley was silent.

"Perhaps you don't feel that it's important to get the answer to these questions. Perhaps you think it's not very significant?"

"Oh, no, sir." The lift opened and Hartley gazed thoughtfully out at the cultivated trees and decorated streets of Opal Residential. "I do want to know why." He turned to blink up at Arno, his eyes half-closed against he strong lights. "Quite definitely, I want to know why."

They reached the Pelagia suite of apartments within a quarter of an hour. "My Lord Cardinal," said Vivian Pelagia, curtsying deeply as she admitted them herself. Vivian always did get carried away, Arno reflected; but one could hardly object, as her flattery was so well-delivered. Iolanthe's mother was not quite forty, undeniably pretty, wearing an electric blue gown that would have been appropriate on a girl of her daughter's age but which she could, just, get away with.

"My assistant," said Arno, presenting Hartley Quince.

Arno hoped that Vivian was unaware of how her face lit up when she took in Hartley's perfect features.

"Officer Quince," said Hartley, with the smile of a trained killer.

"Officer," she breathed. She gave him her hand, and

actually took an unconscious step back when he kissed it, as though she'd stepped too close to explosive material.

Arno cleared his throat. It wasn't Hartley's fault, the boy didn't encourage them, but . . .

Hartley let go of her hand. He kept his eyes locked on hers, though, until she took another step back and Arno said, "I hope Iolanthe's well?"

"Yes," said Vivian, flushing slightly as she shifted her gaze to him. "Er, of course." She paused then, with the uncertain air of one who hopes the question will be repeated. Arno sighed.

"Iolanthe. Perhaps I should go in and speak with her?"

"Oh, yes. I told her you were coming. Would you like any refreshment before we go in?"

She gestured toward a sideboard, where a girl in yellow and white, evidently one of the household slaves, was standing by a selection of cold meats and breads. "Thank you, I'm not hungry. You know, I don't think, my daughter, that you should come with me; I believe it would be better if I spoke to the child alone."

She blinked. "But, my Lord Cardinal, she's been in a stubborn mood for days now. Her father won't do anything, he won't even come home and talk to her. I don't think you'll get far with Io unless I'm there to—"

"My dear." He forced a smile. It did not seem to affect her the way Hartley's had. "I'm sure that as a mother, you're quite properly concerned. But I think that as her confessor, we should be alone."

That ought to be enough for any church-going woman, he thought. She frowned. "There's nothing Iolanthe can say to you that I, as her mother, shouldn't know as well."

Arno prided himself on patience in dealing with the laity. "Officer Quince, perhaps you could stay out here with Lady Pelagia and fill her in on some of the customs of the City of Diamond."

"I would be happy to, sir."

"Well, I suppose that would be all right," admitted Vivian, dropping her maternal concern like a piece of fruit that had been kept a few days too long. "You'll let me know, Lord Cardinal, if you want anything."

"Of course." He hoped Hartley could deal with the situation. Naturally, the boy was essentially chaste, or he

wouldn't have asked to take deacon's orders; such encounters must be tedious for him. *The trouble is that he's
just too obliging,* thought Arno. *I take advantage of him.*

Behind him, he heard Hartley's voice saying, "Would
you care to sit, my lady? This may take some time."

The Cardinal knocked on Iolanthe's door.

Iolanthe was lying in the dark, feeling miserable. Her
headache had passed two days ago, but a bad medical history presented such a handy excuse for staying away from
people. Not that half her relations didn't think she made
up the headaches to begin with; she might as well use the
deceit for once, since they charged her with it anyway.

There was a knock on the door; a heavy, authoritative
knock, not her mother's impatient series of raps, designed
to irritate. Oh, lord. Io sat up in bed, aware of her wrinkled clothes and her uncombed hair hanging halfway
down her back. She'd thought the Cardinal wasn't coming till four.

Another knock. She cast a desperate glance toward the
vanity, but there was no time to do anything. She stood
up, smoothed her dress, and opened the door.

"May I come in, child?" asked the Cardinal, coming in
as he did so.

She curtsied and moved aside. "Forgive me, Lord Cardinal, I had a ... I wasn't feeling well." After all, one
couldn't lie to a priest.

"You do look a little pale. Although it's hard to tell in
this light."

"Oh, I'm sorry! Just a minute—" She raised the dimmers and watched Arno's face spring into full eagle
prominence.

"There we are," he said, smiling. "Not so bad, after all.
That dress becomes you. I wonder if you have a chair for
an old man?"

"Certainly, Lord Cardinal." She pulled out the chair by
her carved wooden desk, laden with stacks of books assigned by her now-unemployed tutors. A frieze of walnut
ran around the desk's borders, showing the loading of the
Three Cities in the days of Adrian Sawyer: a line of
Curosa worker-beasts, carrying materials on their backs;
Adrian Sawyer leading a family into the hatch of a ship;

one of the Curosa themselves, preaching the Story of Life. It was beautiful carving work.

No doubt they wouldn't let her take it off the City of Opal.

"What a frown, my dear," said Arno. "I hope your headache isn't too bad?"

"No, really, Lord Cardinal; I'm much better."

"I'm glad to hear it. Frowns and young ladies do not go together. Can I have a smile from you instead?"

Iolanthe forced a smile, wondering why no request ever seemed as humiliating as that one always did.

"There!" said Arno, evidently pleased at having lightened the atmosphere. "Now, no more 'Lord Cardinals' from you, my dear; I want to speak as your confessor."

"Yes, Father," she said obediently.

"Tell me, what are your feelings about this match?"

"My feelings?" Her voice was wary.

"What do you think of it?"

"It's a great opportunity for the family," she said carefully.

"No doubt. But you'll be leaving all your friends, going to a new place, marrying someone you've never met . . . this must be on your mind."

"The thoughts had occurred to me, Father."

"It's only natural that they should. You know, Iolanthe, all young ladies worry about what marriage will bring, and it's proper for them to do so; modesty prompts it, and natural feminine fears."

At times like this Iolanthe wondered what unmarried clergymen knew about "natural feminine fears," but she had to acknowledge that there was a lot she didn't understand. "Yes, Father," she said. This was a phrase she knew could get one's boat safely through whole vast seas of lecturing. No one, fortunately, ever seemed to want to hear more from her than the affirmative. Of course that "what are your feelings" question had been a bit alarming; but one hoped it had been an aberration, and that the conversation would soon return to a normal pattern.

"I was wondering, my dear, if you'd heard anything about your future husband."

Io had the expression of a startled forest animal. "Heard anything?"

"Anything that disturbed you, I mean. Your mother's worried about you, you know."

"*Oh.* Lord Cardinal—Father—I've heard very little about him at all, really. Just that he's the new Diamond Protector. Which I'm sure is a great opportunity for me, and I should be very grateful."

This last came out so like a rote lesson that the Lord Cardinal chuckled. He recited, as though it were the other half of a textbook exercise, "And you'll have lots of fine dresses and jewels. . . . I'm sure they told you that, too."

She looked up, startled. "They did."

"Well, of course they would. They don't want you to have hysterics on the way over."

Io was thrown completely off-stride by this sudden acknowledgment of reality. Even so, it was bracing; like having layers of cotton wool unwound from one's soul and finding it healthy and sane after all. She was aware of a feeling of gratitude toward the Cardinal, which worried her.

"Do you want to go?" he asked.

"I know my duty to my family," she said, stepping delicately around the chasm of honesty which had suddenly opened up between them. "A life of service to the City is one of the highest things anyone could aspire to."

A dangerous glint of humor had reached the Cardinal's eyes. She'd never even known he possessed the quality. "*Beautifully* spoken, dear Iolanthe. It pleases me to hear you say so. You're certainly not the kind of young lady who just blurts out whatever is on her mind, are you?"

She was uncomfortably silent.

He chuckled again. "I'm not unhappy with you, dear, I promise. In fact, I'd like to talk with you seriously for a moment."

She looked up at him. It was becoming clear now that he had something on his mind, and she was only incidental to it; that was reassuring. She could still retrieve the conversation. The role of listener was one she knew how to play. "Please go ahead, Father."

He sighed as though he regretted something on her behalf. "There are many lessons still ahead of you, but you're a bright young lady, Iolanthe. I've seen the reports of your tutors; you mastered all your subjects in record time. Tell me, which was your favorite?"

"Paperfolding," said Io, whose favorite had been history. Although the boys' books her brothers had studied from had been much more interesting than her own in that area.

"A becoming accomplishment," agreed the Lord Cardinal. "In your other lessons, however, you no doubt learned a little about the City of Diamond—enough to make you nervous perhaps, yet not enough to give you the security, at least, of knowledge?"

Was she actually going to learn something? She clasped her hands modestly and tried not to look too eager.

He said, "Let me tell you about the City you're going to. You're going to have to get used to all sorts of things; men and women dining at the same table; church services of a rather heretical nature—all sorts of unnaturalness. I know a level-headed girl like you can learn to handle these things, and I want you to know, child, that I'll see there's always a proper Opal priest in our group there to act as your confessor. You won't be alone."

"Thank you, Father."

"As to your husband." The Cardinal coughed. "Of course, his reputation may not be the best, but you have to make allowances for the prejudices of distance. They tell me he's quite popular on the Diamond. In any case, there is no way he could fail to be charmed by your lovely self, dear, and I don't mean that as some meaningless compliment."

He saw that he had her complete attention. "You're a fine, loyal young lady, and I know I can count on you. If there's anything that happens to come up that you think I ought to know about—personal, political, anything at all—I want you to get in touch with me immediately."

It all became clear. Her eyes lit up as every melodrama she'd ever read appeared before her and then paled by comparison. She barely noticed when the Cardinal took her hands between his own two huge palms, the band of his ring digging into her. "I can depend on you, can't I?"

"Oh, of *course,* Lord Cardinal!"

He sat back and sighed. "I really never doubted it. Listen, my dear, I'm going to leave my assistant here today; you'll see him on the Diamond often enough, and he can spend the next few days with you filling you in on Diamond custom. He's the one I want you to go to with any messages you may have for me. You can trust him, Iolanthe; he's a fine young man, of unquestionable character, and absolutely discreet."

She nodded. He went on, "Now, I won't bore you with affairs of state, and Officer Quince will be giving you plenty of details anyway. But I do want you to remember that anything you hear about Baret Two will be significant."

She looked blank. "What's baret-too?"

"My dear, it's our next trade stop. We're in Baret System now." He smiled. "I see that Officer Quince will have a great deal to go over with you. Never mind; I know you've always done well in your tutoring, and at least now your keenness will be better applied."

He stood up, and Io followed suit. "I'll be leaving you now to the care of . . . hmm, hasn't your bodyguard arrived yet?"

"My what?"

"Obviously not. I'd understood he was coming today. You're on your way to being a great lady now, Iolanthe; you'll have to get used to these things." He extended his hand for her to kiss.

At the door, he paused. "But, child, I never got your answer about the marriage. Do you want to go?"

"Yes, Lord Cardinal, I do."

"There, I knew your mother had the wrong end of the stick. Gets a bit confused sometimes, doesn't she? Fond though she is of you. Sometimes a friend can see these things better."

And he left, having gifted her with so many things to think about that it was almost like having indigestion. Mechanically, she combed her hair, pinned it back, and tied a dignified, tail-cut jacket over her long dress. She looked at herself in the mirror and started to laugh. This new way of seeing things certainly made her family's betrayals dwindle in the mind. Already her parents seemed like tiny figures on some platform a long distance away.

Until she opened the door to the sitting room, ten minutes later, and found her mother sitting with a rather distastefully beautiful young man, just her mother's type, who had to be Officer Quince. They were sitting far closer together than convention allowed, and none of the household slaves seemed to be in the room, which could only mean they'd been dismissed. For a moment Io felt a reflexive stirring of rage, then banked it. What did she care, anyway?

"Officer Quince," she addressed him, reminding herself that although she was seventeen and female, she was the star of the piece. "The Lord Cardinal said you had some information to give me?"

Hartley Quince rose, sketched a bow that the bravos who'd been haunting the Pelagia residence for the past two years would have killed for, and came up with a gorgeous smile. *Wasted on me,* she thought. Finding him with her mother had permanently destroyed any allure he might have had, even if she'd been in a mood to look kindly on any grown man this pretty.

But she was gratified by the way he dropped her mother's hand and gave her his full attention.

She was less gratified two days later, head stuffed full of ridiculous Diamond customs; suggestions for dinner conversation, indeed! A woman shouldn't have to make such an effort over her meals, that was the whole point of segregated dining. "It's far easier than it would be if you were marrying outside the Three Cities," Officer Quince had said, but what of it? Whoever married outside the Cities?

And then there were the alarming statements that Quince would come out with, *sans* preparation, offering them like a cold dish for lunch: "Of course, you know about the demon," he'd said yesterday.

"I beg your pardon?"

"Adrian keeps a demon on his personal staff. You'll have to remember to be polite to him; he'll probably be seated near you at state dinners."

Iolanthe actually put out an arm to the back of a chair to steady herself. "Demons," she said finally, "are in books. I mean, I'm sure they exist, but—you don't *see* them, Officer Quince. You don't have dinner with them!"

Quince smiled lazily. "Speak for yourself, my dear

lady. I've *had* dinner with this one, actually. He's not a great talker, but I'm sure you can find something to say between the soup and the fish."

She sat down, at a complete loss as to where to begin seeking common reality. Quince finally took pity. "My lady, it's like this. Tal Diamond is an Outsider whom Adrian picked up at a trade stop. He's a product of engineered Elaphite/Human mating, an illegal being in the Republic and Empire. Under sentence of death, at least if Republic authorities discover him—you can see why he'd find life in the Cities more comfortable."

Iolanthe blinked, but she was taking it in; her first remark was to the point. "Why does that make him a demon?"

Quince answered as one would answer a mathematical query. "Because he's a soulless being with no sense of right or wrong. Because he has eyes that are yellow or gray, as classical demons should. Because no true companionship can exist with him, as with any creature of hell." He smiled again. "Because the Lord Cardinal says so."

"I don't understand why he's under sentence of death from the Outside."

Quince said patiently, "Because Elaphite/Human mating is forbidden. Marriage is allowed, but never children."

"Why?"

"Because it produces demons. Haven't you been listening? They don't call them demons, they call them sociopaths, but it comes to the same thing. 'Children who never learn to socialize properly.' I've been reading up on the subject—what a lot of words Outsiders take to get to the point."

She hesitated, not sure she wanted to know. "What do Outsiders mean by not socializing properly?"

He smiled charmingly. "One six-year-old drowned another child who'd taken a stuffed horse from him. Another pushed a female caretaker into a compacter in order to steal her wallet and run away. Acquisitive little buggers, aren't they? He was actually on another planet when they found him, I gather. And that was just in the first half-dozen demons who were born before the laws went into effect. In fact, there are many other stories—"

She swallowed, hoping she didn't look pale, and tried to rally. "He's not a child, though. How old is he?"

"Ah, there you have me. There are four things all Apheans—that's what they call these Elaphite/Human products, by the way—have in common. Genius IQs, the inability to socialize normally, and a theoretical lifespan that goes on for miles. This one seems about your age; but who knows?"

Iolanthe looked at him with forced coolness; she was nothing if not thorough in her scholarship. "That's three things. You said four."

"So I did. The fourth thing is that none of them ever manages to turn theory into practice in the lifespan department. Every one of the little criminals listed in my research managed to get executed by the state or just plain killed by some outraged person before their fortieth birthday—a fair number while still in adolescence, in fact. Makes you wonder what they were like as toddlers, doesn't it? Talk about hiding the kitchen knives."

Io had a sudden, horrifying thought. "You're not making all this up, are you?"

He seemed amused rather than offended. "My lady, may I ask what prompts this paranoia?"

"Well, you don't seem very ... *serious* about this. You're telling me about a creature of hell."

"Oh, a bit of hell here, a bit of hell there." He shrugged cheerfully. "One gets used to it." This left her feeling more alarmed than ever, and it must have showed, because he chuckled and said, "It's just my way, lady. Pay it no mind."

To cover her embarrassment, she said, "Well, why should we be troubled by a demon anyway, even if the Diamond Protector did invite him? Why doesn't the Lord Cardinal notify the Empire, or somebody, at the next stop to come and take him away?"

"Invite Outside troops onto Three Cities territory? Are you out of your mind? My dear lady—"

There had followed a long discourse on the inadvisability of setting any precedents that gave over sovereign power, especially for so petty a reason as the wish to annoy Adrian by throwing out his demon. Annoying Adrian had not been one of Iolanthe's aims at all; she'd been thinking solely from a moral point of view. The weather of adulthood was going to be choppy indeed if Hartley Quince was anything to judge by.

Well, at least her bodyguard had finally shown up, this very morning, with an order currently dated; so he wasn't, technically, late. Sergeant William Stockton, said his ID; City Guard. "Sorry if you were expecting me earlier, my lady. I was reassigned here pretty suddenly. Maybe they had somebody else in mind, and it didn't work out." Io held out her hand so she could practice being gracious with him. Tall, dark, and striking, if not classically handsome—this was far better than Hartley Quince, who was like extra-sweetened tea in a china cup. And here the heroic-looking fellow was, escorting her to some other man, like the stuff of legend. If this was a book, she and the sergeant would fall irrevocably in love and be doomed together to some awful fate.

"Mind if I look over your quarters, m'lady?" The prosaic request made her grin suddenly. So much for Tristan and Iseult.

"Please feel free, Sergeant. Someone will be coming to tutor me in a few minutes, though—that won't be a problem, will it?"

"No," he said abstractedly, opening the door to her bedroom and stepping inside. "Just go on with everything as though I'm not here."

Even with her sheltered life, Io knew that this would not be quite possible. However, they could pretend. At ten o'clock she admitted Hartley Quince for their daily lesson, wondering when her mother would sweep in with hospitable suggestions for the officer's comfort. Fortunately it took Vivian at least two hours each morning to get her hair put up to her satisfaction; without that, these sessions would not have been productive at all. "Good morning, Officer Quince," Iolanthe said firmly, following her new instructions to initiate greetings.

Hartley Quince grinned, an expression of complicity that reminded her of how long it had taken to get over being silent until she was addressed. It was a wicked grin, and Io had to force herself to resist it. Her mother and

Aunt Bella had been "out shopping" for interminable hours every afternoon this past week, and Io had wondered more than once where Officer Quince was during that time.

"Please be seated," she went on. "My bodyguard is here today—oh! He was here a minute ago, Officer Quince, I assure you."

"Probably checking the entrances and exits, like a good bodyguard. Perhaps you should call him in, my lady, so I can get used to him." Hartley Quince seated himself in a plush green chair, stretching his legs out over the embroidered carpet. These two limbs were fashionably attired, in smooth silk breeches of an uncriticizable shade of beige, that nevertheless showed a perfect line of male leg. He smiled at Io, a pure-cream smile that had no reason she could see.

"Yes, I'll call him," she said slowly, though of course no young lady would "call" for anybody, and there were no slaves about. And although she could have tried the doors to the kitchen or the slaves' quarters, she first tried her own bedroom.

There he was, an improbable object indeed; over six feet of broad-shouldered muscle, armed and uniformed, sitting on her pink vanity stool with the silk ribbons, an expression of profound melancholy on his face.

"Sergeant?" she said uncertainly.

He started. "My lady? Aren't you having your lesson?"

"Officer Quince asked to see you before we began."

It was as though she'd propounded some esoteric theory of philosophy. He shook his head very slowly, not in a negative way, but more as a student might who was ill-prepared to respond to the teacher's question. "Surely that's not necessary, lady Iolanthe. I'm not an officer; it's not required that I be introduced. And I do have my work to do."

The idea of returning to Hartley Quince without what she'd been sent to get was alarming. And besides—she looked around her bedroom, with its conspicuous lack of exits. "Are you doing your work in here, Sergeant Stockton?"

He sighed and rose to his feet without responding. They marched out into the sitting room, more, she

thought, like two children on their way to a spanking than
a pair of adults.

Officer Quince glanced up idly from a dressmaker's
book that Io's mother had left in the sitting room. "A sergeant of the City Guard," he said. "Good choice. Have
you filled the lady Iolanthe in on your qualifications, Sergeant?"

Io turned to the sergeant, wide-eyed. It would never
have occurred to her that she had any right to ask for
qualifications. Sergeant Stockton was looking at Quince.
"She knows my name and rank, sir."

"Surely she should know more, since you'll be so close
in the coming weeks. You know, Lady Iolanthe, the sergeant here will accompany you to the Diamond."

She hadn't known that either, though it seemed to come
as no surprise to the sergeant. Quince said, "Why don't
you fill her in, Sergeant? Age, place of birth, years in service? Awards and commendations?"

The sergeant's mouth set grimly. He was still looking
at Quince. "Age twenty-six. Place of birth, Sangaree Section. Three years in serv—"

"Sangaree?" Io was startled enough to say it out loud,
and civilized enough to regret it.

He turned to look at her. "Eight below Z, Sangaree
Section. Would you prefer to ask for another City
Guard?"

"Oh, no! Of course not. I was just surprised. I mean—"
Her tutors had assured her that prejudice did not exist on
the City of Opal; but they hadn't prepared her for situations like this. "It was unexpected, that's all."

They seemed to be staring at each other through a silence like lead weights. "My singing master told me that
without Sangaree, the songs of the past would be lost,"
she offered. "I can play two on the harmium flute—
'Greensleeves' and 'Hey, Jude.' "

He started to chuckle, which startled her again, because
she had meant to be perfectly serious. He sketched her a
bow; not as graceful as Hartley Quince's, but more winning. "With such accomplishments," he intoned, "my
lady could perform in any Sangaree establishment on
Tanamonde Street."

Tanamonde Street was the most respectable place in

the section, she knew; at least, it was where everybody went to hear real Sangaree music. "I've always wanted to go to a Sangaree bar, Sergeant, but nobody would take me. Before we leave the Opal, do you think you could—"

"It wouldn't be wise, my lady," he said firmly. Just the sort of door-closing thing her father would say.

"Harmony again reigns," said Officer Quince. "Did you know the sergeant and I have met before, my lady? How are you, Willie? Can you take a seat with us, or does duty require that you hover about the edges while we work?"

You wouldn't think, thought Io, that a person's name could make him wince like that.

"I prefer to stay on my feet, sir."

"Always the overachiever. You know, there's nobody here but friends, Willie, we're not on admin deck now. I'd prefer that you call me Hart."

When the sergeant hesitated, Quince said, "That's an order."

The sergeant said tonelessly, "Hello, Hart."

"It's good to see you again. My lady, I wonder if you'd do me the favor of bringing my regards to your gracious mother? It would give me the opportunity of catching up on old times with my friend here."

Iolanthe couldn't refuse, but she lingered in the doorway, openly unhappy with leaving the puzzle unanswered of how a high-ranking officer on the Lord Cardinal's staff and a Sangaree sergeant knew each other. Finally she turned, and she heard Hartley Quince's laughter, cut short by the closing of the door.

"She's a nice girl," Hartley said. It didn't come out with the air of a compliment.

"She is," said Will. His own voice was serious, even warning.

"Well, she'll have you to look after her." He was speaking to Will in pure, lively Sangaree speech; Will was answering in a clipped court/admin accent.

"Hart, did you have something to do with my being assigned here?"

"Lord, you've gotten over your standoffishness in a hurry. I'd almost have thought you were avoiding me, the way our Iolanthe had to go in and drag you out by your collar." Hartley Quince stood and looked Will's uniform up and down. "And just see what you've made of yourself. Most of Sangaree thinks of nothing beyond this year's survival and making a buck, and here you are— alive, out of the section, and with a berth in the City Guard. I'm proud of you, Willie."

It was impossible to tell from his tone whether he was serious or sarcastic. Will took the safer road and made no answer.

Hartley said, "Tell me, when I left Sangaree, did you ever think you might see me again?"

Entire nights had been given to it. "Yes," said Will.

Hartley laughed. "I suppose you pictured me in jail, or a holding cell on the way to the pens."

"No," said Will honestly. "I imagined it would be something like this."

The amusement drained from Hartley's eyes. For a brief second, he looked like a man who'd taken a step that wasn't there. Then he smiled. "God, but I've missed you. You're not quite as talkative as you used to be, though. We'll have to work on that. How's your sister?"

"Fine."

"And the job?"

"Fine."

"How's your mother?"

"Fi— Hart, you know my mother is dead."

The sound of a door closing in the interior apartments suggested that Iolanthe and Vivian were on their way. Will stepped closer to Hartley.

"You *didn't* have anything to do with my being assigned here, did you?"

Hartley Quince raised one perfect golden brow. He was good at that. Will recalled seeing him practice it in a mirror at the age of twelve. "What for? We haven't exactly been in touch, Willie."

"I know." *And you haven't exactly answered the question.* Damn! Being around Hart was like being around an Oracle, only more unsettling.

The door to the sitting room opened, and the two Pelagia ladies entered. Hartley took Vivian's hand with a possessive air, and Will moved unobtrusively to the other side of the room, where he practiced blending in with the piano and artwork. It was no small talent in a man of his size. Vivian's light, excited tones filled the sitting room, the verbal equivalent of a bunch of spring flowers. Like any well-brought-up gentleman, Hartley solicited replies from Iolanthe as well, and a lively conversation commenced among the three of them. Will's face was professionally blank, but he promised himself several good beers just as soon as he could manage it.

Chapter 4

Keylinn O'Malley Murtagh:

After my sixth birthday, when I rejected my older brother's quite accurate description of sex with the righteous scorn I felt it deserved, I resolved I would never make a fool of myself again. As you and I well know, this was a resolution doomed to failure. It's in our genes, it's in every society we fashion, it's scrawled across our foreheads in glowing green letters: If you're a human, you're socially awkward. I don't care how charming you are or how often your audience applauds; there comes a day, and more than one at that, when you know yourself to be standing there naked with the shivery winds of cold observation blowing over you, all four corners of your idiocy exposed.

When I was nineteen, I made a slight mistake. We can skip past the details, thanks; but my elders and betters at the Academy got together and decided some sort of notice had to be taken. I really can't blame them; my mistake had been rather flashy. So flashy that I became the first Graykey in a hundred and ten years to be exiled offplanet. Not that they did it in any nasty way, mind you. I was quickly promoted to GK Seventh and put under contract to an offworlder, Cyr Elizabeth Vesant, for the standard period of seven years.

I still remember how she looked at me when they

brought me in. Elizabeth Vesant was an Empire citizen, forty-six Standard, who wore clothes that could have paid all the teacher's salaries at the Academy for more than one semester. She was a trader who knew she was in a superior position to trade and didn't trouble to keep that knowledge from the slight curl of her lips. She didn't speak to me at all, just turned to the Dean of Students. "I brought you eight crateloads of pure powdered antitoxin and instructions on reconstituting it. I've saved your fucking lives, is what I've done. Weren't you people dying, or was that bullshit?"

Her Empire accent sounded strange in the little room with its wooden floor and desks.

"We're very grateful," said the Dean in his usual toneless voice.

"I didn't want to come here, you know. *You* asked *me*. You couldn't meet my price in units, or I'd've taken units, all right? I told you what I wanted—a Graykey of my own. A Graykey of my own, like some fucking storybook, since you couldn't give me money, and what do you bring me? A *girl*. How old is she, anyway? Seventeen?"

"Nineteen," said the Dean of Students.

"Nineteen! She has *student* written all over her! What kind of thanks is this? And why can't I get a male? Where are your other people?"

"She's a full Graykey," said the Dean calmly. I'd been promoted the night before, in what I can only describe as a rather hurried ceremony. "And she's willing to go with you. I would advise you, for your own safety, not to try to make your own choice."

If you'd heard his voice when he said that last sentence, it would have given you pause, too.

Cyr Elizabeth Vesant blinked. Then she gave what I later came to know she referred to as her "country girl smile," and said, "Well, sure, my friend, if you insist. The Vesant Group likes to make friends, not waves. I get her the full seven years, right?"

"The full seven," agreed the Dean. And he led me to Cyr Vesant, placed my hand on her shoulder, and the contract was made.

It wasn't as bad as it might have been. All that "I've

been robbed" business and its accompanying profanity
was an act that my contract-holder liked to put on from
time to time, to test the waters when dealing with strangers. She was a lot sharper than she'd appeared at first
meeting, and a good deal more sophisticated. And because of a special clause in her arrangement with the
Dean, I gave her fair warning when she was treading too
close to a violation; she never needed a second hint. It
was educational, in fact, to be this close to someone
whose survival instinct was so finely honed.

Six of the seven years had passed when she brought me
to Baret One to back her up on her last deal. She had a
case of lorine, perfectly legal in the Empire, and wanted
to sell it to some folk on One, humorless Republic types
who needed it to relax. This done, we boarded the Republic Ship *Kestrel* to swing back to Baret Station, where her
pharmaceutical company kept storage facilities.

I checked her stateroom, pulled out the jammers we always carried, and set one on the polished dresser by her
bed. She sat on the side of the bed, her bare feet touching
the soft ship's carpet. Her silver hair was spread over her
back.

"Keylinn," she said.

"Cyr?" I inquired.

"That thing is on, isn't it?" She cocked her head toward the jammer.

"Of course."

"Good. Sit here." She patted the spot beside her.

I sat. She said, "You have another year on your contract."

"Yes," I agreed, to this somewhat obvious remark.

"Keylinn, I'm retiring. I've played out the situation in
this system anyway; and I've gotten enough banked over
the years that the rewards are no longer worth the risks.
I'm going home to Vakrist."

My stomach went hollow. "When?"

"After we dock on Baret Station; after I get some of
my affairs together; after I arrange booking at Baret
Gate."

"I see."

"Vakrist is several sector-gates away. It would be difficult for you to return to your people if you went with me. I'd be within my right to take you, though, wouldn't I?"

"You'd be within your rights."

"Though perhaps not very wise," she said, with a wry and not entirely friendly look. "I think I've become as familiar as anyone with the negative aspects of keeping a personal Graykey. Tell me, did you plan for that meeting in Tin City to fall apart?"

I said, "It worked to your advantage in the end."

"It wasn't what I told you to do. Aren't you supposed to obey me?"

"It was a gray area," I said.

"The world is full of gray areas for you people, isn't it?"

I didn't reply. It didn't seem called for.

She said, "And those aren't the only kinds of gray areas I have to watch out for, are they? How many times have I come near death at your hands in the last six years?"

"Four," I said at once.

She laughed. "I'd only spotted three." She stood up and began pulling her nightclothes, soft and expensive, from her case.

They teach us to wait, in the Academy, but I couldn't. "Does this mean you aren't taking me with you?"

She turned to look at me. As in our first meeting, she didn't bother to keep the smug expression from her lips. "It means I'll consider the situation," she said. "And I'll let you know what I decide." She rooted around in her case, looking for something. "You know, it's like teasing a leopard. Ah, here we are!" She pulled out her alabaster hairbrush and handed it to me. "Brush me out, Keylinn, before I go to sleep."

I took it; I brushed her hair; I turned out the stateroom light. She said, "Good night, Keylinn." I left, making sure her door was solidly locked.

They'd be proud of me at the Academy. *Good night,* I thought, in my own tongue; which means, literally, *safe until morning.*

Chapter 5

Tal stood before the looking glass in his quarters, a half-dozen sets of lenses spread on the polished dressertop before him. Three needed cleaning, and he hadn't time for that. Two were brown, and the remaining one was gray. Adrian seemed to prefer gray; perhaps he should wear it more often. Although, where Tal was going today, nobody would get the joke.

He lifted a lens to one eye and paused. The yellow-eyed Aphean in the glass stared back at him, troubled. Why did his natural iris color disturb humans so? Half his genetic heritage came from the Elaph People, gentle and golden-eyed, and humans loved them. Not that Tal had any great respect for, or interest in, a species of such neurotic pacificity as the Elaphites. Ask them to walk en masse into the core of a healthy sun, and they would be happy to oblige you. No; humans, while treacherous in the extreme, were much better company.

Adrian was, at any rate; though an enigma. For one thing, he kept Tal around, in spite of attaining no immediate advantage from his company. Of course, he kept Brandon Fischer around, too, and a more useless piece of encroaching senility would be difficult to find. He remembered his first meeting with the Chief Adviser, and the appalled look on the old man's face when Adrian had announced that Tal was to be given asylum.

What he'd actually said was, "I brought him home, Brandon; can I keep him?" Feeling pleased with himself, Adrian was, eyes shining with his own cleverness in getting Tal past the local police and into the Brevity port.

And Tal remembered the first time he'd heard that voice, in the snow behind the Three-Pint Bar, in Kellogtown on Brevity. His quest had not gone well that day. His informant had lied, as his informants seemed to do with such tedious regularity, and Tal had had to shoot him. It was unfortunate the man proved to be so well-connected.

Tal remembered looking down dumbly at the two armed men he'd just sent unconscious into the snowdrifts behind the bar. They were gangsters, pure and simple, but the police were also out searching, and Tal saw no point in differentiating between groups that were trying to end his life. Shouts and questions coming from the bar suggested that more such people would soon be on their way. Well, didn't they say that Apheans all died young? So his quest was unfulfilled—it probably would have failed anyway, even if he'd had five hundred years—

And then a voice had said, "Excuse me! Do you need a hand?"

He looked up into the wildly blowing snowflakes. A figure was lying atop the high concrete wall that surrounded the back yard. "What?"

"I said, do you need a hand?"

It was a human male, perhaps twenty, dark-haired and underdressed for the weather. A number of things went swiftly through Tal's head, but what he said was, "Yes."

"How many are coming after you?" asked the madman on the wall. "Can we take them?"

"It would be best not to try."

"Oh." The voice sounded disappointed. "Well, never mind; here, let me help you up, and we'll softly and silently vanish away."

It sounded like a quote, the way he said it. Tal was about to die in the backyard of a sleazy port bar, and this lunatic was quoting some other human lunatic.

"You don't understand," said Tal. "The only way out is the port, and the police will have been told to detain me."

"Oh, tarradiddle to that," said the young man, confirming Tal's estimate of his sanity. "Come on up; we've got a certain amount of diplomatic immunity, and maybe I can pass you for one of my aides. They're tramping about here in the snow looking for me now; it'll be hours before they all get back." His grin showed through the slanting snow. "You'll be on board by then."

"On board *what?*"

Sounds from the bar increased.

"Do you *care?*" asked the young man swiftly.

Tal took his hand.

And that is how, thought Tal two years later, you entered an entire culture of lunatics. At least they were traveling lunatics, and he could continue his search at each stop.

He finished inserting his gray lenses and examined the results—a totally forgettable human male. Excellent.

He rose, put on the dress helmet of his rank, and took the twenty-minute walk to Transport. That deck was, as ever, a haven for Outsider techs on contract; the walls were full of them, programming the shorties and capsules that were operating between the Diamond, the Opal, and Baret Station. He ignored the admin assistants and approached the dayshift duty officer.

"Officer Diamond," he said. "There should be a station pass waiting for me."

The duty officer, a middle-aged man in Transport yellows, stared at him openly. Diamond was a ship's name, not a proper form of identification. Tal could see the question in his eyes: Was this Adrian's tame demon?

Finally the officer said, "They use tattoos here."

"That's not unusual," said Tal.

"Not as such, sir. You got a double-shift pass, sir; the station charges fifty units for it, and it'll fade in sixteen hours. That's when your air rights terminate, so don't be tardy getting back."

"What's the Baret Station penalty for letting a pass lapse?"

"They space you, I think. A charming bunch, from what I hear. Step over here, if you would, sir; you'll have to take off your helmet. They do the forehead here; easier to spot. By station law, your hair has to be short enough not to hide it."

Tal removed his helmet and handed it to the man. "See that it's returned to my quarters."

"Yes, sir. Please close your eyes, sir."

Tal closed his eyes and felt the tattoo gun touch his forehead.

"All done, sir. You can wait on the line over there."

Tal looked eloquently around at the enormous space of Transport, bays filled with ships. "Why do I need to wait?"

"No pilots available, sir. We've only got shorties on-line now, and they need a human to pilot."

"They need *something* to pilot. Is that one in Bay Orange available?"

"It's okayed for service, sir, but we don't have a man—".

"I'll take it. Plug me into Departure."

Tal turned on one heel and left, not being one to waste his time on social pleasantry. His orders had been sufficiently clear.

Five minutes later he was sitting inside the shortie, waiting for the departure program to fling him away from the City. Recalling the way the duty officer had stared at him, he considered again that it might have been better, on the day he agreed to stay on the Diamond, to have made up some plausible Empire surname. But Adrian had saved his life, and for some reason Tal had not wanted to lie to him at that moment.

Then his pod burst from the line of shortships with a welcome kick of speed; good-bye, for the time being, to the museum of eccentricity that was life in the Three Cities. Back to the real world, the mainstream of human culture that he hunted in, and was hunted. A line from history came to him, the sentence of some ancient queen: "Keep her close confined." They keep you close confined in the universe at large, thought Tal, as he pictured the long, dusty road ahead of him. He used to think that fatalism was no more part of his nature than optimism; but his compass was beginning to swing around to the acknowledgment that his human genes would have their say. He no longer approached his quest with any expectation of success—he no longer approached it with any expectations at all. He approached it like some charwoman on her way into the quarters of a messy nobleman with bucket and broom, looking forward to quitting time.

His station pass was good for sixteen hours. It was frustrating, then, to spend the first four of them in Incoming Detainees, waiting to be interviewed by Security. Three ex-Cities people waited with him, all cargo handlers, all born on the Outside and trying to get back out there—forever or for holiday, not that the Cities cared.

They could always buy more techs to run the machines they thought were beneath them.

"Got any cigarettes?" asked the cargo handler nearest him, an unshaven man with a tattered shirt and light-weight traveling pack.

Tal glanced at him. "No."

The man blinked and said no more. He sat there for five more minutes, then got up slowly and moved to the other side of the room.

The doors slid open and four security guards entered. "Clinton, Emily?" asked one, and the only woman among the detainees stood up and followed the guard into one of the bank of interrogation cells lining the left end of the room.

"Diamond, Tal?" said the shortest of the security guards, a woman who could not be more than nineteen, with a mass of rough black hair pulled into a long mane of ponytail. The tattoo adorning her brown left cheek was a thing of incredibly delicacy: A coal-black stallion rearing up, and a red rose. From his attitude, the stallion seemed to be protecting the rose rather than crushing it. Tal recognized the official symbol of State Security for Baret Two's current ruling family. He knew what was on his own forehead: JOHN, stationer's slang for a passer-through. It wasn't meant to be respectful.

Tal got to his feet. She jerked her head toward the cells on the right, and he followed her into the nearest and sat down at a bare table.

"Unusual name," she remarked, taking the chair opposite.

"Not really."

"For one of you people, I mean. From the City of Diamond, your name is Diamond—see? You're not one of their royalty or something, are you?"

"They don't have royalty."

"That's not the way I heard it. Doesn't the Diamond have some big mucky-muck in charge?"

"Not in charge in a monarchical sense. And it's not a hereditary post."

"Well, not that I really give a shit. Why 'they'?"

"Pardon?"

"You said 'They don't have royalty.' Aren't you one of them?"

He paused, very briefly. "I was born on the City of Pearl. You were talking about the Diamond."

"Pearl, huh? We haven't seen many of them here. I think you're the first."

"We don't travel much."

"Uh-huh. You've got a good accent for a Blood Christian."

"Some of us go to school."

The woman of the stallion and the rose looked at him sharply. There was something about his voice— This kid couldn't be more than a teenager, and yet this was not the way an interview with a Cities hayseed ought to progress. In spite of what he said, could he be some VIP? Maybe she shouldn't have called him a Blood Christian; she knew these Redemptionists didn't like that. "No offense for the long detention. We wouldn't want to let terrorists in, like Cathal Station, would we?"

He said, in a voice without inflection, "Firstly, the Three Cities have no great incentive to blow up your station. Secondly, if your scanners hadn't passed me as harmless, I wouldn't have been kept in your lounge for four whole hours. Thirdly, Cathal Station was destroyed by a longship on a suicide run, and two hundred crew had to die with her for it to work. I can assure you that I'm personally unacquainted with a hundred and ninety-nine such hardy souls, and I myself am definitely not one. I only have a sixteen-hour pass, officer; could we move this process along?"

Baret Security Officer Tersha had had a short, but not uneducated, life. Never in the course of it had she met anyone who could string a bunch of sentences together like that. It rolled out of this kid like it came straight from a book, with no passing through heart or mind or vocal cords.

She cleared her throat. "May I ask what you're doing on Baret Station?" she said, striving to put more authority into her voice. This was her first month on the job, but she'd been on the Security track for the last four years of training. If he'd pulled out a weapon, she would have been able to handle it, but this . . . this undefined *impres-*

sion that she would never be able to explain in a written report . . .

"I'm a tourist," said Tal Diamond.

Looking into his flat gray eyes, Officer Tersha suddenly remembered a line from an old song, something about loneliness and the weaponlike hardness of diamonds. It was supposed to be a song about space, but she saw it now in a new context.

It wasn't this one's easy assumption of authority, his taking for granted that he was in control and his apparent talent for forcing that point of view onto a situation. Much worse was the tone of voice, the rhythm of his speech. That was what was throwing her off-stride. It was bloodless, it was mechanically precise; but behind it and through it was a kind of jaded exhaustion, a just-plain *tiredness,* that was frighteningly inappropriate in a seventeen-year-old. Officer Tersha saw that she didn't understand the quality of what she was facing, and saw, too, that she didn't want to understand it. She suddenly wanted to get as far away from it as possible.

She stood up. "Well, that will be all, Cyr Diamond," she said, "please limit your time strictly to what's on your pass and enjoy-your-stay-on-Baret-Station."

"Thank you, Officer Tersha."

He started to leave. She said, "Wait a minute! How did you know my name?"

"It's on your lapel pin." He pointed to the round decoration at her throat with its random scattering of dots and whorls.

"But that's in modular machine language."

"I know."

She reached out blankly, coded open the door, and watched him walk out of detention, onto the station proper.

Well, why not? She was within the scope of her job. He was right, he wasn't going to blow the place up. These interviews were a formality, to push the incomings and see if anything shook loose; stars would birth and die before anything shook loose from Tal Three-Cities Diamond. She went out into the detainees lounge and shut the cell door. Then she suddenly raised her arm and slapped the durasteel surface, hard. Her hand ached.

One of the other security officers was in the lounge, waiting. "What's wrong with you, Tersha?"

She glared at him. "What business is it of yours, anyway?"

By the time she reached her next interview, she'd worked herself up to a splendidly foul temper.

There were a good three-dozen lace shops on Baret Station, which was no surprise, since Baret Two was known for lace, and any number of Gate tourists passed through the station halls. Tal gathered that much of the lace was machine-made in the bowels of the station itself, but the prices seemed acceptable, and nobody was complaining loudly.

With a clean bill of health from Baret Security, getting onto the Republic Ship *Kestrel* as a visitor should not be too difficult. The Republic tended to prefer letting outsiders in to letting its own folk out. He applied from the station link, got permission to board at fourteen hundred, and decided to use the interval at hand to shop.

"Bring me back something nice," Adrian had said the first two times he'd issued passes to Tal, but he'd soon given that up. Gifts for other people were so low on Tal's priority list that he somehow never got around to them, and on those rare occasions when he did come through, his presents were known for their inappropriateness.

He stopped at a plate glass window on the tourist level and peered inside a branch of The Chi, a widespread net of tech supply shops. The place looked run-down, cost-conscious. Signs proclaiming bargains covered the walls. A middle-aged man and a girl of about thirteen were working inside; otherwise, the aisles were empty.

There were possibilities here. He entered the shop.

The girl, who had hair of bright gold feathers, ignored him. The man, who was bald and unhappy looking, followed his progress as though he expected Tal to pocket the merchandise at any moment. They both wore complex tattoos on their foreheads that suggested ancient circuitry.

Tal made his way gradually to the glass case in back where the expensive items were kept. The man left his post and joined him there; they reached the case simultaneously.

"Service to you, John?" asked the man. His expression remained unhappy.

"I'd like to buy a riccardi," said Tal.

The man's jaws had been working away as though he were chewing something; they stopped abruptly. "You got a license, John?"

"I've got cash," said Tal. "How much are they?"

"We don't take dollars or yen. Get your money changed at one of the banks—"

Tal lifted a gold unit chip, imprinted with the station logo. The man glanced toward the golden-feathered girl. She was across the store, unpacking boxes, her back to them. Tal said, helpfully, "Why don't you just tell me about them, as though I did have a license, and we can iron out the details later?"

The man nodded, not looking Tal in the face, and pointed to the case. "We got three. Those there on the left, they got full sensory input, but they dissolve after six months. That chip on the right's a permanent. You don't want it anymore, you got to get a pro to take it out. Okay?"

Tal nodded.

He went on, "One on the right's designed for the best companies, lifetime employment. You won't find any side-effects there, John; they have to be real careful when it comes to putting something together that's got to be accurate for decades."

"I take it that's the most expensive."

"Happens it is. This one's fifteen thousand units. Others are four thousand, eight hundred. But you got to figure, you need a new one twice a year. So you're really saving money with this one, aren't you?"

"Are any of your riccardis two-way? Send and receive?"

"*Send?* There's no such thing as a two-way riccardi, John. You don't know a lot about the field, do you?"

Tal smiled a humorless smile. "Can I get it within the next ten hours?"

The man's gaze flicked back toward the girl, who had finished with her boxes, and was glancing their way.

"You leaving, right?"

"You'll never see me again," Tal assured him.

"Cost you twenty, to get it so fast."

"Done," said Tal, "but I'll need the service of an installer."

"You crazy? Get your own damned installer."

Tal shrugged and started to leave. The man took a couple of steps toward him and said softly, "I'll walk you to the door. Come back at nineteen hundred. I can get somebody to meet us then."

"You don't understand," said Tal quietly. "It's not for me. I need the installer to come out to the City of Diamond to do it, that's where the person is."

The man made a sound like a laugh. "Forget it, John. Nobody's rowin' out to that ship, I'll tell you right now."

"It'll take him all of an hour. And I'll give him another twenty."

They were at the door to the shop. The man blinked, as though there were sunlight in the entranceway. "Come back at nineteen, John." Then he turned and went back into the badly lit interior. Tal heard him say, "Kit, you don't know how these window shoppers waste my time."

The RS *Kestrel* was another story. Clean, precise lines, efficient processing of his boarding request; Tal approved. He was shown into the lounge, the only area open to visitors, within minutes. It followed a typical Republican aesthetic: utilitarian furniture, least-common-denominator pictures on the walls, beige carpeting. The atmosphere brought back memories.

And there, on one of the soft brown chairs, was Cyr Elizabeth Vesant, an olive-skinned, silver-haired, human woman of middle age in an emerald cape and tight blue pants, perched like a bird of paradise in this island of respectability. "Empire" was written all over her; certainly she made no concessions to her fellow passengers.

But then, at the moment, there *were* no fellow passengers. Except—as he came closer he took in the somewhat less flashy companion sitting at Cyr Vesant's plastic table. A young woman in a white leather tie-jacket and forest green pants, with a sober expression on her face. She had a straightforward, intelligent look, skin just a few degrees darker than snow, and red-gold hair tied back in a braid. He'd never seen a woman with skin and hair of such shades, even in the Three Cities, which were notoriously inbred.

He stopped at their table. "Cyr Vesant?"

The silver-haired woman extended her hand and they shook, Empire-style etiquette for business dealings. "I see my description was no problem."

"That, and the fact you're the only people in the room."

She laughed, a belly laugh. "Sit with us, youngster. There aren't many on this ship who can get a total for two plus two, in any base. It's been a damned long trip from Baret One."

She spoke perfect Empire Standard, but to Tal's ear there was something about the way she put her grammar together, and a slight accenting of certain words, that suggested she was a long way from home. Empire Standard left a lot of room for variation ... where had he heard that style before? Vakrist?

He took a chair. "I doubt that you had an enjoyable time while you were on Baret One either. You must be glad to be returning."

"Oh, I'm not taking ship here for Baret Two. Nor do I return to the place of terminal boredom we just left. I'm from out-sector, youngster; I'm waiting for the sector-gate."

"I see." Gate travel was wildly expensive; Tal had had to take that route before he met Adrian, but it had meant major conniving.

"Not that I've told the ship's steward yet. I figure to wait till the last minute, then walk out—so much easier to deal with Republic paperwork that way."

He said, "Forgive me for attending to business, Cyr Vesant—"

"Ah, an efficient youngster! He listens to his elders maunder on, but brings the conversation back to its goals. Bravo. You know, I was quite surprised when my companion here told me that someone was asking the sorts of questions you were asking. You're not a Baret native, are you?"

"Not precisely."

"Did you know that the Three Cities have come to Baret System? You must have heard something of it, my friend. Three enormous ripe peaches, hanging low on the branch beside this very station. Such excitement when they appeared! Such accents when they speak, I'm told. And it's fascinating, is it not, to imagine so many people traveling so far, without ever passing through a gate?"

"I suppose."

"Not that you care! You make it plain in your voice. Well, no doubt you're right; since gate travel is so much more efficient, why should we pay attention to a backwater of ancient culture, regardless of how it chooses to stroll the universe? Your own accent is quite good, cyr."

"Thank you. May I ask—"

"Still, one cannot help but wonder about a people who follow an unholy mixture of Old Earth myth and alien missionary teaching. Considering the Curosa went on their pretty way centuries ago, our Three Cities friends might be pardoned for cultivating new concerns. As you yourself have, evidently."

"Cyr, your message—"

"But it is time we got down to business," she said. "You asked about Belleraphon."

Tal blinked. "Yes."

"I've not met this Belleraphon, mind you, but I have heard of him. I cannot tell you where he is; but I can tell you where he was." She paused.

Tal lifted the perfectly legal traveling pack he had brought with him from the Diamond, and opened it on the table to reveal stacks of genetically imprinted NetBank notes. "Actual living paper," he said. "It's so much more transportable than account credit."

Cyr Vesant's eyes widened. Her companion showed no reaction. Cyr Vesant's hand reached toward the notes in a movement that seemed involuntary. Tal closed the pack. Her eyes went to his face. "My young friend," she whispered, "where did you come by all this money?"

Tal was silent.

Cyr Vesant continued to stare, and he saw a frown form on her face. "My friend . . . how old are you?"

He made no answer.

She leaned back in her chair. "Well, well." She turned to her companion. "An interesting acquaintance we've made, don't you think?"

The red-haired woman did not reply. Cyr Vesant addressed Tal. "I have a proposition for you, my friend who may not be so young." Her eyes shifted back and forth between him and the red-haired woman. "It's a cold, lonely universe. Allow me to remedy this for you."

"I beg your pardon?" Tal said.

"Tell me," said Cyr Vesant, lounging back farther and crossing her legs, "have you ever heard of the Graykey?"

"I've heard what the Imperial Encyclopedia has to say about them. Will that do? Is this to be a history lesson, cyr?"

"Bear with me, please. Yes, the great Encyclopedia— had I several lifetimes to live, I would begin reading it. You must pardon me, therefore, for not knowing how much you may have gleaned from that venerable source. No doubt you've heard that they were great fighters and scholars, that they knew secrets of weaponry, of arms, of combat—some say of magic, if you will forgive my romance. That each Graykey lived by his 'contract,' sworn to serve one master while that contract was in force. Perhaps you even know that it was fashionable, a few hundred years ago, for every man and woman of importance to have their own Graykey."

"Forgive me, but does this bear on our business today?"

"It does, and you will do me the honor of being silent, my most dangerous friend."

Tal sat back, biting his lips.

"Now. The Encyclopedia, being a respectable source, no doubt told you how the Graykey were turned against three hundred and ten years ago. That they were blamed for the assassinations and the proscribed weapons that leveled systems in four different wars. That they were hunted down and killed."

Tal nodded with a minimum of patience. She knew he needed her; this was just the sort of human he hated to deal with.

"Ah, I thought so. Well, your so-respectable source was not entirely accurate, as respectable sources often are not. A few of the Graykey were killed, it is true; but most simply left the civilized net. Just as we turned against the Graykey, blaming them for the terrors, they turned against us with the same accusation. For each Graykey, you see, considers him or herself a mere weapon in the hands of their contract-holder; and they blamed the contract-holders for their lack of discipline. They therefore retired to their own society. Their own planet, chosen by them, where they could practice their arcane philosophy in peace."

"I hadn't heard that."

"It was a secret." She smiled. "Even I do not know the location, though I've set foot on its surface. Several years ago I had occasion to do the Graykey a great service— there was an item they were in need of, which I was able to provide. And they paid me in the traditional way—in contract-time." She motioned with her hand. "Allow me to introduce my Graykey to you, cyr. Keylinn, may I present this nameless gentleman with many banknotes."

The red-haired woman inclined her head. "How do you do," she said. They were the first words she'd spoken.

Tal said, "I don't believe it."

But he thought that perhaps he did.

Cyr Vesant leaned over, resting her chin on two fists, elbows on the table. "I will honor you with my confidence," she announced, like a teacher declaring a picnic outing.

This was mildly alarming. Tal said, "You've really shared enough with me—"

"I have enjoyed a successful career," she said. "I wish to retire while I'm still ahead of the game; I wish to go home. I wish to begin a garden, with many different colors of roses. I would like to think there will be no use for a Graykey in my quiet future." She tapped the edge of Tal's pack. "Would you be interested in buying one?"

Tal said, "Slavery is illegal in the Republic and Empire both."

"A lot of things are illegal, as I'm sure I don't have to tell you, cyr. Besides, don't think of it as slavery (unless the thought appeals to you). Think of it as a service contract; that's how they think of it. You'd only get her for a year, I should say, unless you renew when it expires. My arrangement was for seven years, and she's served six."

Tal watched the woman called Keylinn. She appeared

uninterested in the conversation, as though she were here to be polite. After a moment he said, "No. Thank you very much. But I'd rather stick with our original arrangement—money for information."

Cyr Vesant pulled out an exotic-looking cigarette and lit it. She took a deep drag and said, "Alas. I've decided I wish to make arrangements for the care of this Graykey before I go. It's like having a pet, you know: a responsibility. We've grown close. She's part of the deal, cyr. I don't increase the price, but you take Keylinn with you when you go. She's a gift."

The room began filling with blue cigarette smoke, just the kind that ship administrators hated and forbade passengers to bring on board. Somewhere in the distance Tal heard air-scrubbers switch on. He considered the offer.

There would be advantages in having another spy on the Diamond, especially one with technical skills. Spider's abilities didn't seem to extend much beyond electronic forgery. And this business about contracts was interesting, though it wouldn't do to put too much stock in it, humans being unreliable by nature. Cyr Vesant obviously had her own reasons for passing this "gift" on, but he might never know what they were. And beyond anything else, he needed the information she had.

Cyr Vesant put in, "Your personal gladiator, you might say. A Samurai. A true and gentle knight. A perfect slave."

The woman Keylinn spoke in a neutral tone. "Cyr Vesant, it's my duty to warn you when you're approaching a gray area."

A flicker of irritation, and something else, passed over Cyr Vesant's face. She turned again to Tal. "It's possible that some of my terms may be misleading." The eyes flicked to Keylinn and back again. "In any case, you'll find an obedient and helpful companion, paid for in advance. It's expected that you feed and house her, but if it's not in your power, then even that is unnecessary— she'll use her skills to feed and house you both, and still provide excellent service."

"Graykey really make a practice of this? It's hard to believe they could get paid enough. What do they get out of it?"

"Now that is something I've never understood, though I've read as much Graykey philosophy as I could stomach—"

He turned to Keylinn. "What do you get out of it?"

"That's not a question I have to answer," she replied in the same neutral tone as before.

"I thought you had to answer all questions."

"You were wrong."

Cyr Vesant broke in hastily. "I'll handle the questions, Keylinn."

"Not yet," said Tal. He said, to Keylinn, "Is this what you want?"

"I'll follow my contract," she said.

"That's not what I asked."

"Yes," she said, meeting his gaze. "I'd like to go with you."

He said to Cyr Vesant, "All right. We have a deal."

Cyr Vesant chuckled. "What if she'd said no, she wanted to stay?"

"I don't have to answer all questions either," said Tal. "Where is this contract, is it written, computerized, what?"

"It's verbal. It's the standard contract, am I right, Keylinn? Some of the particulars we added for me would not apply to him."

Keylinn nodded. "Don't worry that it's not written," she said almost kindly, in the first touch of humanness she'd shown. "We consider it a matter of honor to obey verbal contracts above written ones."

"I can see we'll have many interesting hours of philosophical discussion ahead of us," said Tal, but not as one who was interested. "Meanwhile, as to Belleraphon—"

"Yes," said Cyr Vesant. She leaned over and tapped the money case again, with a more proprietary air. "I have had business dealings with a number of Republic citizens during my stay on Baret One. One of these citizens is a crewmember of this very ship. I'm in the export business, cyr; I provide various items of chemical nature which a puritanical government may make difficult to obtain." She smiled, and her Vakristian accent seemed to broaden. "We all know what dayzoosies and lagtails they are, the Republic government. Well, this crewmember put in an order for quite a large amount, and when I inquired about it, he said he represented another party, one Belleraphon, who handled distribution on Baret One."

Tal felt his fists clenching under the table. "Is this crewmember on board now?"

"This very second? I wouldn't know, he might have a station pass. But he made the trip here, and I assume he'll make the trip back."

Tal put his hand on the tabletop and drummed his fingers with a deliberately slow rhythm. Cyr Vesant said, "Our interaction has been so pleasant, I feel it my duty to tell you that in all the time I spent on Baret One—and I've spent quite some time, all told—I never heard of this Belleraphon before or since. And I had occasion to meet many distributors."

The drumming continued. Tal said, "Describe this crewmember."

"Height shorter than mine—about to my chin, for as you see, I'm quite tall. Very light hair, grayish white, cut very short. Brown eyes. Skin gold-brown—about the shade of that picture frame over there. His name is Peeskill." She smiled. "I know because I checked the door to his quarters. The names of passengers and crew are neatly labeled on each; how like the Republic."

"Anything else?"

She shook her head. "That's all I know. Sufficient?"

Tal opened the pack and counted out about a third of the notes. "Second-order information," he said. "If you could bring me face-to-face with Belleraphon, you'd get it all."

"As I expected," said Cyr Vesant. She stood up and stretched unself-consciously. "What a lovely retirement bonus. This system is so unusual—two habitable planets, half Empire and half Republic—it cried out to be exploited. I almost hate to go home." She fastened her emerald cape. "But I would be pressing my luck. It's only a matter of time before Baret Two drowns under the Republican tide, and then where's the point of smuggling? Keylinn can leave as she is; any possessions she has belong to me in any case."

Tal rose, too, and Keylinn followed suit, lifting a small pack. Had she been expecting this? Cyr Vesant said, "Or-

dinarily I would not ask, but as I'm leaving this sector
forever, I believe I'll indulge. What will you do with this
Belleraphon when you find him?"

Tal smiled, an Aphean smile that held no reassurance
for humans. He said, "You wonder if you've targeted
someone for murder. Does it matter to you, cyr?"

"Not enough to give the money back. Well, my friend,
good-bye; and a word of advice—don't keep your broadcast jammer in your vest pocket, it makes a bulge. Or else
get a smaller model." She yawned delicately, raising the
back of her hand to her mouth. "I'm not clairvoyant, it's
just that you'd be a fool not to have it running on a Republic ship. Between yours and mine, this whole lounge
must have come out as one great white noise."

She pushed in her chair and shook herself as though to
wake up, like a child who'd fallen asleep during the conversation of grownups. She smiled with deliberate sheep-
ishness and Tal thought, Mercati or not, Adrian could
learn a thing or two about charm from this one. She said,
"You know, I think I'll take a nap in my cabin. I don't
have to disembark till tomorrow. Good-bye, Keylinn."

"Good-bye, Cyr Vesant. Pleasant journey."

She shook hands again with Tal, and left.

He looked at Keylinn. "Do you have a station pass?"

"No."

"Then we'll take you round by way of Quarantine. You
can't leave the docking area, but my ship's not far."

Later, in the shortie, he checked their course and
looked over to where Keylinn sat, silent, in the copilot
seat. He said, "Have you ever piloted a short-range?"

"Yes."

"Then with manuals you can probably program these,
and City capsules. Good. We can get you taken onto the
Diamond with skills like that. I'll say your pass was running out, and you couldn't wait for our recruiters to interview you on the station. I warn you now, there'll be
language difficulties, and no tapes or pills or implants to
get you over the hump. But you'll find when you're used
to them that they're not insurmountable. The Cities use
what's actually a variation of Empire Standard, hard
though it is to believe when you first hear them. It's a

number of centuries out of date and splintered off." He looked openly at her profile. A large, very slightly askew nose, a scattering of very faint freckles—unusual—and eyes somewhere between green, gray, and blue; *sea-colored eyes,* he thought, or at least the color of the sea where he'd grown up, anyway. *We can cancel that memory.* He said, "Tell me what I can expect, Graykey."

"Pardon?"

"What do I get with my contract?"

"I'll obey orders, answer questions truthfully, and serve your best interests ahead of my own life for the next two-hundred and ninety-three days."

"Cyr Vesant said a year."

"She was making an approximation. Two hundred and ninety-three days remain on my contract."

"I see." The Diamond was ten minutes away. There was still time to call a halt—there was a Keith pistol in his other vest pocket—but the situation was too interesting to let go. "I suppose it's educational to meet a footnote in galactic history. I'm rather a footnote myself. Are you familiar with Apheans?"

"Somewhat."

"I am one. It's no secret where we're going. Is that a problem?"

"Definitely not."

Why "definitely?" "How much do you know about Apheans?"

"Like you, I've also spent time with the Imperial Encyclopedia. That's the extent of my knowledge of Apheans—and Belleraphon."

Tal's fingers went toward the pistol. He drew them back again. "I suppose I should be glad so few people have the time or inclination to slog through the nonessential data in the Encyclopedia, although I note you don't claim to have gotten past the A's—or possibly the B's. Tell me what you know."

"I know that 'Belleraphon' was the study code name given to one of the first Aphean children, to protect his privacy in growing up. That he was born two hundred and sixty years ago, which, given the potential Aphean life-span, means he may still be alive. That he disappeared over two centuries ago. That's all the official information states. . . . Am I right in assuming that Belleraphon is the only known Aphean whose execution has not been witnessed and recorded?"

Tal was silent. Keylinn said, "Excepting, of course, yourself. Though I'm not sure you qualify as a 'known Aphean.' "

Tal said, "Did you tell all this to Cyr Vesant?"

She shook her head. "It wasn't relevant, and she didn't ask."

The water was rapidly getting deeper, Tal thought. She said, "I hope you'll tell me soon why you're looking for him. The more I understand you, the better I can serve your interests."

Tal slowed the approach to gain time to think. In an effort to prompt her further, he said, "I see possible conflicts. What if your contract-holder believed something to be in his best interests, and you knew it wasn't?"

"That would be a gray area."

"Ah, yes—the gray areas."

She said, with a touch of defensiveness, "Everything in life is subject to interpretation. I've been taught to interpret."

"All right, Order Number One: I don't want anyone in the Three Cities to know you have a contract with me."

"Very well."

"You'll have to come on board under the same circumstances as the Outsider technicians. If I can get your stay extended through the next Blackout—that's a sector-jump—there'll be an oath of allegiance to the Diamond; can you take that?"

"Most likely. It would depend on the wording."

He said, with some irritation, "You're being very agreeable, aren't you?"

"I'm an agreeable person."

"How can you manage your life that way? What if your contract-holder ordered you to sleep with him?"

"Are you speaking hypothetically?"

He had been, but now he hesitated. "Probably."

"Hypothetically, then, that would be a violation of contract, punishable by death."

There was a momentary silence. "I can be in violation of contract, then."

"Yes."

"And you make the judgment and pass the sentence."

"Yes."

"You know, for an agreeable person, you're not very forthcoming."

She turned to look him in the face. "I'm shy around strangers."

They sailed on wordlessly for several minutes. The Diamond had long ago filled the viewscreen; now he could see the lights of the Transport docks. Tal said, "Can I ask you a few things about Cyr Vesant?"

She shook her head. "Nothing that might be considered confidential, I'm afraid. Past contract-holders are under Graykey privilege. How else could they trust us with their secrets?"

"But your contract is mine now. If I insisted?"

Something in the movement of her eyes made him anticipate, and they spoke together: "Violation of contract."

He added, "The penalty for which is—"

"The penalty for contract violation is *always* death."

Not so much a personal gladiator as a tiger by the tail. "If, in the future, you saw I was about to violate contract, would you warn me?"

She smiled. "I might, but I'm under no obligation to do so."

It was a predator's smile. She added, "Thank you for taking me out of there."

Tal thought: And they returned from the ride with the demon inside, and the smile on the face of the tiger.

"I picked her up on the station," Tal told the Transport supervisor. "She couldn't wait, her pass was running out. Do we have any other candidates for admission?"

"Over there." The supervisor jerked his thumb toward the section below Bay Green's control booth, where two young males, perhaps fourteen or fifteen, obviously brothers, were waiting nervously. No tattoos, they must have come off some passing ship. If the Cities didn't take them, their airclaims on the station would be terminated.

"Good," said Tal. As he and Keylinn walked toward the brothers, he said, "Your competition doesn't look like much. They don't like taking women on to work here, but they can't afford to be choosy when good tech help is scarce. Remember, whatever they need, you can do it—I'll coach you later, if it's necessary."

"All right."

All right. Always all right. Cut your right hand off, would you, Keylinn? *All right.* What was going on in her mind?

He said, not knowing why he chose this out of all possible topics, "Keylinn? Why were you chosen to satisfy Cyr Vesant's contract?"

For the first time she looked embarrassed. A faint flush suffused the pale skin, eclipsing the freckles. She said, "I had some trouble with my sense of humor." Then she increased her pace and walked swiftly toward the waiting area, visibly working to maintain her dignity.

Tal blinked. He turned and headed out of Transport, suddenly feeling more out of his depth than he had in three decades.

An hour later, the job assignment interviewer was speaking to Keylinn. Apparently he was an Outsider himself, for he spoke with an Empire accent. "Good," he said, "we can use capsule programmers. You scored well on the sample questions. How are you on communications protocols?"

"Excellent," said Keylinn, who figured she could learn.

He checked another box on a list. "Good," he said again absently, then added, "Excuse me a sec." The interviewer took a few steps toward another man in Transport yellows and called, "Doug! We're up to quota. You want to go to Lane's after shift?"

"Suits me," said the man. "Do we need to do any more with the boys?" He nodded toward the young brothers who stood miserably nearby.

"Nah." The interviewer waved a hand toward a couple of security officers standing near the exit and called, "We can dispense with them." The security officers came forward at once to lead the boys toward the return ship. One of them started to cry.

The interviewer said to Keylinn, "New hires claim to have a lot of trouble understanding Cities folk, but ask them to speak slowly and you'd be surprised how much you'll pick up. Most of the supervisors are used to talking to your kind, anyway."

Keylinn noted that, from his wording, he no longer quite identified with Outsiders. She wondered how long he'd been on board.

A third security officer joined the pair who were forcing the boys up the ramp of the return ship. Her eyes went involuntarily toward the spectacle, then snapped back to the interviewer.

"Yes, sir," she said.

"Oh, and what's your name?" he asked, pen poised.

"Gray," she said, aware out of the corner of her eye of the struggle that was presently taking place on the ramp. She smiled politely up at the interviewer. "Keylinn Gray."

Chapter 6

"A check of the Cities calendar will show that it was an ordinary Saturday: shiftwork, early dismissals for Sunday worship, a rather tedious meeting of the Diamond council. And yet, looking back, March 30, 545, was a day of reverberations for the Redemptionist historian. Two women came to the Diamond: Iolanthe Pelagia of Opal, and Keylinn Gray."

GABRIEL, his private books

Partial text of a letter from Keylinn O'Malley Murtagh to Sean Reagan Murtagh, written in Graykey Old Tongue:

To Sean Reagan Murtagh
Cold Hill Farm
c/o Graykey Academy
PRIVATE

My dear, my darling Sean,
    I've been aboard the City of Diamond for a day and a

half now, and I'm still reeling from culture shock. Fortunately I don't think anybody's noticed. My contract has passed from Elizabeth Vesant to a personage who shall remain nameless, but whom I can sum up to you by telling you he's a born gathrid. I narrowly missed being taken several sector-gates away, my boy, so don't tell me life out in the wide universe is dull compared to home!

I slept in an assigned cell on the Transport deck, and next morning (this morning, that is) found a free pass to the City proper left by my patron. There were some funny looks from the guards on duty—apparently Outsider techs are generally restricted to the deck where they work—but I had no intention of staying confined if I could help it.

Sean, it's amazing here. I had no idea that an engineered environment could be so gaudy, so flamboyant with life. Coming off the *Kestrel,* it was like stepping from a desert waste into a teeming jungle. Mercati Boulevard, the "main street," cuts through a dozen levels, disappearing abruptly at locks along the way and then reappearing at the next higher. I was going to compare it to a sunken river, but it's more like something out of the theater. Colors, noise, songs . . . the shadows of wind-chased, illusory clouds constantly pass over the storefronts, and the roof overhead pulses with Earth-sky blue. You're caught half in pure nature, half in techno-drumbeat, and I think it comes out in the footsteps of the pedestrians—all on their way to someplace *fast.* I was crossing a walkway, heard somebody yell, "Ware below, sweetheart!"—at least, I think that's what he said under the accent—and just missed being splat by a sack of garbage, ready for the noon maintenance teams. This is nothing like a station as you or I have heard of it. The first few months I spent on Baret Station with Vesant, I started to go green-crazy, aching for leaf smell and dirt smell, longing for trees. (There should be a name for that in Old Tongue, Sean, "the longing for trees." Let me think about it.) Any road, it wears off eventually, but I'd touch down on Baret One for a week and it'd be back again, virulent as ever. Baret One's only half terraformed, but it's enough to raise the genie from your cells, believe me. I can *live* in space, Sean, but I was designed for planet-side.

Gray walls and cafeterias, that's Baret Station. Not here, my boy, not here: Variable lights, banners, plants, parks, neighborhoods, dialects, and bars, bars, bars. All with people arguing inside. Do they argue ball-playing, Sean, do they argue love? Do they argue status, insult, hierarchy? They argue the most obscure points of theology that ever danced on the head of a pin. I counted the number of times I heard the word "heresy" spoken inside the Green Lion Tavern. Thirty-six. I suppose a Graykey shouldn't complain, since nowhere outside of home have I heard the fine points of contract duty debated as we do in our off hours, but still I do complain.

The truth is, I complain because they don't allow unescorted women into the better taverns in this city. Oh, don't look disapproving, love, I wasn't going to knock off a half-dozen pints; I just wanted to feel comfortable for a while, and I thought a tavern would be the place to do it. On sparkling water, Sean, I know very well that I'm on duty.

But I get ahead of my story. My first morning, I made my way up Mercati Boulevard to what they call here the admin levels, where the government offices are. Theoretically, they tell me, I could keep cutting through the levels along the Boulevard until I reached court, assuming they let me through the last few series of locks (improbable). The first neighborhood I scouted, where the garbage just missed me, was loud and cheerful sounding enough. I passed two full-color posters of the lad who they tell me runs this place, along with announcements of his wedding. No pictures of the bride, though. I looked. Anyway, I considered, purely as an academic assignment, how I would go about killing the fellow, and decided in the end that the main problem would be not the task itself but getting to Transport afterward.

I passed a few public recyclers, always a sign of civilization (the loud noise they make here, for all the world like a hawk-and-spit sound, made me jump the first time I heard it), and found myself peering at the notices pasted to the outside. Just call me "Nosy" Murtagh. I wrote one bunch down for you:

REWARD!!!!
FIVE HUNDRED (500) DOLLARS
For information leading to any of the following persons:

George Paxon
Beryl Smith
Maryanne Fouquet

All wanted for lottery fraud.
Contact your nearest citycop or security station.

Underneath this was a notice saying:

FIVE THOUSAND DOLLARS
$5,000
FIVE THOUSAND DOLLARS

For information leading to the arrest of

Nicolet Foulard
A notorious ghost
murderer and thief

A rather rough sketch of a man's face followed. And beneath this:

The Diamond Repertory Players
present

Henry IV
A Play in 5 Acts
by William Shakespeare
Now through Christmas at the Starhall Theater
Old version, subtitles provided, full refreshment bar

Naturally, I made a note of the theater. You know how I am about historicals, partic. with live actors. I'm not sure what they mean by "old version," but I can't wait to see what they do to it with their accents.

Meanwhile, did you catch that reference? "Christmas"! Isn't this place a treasure-trove? The calendar here corresponds rigorously to Old Earth's year—do you think that means I'll soon see spring fertility rites? Garlands and May Queens and egg hunts? I do have hopes.

And the language, Seanie, the language! The Old Tongue is nothing to it, though they share a certain rough spirit. You don't say, "I/me eat three apple yesterday"—that would be too easy. You say, "I, the subject, ate, in the past tense, three, apples, in the plural, yesterday." So many gloriously unnecessary things! Articles and tenses thrown around with abandon, and logic a bare afterthought tapping on the windowpane.

I can do out my exile here standing on my head, I assure you. I'm in good spirits, I'm in no more danger than is to be expected, and of course I miss you all very much. I will *not* be writing to Father, so I trust you to fill him in. (I always imagine you standing over me, telling me to write myself. It was his decision, my love, as you well know.) Please tell him not to be alarmed that my contract-holder is a gathrid. It's less than three hundred days, after all; how much can happen?

I will be leaving this letter with my official one to the Graykey Circle. I'm marking it "private," and assume they will so honor it. It's hard to write to you, watching the years go by, and never hear back. Do you know, I had to do some calculations to figure out what the season is there; if I'm right, it must almost be Year End Day. Tell Janny for me that she can wear my yellow gown and scarf to the Academy Ball. She must be quite the young lady now.

                              Your loving sister,
                                         Keylinn

PS: There may be a bit of trouble-rousing over my letter to the Circle. You'll be relieved to know I've finally gotten around to apologizing to Bantry, as Father wanted, a mere six years after the fact—but I don't mention Perrin at all. I can see you shaking your head from here.

In truth, I always had paranoid thoughts before sending off one of my rare letters to Sean. I tried to make them as cheerful sounding as possible, but I'd think: Maybe Janny was killed six years ago in a hiking accident and every note they get from me is like salt in the wound. Maybe Father's dead and I should have broken my silence to him long ago, regardless of what he'd said. Maybe Sean himself was dead and my letters were piling up, unread, at the Graykey Academy. Of course, there was no reason to believe any of them were dead.

But I had no way of knowing differently. Not even the Circle ever wrote back. Naturally, my letters to them were quite different.

To the Honored Dean
Chief Ranked of the Graykey Circle
The Academy

Sir:

This is to inform you that my contract has passed into the hands of a resident of the Three Cities. It may be some time before I can get this letter to our maildrop on Baret Station; I shall do so as soon as possible, of course.

Cyr Vesant declared herself satisfied with her contract and is returning to her native sector.

My present contract-holder has expressed a wish for anonymity, and as I do not want to bring up the matter of letter-writing with him, for fear he may misguidedly ask me to stop, I must interpret his ban on names as encompassing even the Circle.

Your obed. servant,
Keylinn O'Malley Murtagh

PS: Please express my regrets to Instructor Bantry.

I wasn't really capable of constructing a letter in hard copy without a postscript. Believe me, I tried. I tried because I read once that this was a sex-linked characteristic, and I resented any form of implied predestiny. But surely there was nothing wrong in itself with a friendly little postscript, a last wag of the tail, as it were?

I hoped my letters to Sean didn't sound phoney. Anyway, all that would be over in just another year, when I'd come walking over the hill to his farm and test whether he'd lost the knack of noticing when people were sneaking up on him. Ah, but I knew he'd straighten up from his hoe and have his arms out when I was still *leagues* away. That's why he has O'Malley blood.

Meanwhile, life in the present tense: When I could finally tear myself away from Mercati Boulevard, I made my way through the admin levels until I found A83C, an undistinguished door among acres of forgettable corridors, where I put my hand on the IDMat and announced myself.

The door slid open, showing a room with a sofa, chair, desk, and doorway to another room; and reclining there on the sofa, a plump, middle-aged man in a green uniform, who looked up and smiled the smile of one to mischief born. He rose at once, bowed a charming bow, and said, "You must be Keylinn Gray. Tal told me you were coming." He put out a hand, which I took automatically, and he bent and kissed it. "Stratton Hastings," he added, "but call me Spider like all my other friends do."

I didn't know if the handkissing was customary, or he was merely taking advantage of the situation. In any case, I'd not been prepared for him—Tal certainly hadn't told *me* anything. I said warily, "Hello." A wonderful word, which commits you to nothing.

"Hello back. Tal's late, you know."

"Oh."

"Care to join me for tea? There's a little heater over by the link."

"No, thank you." It went without saying that I never accepted drinks from strangers.

He just grinned, taking no offense. "I'll have a cup, if you don't mind, sweetheart." He started to busy himself with the water. "Tal tells me you came aboard through Baret Station. What's it like there, if you don't mind my asking? I've never been off the Diamond in my life, and asking Tal is like calling for a printout of their imports and exports."

I took the yellow leather chair by the desk, moving slowly. There was no reason to believe the area wasn't under audio scrutiny, and I was brought up to be discreet. For all I knew, this was a test of some kind. Finally I said, "To tell you the truth, Spider, Baret Station is boredom itself next to the Diamond. This place is a marvel."

He'd beamed when I said "Spider." Now he tilted his head a bit to one side, as though he weren't quite sure whether to believe me; but he didn't seem displeased. Before he could ask more questions, I said, "Are you a friend of Tal's?"

"More or less."

"Does it vary with time? Which is it today—more or less?"

He grinned. "Sure you don't want a cup? If you're paranoid, you can use the same teabag as me. It'd be an honor, sweetheart, to be in hot water with you."

"Sweetheart yourself," I found myself saying, unable to keep down a smile. The man was outrageous. "But no thanks."

"Best think about it," he began, when a voice spoke from the doorway.

"By all means think about it." Tal stood there, carrying a load of loose papers. "Spider's an expert at living in hot water." He walked in and dropped the papers on the desktop. "Sorry to keep you waiting," he added, in a voice that I really don't think knew how to *sound* sorry, "but I had some arrangements to make. I wanted you to know where this office is, Keylinn. It's not technically mine, since I don't have an official administrative post, but I told Adrian I wanted a place off court level where people wouldn't know where to find me. You may assume its existence is a secret." He glanced toward Stratton Hastings. "Spider finds it useful, too."

"True," said Spider.

"And I wanted you two to get used to each other before I left."

Spider's head swiveled round. "Where are you going *now?*"

"I'll be gone for ten days, maximum. Feel free to use the office, Keylinn. I want you to familiarize yourself with it and with the City. I got you a free-range pass; most Outsiders never see them. Take advantage of it." He was walking into the other room as he talked.

Spider turned to me. "I don't consider this good news,"

he said gravely. Then he peered at my shoulder, making me nervous. "What happened to your uniform?"

"Oh!" My hand went to the tear in the yellow jacket that marked me indelibly as Technical/Transport/Hired Outsider. "It wasn't in good shape when I was issued it, but I didn't realize till I got it back to my quarters. They told me to turn it in for a new one, but it seems a waste."

"You should've told me," he said, "I'll mend it for you, if you like. Only take a minute." He held out his hand, and I stripped it off and gave it to him, not without misgivings. He smiled again, this time rather shyly. He sat down on the sofa with the jacket and produced a needle and thread.

"You can sew," I said, impressed, for not many in the wide universe can.

"Oh, Spider's very good with his hands," called Tal's voice from the other room. For some reason this brought a blush to Spider's cheeks.

"His hearing's practically inhuman," I commented, testing it with an even lower tone of voice.

"So's he." There was no immediate comment from the other room.

A few seconds later Tal's head appeared at the door. He had a pinning gaze, I noted; Spider knew at once that he was the one wanted. "Be in Transport at midnight tonight," Tal said. "And be punctual. I want to leave by twelve-thirty."

Spider looked wary. "Why?"

"There's something I want you to do." He seemed to see no need for further explanation.

"Does it involve leaving the City?" asked Spider, after a moment, for all the world like: *Is it bigger than a breadbox?*

"No." Tal disappeared again into the other room. The sounds of packing came faintly through the door.

Spider looked blankly at me for a moment, then sat back on the sofa, his needle flashing. After a minute or two he cut the thread with his teeth, tied it, and held out the jacket toward me.

I took it. "Thank you."

He leaned back against the cushions, closing his eyes. I wondered if he was thinking about midnight and the

Transport deck. "Sure you don't want some tea?" he said, finally.

"Oh, what the hell," I said, and got a cup off the desk.

Chapter 7

I have seen some Rings made for sweet-hearts with a Heart enamelled held between two right hands. See an Epigramme of G. Buchanan on two Rings that were made by Q. Elizabeth's appointment, which being layd one upon the other shewed the like figure. The Heart was 2 Diamonds, which joined made the Heart. Q. Elizabeth kept one moeitie and sent the other as a Token of her constant Friendship to Mary Queen of Scotts.

—JOHN AUBREY

"Don't expect to be happy."

Her mother's last words reverberated in her head, repeating with each footstep. Iolanthe Pelagia made her way from the sedan chair down the echoing length of the Opal Transport deck, without benefit of emotional escort—father, mother, cousins, and friends were all absent. This was partly for security reasons and partly, she knew, because she had made a prize bitch of herself to them ever since her wedding was decided on. Not that they didn't deserve it; not that that lovely moment when she'd thrown Aunt Bella's priceless greenglass Curosa figurine against the wall had not been worth it; but the walk down the expanse of Transport was a remarkably empty one. Hartley Quince accompanied her, as did William Stockton, along with four armed City Guards who spoke only to the sergeant, and then in accents of purest Sangaree.

She turned to Will Stockton. "Not a lot happens here, does it," she said, for the sound of their footsteps was beginning to make her nervous.

The sergeant continued giving his attention to the walkways and exits. "The deck's been cleared out for you, my lady. Generally it's a pretty crowded place."

"Oh." She felt her face get hot. Of course the deck, with its bays of ships and equipment, cried out for more personnel. Where did she come by this gift for saying such obviously stupid things? And to the sergeant of all people, whose respect she would like to have, and before Hartley Quince of the cutting tongue.

What incredible embarrassment would she perpetrate in front of Adrian? She brooded, certain that the two men walking beside her were turning over her idiocy in their minds, too polite to comment on it.

Hartley spoke. "Ever been in a short-range?" The question seemed to be aimed at Will Stockton, who shook his head.

"Not much call for it in City policework."

Hartley, not quashed at all by this leaden response, transferred his smile to Iolanthe. "Lovely gown, if I may presume to say so."

"Thank you." It came out as leadenly as Will's reply. Hartley had chosen the gown himself in tandem with her mother, during one of those mystery shopping trips that took all afternoon. It was midnight blue with fine lacework, and depressing in its clarity of purpose: Chosen to please Adrian, not her.

"It suits your fair skin."

"I prefer lighter shades." *As well my mother knew.*

"One dresses for onlookers, not for oneself. Wouldn't you agree, Willie?"

"No," said Will Stockton shortly. Io glanced from one to the other of her assigned escorts. What in the world was going on with them?

"There speaks an honest guardsman," said Hartley. "You will find, Iolanthe, that an awareness of one's audience is a prerequisite for success in any project. If they consider painting the face blue and spitting pomegranate seeds to be the height of charm, then start painting and learn to spit."

"Words to live by?" inquired Will.

"If you like."

They had reached the ramp of the private Council

short-range. One of Will's Sangaree guards detached himself from their group, entered, and returned.

"Pilot's in place, sir," he said to the sergeant.

Io could barely make out the words, his accent was so
thick. She determined to listen more closely; she was
tired of having things talked of around her, decisions
reached without her knowledge. She took Will's arm and
climbed the ramp beside him.

At the top she stopped and looked around. Opal Transport Deck: Good-bye to all that. Hartley Quince paused
by the sergeant, just inside the doorway.

"Heard any good heartsingers lately?" The Lord Cardinal's assistant was speaking in Sangaree, she realized
vaguely, the knowledge drifting smokily through her
brain as though from another country. Up and down the
deserted deck, panels sat gently glowing. She'd left her
room so quickly this morning, there'd been no time for
any last looks.

"Never listen to them," said Will, in flawlessly correct
court speech.

"And you a product of Tanamonde Street. Where do
you go for recreation, Willie? I know you keep away
from the smokeshops."

All her plush dolls and animals had been left on the
quilt, just as if she were coming back. The silk doll's
clothes she'd helped to sew when she was seven; the miniature umbrellas, the complicated headdresses of velvet
and feathers. A new one each birthday, bought by her father from the old man who ran the shop in the most exclusive district of the City. The smell of sawdust and
paint in his studio.

She'd *meant* to take a last look.

"Don't expect to be happy." The soft swish of her
mother's silk gown as she lifted the material and ran it
through her fingers. The satisfaction in her eyes. *"Io, darling, have I warned you about what he'll expect from
you?"*

Will's voice was at her ear: "Come inside, my lady."

She felt him change position, moving so that his body
was between her and the deck. Cutting off her view.

Hartley's voice, then: "What about The Caravanseri?"

Will looked past her, and spoke in the tones of one

goaded into the truth. "If you think that sucker-joint for bored aristos is a real Sangaree bar, Hart, you're more out of touch than you know."

He'd answered in Sangaree dialect. Iolanthe finally responded to his tugging, stepping into the ship, as Hartley Quince began to laugh.

Adrian took his seat at the head of the marble-topped conference table in the Flux Chamber. The chamber, built into the heart of the Diamond, was a translucent square suspended within the sac of irrationality that was the Curosa flux drive. Its walls pulsed with rainbow pastel shades, a constantly shifting pattern of color. "What do they mean?" he'd asked Fischer, the first time he ever chaired a council meeting there.

"What?" the Chief Adviser had replied blankly.

"The walls. What do the patterns mean?"

Fischer looked around, as though Adrian had suddenly asked for a definition of light and dark. "Something to do with the drive, I suppose."

"But what? Look there—they're going faster now. Did something change in the drive?"

"I wouldn't know. Adrian, do you want to go over what I told you about Lord Muir—"

"Hmm. I suppose if the drive explodes or something, we'll be the first to go, but it won't really matter since everyone else will die, too. What if it just breaks down, though? Do you know, I've never really considered that? Brandon, what if the drive just sputters out one day, in the middle of the afternoon? Nobody in the Cities knows how to fix it. We couldn't even call for Outside technical help, since they use their Gates and their short-ranges—"

"The Curosa guaranteed their drive for a million years." Fischer rustled his notes impatiently.

"Do years mean the same for them as they do for us?"

The Chief Adviser paused. "I don't know." He looked thoughtful, then said, "Well, there's nothing we can do about it anyway."

Adrian thought it over. "I suppose not." He sighed. "So what about Lord Muir?"

Numberless council meetings later, Adrian barely spared a glance at the alien energies that cast their glow on the walls. "Pretty colors today," he murmured, push-ing some hastily penciled notes toward Fischer.

"Umm. Yes, aren't they." Fischer glanced at them, and said, "Have you seen these trash collection figures?"

"Uh-huh. You think Muir is making them up, or—"

He broke off as the eight other council members began filing into the room. Fischer rose to his feet. When the ta-ble was full, Adrian said, "Please be seated, gentlemen."

Half an hour later they'd passed without incident through a request from the chef's guild for a new uniform insignia (granted), a suggestion for a curfew to lower crime on decks below G (turned down—"Good lord, Stephen, people have to go to work. It's not like the cur-few on court level during the Troubles. It's just unen-forceable, and why show them how powerless we are?"), a bill to raise the tax on candy by three cents for every five pounds (passed, without comment from Lord Muir, who was sensitive about his weight).

All this was well enough. But just when Adrian was looking forward to a shower and a free forty-five minutes until his scheduled dinner, Lord Baltis stood up.

This was alarming in itself. Members of the council were generally comfortable with speaking from their seats. It suggested that Lord Baltis had something of ma-jor importance to say, and Adrian, who had dedicated his few years of public service to seeing that nothing of im-portance was *ever* brought up at a council meeting unless it had already been settled, moved with the speed of a for-est hare who had wandered into the sights of a cougar.

Pretending to have suddenly gone blind, Adrian fo-cused his gaze toward the corner of the room farthest from Lord Baltis, and said, "With no new business, I think we should return to the question brought up by Lord Muir—"

Lord Baltis cleared his throat.

"A-most-timely-rethinking-of-our-maintenance-proced-ures—" said Adrian, the words tumbling out with remark-able speed, leaving no room for courteous interruption.

"Sir!" said Lord Baltis, who had left courtesy behind long before his fiftieth birthday, and who now, at the age of sixty-two, considered himself more than entitled to

break in on anyone under twenty-five, even the Diamond
Protector. Well, at least at a closed council meeting,
where things were informal. "Sir, I'd like to question the
protector regarding our strategy for a trade agreement
with Baret Two."

There were groans from several members. "We've been
through all that, Ned," said the young Lord Messina. He
made a sour face toward Datchett, the recording secretary,
with whose son he had a tennis engagement in half an
hour.

"Not to my satisfaction, we haven't," said Baltis
grimly. "With our basic stores down fifteen percent, I
want to know why we picked a nonagricultural trading
partner like Baret Two. With all respect to our lad here,
if he wanted wedding lace for his bride, he could have
gotten it more cheaply."

"We're here now, Ned," said Messina. "Can we pass
on to other things? You didn't vote against the destination
when it was proposed."

"I was home with the flu!"

"You voted by proxy," said Datchett, consulting his
notes.

"They told me it was to be a short-term trade stop! Not
a long-term one!"

"Oh, wake up, Ned! We're already in-system! You
want us to move?" Messina draped one arm over the back
of his chair and turned it slightly toward the door, a move
verging on rudeness.

"Gentlemen," said Adrian, in a voice that suggested he
had no opinion on the matter one way or the other, "is
this a proper use of our time? I'm surprised at you,
Roger." Roger Messina looked down at the table. "Lord
Baltis has brought up a valid point. A bit tardily, I'll admit, but certainly he has a right to express his views."
Adrian smiled tolerantly. "But first, I think we're doing
our colleague Lord Muir an injustice. He had several
points to make, as I recall, about our waste recycling procedures, which were very well taken. I don't want to cut
him short. Lord Muir—"

Lord Muir, a florid-faced man with a white mustache,
the very picture of aristocracy, rose to his feet, not to
be outdone by Ned Baltis. "First," he said "may I draw

the attention of my honorable brothers to the schedules presently published by the Department of Waste Management?"

Lord Baltis looked around and then sat down uncomfortably. Lord Muir continued in his driving, enthusiastic tones for a good quarter of an hour, while Adrian, the only person with the authority to shut him up, sat with a faint smile. Lord Muir was known for his desire to enlarge the status of his family through the design of pointless public projects. As the table chimes announced the new hour, Roger Messina looked very close to bolting from the room, but contented himself with staring grimly at Adrian, whose gentle smile never wavered.

Finally Adrian spoke kindly, "Lord Muir?"

"—the teams of the alternate day—"

"Lord Muir?"

Muir halted, looking confused. "I haven't fully explained—"

"I know, but I'm afraid our time grows short."

"But this is an important project, Adrian."

"It is, it certainly is. That's why I'd like to ask—if you wouldn't mind—if you'd consider submitting an official paper on it."

Lord Muir's face beamed with pleasure, becoming even redder than before. "Really?"

"I definitely feel it's called for."

"I don't know ... I've never written a paper before."

"Why don't you go to the head of the administrative procedures department—what is that man's name—"

"Teal, sir," said Fischer, giving the name of the man who actually ran the department, as opposed to the aristocrat whose territory it officially was.

"Teal. An excellent fellow. Ask him to help. No, order him to assist you—say it was a directive from the Protector. His department falls within your jurisdiction, doesn't it?"

"Yes, it does! I'll see him at once." Muir began stacking his notes together again, out of order, oblivious to the wide smile painted across his features.

"I suppose we'd better call it a day, then," said Adrian. "Unless anyone has further business to bring up."

Nine pairs of eyes turned to burn into Lord Baltis, who stayed where he was, brooding silently.

"Fine," said Adrian. "Thirtieth of March meeting, two-thirds of the members being present, is over. As always, thank you for your counsel."

Roger Messina grabbed his notebook and was out the door, followed by the rest of the council at a more leisurely pace.

When they were alone, Fischer looked over at Adrian. "The Teal thing was a stroke of genius."

"Thank you. I couldn't help remembering how he destroyed the first five ideas I ever came up with. He focused his beady little eyes on them and melted them down with a beam of white hot logic. Very painful, it was."

"He won't be logical with Muir, I trust."

"Oh, no. He'll just help Muir flesh out his ideas on paper, and by the time they're finished Muir's plan will be identical to the system that now exists. I'm very fond of Teal, you know."

The table chimes sounded and a feminine voice said, "Information level five."

Adrian sat up straight and put his feet back down on the floor. "Accepted."

"The lady Iolanthe Pelagia is waiting at the Cavern of Audience."

"She's *what?*"

"The lady Io—"

"When did she arrive? How long has she been there?"

"She requested audience twenty minutes ago."

"Good God! Doesn't anybody call me?"

"Interruptions below level six are not permitted during council sessions. The session only ended forty-five seconds ago."

"Why wasn't it classified a six? No, don't tell me!" To Fischer, he muttered, "Nobody wants responsibility for *anything.*" He raised his voice. "Please inform the lady Iolanthe that I will be there presently."

He turned to Fischer. "God, what do I do now? She wasn't supposed to arrive today!"

"Arno, being a pain in the rear quarters."

Adrian got up, walked impatiently back and forth, then

stared at his ghost in the Flux Chamber wall. The wall
gave back only a vague outline. "How do I look? Where's
my comb? Where's Lucius? Is he on duty this afternoon?
Do I have time to stop at my quarters?"

"My dear boy, she won't turn you down, you know.
She can't."

"That only makes it worse."

He paced up and down again, and a faint look of alarm
came into Fischer's eyes. "Adrian, you're not getting into
one of these moods—"

"No, I am not getting into one of these moods! Dammit, Brandon, could you show a little compassion? Could
you give me a straight answer on how I look? —Oh, why
is Tal never here when I want him? Damn the fellow!"

"Adrian, you look fine. I swear it. I'm not unsympa-
thetic, but for heaven's sake, why are you nervous?
You've just handled the council beautifully, and they're
eight grown men!"

"Grown men are nothing, Brandon. We're talking
about the woman who's going to be my wife."

Occasionally, it dawned on Fisher that there were times
to abandon logic even when talking to his friend and ex-
protégé. He said, "You look excellently well today, in
fact. That sand-colored jacket suits you. I meant to remark on it earlier."

Adrian's pacing slowed. "Really?"

Good lord, thought Fischer, he sounds just like Muir. I
hope Opal never finds out how wide his weak spot is
when it comes to appealing to women. "My Jane saw you
in it last week at the river festival and told me how well
you looked. Piratical, I think she said; meaning it in some
romantical female sense. Were you wearing your white
silk shirt with it?"

"Light blue."

"Good choice, but I like the white you've got on now
better."

Adrian stopped pacing. "Well, there's no need to make
a fuss about a premature meeting."

"Certainly not."

"I mean, we have to meet *sometime*."

"Of course."

"Opal only wants to irritate me, and why give them the satisfaction?"

"Exactly."

Adrian stood in thought. "And of course, she might not be in any position to carp. I mean, she might be a crone."

Fischer rose purposefully. "I think it's time we met her."

"Yes," said Adrian. He straightened his shoulders and strode toward the door. Just across the threshold he stopped, nearly causing Fischer to bump into him. "You don't think one of my dark suits would be more appropriate?"

"No," said Fischer, the word coming out between his teeth.

The door slid shut. A kaleidoscope pulsed against the walls of the empty room.

Io was getting near the edge, and she knew it. She'd felt the ghost of the migraine aura several times and understood that she was in for a very bad time, very soon. And then they'd had to wait, all seven of their party, standing conspicuously outside the audience hall while gentlemen in capes and silk jackets and ladies in hats of feathers kept whispering among themselves. She considered the fact that this was the pattern her life was to take: the misery of public spectacle, forever and ever.

It was interesting, at the age of seventeen, to have nothing whatsoever to look forward to. She glanced at Hartley Quince, lounging against the wall. He'd gotten a smokeless from one of the Diamond courtiers and was trying to engage one of the servers in conversation. How easy it was to hate Hartley Quince. Will Stockton, on the other hand, stood ramrod stiff beside her, giving every evidence of official obliviousness to the stares they were getting. But it was clear to her that he was aware of every one.

How could Adrian leave them out here? Was he trying to humiliate her? They'd never even met, how could she have offended him? Maybe he was one of those men who like to humiliate women and don't need a reason for it. One of her brothers' friends was like that. Or maybe Adrian just didn't give a damn one way or the other; that would be immeasurably better. Perhaps, if she found favor with God, Adrian would just ignore her for the rest of their lives.

Maybe he was sending some message to Opal by ignoring her. Yes, maybe that was her fate: To be a living communications system, and the two Cities could take their cue for their relationship by how well she was treated. A slap, a black eye, and committees would form on Opal to review their treaties. . . .

Io, darling, have I warned you about what he'll expect from you?

"My lady?"

Iolanthe found herself facing a woman of about thirty, with twinkling blue eyes and blonde hair pulled up into a net of pearls. Her gown was sky blue, with glossy sleeves, and it made Io suddenly very conscious that perhaps her own dress was over-dark for daytime wear. Maybe that was one of the things the gossips were whispering to each other.

"I'm Prudence Favvi. Adrian was running a bit late, so he sent me to take care of you. I hope you've been well-treated."

"Yes, thank you," said Io, who understood what it was she was supposed to say.

"Is this your whole party? Shall I have chairs brought? Would any of you like something to drink? We have coffee, tea, and water in that little room there just off the corridor." Prudence Favvi pointed to one of the carved wooden doors to the left of the hall entrance.

Hartley Quince had quitted his lounging and walked over to stand beside the Favvi woman. "Thank you," he said, "but we're quite well as we are. That is, assuming we don't have much longer to wait."

She smiled a professional smile toward him. "Certainly not. Adrian has been looking forward to your arrival. And I'm sure that he would have been here to greet you on the spot—if anyone had thought to let him know you were coming."

They exchanged warmly insincere looks. Then Prudence Favvi curtsied toward Iolanthe, and withdrew.

* * *

Prudence entered the Cavern of Audience, which had been summarily cleared of spectators. Brandon Fischer stood there beside Adrian, who had returned to his vocation of pacing restlessly across the floor. He was still wearing his sand-colored jacket.

"You do look marvelous," said Prudence warmly to him, for like Io, she understood her role here, and she and Adrian were old friends. "Let me straighten your collar."

He stood obediently while she did so. "Well?" he said.

"Just first impressions, Adrian. But I don't think you should meet in the Cavern."

"Why not?" asked Fischer.

"She's scared, I believe. And possibly the least reassuring thing I can think of is to drag her in before the court and exchange those meaningless pleasantries of state that have to be said at times like this."

"The advantage of meaningless pleasantries of state," said Adrian, "is that nobody has to think about them. They may be less of a strain on all concerned."

"In my opinion, she's been stared at enough for one day. She's only seventeen, and she wasn't brought up to it the way you were."

"I wasn't—never mind. Prudence, that wasn't my first question."

"What question—oh!" Prudence Favvi smiled widely. "She's lovely."

His eyes widened. "Is she really?"

"Dark-eyed beauty, straight out of a storybook."

He started to pace again. Prudence could almost see the nervous energy crackling in the air around him. "Dear me, perhaps I should have told you she was a hag."

"Why?" he said, startled.

"Well, I don't know that if I were your designated bride I'd want to meet you this way. She's off balance enough already. You look like you might scoop the poor girl up and fly her to your aerie on the mountaintop at any time."

"That's ridiculous. I don't scare women. Brandon, tell her that I don't scare women."

The Chief Adviser stepped away. "I'm staying out of this."

"Coward. Wait, does that mean you agree with her?"

"Adrian," said Prudence, "she's waiting outside."

"Yes, yes, I'm very aware of that. All right. We'll meet in the tea room, how about that? Does that please your feminine sensibilities, Prudence? We'll clear out the servers and just bring in her and—well, I suppose we'll have to include the highest ranking escort in her party—"

"Not the man I just met out there. Troublemaker, written on every pore."

"Really? Very well, we'll include her chief bodyguard, then. How about that, my Prudence? Does it satisfy your intuitive heart?"

"I think it may do," she said airily.

"Well, I'm sure we're all relieved to hear it. Should you have any new insights on state policy, you'll be sure and bring them to us, won't you?"

"You're fortunate I'm here giving you my support," she said, with some tartness.

"Yes, I am." The edge of mockery left his voice. He lifted her hand and kissed her fingers. "Thank you. In future, when I'm difficult, I hope you'll remember that I did once express the gratitude you deserve."

He was indisputably sincere, and for a second Prudence felt her eyes sting. This was not the time, so with an effort she threw off the feeling and forced an easy smile. "Adrian, only you would take an occasion of gratitude and use it as a bargaining chip for future favors."

He laughed, startled. "Blame Brandon, it's the effects of his training."

"I'll go clear out the servers," she said, curtsying with her old pertness, and withdrew.

The room was small, not well-lit, and warm from the effects of coffee urns and heaters and closed trays full of toasted muffins. A black-and-white-striped lacquer chair had been placed by the table for Adrian, but he was not in it. Brandon Fischer sat in a folding chair in the corner watching his lad circle the muffin table. Fischer opened his mouth a few times, but then closed it before saying anything. Silence was the only feasible route here, though the temptation to useless speech was strong.

Prudence Favvi had done well, he thought. She was the strongest and best of Saul's distant cousins, and had always been a friend to the boy. If Adrian's marriage turned out to be a tenth as good as the one between Prudence and her husband Michael, he, Fischer, would be more than satisfied with it.

The door to the tea room opened. Prudence came forward, leading a dark-haired girl. Fischer's first impression was simply that, a young girl looking insecure and uncertain; his second impression, directly on its heels, was: *Good heavens, this is possibly the most beautiful young woman I have ever seen.* A tall young man in City Guard red followed.

"My dear," said Prudence gently, in defiance of all scripted etiquette, "this is Adrian." She patted the shoulder of the dark-haired girl, her voice low and calm, with the steady reassurance of a nurse. Her actions seemed so natural, it was only a moment later that Fischer realized that Adrian should have spoken first.

Adrian stepped forward from the jungle of old tea urns. The light of the heaters suffused his face, giving badly needed color to his paleness. "I'm very glad you've come," he said.

A good beginning, thought Fischer, but then the boy stopped. After a moment, Iolanthe Pelagia said uncertainly, "I hope—"

Simultaneously, Adrian had begun to speak. They both fell silent.

Fischer felt his toes curl up in empathic discomfort. This was Adrian, the charmer of every young lady from court level to Requiem Row? Damn, the occasion was too important, that was the problem. If the boy only cared a little less, he could have been his usual self and given this girl the reassurance she so clearly needed.

"Please go on," said Adrian finally.

"I hope," said Iolanthe, with a trace of grimness, "that the amity between us will become a bridge across the stars between our two Cities."

Oh, heavens. Even Prudence looked appalled. You can get away with that kind of thing in a hall of audience, when you were playing to the crowd anyway; it fell miserably flat here in this tiny room, particularly in the school-lesson voice that the Lady Iolanthe dragged it out in. Adrian might have pulled it off, barely.

Iolanthe Pelagia bit her lips, looking a little horrified herself, but wearing the expression of one determined to enter Purgatory. She said, "The essential unity of the heirs of the C–Curosa—" Her voice cracked just then, making her stumble over the alien name. She stopped short. A pink flush spilled over her face, starting at her neck and reaching her hairline in less than a second.

It was completely enchanting. And her cracking voice had removed any authority her undeniable beauty had lent earlier. Secure in his one-upmanship, Adrian suddenly found his tongue.

"I know we hope the same," he said kindly. "Do you know, I think you should sit down and have a cup of tea. We have lots of them here."

She blinked at him, confused, through eyes that were shining with moisture.

"Prudence," said Adrian, "do you think you could pull over a chair here? And what about your escort, my lady?"

"What about him?" she echoed blankly, leaving the world of diplomacy behind.

Adrian grinned. "Does he want *tea,* my dear." He was addressing her the same way he addressed his legion of ex-lovers, but fortunately Iolanthe was unaware of that.

"He's not an officer," she said, a little shocked.

"Well, no need for us to be inhospitable. What's his name?"

"Will Stockton."

"Will Stockton, would you like a cup of tea? Or coffee?"

To Iolanthe's clear amazement, the sergeant said calmly, "Tea, please. I never drink coffee." And he pulled over a chair.

"Excellent choice. The coffee here has been standing for at least an hour that *I* know about," the Diamond Protector said darkly.

Fischer started to chuckle. The others turned to look at him.

"Sorry," he said. A few more chuckles escaped. "Sorry," he said again, to Adrian.

The Protector shook his head. He pushed his chair a bit closer to the heating table and lifted a traytop. He glanced over at Iolanthe and Will Stockton.

"Now," said Adrian, as though he were putting a question to the council, "how do we feel about muffins?"

Chapter 8

Io did not know what to make of him. He didn't seem particularly frightening, but then Lord Cardinal Arno also went out of his way to reassure, and it was wise never to relax around people like that. And yet . . . Adrian seemed so pleasant. So normal. As Prudence led her through corridor upon corridor, flanked by all five of her bodyguards, Io turned to the older woman. "Was that . . . usual?"

Prudence dimpled suddenly. "Usual in what way, my dear? He's never been engaged before, so I have no yardstick to measure."

Io tried to match Prudence's brisk pace. She noted an occasional well-dressed lady, but no gentlemen, except for her five, and they seemed to draw unhappy looks from the ladies the group did pass. No sedan chairs either, and she could have used one. She put a hand to her forehead. The headache was hovering nearby; she could feel it watching, sizing up the situation. If only she could retire to her room for a few days, the way she used to at home.

"You look tired," said Prudence in a businesslike way. "When we get to your quarters, why don't you take a nap if you want one? I won't let anyone disturb you for the next four hours. Dinner's at eight."

"Will Hartley Quince be there?"

"I don't know—may I call you Iolanthe? Call me Pru, if you like. I don't know if he's been invited."

"Do you think he was angry at being sent to quarters in the Jade Court?"

"I don't see why he should be, that's where the rest of the Opallines are. We can hardly put you up with them, Iolanthe. You're the Protector's wife, practically. Anyway, what does it matter whether he's angry or not?"

"It matters," said Iolanthe, who had grasped that fact at least from her mornings of tutoring with Hartley.

"Oh?" Prudence made a face. "I'll be glad if he stays away. I took a running dislike to the man. Though, to be honest, I suppose I could change my mind. He is *extremely* good-looking."

Io turned to her in surprise. She had not been brought up to discuss the physical merits of gentlemen quite so openly. Their reputation, their wealth, or their family inheritance, yes. But . . . suddenly she decided to dabble in these waters.

"I never could see it, myself," she said tentatively.

"No? The face of an angel, and my, he does fill his pants well."

Io immediately felt her face get hot, for the second time in an hour. The conversation, she decided, was getting too advanced for her. "Will there be other ladies staying with me, besides you?"

"Not right away. Adrian thought you'd like to choose your own companions. I'm just here to get you started, Io," *Io* already, Iolanthe noted, "and once you've settled in, I'll be on my way."

"Why?" The question came out more forlornly than she'd meant it to. She'd only met Prudence ninety minutes ago, but she was the only friend Iolanthe had.

"My dear! I won't desert you. But I have a husband and family, you know. I'm just doing Adrian a favor, seeing you off till you can fly on your own. We can still see each other, if you find you want to." Prudence stopped before a copper-covered door etched with squares, a summer apple tree engraved in each. "Here we are."

As Prudence entered the command code, she said, "Now, if you get lost, remember this is the ladies' wing of the Boxwood Court. Adrian's quarters are three sections over that way," she gestured vaguely toward her right, "so this should be respectable enough."

The door opened. "One moment, my lady," Will Stockton said, and he vanished inside. Two minutes later he was back. "All right."

Iolanthe stepped inside. The room was hung in shades of lavender and mauve, with tables of black lacquer, pillows, several chairs, and a deep carpet woven with the Curosa breath-of-life symbol entwined with fruit trees, picked out in violet on an ivory background. "Oh, my," she said, and Prudence looked pleased.

"Your sitting room," she said. "Writing paper's here, and invitation cards; link's over there by the long table. Your bedchamber's through there."

Iolanthe walked into the bedroom and out again. "It's lovely," she began, then winced, putting a hand to her forehead.

"Headache?" asked Prudence sympathetically. "It's not surprising, given the day you've had. Why don't you take that nap? I'll be back in plenty of time for you to dress for dinner."

Io did desperately want some time to herself, though she understood it would be useless in fending off the headache. But she also knew it would be useless trying to explain that; somehow, the definition other people used for the word "headache" signified some different order of creature from the thing she knew. "Thank you," she said, being the best she could come up with.

Prudence activated the front door. Will Stockton appeared there; he bowed an inch and said, "My lady, I'm going to get my men settled into quarters in the Jade Court. Two of them will be outside your door at all times."

"Thank you," she said again, dully, not really caring if they were outside her door or making up a singing party to welcome the spring.

"Io's going to take a nap," said Prudence firmly. "Come along, Sergeant." And she turned the sergeant about and exited the room, pulling him along.

"She's gorgeous, she's totally gorgeous. I can't get over it."

"I know you can't get over it, you've been repeating it for hours." Fischer cast an unhappy glance at Adrian, who was spread-eagled on the couch in his quarters, staring euphorically at the ceiling and ignoring the dinner attire Lucius had draped over the chair.

"Well, can I not have my moment of joy? What's your problem, Adviser? You thought the wedding was a fine idea."

"I thought it was an appropriate idea."

"So it's merely that you object to my taking any pleasure in my duty?"

Fischer sighed. "You know that's not it."

"Well, speak up, guide of my youth! Unveil this difficulty, and we will pummel it until it's stunned, melt the remains with a light-rifle, and hammer down any loose ends with carpet tacks. What do you have to say?"

"I wish you weren't so *happy*."

"Oh, *lord!* This is what I long to hear from my friends."

Fischer tapped his feet uncomfortably on Adrian's snowy carpet. "I express myself poorly. I only mean to say that any elation may be premature. We don't know this girl—"

"We know she's charmingly shy. Delightfully beautiful. No obvious signs of imbecility, though it's early days to be sure. And, Brandon, we both know that if she were a lot less, I'd marry her anyway. I feel a little happiness to be *completely* justified."

"I only mean to say," said Fischer, and stopped.

"Yes?"

"I only mean to say that she was clearly chosen by Arno and his cronies for her looks."

Adrian laughed. "And a fine job they did!"

"Perhaps, having heard of your reputation with the ladies—"

Adrian sat up suddenly, swinging his feet onto the floor. "What reputation are we talking about? I have been as discreet as the day is long, Brandon. I haven't visited Requiem Row in *months*. And I always used a false name, always!"

"Oh, come now. As though every house on the Row didn't know who you were."

Adrian glowered. "In any case, regardless of this reputation—which I hold is entirely in your overly sensitive mind, Brandon—I don't see what dreadful results will come from my marrying Iolanthe Pelagia."

"Not marrying, falling in love. That's the danger."

"Oh, who's talking about love? This is a marriage treaty."

"I think that, given your—uh, well-known proclivities—that falling in love is, in fact, a clear and present danger, given time and exposure. And that such a bond with a product of Opal propaganda would be a major weakness."

"Opal propaganda! She's a seventeen-year-old girl, Brandon! What are you saying, that she's some kind of trained seductress?" He shifted uncomfortably in his seat. "I feel silly even saying the word."

Fischer said, calmly, "If I had to guess, I would say she's a shy, socially unprepared girl with no pretensions toward politics, at least at the moment. That is exactly my point. Sincerity is a terrible weapon, Adrian. I've seen you use it often enough."

The square of light over the front door beamed on and off, lending a hearthfire glow to the ivory silk wallpaper of the room. Adrian looked up. "Who?"

"Tal Diamond seeks admittance," said the door.

"Let him in." Adrian glanced at his friend. "Let's see what the most cynical man on the Diamond has to say about your scenario."

Tal entered, still wearing his station tattoo. He carried a brown leather bag and wore a newly pressed officer's jacket. Adrian said, "Well-met! Tal, I want you to listen to the tale of romance that Brandon is . . ." He stopped. "What's the bag for?"

Tal set it down on the carpet. "I want another station pass."

Adrian started to laugh. Both Fisher and Tal waited patiently. At last, Adrian said, "Don't ever change."

"I beg your pardon?" inquired Tal.

"You make the most open use of your relationship with me of anyone I know. How many passes have I given to you over the past two years?"

"Six," said Tal reasonably.

"Do you understand, do you grasp, that most people never leave the City for any reason, unless they're sent on state business?"

"Yes," said Tal. He waited for anything further, and when it did not come immediately, he said, "I'll need a fifteen-day pass this time."

Adrian sighed happily. He said, "Brandon, give Tal a fifteen-day pass. —Oh, would you like to tell me what it's for? If it wouldn't be prying."

"I'm going to board the *Kestrel* on-station and ride with them to Baret One."

Adrian's smile vanished. "Isn't that a Republic ship?"

"Yes."

"Then aren't you playing with fire?"

Tal said, "As you know, I've been working on a personal project. It requires that I be on the *Kestrel* for several days. At Baret One, I'll take the next available ship back to the station—I won't even pass through Customs."

"But you'll be on official Republic territory for the length of the trip."

He shrugged. "It's unavoidable."

Adrian stared at him. He stared back. Finally Adrian said, "If you get killed, who will entertain me?"

"As I understand it, you *are* getting married."

Adrian invested in a sharper stare. When neither of them seemed inclined to speak, Fischer said, "Perhaps we should consider—"

Adrian said calmly, "The Chief Baboon is still collecting his thoughts; therefore, the rest of the troupe will be silent."

Fischer and Tal exchanged a glance, momentarily united in status. They waited.

Adrian looked at Tal. "So be it, you know I don't interfere with your personal life. But you don't leave until after the welcoming banquet tonight. I want you to meet my wife-to-be, before she hears anything about you that might . . ."

"Might mislead her?"

"How excellently well you phrase it." Adrian grinned.

"Corporal Hastings!"

Spider jumped. The Inventory Two-Shift Supervisor strode over to where he stood, entering box numbers onto an asset sheet.

"Sir?" said Spider.

"What do you think you're doing?"

Spider swallowed. "I'm reconciling our syntho-cotton blankets with the amount that Purchasing ordered."

"Why the hell are you doing that? Get over to Foodstuffs, you imbecile! We've got ten thousand orders coming in! Who the hell cares about syntho-cotton blankets?"

Spider tucked his asset sheet inconspicuously into his shirt pocket and started walking toward the food and beverage area, pursued by his supervisor, who seemed to feel a need to continue the conversation.

"It's spring! The temperature is being raised every day! Nobody is going to get on our tails about syntho-cotton blankets! Will they call us if their wine shipments are not delivered? Yes! Will they call us if their petit-fours are not in place? Yes! Do you know how many parties are already scheduled in court territory to introduce Adrian's bride? Sixteen open and twenty-two closed! Orders are pouring over us like solar radiation! And what are you doing, Corporal? Counting the blankets! Are you doing this to ruin my health, Corporal? Is this deliberate? Is this some form of superior-officer assassination?"

Spider understood that the questions were rhetorical. He walked over to the flour pile and joined Private Smollet, a young man with a rather prominent Adam's apple, in separating eight sacks from the pyramid.

The supervisor said, "Smollet, what's the total for this order?"

"Eight flour, twelve wine, eight sugar, six sakish."

"And when do they want it by?"

"Two hours. There's some kind of banquet tonight."

"Two hours! And do you know what Corporal Hastings was doing while you and others here were trying to fill requests from the court larder?"

Smollet, who was a good-tempered sort, made no answer.

The supervisor glared at Spider in disgust. "Blankets," he muttered again, and turned and walked away.

Spider and Smollet counted a while in mutual silence. When the shipment was ready, Spider said, "I'll enter it at the link-station."

"Thanks."

Spider went to the nearest station, sat down, and picked up the pen. He called up the inventory debit sheets. Then he entered, "12 flour, 16 wine, 12 sugar, 9 sakish," multiplying each by a discreet factor of about one half and adding that to the total.

"Signature required," said the link. "Sergeant or above."

Spider hesitated, holding the pen, and let himself, as he liked to think of it, "go Zen." Then he wrote, with a flourish, "Sergeant Roderick Northerby, Two-Shift Supervisor."

He waited. If the signature did not match the template, not only in handwriting but in pressure-to-paper and time to write, alarms would go off and people would come to take him away.

"APPROVED," read the debit sheet. It swirled away.

Spider put down the pen and took a deep breath.

"HASTINGS!" yelled Northerby.

He jumped. "Over here, sir!"

"Where the hell are you? Have you finished your order? Did you go to sleep? Maybe we should wrap you up in one of those syntho-cotton blankets, Hastings—"

When Iolanthe woke up, she saw that her bag had been left by the door to the bedchamber. Prudence was standing in the doorway. "Feeling better?" She walked in, stood over Io's bed, and frowned. "My dear, you look terri— You look tired. Is anything wrong?"

"It's just a headache," said Io, in a voice of doomed resignation that would have suited "it's just an earthquake."

"This will never do," said Prudence thoughtfully. "You wait here just a minute; don't move." She left, said something unintelligible to the guard at the door, and her footsteps faded. Fifteen minutes later she was back, carrying a china cup and saucer with the care one gives to very hot water.

"Couldn't remember which purse I left these in," she said. She took out a colored packet and emptied some crumbled leaves into the cup. The steam took on an earthy aroma.

Io pushed herself up on one arm. "What is it?"

"Headache medicine. I brew it for my husband all the time, poor dear. Drink it down, now."

Io regarded the cup with suspicion. "Where did you get it?"

"From a witch I know on Mercati Boulevard. Very reliable. Go on, drink it, sweetheart. The banquet starts in an hour."

Io took a few sips. "It doesn't taste bad."

"It doesn't taste good, though, either. At least, that's what Michael always tells me. There you are, now. Finish it off. Good!" Prudence retrieved the cup. "Now lie back and finish your nap, and I'll be back in half an hour."

"I'll never be ready for the banquet on time."

"Oh, phooey, they're longing for you to make a big entrance anyway. Let me worry about that nonsense."

Iolanthe settled back down. "You were joking about the witch, weren't you?"

"My dear child." Prudence dimmed the lights and stood at the door, cup and saucer in one hand. "Whatever your nurse used to tell you, you're a grownup now, sink or swim. You can't afford to be a stickler about form."

Iolanthe turned to the doorway, startled, but Prudence had already gone.

"She's late," said Tal.

Adrian, sitting beside him at the long banquet table, smiled. "That's as it should be. Anticipation is half the fun for us mortal human types, Tal. Look around the table—the gossip level is volcanic, and we haven't even been served the soup. I think they're half-inclined to like her already, just for the drama she's helping to invest in the situation."

Tal glanced across the damask tablecloth, where Fischer sat beside Sophia Messina, a distant cousin. She was talking animatedly, gesturing toward Iolanthe's empty seat. Her tight brown curls were starting to fall into her eyes.

"Will they slam their cups against the table," Tal inquired, "and demand that the show begin?"

"All right, perhaps it's not the most gracious attitude, but at least it's relatively positive." Adrian dug a finger around his dress collar. "This isn't leaving red marks on my neck, is it?"

Tal looked at him.

"I'm just asking. I suppose she wouldn't be able to see them by candlelight anyway. —Tell me, what would a banquet be like outside the Cities? I hear the Republic and Empire tend to use artificial meat. Is it true?"

Tal was accustomed to his sudden dips into anthropological speculation. "True enough, most of them do."

"So they might consider us barbaric?"

"The Empire would never say so. They believe in polite deceit."

"But you don't. You come right out and tell me anything I ask. Is that because you're Aphean, or because you're from the Republic?"

Tal looked badly startled. Adrian missed this rare sight, because he turned just then to see Iolanthe Pelagia enter the room.

"I never said I was from the Republic," Tal said, and stopped, because Adrian was so clearly not hearing him. Iolanthe walked slowly down the length of the hall, flanked by Prudence Favvi, wearing a gown that every woman present know was borrowed, for it was a magnificent sky blue, Favvi's trademark color. And Prudence herself was wearing dark midnight, which was plainly ridiculous, as well as making her look at least five years older.

"They've switched gowns," Tal heard Sophia Messina say in her alto voice, clear as a bell across the table. Tal glanced toward her briefly, reliving one of his occasional paranoid thoughts that human women were telepathic.

"But what does it *mean?*" old Lady Baltis hissed toward Sophia. The latter woman shrugged the pair of lovely shoulders that showed above her low-cut gown. From the intensity of the whispers, Tal judged that if Adrian's gossip-formula were correct, Iolanthe's popularity must be growing by leaps and bounds.

"Pity she's a spy," said Adrian, and Tal turned to stare.

"I thought you disagreed with Fischer's assessment."

"Don't be silly," said Adrian, his gaze still fixed on the vision in sky blue. "Of course he's right, but I refuse to accept Fischer's crushingly obvious advice on personal matters. Sometimes he thinks I'm still twelve years old. He should learn to hide it better."

Iolanthe halted just across the table from Adrian, and performed an impeccable curtsy toward him as giver of the feast. Adrian stood. "How beautiful you look," he said, a sentence he had always found welcome, though never as appropriate. "Won't you please grace us?" He gestured toward the seat at his left.

She circled the back of the table and took her place, Prudence next to her. As she crossed behind the chairs, she saw the young man beside Adrian turn and stare at her in a way that was discomforting. He had gray eyes, eyes that seemed "off" in some way. *Well, all in a row,* she thought, sitting down; *the Demon, the Protector, the Misfit, and the Sophisticate.* She turned toward Prudence for a moment to observe how she unfolded her napkin.

"Thank you so much for the medicine," said Iolanthe to Prudence, as the soup was taken away. "I feel so much better. A little disoriented, but there's no pain at all; I can't get over it."

"I'm glad you're feeling better," said Prudence, "but you know, you really have to talk to Adrian. One course devoted to me is acceptable, but two would look very strange."

Io peered down at her blue-and-white plate. Another breath-of-life symbol, feathery strokes hand-painted on thin china.

Prudence sighed. "He can't talk to you until you turn to face him. You're the lady, you have to signify that his attentions are welcome."

"They're welcome enough," Io said to the plate.

"Don't tell me, tell him."

Io waited until the rumblings of Adrian's voice, addressing Tal, had stopped for a moment. Then she turned tentatively to her right.

And found her eyes looking straight into Adrian's brown ones. He said, "I hope the soup was acceptable?"

"Oh, yes. Very nice."

"And the mint-roll?"

"Yes. That was very nice, too."

A brief silence ensued, and Io felt herself starting to panic. The momentary ease of this afternoon, over muffins and tea, had clearly been temporary. Her mind was a glaringly blank field, seared empty.

"May I ask how you spend your time, my lady?"

"My time?" She was puzzled. "I took a nap."

"No, I mean at home. What do you like to do?"

"I don't know. I studied with my tutors. I read books. I had a doll collection," she offered, though nothing new had been added to it for the last several years, and she'd never been really engrossed by it, even as a child. She couldn't think of anything else. She was terrible at this. Why had they sent her?

"Would you like to tell me about your collection?"

Io looked down at the plate again. "You wouldn't be interested in that."

"Probably not," he agreed disarmingly, "but I do like to hear your voice."

He appeared to mean it. She picked up her fork and moved it randomly around on the plate, writhing inwardly with pleasure and acute discomfort. When she didn't continue, Adrian said, "I wonder if I might take this opportunity to expand your acquaintance with City society. May I introduce you to my friend, Officer Tal Diamond? Tal—"

He turned to get Tal's attention, and failed to see the way Iolanthe gripped her fork as though she might need it as a defensive weapon. Then he pushed his chair back an inch, so that Tal and Iolanthe might exchange words more easily.

"I'm honored to make your acquaintance," said Tal, who had been extensively coached by Adrian on how to open social conversations. His encounters tended to be such that he was rarely called upon to close them.

"The honor is mine," said Iolanthe.

One would not have thought so, from her tone of voice. Adrian said, quickly, "Tal was just filling me in on dinner customs in the Empire. Did you know, my lady, that people above the rank of 'cyr' are judged on how lavishly they entertain? The poor souls have to give huge parties on their birthdays, with presents for the guests. Not to mention hired singers and dancers, that sort of thing. Turning fifty can set a bank account back years, apparently."

Iolanthe was thrown off-balance. She had always been led to believe that the Empire was a sinkhold of depravity, and here Adrian was, teaming up with his demon to present her with a full-color picture of their heretical customs. The degree of jadedness they had so casually reached was rather daunting, and they hadn't even gotten past the soup yet. *I don't think I'm advanced enough for this, regardless of what the Lord Cardinal says.*

"I'm afraid those sorts of ideas go over my head," she said, hoping to change the subject. To her horror, she heard it come out in what she would have called a "snippy" tone of voice, the voice of one trying to administer a snub. She froze. Adrian looked merely puzzled, but the demon's gray eyes fastened on her with polar attention.

"I would be happy to clarify them for you," he said, in a tone that made it clear what a snub really was.

Adrain's chair slid abruptly back into close proximity with the table, cutting off the view between Tal and Iolanthe. "Well!" he said heartily. "Ivan! Are those fish-rolls? Bring one over here, will you?"

"You hate fish-rolls," she heard Tal's voice say.

"Shut up," Adrian replied.

It was ten past midnight on the Transport deck when Spider finally located Tal at the entrance to Bay Blue. Three-Shift had just come on duty; he'd passed any number of yellow-suited techs before spotting Tal's dark jacket across the floor.

"You could work on your punctuality," said Tal.

"You didn't tell me where to meet you. It's a big place." Tal had a briefcase and a luggage bag on the floor beside him, and was reaching for the briefcase as Spider spoke. "So how was the banquet? You were there, weren't you? What did you think of Adrian's bride?"

"Is she worth thinking about? Here, hold this." He handed Spider the briefcase and turned, apparently looking for someone. "Mynor!" he called. "Over here."

Spider followed his gaze to a man standing by the side of the bay, looking out of place in a soft velour bodysuit colored in black and white zebra stripes that curved in a pear shape below his waist. "Who the hell is—"

"Mynor Cat Eshlava," said Tal, introducing him to Spider with the Empire honorific denoting a middle income. At least one knew where one stood, financially, with Empire citizens. "He's from Baret Station, an installer of technical devices."

"Hello," said Spider politely. Mynor Cat Eshlava was past his prime, with watery eyes and a belly that made Spider work to keep from glancing at his own growing paunch. He'd thought there were pills Outsiders could swallow that took care of that kind of thing. Maybe the poor guy was allergic or something.

"Honored, cyr," said Eshlava, shaking hands. There was a tremor in his grip, and if he'd been a Three Cities man, Spider would have sworn he was a drug addict or an old alkie. He'd thought Outsiders had clinics that took care of that kind of thing, too. It was nice of the fellow to call him "cyr," very polite, but it suggested a level of financial backing way over Spider's head. He hoped Tal hadn't been flashing money around.

"We've brought you a gift," said Tal to Spider.

"Thank you," said Spider warily.

Tal took a small green case from his pocket and thumbed it open. "This contains several riccardis."

"Several what?"

"Riccardis are short-range communication devices. They're easy to carry and virtually impossible to eavesdrop on."

"That's interesting, I suppose—"

"The receiver, you see, is implanted in the brain, and it's tuned only to one sender. Nobody else even knows when you've gotten a message."

Spider was not slow to see where this was going. "Thanks for thinking of me, really, but I'm due back in Inventory—"

"It's not your shift," said Tal, with a relentless grasp of his minion's schedule.

"—all this overtime for the Food and Beverage sections—"

The installer looked from one of them to the other uncertainly. "Do I have to come back?"

"No," said Tal. "Ignore him. Get your instruments ready."

Eshlava set the briefcase on a countertop and flipped it open. Over his shoulder, he said, "This will only take a moment, cyr, I assure you. It's quite a routine procedure."

Spider eyed the briefcase, with its forest of gleaming metal tips inside, then walked over, grabbed Tal by the arm, and pulled him away. "This is proscribed technology, isn't it?"

Tal appeared faintly amused. "I suppose if you want to be literal about it."

"I do!"

Tal gave a distant nod to two passing Transport sergeants. "Picky, picky," he said, using a phrase Adrian had turned on him often enough when he objected to the Protector's plans. It was pleasant to throw it back at these humans.

The effect on Spider was certainly satisfying. A look of acute frustration came over his face, and he grabbed Tal's elbow again. "Is it Outsider-generated? Then it's a tool of Satan, by definition! I'm educated, Tal, I went to school, I know what the rules are! Damn it, the priest'll have me standing in line at the recycler again, and I didn't like waiting the last time—"

"Spider. Relax. Nobody will ever know. This nice gentleman will go into that empty supervisor's booth with you, install the riccardi, and five minutes later I'll be taking him back to Baret Station. He hasn't even been registered as a visitor."

"And that's another thing!" He lowered his voice dramatically. "This guy's a nathy, Tal—I don't know what he's been taking, but he's been on it too long."

"His hands don't need to be steady. His tools will take care of the fine points. Now let's go, I've got a lot to do." Spider didn't move. Tal sighed. "Who got you off the recycler line last time?"

Looking as though something were stuck in his throat, Spider walked over to the installer. "Will it hurt?"

"No," said Tal and the installer together.

Then Spider and Mynor Cat Eshlava, and Mynor Cat Eschlava's black briefcase, all went into the supervisor's booth. As they walked away, Tal said, "Stay in the booth once you're outfitted, Spider, and call me on the link. It's a visual. I'll be in Bay Blue."

Spider nodded, palely. In a we-who-are-about-to-die spirit he gazed frankly at the installer's face, where the image of a slender power driver was etched in silver, crossed by a red quill pen whose point touched a microchip. He said, "That's an interesting tattoo. Would you mind if I examined it more closely when we got in the booth?"

"Not at all, cyr, not at all. You're most flattering."

Ten minutes later Tal stood in Bay Blue with the installer at his side. Spider's face was on the screen.

"Well?" asked Tal.

"I'm alive," said Spider. Tal reached over to the link and cut the outgoing sound. He took a small disk from the case in his pocket.

The installer said, "I could implant a receiver in you, too, if you like."

"I don't need one." Into the disk, Tal said, "Can you hear me?"

"Of course I can," said Spider. "You're standing right next to the link."

"You don't need to speak so loudly," said Eshlava. "If you like, you can hold the disk to your throat and subvocalize. It makes quite a secure arrangement."

Tal put the disk to his throat and spoke very quietly. "Riccardis are useful devices, Spider. They're for organizations who don't want their employees to have any personal life to speak of."

"Thanks. Thanks very much."

"It could be worse. There are versions with pain and pleasure enhancements. Wasn't I nice not to pick one of those?"

"Probably cost more," said Spider.

Tal turned to the installer. "It seems to be working. Thank you for your time. What do I owe you?"

"Five hundred units," said the stationer cheerfully. "And, of course, a ride back."

They turned away from the link and began walking toward the shuttle in Blue. "Hey," called Spider. "What about me?"

They reached the edge of the bay. The door to the supervisor's booth clanged and footsteps scrambled over the walkway. "What about me?" called Spider, pausing halfway down the steel steps that led to the deck floor.

They looked up. "Nothing," said Tal.

"What do you mean, nothing? My life just changed, didn't it?"

The installer glanced up at him, his watery eyes sympathetic. "I assure you, cyr, there are no lasting medical effects."

"Just a voice in my head I can't shut off."

Tal said, "You won't be able to hear me from the station, Spider. Of course, when I come back," he smiled, "you'll be the first to know."

"Well, the hell with you, too." Spider finished descending the steps and walked swiftly away toward the exits. "Enjoy your vacation," he threw over his shoulder.

"My, your friend is volatile, isn't he?" Cat Eshlava watched Spider stalk across the Transport deck. "Is this your vacation, cyr? I can't say I ever thought of Baret Station as a holiday spot for tourists."

They'd reached the ramp at Blue, and Tal motioned for Eshlava to precede him. "Oh, you don't do it justice," said Tal.

The installer looked puzzled. "Well, your tastes are certainly in the minority. Unless I misunderstand you, cyr. Perhaps your friend was joking?"

"Tell me, mynor, speaking as a technical expert, have you ever heard of a two-way riccardi?"

Eshlava frowned. "There's no such thing, cyr, I certainly would have heard of it if there were. I'm afraid you've been misinformed."

"So they tell me. You'll have to pardon my ignorance, mynor."

Eshlava smiled benignly, apparently pleased at the proximity of the ship that would return him to Baret Station and the five thousand units that would soon be in his possession. He patted the arm of the odd gray-eyed youngster beside him. "It's no dishonor, cyr. You people in the Three Cities are just not technically inclined."

Tal's lips quirked. "Yes. I suppose we simply must face the facts." And he entered the ship behind the mynor, to take up the hunt once again.

Chapter 9

"You, whosoever or wheresoever you be, that live by spoiling and overreaching young gentlemen, and make but a sport to deride their simplicities to their undoing, to you the night at one time or other will prove terrible, except you forthwith think on restitution; or if you have not your night in this world, you will have it in hell."

THOMAS NASHE

Spider's bed was wet with night-sweat. In Spider's dreams, he pounded through the streets and back alleys of the underdecks. He climbed the walkways, shinnied up pipes, and dived behind garbage cans—in his dreams he was skinnier. He wasn't always sure who was after him; sometimes it was the citycops, as real as they'd been twenty or thirty years ago when they'd terrorized the kids from Spider's neighborhood. More often it was the ghosts, the spikes beneath the carpet of his present comfortable existence.

Tonight, in his dream, he'd entered a ghost road, one of the old secret ways through the ship that only deckrats and other lost souls knew, and found the gang waiting for him. Why he'd entered the road was incomprehensible, for in waking life the thought of being trapped in one of those places terrified him. And now here was his worst paranoid fantasy standing at the twist in the blue metal corridor, Fox and Breaker and Snake and the Salamander, all the ragged bunch of them, with only Nicolet missing. If Nicolet had been there, Spider's heart would have crashed to a standstill on the spot. Nicolet hated him.

Spider recalled once seeing what was left of a ghost Nicolet had taken a dislike to. He'd had no idea skin looked like that when it was stripped off, like some kind of bloody pile of old trouser hems. Ghosts couldn't tolerate the appearance of disloyalty, they couldn't afford it; they feared it in themselves and were vicious when it appeared in others.

But I didn't do anything! he thought helplessly, and jumped as the Salamander lunged at him. The Salamander tipped his fingernails with nerve poison from the barracks warehouse on P level. He didn't seem to care if it meant crossing the radiation barriers. He was nearly as crazy as Nicolet.

Spider dived past Fox and Breaker and ran blindly around a corner of the ghost road. He recognized where he was now; there was an exit here, somewhere, that came out behind a Vance Alley restaurant on G deck. If he could make it out in time . . . his heart was pounding dangerously. His side hurt. Oh, God, he was going to die before he got there—

He burst out of the alley. His blind run took him straight into the arms of two citycops who were standing by the back entrance to the restaurant, eating rolls. If they hadn't been armed, or if he'd had as much as a shred of strength left, he might have been able to do something about it. . . . *Wait a minute,* he thought, as they took him away. This had happened before, hadn't it?

The scene shifted, tearing that thought away. Now he was standing in the goat line at the recycler, next to two lottery losers. The man behind him wore a red cheek brand, marking him as a three-time convicted thief, born cycle fodder. Not like Spider, dammit, who'd only been caught once in his life, whose number only came up through a fluke of perversity on the part of the universe. . . . They took the man ahead of him, escorting him gently to the civilized room on the other side of the door, where two priests waited to give him final rites before he was reduced, alive and aware, to his respective components.

Which was, at that moment, fine with Spider; it gave him five more minutes. He glanced over to the glass-enclosed walkway where a group of citycops were standing. There was an officer-rank there, a young one— couldn't be more than seventeen, had to be somebody's kid with a bought commission.

The tumblers in his head clicked, and Spider smiled.

Tal. He remembered, he knew what happened now. Tal would point him out to the supervisor, show his pass from Adrian, and Spider would be summarily plucked from the line. Then Tal would introduce himself, and Spider would accept a cup of coffee that his hands would be shaking too much to drink. He knew this story. The relief from his previous terror was like waking up from a fever, whole and remade.

Tal was pointing toward the execution line. The citycop descended the steps from the walkway, strolled past Spider, and began untying the hands of the man with the cheek brand who stood behind him. Spider stared in disbelief. His heart started hammering again. He threw a look of pleading up toward the walkway, as though by sheer force of will he could penetrate the glass and make Tal *see.*

Tal was turning now. He was examining the entrance to the recycling room with interest. *Me,* look at *me,* Spider thought! The escorts approached him, clubs discreetly at the ready. This wasn't how it was supposed to be, this wasn't the way— He looked up at the door to the room. He turned, planted his feet on either side of the doorway, and twisted wildly, trying to dislodge the hands that reached now for his arms and shoulders, pushing him along. "It's not fair!" he yelled. "This isn't what happened! Ask *him!*" He yanked his head toward Tal. After all the things he'd done for that ungrateful demon—

His feet lost their purchase and he flew through the door.

—Spider sat up in bed, his chest jumping like an overheated engine. He wiped some of the sweat off his face and sat quietly for a few minutes, taking stock of himself. Perhaps he'd screamed in his sleep, but the drunks whose rooms bordered his were used to that. He waited till his heartbeat had slowed somewhat and his hands were under partial control, then rose, pulled the damp sheets off the bed, and methodically went about replacing them with the set that was waiting on the chair. He went to the bottom drawer of the bureau against the wall, opened it and removed another set of sheets, which he dropped on the chair. Three bedchanges this week; that would be average, but the week was still young. He blamed his midnight meeting with Tal on the Transport deck for breaking his statistical mean.

He checked the clock: Four-twenty-five a.m. He poured a glass of water from the pitcher that stood on the bureau, drank it down without pausing, poured a second glass, and returned to bed. The lights, as always, remained on. Spider had had an acquaintance tinker with them so they couldn't be turned off, even from the main switch outside. Especially from the switch outside. When they did finally come for him, he didn't want it to be in the dark.

He sat for a few minutes in the bed, staring straight ahead. Then he lay down on his side, pulled up the clean sheets, and closed his eyes.

Will opened his eyes to a blue ceiling. He was immediately disoriented, not recognizing the white of the City Guard dorms or the faded yellow of the compartment he'd grown up in with his sister. A long, black second later it came to him: *The Diamond.* Will did not like uncertainty about his life, and he supposed the jarring, stomach-twisting couple of seconds he woke up to here was the price he paid for sleeping on his back. People who sleep on their stomachs, his sister used to say, always wake up in the same place: facing the pillow.

Somewhere to his left a gentle snore erupted. Will smiled, rolled up, and swung his feet down off the cot in one smooth motion. Three feet away, Barington Strife, City Guard Corporal, lay sprawled on his side. Barry's pillow was on the floor. Three other cots were set up in the room, a medium-sized chamber with a floor of inlaid marblewood and wall hangings of shimmery forest green. *Jade Court,* he thought. *I never thought I'd wake up on court level.* His four Sangaree guards had been impressed, though it was Will's private opinion that this chamber used to be a wardrobe closet for some court lady. He'd found a tangle of hangers stuffed behind the dresser and a rather delicate pair of rose-colored underpants.

Will got up, passed the two empty cots belonging to the guards still on twelve-hour shift outside Iolanthe's door, and went into the adjoining spit to wash. When he came out again, he slapped the side of Barry's cot.

A groan issued from Corporal Strife.

"Get up, Bar," said Will.

Strife sat up. He was thin and dark, with a sharp nose. "What time is it?"

"Six-thirty."

Strife immediately collapsed again upon the cot. "It's three hours till relief."

"But you have things to do first." Will glanced at the other occupied cot, where a stocky young man lay motionless beneath the covers. "You too, TJ, I know you're listening."

"Oh, shit," said TJ. The youngest of them, only eighteen, he slowly pulled back the sheets, then lay there motionless again as though waiting for Will to change his mind.

Will smacked him on the anklebone. TJ got up and headed for the spit. "Hang on a minute," said Will, "I have to be out of here in ten minutes, I need to give you your orders. Teej, there's a full level-by-level map of the Diamond in a chamber off the Hall of Audience. I want you to go there and start memorizing it. You can study till it's time to change shifts."

TJ waved acknowledgment and proceeded into the spit. Will said, "Bar, I want you to attend the breakfast reception being given by the Chamber Music Society in Malachite Court. It'll get you used to the customs here, and I want you to start recognizing some of the important people."

Strife looked horrified. "Why does TJ get the easy assignments?"

"He was the first one of out bed. Take it to heart." Will started pulling on his uniform pants.

Strife sat there, looking unhappy. Will said, "You'll get free food. And they serve real coffee here all the time, to everybody on court level. Take advantage."

"As though you care. The way you look at a cup, you'd think it had poison in it."

"We all have natural food preferences, Bar. I like tea."

Strife continued looking miserable. Impatiently, Will said, "What?"

Strife didn't meet his eyes. In a low voice, he said,

"Willie, you sure you made a good choice with us four? We're not exactly the breakfast reception type."

Will paused in buttoning his crisp white uniform shirt. He stepped over to the wall and leaned against the ornate, overly baroque bureau that had been hastily shoved into the room when they were assigned to it. Neither of them spoke for a full minute. Then Will said softly, "Maybe I didn't feel like depending on four admin kids who'd only be putting in their time until promotion."

"Your four admin kids would probably go over better with the people here."

There was a profound silence between them, without even the sound of water from the next room. Finally Will said, "Sangaree doesn't define you unless you let it. It's a fucking game, Bar, that's all it is. If you're afraid to play, you're screwed from the beginning."

"You can say that."

"Me? Did somebody come down and tap me with fairy dust? I'm in the same position you are, Bar." He walked over and stood in front of the cot. "We're in enemy territory here. I wanted four people with me that I could trust."

Strife continued looking at the sheets. Will added, "Hartley Quince is supposed to attend the reception. Let me know who he spends his time with."

"Isn't he on *our* side?"

"Just do it, Bar."

In the next room, TJ must have completed his use of the toilet, for the sound of a massive hawk-and-spit coughed at them with the activation of the recycler. Finally Strife glanced up and met Will's eyes. "Jeez," he said, "these are worse than the ones at home."

Will laughed. He went over, took his red uniform jacket from the peg by the door, and started pulling it on. He wondered how Iolanthe was taking her first morning on the Diamond.

That brought to mind his own responsibilities—but if there'd been any trouble, he would have heard about it. He checked his reflection in the glass on the opposite wall. Tall, clean, hair combed, perfectly respectable.

"You're a gift from heaven," said Bar, deadpan, and Will realized he'd been staring.

He laughed, uneasily. Powder-red, they called this uniform. It always reminded him of dried blood. *God, you're a morbid sonofabitch,* he thought.

"I'll see you at the shift-change," he said to Barry.

Having Tal out of town had its advantages, Spider thought, though it was nervous-making in other ways. While good folk in the upper decks were preparing for Sunday church, he guided the freight carrier through the doors of the main court larder and storage house. He glanced over at his companion, O'Connell, and grinned at the knowledge that no imperious summons would come over the thrice-damned riccardi gadget to interrupt this venture. "Not falling asleep, are we?" he asked O'Connell.

"It's early in the morning."

"The better to profit by," said Spider. O'Connell was a slender, light-haired man of about forty, an ex-admin thrown out of the ranks six years ago in a petty official's backtracking to cover his own incompetence. O'Connell was a survivor, and a good man to drink with.

He knew the right way to wear an admin uniform, which was more to the point today. They halted the freight carrier in the larder's loading pad. A kitchen clerk started toward them, a low-ranking apprentice from the look of him, but already angry and letting it show. Tsk. Patience, thought Spider; you'll never rise in the world without it. He pushed open the door of the freight carrier, stood on the edge for a moment, and dropped to the ground.

"Hey there, friend!" he called. "You have our shipments for us?"

The kitchen clerk was very young, Spider saw. He could almost pity him. "What shipment?" The boy's voice started to rise. "Is Inventory screwing *everything* up now?"

"Why, what do you mean?"

"We already got one set of wrong orders last night! They showed up with the last freight carrier and we couldn't send them back! And now you idiots show up, and you're not even on the roster!"

Dear, dear, dear. Spider turned his face up toward

O'Connell, making his voice louder. "Sir, they say we're not on the roster!"

"Do they?" O'Connell opened the door on his side and stood on the edge of the freighter, letting his lieutenant's uniform be seen. The clerk gulped. "We damned well *better* be on the roster, son. I didn't get out of bed early today for us not to be on the roster."

Spider said, "I'm sure it's not a problem, sir." He said, more softly, to clerk: "We're supposed to clear up things from yesterday, my friend—that's why they sent the lieutenant. Maybe you didn't notice, but you had more food-stuffs delivered to you than you ordered—"

"Of course we noticed! I told you, we tried to send it back. We don't have that much free space here, and our department can't incur any more storage costs."

"Then we're here to *help* you," said Spider soothingly. "We're to pick up the extra deliveries and take them back to the warehouse for redistribution." He made his voice confidential. "Somebody up there made a mistake. And you know how it is—mistakes don't happen. So we're here to make sure it *didn't* happen."

O'Connell's voice came down like an iron bar. "In fact, it never happened, if you know what's good for you."

The clerk looked uncertain, but he was the only one on duty on Sunday, a decision had to be made, and their story was all too likely. And then Spider produced a list he unfolded from his pocket, with precisely the amounts they'd been overstocked with. "Well," said the clerk.

"Believe me," said Spider, "if you ever want to get to the next rank, you won't offend the higher-ups."

The clerk threw up his hands. "Take it! Just make sure we don't get charged for it."

"Trust me," said Spider. "I'll do the paperwork myself."

A few minutes later they were piloting a much heavier freight carrier out of the larder. O'Connell said, "I can find buyers for most of the stuff, particularly among the ghosts. But what am I supposed to do with the salt? It's much more than I can use."

"I have an idea," said Spider.

"Lord save us all from your ideas," said O'Connell. He glanced behind them at the vanishing freight doors of the court storage house. "We could do this again in about six months."

Spider shook his head. "Might get the same clerk."

"What of it? Mistakes happen. We could call ahead, and I'll bet he'd *ask* us to come by and pick up the surplus."

"I sort of know him now. I have trouble lying to people I know. It's a problem I have."

"Since when? You lie to your supervisor all the time."

He shook his head again. "I lie to the electronic records. I just don't volunteer the truth to my supervisor."

"Good God," said O'Connell.

They drove on toward the level freight locks. O'Connell said, "You're a much more dangerous person to be with than I ever thought."

"I know," sighed Spider.

Iolanthe entered the Cathedral of Saint Thomas the Doubter flanked by Will's two night-shift guards. Will himself walked behind her, and Prudence Favvi and three ladies preceded her. All in all, she thought, it ought to be sufficient reinforcement to keep her bravery up through the ceremony.

Bravery was needed, for one thing, because every soul in the cathedral was craning a neck to see her. Ladies in their service-going hats of sheer, pearl-trimmed lace; gentlemen in capes and admin jackets; the rows of the children's section, where skinny arms and legs made the fine clothing look as though it had been awkwardly fitted to dolls. A mass of satin and cotton and noses and elbows and hats and the sideways flash of eyes, not as though they were people at all, but part of some collective, organic creature whose parts were wriggling about, displaying a frightening interest in you.

The aisle lasted forever, and then she had to join Adrian in his box on the side. A tall mosaic of Saint Thomas ran up the length of the wall behind them, Saint Thomas Ruiz Brennan, the friend of Adrian Sawyer who had first doubted him and later helped to build the Three Cities. Io took her seat beside Adrian, pausing to kneel and touch her thumb to her left arm in the sign of sharing.

He gave her a sideways smile. "Buck up," he whispered as she got up, not moving his lips. "It's only an hour."

She was so startled she nearly lost her balance getting off her knees. Nothing in her past experience had led her to expect anyone to understand that this event might be a little frightening for her. Or was it glaringly obvious from her face? Oh, God, she hoped not.

The service wound out its routine ritual; she barely noticed it. The gospel that day was the Curosa creation tale, enacted by two priests in costumes of blue and yellow feathers, who danced precisely across the marble floor before the altar, pantomiming the old story. There was no need for Io to pay attention. She could almost have danced it herself.

She tried to stir herself for the sermon, curious as to whether something heretical would be pronounced. But it was only the old Diamond archbishop, whose name she didn't recall, reminding the congregation of the wonder and joy that Adrian Sawyer knew when he realized the Curosa blood-sharing was simply the Christian Mass under alien guise. Iolanthe felt her thoughts drift off and made no effort to hold them back.

". . . and so, brothers and sisters, if Adrian Sawyer, in his inspired wisdom, could see the unity between Curosa and human, how much more should we see the basic unity that exists between our way of Redemptionism and that which is practiced in the City of Opal? Twisted and confused though it may be . . ."

Io sat up straighter. This was more like it! If Arno were here, he would have a stroke.

She looked around the cathedral. There were a number of dissatisfied faces; evidently even a backhanded compliment to the City of Opal was considered unpopular. Adrian's expression was unperturbed.

When the service concluded, Io followed Adrian out to the vestibule, a good five minutes before the rest of the congregation was dismissed. She could hear "Blood of Our Fathers" thundering distantly through the walls. "Holding up?" inquired Adrian. "Breakfast and coffee in a minute." She opened her mouth to reply, but he'd already taken the first steps up the broad stairway to the re-

ception hall, and Will had touched her arm to guide her
along behind.

Prudence met them at the entrance; when on earth had
she slipped out of the service? She smiled at Iolanthe, and
indicated the rest of the room with a sweep of her hand.
"Better get in a few bites while you can, before the
hordes arrive." The room was lined with long tables, set
out with warming plates filled to the brim with sausages,
eggs, toast, bacon, rolls, muffins, and four kinds of juice.
The smells were making her weak.

"Come on," said Prudence, pulling her by one satin
sleeve, "take something in before you faint. You're looking a little pale."

Io found her hands suddenly full of breakfast plates.
She rested one on a table, took a cup of coffee, and began
eating ravenously, glad that the silk and beribboned invaders had not yet arrived from below, and nobody was
judging her on table manners.

"How are you taking it?" asked Prudence. She leaned
against a table, holding a china cup delicately in one
hand. Prudence never seemed to *get* hungry.

"These shoes are killing me," said Io, her mouth
stuffed with a roll.

Prudence glanced down at Iolanthe's specially ordered
white snakeskin shoes, with their crystal heels and their
tiny diamonds sparkling at each eyelet, tied up with pink
lace ribbons. She sighed. "I know. Mine are a preview of
hell, as well." She slipped a muffin onto Io's plate.
"Adrian failed to consult me about today's breakfast. I
must say, it's just like a man to think of a stand-up
buffet."

They glanced over to where Adrian was standing beside a coffee urn, talking to Brandon Fischer, who'd materialized along with several more security guards. "Men
are genetically incapable of grasping the Shoe Problem.
You know what my idea of the perfect state dinner is, Io?
A table with padded chairs, and a servant to crawl along
beneath the table, massaging everybody's feet."

Io started to giggle at this scandalous image. "A man
or a woman?"

"Well, I suppose proprieties must be observed. A
woman to minister to the ladies and a man for the gentle-

men. We'd have to take their word for it, though, since no one would injure their own dignity by lifting up the table-cloth to check."

The doors to the reception room were opened and a stream of hungry churchgoers began pouring in. Iolanthe found that Will had reappeared by her side. There was a spot of bacon grease on his collar.

"Do you want a chair?" he asked. "Those shoes must be killing you."

She stared at him. Adrian came over then, took her hand, and said, "Let me introduce you to some people you should know."

An hour later found her leaning, as discreetly as possible, against the corner of a table. Prudence and Will immediately closed ranks on either side. "It's nearly over," said Prudence. "Come on now, smile at me; you can't afford to look weak, not as a first impression. ... That's better. We'll just stand here and talk for a bit and pretend we're all having such a good time—oh, lord. Here come the Muirs. Heads up, Io. He's Lord Timothy Muir, ultra-respectable, he was in the War and he never misses a council meeting. I understand he's a major pain in the butt. The long-suffering bore with him is his wife Judith. They're trying to get their children administrative posts, and poor Adrian— Timothy! How lovely to see you. Judy, darling, what a magnificent veil, those rubies are almost frighteningly large. What's it like to have a husband so generous?" Prudence babbled on, as she had through many of Iolanthe's introductions this morning, making Io's brief replies seem mature and thoughtful by comparison. Io suspected that this was a deliberate strategy on Prudence's part.

Adrian glanced over from the knot of people who'd cornered him—he hadn't even attempted to have breakfast—and saw what was happening. Iolanthe met his eyes with a look of quiet desperation. He disentangled himself from the group, amid a series of apologetic smiles, and made his way over to her.

"Adrian," said Lord Muir heartily. "I just had the honor of making your promised wife's acquaintance. A

charming young lady. I was telling her about my son
Harry."

"Oh?" said Adrian noncommittally.

"He's out of the knight's pilot school, you know."

"Really."

"He hasn't yet declared an interest in any particular
sphere of public service. This would be the time for a
sharp administrator to pin him down, I thought. Before he
got into somebody else's ministry."

Adrian sent a wry look toward Io over Lord Muir's
shoulder, then faced him. "I know Harry would be an or-
nament to any post he took. But as you're aware, there
aren't many available just now . . . and didn't we give the
assistantship of the Climate Control Ministry to your elder son George? It was just two months ago, wasn't it?"

Lord Muir stroked his mustache thoughtfully, as though
this had not occurred to him. He looked, Io thought, the
way an aging bravo ought to look; strongly framed, aristo-
cratic, stern but approachable; you could believe he'd been
in the Civil War. No actor could have done a better job.

"But, Adrian, surely room can be found for a bright
young man who's so ready to make his contribution. If
we were fortunate enough to have a war—excuse my
phrasing—I know he would distinguish himself. As it
is—"

"As it is, my good friend, there are no posts available."

"Well, now, not to be premature, but the position of Security Chief is bound to open up soon, isn't it? Old
Farnham can't hold on forever. And once he goes, there'll
be a lot of shuffling 'round and moving up, won't there?"

Prudence put her mouth to Iolanthe's ear and whispered quietly, "Farnham's been on his damned deathbed
for years now. We're starting to think he's immortal."

Io lost the thread of the conversation in wonder over
hearing a woman say the word "damned."

"I wouldn't like to speculate on that," said Adrian
firmly. "Bad luck." And bordering on bad taste, his voice
implied.

Lord Muir backpedaled quickly. "Well, now. Well, now
. . . I just wanted to suggest that Harry would do well in
any posting. Not necessarily Security."

"Oh, I'm sure he would. Although, you know . . . he doesn't really have any experience in anything, does he?"

"Experience?" Lord Muir chuckled a perfect man-of-the-world chuckle. "When does a fine aristo lad just starting out need experience? The damned admins can do the day-to-day work, that's what they're there for, hey?"

"That's certainly been the custom." Adrian smiled. "You might mention to Harry that if he's seriously interested, he might spend less time hell-raising with Jason Speluker's crowd—I've been getting complaints—and more time behaving as a ministry candidate is expected to. And Timothy—" he lowered his voice. "I'm afraid I really must ask you to watch your language in the presence of my bride."

Lord Muir looked stricken. "Pardon, I'm sure. Forgot myself. Terribly sorry—my lady, truly—" He began backing away, taking his wife with him.

"Well done," said Prudence, under her breath. Iolanthe saw a slight smile trying to fight its way onto Adrian's face. He turned hastily so his back was toward the departing Muirs. Io met his eyes; suddenly he looked all of about seven years old, pleased and guilty together.

She giggled. A look of delight washed over him. "I'm sorry," he said to her, "but I was under the impression you wanted to leave as much as I did."

She nodded. "You were right."

"God, I love being right!" He took her hand, lacing his fingers between hers. "Now I must take you to a high mountain and show you the treasures of the earth."

"I beg your pardon?" she said, no longer alarmed at all by his verbal balletics.

"No, I beg yours. You would never require my pardon. I meant only that the first phase of your grand tour of the Diamond begins this afternoon, and I would not want to make us late."

"Am I coming?" asked Prudence. "No one warned me."

"Do you want to come, Pru? It's the traditional gemfarm tour."

Prudence made a face. "If you think I'm wearing satin and lace to a gemfarm—"

"It's expected that we go. The Protector's wife gets to

witness one of the economic bases of Diamond trade, not
to mention picking up a brooch or comb along the way."

"It's hot down there, Adrian. My hair will frizz up."

"May I remind you, wisest and loveliest of my advisers, that you invited yourself?"

"Well, if you put it that way, Adrian. Of course I'll
come."

"Good. Now where did Brandon get to—" He looked
around and spotted the Chief Adviser. "My next victim.
Excuse me, Iolanthe."

When he'd gone, Io turned to Prudence, frowning.
"What's a gemfarm?"

Will envied Chief Adviser Brandon Fischer, whom he
overheard begging off the gemfarm tour. "If you love me,
Adrian, don't make me come along on one of those
things. The boredom is matched only by the discomfort."

"You'd add a welcome fourth to the group. As it is, it's
only me, Iolanthe, Prudence, and a dozen guards."

"It's ninety-eight degrees down there, Adrian!"

"All right, all right. Don't whine, it lacks dignity in a
Sixteenth Rank. Go, spend the day with Jane and Emily
Rose. And think of me suffering as they bring you cakes
and iced beer."

"Easy to see you've never been married, lad," muttered
Fischer, but he took himself off with alacrity.

Will approached the Protector. "Sir?"

"Yes ... Stockton, isn't it?"

"Yes, sir. May I take my men through the farm before
the party enters? We didn't hear about the tour schedule
until this morning."

Adrian sighed. "Neither has anybody else, that was the
plan. Do you really find it necessary, sergeant? Besides,
while you three sweep the farm, do you want to leave the
lady Iolanthe with only two Diamond escorts? Who are
perfectly capable of handling any situation that arises, I
might add, but I was under the impression that the Opal
was to retain security control until after the wedding."

Will bit his lip, looking unhappy. Adrian said, "I assure
you, a couple of suitably paranoid Diamond fellows are
looking the spot over at this very moment." When Will
still hesitated, Adrian added, "Let me give you a piece of

advice from the last Protector that's stood me in good stead. When anything you do is wrong, do nothing. Fewer people will criticize you later."

Will spread his hands in a gesture of surrender. He returned to Iolanthe's side, glanced at his two Sangaree guards, and shrugged.

They emerged out of a blue haze, the transparent walls of the lift bullet showing a patchwork of green and brown fields spread out below. An arc of sun-lights ran over the orb of the sky. The bullet descended for a good fifteen minutes, giving Iolanthe time to reflect that it was fortunate she had a head for heights. The ride was lovely, in fact. "I never saw the inside before," she said.

"We all live inside," said Adrian. "This is just a bit farther in. The Flux Chamber's not far from here; another five levels below the ground. The farmers claim they can hear the earth humming."

Below them, the hills resolved themselves into rice paddies. The golden line of wheat stubble in the distance disappeared. "Is it dangerous?" Io asked. "Being so near the flux?"

"If it were, I'd never get anyone to a council meeting. Though that's an idea—maybe I ought to start a rumor, it would make civil action so much easier if there were nobody else in the room." He seemed to be thinking of something else for a moment, then said, "Don't let it bother you, my lady; exposure is only a problem in the long-term. It's the people on the outer shell who total up the real radiation count; that's why we try to keep rotating them. —Look, pearl farms around the ponds. That's the Old-Earth kind. And that building there, that's the gemfarm."

She looked down at a long, rectangular roof that seemed to go on for miles. "They grow rubies and diamonds in there?"

"The treasures of the earth," said Adrian, "as promised." The lift slowed. When they reached bottom and Iolanthe stepped out, her first thought was that the treasures of the earth required a lot of moisture. The air was humid and heavy. A supervisor in white shirt and short trousers met them at the entrance to the lift, bowed, and said, "We're honored." He was in his thirties, with fair skin and an open face. His shirt was damp against his back and beneath his arms. "May I escort you inside? We only had word you were coming half an hour ago, or we would have made better preparations."

"Not necessary, Roger." Adrian smiled. "Somehow I thought this farm would be the most appropriate to introduce the Lady Iolanthe to one of our best Curosa legacies."

"And I must agree. What has it been, five years?"

"Six. And a half."

"Well, you were never forgotten. So much gossip blew through here during the Trouble, we got no output done at all—everybody from the grannies down through the prentices bet the Sawyer kid would end up on top. None of us took those Verities seriously."

"You knew more than I did, at the time. Though I always expected you wouldn't stay in the planting line, Roger. Whenever I turned around, there was a new idea from your section about cutting production time."

Roger beamed. The group started strolling toward the gemfarm doors. Io was walking behind Roger, and she heard him say, in a lower voice, "Adrian?"

"Yes, my friend?"

"Can we advertise the fact that this was the farm the Protector's wife was shown?"

Adrian started to laugh. They went inside.

A blast of hot air hit Iolanthe as soon as she went through the door. The temperature outside had been a delight by comparison. What's more, she noted at once, there was no floor to the building; just dirt. Soft, damp, black, squidgy dirt that was not far removed from mud. She could feel her crystal heels sink with each step. Her shoes—perfectly suitable for morning service—had cost more than most Three Cities families earned in a month. *White snakeskin,* she thought ruefully. *Prudence was right about men not grasping the Shoe Problem.*

The workers had dispensed with uniforms, including shoes, and one could see why. Long tables of rough wood led into the distance, bordered by conveyors down the center. The table legs looked as though they sank down into the earth at least an inch. The ground to the side of the tables was punctuated by rows of large, swampy bogpits that issued forth unfamiliar, but recognizably animalistic, smells.

A young girl sat on the end of the bench nearest them, her dark head bent over her work. She wore a light yellow dress and no shoes, and though the idea of going barefoot in all this muck was a little off-putting, the thought of touching the coolness of the earth was not without appeal. Among the men, rolled sleeves and open shirts were the order of the day.

So these were dirt-dwellers. She'd never thought to be so close to any. She touched Adrian's arm, and he swung around at once to face her. "How do you know that man?"

"Roger? He worked here the summer I was sent down." Seeing her puzzled look, he said, "It's the custom for court-level children to be sent here for a few months to gain experience. To grasp what goes into gem-farming, and how long it takes to build up a trade output, and what life is like outside of the courts. It's more honored in the breach than the observance, but Saul wanted me down here, so down I came. Of course, as an orphan I didn't have parents to make a fuss and keep me out."

"You lived down here?"

"For a few months. Why do you look so surprised?"

"I'm not surprised. I'm— I don't know, I just never saw any people from the agricultural levels before. I thought they would be different."

"Different how?"

"Well . . . they die more, don't they?"

"One death for each man or woman, I assure you."

"Oh, but you know what I mean."

"Yes." His smile was one of such tenderness, and came so out of nowhere, that she hardly knew what to think. "Their life expectancy is about nine years shorter than that of the middle levels, on average. It's the result of all those years of cumulative exposure. Added to by the number of accidents that can happen in a place like this."

Io glanced around hastily, wondering what *did* happen in a place like this. "They don't seem upset. How can they be normal people?"

"They're not happy about it, believe me. Their options are limited."

Iolanthe considered this. "You're the Protector. You could order that people be drafted to work here in shifts."

"What an unusual political agitator you are, my Lady Iolanthe. A seventeen-year-old court beauty, and from the Opal, too. What would the Lord Cardinal say?"

She felt herself flush. "I merely meant to wonder, sir."

"Oh, well, if you call me 'sir,' my heart will be broken in any case, and nothing will be left for you when you lead the revolution against me."

She saw that he was not really offended and said, "Then—Adrian—would you tell me why there's no draft to bring in new workers here?"

He laughed. "I once knew a small dog with very sharp teeth who was much like you. He never let go. One day the Lady Prudence had to cut off a piece of her gown in order to separate herself from the creature." He glanced over to where Prudence stood gingerly beside a table, holding her skirts well above the dirt. "The truth is, we have a hard enough time filling the high-radiation levels. The council doesn't consider the farmers' problems to be as extreme."

"Is that what you think, sir? —Adrian?"

"What I think . . . What I think, my lady, is that I will have to call you Pouncer, which is what we called the dog, and that in your spare time we will have you interrogate prisoners for State Security. As for the farmers, it occurs to me that much of the work could be automated—"

"But the Book of Sawyer says that all Curosa legacies must be worked by human hands!"

"So it does. I merely made an observation. Besides, this is hardly unskilled work, and rotating new people in here every few months would lose us an enormous amount of output. Watch."

He nodded toward the dark-haired girl in the yellow dress. She reached for one of the vastules going by on the conveyor. Io stepped closer; she had never seen one before. It was flat-shelled, grayish white, and about the size of a spread hand. The girl very quickly forced it open, inserting a metal stick to keep it that way, and moved her hand warily past the sharp, pointed teeth. "Cuts from these can take weeks to heal," said Adrian, over her shoulder. "And the buildup from anything above twenty or so is fatal." Now the girl took a tweezer, reached into the shiny bowl beside her, and removed a tiny, glinting diamond chip. She maneuvered the chip past the teeth and dropped it well back in the vastule's throat—or body, depending on how one looked at it. Then she removed the metal stick with a well-practiced swipe, narrowly missing the snap of the closing jaws. She marked a red diamond-shape on the top of the shell and placed it back on the conveyor. The whole process took less than thirty seconds.

People were working with a similar quiet efficiency all down the row. Roger appeared across the conveyor, waving a closed vastule. "Care to try one for old time's sake?" he called to Adrian. "We could time you against one of the apprentices, as we did before."

"You're too kind," said Adrian, in the voice of one who suggests that an experience of the past has not been forgotten.

Roger laughed. "Perhaps later." He replaced the vastule.

Iolanthe said, "I'm surprised that Saul let you work here. What if you'd been bitten?"

"I was," said Adrian. "But less than twenty times."

She blinked, considering this, and followed him down the rows. Saul must have been very peculiar man.

"Come over, my Lady Pouncer, and see the vastule pit." Adrian crouched beside one of the bogs. Prudence followed, still carefully clutching her skirts. "This one is a diamond pit, I'm pretty sure; we've got ruby and kylite and emerald in this building. The kylite's mainly for industrial uses. Stations and ship builders will pay top dollar for it, and they don't bleat about how it was created artificially, the way some of our customers do."

A man in a red headband was leaning out over the bog. "See what he's doing? He takes the packed vastules off the conveyor and plants them in the pit. In about four months or so they'll be removed and checked to see what we've gotten."

The man did one creature at a time, reaching for it,

then feeling around in the bog as though searching for the proper spot. Occasionally he leaned out far across the pit, holding onto a metal strap on a rod above. Adrian said, "They have to be spaced properly, or they won't grow anything. And look what he's wearing."

Io looked. She was puzzled. "A headband, a shirt—"

"No, on his hand. The one that goes into the bog. He's wearing a Curosa glove."

Io peered closer. It was true, on his right hand there was a black, shiny glove that ended at his wrist—no, it went back to mid-forearm— "It's changed its length!"

"One of the biological legacies of the Curosa. Most people only see the blood-sharing in church, but we really depend on any number of inheritances from our teachers."

"May their mission forever continue," said Iolanthe automatically.

"Indeed. You'll note the glove is alive, made up of thousands of tiny parasites. They consume a very small amount of the wearer's blood, and in return they function as a flexible, fully sealed barrier. Otherwise, the material in the bog would damage him." They watched the man swing back from the strap, choose another vastule, and turn again to the pit. "See, the glove starts to lengthen as he puts his hand inside. I'm told they're highly sensitive, and allow for very fine work."

Will Stockton squatted down beside them. Forgetting he was only there to observe, he said, "Is it true the vastules can duplicate any molecular structure?"

Adrian glanced at him, the surprise plain on his face. "You're very well-informed, Sergeant."

"I read a lot," said Will defensively.

"And why not? They can duplicate any we've tried so far, but then, we haven't tried that many, being limited by reasons of practicality. Gems happen to be the most efficient and lucrative for the size. By the way, we've got a real pearlfarm a few miles away—the old-fashioned kind, with oysters. That's why you won't see us wasting any effort on pearls in here—"

As he was speaking, the man planting the vastules fell to his knees suddenly. Adrian grabbed hold of his arms to keep him from tumbling into the bog, then quickly pulled off his shirt as a small crowd of workers gathered. The man's chest was flushed an angry pink, ringed with tiny rashes. Adrian held him gently, turning him to examine his back, where more rashes showed. The supervisor arrived then, breathing heavily from his sprint across the room.

"Sorry—" began the planter, from his vantage point on the floor.

"Gemsickness," Adrian cut in, looking at Roger. "An advanced case. You'd better get him home."

"No!" The man on the floor stirred. "Don't send me home. I've got a perfect record."

"Shut up, Nickel," said Roger. "It's gone too far for me to do anything. The Protector says you've got to go home."

"I can't afford to go home—"

"To hell with your perfect record, man," said Adrian. "You need at least a week off. Another hour, and you'd have fainted into the damned pit, you idiot. What were you thinking? You should have skipped a day as soon as the symptoms showed."

The man twisted uncomfortably and sent a despairing glance toward Roger. The supervisor knelt. "Things have changed since you were down here, Adrian."

Adrian sat back on his heels, his voice suddenly cold. "Changed how?"

"No paid time off for gemsickness. Everything is piecework. If you don't do it, you don't get any money."

Roger and Adrian looked at each other. Roger said, "If you recall, there was a time a couple of years ago when things in the City were, shall we say, confused? The council wanted to boost output. We had no one on hand to explain the facts of life to them. You were busy at the time, Adrian."

"A policy such as you describe would lower output in the long run."

"You know that and I know that, but the rules are still in effect."

The gem planter was being helped to his feet and led away. Adrian stood up and stepped back from the pit. "You should have sent me a petition of notice."

Roger's face was blank. "I didn't know if you wanted to hear from us."

Adrian's jaw clenched noticeably, but he did not reply. Prudence Favvi spoke up. "Let's finish the tour, Adrian."

"By all means," he said. "The tour."

Roger's smile was ever so slightly forced. "I think it's time for the Protector's wife to choose her good-luck gift."

Io was unhappy to note everyone turning to her. "What is it I must do?" she asked quietly.

Adrian was staring down at the pit. "You choose a vastule from a ripe bog and we open it. If there's a gem inside, it's considered a good omen. If there isn't, we don't mention the incident to anyone."

"Ah," said Iolanthe.

"The pit at the end is ready for harvesting," said Roger.

They proceeded to it. Iolanthe stood on the edge, looking distrustfully down at the liquidy brown muck and the shadows of vastules within. Adrian said, "The ones in the center are more likely to have formed something."

"True," said Roger. "Although one can never tell."

The stench was repulsive. But Io was determined that, if they didn't come out of this with a good-luck stone, it wouldn't be for her lack of trying. She reached for the metal strap overhead and leaned out slightly, pointing toward a shadow in the center. "I think—"

The strap pulled off its track, releasing itself completely. She shrieked in panic, flailed, and tumbled over into the bog, which accepted her at once with an undertow like the suck of a giant carnivore. The strap was still in her fist.

In less than a second, hands were reaching for her, finding purchase under her arms, lifting. She felt the bog resist, not wanting to let go. Then came an ugly popping sound, and she was dragged out onto comparatively dry land.

A rag was wiping her face. She opened her eyes and found herself looking at Will Stockton. A red streak was on his left cheek and his uniform sleeves were coated with muck. The hands that were wiping her face were a horror: raised red welts covered them like some abstract engraving. Seeing her reaction, Will stood up. "I'll send for a chair, sir, so we can get her back to court level—"

But even as he was speaking, the logic of the situation

was presenting itself to Iolanthe's mind, frightening her far more than a brush with death in a vastule bog. His hands . . . She looked at her own. They were even worse than Will's. She put her palms to her face; it felt like a corridor map there. She moved her hands compulsively over her forehead, her chin, her cheeks—

She started to cry. They had made it very clear to her at home that beauty was all she had, and it was gone forever. She was trapped among strangers with nothing at all to offer them that would save her from being trampled in their own plans and stratagems. A figure of mockery, a disgrace to her family, a thing from a horror story—

At once Adrian knelt behind her, circling her in his arms, holding her as though she were a small child. "No, don't cry. My dear, my sweet Iolanthe, my darling Pouncer." She had an overpowering urge to weep even harder, knowing that she would be nobody's darling when they all saw her face. She started to choke, forcing down the sobs. "Sweetest child, it will be all right, I swear."

"My *face*," she said, barely intelligibly.

"It'll fade. It'll be all right. It's only a matter of time."

She had no faith in his assurances. He was a man who lied to get his own way, as all men did, her nurse had warned her, but this one more than most—all his verbal playfulness was now weighed against him, and she condemned him in her heart. He would say what he liked to get her to behave, then he would send her back to Opal in disgrace, or marry her and let her be the laughingstock of the court—

Will Stockton knelt before her. The welt on his left cheek throbbed. "It's true, Io. Do you hear me? It's just a skin irritation. It'll go away."

Stolid, dependable Will. Opal-born. He wouldn't lie to her. "Oh, *Will*," she said, and reached out her arms to hug him.

The hem of Prudence's gown appeared in her line of sight. "I've called for a chair," said Prudence's voice. "A closed chair, Io, nobody will see you. We'll take you home and put you in a cold tub, to get the swelling down. Io, *let go*."

Iolanthe released Will from her hold, wiping her nose with the sleeve of her gown. There was no self-consciousness in the movement. There was freedom in being a troll instead of a beautiful woman.

Will stood up, facing Adrian. "She was upset."

"Yes," said Adrian. "Will you step aside a moment with me, Sergeant?"

Heart pounding faster, Will followed him to the other side of the table. Adrian regarded him for a moment. Then he said, "Was the pit in your line of sight most of the time you were here?"

"No," Will said, relieved. "I'd already thought of that. I'll be checking with my men, and I presume you'll check with yours, but my impression is that nobody was watching it that closely. When the planter fainted, that drew everybody's attention. I did do a visual scan a few times while that was being dealt with; but this building is a big place."

"And there are a lot of people in it."

"Yes, and a lot of them moving around in the course of their business. Any number of water-carriers would have passed by the pit on their way farther down the line."

"But you couldn't guarantee it would have to be a water-carrier."

"I couldn't even guarantee it was sabotage, at this point, but I want the strap attachments checked."

Adrian glanced thoughtfully toward Iolanthe, who was being helped up by Prudence. "Are you putting through a formal request to have the bog swept for the strap?"

"No need." Will reached into his mud-caked jacket and withdrew the strap in question. Adrian looked at him in surprise. "She was still clutching it when we pulled her out. I had to pry her fingers off it one by one—I don't think she was even aware she was holding the thing."

Adrian met his eyes. "Sergeant, I would like to ask a favor."

"Yes, sir?" Will's voice was noncommittal.

"Appearances are an important thing at court."

"Sir."

"We could never hush this up, though that would be my first preference. My second . . . I would like to present this to the Diamond not as a plot to embarrass Iolanthe—which I'm sure you'll agree is more likely—but as an attempt to kill her."

"Another few minutes and she *would* have died. If we weren't here—"

"But we were here. Nevertheless, I want to stick with the more serious scenario. Your own folk on Opal will yowl, but—" He looked over again toward where Iolanthe stood huddling beside Prudence, her face down, every aspect miserable. "She has to live at court a long time. For her sake, I'd rather present this as an unsuccessful murder try—there's dignity in that—than as a *successful* attempt to humiliate her."

Will followed his gaze, a lot of thoughts tumbling through his mind: his guardsman oath, the Opal council, his sister at home, the way Iolanthe had stood up to dealing with Hartley Quince. Earlier than he would have thought possible, he found himself saying, "I'll back you up, sir."

"Thank you." They walked back toward the two women. "Besides," said Adrian, "I see no reason for you to go into *enormous* detail about the event, particularly in this City, where you have no official superior to report to."

Will felt himself reddening, recalling the feeling of Iolanthe's arms clasped around him. "No, sir."

They reached the place where Io and Prudence stood holding each other. Adrian stopped abruptly; Will thought he heard him say something under his breath, something nearly unintelligible; "poor little gargoyle," it sounded like. His voice carried a weight of tenderness that was almost shocking.

Then Adrian stepped forward; he touched Io's cheek, raising her face, and carefully showing no reaction when she did so. She was flushed and sodden from weeping, the redness filling in the spots where welts had not cut. She stood straight, in a doomed but wrenching attempt at dignity.

"My lady," said Adrian more clearly, "the chair will be here soon. They may have difficulty bringing it past the benches and tables. I believe it would be better to wait outside, where the air will be cooler. May I assist you?"

Will took her arm on the other side, and they made their way down the aisle, past the benches, to the front doors of the gemfarm. They passed Roger, who stood aside with a helpless, appalled look on face. The supervisor clearly had no further ideas about advertising today's tour to anyone.

They gathered outside, blinking in City daylight. Will glanced up at the artificial ring of suns, then over at the gleam of the lift; it was such an ordinary day. The group huddled in unhappy silence.

After a moment, Adrian said, "I owe you a debt, Sergeant."

That startled him. "It was my job."

"Not only pulling her out, though that also, of course. I'm sorry I can't reward you properly, but you don't work for me. Still, if you put in a request for, say, a diamond-and-ruby ring from the treasury, it would be honored."

"Sir, I can't. It wouldn't look right."

"You're a hero, people would expect me to do something. And it's to the credit of Opal, so *they* can't object. Don't think of yourself, Will; wouldn't your wife or girlfriend be happy to receive something like that?"

It *was* good Opal PR, now that he thought of it. Besides— "My fiancée would like it, yes, sir. Thank you."

"Ah, you're engaged. Welcome to the club. We're an exclusive band—"

A sound like a small sob came from Iolanthe. They turned to her. "Sweetheart?" said Adrian at once. "Does it hurt?"

"I think I was holding her too tightly," said Prudence. "I'm sorry, baby. They'll be here in a minute."

Iolanthe made no reply. She looked up, met Will's glance, and started crying again.

This time none of them commented on it.

Chapter 10

Will strode purposefully across the public space of Rose Court. He climbed the winding staircase behind Glassfall Cascade, crossed the arboretum, and walked past the entrances to the quarters of the lesser nobility without a second look. It was early Sunday evening. Ladies and gentlemen strolled the esplanade, flute-boys and small dogs walking behind. A number of the passersby glanced curiously at the angry red welt that cut across his cheek, then glanced away when they took in the expression on his face.

At the entrance to Lord Muir's he stopped, debating for an instant whether the tradesmen's door or the family door would get him to his goal the sooner. He took the family door, presented his credentials to the servant, and was shown to an anteroom below the main quarters.

He paced beside a small carved oak table with a greenglass figurine on it. In less than a minute, the door to the room beyond opened and Hartley Quince stepped out. Behind him, Will could see several young men of good Diamond family lounging amid a haze of smoke, among them Harry Muir, who was stretched out on the expensive carpet with his eyes shut. Will felt his lip curl into the sneer of contempt that one who came up the hard way can feel for those who toss away their birthright. Beyond this, he gave Muir and his friends no thought at all. Hartley closed the door.

"What is it?" he asked.

Will, feeling as though he were the mere final expression fo the momentum that had carried him through the levels to Rose Court, walked into Hartley's personal space, grabbed him by his collar, and pushed him back into the wall.

Hartley's hands went at once to Will's, trying to pry them off, but Will was stronger. "What the hell are you doing?" Hartley demanded. In answer, Will tightened his grip on the collar, causing a most satisfying paleness in Hartley's countenance. "Tell me," he got out, with difficulty.

"Somebody just tried to kill Iolanthe Pelagia."

"Really?" Hartley's eyes widened with interest. He seemed to forget that he was being strangled. "Where? What happened?"

Will released him. "At a gemfarm tour, on the agri levels. Somebody loosened a strap, and she fell into a vastule pit."

"I take it she's alive."

"Yes."

"A public tour? That would seem more like an attempt to humiliate her."

Will took in a deep breath, remembering abruptly how quick Hart could be. Unless— He took hold of his collar again. "Did you arrange it?"

Hartley made no attempt to loosen Will's grip. "No, Will, I did not." He said it quietly, with none of the heat a person being pushed against the wall ought to have.

Will let go, suddenly feeling silly. He hadn't thought ahead of physical violence, and now the impulse to fight was ebbing, robbing him of that sense of invulnerability, leaving him feeling smaller, more open, less sure of himself.

"How did you know where I was?" asked Hartley.

Will paused. He'd had at least one of his group of four keeping tabs on Hartley at all times, but that was not the kind of thing one said to an Opal superior. Hart grinned. "Come on, there are some chairs in the next room."

They entered a small drawing room directly across from Harry's door. The walls were covered in gatherings of pink brocade. Will sat in a delicate cushioned chair carved with rosebuds. Hartley pulled over another to sit beside him.

"Tell me everything that happened," said Hartley.

Will related the day's events, leaving out only Adrian's request for a favor. Hartley tilted his head back in the chair for a moment and squeezed his eyes shut, as though trying to focus on some obscure internal principle of philosophy. "You don't have any candidates to blame in this thing?" he finally said.

"No, or I would have mentioned it. —Hart? Are you selling interdicted drugs to these aristo kids?"

"Don't be silly," said Hart, with some acidity. "I'm letting them sell interdicted drugs to me."

"And making a list of names for later blackmail purposes."

"That goes without saying. Shut up a minute." He closed his eyes again. Then he opened them and looked at Will quizzically. "How did Adrian take it?"

"I told you what he did. He helped her to the chair—"

"No, no. You were there, Willie. You were standing next to them both. We both know you notice things. What was he feeling? Do you think he'll try to call off the wedding? Is he trying to be polite to damaged goods?"

Inwardly Will cursed himself. He ought to have anticipated that Hart would want to turn the direction of this interrogation around. It was obvious. He'd let his emotions sweep him in here, while he knew very well—Hart himself had explained it more than cogently, at the age of twelve—that he was at his weakest point when he was emotional. Some people did well in the grip of violent feelings, but Will was not one of them.

"You're asking for an opinion."

"Of course I am."

"I think," Will said, "that he is fonder of her than ever. I think he was concerned about the accident. I think that the experience may have added feelings of protectiveness to good old simple lust. I think this is all speculation."

They were conversing in court speech. Hartley smiled gently. "How nice for us," he said, in an aristo accent so pure it was almost repellent.

"How do you figure that?"

"Willie, anything that makes Adrian more vulnerable is to be encouraged. These protective instincts are an excellent thing. Human beings tend to trust those who are entrusted to their care. Certainly they don't perceive them as a threat. How much easier it will be for Iolanthe to gather information for us!"

"Have you ever noticed that you talk about human beings in the third person?"

Hart chuckled. "What a good day it's been all around. The aristos love me, you've been a hero—we have something to complain to the Diamond about, and yet everything's going perfectly."

Not for Iolanthe, Will thought. "But you say you've had nothing to do with it."

"Cross my heart, Willie. 'Fate turns the mother's face toward us; she saves the dagger for tomorrow.' We've just been lucky. Have you had dinner?"

Will rose to his feet. "Not yet. I didn't feel like eating."

"Nor did the drugheads in the other room. Care to try the Malachite Common with me? On second thought, I think I'll order in my chamber. Cold chicken and spiced salad, a bottle of wine—better than what they serve the City Guard."

"You must be joking." Will walked to the doorway, feeling the tiredness of the day suddenly settle over him.

"As you like. Oh, Willie? What on earth made you think I was involved in this thing?"

"I don't know," said Will. "It must be force of habit."

He left Hartley sitting there in his carved brocade chair.

Granny Seaton dipped her scented cloth in the bowl of liquid beside Iolanthe's bed, and reached out toward her face. Io turned toward the wall.

"Child, I've told you the marks will fade. This will help, and it'll keep them from becoming infected. You have to be a big girl and let me wash you—"

Iolanthe tensed. A big girl, indeed! She felt all of six years old around this ancient lady, and it was clear the lady took her for about that age in fact.

She turned abruptly and faced the woman. Granny Seaton was wearing a long, plain brown dress, her white hair done up in braids and her face shining with the patina of very old age, like an ancient piece of ivory. The edge of a strand of pearls could be seen poking from beneath the first open button of the dress.

"Are you a witch?" Io demanded.

Granny Seaton regarded her for a moment. "Yes, I am, dear," she said tartly. "And fortunate for you that I am, and you're not facing some half-baked boy of a doctor, who'd cause you twice as much pain and do you no good at all."

"Witches are evil company, and their spells are useless in any case." It was a rude thing to say, but Iolanthe felt justified by circumstances. Also, she was a little afraid of this witch, and wanted her to leave.

Granny Seaton did not seem offended. She said, "Well, I've been able to ease dear Prudence's way with her husband's headaches; and I've helped the boy from time to time, too."

"The boy?"

"Adrian. A nice boy, very polite."

They looked at each other. "It won't hurt," said Granny finally.

Iolanthe sighed. "Just the face," she said. She tilted her head up toward Granny, eyes squeezed shut as though expecting a blow. The cloth was cool, damp, and gentle. After a moment she opened her eyes. "I suppose you could do the arms as well."

"That seems to me a good plan."

A quarter-hour later Granny wrung out her cloth for the final time. "When do you get married, sweetheart?"

"I don't know. Within a few months, I suppose. Or perhaps sooner."

The old woman pursed her lips thoughtfully. "Have you been examined?"

"Examined?"

"Inside and out, as they say."

"Certainly not!"

"Well, this would be a good time for it. You have your clothes off, and I don't come to court all that often—"

"No!" Io squeezed her legs together.

The witch sighed. "Sweetheart, we won't do anything that would upset you. But you're a bright child, aren't you? Let me tell you why an examination is a good thing—"

Adrian rose to his feet when Granny Seaton entered the sitting room of Iolanthe's quarter, as he would for any lady of court. "How is she?"

"As you said, the marks will fade. She's had a scare—in a strange new City, that she didn't want to come to in the first place—and that may take longer to get over. I've given her something to put her to sleep."

"Did she say she didn't want to come here?"

"Don't interrupt me, youngster. You may be the Diamond Protector, but I knew you when you were a lot younger, and a hell of a lot less confident." She dug around in one of her large pockets, pulled out an enormous white handkerchief, and blew her nose enthusiastically. "Let's sit down."

Adrian sat. Granny Seaton let herself down onto the sofa cushion beside him, sighing as she did so. "Ah, that's better. You could offer an old woman a glass of spirits, boy."

"You know that I asked before you went in to—"

"I'm an old friend of the family, not to mention the representative of the Past Days Goddess—"

"*Please* don't say that where my counselors might hear you."

"What, are they hiding in the walls? Nervous youngster, aren't you? The Mercatis always were a skittish lot. Thoroughbred nerves, my old aunt used to call it."

"Could we talk about Iolanthe?"

"Yes, that we must. As her promised husband, this is a problem for you."

"What? What does my being her promised husband have to do with anything?"

"I took the opportunity, my darling boy, to give her a thorough examination. And it's fortunate I did. For one thing, I don't think she has any idea of her woman's parts."

"Wait, wait. Are you talking about the sort of examination where—"

"I am. I did. The child tried to tell me they used dolls for that sort of thing at home—can you believe it? They point to the part of the doll's body where the problem is, and have the physician diagnose from that. Of course, I put that nonsense out of her head at once."

"Of course," said Adrian, with a slightly cornered look.

"And now I must be specific. I was searching, of course, for those things relating to marriage and child-bearing—"

"Granny, wait. Are you about to tell me about her private, that is, her personal—"

"Of course I am, youngster! Who else would I tell about it?"

Adrian stood up. "One moment, please." He walked to the door of the small chamber that lay off the drawing room, and called, "Prudence! Would you come in here?"

Prudence Favvi entered, wearing a light blue house gown, followed by Brandon Fischer. She smiled at the witch. "Hello, Granny."

"Hello, sweet girl. My compliments, Chief Adviser." The second greeting was coldly formal; all of them knew

Fischer did not approve of Adrian's more eccentric contacts.

"My lady," said Fischer stiffly, bowing.

"Granny has something to tell you," Adrian declared, as though announcing a public proclamation.

"To tell *me?*" Prudence was startled. "Is Iolanthe all right?"

"She's fine. Why don't you two go back in the other room, you can discourse in more comfort."

Granny eyed him narrowly. "You'll have to discourse yourself, sooner or later, my boy."

"And Brandon will keep me company while you two speak," Adrian said firmly.

Fischer seated himself on the sofa, looking confused but interested. Prudence shrugged and began moving toward the other room. Granny Seaton joined her. As the door closed, Adrian and Fischer heard her say, "Pay him no mind, my dear, his whole family was like that. I could tell you stories—"

The door shut. Fischer turned to Adrian. "I wish you wouldn't bring the old lady onto court territory at your whim. We're not as secure in public opinion as you seem to think."

"Really, Brandon, I don't know what you do in your spare time. Granny provides services for half the aristo wives from Jade Court to Tourmaline. True, most of them go to see *her,* but she's been known to pay house calls before. She went to see Jane last month."

"She did? Are we talking about *my* Jane?"

"She didn't mention it?"

Fischer, looking distracted, did not reply. Adrian went on, "In any case, I wasn't going to have one of those damned doctors poking her. You come from their hands in worse shape than you went to them, and then they shrug and say suffering is God's will. The girl's been through enough."

Fischer's gaze was still distant. "Brandon?"

The Chief Adviser pulled his attention back. "Yes."

"Have you given thought to the investigation?"

"Naturally. But you need to tell me who you want to run it."

"There isn't much choice, is there?"

"Well, obviously not the Ecclesiastical Police. It falls outside their jurisdiction. But do you prefer the City Guard, or Special Security?"

Adrian grimaced. "If we give it to the citycops, it'll be all over the Diamond tomorrow, and maybe not in a version we'd like. Which leaves—"

"Special Security."

"Who will spend eight or ten months investigating until someone on staff pulls it together long enough to frame some other poor idiot. God, I'll be glad when Farnham finally dies and frees up the Security Chief posting. The admins are on holiday over there. They answer to nobody but themselves."

"Don't say that to Lord Muir. He'll have Harry on your doorstep in seconds."

Adrian smiled. Fischer hesitated, then said, "There's another matter I should bring up, while I have the chance."

"Oh?"

"You have a jammer on in here, don't you?"

"Brandon, would I bring in a witch without having a jammer on?"

Fischer looked troubled. Adrian said, "Well, what?"

"Hartley Quince."

"The Opal representative? Has he been making a pest of himself? There's not much I can do about these people, Brandon, they have the freedom of the City."

"Not a pest, exactly." Fischer paused again, maddeningly. "In fact, in some circles he's gotten quite popular. It's more . . ."

"Spit it out."

"Gossip, Adrian."

Adrian laughed. "Is that all? Tell me, then. Who's been sleeping with whom?"

"It's more . . . who *slept* with whom, in the past. . . ."

"Brandon, my dear friend and counselor. The point."

"The point is, he certainly *looks* like a Mercati."

Adrian's smile vanished. "You're losing your mind."

"I didn't think you'd take it well."

"I'm the last Mercati in the Three Cities. It's a well-known fact. I have no brothers, sisters, cousins—I was an orphan—there was supposed to be an uncle who went to

Pearl thirty years ago, but since nobody's heard of him since, we may assume he's out of the picture. There's never been a Mercati on Opal that I know of; where's this Quince supposed to have sprung from?"

"I don't know. I can't get any good information on his past, but he's risen through the ranks in a very suggestive way for someone with no apparent family."

"Somebody's bastard? Not my family's, I assure you. Where are you getting this information?"

"I've been making discreet inquiries."

The Protector's voice was appalled. "How discreet?"

"As discreet as possible, Adrian, a lot of people are talking!"

Adrian stood up, glanced toward the closed door to the room where Prudence and the witch were consulting, and paced unhappily on the carpet. "This is not the best time for something like this to come up," he said at last.

Fischer looked alert. "Something's brewing, isn't it?"

"Why do you say that?"

"Does it have to do with Baret Two?"

"Why do you say this, Brandon?"

"You rammed that schedule change through the council as though it were the only important thing on earth. And yet you never openly sponsored it yourself."

"Well, don't I have the right to set trade schedules?"

Fischer did not reply. Adrian stopped pacing and said, "Yes, it has to do with Baret Two. But nobody—without exception, nobody—must know about it."

Fischer said quietly, "Let me help."

They looked at each other. Fischer said nothing more; either the boy would trust him, or he wouldn't.

"Yes, it's time." Adrian spoke as though he were deciding it at that very second. "In fact, it's past time, and I apologize for that. Listen: When Saul fell ill, he called me to his room and spoke to me."

"Yes, we all knew for certain then that he'd designated you to follow him."

"We were alone for no more than ten minutes; people were pouring in and out, already there were rumors of rioting on court level. You don't know how often I've wished that we had longer. Brandon, Saul told me that he had reason to believe that the Sawyer Crown is on Baret Two."

It was a moment before the Chef Adviser could take this in. "*The* Sawyer Crown? The Sawyer Crown we hear about every Fire Sunday?"

"The same."

"But the Curosa took it with them when they left to continue their mission of conversion."

"But they also promised it would be found one day."

"That was meant metaphorically. That we would one day achieve the spiritual sharing the Curosa had reached."

"Yes, I always thought that sounded plausible, too. But Saul had evidence that the Crown was on Baret Two."

"What evidence?"

Adrian looked frustrated. "I don't know."

"You don't know?"

"We only had ten minutes!"

"All right, I see. Well, where on the planet is it? Is it in the keeping of the Imperial Governor?"

"I don't know."

"You don't—"

"Ten minutes, Brandon!"

"Yes, all right. So once we've finalized negotiations, you're planning to institute some kind of search—"

"A quiet, private, clandestine search."

"I should think so. Why, if Opal heard about this, they'd be scavenging over the whole planet. Do you realize what the Crown would mean?"

"It means," said Adrian, "that I would be accepted by every man and woman in the Three Cities as the spiritual heir of Adrian Sawyer."

"Talk about managing public opinion. Why, you could do what you liked."

"Whereas if Lord Cardinal Arno got hold of it, we would see some purges that would make the Black Century look like a boating party on the Katherine River." Adrian sat down heavily on the sofa. "Purges, by the way, that I don't think anyone in these three rooms today would survive, with the possible exception of Iolanthe."

Fischer turned to Adrian. "As your adviser," he said, "I consider that perhaps we should let negotiations break down, and exit Baret System. Leave the risk behind. Political reality as we now know it begins to seem not so bad."

"No."

"Think about it, Adrian."

"I want the Sawyer Crown."

His tone held a finality that silenced Fischer. The two men sat together silently. After a moment, Adrian said, "What can they be talking of in there?"

He was looking toward the door to the other chamber. Fischer blinked, like a man waking up. "I'd forgotten they were here. How can you think of anything else?"

Adrian smiled, knowing he meant "anything but the Crown." "I've had a lot of time to get used to the idea," he said. "But you see, don't you, why I don't want to have any scandals chipping away at my family's memory, not while I'm working on this, and preparing for the wedding, and supervising the station negotiations."

"And then there's Baret Two's present . . . unsettled nature."

Adrian met his glance.

"It must have been a shock to you, when we broke from Blackout and found half the system had gone Republican."

"It was." Adrian let out a breath, as though it was a relief to speak. He smiled wryly. "But it could be years yet before civil war reaches Baret Two."

"Or it could be tomorrow. You're short on time, boy."

The faint whitening of Adrian's lips was the only clue Fischer could discern as to how close to his soul Adrian was playing this one.

"Tell me," said Fischer, "why do you—"

The door to the other chamber opened, and Prudence's blond head appeared. "Adrian, I think you need to hear this."

Adrian stood, suddenly looking young and uncertain. "Are you sure?"

"Yes, Adrian, I'm sure."

Fischer grinned as he watched Adrian cross the room like a ten-year-old about to be reprimanded by his tutor. The door closed behind him.

Fischer shut his eyes and leaned back on the couch, the better to rest and consider.

* * *

In her bedroom, Iolanthe moved sluggishly away from the door, feeling the effects of her sedative. Surely they couldn't have meant the actual Sawyer Crown, the one the Curosa made for human use and then took away on their ships when they left. That was something out of history and legend; it wasn't anything one would ever meet in real life. Adrian must be misinformed.

She climbed into bed and pulled up the covers. This was, quite definitely, something the Lord Cardinal would want to know about. She shivered, turning onto her side. It suddenly occurred to her, as it never had on Opal, that reporting back on the private conversations of one's husband, or even one's promised husband, was not—she could think of no other word—nice. And yet, the Lord Cardinal was right, wasn't he? And beyond that, he was bound to ask to see her sometime soon, and ask for her confession, and the cold and horrible truth was that she could see no way in the world he wouldn't be able to get the information out of her.

She stared at the patterns on the wall, wondering why she felt so depressed. *It must be the effect of the witch's drink,* she thought, as she fell asleep.

"Well?" Adrian pulled out one of the embroidered chairs beside Granny Seaton.

"Granny, tell him," said Prudence.

The witch turned to him. "You'll not like this, boy."

"Then don't make me wait, Granny."

She shrugged. "You've heard of masking?" His expression was unenlightened. "Some call it 'hooding.' "

Adrian turned to Prudence, eyes wide. "That hasn't been done in centuries. It's against the laws of the Church."

"Not on Opal, apparently."

Granny Seaton said, "It's been done hereabouts, too, once or twice that I know of. A simple enough procedure, after all. A shield of plastiflesh is placed around the clitoris, tied in place for a few minutes until it starts to attach. . . . I don't believe the child even knows it's there, though from the looks of things it was done in the last few years. It must have been some time when she was deeply unconscious, probably just after her Confirmation. It would've been a painful and highly memorable experience, otherwise."

"Barbarians," Adrian muttered.

"Oh, there's plenty more on the Diamond who would do it if they could. It's so easy to trust a wife who gets no pleasure from sex."

"Any at all?" asked Adrian.

Granny's silver-buckled shoe tapped the floor. "Well, I suppose there's the pleasure that comes from doing one's duty."

"Damn!" said Adrian.

"Yes," Granny agreed. "They ought to have told you. I expect there was no insult in mind when it was done; they only thought to increase her marriage value. I even wondered whether to speak up—by now, you know, the sheathe will have permanently joined with the flesh, and it would be a nightmare to remove. But then, I thought, it's the Protector, after all! And a hooded wife? Not to be tolerated! What could they have been thinking of?"

Adrian felt his face grow warm again. By folk tradition, a certain sexual prowess was associated with the Protectorship. "Well, thank you for your attendance, Granny. I'll give the problem some thought."

"Now, as to other matters," she said briskly. "Things look auspicious for the wedding night; she's a virgin, of course, but the passage is fairly well-sized, all the messing about they did must have stretched it."

"Thank you, Granny." Adrian stood up and took her hand firmly. "I'll escort you to Brandon Fischer now, shall I, and he'll see that you get home safely."

"I'm not finished."

Adrian swung open the door to the main sitting room. "Brandon, would you see that our honored visitor has an escort home?" He threw a look over her stooped shoulder that said, *Brandon, please.*

Fischer grinned. "This way, my lady, if you would."

Adrian went back inside the other room, where Prudence now sat perched on the arm of a heavily stuffed chair. She was also grinning. "Considering all the time you've spent with the girls on Requiem Row, I'm amazed you can still be shocked."

"On the Row they don't talk about things so . . . clinically."

"So plainly. No, I imagine they use more colorful terms, at least until the customers leave. You know, my dear, in your own way you're something of a romantic."

Adrian frowned suddenly. "Anyway, who says I spend time on Requiem Row?"

Prudence laughed. "Without gossip, court life would be intolerable."

His answering smile faded. "What am I to do? You know the statutes about using anesthesia in reproductive operations—"born in sorrow," and the other sections of the law. I'm not putting Io through that. The reasonable thing to do would be to smuggle her to a medic on Baret Station—I'm sure Tal could arrange one quietly—but should anyone find out, I'd have no excuse for taking her there. I could try to bring a medic in, but we could never keep it quiet."

Prudence gave him a sympathetic look. Adrian said, "Maybe I'm overreacting. Aren't you going to tell me that women don't care about that sort of thing as much as men do?"

She kicked off her slippers, slid down into the couch, and curled her legs underneath herself. "My dear friend, I can't speak for other women. But judging by my relationship with Michael—"

"Yes?"

"Well, were I you, I would go out and try to solve this problem, Adrian. Brandon and I, and possibly your demon, are all your friends. You don't lack for supply in that area. I thought you were looking for a wife."

Adrian was silent. Then— "I am," he said.

"And is she one you could accept? Myself, I like her— but how is it for you?"

He gave an unhappy laugh. "She's a beauty, I saw that right away. My heart beat faster at once. Of course, my heart has beaten faster many times."

"A strong cup of coffee will do it," said Prudence tartly.

"As you say. She has skin you could get lost in, like the snow at night in Helium Park. One could gaze for hours. Her hair is like a silken gown left tumbled on a bed, asking to be gathered up—"

"I grant you this," said Prudence, "but I note that, as yet, you've said nothing of love."

"I would have thought, yesterday, that I was speaking of love."

"Ah. Then did something occur today of an educational nature?"

He smiled, not happily.

"I see it did," said Prudence. "Go on."

"It was after she embraced Will Stockton."

"Oh, how like a man!" The ancient cry came out without thinking, and it did not sound pleased. Then: "Forgive me, my dear, please continue."

"But it wasn't that. It was when the sergeant and I returned and saw you comforting her, and she stood up with such a vain grasp at dignity, and she'd been weeping like a five-year-old, without any thought for her appearance. . . ."

He trailed off. Prudence said, "Yes?"

"And her face was like a gargoyle on a column in Saint Tom's." The unhappy smile came back. "Oh, she was trying *so hard*. She was an inch away from breaking down completely."

"I could feel it, when I held her."

"And I suddenly thought," he said quietly, "that if I could not comfort her, life would not be worth living."

Prudence was struck dumb, at least for a moment. "I am very impressed," she said finally, "with this news."

"I thought you might be." His habitual tinge of irony had crept back.

"This changes everything."

"It does for me, but I don't see how it does for you."

"Obviously the wedding must take place. And obviously this hood will have to go. We cannot allow half-measures."

"I'm glad you see it this way."

Prudence thought with a concentration that was visible. "You know what alternative this leaves us with," she said.

"The witches. A surgical coven."

"Yes, and as soon as possible, so she'll have time to heal before the ceremony."

"The arrangements would have to be on a par with strategy for a declared war. If word got out that I was using witches—"

Prudence smiled. "Remember the motto of my natal family, Adrian. Prudence, valor, and *discretion*."

He crossed the room, sat down beside her on the sofa, and linked his arm with hers. "I want you to stay by her, Prudence. I have reason to believe life is going to become very complicated around here."

"Haven't we just agreed on that?"

"More complicated even than arranging for a secret surgical coven."

"Good heavens." She turned wide eyes to Adrian. "The mind stops short, as though at a blind corridor. What can you possibly be planning?"

He chuckled. She said thoughtfully, "Perhaps we should have asked my younger sisters along as ladies-in-waiting."

"Well, I enjoy Discretion's company, but your middle sister should be avoided, I think."

"Valor's often uninvited, but she shows up anyway. What a summer season this will be!"

"Umm." The thought did not seem to excite him the way it did Prudence. "But you'll watch over Iolanthe, when I can't be there? You'll stay close to her, you'll be her friend?"

"I will."

He turned her hand over and kissed it.

Much later, after she had spent some hours crying, Iolanthe rose from bed in her darkened room and made her way to the door. She had never slept in any bed but the one in her own room in her father's house, with all the familiar decorations she had placed herself, over the years; she still thought of that as "her" room, and this other place as some temporary land. She had never been so surrounded by strangers. She had never felt hatred directed at her, as it had been at the gemfarm if the whispered bits and pieces she overheard were true. She had never been ugly before. Or almost died before. Or had so much responsibility before.

Or choices to make. They had all used to have been made for her.

No one had ever used the word "homesickness" to her, and she did not connect her new proclivity for tears with her situation. No, it must be that there was something wrong with her, some flaw that made her even more useless a vessel than she had been brought up to believe.

There was still, however, duty. She moved through the dark sitting room to the front door and opened it.

Two of Will Stockton's men stood there. They turned to her in mild surprise.

"Strife, isn't it?" she asked the one on the left.

"Yes, my lady," he said, blinking. She had never addressed them before.

"Will you take a private message for me, when your shift is over? I would be most grateful."

"Of course, my lady." He looked toward his companion in bewilderment.

Say it, the voice in her head ordered. But once spoken, all choice ended.

So much the better.

"Please tell Hartley Quince that I want to speak to him. As soon as possible."

He nodded and she closed the door, returning inside. She leaned against the wall, breathless, as though she'd been running.

No one ever told her how bad it felt to do the right thing.

SECTION TWO
R.S. Kestrel

Chapter 11

Ask the pine if you want to learn about the pine, or the bamboo if you want to learn about the bamboo. And in forming your question you must abandon your subjective preoccupation with yourself. Otherwise you impose yourself on the object instead of learning from it. Poetry will rise of itself when you and the object have become one—when you have plunged deep enough into it to perceive the shape of the concealed treasure there. Your words may seem well-phrased to you, but if the object and yourself remain separate, then your poetry is not true poetry but merely your subjective mimicry.

BASHO

You have read the ancient poets who sought tarethi, *although not under that name. We say that we will teach you* tarethi *here, but that is just a manner of speaking for those who do not understand. Tarethi is a way of life, a habit of being. Never forget that the gathering of* tarethi *is essentially selfish. . . .*

Imagine that you are lying in your bed on a rainy spring night. Outside the rain is falling, the wind is cool and damp, tree branches move; every blade of grass and piece of earth and nesting bird feels the weather and responds to it. Humans only are cut off. Now open the window. Suddenly the sounds and feelings of the night invade. . . . suddenly the barriers between inside and outside are no longer certain. Lie in your bed, then, be aware of where you are, but now be aware of everything moving in the night. Listen.

Greykey Exercise One:
The Rain on the Roof

Keylinn:

My shift in Transport was over. Spider's still had two
and a half hours to go, at which time he'd promised to
take me to a matinee at the Starhall Theater, an interest
we seemed to have in common.

I was glad that Tal Diamond had gone off to the *Kestrel,* for there was business to take care of. Two and a half
hours would not be enough, not even to make a good beginning, but I might start to get my feet wet. Anyway, my
survival as a Greykey required that it no longer be put
off.

I entered my room, pulled off my boots, and tossed
them in a corner. The quarters were spartan—narrow bed,
chair, a small table for my personal books. No provision
for clothes, but perhaps Outsiders weren't expected to
come with much or stay for long.

I turned off the lights, sat on the floor in the middle of
the room, and began the Exercise of Incorporation.

I began with the physical: Imagined being 180 centimeters tall; imagined being male in a familiar sense, so
that one was aware of it but didn't have to think about it;
imagined walking with Tal's walk, how that felt, what it
meant. He walked very quietly.

Imagined being without kin. Imagined looking like
one's fellows but not being of them. Imagined being
under sentence of death outside the Three Cities.

Aphean, Aphean . . . how to deal with that. This was
tricky. I had been many people in my time, but all of
them had been people. Even the wolves in the hills are
people, part of a continuum of clan, with postures of defense and attack that are clearcut.

After an hour I got up and paced about the quarters,
still meditating. I took care to walk very quietly. It was a
pity I didn't know more of his childhood—usually that
was not necessary; the pattern existed, how it came into
being was interesting but irrelevant. Clues would be helpful here, though. I was working without markers. They
expected too much of me at home. . . .

Intrusion of self. Bury it.

And I was still in the trap of objectifying ... face it, cadet, because you are reluctant to enter Tal's viewpoint. It would not be a pleasant universe, but it did have points of congruity with my own, and it was to these points I must fasten myself and revolve the world at an angle until I was in that other universe.

I sat down again and pressed my hands against the floor. Sentence of death. Different species. People were, on the whole, hostile and unpredictable, so where could correct data be found? The Republic ... dangerous. And over here, in one small corner, were the handful of people whose interests coincided with one's own. A pitiful few. If not for them, social life would be unbearable. I considered the paradoxes involved; Adrian must be one, Spider another; where did that put an unknown Greykey?

And what of Belleraphon? I tested the name, briefly imagined killing him, how I would react emotionally. The vision had a pointless feel to it. But here was an interesting scenario: To be surrounded always by full humans, unreliable and deceitful but not even predictable enough to be motivated by their best interests ... Perhaps ... perhaps he wanted to find Belleraphon just to ask him some questions. Just to talk to him. Just to see what the future might hold for an Aphean with every intention of growing older.

I became aware of a pounding at the door—Spider, come to get me for the theater. I sighed, got up, and turned on the lights.

But probably I was way off base.

Chapter 12

I have something more to do than feel.

CHARLES LAMB

Tal's stateroom aboard the *Kestrel* was terribly correct by Republic standards: The walls were off-white, the table was off-white, and the bed sheets, in a fit of eccentricity, were sand-colored. He remembered someone explaining to him long ago, "The Republic gets nervous when people have too good a time." Tal cut that association off; the past was painful and irrelevant, a drag on clear thinking. He did not choose to indulge it.

On his papers the "reason for travel" was listed as "pleasure." Which didn't really explain why he was scheduled to return to Baret Station so quickly, but also didn't necessitate the creation of a false business connection that wouldn't hold up under scrutiny.

He stowed his things in the cabin and headed for the dining salon. Whoever the SP was on this voyage, he'd want a look at any new passenger, and staying out of sight would only cause attention. The Secret Police were a nosy lot. "Lunch" was the meal they claimed to be serving at this time; by Tal's internal clock it was closer to midnight.

He slid onto a bench beside a man in a brown jumpsuit. There were a few obvious Empire passengers sitting here and there, but it would probably be better not to sit by them—the SP might think he knew them, and one never knew what got under the skin of an SP.

He glanced over at the crew tables, searching for Cyr Vesant's contact. Nobody fit the description. A group of senior officers sat with passengers at the other end of his own table; to be safe he looked them over, too. Nothing. He pulled the cover off his "lunch"—preconstructed meatloaf and a baked apple, all produced by Intercorp. He ate slowly. Ten minutes into the meal there must have been a shift change; crewmembers started filing out and new ones came in and pulled out benches, laughing and digging happily into their food. The Diamond had spoiled him, apparently, when it came to artificial meals. None of the new people matched Cyr Vesant's description. Could he have gotten off at the station? Why? Or had Cyr Vesant handed him a story? How much did Keylinn really know about Cyr Vesant's business, and how much was she willing to tell?

His gaze lingered a little too long on the crew table as he considered the matter. A voice said, "A problem, Officer Diamond?"

He turned. Four seats down, on the other side of the table, sat an officer of the *Kestrel*. She was perhaps seventy years old, and she wore an orange neckerchief and a pink-and-purple sash, and there were traces of sparkle in her white hair. The Republic made a place for its eccentrics, especially when they were older and nonpolitical—maybe it made up for their system being so boring the rest of the time. The officer regarded him steadily.

"I beg your pardon," said Tal, "but you have the advantage of me."

The *Kestrel* officer grinned, showing yellow teeth and a light of mischief in her eyes. "Captain will do," she said. "Captain Nestra."

It *would* be. How did he always end up coming to people's notice? And dammit, if the Republic would just be a little more openly hierarchical, people like her would be sitting at the head of the table and he could watch out for them.

"I'm impressed that you know my name, Captain."

"I know the names of all my passengers. There are only sixteen of you this trip, after all. Do you have a problem? I see you watching my crew, there."

Conversation had ceased around his immediate area. He said, "I'm curious, I suppose. I don't mean any offense. I'm from the Three Cities; we don't travel much among other people."

"The Three Cities."

"Yes." She'd said it as though she didn't quite believe it. Tal felt his palms starting to sweat. Luckily full-humans rarely seemed able to pick up on his emotions. "It's on my ticket, Captain. I don't know how you avoided seeing it, if you saw my name."

She passed over that topic. "It must be a fascinating place, the Three Cities. Marvel of engineering, and all that."

"Yes. I'm afraid we rather take it for granted."

"They must feed you up there, at least—you're not eating much here."

He shrugged. God, she was worse than the Secret Police. Was this some kind of curse? He'd only been on board an hour!

"Are you traveling to Baret One for business?"

"Tourism. I've never been on a planet surface before."
She opened her mouth and he forestalled her. "It's true it
would have been a lot faster to go down to Baret Two,
but we haven't opened up official negotiations with them,
and I thought it would be more discreet to do things this
way."

"You're very thoughtful," she said, "with your superi-
ors, at least."

In a second she was going to ask him how long he was
booked to stay, and why. He pushed his tray in, signifying
that he was finished with his lunch. "I suppose you're
right, I'm not very hungry. Tell me, Captain, does this
ship have a gym? Or any area where passengers can work
out?"

"Of course. Didn't we give you a passenger map?
Choris, show this gentleman where the fitness room is.
And give him a map. He's carelessly lost his own."

Choris, a young female officer with close-cropped
black hair and a prominent security badge, rose at once
and accompanied Tal to the door. As they left, he heard
the Captain's voice continuing. "Well, citizens, I see
they've cut the beer ration again. I think we all know
whose fault that is. . . ."

Somehow it was always the women who were the
worst, he thought, as he lay in his bunk that night. Even
Republic women, who were brought up the same as men,
and ought to behave no differently. They all seemed to
know something he'd never been told. As for Diamond
women, there was a slight nervousness in everything they
did around him, as though they didn't know what horrifying act he might perform next. Clearly he was not giving
off the right signals, but just what the right signals were
was a mystery. There was some subtle range of human
behavior he wasn't getting, he'd been aware of that for
years. Sex was particularly bad. The males around him all
seemed to know how to proceed, but the last time he'd
suggested something to a Diamond woman she'd slapped
his face and her brother had almost had to be killed.
Luckily Adrian had smoothed things over. And Tal had
only chosen her to approach because she seemed less ner-

vous around him. Well, at least he'd been accurate in that—she's shown no hesitation about hitting him.

This Captain Nestra had the same terrible assurance he'd seen in other women down the line, the ones who'd troubled him the most. The fact that it wasn't sexual didn't help. At least, he thought it wasn't sexual. God, who could ever be expected to know what full-humans were thinking? It wasn't rational thought that went through their minds at all, they were in some kind of bizarre psychic attunement with the cosmos, or something equally meaningless.

He turned over in the bed. Tomorrow he would have to show up in the dining area at different times. Cyr Vesant's contact had to be on another work schedule from the people he'd seen there today.

Besides, there was less chance of running into the Captain again.

And breakfast brought success. Sitting alone at the crew table, very early on the ship's "day," was a youngish, white-haired worker with skin of golden brown. Tal followed him when he left the dining area.

He vanished into a maintenance hold. Tal spent the day walking purposefully up, down, and near that corridor. His target came out again—alone—four hours later, when he returned to the dining salon. Then back to the hold, a break a couple of hours later (spent in the fitness area) and another trip to the hold. During this time only two other people entered the hold, briefly, during the first quarter of this shift.

The target disappeared into crew residential territory later. Tal returned to his stateroom.

The next day Tal waited till midshift, then pushed open the hold door and found himself at the head of a steel stairway. He followed it down into a dark, rather dirty area, where swollen energy sacs bulged from the walls. A feed-station for the drive. He saw his target measuring out chak for the energy sacs, his back to the stairway, the chak dripping orangely from his hands—a mindless, low-status task, but more accurate when performed by a human than by a machine, since observation and maintenance were part of it. Tal considered shoving his target's head between the energy sacs as a preliminary introduction, but though it would convey the upper hand temporarily, it might be better to keep things on a friendly footing. There were several more days to go till Baret One.

Therefore he said, "Excuse me."

The man whirled around, spilling chak, which hissed as it hit the metal flooring. The voder by the mouth of the feed-station clicked twice, and the *Kestrel*'s drive spoke up: "I'm hungry," said a childish, mechanical voice. "Don't stop."

The worker ignored this plaintive comment. He glared at Tal. "Who the hell are you?"

"I'm a passenger, and I'm here to offer you money." It was always best to get that in at once.

"Get the hell out of here." He didn't talk like a native Republican. Maybe that was why he ate alone.

"I'm *hungry*," said the drive again.

"Shut up," said the man.

Tal pulled out two NetBank notes and held them up for inspection. The man was quiet for a moment, glaring at them suspiciously. Then, "What do you want?" he said.

"Information."

"I don't know anything." He took a step back and looked, if anything, even more hostile.

"You could tell me your name." When the man hesitated, he continued, "Surely it's not a secret."

"Maintenance Worker Peeskill."

Tal handed him a note. "That wasn't so bad, was it?" He help up the second one. "Now maybe you could tell me about Belleraphon."

For a second the man looked disoriented. Then he said, "Get the hell out of here."

"We can always raise the amount—"

"Get out!" He picked up a steel gripper and took a step toward Tal.

"Certainly," said Tal. "I hate to be rude." He backed up to the stairway and climbed it to the entrance, aware every second of the man standing there, violence ready to break out of him. Tal reached the top, opened the door gently, and found no one in the corridor.

And some people think that I'm unstable, he thought.

Some hours later during afternoon shift, when the fewest people were in their quarters, he entered the crew residential section. Charmingly, the administratives had put names on the crew doors. Well, it wasn't as though the names were a secret, in a crew this size. They probably thought it did something to combat the depersonalization that was rampant in Republic life. At least, it did something without really doing anything, a strategy always popular with administratives.

Maintenance Worker Peeskill's quarters were the farthest from the showers of anybody's, another mark of the regard in which he was held on this ship. Tal made use of skills his search had made necessary over the years, and opened the door.

The room was drab and messy, no surprise. Used shirts were thrown in balls on the floor. The maintenance worker's quarters were as confused as his alleged thinking processes. Tal looked though his drawers, under and around his bed, and through his duffel; then he pulled out the drawers one by one and checked the inside of his furniture. On the bottom side of one drawer he found four packages stuck with adhesive. In his own quarters, and not exactly well-hidden. The man was lower on the evolutionary scale than Tal had thought.

He checked the contents quickly; the light blue color of the powder suggested taxmal or veridh'n, the latter less likely for Baret System. He'd have to test it more thoroughly later. Taxmal was reputed to give its users, if human, a sense of power and the belief that they were telepathic. The sense of power was illusory, but the telepathy was real enough. Temporary, though, as he recalled; about four or five hours maximum. What would be the effect on an Aphean? ... Might be useful to have on hand, humans being the unpredictable masses of contradictions that they were. He pocketed the four packages and left.

Now he had something to negotiate with. He spent the rest of the day in his quarters, to give Peeskill time to become nervous. The next day at midshift he climbed down to the feed-station again.

"Missing anything?" he called when he reached the bottom.

Maintenance Worker Peeskill looked up from his task,

flushed a very dark red, and ran toward him with murder in his face.

Damn. Never underestimate the intelligence of a human. Tal stepped aside, grabbed hold of him, and added his own strength to Peeskill's momentum, pushing him headfirst into the space between two energy sacs. Clearly he should have begun this way yesterday. There was a wicked crack as Peeskill hit. Tal did not wait, but pulled him out, spun him around, and delivered a blow to the other side of his head. Peeskill blinked, looking dazed, and sank to the floor, where he sat blankly. Tal squatted down beside him.

"Maintenance Worker Peeskill?" he said politely.

Peeskill did not answer at once.

"Get hold of yourself," said Tal irritably. "You're perfectly all right." And he was, basically—there should be no permanent damage. Peeskill's forehead was turning pink and his right eye should be black in a short time, but that was all. Well, aside from the bumps on his skull . . . "Peeskill?"

"Yeah."

"Maintenance Worker Peeskill, I'm looking for someone named Belleraphon. I understand from a mutual friend that you've had some contact with a Belleraphon. Could you tell me about that?"

Peeskill looked at him blearily. "Who the hell are you?" he asked, with a complaining note in his voice.

Tal slapped him, twice. "Belleraphon. Tell me about him."

"Wait . . . will you give me my stuff back?"

"I'll consider it."

"I gotta have it back. You don't know what they . . . what are you doing?"

Tal had taken hold of his left hand and put it against the floor. He said, "I'm going to take your gripper here, and use it to crush the bones in your little finger."

"What the *hell!*" Peeskill tried to drag his hand away and found it trapped in a machinelike vise. "Look, you're out of your—"

Tal maneuvered the hand into a more efficient position. "Then we can work our way up. The human body has plenty of bones." He lifted the gripper.

"Wait, look—*stop!* All right, stop!"

Tal paused. Peeskill said, "I'll tell you. I'll tell you. God! You're crazy, you know, you're not normal."

"I know."

"You're not even *mad* at me!"

"I'm seriously annoyed with you. You can consider that enough to get you killed, Maintenance Worker Peeskill."

Peeskill put his other hand up to his face, and took it away again when his face hurt. He said, "I never met Belleraphon. I only heard about him . . . before my time. Maybe thirty, forty years ago, Belleraphon was supposed to be running the underground on Baret One. All the illegal stuff . . . drugs, proscribed music, weapons, nonapproved sex. I don't even know if he was real. People say he was. A couple of my off-planet contacts wanted a name from me, and, hell, I'm not supposed to give them any. So I said Belleraphon. That was all! I made it up. I'd have made up someone else if I thought anybody'd be so damn interested."

"Just out of curiosity," said Tal, who had not put down the gripper, "what is the name of your employer?"

Peeskill met his eyes. Something he saw there made his fingers throb with unpleasant anticipation. Peeskill said, "My direct contact is Warek. I don't know his first name. He never trusted me enough to tell me who he works for."

"Very sensible," said Tal.

He stood up. Peeskill said, "Are you going to give me back my stuff?"

"I said I'd consider it."

"I told you the truth!"

"I know you did." Tal smiled. "That was taxmal, after all."

Peeskill looked down. "God." Then he said, "How am I supposed to explain *this?*"—gesturing to his swelling face.

"Tell them you fell down the stairs. Does anyone really care enough about you to pay attention?"

"No." He said it without bitterness.

"I didn't think so." Tal dusted off his hands and went upstairs.

* * *

He woke up suddenly. Someone was in his stateroom. Tal lay very still for a moment, breathing lightly, listening. Then he rolled off the bed and came up on the floor holding a pistol. At almost the same second someone came down on his bed. Tal maneuvered between the intruder and the control for the lights; he saw better in the dark than humans, and if the lights came on, he would be momentarily blinded.

It was Peeskill, of course. Threats to his bodily safety were about the only thing that could make Tal genuinely angry; at this moment he was aware of a strong wish to tear Peeskill apart. Then Peeskill lunged at him, and Tal saw the glint of a knife arcing through the darkness. Tal fired his pistol.

Peeskill went down, and his knife hit the floor. Tal kicked it away. He wanted to be sure only Peeskill's fingerprints were on it, because he was well aware that that shot had done it for both of them. An energy weapon had been discharged aboard ship, and Security was on the way. He flicked on the lights, blinked for a moment, then went over to inspect Peeskill. Unfortunately he was still alive. Tal indulged himself enough to give a vicious kick to Peeskill's side—Tal had strong feelings about people who tried to end his existence, and it might have the added benefit of killing Peeskill before he could talk to Security. If he had any sense, of course, he wouldn't tell them the truth, but Tal had no faith in Peeskill's intelligence.

The door slid open and six security guards entered, fanning out quickly. Within seconds they separated Tal from his pistol, checked him for other weapons, and examined Peeskill. "He's alive," said one of them. He looked up at Tal. "Want to tell us what happened?"

"Better wait for the Captain," said another.

"Can I sit down?" said Tal.

"No," said the guard.

A few minutes later Captain Nestra appeared. From her crimson dragon-robe and slippers, she had clearly been off-duty. Her white hair hung in a braid down her back, and her captain's cap had been hastily stuffed in one of the robe's pockets. She paused at the doorway and inspected Peeskill, who was being helped to sit up, and then Tal, who stood against a wall. She raised an eyebrow.

"Had a busy shift, have we?" She stepped inside and walked over to Tal. Keeping her eyes on him, she said, "Officer Rami?"

Choris Rami, who had so kindly given him a map of the ship his first day out, appeared to be highest ranking security guard present. She glanced toward Peeskill and said, "He's going to be all right. He's got a burn down his right shoulder and arm, and some bumps and bruises. Neither of them's said anything yet."

"Very good, officer." She said to Tal, "Would you like to make a statement for the record?"

"I don't know why he was in my room," said Tal. "I think he was trying to rob me."

"That's a lie!" said Peeskill.

The captain turned to him. "Yes?" she said. "Why were you in his room?"

Peeskill looked around at several pairs of eyes, all waiting for him to go on. He dropped his gaze. "This cargo said he wanted sex with me. He said men can't do it in the Three Cities. Said he was curious."

Tal noted the eyes turning back in his direction. He said nothing. It wasn't a bad try on Peeskill's part, after all. Experience had led Tal to believe that money or sex were understood as reasonable motives for anything humans ever did. This story contained both, so it might be acceptable.

The captain said, "Well, nonapproved sex is a misdemeanor, but robbery is a felony. Want to change your story?" Tal did not reply at once, and she said, "Still doesn't explain the fight, boys."

Peeskill said, "He refused to pay me afterward. I got mad, and he drew a pistol. I tried to defend myself."

The captain walked over to the bed where a knife slash was more than visible, running down the front of the sheets. "So I see. If he had his pistol out, I'm surprised you got so far."

Peeskill was silent. The captain looked to Tal, who also did not speak. She sighed. "I'm not fond of excitement on my trips." She walked up to Tal and said to him gently,

"You know, I once knew a first lieutenant who had eyes like yours."

Tal froze. "A lot of people have gray eyes," he said.

"I wasn't talking about the color." She turned and said, "Take Maintenance Worker Peeskill to Medical. Tell Darla I want a full report on his injuries waiting for me when I go on-shift."

They began helping Peeskill out. The captain turned back to Tal. She lifted his pistol in her hands, inspecting it. "I assume you brought this on board in pieces, but that still doesn't explain how you got charges for it."

Tal said nothing. This Captain Nestra felt very dangerous. Why was it always the women?

She sat on the edge of the bed. "Let me put it his way. As far as the Secret Police are concerned, I'm sure they consider you a spy. They consider everybody a spy. Now, regardless of what caused this little brouhaha, I'm gong to have to turn you over to the port police when we reach Baret One. You may or may not be able to talk your way out of this then. Meanwhile, we can put you in the brig, or we can confine you to your quarters. Which is it?"

Tal said, "I charged it off the packs in your storage cabinets."

"They're the wrong size for a pistol."

"I resized one."

"Great flying elephants," said the captain, reverting to a childhood oath she hadn't thought of in sixty years. "You could have blown us all up!"

"It's perfectly safe if you know what you're doing."

"And I thought we had the option of not putting you in the brig. It would be for the safety of everybody if I did."

"Well, you've got the pistol now. And you did imply you wouldn't if I spoke."

"So I did." She rose. "When I consider that first lieutenant I mentioned, I should have known better. Meals will be brought to you here. Do try to stay out of trouble."

"Captain? This officer you spoke of. What happened to him?"

She paused at the door. "We were married, briefly. He's dead now."

The door slid closed behind her. Tal went back to the

bed and sat on the slashed sheets. Somehow that last sentence did not surprise him.

This officer would be dead, too, soon after they grounded at Baret One. All it would take would be the medical check.

There was a hissing sound outside as Security sealed the door.

Chapter 13

Iolanthe woke feeling groggy, her body one huge ache, as though all her muscles had been engaged for hours. This alarmed her, distantly, for she was obliged to do something today, either with Adrian or with some party of courtiers; she couldn't quite recall what, but she was obliged to do something *every* day.

She forced herself to sit up. No, that wasn't going to work. She lay back against the pillows and managed, as Prudence came sailing in bearing tea, to make a pitiful sound in her throat.

"Darling!" said Prudence, who set the cup on the table at once and placed one cool, perfectly manicured hand on Iolanthe's forehead. "No fever, but not quite the thing, are we? Do you want to stay in today?"

"*Could* I?"

"Poor baby, you say it so disbelievingly. Of course you can, you're not a prisoner, this isn't a life sentence ... well, I suppose it is, but even God rested one day a week." She adjusted Io's pillows efficiently and said, "Let me go and tell them to change your day-book."

And she whirled out, sky-blue gown swirling. Io lay back, looking at the ceiling frieze, wondering at the distinct, sharp sting of misery that clung to her today like some too-strong perfume. Why in heaven's name ... suddenly an image flashed through her mind—people, or demons, in masks, one of them with a knife. And a heavy smell of strange incense, and voices ... praying?

She understood abruptly what people meant by one's

blood running cold. Goosebumps raised themselves all along the square of skin outside her bodice. Because that image had been, somehow, *familiar.*

Adrian came in to find her shivering. "I'm sorry you're not feeling well," he said, as harmlessly and reassuringly, he trusted, as any well-brought-up bravo from the Opal would have. "I brought you this."

He offered her a silk doll, much like the ones Will said were in her room on Opal. Dolls were an appropriate gift to take to a sickbed, at least here on the Diamond; he hoped she didn't think he was making some comment on her maturity.

My, but he'd gotten defensive around Iolanthe, hadn't he? Checking everything he said and did. . . .

"Thank you, sir."

"Adrian."

"Adrian," she said obediently, making him wonder whether he was browbeating a sick woman. Surely he could work on this "sir" thing later.

"Thank you for not being upset with me," she said, with a contrite sleepiness. "I'm just so tired . . . I don't know why. . . ."

"That's quite all right," he assured her, ignoring the arrows of guilt that were raining down. "Just rest for as long as you like. A day, a week, it doesn't matter."

"You're very good to me . . . considerate. . . ." She trailed off, her eyes closing as the drugs took effect.

Adrian closed the door on the way out. In the outer room he found Brandon Fischer with a tall, middle-aged woman who wore her court dress as though it were a disguise.

She glanced toward Adrian with the equality of one who considers herself a mistress of her own world. "How is my patient?" she said.

"Tired. And I suspect, sore."

"Painkillers, as I've said, for at least ten days—"

"Yes. So you've said. You pumped enough into her last night, and there was more in the tea this morning."

She looked at him narrowly.

"I promise you, madam, we are giving her the best of care. She's my wife, isn't she?"

Her voice gave him back nothing in trust. "I've never taken a patient before who didn't come to me of her own will. I've never walked into a room with a coven circle to take a woman already drugged senseless—"

Adrian's wince was imperceptible.

"And none of us would have done it for anyone but the Protector. Nor for any reason but that she'd been violated before."

Now Fischer was looking at him, too. "You didn't tell—" He cut himself off.

Crossly, Adrian said, "Satisfy yourself, madam! I insist." He gestured toward Iolanthe's room. "You'll find her sleeping peacefully."

She took him at his word, leaving them there.

As soon as she was out of the room, Fischer said, "You didn't tell Iolanthe?"

"She wouldn't have liked the idea, Brandon."

"But you didn't tell her," he continued, monomaniacally. The concept, Adrian saw, left him completely at sea. Was this what marriage reduced one to?

"I had the right to insist the operation take place."

"That's my point, Adrian. You could have ordered her to go through with it. She would have, I'm sure."

Adrian paced uncomfortably. "I refuse to have her *looking* at me. With that look women get, as though you've failed them entirely and ought to be taken out with the spaniel who's left something on the rug."

"Iolanthe wouldn't—"

"Look who speaks for her now! The man who tells me the obvious, that she's a product of Opal!" Abruptly, his anger passed. "She doesn't trust us, Brandon. She would have been terrified. I make choices for four million people—it's a little late to decide I can't make one now."

Fischer regarded him silently. At last he said, "We must pray she never finds out."

The witch-surgeon returned. She closed the door gently and brushed her hands together as though disposing of chalk dust.

Adrian waited, then said, "Well, madam?"

Her face expressionless, she said, "I wish you joy of your marriage, sir." She inclined her head to them, and left.

"Witches," said Adrian.

Fischer made no comment as they left Iolanthe's rooms. Out in the corridor they were met by Will Stockton. "Sir, I must lay an objection," he said formally.

Adrian sighed, knowing what was coming. With the two Opal security guards, his own two, Brandon and now Will, quite a knot was forming in the corridor, all to listen and participate in a discussion that would be better not happening.

Will spoke with stiff earnestness. "With all respect, why wasn't I informed that a party was taking place here yesterday? I was under the impression the Lady Iolanthe had retired for the evening. Sir—I don't like to hear this sort of thing from my own guards after the fact."

Adrian gave him a look of well-bred surprise. "It was a simple tea party, from what I was told. Ladies only. I don't think you'd have been welcome."

"Sir," Will said doggedly, "the point is that this is a security issue. I should have lists of attendees, times, places—"

"Yes, yes. You're quite right. We'll be more careful in future. No harm done this time, though, was there?"

Will's expression was pure dissatisfaction, the look of one who wanted to fight for his point and was balked by unfair capitulation on the part of his enemy. Finally he said, "I must insist on being informed, sir, really."

"You're absolutely right, Sergeant. I'll speak to someone about it."

He heard the tiredness in his own voice and was surprised by it. *Guilt can be wearing,* said an imp in his head, nastily. *Oh, shut up.*

"That poet was a liar," he muttered to Brandon as they walked away from the tangle. "Love does not make all things simple."

"Would you like my advice?" Fischer said. He opened his mouth.

"I shall become violent," said Adrian, turning to look at him. "This is fair warning."

Fischer closed his mouth. They continued down the corridor, Adrian hearing the pace of his security guards like the tramp of every bad decision he'd ever made, treading on his cape.

* * *

Hartley sat in Rose Court, behind the Cascade, hidden by the staircase. He peeled off an exquisitely thin silk glove and inspected it for tears. The truly creative, he thought, are never bored, but this is pushing the theory. He'd been waiting for over an hour.

The expanse of the courtyard was nearly empty now; partygoers, pleasantly drunken, had swayed gently from their gatherings and made their way home again, guided by pages. It was dim and quiet—only the distant murmur of a private dance, talk and music together, blended on the periphery of hearing.

A man approached him. A young man, Hartley thought, from the way he moved. He wore a party mask, a scarlet bird's head with crepe streamers.

"'Out of the night that covers me,'" the young man offered, his voice uncertain.

The truly creative are often *tested* by boredom, though, Hartley said to himself. The young man's mouth was just visible beneath the top half of beak, and as Hartley watched, a tongue emerged to wet dry lips.

"'Out of the night that covers me,'" the young man said again, more uncertain than ever.

"'Black as the pit from pole to pole,'" said Hartley obligingly.

"'I thank whatever gods may be—'" Slight note of relief there.

"'For my unconquerable soul.' Pleased to be of service. Have we met?"

The bird-man goggled at him. In the same mundane tone, Hartley continued, "Do you know, I believe the man who wrote that poem killed himself soon thereafter. It hardly seems fair that you have such a splendid mask, and I have only my skin. Would you care for a peppermint? I have some in my pocket."

You wouldn't think a mask could look so horrified. "Oh, never mind. Sit down," said Hartley.

The bird-man sat. He landed with a thud, as though air had been let out. "I've come with important information."

"I was sure you had," said Hartley, smiling with all friendliness. "I hope you're not going to share it right away. That would take all the artifice out of the thing—it would be too much like real life, then, and who would be interested?"

Two brown eyes stared at him blankly. Hartley sighed. "Well, if you insist. Tell me, what is your important information? I'm all eagerness."

He turned a face of polite expectancy to the bird-man, who seemed taken aback.

"I don't . . . I wasn't planning . . ." The bird-man coughed. He got hold of himself. "Officer Quince," he began daringly, with a glare through the slits as though challenging his companion to stop him from using names.

"Oh, call me Hartley, please."

Another wipe of the lips. "I didn't mean that I have information *now,* dammit! I meant that I could easily, in the future . . . what I mean is, I could place myself at Opal's disposal. If you see what I mean, sir."

Hartley smiled, angelically this time, and left off tormenting him. "I do see, and you would be most welcome."

"I would?" This took him by surprise. "We haven't spoken of money."

"Oh, don't let's talk of it. I don't doubt that whatever you think is fair would be just compensation for one such as yourself, who places himself in danger for the good of all."

The mask examined him through sideways eyes, but Hartley's voice was entirely sincere. "Danger. Er, yes. You see, I can't reveal my identity . . ."

"Certainly not," interrupted Hartley. "Why put your destiny in the hands of those who may lack your moral stamina?"

After a puzzled silence, the masked man said, "Um, yes. Exactly."

With a smile of all sweet accord, Hartley said, "Well, run along, then."

"Run along? I, uh . . ."

"You've placed yourself at our disposal. We're happy to accept. Don't want to keep you up late."

The bird-man rose to his feet uncertainly. "But shouldn't we . . . I don't know . . ."

"Come here again on Saint Jean's Day, and I'll have a

token of our esteem. And you can tell me how many more tokens you'd like."

"Oh." He took a few steps away, then turned back.

Hartley waved. "Well-met, we must do it again."

The bird-man spy walked away, his red crepe streamers lifting behind him in the air. His shoulders were hunched and he seemed to be thinking hard.

Well, thought Hartley, that was mildly entertaining. Would Lord Muir ever find Harry a place in the administration? Hartley had known that Harry Muir hated his father, but he hadn't known it was deep enough hatred for treason as spite.

Heigh-ho. Time to get back to his quarters, where a lovely girl was waiting who would require a lengthy apology.

Hartley was nothing if not polite.

Chapter 14

"Graykey truth has a different color every day."

"When a Graykey swears, cover your ears."

"Trusting a Graykey is like picking up an alleycat."

The aphorisms about distrusting the Graykey are numerous, and I must begin by saying that I do not believe they deserve their reputation for deceit. On the contrary, they are the most obsessively honest people I have ever met; clear and plainspoken, and scrupulously accurate about almost everything that comes out of their mouths. Ask a Graykey in passing how he feels, and he has to stop a minute, think, and give you the most perfect summing-up he can.

Having said all that, I must now add that I do not trust them either. And the reason for this is simple: Ethical behavior is hierarchical among the Graykey, and the Contract comes before all. Where it does not conflict with his Contract, a Graykey will be the most openhearted and accommodating of companions. Where it does, they are totally without mercy.

*Ironically, their reputation for trickiness really stems
from their ingrained honesty, for they try to tell the truth
wherever possible—leading them and their listeners into
some twisting verbal bypaths. "Jesuitical" is the first ad-
jective you will find listed in the Imperial Encyclopedia;
and that source will tell you also that the Graykey are
great practitioners of the game of casuistry.*

*From my personal experience among them, I believe
this reputation depresses them terribly.*

Keylinn:

I saw Spider putting down Caudlander's *A Tourist Guide
to the Graykey* as I entered the office. He lifted his head
from the sofa pillow and smiled at me without a trace of
shame.

"I stored those books here for safekeeping," I said,
"not to provide you with a personal library."

He grinned. " 'Jesuitical'?" he asked. "And what in
heaven's name is 'casuistry'?"

I walked over, took the book from his hands—I'd hard-
copied them for convenience, since this was a long-term
assignment—and checked what page he was on. "Mostly
nonsense," I assured him.

"Oh? Why do you keep it around?"

"To remind myself of how strange some people's
mindsets can be." I sat on the sofa beside him. "Present
company excepted, of course."

"Thank you." He did not appear offended at all.

I decided not to pursue this topic. There was no reason
for him to believe that my interest in the Graykey was
anything but intellectual. Unless Tal had told him, which
I would not assume. I said, "I go on-shift in two hours.
Where is it you wanted to take me?"

"Ah, yes." He got up and put on his good jacket. "You
really liked the play yesterday?"

"I said that I did."

"And you really liked the fellow playing Falstaff."

"Yes, I really did. Why, do you want to see it over
again? It's not playing today, and I wouldn't have time
anyway."

Spider said, "He's a friend of mine, and we're due to

go have tea and cookies with him and his friend, right now."

He seemed to enjoy tilting me off-balance. "We are?"

"We are." He touched the door open and bowed for me to go first. Out in the corridor he offered me his arm. A gentleman and a forger, I gathered.

We took a lift to a Mercati Boulevard lock, and walked the street arm in arm, a decorous couple considering that Spider kept glancing at my uniform as though I were not quite dressed for my part. We descended through the levels, and around G I became aware that Spider was ... well, becoming aware himself.

"Anything wrong?" I asked him.

"No, what could be wrong?"

"You keep looking around. I thought I was the tourist."

"Ah, well," said Spider. Then he said, "There are some people down here I'd be better off not meeting."

His arm, still in mine, seemed to have stiffened to wood. I said, "Do you go through this every time you come down past G?"

"Go through what?" asked Spider.

"Spider, if it makes a difference—" I lowered my voice. "—I'm armed. I know I'm not supposed to be—"

"So am I." His voice was curt, as though he were not quite comfortable with having a lady he was escorting tell him that she was armed. I did think that he needed to know, however, so I added, "It's a Wender-three, relatively accurate over fifty meters, and then it dissipates, so it's perfectly safe—"

"All right, all right." After a minute he said, "Thank you."

We began climbing a walkway to a side street. I said, "If there's anything I can do, please let me know."

"So," said Spider, "you're a Graykey."

I shut up.

He said, "Fascinating subject, the Graykey. Do you know there was another Graykey on the Diamond about a hundred years ago?"

"Eighty," I said under my breath. I was looking down at my feet by then.

We reached a door, and Spider stopped. There was no bell or alert light visible; it looked as though the quarters

on this street had once been storage rooms. A lot of
places below G were like that. Spider knocked. He said,
"Are you here on your own, or does Tal have your contract?"

"I'm here for my own purposes," I stated. This was a
true statement as far as it went.

Spider opened his mouth as though to say something
else, but then the door swung wide and a tall, stocky man
grabbed Spider in a bear hug that made me feel for a
weapon before I saw it was friendly. "Spider! Sweetheart!
Where the *hell* have you been? It's been months!" He
pulled Spider inside as they balanced precariously, both
grinning, though Spider with more embarrassment.

"Is this your friend?" asked the stocky man.

"Yes," said Spider when he could talk. "Keylinn Gray,
this is Howard Talmadge Diamond—Falstaff of yesterday."

"Miss Gray," said Howard Talmadge, bowing. He took
my hand and kissed it with due ceremony; not a practice
followed among the commoners of the Three Cities.

"Heavens," I murmured, feeling the tingle up my arm.
They usually called me "Tech Gray" here, but I wasn't
about to correct him.

The room, I saw when I could look around, was pleasant and comfortable, but clearly makeshift. Crates served
as tables, with brightly patterned cloths thrown over
them; lamps had been brought in, for the overhead lighting was scarce—lamps with sculptured bases and colored
tops. It was all of a piece with the manual door; a jerry-
built sort of nest, upgraded to live better than it was
meant to.

And there, in a dark corner, was someone else. A man
sitting in a chair with wheels, I'd never seen such a
thing—another conceit of furniture design? He wheeled
himself out and extended a hand. "Miss Gray," he said,
and I placed my hand in his. He kissed it also, only bowing his head, for he did not stand up.

His kiss, like his appearance, was less dramatic than
Howard Talmadge's; he was thinner and somewhat older,
and right now he looked more tired.

Spider said, "Keylinn, this is Dominick Potyevsky."

"Hello, Mr. Potyevsky." This was the polite way to meet nonranked civilians, Spider had said.

Spider tossed Howard Talmadge a package wrapped in paper. "I brought a present," he said, and flopped down in a chair.

Talmadge sighed in relief. "Thanks, my friend; we've been waiting." He carried the package to Dominick Potyevsky and dropped it in his lap. "You're excused," he said firmly to Mr. Potyevsky, and the latter smiled and wheeled away into a back room.

He didn't do that as though he were playing, I thought abruptly. It was more as if he really couldn't walk—where had I come, to the dark ages? And even if the loss of mobility were temporary—a chair with wheels? What was the point? He'd never make it down the walkway.

Talmadge said, "It's been getting worse. I appreciate this, Spider, I wish you'd let us do something for you."

"Please," said Spider, pushing away with his hands while his feet did a little dance of embarrassment.

Talmadge turned his smile on me. "So this is the young lady who likes historicals. How did you enjoy our Henry-four?"

"Very much. Especially the fat fellow with the beard."

His smile was eloquent; now it suggested that if I were lying, it was a charming thing to do. "Have you seen much Shakespeare?"

"We do some at home. Tell me, do you always do it that way? Traditional format?"

"In general. Unmodified, with subtitles, that's the usual—but then, there are a lot of people who can't read, you'd be surprised; so we slip in a modified version every few years for them. More fun, in some ways—the laugh comes when you speak the line, and not when the titles come up . . . they're not always timed just so. Especially if the title-runner's been at the bottle too early." He smiled and added in a booming voice, "One ha'penny of bread to this intolerable deal of sack." He said it in Oldstyle English, and Spider looked left out. I laughed. "A linguistic sophisticate, I see. Where's 'home,' if I may ask, Miss Gray?"

"I'd prefer to be called Keylinn, if that's all right. I'm

still not very sure of your customs, so if I say anything wrong, I hope you'll forgive me."

Dominick Potyevsky was returning from the other room, looking considerably more cheerful.

Talmadge turned to him and said, "And we're Dominick and Howard, to any friend of Spider's, right?"

"If you would," said Potyevsky. Dominick. "Would you like some cookies, Keylinn? We always prepare when we know Spider's coming." And he patted his belly with a wicked look in his eye.

Spider sat up straight. "That's not fair! Who played Falstaff yesterday?"

"I used padding," said Howard Talmadge. "It would be superfluous in your case."

"See what happens when I bring a lady with me?" Spider turned to me and shook some crumbs off his palms. "This is the story of my life: Constant abuse at the hands of my friends."

". . . oh, I don't know. I guess the greatest disappointment—second only to the fact that we've run out of cookies—is that I never got to play in *Othello*. I made a nuisance of myself for years over it—you see, Keylinn, we do one quarter year Shakespeare, and one quarter Ayscough, and one Gleisner, so I hoped eventually—"

"You've left out a quarter," said Spider.

"That's the quarter for new plays. Whatever we can get past the Censor. —Dominick does those, did you know that, Keylinn? We put on one of his four years ago. . . . Where was I?"

He would probably be clearer on where he was, I thought, if whiskey had not begun to replace the tea about an hour ago.

"You know," said Dominick, "you always say that. *In Othello*. I've always meant to ask you, do you want to play Othello or Iago?"

Howard Talmadge blinked at him. "How can you ask that?"

"Well, I know you love a title role, Howard, but Othello's really a very silly fellow at bottom, and—"

"There's a writer for you." He gestured toward Dominick with the whiskey bottle. "They're all got a soft spot for the villain. Go miles out of their way to pay you back a quarter—well, some of them—but the more corpses pile up around a character, the better they like him."

"I agree with him," I said. Howard put on a look of betrayal, while Dominick lifted a teacup in acknowledgement. "Othello was an awful man. Iago only tried to hurt what he thought were his enemies; Othello killed his wife, and on the basis of—what was it, a handkerchief? Next to him, the bad guy can't help but look good."

From his place on the sofa Spider said archly, "Maybe he thought she violated a contract. The marriage contract."

Oh, you're treading close to the tide, Spider-my-boy.

"He should have ascertained that as a fact," I replied cooly. "No, no mercy for Othello in my book. He deserved what happened to him."

"The lady's harsh," said Howard. "But at least Spider agrees with me."

"Not really," said Spider.

"I'm alone!" He tilted back the bottle and emptied the last sip.

"A husband has duties to his wife," said Spider. "Call me old-fashioned, but *not killing her* comes somewhere near the top of the list."

"Well, you're statistical anomalies, the three of you, and I'm glad all audiences aren't like you."

I knelt beside the sofa to retrieve a glass, and whispered to Spider, "I go on-shift in twenty minutes."

He sat up. "Howard, Dom, we'd better start moving. I'll be back in two weeks with whatever I can get."

They exchanged good-byes for another five minutes, and I promised to return with Spider.

On the other side of the door Spider asked, "Did you have a good time?"

"Yes, I did. I like them." And I'd fallen hard for the handkissing, which in Howard's case had an impressive engine behind it for someone I didn't believe was primarily hetero.

"You didn't say much."

"I'm shy around strangers. I get over it." Partway down the steel steps, I thought to ask, "What's wrong with Dominick?"

"Basically, he's dying."

"Oh." I wondered if that kind of statement would always be so hard to reply to.

"It's taking a long time, and meanwhile he's in a lot of pain. Particularly his back—sitting in that chair all the time really puts a strain on it. Howard and I do what we can for him—although I can't really compare with Howard. He does everything, every day." Spider's shirt came untucked as he hit the last few steps; he lifted his jacket, stuffed it back in unself-consciously, and offered a hand to me for the final step. As though I hadn't made it perfectly well down the rest of the stairs; this was charming. I liked Spider more and more.

We walked to the Boulevard. The dimmers were coming on, and the store signs with them. I considered the state of medicine on the Diamond, and what I might or might not do as a Graykey to assist Dominick Potyevsky. There was nothing I could think of that did not violate Diamond policy and either endanger my contract-holder or invalidate the contract. Spider, I had noticed, generally found silence awkward after a time. Now he said, "You'll have to take a train if you want to reach Transport by your shift. Sorry."

"That's all right, it was a pleasant afternoon. I wonder what Tal's doing now?"

He snorted. "It's pointless to even speculate, believe me. . . . Does he really not have your contract?"

"I give you my word, Spider, I'm not under contract to anyone on the Diamond." Tal was at that moment quite some distance off the Diamond.

"Well, do you know this thing of his about Belleraphon?" We reached the track steps, and stood there for a moment facing each other.

"I've heard the name."

"Do you know why he's looking for him?"

I said carefully, "I just came on board, Spider, you're supposed to be the expert. What do you think?"

"Not a clue. I don't get paid to think." The vibration of the railing announced that a train was coming, and he said, "Best go up or you'll be late."

"Thank you for a lovely time," I said, and kissed him on the cheek.

He touched his cheek, looking nonplussed, and I ran up the steps.

Up top, I threw myself into the train and onto a cushioned seat, ignoring the stares from Cities folk at a woman tech in this part of town. The Boulevard began to flash by the windows.

I thought: I wonder what's happening on the *Kestrel*.

Chapter 15

Aboard the *RS Kestrel*, trouble was happening. Captain Nestra stood in the power room, assessing the damage. "Whatever happened to quality control?" she inquired laconically.

The power room supervisor felt his earn burn. "This is hardly my fault, Captain. It's a new panel. They're supposed to be good for a thousand entries."

"It wasn't, though, was it? All right, citizen, why don't you see what you can salvage of the mess. Officer Rami?"

Choris Rami, a set look on her young, well-scrubbed face, came over to stand beside the Captain.

"It looks like we're not going home this way. We'll have to turn back to Baret Station, we'll never make a gravity landing. You know what this will do to the schedule."

"Yes, Captain."

"We're gong to have a bunch of unhappy people here. Let 'em vent as much steam as they want, and assist them in filing their complaints. At least half of 'em will want to. Right?"

"Yes, Captain."

"And now we'll have to send a message to those other unhappy folks, back home, and listen while they tell us it'll go on all our records." She sighed and turned to leave, but Officer Rami spoke up.

"We can't notify them, Captain, the transceiver's on the blink."

The Captain stopped. "Since when?"

"It was reported two hours ago."

"Rami, m'dear, what are the odds on a landing panel and a transceiver going out at the same time? Hmm? And you didn't think to tell me about it sooner?"

"Captain, the transceiver is down about half the time anyway. It's a piece of junk, sir—I'm quoting yourself."

The Captain stood there with a look of distant thought on her face more appropriate, Rami thought, to a garden back home than a system transport. Then she said gently, "That spy I like. Teal, or Tall—"

"Tal Diamond."

"Bring him out here, Rami."

"Yes, sir."

Ten minutes later Tal was brought in. His hands were bound, humanely, in a stretch-loop. Rami said, "He hasn't been out. I checked the door-seal—there was a mark we left when we closed it up, and it was still there."

"Hello, Officer Diamond."

"Hello, Captain."

She glanced to the panel. "We've had a bit of trouble here."

Tal took a step closer an looked it over. "It doesn't look good. I'm not much of a technical expert, though, being from the Three Cities. Sorry I can't help you."

She smiled. "I wasn't gong to ask you to repair it, officer. We don't put prisoners on work detail here. It's against Bureau of Transport rules."

"Oh."

"Besides, repairing it will give my power room supervisor something to do while he's thinking of how to make this sound plausible in his record." The supervisor glanced over at them from where he stood by the panel. He did not look happy, or patient with the Captain's style of speech.

"Then, may I ask—"

Just then the supervisor pried open the panel door with a metal pick, in one massive levering-off that contained all the frustrations of his day. The panel fell open. The circuit-glow inside ignited into a fireball, and pieces of red-hot metal and melting plastic exploded over the room.

A jagged piece of metal, about the size of a large ring,

was on a trajectory for Tal. He knocked it aside, simultaneously reaching with his other hand to deflect a piece of inner paneling that was about to hit the Captain's face. He dropped the piece a half-second later, and clasped the burnt hand with his other one.

Captain Nestra and Officer Rami hit the floor, a bit late. The explosion was over. They lay there for a few seconds, then looked up at Tal, who said, "I think that's it."

They stood up again, the Captain with some difficulty. She got to one knee and held out a hand for Tal to assist her the rest of the way. He did so.

Officer Rami was untouched. The supervisor had a piece of metal half-buried in his shoulder. "Call Medical," said the Captain.

Tal said carefully, "I believe that significant portions of equipment are booby-trapped by your own government. As a guard against terrorism. I've heard that your people are supposed to follow certain procedures in opening up such equipment, which I did not note your supervisor to do, or the results—"

"Shut up, Diamonder. I'm not blaming you for this one."

Tal shut up. The Captain continued to stand there, obviously playing back everything in her mind. "You saved my life, or from certain injury."

It was not phrased as a thank you. Tal did not reply.

"You shouldn't have been able to, Officer Diamond."

He shouldn't have been able to. He'd reacted too quickly for a human—so quickly that they hadn't even been able to take in what he'd done till now. No doubt he should have let that piece hit the Captain, but he'd been acting on reflex at the time. The Captain continued, "Officer Rami, check his bonds."

Rami looked over from where she'd been examining the supervisor's wound. "They're not broken, Captain."

"They're stretched beyond the point they should be. He needed both hands a certain distance apart, to help both himself and me. Was this loop set for humans?"

"Of course, Captain." But Rami came over, felt the loop dangling from Tal's wrists, and looked at him, puzzled.

"And there we are," said the Captain softly.

Sounds came from out in the corridor; Medical was already on its way. The Captain said, "I want our guest to have a full physical examination, Rami. And a security watch."

Tal waited, feeling as naked as if he'd taken out his lenses in public—something he had never done, even as a child.

Rami said, "Captain, that seal on his door was unbroken. If there's somebody else running around the ship doing sabotage—"

"I know. We're going to put a watch on all vital pieces of equipment. If Security doesn't have enough people to go around, we'll have the general crew take turns. But meanwhile—" she reached out and tapped the back of Tal's hand, as though testing an unfamiliar piece of merchandise. "I want to know what we have here."

Chapter 16

Things do not change; we change.

HENRY DAVID THOREAU

"What is it, sweetheart?" Prudence made sure the bedroom door was securely shut, and moved to embrace Iolanthe. "What's wrong?"

Io's face with tight with unhappiness. "You have to help me, Prudence. I have to see the witch who was here ... the old woman ..."

"I know whom you mean, darling, but why? If it's the headache again—"

She shook her head. "It's a personal matter."

"A personal ..." Prudence's voice trailed off. She inspected Io, then took her hand and led her over to a pile of embroidered pillows. "Sit."

"Prudence—"

"Sit." Her hands pushing on Io's shoulders made it difficult not to. They sat and Prudence smoothed her dress.

"Now, darling, listen. If anything has happened to you, I just want you to know that we can deal with it. Adrian will never back out of the marriage at this point. You're perfectly safe."

Io looked up, startled. "What?"

Her companion was businesslike. "Has Adrian been anticipating the wedding? He's a Mercati, I don't expect a saint of abstinence."

"No! Of course not! Adrian . . ." Words failed her.

"Our tall sergeant, then? I swear to you, Io, we can deal with it."

"No!"

"Then what is it?"

Iolanthe swallowed. "There's something wrong with me."

"You mean . . ."

"Here, there's something wrong here." Her hands circled nervously, an inch from her crotch. "It *hurts.*"

Prudence hesitated. "Since when?"

"Two days. And I had some terrible dreams—like fever dreams. I think I've caught some kind of sickness."

Prudence stood then and began pacing, a general faced with a new tactical problem. Finally she turned to Io. "You're probably right, we should call Granny. But we can't bring a witch here without preparation. It must be done discreetly. We need Adrian's permission and help."

"I don't want to talk to him about this."

"Look at me, Io. It won't lessen your value."

"No."

"Then I'll talk to him."

"No."

"Sooner or later, somebody has to talk to somebody. Be sensible."

Io met her eyes. "Ask Lord Fischer."

That stopped her. Io was perfectly right; Fischer could arrange something discreetly, if anyone could. And he was behind the marriage, and was a reasonable man.

"Hmm. For a stranger to court, you have better ideas than I do, sometimes. All right, stay here and wait for me. I'll sound out the weather in that direction."

Io smiled wanly. Prudence kissed her and went off to find Brandon Fischer.

* * *

When she returned to the room an hour later, she was fuming. She would kill Adrian. She would pummel him to the deck and set her dogs on him.

"Prudence? What did they say?"

She sat down beside Io and took her hand. "I spoke directly to Granny Seaton, dear heart. She said not to worry, that this is perfectly normal."

"It is?"

"Yes, it's something that happens to some women when they reach maturity. Just a phase. I means your, er, womanhood has developed properly." Surely that didn't sound at all plausible, did it? Fortunately Io's complete ignorance was an advantage.

She looked distrustful, though, Prudence noted. Yes, she would have to kill Adrian. After her dogs were finished, she'd torture the remnants. Like all Mercatis, he took the easy road when it came to personal relations—when charm wouldn't do the trick, perhaps abdicating responsibility would. . . .

"But it hurts, Prudence. That can't be right."

"The hurt will fade, dear, I promise. In a few days."

"Really?"

How typical of the man. He was as in love as he'd ever been, and yet the idea of respecting the wishes of his beloved never crossed his pointy little mind. It might be a bad PR move to tell her the truth, after all.

Prudence put her arm around Iolanthe and rocked her gently. "Of course."

There was a whole person, a whole world in there, Prudence thought. Young and naive, but with glimmers of good sense. One day Io would say something wise to the poor boy and he'd be caught in a rainstorm of surprise. For Adrian, loving a woman and acquiring a new puppy—or a pet demon—were somewhere on the same scale, and Prudence longed to see that scale get too heavy for him to handle.

"And do you know," she murmured, kissing Io's forehead, "I think we're heading in that direction." After all, puppies grew into hounds that could lick your face or tear out your throat. Who knew what Iolanthe would grow into?

"What direction are you talking about? And why are you smiling?"

"I like surprises," said Prudence cryptically.

Several days later, following the instructions she received from Hartley Quince, Iolanthe made known her wish to see the Helium Park Zoo on a day when Adrian's schedule was impregnable. Brandon Fischer could not be spared either, and Adrian sent sincere apologies. But was there any reason, Iolanthe inquired, she could not visit the zoo in the company of her bodyguard and one or two old friends from Opal?

She was assured there was not. And so on this pleasant spring afternoon, sent to them by an obliging Helium Park Climate Control division, she crossed the river in a water-taxi to Zoo Island. Hartley Quince stood on her right, licking a lemon ice. His eyes scanned the banks of the river. Will Stockton sat beside her on the bench, his back to the water. The driver glanced at them from time to time; the boat purred gently as it moved; the air was warm and deceivingly fresh. A simple day on the river.

The taxi had room for about seven passengers, but they were the total complement; Will had paid the driver to leave ahead of schedule. Behind them the endless greenery of Helium Park extended for miles, with here and there an obscure government monument poking above the treetops. Conversation languished until they put in at the small dock on the island, got out and stood watching while the boat turned and grew steadily smaller on its journey back. There were booths around them of red and green and gold selling sugar candy and sweet drinks, and a handful of people wandering about them. A slow day, early in the season. None of them looked at Iolanthe, whose face had not acquired Adrian's notoriety, and on whose skin red welts were still healing—nobody's idea of a princess. A path led from the dock to the zoo proper.

Iolanthe was feeling very responsible for calling these two ranking males from their duties, and she began to wonder if anything she had to say could possibly be worth it. The sound of their bootheels crunching on the gravel path became progressively more unendurable. She said quietly, "I'm sorry to have disturbed your schedule, Officer Quince, but I—"

Hartley Quince put a pale hand on her wrist in a perfectly friendly way that nevertheless said—although she could not have said how—*not now.* He smiled. "It's always a pleasure to have an excuse to take a day off. The zoo was a delightful idea, and I'm only glad to know you haven't forgotten me, my lady."

Io looked at his smile and the words *above reproach* came to her. She definitely preferred Will. It was reassuring to think that, whatever the problem was, Hartley Quince would handle it; but what if the problem were her? Talking to Quince was like entering a fencing contest armed with a paring knife. *I wonder if he's slept with my mother,* she thought.

They walked up the path to the habitats. "Earth animals first, then mixtures, then alien species," said Quince, reading from a plaque. he looked up. "Alien species aren't mentioned on my map."

"They're new," said Will. "Adrian's been bringing them in for the last few years. He's starting a collection."

"You do keep on top of things, don't you, Willie?" Quince spoke with good humor. "I'm sure the lady is glad you were assigned to her." He glanced at Io.

She spoke up loyally. "Oh, yes! That is, Sergeant Stockton has been handling things wonderfully."

"He always does," said Quince, watching Will's face darken slightly.

"This is the elephant house," said Will. "Would you like to see it, my lady, or should we keep walking?"

"I've never seen elephants."

"Then we can stop on the way back," said Quince. "I believe you had something to say to me, my lady, and this would be an excellent time."

There was no one on the path ahead or behind. Io ducked her head, feeling very uncomfortable. "I . . . Adrian said . . . when I was sick I . . . ." She stopped and sat down on a bench.

Quince sat down beside her, all polite attention.

She pursed her lips. Getting these words out was like bringing up stones. At last she whispered, "I think I'd like to see a confessor." It came out barely audibly, shaming her further.

Quince said, in a voice of normal friendliness, "I take it my lady means outside of her regular confession-time, which is probably not till next Saturday."

"Yes. I'd like to see someone right away. I'm having a . . ." She balked at the words, then said, "spiritual crisis." The words were almost too pompous to pronounce, but all the holy books agreed that anyone having a spiritual crisis could gain access to a confessor right away. Perhaps the hierophant who'd accompanied the Opal envoys could speak with her; he had a kind voice, and God knew she needed to tell someone.

Quince said, "Lord Cardinal Arno will be on the Diamond the day after tomorrow. I'm sure he would make time to see you."

Io looked swiftly away. Arno would have her for breakfast and wash it down with coffee after. As a sick person knows what they crave for a cure, she could feel in her bones what she needed—to talk and think, with someone she could trust—not have someone else's thinking forced on her.

Will Stockton spoke up. "Hierophant Bell is with the Opal delegation already. If my lady doesn't want to wait." Io looked up at him. "He's a very good man, I use him myself."

"Yes, I—"

"What a pity he's leaving today," cut in Hartley Quince. He glanced at his timepiece. "Probably already on his way. That's why the Lord Cardinal is coming: to see to our needs until a new hierophant is assigned."

Will looked at Hartley. This had *lie* written all over it, but there was nothing he could do about it.

"So it will have to wait for the Lord Cardinal, I'm afraid," said Quince, when Io did not respond.

She nodded tiredly.

"Was there anything else? I'm here to serve you, my lady."

"I'd like to see the elephants," she said. And not looking at him, she gave her hand to Will.

* * *

Hartley knew a cold shoulder when it was presented to him, and he extended himself to be nice to Iolanthe. They visited the monkeys, the tropical birds, the bears, and the seals. He offered her ices when she looked thirsty and benches when she looked tired. But he was only partly attending; the greater part of his mind was elsewhere. If his efforts had no effect, it really didn't matter—her liking for the sergeant was plain, so he could always approach her through Will.

"Panthers," said Will, as they came upon an enormous, many-leveled cage. "A mix. Asian leopards from Earth and tree cats from Osiris." He bent over the plaque. "They're called marble panthers."

One could see where the name came from. The panthers seemed almost black, but closer observation showed the pelts to be a dark, rippling green—like looking into a deep and shadowed pool. Or a smooth piece of marble.

"Adrian's famous panthers," said Hartley. "I've heard he likes to semitranquilize them and give them the free run of the Hall of Audience, upon occasion."

Iolanthe's eyes grew round. "I can't believe that," she said, and her tone added, *even of Adrian.* Hartley grinned.

"I heard it, too," said Will, "but I thought it was just a story. They say he throws out the courtiers, even his bodyguards, and locks himself in the Hall with them."

The beasts were heartlessly beautiful. One of them flowed over to the front of the cage and regarded Iolanthe with an unblinking black stare. She took a step back before realizing she'd done so. She found herself saying, "He seems like such a normal person."

Hartley yawned and examined his nails. "I suppose he likes the aesthetics. Marble on marble."

"Even so—good heavens, people could get killed. *He* could get killed!"

"I heard it from a man who claimed to have been there. That's all I can answer for."

"They say the Mercatis were all a little crazy," said Will.

Hartley looked at him sharply at that, but he seemed not to have meant anything by it.

"Not 'were,' *are,*" said Io softly. "Adrian won't be the last."

It was her turn to receive a sharp glance, but she was looking down at her stomach speculatively; then she became aware of the vulgarity of such a gesture, and raised her head again.

"I'm sure you'll do your duty," said Will, with a mix of directness and discretion that was as trained as his reflexes. "Shouldn't we be leaving? The lights are going out."

They were standing at the top of a steep path leading down to the docks. The radiance overhead had diminished, and in the distance the immense expanse of greenery that surrounded Zoo Island was darkening. "We don't want to be in Helium Park at night," he added.

"No," agreed Hartley. As they descended the path, he said, "Did you know that the Royal Hunt takes place in the park? A barbaric custom."

Will was helping Io negotiate around the pebbles. His attention was not on Hartley when he spoke. "At least it's a custom that only hurts the Protector; unlike some of our own barbaric customs."

Hartley looked thoughtful. They reached the dock in silence; by the time they stepped in the water-taxi, colored lanterns had been lit, and the water rippled with them.

Iolanthe was seen safely home, and her quarters left in the care of Barington Strife, of the Opal City Guard. The Diamond was on night-time; in the dim corridor outside the women's wing, Hartley Quince pulled Will aside. He spoke in Sangaree.

"Did you hear her?" he said happily. " 'I . . . Adrian said . . . when I was sick . . .' When they talk like that, it's always the pure product."

"She didn't seem pleased at the idea of talking to you, Hart."

He was unoffended. "Of course not. She has the ability to string sentences together under normal conditions." He glanced at Will sidelong. "I'll let it pass this time, but don't do it again."

"Do what?" asked Will, with a studious blankness.

"You knew I wanted Arno to see her. What was that Hierophant Bell shit? Now I have to get him off the Di-

amond tonight and arrange for a new priest. Don't pull
anything like that again."

"Yes, sir."

"All right, Hart."

"All right, Hart."

They walked on. After a minute, his good humor re-
stored, Hartley said, in Sangaree, "He's an old guy sleeping in his underwear, Willie, and now I've got to roust
him out of bed. You could have more consideration."

If I didn't know you, Hart, I'd almost think you cared.
Will bit back the words.

Twenty hours later, Willie Stockton sat back in his seat
on the train, leave notice in his pocket, with a contented
smile. *Home.* Outside the windows he saw the Opal
neighborhoods changing, the streets and tunnels of the
upper decks with their ladies in closed chairs and men in
capes and uniforms of rank metamorphosing gradually
into the tumbledown stores and makeshift residences of
Sangaree.

Hart had spent the last few days arguing with him over
the leave. But he'd pointed out it was his sister's wedding, unassailable grounds. And when it came to it, Hart
didn't mind doing favors for people, because he could always remind them of it later.

Three days off. It was too bad regulations required he
wear the uniform—sometimes it started fights in Sangaree, and he didn't want to upset Bernadette so near her
wedding. He straightened out his long legs so they extended into the aisle, feeling a welcome stretch in confined muscles. It was a long ride from court territory and
for the last two stops he'd been the only person left in the
car.

The squatters' compartments outside showed they were
nearing the Brissard Street stop. The warehouses just beyond were either cannibalized into skeletal hulks or transformed into strange new places with different purposes,
sheets of steel welded over what used to be open doors
for trucks, laundry hanging off old pieces of equipment.
There could be few gaps greater than the one between the
spectacle he'd witnessed just twenty hours ago at Helium
Park, with its comforts and cleanliness and extravagant

display, and the environment presently passing his train windows. It was a difference to warm the heart of professional provocateurs, like those operating in the name of the Republic on Baret Two. But Will never dwelt on such comparisons; things were as they were, and he dealt with the universe on that basis. Instead he soaked in the comfortable pleasure of coming home, of the anticipation of a place where his welcome was fully assured, where everything was familiar and ordered by rules he knew by heart.

He stepped off the train at Brissard Street, carrying a package wrapped in brown paper under one arm. The street stank as it always had. Will passed the almshouse at the corner, then the games hall under the abandoned recycling station, where a curl of blue drugsmoke came through the bars (creating smoke in an unsupervised area, said part of Will's brain, punishable by confiscation of goods for first offense, death for second—though there was absolutely no chance of confusing the automatics into thinking there was a fire here, because the automatics had been ripped out years ago), then the clothing exchange, where a handful of old men and women pawed through secondhand goods, and then on the corner the Cafe Bordo. There was a dirty plex window in the front of the Cafe Bordo, and a hand-lettered sign reading "Stretch's Chicken Savoy." The sign had been there as far back as Will could remember; nobody he'd ever spoken to knew who Stretch was, or had been. The Chicken Savoy, on the other hand, was legend—full of unnamed and unnamable bits of reused things, and greatly to be avoided.

At the corner of Brissard and Schliemann he climbed to the second level. Far, far down the walkway he saw a small, plump girl-shape running for exercise, her hair the color of mahogany. A far cry from the veils and litters of the upper decks, thank God. Will smiled. She slowed to a walk, clearly exhausted, rubbing sweat from her forehead. She ran, slowed, and ran again, determined, but with an endurance level somewhere near ten or fifteen seconds. A young man was strolling the walkway ahead of her, and as she passed him, she speeded up and kept on running. *Put on a good show it if kills you.* Will's smile grew into a grin. Would exhaustion overcome dignity and force her to slow again before she reached the end of the walkway? As the plump figure drew close, pouter pigeon breasts pumping, he said, "Jeez, Bernie, don't say hello."

She blinked at him disorientedly, then screamed "Willie!" and threw herself into his arms. When she'd gathered enough breath, she said, "I knew you'd come, I knew you'd come, I told them all, Willie'll be here." Then when the litany ended, she drew back and stamped on his foot. "You missed *every* rehearsal!"

"I'm sorry, I was on duty."

"You should've gotten off!" She glared at him, then threw her arms around him tightly, and he grabbed on, too. Their heights were so dissimilar that they overbalanced, doing a little involuntary dance over to the edge of the walkway. They'd lived all their lives together in the same two rooms until Willie joined the Guards, and here it felt to him like ages since they'd hugged, as though that had all been in some ancient era of mankind.

"Anyway," he said, "I'm not late."

"Lucky for you," she said. She took his hand and pulled him along. "Come on, Jack's upstairs, and Johnny Black and Antonia are here, too."

Will resisted the pull slightly. "Is anybody mad at me?"

"What for, dummy?"

"For being in the Guard. For going to the Diamond." For not being dead or drafted.

"Shithead," said Bernie, whose language was pure Sangaree. "Nobody cares if you went to the Diamond. And you've seen Johnny and Antonia since you joined the Guard."

"No, I haven't. I saw Johnny once, but I didn't have a chance to talk to him. And I didn't see Antonia."

"Really? You haven't seen Johnny for two years?" She stopped, as if calculating the time. "But you've been here a few times since then."

"Just to see you, Hell-on-Wheels. And I never had long."

"Well, never mind. It'll be okay—you know Johnny." As for Jack, there was no need to mention him. Bernie's fiancé came from the middle class, and wouldn't look at the Guard the same way a born Sangaree would.

He let his sister lead him up to the third level above the street, where she took out three keys and opened the door to their compartment. Odd, he thought; he'd gotten so used to voice and print and combination locks. And yet he'd grown up with these rusty metal keys. He could still feel their ghosts hanging around his neck under his shirt, pressing into the skin. It was a game at school to try and take kids' keys away ... he must have had ten thousand fights to keep his set. Thoughtfully he ran a hand over the square seal at the side of the door. The connections were still there, he could get it activated again for Bernadette, record her prints and voice in the Security banks. He had the money now.

It was a sudden feeling of double vision, looking at something like the keys that were so normal they needed no thought at all, and seeing instead something that said *poverty* and *inefficiency*. Then the door opened onto the small room beyond, where two young men were sitting on a makeshift sofa, and he was enveloped in a cloud of rowdy welcome.

They were off the sofa in a minute, and one of them grabbed Will in an embrace. "Willie-oh," he called as he did so.

"Johnny!" And another hug came, followed by mutual punching on the arms. Johnny was black-haired and black-eyed, with pure Sangaree good looks and a gentle spirit. The initial euphoria of meeting over, he ducked his head shyly. "Willie, welcome back."

Jack Freylinger stood beside Bernadette, and Will reached out to shake hands with his sister's fiancé. "Jack."

"Hello, Will."

Jack was tall and well-muscled, as though he'd come out of City Guard training himself; but he was a silk trader and tapestry merchant from deck F. He brought together buyers and sellers, both Inside and Outside, and took a cut from each transaction. His grandparents had been Sangaree. Will liked him, even if he did pronounce his name "Freelinger" instead of "Fray-lone-jay," the old Sangaree way.

Once there had been Freylingers all through this part of the Opal. But families died out in Sangaree all the time.

"Where's Antonia?" Will asked.

"She had to get back to work," said Johnny. "We didn't know you were coming—"

"He didn't send a message!" accused Bernadette, hitting him in his upper back with her small fist. Willie grinned; he'd missed Bernie's little love taps.

"What's in the package?" asked Johnny, pointing to the parcel Will had managed to hold onto through this series of affectionate displays.

"Wedding gift," he replied.

"Can we see it?" said Johnny.

Johnny was interested in everybody and everything; if he weren't so empathic, he'd have made a great spy. "Try and open this," warned Will as he pushed it into a corner of the wall shelves, "and alarms will go off at the nearest guardstation."

Johnny looked taken aback for a moment, then he laughed. "You know something? With you, I'm never entirely sure it's a joke."

It was Will's turn to be taken aback. This was a thought he had often had about Hart. *Relax and enjoy your friends,* he told himself, *and stop worrying about Hartley Dynamite-for-Brains Quince.*

Bernadette started getting dinner out of the hotbox. Johnny got up at once and joined her. "You're still tired from running," he said, "I know you'd like to shower. Let me start this."

"You don't mind? Thanks." And she brushed the hair out of her eyes with a weary gesture.

Bernadette hated to be in sweaty clothes, Will thought. Her fiancé hadn't noticed, but Johnny had.

As she crossed to the other room and Johnny bent over the hotbox, she pulled Will aside. "Talk to him," she said, pointing to Johnny.

"Why, what's the matter?"

She shook her head.

"Verx? You said he'd stopped."

She shook her head again, tiredly.

"Okay, go shower." Will gave her a peck and a smack on the rump as she left (why is it the aristos never seem to touch each other? asked a part of his mind) and turned back to the table. "Let me help you, Johnny."

Beneath the clatter of dishes he said, "You have anything for a headache?"

Johnny's eyes met his. The pupils were dilated.

"Really?" he said tentatively.

"Sure."

Johnny turned toward the sink and pulled a small bottle from his pocket. He started to open it, but Will took it from him, and Johnny made no effort to stop him. Will removed one of the thin white pills and touched it to his tongue, where it immediately began to dissolve in sourness. He made a face.

"This is pure aspirin, Johnny."

"Absolutely pure," said his friend.

"You know the penalties for trafficking in pain relievers? The EPs will have you up on charges of tampering with God's will."

"I don't traffic, exactly. I just sell it to people I trust. Old folks with aches, and people just off the radiation levels."

Will looked over to where Jack had gone to stand by the door, apparently very interested in the wall design. Jack couldn't hear what they were saying, but it was clearly private and he would let them have what privacy a Sangaree compartment afforded. Jack wasn't a bad person, Will thought. Bernie could have done a lot worse.

"I need the money," said Johnny.

Of course he did. Looking into his face, Will could see he was playing with vert-reves again, he should have seen it the second he walked through the door. "Johnny," he began. *Johnny, you believe everything people tell you. Someday you're gong to sell aspirin to a nice guy who'll be from the Ecclesiastical Police. Johnny, whoever's selling the stuff to you is shortchanging you, because you're too far down the pole* not *to shortchange. Johnny, don't be an idiot and live this way, because I'll be very upset if you die young.*

"Johnny," he said again, and stopped.

His friend looked at him with a quizzical smile. "Want a beer?" he asked. "Bernie has some on hand."

Hell. At least Johnny was snorting it as verx instead of injecting pure vert-reves. Of that they were all sure, because as Bernie once put it when she stopped laughing, "Johnny's too big a wimp to use needles."

"Yeah," he said, "why don't you get me one."

Anyone else Will would seriously have considered turning in. Officers were sent to the radiation levels for looking the other way. But it never would have entered Will's head to turn in Johnny—he was Sangaree.

As Johnny fetched the beer, Will examined the pill bottle. "You know what they say," he commented. "It's a short, straight line between aspirin and vert-reves."

"Is that what they say? I wouldn't know, I never tried aspirin."

Then they both started to laugh because, being Sangaree, Will and Johnny considered "what they said" of drugs to be about on a par with what they said about everything else. Life below the letterdecks encouraged skepticism, if nothing else.

"No, but listen," said Will. He hesitated.

Johnny looked at him, saying nothing.

Will said, "You're going to get killed one day doing that."

"I'm careful."

"I *know* you're *careful*," said Will, as he punched Johnny's shoulder affectionately and Johnny ducked his head the way he always did, embarrassed.

Then he looked up at Will. "You think Jack knows?"

"How do I know what Jack knows?" Then Will said, "I don't think so." He raised his voice. "Jack, care for a beer?"

"Not for me, thanks. Go ahead if you want to."

Johnny said, "As if I needed an invitation." He was shutting the cooler when there was a knock at the door.

"We expecting anybody?" said Will. The other two shook their heads. Will hated the lack of security in a mechanical lock; there was no way to check the identity of who was outside.

Bernadette came out of the other room, wrapped in a robe. "Did I hear—"

"Yeah. Want me to open it?"

She nodded.

Will's hand was on his pistol as he opened the door.

Teams of people—even ghosts, sometimes—broke into compartments for everything they could steal.

It was an elderly and stooped man, well-dressed in secondhand clothes that did not quite fit. He held a chrome cane.

"Yes?" said Will, a little ashamed of the suspicion in his voice.

"Mr. Teksa!" said Bernadette, coming forward. She put out her hands and drew him inside. "Will, you remember Mr. Teksa."

Will did, from years past, but he certainly didn't remember him this frail and uncertain. And didn't he have the vague impression that the Teksas weren't living around here anymore? "Sure I do. You moved back to the neighborhood, Mr. Teksa? And how . . ." He was going to say, how is Mrs. Teksa? But his ingrained knowledge of Sangaree lifespans made him hesitate, and seeing Bernie's slight headshake he finished, "are you doing these days?"

"Very well, thank you. How tall you are, Willie! But I just stopped by to ask if you could help me. I'm expecting a message from the link-boy, but I *have* to go out—"

"Say no more, sir," said Bernadette. "We'll take it for you."

Will wondered where somebody of their neighbor's age had to be so urgently. "Going far, Mr. Teksa?"

"To Tarragon Street," he said, bowing as he left. "I have an appointment to see the physical terrorist. Thank you so much." He closed the door behind him.

Will looked at Bernadette. " 'Physical terrorist'?"

"He meant therapist. He meant Tanamonde Street, too. He's had a lot of trouble with words since he came out of the holding pens."

"That old guy was in the pens?" Will stared toward the door with new respect. "How? I refuse to believe he's capable of any great crime." Disloyalty? Heresy? The Teksas had fallen to Sangaree long ago, from some other level; they were too timid to even speak up at street meetings.

"Someone denounced him. I don't know . . . some peo-

ple said the Eigerlys denounced him because they wanted
his compartment."

"They moved in after the Teksas left," said Johnny. He
was taking out another beer.

"They didn't stay long, though, did they?" said Bernadette. "The lock kept getting torn off their door. And the
maintenance teams wouldn't pick up their garbage, so
they had to drag it to the Belt all by themselves."

"'Cause when they didn't, they got fined." Johnny took
a long drink.

"They had to move out finally. So the place has been
empty till the Teksas came back ... Mr. Teksa, I mean.
Mrs. Teksa didn't come back."

Will was glad he hadn't asked after her.

"He talks funny now," said Bernadette, "and he has to
keep going to the meds. But he seems okay."

And to think that Hartley Quince had been in the same
holding pens, for years, and like Mr. Teksa, he was one of
the few to come out again. But there was nothing wrong
with *his* speech patterns, nor his intelligence, nor any
other ability Will could think of; and he found himself
impressed again by Hart's achievement: escaping the pens
unscathed. Then Will shook himself mentally—what was
he thinking? Probably Teksa was a thousand times more
healthy than Hartley Quince.

"You want your beer?" Johnny (whose mind had held
onto essentials) was asking.

"Sure," said Will. And how healthy did that make him
for hanging around with Hart? Not that there was a lot of
choice involved.

Since Johnny and Will hadn't progressed very far with
dinner, and Will's homecoming had imparted a festive
mood, they decided to go out to eat.

"Why the hell not?" said Bernie. "We'll put this stuff
in the friggin' garbage. You only live once."

Jack, who had a disturbed look in his eyes, led
Bernadette gently away and whispered to her. Will hid a
smile. Jack had a romantic view of things, and didn't like
to hear words like "friggin'" come from the lips of his
beloved. Willie knew this because his sister had told him
how once, as they stopped to buy peaches from a street

vendor, Jack had turned to her, gazed deeply into her eyes, and said, "Darling, I'd really like for you to spend Christmas with me and my family."

"You're out of your friggin' mind," said Bernie. "It's still June."

Now she and Jack returned to them, and she said, "All right—but I want to go to a Sangaree bar."

"No," said Jack.

"Absolutely not," said Will.

"I don't know—" said Johnny, only to receive glares from the other two.

"*Lysette* goes to Sangaree bars," said Bernie.

This reference to his fiancée only annoyed Will. "Lysette has to, she's a performer. And she only goes where the management guarantees her protection."

"The three of *you* can guarantee my protection, can't you?"

Put that way, she had a point. Will had a high opinion, not entirely unjustified, of his own abilities in a fight. And although he knew his sister was pressing his "respond to challenge" button, he responded anyway. "Maybe," he said, "but we sit quietly and eat and then we leave."

"Wait a minute—" said Jack, looking startled.

"It'll be all right," Will told him. And it probably would. Taking one's sister to a Sangaree bar was a little daring, but the truth was that Bernadette Stockton was well-known through most of the area. She could probably walk into a bar now, unescorted, and not get hurt—as long as it was in the neighborhood. Flanked by three fair-sized males, the problem shouldn't arise.

Will went quickly into the other room, where he stripped off his sergeant's uniform and put on a red jacket and gray pants. He didn't want to be challenged for wearing the uniform, or reported for not wearing it. This was non-reg, but close enough to the uniform that it might confuse observers in a dark bar into leaving him alone.

As they trooped out the door, Bernie patted his hand and favored him with a smile. "Next time it'll be the Cafe Bordo," she said.

"Yeah," said Will. "Maybe we'll run into Stretch."

* * *

"You mean you never heard of Stretch?" asked Johnny. They were sitting at a round table in the Coeur de Noir, far from the singer's spot and close to the door.

Will had chosen it. Coming inside, looking around the interior of the bar, there was another moment of double vision: the opulence of Adrian's court coming between the image of the bar as familiar comfort and the image of it as dark, cramped, and poor. Will found himself choosing the table for Bernadette as he would have for Iolanthe, for security reasons. A tattered sign hung in the darkness above the door, reading: Coeur de Noirceur. Somewhere over the years the final syllable had gotten lost from people's speech; maybe in the future the name would shorten even further.

"Stretch worked at the Cafe Bordo in my father's time," Johnny was saying. "He was a bouncer. Chicken Savoy was the only thing he could cook. When he was drunk, he used to insist that at least one person in every party order it. And boy, did they. He was a big guy, my father said—practically a legend."

Sangaree was full of legends. Maybe it was the compression of time. The heyday of Johnny and Will's parents was only twenty years ago, and they were all dead now, to no one's surprise. That was the way things were in this part of the Opal.

The singer was coming out now, and the patrons applauded. Bernie, glancing around the room, leaned over and hissed to her brother: "See, there are women in the audience." Will glared at her. There *were* women in the audience, but not the sort a good Cities boy would choose to associate with his sister. The singer, however, was another story, and one far murkier. She was a woman on the verge of middle-age, with brown hair and a sharp nose and sharper eyes. She wore a black shirt and skirt, and carried a portable keyboard, which she set up in the spot. Clearly she was a heartsinger, and Willie wished he were elsewhere. He hated heartsingers and their black visions. He was glad to his bones that Lysette wasn't a heartsinger.

"My name is Elinor," said the woman, in a gentle voice. And she touched the keyboard, enhanced in the range of melancholy and delighted irony that heartsingers loved.

And distraction from the song came, though not in the form he would have wished.

"I'll be damned!" cried a nearby voice. "It's Willie Stockton, gone slumming. We're out of uniform, aren't we, Willie?"

Timothy Lee, every hulking foot of him, came over to their table and stood between Bernadette and Will. Will looked back and saw that Timothy Lee had come from a table where he was sitting with Parry Winzek, yet another old schoolfriend. And although Parry looked at him with dark, unhappy eyes that had a trace of hatred, Will knew that Parry wouldn't fight him. Although perhaps Timothy was too drunk to realize that.

Bernadette twisted her head to look up at Timothy Lee. "You're a little drunk, Tee-lee."

He ignored her. "You bring your sister to places like this, Willie? No wonder you're such a popular guy. Hey, who's this?" His glance had fallen on Jack Freylinger.

"Jack, this is Timothy Lee." Bernie's tone was short.

"This your husband?"

"Fiancé," said Jack, offering his hand. Because there had been no church declaration of intent to wed, they could not officially refer to themselves as husband and wife. The aristos were free and easy about these things, and so was Sangaree; but on F deck, Jack made it clear, they waited for the actual ceremony.

"Fee-onse," repeated Timothy Lee, making the word sound ridiculous and alien. "You know, I thought that Willie here was the bastard, taking the Guard's way out. But I always believed this his sister was one of us. And here you are, as ready to climb into the laps of the letterdecks as anybody. Your fee-onse likes Sangaree bars, does he? Did he bring you here like one of his whores?"

That was it. Will stood up. Jack was pushing back his chair, too, but Bernadette grabbed his hand. "It's Willie he wants," she said.

"That's right, letterdeck, it's Willie I want. How about it, Willie? Tell you what—if you can beat me, maybe I won't turn you in for being out of uniform."

Will's eyes were blazing, but he'd learned a long time ago that he was better off fighting in cold blood. The bar was quiet; the heartsinger, with a look of annoyance, had retired from the field almost immediately. There were bars where fights—and other things—went on below the music all the time; but the Coeur de Noir was not one of them. Will raised his voice. "Parry, did you hear what your friend just said?"

"I heard him," said Parry Winzek.

"You want to join in this?" asked Will.

"No."

"You shit," said Timothy Lee. He glanced toward his companion and then back to Will. "So what? You don't even come up to my collarbone, Stockton."

Parry Winzek had stated in front of witnesses that he'd heard his friend agree not to report Will if he lost. Public opinion would be against Timothy Lee if he reneged; and in Sangaree, public opinion could be violent.

"Everybody heard you," warned Will.

"Think that bothers me? You don't trust my word?"

"Maybe Parry doesn't trust your word either," said Will, and when Timothy turned his head to look at Parry Winzek, Will hit him a hammerblow in the gut.

In Sangaree they don't wait for you to take your glasses off, Will's father used to say; and he should know, he'd died when Will was twelve, in a knife fight over a heartsinger. Though why anybody should be carrying drinking glasses on them, Will had not understood—he'd never seen a pair of spectacles till he left Sangaree.

A look of startlement and agony had come over Timothy Lee's face. It was a vicious blow, aimed at the solar plexus, and he stopped in the exact position he'd been standing in, with the wind knocked out of him. His knees buckled slightly. Will seemed to have a thousand years in which to move and a clear field to do it in; he reached out in dreamlike fashion and jabbed his thumb forcefully just above Timothy Lee's adam's apple. This completed the cutoff to his air supply. Timothy Lee's trachea collapsed, and so did he. With a gasping sound he dropped to his knees. A second later he was unconscious on the floor, still making fishlike sounds.

Bernadette was gathering her things, and Johnny was

rising from his chair. Will was suddenly conscious that he'd been sweating, and hoped he didn't smell as rank as he felt. Jack took Bernie's arm and headed for the door. Will and Johnny followed, leaving Timothy Lee to the care of his friends and enemies in the Coeur de Noir.

Outside, Jack turned abruptly to Will. The words tumbled out as though he had no control over them. "Is it true that nobody can graduate into the Guard who hasn't killed someone? Performed an execution, I mean?"

Bernadette looked horrified, and even Johnny, who tended not to register any emotion beyond a vaguely benign affection, appeared to be appalled.

Jack was too excited to realize he'd committed a faux pas. "Is it true?"

"Come on, sweetheart," said Bernadette, and she pulled him down the street with little ceremony. "You've had a long day."

"We still have to eat," said Johnny, joining loyally in the effort to get Jack off this unfortunate line of talk.

"Just a minute," said Will. He looked distracted. "I'll be right back," he said, and reentered the bar.

Timothy Lee was still on the floor. Parry Winzek stood near him uncertainly. Will knelt down, lifted Timothy Lee's head, and took out his knife.

"Hey!" said Parry.

Somebody else called, "He couldn't say you won—he was dropped too soon. You can't kill him now."

But no one moved to stop him. Will put the point of the knife at the spot he'd hit, made a cut, and twisted. Timothy Lee's breath entered successfully in a long whistling gulp. Will wiped the knife on his pants and put it away.

He stood up. "He can breathe through the hole for a while," he announced. "But he'll need a doctor or a witch." He looked around the bar at Parry Winzek, at the spectators; none of them moved. There were only some blinks at the picture of a City Guard talking openly about witches.

He shrugged and left the bar. It was up to them.

They were still waiting outside. Bernie gave him her purse to hold just as if it were any other evening, and Jack was silent and chastened. She said, "Let's go someplace closer to home."

And so, emotionally buttressed by his sister and his friend, Will let himself be taken to the Cafe Bordo.

The Guard had only put the finishing touches on training already begun. There was a time many years ago when Will would have jumped on Timothy Lee without thinking, in a raw effort to bang his head against the wall. Will would probably have lost the fight and possibly his life, but each successful blow would have brought a deep, red pleasure. Now he won the fight but felt absolutely nothing.

The heritage, he thought, of being trained to fight by Hartley Quince.

A short time later, with Johnny and Bernie's unconditional support and the support of the hard liquor made available by the owner of the Cafe Bordo, Will let Timothy Lee and all related problems float away.

No heartsingers sang at the Cafe Bordo; no musicians played. There was only the background sound of dishes and cutlery and people talking, softly, in the distance. An occasional child cried, but Will didn't mind that; he missed it when he was on court level, where the children were all tucked away in nurseries.

"Besides," said Johnny, "you're here for three days. We can go to another bar tomorrow, and you can smack somebody else."

"Thanks—that really cheers me up."

Jack looked puzzled. Irony, Will had found, was not in general use in the upper decks of Opal. He'd grown up with Sangaree ways—saying just the opposite of what was meant, in a certain tone of voice—everybody understood.

Then one day in training he'd taken a tumble from trying a new hold, and said as he got up, "Well, *that* was a good idea." And his partner had looked as confused as Jack, here, and said, "I don't think it was a good idea at all."

He'd had to watch himself after that. Though he had to admit that once or twice he'd said that sort of thing to Adrian, and Adrian had had no difficulty understanding. Maybe the Diamond was different.

And Sangaree was different. He didn't have to watch

himself here. He looked around at the tattered hangings on the wall of the cafe and leaned back in his chair.

Will felt a sigh of contentment leave him, a sigh that encompassed Johnny and Bernadette and the Cafe Bordo and all things worn with handling; and he said to his sister, "God, it's good to be here. Are you guys really going to live on F when you get married? Maybe you can talk Jack into moving here—there are some fairly ritzy places on Tanamonde Street."

And then Willie Stockton felt an ache in his chest, because his sister, who'd shared every thought with him until he left for training, said, "Are you kidding? Once I get out of here, I'm never even coming back for my mail."

She turned casually back to her fiancé, who was having trouble choosing from the menu, and through the distance Will heard her laugh because he was pointing at the Chicken Savoy.

Chapter 17

Keylinn:

The truth was, I felt quite satisfied with myself when my transport docked in Baret Station. Volunteering to supervise the transfer of minor cargo was a minor stroke of brilliance; there were no contenders for the job because nobody wanted to work third shift. The metabolism of most of Transport's personnel had adjusted to the Diamond's use of dimmers between 2000 and 0400, "spring time," and they wanted to be home in bed. That was why Baret Station, like the sensible place it was, kept its brights on round the clock—everybody was equally uncomfortable.

Baret wasn't new to me; I'd been on the Station proper once before, with a forged passport from back home. That was six years ago. Cyr Vesant, cognizant of the station penalties for forged passports, tended to keep me in the docking area on our regular trade runs. This time I was free to wander—as soon as the cargo was arranged for, and as soon as I could make sure my maildrop was still functional.

I located the cafeteria, a down-at-the-heels sort of place that probably hadn't had a washing in the six years I'd been gone. Nor a change in clientele, either—it was still marked by pockets of druggies and bronzers, some of them johns just passing through and some with tattoos that placed them in the lower rungs of station life. Ninety percent of them must live on the borderline of airspace cancellation.

"Is Milo Veridia here?" I asked the counterman, fully expecting to be told he was dead or at best off-shift. But the man shrugged and pointed to a young and pimply fellow who was spooning mashed potatoes into small bowls. I moved down the counter toward him.

I waited. "Remember me?" I asked finally. His tattoo was a knife and fork—no promotions since I'd been here last. In his own good time he looked up briefly and down again.

"Ai," he said.

"I have another package."

He seemed uninterested. Still looking at the bowls, he said, "Sixty."

That kind of bargaining always made me uncomfortable. I felt vulnerable where my mail was concerned. "I don't pay you," I said.

"If you don't pay me, who does?" he inquired, in the nasal Baret accent I was beginning to dislike.

"How should I know who pays you? But not me." I had a list of names and places, given to me before I left home. Who paid whom and how it was managed, not to mention how my packages got sent, were details that interested me rather less than computing all the digits of pi. I just wanted the mail to go through.

The spooner of potatoes was silent. I said, irritated, "You want to keep getting a fee? I can send word through someone else about what a dead loss you've become."

He spooned out two more bowls, and said, "You got it on you?"

I reached into my jacket and he went into a seizure.

"Not here, not here! Around the side." He gestured to

the end of the counter, and I passed it to him out of sight. I sincerely doubted anybody cared what a techie from the Diamond did with her mail, except for Tal, and he was busy elsewhere.

"That's all for now," I said. "You don't think you'll have any trouble?"

"Why should I have trouble?"

"Beats me." I turned and walked away. Outside the cafeteria I considered how long I had to play before return transport to the Diamond, and decided to find a saloon. Preferably one patronized by a higher order of life.

Tourist Information listed three possibilities, and I took the easiest to reach. As I walked I occupied myself by analyzing the ethics of dealing with my potato-spooner. He was, of course, sludge; because living up to one's agreements was what life was all about ... still, anyone who was a bottom-rung cafeteria worker for that many years probably needed an extra sixty. This sort of charitable excuse went strictly against the Code, but having just offloaded my mail, I was in an excusing mood. I was, in fact, practically glowing with the knowledge that my letters would soon be in the hands of real, beloved people, people who didn't require constant analysis, who understood what was real and what was transient. Sean and Janny and Uncle Bram ... and they'd see Father knew I was all right. I smiled.

The Ginza Bar was well-located, well-padded in plush cushiony booths and chairs with soft arms and backs, and with eight different holowalls. I sat against the one that simulated the space around Baret Station, since I thought it deserved something for faking reality best.

Two shots of straight whiskey later, my thoughts began taking on a different tinge. Sean and Janny and Father ...

There I was, Keylinn O'Malley Murtagh, first-rank Graykey, occasional killer, the hero and disgrace of Nemeter Training School, sniffing back a threatening sob and feeling my eyes well up.

When was I going to get to go *home?*

It was three hours later and I was moderately drunk as I strolled along the corridors of Baret Station. I enjoyed the sensation; it had been a long time. I would never have ordered the two extra whiskeys had not my contract-holder been far, far away from any demands of duty.

It was a matter of pride, however, that nobody *know* I was drunk; and apart from the flush that I felt like a warm dishcloth on my skin, I sincerely hoped that nobody guessed the way the walls moved gently out of kilter as I walked.

I was partway to the docking area when a man's voice came booming mechanically through the corridors.

"Attention. Attention. This is a level-three emergency. This is a level-three emergency. A ship has turned back to us, coming in without docking ability. All transport shift-supervisors report to the docking area; all blue-team medical personnel report to your stations; all media personnel wait for further news. No media personnel will be allowed in the docking area at this time. I repeat, no media personnel will be allowed in the docking area at this time. Any media personnel blocking corridors between the docking area and medical areas will be held for possible later airspace termination. End of message."

I found I had frozen. It was like being hit by cold water. *They didn't say the name of the ship,* I told myself. But how many ships had left the station in the last few days? If it had been a Cities transport, it would have tried to make the docking at Opal or Diamond. No Baret Two ships had left in the past ten days. So what did that leave?

Suddenly I was running down the corridor.

The docking area was blocked off. The sight of armed guards did not stop me from trying to enter anyway—first with faked casualness, alongside a medical team, and then by brute force.

Within minutes two Baret Station security guards held me against a wall. They were firm but courteous, for although station security would "terminate airspace" without any hesitation, they were expected not to annoy paying transients. Not until they were told to, anyway.

"I'm sorry, Mynher Diamond," said one of the blank-faced pair. "No one may enter without authorization."

"All right, all right! Put me down. Where do I get authorization?"

They released me. "The governor of Station," recited

the man, "or the emergency measures supervisor, or the docking area supervisor, or the medical team supervisor provided you're a licensed health dispenser."

Right, who were all very busy right now. I said, "Look, just tell me one thing. What ship is it?"

The uniformed hulks regarded me silently.

"Come on, how big a secret can it be? It's the *Kestrel*, isn't it?"

The guard who had not spoken made a pursing gesture with his lips, as though to say that he couldn't speak, but wouldn't contradict me.

I turned and starting running again, this time to find the administration offices.

A totally useless task, as I knew. And as I ran, the purposelessness and the shame overwhelmed me. The bureaucrats of Baret Station would never pay any attention to a transient worker on a temp-pass from the Diamond. My contract-holder was in imminent danger of death, and I couldn't even get to the site! One's own *tarethi-din* killed while in one's custody ... the thought was enough to turn bone to powder. How could anyone ever explain failure of this magnitude?

It was a while before I realized I was crying as I ran. That would have been another shame; my people have no taboo against tears among themselves, but we like to put up a brave front to outsiders. Too young for this assignment, I thought—that's what everybody had said. She hasn't even graduated yet, they said. Oh, but never mind, said the Chief Judge—we'll bump her into the first rank, and she'll live up to what's expected. And now weren't they all proved right, the damned critics, and the faith of the Society sorely misplaced? My thoughts, I discovered, were falling not into the dry and logical, created tongue of the Graykey, but the older and more lyrical language we still used for poetry, love, and cursing.

And as I ran on, half-blinded, I rammed against another person walking in the opposite direction. The young man in question was knocked forcibly into the wall and, entangled with a maddened Graykey, understandably fell over. "Terribly sorry," he said, showing impeccable training in manners, since he was the clear victim. He reached out a hand to assist me, and as the cuff pulled back from his wrist I saw a blue tattoo there. Not a stationer's tattoo, which would be plainly displayed on the face in any case. It was the Circle of Seven Stones—the Graykey symbol of wisdom.

I looked up into a freckled face that returned the gaze with a friendly one of its own; into green eyes and sandy hair. You may well believe that I did not, as I would at any other time, delve into the major statistical improbability of finding another Graykey here. Nor did I waste seconds even considering that the tattoo might be a coincidence. I looked up through blurry eyes and said, "Help me, brother."

The young man blinked. "Sister?" he asked, in Graykey.

"I must get into the docking area. I must get to the ship that's coming in."

"It's closed off—"

"You must help me! My *tarethi-din* is aboard that ship!"

His eyes widened, and he was silent a moment. Then he said, "Wait."

He moved down the corridor to a station phone. I saw him speaking into it. I sat where I was, not knowing what else to do, afraid of hoping. My honor was hanging by a thread.

Eventually he returned. "Sorry it took so long," he said, "I had to wait to be connected."

"What happened?"

"I called my own *tarethi-din*. He has influence with the people who run the station. By the time we reach the docks, the guards will have been told to admit us."

"Thank you, brother." I kissed him on the cheek as he helped me up, as I would have a comrade at home in the same battle-section. "I won't forget your mercy."

"We would be the poorer by your death," he responded politely. Then, in Standard, he said, "We'd better hurry."

The *Kestrel,* we found, was already docked, and with no apparent damage. "A miracle," said my new companion, "if the docking gear was really damaged." We looked at each other calmly—Graykey do not believe in miracles. The outer doors of the *Kestrel* had to be forced open.

The moment they parted, gray and white smoke billowed forth over the docks, sending the transport workers back. My friend and I wore green station medical badges, by virtue of the compromise that gained our entry onto the docks; we had to wear *some* kind of authorization, and local Transport badges would only have made trouble. All the Transport workers knew each other. The chief of the medical teams began handing out masks to all his people, and when I found one stuffed into my hands, I did not object.

Transport was finding its own masks, a little late; but with the *Kestrel* fully docked it was really in Medical's hands now, in any case.

"Come on," said my gift from the gods, who had made this possible (though the Graykey do not believe in miracles); and I followed. Walk with enough assertiveness, I told myself, and each team will think you belong to one of the others. Be a stationer for a while; you've been so many others. We entered the ship with the first of the medical people, stumbling through the smoke.

There were plenty of bodies. Apparently the entire ship's complement had been heading for the exits when the fires broke out. I dropped down by each newly felt body, peering at it through the haze, feeling my eyes burn even through the mask, pulling each body toward the exit if there were any doubts as to identity ... none of them was Tal.

None of them was outwardly hurt either. "No evidence of explosion," said my companion. "I think they're all out from smoke inhalation."

"Just as dead," I responded briefly. I meant, we both knew, that smoke was just as lethal to one's *tarethi-din* as any other form of death; for a great many of the people we were stepping over in this methodical search were, in fact, still alive.

"There must be more exits," I said.

We made our way farther in, following the outer corridors near the hull. There were no people along this way. "Cargo exit would be below," said my companion.

"I know," I said. Amazing how calm I sounded. As though it were an exercise at home. No, more calm than that; at home we put blood and bone in our exercise.

There were two bodies at the top of the steps leading down to the cargo exit. My companion turned one over; there was less smoke here, and no need to kneel down to see the face. It was a woman's face, what was left of it, ripped open. The walls around the bodies were splattered with tiny holes and bits of plastic that had melted and solidified. "Here's our explosion," he said, as I climbed down the stairway beyond him.

Tal's body was at the bottom of the steps. I felt for a pulse, found it, turned him over and checked his breathing. Just unconscious; though there was a nasty bump on his head. It must take a lot to take out an Aphean, I thought, and looked up at my companion. "Get a stretcher," I told him.

"Easier to open the cargo doors," he said.

"Then do it."

As he searched for the door controls, I pulled open one of Tal's eyelids, then the other. His lenses were still in. So I got up and walked over to the controls, where I'd spotted them earlier, and opened the doors.

The sound of them opening caught my companion's attention, and he looked up from his search. "Ah," he said. We both took hold of Tal and started to pull him down the ramp onto the deck.

A medical team approached at once, with a stretcher-glide and an alarming amount of equipment. They loaded Tal onto the glide, and that was all right; but when they started linking their equipment, I felt the need to speak up loudly.

"This is a Three Cities citizen, and I'm a Three Cities representative. We don't wish any further medical treatment, it's against our religion."

"Look, cyr," said one of them politely (I'd been promoted from "mynher," I noted), "this person may be seriously hurt. He clearly has a head injury—" The rest of the team were ignoring me, continuing to link up their monitors, while this fellow performed his distraction.

I stepped over to the glide and unhooked a monitor. "I'm a Three Cities representative," I repeated. "We will regard this as an unfriendly act. If one of you will send word to the Diamond Protector that Officer Tal Diamond is here, our own medical people will handle things."

"Security!" yelled one of the team. One of the others—of a higher rank, I think—put a hand on his arm and spoke softly.

"What are *we* supposed to do?" asked the first man angrily.

"Keep him in medical quarantine," I replied at once. "The Diamond will guarantee all his bills. We're very grateful for your prompt attention. It's just . . . against our religion to have unbelievers perform unsanctioned medical practices."

"You'll take responsibility if he dies?" said the one who had restrained the first man. Turned to me now, I saw an insignia marking him as team leader.

"I take responsibility in all circumstances," I answered simply.

The team muttered among themselves. I added, "If you wish, you can add the procedures you would ordinarily use to our bill. The Diamond will pay it. We're aware of the trouble you took in getting yourselves and your equipment here so promptly."

Amid the mutters I heard one older medtech say to another, "He's just a kid. We ought to at least check—" And another answered, "Shh."

Just a kid? It was a second before I realized they meant Tal. I'd been planning to call Adrian myself, but it occurred to me now that it would be better to stick with Tal in case anybody tried to be charitable. I looked around for the other Graykey here. "Brother!" I called, and he stepped over. "In light of the *tarethi* we have gathered here together, would you do me a service?"

"If it proves practical," he said, with the usual reluctance of our people to commit.

"Would you call the Diamond and leave a message for Adrian Mercati? I'll reimburse you for the call. Tell him what happened here and everything I told these gentlemen, word for word." I knew he could do that; language is what defines our bonds, and Graykey are taught to pay great attention to the exact phrasing of the conversations around them.

"As you wish, sister. And will you honor me?"

I looked up from Tal's body, startled. "How?"

"Meet me in the Ginza Bar when your present obligations are fulfilled."

"For what purpose?"

He said gently in the Old Tongue, "To drink to old times, short sister with the big voice, who doesn't watch where she runs."

I smiled. "I will if I can." ... Rude brother who is overconfident. But that pleased me; the males of my clan are all like that.

On the glide, Tal's eyes blinked. He tried to sit up on one arm, and at once three medtechs were around him. "Take it easy, boy," said one. "Lie back down."

He got a good careful look around the docks before they forced him back down. That Keylinn was there somehow did not surprise him. She stepped away from the young man she was speaking with and came over to the glide. "I've informed these gentlemen of our scruples concerning medical treatment by unbelievers. Perhaps you'll emphasize this to them."

"Yes," he said, coughing. "If you please, cyrs. I officially refuse any medical treatment. Thanks, anyway. . . ."

"Look, son," began the medtech who had spoken before, but the gaze Tal fixed on him made the words trail off. Tal had found that his stare often had this effect, although he didn't have a clue why.

In the same hoarse, raw voice he said, "Keylinn."

"Here."

"Find out the death list. Particularly the captain. Tell me if she survived."

"She did," said a medtech standing nearby. "If you mean Captain Nestra. She's with a team that left ten minutes ago."

"Good," said Tal. He relaxed against the cushion on the glide. A long curl of smoke snaked overhead.

The image he'd seen when he looked around replayed itself: The docks in chaos, the noise of the air-scrubbers, the medical teams still pulling bodies from the smoke.

Before things went black again, he had time to hope that Adrian wouldn't be too upset.

* * *

He didn't expect Adrian to actually come himself. Nor did Keylinn, from the look on her face when she relinquished her place several hours later and left them in the hospital room.

"I just can't leave you alone, can I?" said Adrian, and Tal relaxed. Eventually he might reach the point where Adrian threw him out, but apparently this was not that time. As always, Tal found Adrian's motivations unclear at best.

Adrian pulled over a chair to the bed. "Somehow I expected more," he said gesturing to the simple cushion and pillows.

"Most of the other beds have built-in monitors. Keylinn made them fetch this one."

"Ah."

Tal waited; the subject of Keylinn was going to have to come up. Adrian would be wondering how she knew to keep him out of the hands of the station's medical establishment. True, Tal's nature was an open secret on the Diamond—but among the court levels, not among hired Outsider techs. Adrian said, "You inquired after the *Kestrel's* captain, I understand."

Tal blinked. Would he ever get used to human thought processes, and Adrian's in particular? "I did. They tell me she's alive."

"Alive and talking. Insists you're Republic property. Wants you released to her for the next trip to Baret One." Adrian's eyes met his. "Somehow, even under a fresh identity, you manage to accumulate criminal charges."

Tal gazed back without embarrassment. "I hope you don't consider it a personal reflection on yourself."

"Is that a reference to my ego or my judgment? Never mind. The thing of it is, the politics of this are a little hazy. We do not as yet have a signed treaty with Baret Two or the station. I came over to put a little weight on our side of the question ... technically I'm a head of state, albeit a small state by Outsider standards. I outrank an in-system captain. We're negotiating a trade agreement and neither of us wants to irritate the other ... on the other hand, we'll be leaving eventually and Baret One will still be on their doorstep, so to speak. They have to live with each other. On the third hand, Baret One is Re-

publican, and the Republic is not popular here. Are you
following all this?"

"Perfectly."

"I've made a major fuss. Pressure is on the station governor to release you—to *somebody*—right away. I pointed
out that you had not yet received medical treatment, and
could die while illegally in their custody."

"I appreciate the thought."

"And so, the universe being what it is, I thought we'd
try to walk out of here and see who stopped us."

Immediately Tal pulled back the sheets on his bed. He
stood up, with Adrian's help, and the room teetered. He
took a few tentative steps. "Better," he said, as the walls
ceased virbrating.

Keylinn was not outside the door. Evidently she considered Adrian and the six security guards he'd brought
with him to be competent to their task. They entered an
administration office, where men and women with green
medical tattoos sat busily at desks. The security guards,
chosen for their size, looked out of place.

"I knew it!" said a voice from another doorway; and a
young man in a Republican uniform came in in a hurry,
followed by four members of Baret Station security.

The room was becoming crowded.

"Excuse me," said Adrian politely, as he tried to pass.

"I'm the Republic legal representative on-Station," announced the young man.

"Charmed, I'm sure," said Adrian, who continued making his way toward the exit.

"We have a warrant to arrest this man," said the
Republic lawyer.

Adrian froze. " 'We'?" he repeated, looking at the Station personnel.

"*He* does," said the officer in charge. "We're just protecting the peace."

Adrian relaxed. "There are four of you, and six of my
friends. We can probably subdue this excitable person if
he tries anything. Come along, Tal."

The lawyer said, "Wait a minute! You can't just walk
out with him—"

"That's what you were going to do."

"The hell it was! I've already notified Governor Az-ereti. He's on his way here now."

"Have a nice talk with him when he comes." Adrian was at the door by now.

The officer in charge of the Baret security guards said, "We really ought to have an authorization to let you go."

Adrian sighed. The officer's tone had been apologetic, but one did not fool about with Station security. He turned and strode back into the center of the room. He scanned the people working at the desks, chose one, and looked him square in the eyes. "You! Who's in charge here?"

The man started. "Uh, me? I don't know ... this is Salcor Verona's section. He's off-Station. . . ."

"Who's in charge in this room? Who has the highest rank?"

"Uh ..." His gaze went to an older man at a desk by the door. Adrian walked over to him at once and planted himself in front of the desk.

"You have the authority to release patients," he stated.

"Under usual circumstances, which this isn't," said the man, unimpressed.

Adrian pointed to the Republic lawyer. "This man wants my friend released to his custody. I want him released to mine. We're leaving now, we need a decision."

"You can't just—" began the lawyer.

Adrian said, "Your patient has a head injury for which he needs treatment. Let me get him back to the Diamond where he can get some. If we wait for somebody else to take some responsibility, he could collapse."

The medtech pursed his lips. He turned to a woman at a nearby desk. "Who's paying this one's bills?"

She consulted some papers. "The Diamond."

"Then the Diamond can have him." He turned back to his work.

Adrian started for the door again. The lawyer said, "What are you *doing?* Is this a *joke?* You don't have the authority to settle questions this way." He ran up against the Station security guards as he tried to follow Adrian and Tal out the door.

In the corridor Tal said, "Where's the Ginza Bar?"

"What difference does it make? We're heading for Transport."

Tal pulled away from him and walked toward the simplified level-map that was spread across the wall opposite. Adrian looked up and down the corridor; what with six guards dressed in Three Cities uniforms, they were a conspicuous little bunch. The Governor could still overrule them. He walked over to Tal. "I hate to interrupt—"

"I'll meet you on the docks in twenty minutes."

"You'll meet me in ten, because you're coming now."

They regarded each other. Tal began, "Personal b—"

"Business," finished Adrian. "I think I've been very tolerant of your personal business, Tal. Do you want to make things more awkward for me politically?"

"You don't have to come. Just wait for me at the docks."

Tal seemed to have no human idea of when he was supposed to back down. Adrian Mercati, highest ranking male on the Diamond and possessor of what he was told was great personal magnetism, gave up the matter. "Twenty minutes. No longer, right?"

Tal nodded. Adrian motioned to one of the guards. "Go with him."

Chapter 18

A flock of birds finds simplicity in its pattern. The patterns of humans can tear the unwary.

Graykey Exercise 2: The Flash of Birds
In Forest Branches

Keylinn:

I entered the friendly atmosphere of food, drink, and money that was the Ginza Bar and found my ally waiting at a table. Behind him a holowall showed the Street of

Dreams in Everun, Baret Two, stretching into an infinity of colored awnings. Apparently he chose his backgrounds differently than I chose mine. As I approached the table, he stood up to greet me.

"I don't even know your name," I said.

"Ennis Severeth Gilleys," he replied. "And you're Keylinn O'Malley Murtagh."

I sat down hard. "How did you know?"

"I heard your friend call you Keylinn. How many Keylinns can there be running loose in the Wide World?"

It was a common name at home. But he was right; very few Graykey ever left their planet, and with good reason. I would not have myself, had I not been "volunteered" to pay off Cyr Vesant for medical supplies. "You left after I did, then. I didn't realize my reputation had spread so . . . violently."

"My dear comrade, your name was legend in training school. They're still talking about what you did to Bantry and Perrin. Not to mention a number of other anecdotes—"

"Yes, well, we can skip all that." I felt my face growing warm. Was there nowhere in the universe one could be safe from one's past?

"And I'd like to think I would have known you anyway. The O'Malleys are famous for the 'divine fire' in time of battle. There was a spark of it in your own eyes this day, whether you know it or not."

"I'm afraid the 'divine madness,'"—I gave it its other, less-flattering name—"must have lost its power coming down through the generations. In my own case it merely manifests as a compulsion," I took a breath, "to perform practical jokes in times of stress." There; I'd said it out loud.

"Of legendary proportions. Do you know, Perrin hasn't humiliated another cadet since that night? His class is now known as a soft-pass."

I moved uncomfortably in my chair. "Can we let all this by? It was a long time ago." Six years, and it felt three times as long.

But this Ennis Severeth Gilleys seemed determined to track down all my most tormenting thoughts. "Have you considered," he said, "that they might not have sent you

out as a punishment? You were a top cadet, you know.
Did you ever think you might be one of the Twelve?"

The Twelve: Every eighty to a hundred and fifty years
or so, the Society of Judges sent twelve people to sample
the universe outside, to live among strangers. To see if
the civilizations were ready for the return of the Graykey,
or if we would be courting a disaster like the one that had
sent us fleeing to a secret world of our own. Last time
only eight had returned, among them the famous Deirdre,
who had lived briefly on the Diamond during the Protectorship of Michael Veritie. The verdict was always the
same: The Graykey stayed where they were.

"The thought had crossed my mind," I said slowly, for
even to admit such a thing was hubris; but who else left
with the Society's blessings but the designated Twelve?
"It's useless to speculate about things like that. And I
wasn't exactly in good odor with the Society at that
time." I licked dry lips. "What about you? Why did you
leave?"

It was Ennis's turn to look uncomfortable. "I'm quite
sure I'm not one of the Twelve," he said finally. "Trust
me on that."

It would be rude to press something that might upset
him. I sought another topic. There was his *tarethi-din,* but
since I couldn't discuss my own, it would be impolite to
ask after his. "What brought you to the Station?" I asked
finally.

"Looking for work. Some odd people come through
here, waiting for the sector-gate. I thought it was a good
chance to gain *tarethi.*"

I smiled. "And you were successful."

"Yes." He took a sip of the whiskey he'd dialed up.

I'd tried the same brand earlier; it wasn't as good as
home. Besides, my *tarethi-din* was now on-Station. I
stayed with colored water. "Have you met any Three Cities people here on the Station?" I asked.

"Some. I've even worked with a few in Transport.
They're more or less what I expected."

"Oh?"

"All respect to your *tarethi-din,* of course; but clearly
these people have inbred too long. Scratch the surface,
and they all show signs of, shall we say, mental eccentric-

ities. A very neurotic lot of humans; I'm surprised they've functioned successfully thus far."

Thinking of the people I'd met with Cyr Vesant, I said, "I thought all outsiders were like that."

"Yes, well, even more than usual. Surely you've seen symptoms? Some of them are even a bit frightening. *Unpredictable.*" He said this last word with a grimace of distaste; unpredictability is a major Graykey sin.

Tal chose this moment to interrupt us. Ennis stood up again, as a gesture of courtesy to my *tarethi-din,* whatever his name might be. I'm afraid I simply looked surprised.

"Excuse me," said Tal. "I want to speak to you for a moment," he said to me.

Ennis nodded, and I rose and followed Tal to an empty spot near the bar. "I have to leave here," he said without preliminary. "I want you to do something for me."

"All right."

"Tell me, first: If you were going to blow up the *Kestrel,* how would you do it?"

I raised an eyebrow, but couldn't help smiling. Exercises like this were posed at home all the time. "Undetectably?"

"It would be preferable."

"They use a feed-drive system. I'd sabotage the drive."

"Assume the drive area is off-limits to everyone."

My smile grew wider. "Nothing is off-limits to everyone. I'll bet maintenance workers go in there—and if they can, other people can."

He put one hand on the bartop, as though to steady his weight. "So you don't think the task is beyond you?"

"Of course not." Now my smile faded. "You're speaking hypothetically."

"No, I want you to blow up the *Kestrel* on its homeward run."

I blinked. An unreal burning was in my hands and feet, like stepping unexpectedly into a glacier-fed stream. He was a gathrid, I knew, but even so—*"Why?"*

He said coldly, "Is it part of your job description to ask why?"

"I want to know."

He looked around, spotted a stool, and sat down on it.

"They have medical data on me in their memory banks. That's sufficient in itself. Second, there will be one person on that ship who can interpret such data as referring to an Aphean. That will be the Secret Police spy on board. We have no way of knowing which crewmember or passenger that is, so—"

"So blow them all up!"

"If you have a better idea, I'm open to suggestions." He moved one hand tiredly across his forehead.

I had been taught to have alternatives, and I began to list them. "The police spy might still be here, in Medical—"

"The only person still in Medical is Captain Nestra. She's a highly unlikely candidate."

"By the time the *Kestrel* is ready to sail again, the data will probably have been transmitted back to Baret One anyway. There's no reason the spy can't send a transceiver message from here, you know."

Tal sighed. I sensed that he really wanted to be in bed. He said, checking off on his fingers: "One. The ship is leaving tomorrow. Those were mostly smoke bombs I planted, and they did no real damage."

"*You* planted—"

"Two. Transceiver messages cost money. Baret Station charges a fortune for them. Police spies are on budgets just like everybody else. Why get called in to explain blowing your expense account on a message that won't arrive much before the *Kestrel* itself does? That'll be intercepted and read by station security?"

"You planted those bombs?" I found myself saying again.

He glanced at a clock on the wall, as though he had places to go and people waiting. Quickly and dryly, he broke down for me his experiences aboard ship. No, the docking gear had never been damaged; just the equipment for a gravity landing. Baret Station had misinterpreted the *Kestrel*'s signals—things like that can happen when communications go down. The only real bomb had gotten him into the cargo hold, whose entrance was fused shut.

I must have been staring at him. "How did you get out of detention? The door was sealed."

"The floor, walls, and ceiling were all open to negotiation. I trust I've answered all your questions, Key-linn—"

"What did the Protector say?"

"Adrian is very discreet in his own way. I don't think he wants to know what I do with my spare time."

I was quiet. After a moment I said, "There are over twenty people on that ship."

"Yes, that's true."

"Twenty people."

He said, "Do you know what the Republic will do if they hear there's an Aphean on the Diamond? The next Outsider techs we pick up to do odd jobs will have assassins among them. I'm comfortable on the Diamond, Keylinn; I don't want to leave."

It was all hideously rational. His request was, by contract terms, reasonable.

I went so far as to acknowledge one item. "We have to kill the SP."

"I'm endeavoring to do that, Keylinn."

"Wastefully." I considered the parameters of the assignment. "Can't you eliminate anyone?"

"And you could break their legs before they board. It's a gentle and considerate thought, Keylinn; did you have anyone in mind?"

"The Empire passeng—no." Wearing Empire clothes and carrying Empire ID guaranteed nothing. "Are there any children on board? We could eliminate them."

"Not to my knowledge."

I took hold of the edge of the bar, thinking. There were philosophical games of this sort one played at the beginning of training school. What if your *tarethi-din* asked you to destroy all life in the universe? Or one of many questions similarly unlikely to come up, but which could be debated for hours.

The theoretical answer was: Destroy all life in the universe. Graykey are nothing if not stubborn; they would die as they had lived. Not that our sympathies wouldn't be with someone who disobeyed such an order—but it was the wrong way to go.

The practical answer was: *Don't ever let yourself get in such a situation.*

Of course, that was much easier at home, where everyone understood their obligations.

"Pay for my ticket," I told him.

"All right." He turned and faced the bar counter, as though by looking elsewhere he would distance himself from the intensity of the conversation. "I'll send you a payment order from the Diamond."

My gaze fell on the Graykey sitting at my table, now watching us with interest. Practical jokes in training school seemed a million years away.

"Is this a problem?" asked Tal. "You don't look well."

"I'm all right."

He stood away from the bar counter, straightening himself with an effort, then paused. "I've not violated contract, have I?"

"Oh, no. You're quite within your rights."

"Ah. That's all right, then." He turned and walked away, and I saw a Diamond security guard meet him at the entrance to the bar.

I stayed there for several minutes, before returning to Ennis's table to tell him I wasn't feeling quite up to par.

Ennis Severeth Gilleys was very polite. He sat drinking for a while after Keylinn had gone. Then he went to the docking area, took passage to the Opal, and went to see his *tarethi-din*.

He found him packing a bag.

"Can't trust servants for this," said Lord Cardinal Arno. "I find they always leave out just the thing I want to wear."

"I didn't know you were going anywhere," said Ennis.

"Nor I. I just heard recently that my presence is needed on the Diamond. One of my flock is having a spiritual crisis."

Ennis did not remark on this; outsider religious madness bored him. He flung himself down on a couch and reached for a handful of grapes on a nearby table.

"Guess who I ran into on the Station," he said.

Chapter 19

Let's suppose I go to someone living in a wealthy and comfortable social rung of the Empire, and I say, "There's a famine in Benar." He or she might say, "I know there's a famine in Benar; I am current with the latest news; there is often famine in Benar." But if I took him to Benar and asked him to hold a swollen-bellied, stick-footed child in his arms while the dying mothers are handed their latest rations, he might protest, "But dear god, this is a famine! People are suffering! Something must be done!"

Or let's say I told any one of you that someday you're going to die. You might respond, "Brilliant point—I know I'll die someday, you're not telling me anything new."

But one day something you hear or see—the words of a medtech, or the sight of someone you know dying, the lines of a poem or the year on a calendar—will strike into your heart, and you'll cry, betrayed, "I'm going to die!"

The Graykey would say that you only thought you knew before, but now you really know. The Graykey mark a great difference between knowledge one is taught and this other form of knowledge that cannot be taught, that comes from personal experience and strikes so deeply. It is less marked in other societies, not because it isn't recognized, but because there is no term for it. The Graykey call it bone-knowledge.

Another word for it is tarethi.

from CAUDLANDER'S
A Tourist Guide to the Graykey

Will wanted to walk by himself. He let Johnny and Jack see Bernadette home—or more the opposite, really, as Johnny and Jack had both drunk rather more than their general capacities.

Sangaree's lighting was rarely bright at the best of times, and on night-time it was almost black in places.

Much of this part of Opal had not been intended for human habitation, and the comforts and lighting had been planned accordingly.

Lysette was singing tonight at the Bloodshell. It was too early to expect her to be off, and Will was restless, so he turned into the darker walkways that led down toward his old school.

There was a flash of light just ahead by an entrance-way; Will stopped short. Before it was extinguished, the light showed an old man's face, lined and uncaring, and a white kitchen uniform. There were foosteps, and a man's voice said, "How they hangin', Fred?"

Fred—the old man—grunted. Will made out a huge shape on wheels that Fred was pushing over to the other man. Whether it was laundry, or garbage, or contraband, Will had no idea, nor did he have any intention of asking. He waited until the sound of footsteps and wheels went away, and a small square of light showed that Fred had gone back inside. Then he went on down the street.

Sangaree. The place wasn't so bad if you followed the rules. So what was his sister's problem? No . . . what was *his* problem, that he had this feeling of getting in deeper and deeper water, farther and farther from land? He was using Bernadette as a life preserver, as though she could save him from the complicated mess existence was becoming . . . only to reach for her in the water and see that she was too far away to depend on.

At the end of the street he turned into the tunnel by the recycling plant. People avoided it because of the flooding and the stink, but Will had learned every foot of it, with Hartley Quince, at the age of nine. It led by a shortcut to the courtyard of Blessed Sacrifice School. He had no conscious plans to walk by the school, for he had few happy memories connected with it; but he wanted to avoid any encounters with anyone. Especially at night, the people one met on the streets and walkways of Sangaree were . . . unpredictable. Will's father had been one such; Will didn't remember a lot about his father, but it was clear the man had what they called here "troubles."

Often the "troubles," however they manifested themselves, ran in families. Will thought about this sometimes, especially when he was trying to go to sleep.

He emerged from the tunnel behind a dark entranceway to the Blessed Sacrifice dormitories, where unmarried teachers were housed. And now he wished he'd gone some other way, any other way, by Tanamonde Street and the well-heeled, or by Broken Corner and the jail, where the debtors and petty thieves would be yelling out the bars to their mates and lovers—it was better than a play, at Broken Corner. Whatever had possessed him to come this way? The stench of the tunnel was making him sick, or maybe it was the memories the tunnel called up.

"Nathys are unreliables, riffs are informers." He could hear Hart's nine-year-old voice telling him. Hart was new to Sangaree while Willie'd lived there all his life, but Hart had the structure of power down pat within weeks. Was it a structure at all similar to the pens, was that why he could recognize it? Or maybe he was just a genius at spotting corruption. No way to tell with Hart, he never talked about the holding pens; they were just a rumor that clung to him like a filthy smell, coming out in whispers from the grownups and orders at the breakfast table not to associate with him.

Hart still never talked about himself, Will thought. He'd watched Hart at court. He seemed to answer questions freely enough, but he was always more interested in *you,* whichever *you* he was talking with; he listened with a concentrated attention that worked better than any verbal flattery. And it left people to build up a background for him from their own minds, made of his court accent and excellent manners and social consideration, uncontradicted by anything he actually said.

He'd first seen Hart upside-down, across the playground, while getting the shit beat of him by Parry Winzek. He'd let Parry get to him again, listening to him insult his father until he couldn't take it anymore and jumped on Parry like an awkward sack of potatoes, pummeling and pummeling. Some people fought better when they were crazy-angry; Will was not one of them. This was the third time Parry Winzek had bloodied Will's face on the playground floor.

He'd looked through blurry eyes when Parry got up, and saw the light-haired kid in the neat tan pants and white shirt smile at him quizzically from across the yard. Will lay there for a few seconds, tasting the blood from his nose, then carefully started to get up. Parry walked around him and raised one foot very slowly, aiming for a final kick.

"You already won," said the new kid in the tan pants. He didn't say it like a challenge, or as if he were disagreeing with Parry. He just said it.

"That's right," called one of the circle of kids who were watching Will's latest humiliation. "You're not supposed to do that when you already won."

"He didn't say it," said Parry.

Willie closed his mouth, swallowing the thick, salty stuff that must be blood. No doubt his face proclaimed him the loser he was. He wasn't going to say anything.

Then he met the new kid's eyes. The kid jerked his head to one side, a look of contempt going briefly across his face as his glance ran over Parry. His eyes met Willie's. *Say it, asshole. Why give this shit another chance to hurt you?* And for about a second Willie saw the code of the playground in a whole new light.

"You win," he said. Parry's mouth turned up in a smug smile. And yet Willie felt superior, for the first time. Parry wasn't worth being truthful to. Willie hugged that look he'd seen on the new kid's face to his heart. He'd never seen anyone look at Parry with contempt, but it matched something Will realized he'd been feeling himself, somewhere underneath the code and the confusion of what everybody else told him was right. Parry was barely aware that two and two were four, and his taunts were pretty lame, too, when you got away long enough to consider it. And more importantly than anything else, Will wasn't alone in thinking so.

Parry walked away to be congratulated by his friends. Will heard them praise Parry and talk about how Will "just jumped you, without any reason." The new kid came over and stood by Will as he got up. Then he handed Will a handkerchief, white and neatly folded.

"You're messing up your shirt," he said.

Will looked down to see spots of red on the white material. "Oh, hell. My father's going to kill me." His tone was calm, but to Willie this was literal.

"Cold water's good for bloodstains," said the kid, conveying the first piece of information he bestowed on Will.

"There's leakage over in the recycling tunnel. Come on and we'll soak it now. I'm Hartley Quince." He turned around and began making his way past the knots of ballplayers toward the edge of the yard, and Willie followed him.

Will stood in the dimness by the Blessed Sacrifice dormitories, and wondered what his life would have been like if Hart had been assigned to some other corner of the Opal. Would he himself ever have made that breakthrough, that twist of mind that made him see the codes of Sangaree differently? You couldn't escape them completely, and he didn't really want to; but if not for that day in the playground would he ever have chosen to go into the Guard, instead of waiting to be drafted to the radiation levels? Would he be laboring now with the work teams, or released for a slow death at home, tended by Bernadette?

In a lot of ways he owed Hart far too much. Will started to cross the courtyard, heading for the skinny alleyway he knew ran along the other side, that led by some torturous twistings and climbings to Duquesne Street, just ten minutes' walk from home. A movement in the gray dimness by the entranceway made him freeze, then drop down behind the broken statue of Saint Adrian the First.

Some teacher, bored and restless and out for a stroll? The courtyard was a little small for that, but it was safer than the outer streets. Will pushed his back against the statue's pedestal, minimizing his visibility. He heard footsteps go back and forth, first faint, then near, then faint again. What were the trespassing penalties these days? The last time he'd been here was as a child. What were the penalties for adults? Would they come down hard on a City Guard sergeant? The inevitable and hateful thought followed: Could Hart get him off? . . . He had before.

The bloodstains never did come out completely, but his father had been too drunk to notice for several days; and meanwhile, Will had garnered enough triumph in the playground to see him through one more beating at home. It was Hart who advised him through this new campaign. He suggested that Will pick a fight with Parry, something that had never even crossed Will's mind. He fought when challenged; the idea of *initiating* a fight was alien to his nature. And with Parry? What would be the point of asking to get beat up?

But by God, it worked. He rehearsed the fight for hours with Hart, who had some very direct techniques he'd learned in the pens—most of them unsuitable for dealing with anyone you didn't want to cripple or maim, but still it made one feel better to know one *could.* "I don't know," Willie had said finally. "I'm not mad at him right now."

"Good," said Hart, "then this is the time." And he pointed Willie gently in Parry Winzek's direction.

The encounter was a rousing success. Will couldn't come away from it with the soul-deep satisfaction he would have felt if he could beat Parry Winzek while in the grip of a violent temper—but he had the satisfaction of winning, which was something he didn't have before. Parry seemed beautifully shocked by the whole event.

Hart watched it all. He did not offer Parry his handkerchief. The next day he said to Will, "Beat him up every morning." "But he hasn't *done* anything," said Will. "He's thinking," said Hart; "stop it there." And for the next week Will did so, though without enjoyment. It was like some stupid chore he'd been assigned, and he tackled it as dutifully.

When he discontinued the process, Parry showed no inclination to start it up again. In fact, Parry avoided him entirely.

The teacher, if it was a teacher, turned around at last and went back inside. Will let out a breath. That's what revisiting Sangaree does, he thought; it cuts about forty points off your IQ. To avoid possible danger on the outer streets you walk through the tunnel and end up in a situation just as dangerous. You would think you'd remember the last time you were here—it wasn't exactly a forgettable incident.

Ir was sort of ironic, though. In the dark he couldn't even tell if that teacher were male or female.

Those two years were the happiest of Will's life. He resented thinking of it that way later, but the truth was the truth. Hartley Quince seemed totally without fear, completely unaware of the boundaries normal people knew were there. There were things you could do, and things you couldn't do, and everybody knew it but Hart.

It was like being set free. There were few places in this part of Sangaree that didn't hold memories of the adventures of that time.

Hart in school: a well-behaved, background-blending Hart. His hair was lighter in those days, almost blond, cut neatly, and his shoes were polished. His shirt was pressed enough to be presentable to the teachers and not so much as to call attention to him with the other students; his grades were much the same. Hart before and after school, with Will: dirty-faced and bright-eyed after figuring how to get into the teachers' residence through the branch off the access tunnels. (Hart had gotten into the maintenance rooms and looked at the maps.) Delighted with Will's success in quashing Parry Winzek's companions. ("Don't let him up until he says it," advised Hart from the sidelines.) A face shining with pleasure after they successfully followed the local black marketeer through three levels to find his next contact point—why Hart had thought that necessary, Willie never did find out. Borderline though Hart's activities were, Will was never alarmed by them; Hart's confidence was contagious. And he was never angry, never hated, never screamed at Will the way his family did, never, in fact, raised a hand in violence to anybody, which was like a cool draught of water after the rest of Sangaree. Beating up Parry Winzek wasn't something Willie would ordinarily have thought of doing outside the heat of the moment; but with Hart there was no question of heat. A short temper was an evil thing and adults were unreliable beings who might explode at any time, but Hart was easy and deliberate. How wrong could what they did be?

But one day Willie went solo, and it all went bad.

It was love that did it.

Her name was Miss Smith, and she was his new teacher, replacing Old Miss Deaville who'd died in the night and been taken away. That happened, Willie knew; dead people and bad people got taken away. "They get cut into parts," his father used to say, and he'd look pleased when Willie was scared. But Miss Smith was a revelation: She didn't slap kids who gave the wrong an-

swer, or scream at anybody while they cried. As far as
Will could remember, she never took the rod down off the
wall at all.

She didn't know a lot about math, which Will was
good in, and when the school observer sat in on class they
often did the same arithmetic lesson all over again—
assignment nine, basic multiplication and division. However, this was irrelevant to Will, who was beginning to
see Miss Smith in the light of a saint. It was some time
later that the glow around Miss Smith began to be connected in his mind with her shining black hair and her
dark eyes and the graceful, easy way she walked. It was
fascinating to see the way she crossed her legs under the
long skirt; there was a slidey sound when she did it that
was delightful.

"They say she's riathic," said Hart one day, watching
Will's glance follow Miss Smith from the yard to the
front of the school.

Will didn't like the way Hart said that; it sounded like
something bad. "What does that mean?"

"A neuter," said Hart. "Brought up to be in the Dome
of Service, but got sent away. Maybe she failed at whatever she was supposed to do. Maybe she didn't have a
good voice for the choir or she couldn't hold her own in
prayer meetings. Anyway, sometimes the failures get sent
to teach school."

"Miss Smith isn't a failure."

"I'm just telling you what I hear," said Hart amiably.

Will looked at him with suspicion. He hated to reveal
the depth of his ignorance, but— "What's a neuter?"

"Not a man or a woman. That stuff gets taken out, or cut
off, or whatever. She might have started off as a man."

"No!" said Will, bunching up his fists. For the first
time ever he hated Hart, and longed to throw himself at
him and wipe that superior look off his face. Ironically, it
was Hart's training that stopped him. Will had learned not
to respond to the callings of his temper.

"I didn't know it would bother you," said Hart. "It's
just a rumor."

Will got up and left. He didn't know what he would do
if he stayed. But for weeks the thought tormented him:
That Miss Smith was something *else,* that she might have

been a man! It was in the back of his mind all the time—at school, at home, with Hart—especially at night.

Recklessly, he decided to do something about it. He knew the way into the teachers' dormitories. He would sneak inside, hide somewhere—in Miss Smith's room, or the local spit, or the showers—and he would see for himself. The plan was a little vague, he knew, once he got inside; but there was no hope for that—he had no idea how the residence was laid out.

Cowardice had never been Will's problem. No sooner did he fasten onto the idea than he put it into practice. Late one evening he made sure no one was watching, then he cut into the tunnel by the recycling plant. He climbed up a walkway to some access tubes and crawled inside, first shaking water from his shoes. He knew from his excursions with Hart which tunnels were dry and abandoned, which were messy and dangerous. He opened an emergency hatch at one point and found himself looking quite far down into the teachers' courtyard, above the statue of Saint Adrian the First. "Give me some luck," he said to the saint. He crawled on. The next emergency hatch would be inside the residence.

It opened in the base of the wall of an inner hallway. There was nobody there (for which he thanked the saint); should he take a chance and go out now, or try for another hatch? He would have more chance of locating Miss Smith's room if he were outside.

He pulled himself out and closed the hatch behind him very carefully, making sure that it didn't catch. He made his way down the hall. It dead-ended rather quickly and he took the left branch, wondering if he were getting just a bit far from his exit. At the end there was a big door of dark wood, with scenes from the Book of Sawyer carved in squares all over. It was old and dusty. Will pushed it very slowly about an inch open.

There was a large kitchen inside, with six teachers working. He recognized them all: Miss Tofler, carrying the pot of soup, Miss Ryneth, with the dirty dishes . . . but no Miss Smith. Will backed hastily away from the door and started retracing his steps. People were always walking in and out of kitchens.

At the end of the other hall was a staircase, and Will

Jane Emerson

followed it to the bedroom level. He felt slightly more
confident now; evidently everyone was downstairs doing
the evening chores. He found a row of doors, all unlocked. There was a small cell beyond each, with a cot,
a bureau, and a tiny desk. Books and papers were stacked
in most, and a quick glance at them was enough to say
whose room each must be. The end of the hall was Miss
Smith's room. He recognized the assignments of his own
class lying in a pile on the floor.

Now what? In the back of his mind he'd never expected to be even this successful. He'd anticipated finding a way into the residence (at best) and then making a
quick withdrawal. As for his vague plans of hiding and
watching . . . there was no place to hide in this tiny room.
Not even a closet.

Unlike the other rooms, there was almost nothing of
personal possessions here. The only exceptions were a
box of scented powder on the bureau top and a conservative (for Sangaree) lipstick lying beside it. Will lifted
the powder; it was Miss Smith's scent. He remembered
her bending to assist him with his religion assignment.

He'd better get out of here. Will left the room and
started back down the hall. As he passed, he noted there
was a spit at Miss Smith's end of the corridor. The one
she was most likely to use . . . He'd gotten in all this way.
Should he waste it all now by leaving?

Willie had not been brought up with any sense of spy-
ing on a lady as an ungentlemanlike activity. It was now
a question of success or failure, of what one could get
away with. He entered the spit. There was a bank of four
showers and two spit-seats. There was also a mirror on
one wall, and Will recalled now that he had seen no mir-
rors in the cells.

One part of him noted that he was pressing his luck
into oblivion. That he was crazy. But he'd come so far . . .
and an inspection of the walls showed an entry to the recycling system (no surprise, considering the nature of the
room)—and there, beside it, was the emergency maintenance entrance for major system repairs. Clearly Saint
Adrian was on his side in this. How could he possibly
leave now? He let himself into the access tunnel, leaving
the hatchway open a crack, and waited.

Hours went by. Apparently nobody used this spit. Eventually he heard faint sounds of doors closing and voices saying good night. Everybody was going to bed except Willie Stockton. So much for the great adventure . . .

More hours passed. He was a mass of cramps when Miss Smith came in. She wore a respectable gray jacket and cap, as though she'd just come from the street. She did not use the spit-seat—which did not strike Will as odd, for he hardly expected his heroine to have normal bodily functions—but stood before the mirror and removed her cap, her silver necklace, her earrings, and her blouse.

Miss Smith was not wearing the sort of undergarments Will had seen his mother and his sister wear. In fact, she wasn't wearing any at all. He froze solid, right there in the tunnel. She stripped off her long skirt and slips, and pulled off her thin gray boots. Miss Smith was definitely not a riath, whatever Hart had heard. Will felt joy welling up in his chest—he felt it distantly, in a dreamlike sort of way, as though it were a physical thing having nothing to do with himself.

The whole evening had been verging on the unreal. Will had never done anything so bold, and certainly not without Hart pushing him on. Now the limits of reality started to make themselves felt.

This was a very awkward place to be in. He'd better leave. With great difficulty he managed to move back a little.

And the unreal became the surreal. Will looked out for one last glance, like Lot's wife in the book, and he turned into something else.

Miss Smith was rubbing a lotion over her skin. She put down the tube, raised her left hand and, in a curious motion, pulled off her right arm. She began applying lotion to the arm at the place where it had joined the shoulder.

It was a jolt of electricity. All the laws of life collapsed. He must have made some sort of noise because she stopped. She listened. Willie heard his own breathing. She called, "Is anyone there?"

That was it, he broke. He clicked the hatch shut, turned the inner bolt, and scuttled backward down the tunnel all within a second. He backed into the first main branch and then started headfirst in the other direction.

Behind him he heard a hatchway being pulled open. He went, impossible though it seemed, even faster. There was a branching in the main tunnel ahead. Some people of the Cities had an innate sense of three-dimensional direction that kept them from ever being quite lost; Willie was one of them, though he didn't quite know it yet. He only knew that if he wanted to get back to the route over the courtyard, he had to go right. And he did, without hesitation.

Perhaps it was that; perhaps it was the speed of fear. Perhaps it was the fact, which came to him many years later, that androids have no sense of smell. For when he finally emerged unscathed from the access route in the main tunnel alongside the plant, he found that he'd defecated into his pants. And though he had no memory of doing it, he knew in his heart it must have happened when he heard the sound of the hatchway being torn open.

He ran. He ran all the way to the foot of Tanamonde Street, where Hartley Quince lived with his guardian.

The guardian was a strange old man with an accent, who didn't want to get Hart out of bed; but Hart appeared anyway, in his nightclothes, and asked the man to leave.

And to Willie's wonder, he did leave. Hart looked at him and said, "What's the matter?"

Suddenly Will felt exhausted. "Can I use your spit?"

"Sure. Probably a good idea—you stink." He pointed to a door.

There was a mirror in here, too, and as Willie stood bracing himself on the sink he saw a stranger in the glass: wild-eyed and sweaty and with disheveled hair. He cleaned himself off and splashed water on his face and under his arms and then put his shirt back on, still clammy and damp with sweat. He ran his fingers through his hair, which did a little good but not much. Then he went back out to Hart.

"I'm in the kitchen," called Hart. Will followed the voice to a small room with a table and two chairs. Hart had pulled out one of the chairs for Will. He'd never seen a kitchen in a place where only two people lived.

Will sat down, and Hart gave him some stuff he said

was coffee, and Will told him everything that had happened that night.

Hart put his hand on Will's forehead. "You're not hot. In fact you're sort of cold."

Will jerked his head. "I'm not sick. I'm telling you the truth."

"So she's a machine? Outsider technology? They've got a tool of Satan teaching school in Sangaree? It's not probable."

"It's true."

It did not occur to either of them that the arm might have been a prosthetic device. Such were rarely used on Opal, and when they were they were deliberately made as unlike flesh as possible. Nor were they ever very technically efficient. And somehow it just hadn't *looked* to Will like a false arm—it looked like part of a larger mechanical *thing*.

Hart said, "Maybe all the teachers are machines. Maybe old Miss Ryneth and Miss Hoagland and their complaints about arthritis are just a cover. Maybe—"

Will jumped up from his seat. "Stop it! It's true, it's true, it's true—"

"All right," said Hart quietly. He put his hands on Will's shoulders. "I believe you." Will was breathing hoarsely. "Why would you lie?" said Hart, and Will sat down again.

Hart stared distantly at the walls. "You know," he said, "she's not a very good teacher. She does the same math lesson over and over again."

"So what?"

"She wasn't designed for teaching. I wonder what she *was* designed for."

"Does it matter?"

Hart smiled. "Maybe not." He topped off Will's cup again. "But if she was designed for teaching, she'd've hit us. Right?"

"I guess so. I didn't think of that."

" 'No machine may do a man or woman's proper work.' That's what the Book says. Teaching by machine is against the canons. But I bet her primary work is something else."

"She shouldn't be teaching, though. It's against the law."

Hart looked at him. "And now she knows that somebody else knows."

Will went white.

"And whoever put her there knows that somebody else knows—"

"Jesus, Hart!"

"She didn't see you?" asked Hart.

"No ... I don't think so. Only the back of my pants, maybe."

"But they'll figure it's a kid."

Will pushed away his coffeecup. "I'm never going to school again."

"But you've got to," said Hart ruthlessly.

Hart let him sleep over. Willie was still shivering, and thought that if he went home this late and got beaten up on top of everything else, he'd just die. Not that he did much sleeping.

Miss Smith wasn't in the next morning. Miss Weston, who was supposed to be retired, took the class. Willie got slapped for not knowing the answer to a math problem, but he could no more concentrate on the slap than on the problem.

It was during the afternoon session that the men finally came. They wore the black colors of the Ecclesiastical Police, rarely seen in Sangaree. One of them stood in front of the class and made a little speech about the importance of following the rules of the Church and how they were all expected to grow up to be useful members of society. Then two other men came down the aisle—Will thought his heart would jump out of his chest—and passed him by and stood by the chair where Thomas Vanessa sat. And they asked him to come with them, please. And Tommy, with a funny, held-in look on his face, got up and went with them. He started to take his books, but they said he could leave them behind.

When Tommy was gone, the man who made the speech told them that perversity had to be rooted out at the source, and that Thomas Vanessa had been very, very bad. He wouldn't even want to tell good children what

Thomas had done. And then he left. And Miss Weston came and took up Tommy's books and put them on her own desk. Will's eyes kept going back to those books all during the rest of the lessons.

"They take them away and cut them up for parts," he heard his father's voice echoing.

Tommy hadn't done anything. He should have spoken up. He could still get up how, and tell Miss Weston to call back the men. Tommy didn't deserve to get cut up for parts.

Willie didn't want to get cut up for parts either. He risked an anguished glance back at Hart.

Hart returned his gaze calmly. He looked back down at his religion book, and Will suddenly knew how the men in black had gotten Tommy's name. How had Hart done it? Did he say, "Tommy came and bragged that he was going to try to get into the teachers' residence?" Hart could have done that, he could have talked to those men. He was never scared.

But to give then Tommy's name! If it had been Parry Winzek's name, or one of his hangers-on, Will could almost—almost—have understood it. But Tommy had never done anything to them. They barely knew him.

He couldn't just sit here! Willie hissed, making Hart look up. *Well?* said Hart's look.

And Will experienced one of those moments—like the moment in the yard when he saw the code of fighting differently, but now it was stronger, more precise and intense. He couldn't say how he knew, but he knew it with a force of clarity and logic that matched his knowledge of if-I-drop-this-pen-it-will-hit-the-floor. He knew it in his bones. Hart didn't give a damn if it was Tommy Vanessa or anybody else. None of them were real to him. That brief look of contempt that Will had seen the first day in the yard, that was real. For a moment he felt as if he were in Hart's skin, and his own claim to reality seemed to dwindle.

It was the final gift of traumatic knowledge in a day of traumatic knowledge. His stomach heaved. He held the sides of his chair until his knuckles grew white.

You can still get up and say something, said a voice in his head. *Hurry.*

What?

Tommy Vanessa. He's innocent.

That's right, thought Will, there's still time to do something. And he went on thinking it, more and more weakly, as the rest of the afternoon passed.

To Will's unutterably relief, Hartley's guardian took him out of Sangaree shortly thereafter. They moved to one of the upper decks, and Will assumed at the time that they would never meet again.

The years taught Will that a teacher's residence was a good place to hide an android; certainly the aristo families lived with little privacy, cousins and servants always walking in and out, and the folk in the poorer areas shared space as a matter of course. The teachers lived like monks, in small single cells. He could even see why "Miss Smith" would regularly use a spit nobody else used. He supposed a mechanical body required periodic maintenance, just as a flesh one did. But he'd never, never come up with a reason why somebody had brought an android onto the Opal. And he'd given it an enormous amount of thought, for a subject he tried to push out of his mind.

And now, a decade later, Will crossed the courtyard to the alleyway with a sour taste in his mouth. It was a taste that called up the bitter flavor of the coffee Hart had poured for him on that night. Will had never tried coffee again, though it was available at the Diamond court. He had no reason to believe it had become any sweeter.

Out on the street he took a deep breath. The Bloodshell wasn't far away; he didn't much care if Lysette's set was over or not. He wanted to see her.

He changed direction, then slowed. A thought occurred to him.

It was an open secret that Hartley Quince had come out of the holding pens. But children don't leave the pens on their own, not even genius psychopaths like Hart. So somebody arranged to have him taken out. And where do you put an untrained, unschooled child? Where but in Sangaree, where he can make all his mistakes without any witnesses but the locals, and who cared about them? Then when his initial training is sufficient, bump him to a higher level.

Who was backing Hart, and why? Will had heard the rumors on the Diamond that Hart was some kind of left-hand-born Mercati. But he discounted that; there *were* no Mercatis on Opal—not one.

So what was Hart's story?

He liked to watch Lysette when she didn't know he was there. She was a good singer; straight bar stuff, no heartsinging or anything over the line. She just did the old songs the way her singing master had taught her. That was enough.

She stood in the singer's spot in the Bloodshell and finished up "I Know Where I'm Going." Her brown hair was straight and pulled back on top, long in back. Her eyes, her expression, and her songs were all very clear and direct. Will smiled in the back of the dark bar, knowing that Lysette belonged to him. If she hadn't, she would have made that very clear, too.

Sometimes, as a joke, she finished with "Bonnie Ship the Opal." But that depended on the audience, and apparently she wasn't going to do it tonight. When the light around her faded, Will stood up so she could see him.

She smiled at once and came over to the table.

"Want anything?" he asked. He meant water or sweet drinks; Lysette never went near alcohol.

"You, sugar." She leaned over and kissed him before they sat down.

God, this was just what he needed after a sorry night. If only she would follow through on this, he thought wistfully. But she was very firm—the banns hadn't been read, they still couldn't even call themselves husband and wife, even prematurely. And that sort of thing was saved for marriage. Somehow, he thought, he and his sister had both fallen in with real sticklers for form. It would be hard to find personalities farther from their childhood experience.

"I brought you something," he said, and he handed her the diamond and ruby ring that Adrian had given him the day he pulled Iolanthe out of the pit.

"Willie!" She held it between two fingers, gazing in awe. "Where did you get it?"

"Diamonds from the Diamond," he said, pleased. "Like it?"

She leaned over the table as far as she could go, and Will got another kiss. "I've missed you so much," she said, and his smile vanished.

"I'm going back tomorrow night."

She put down the ring and he saw the glow leave her face. "That soon?"

"Right after Bernadette's wedding. That's the only reason I got off at all."

She sat back in her chair and looked around the bar. She tapped her shoes against the floor. Then her gaze returned to him and she said, "Why can't you ask for a transfer back?"

"Sergeants go where they're told, Lyse."

"Just what do you *do* on the Diamond, anyway?"

"Whatever I'm told. Look, sweetheart—"

"If you hadn't gone into the Guard—"

"I'd be dead, and we wouldn't be sitting here!"

They glared at each other for a moment in silence.

Finally she said, "You'd better go home and get a little sleep. You've got wedding preparations to make."

"Yeah, I'd better."

They sat there a while longer, still not speaking.

He said, "We're still engaged, right?"

"Maybe."

"You're not going to forget me while I'm gone?"

"You won't be gone long."

"Look, I told you, I don't know when this assignment will end."

"Never mind," she said, and kissed him for the third and final time. He smelled her hair and her breath and a faint flowery perfume. She said, "I'll be looking at the moon, but I'll be seeing you."

He left the bar in a daze. It had been a long night. There were no moons over Sangaree, of course, but *the* moon was an old legacy, handed down in a thousand songs and poems. By now it no longer conveyed a barren satellite, any more than the word "heart" in the same poems meant a chamber for pumping blood. In Sangaree more than anywhere else, the old songs were still sung, and Will found himself humming as he walked home.

It was, he realized, from the song she'd quoted. What was the rest of it? *I'll be looking at the moon, but I'll be seeing you.* Then he started to laugh. *I'll be seeing you, in all the old familiar places.* Well, she'd said he'd be back.

You had to love a girl with that much confidence.

Chapter 20

The perfection of simplicity. The perfection of stones. The perfection of art. The perfection of death.
                        Graykey Exercise 2: The Flash of Birds
                                      in Forest Branches

Keylinn:

I knew that in this case I was a long way from the place where understanding and action were one.

Nevertheless I booked passage on the *Kestrel*— somewhat surprised at my own methodical efficiency— boarded, and took my stateroom. I ate briefly in the ship's dining area, unable to keep from noting the faces of the doomed as I did. The food went down like lumps; three bites and I was in danger of nausea.

I'm only a cadet, dammit.

From the table, I went immediately to reconnoiter the area around the drive station; we could not afford to be very far from Baret Station when the explosion was triggered.

It was easy. I felt a distant sense of amazement at how easy it was. My instructors at the academy delighted in presenting every possible scenario of doom; I was, I discovered, overprepared. These people believed they had been through the crisis for this voyage. Some of them were still recovering mentally from the panic that ensued onboard when Tal's smoke bombs had gone off. The response to that crisis might have been to beef up security, but it was not. For one thing, there was little to beef up.

With the absence of the Captain there was one fewer crewmember on a ship not plentifully equipped with crew. And for another, the spy they held responsible had been left behind on Baret Station.

Only in one sense of the word, I thought. Unfortunately, his *tarethi-din* is here in his place.

I ran through my mental list, not attempting to damp down all emotion but simply ignoring it. It is best, of course, one of my old instructors used to say, if you have brought yourself to a depth of *tarethi* in which your action is as instinctive as that of a bird or a hillrunner. But this is not always possible in the time you may have. If need be, do your duty and worry about it later. Worry can be dealt with; failure cannot.

I knew what would be happening in the enclosed world of the *Kestrel*'s officers.

Two hours after departing the station, word would come to the acting captain that the drive was on a positive chain. Past containment, the drive room supervisor would say. An immediate evacuation would be ordered, but the lifeships would be inaccessible. The access codes have been tampered with, they discover. This could be dealt with if there were time; but there will be no time . . . a truth that will sink through their skins in a few unbelieving minutes. . . .

Subjectivity exercises cut both ways.

And then, with the same icepick feeling behind the muscles of my face that had been there since the Ginza Bar, I was in Lifeship #3, leaving the area of the *Kestrel* as quickly as possible. The security board on the *Kestrel* would show that a ship was missing, but under the circumstances nobody would spare much attention.

I headed not toward the station, which would have been suspicious in any case, but toward a point I had notified Tal Diamond of just before boarding. I told him to have a short-range from the City waiting there to receive me. Now he would either comply, or he would not.

If I died, so much the better.

Chapter 21

"We have your signal," said the tech he'd pulled out of Transport.

"Good," said Tal. "Prepare to link up for boarding."

As the tech began the complicated maneuvers that would link them with the *Kestrel*'s lifeship, he said, "It would've been a lot easier if this messenger would just meet us at the Station."

"They prefer anonymity," said Tal. "As do we. Which I trust you'll bear in mind later."

The tech said nothing. His boss on the docks had made it clear that Tal spoke for the Diamond Protector, and if he himself didn't hold on to this job on the Diamond, he'd be returned to the Station. Where he'd already used up his airspace time.

Nor did he really care what the Diamond higher-ups did. He made the final arrangements and noted that the lifeship was matched and linked for boarding. It took a good half-hour of maneuvering and checking, but that was what they paid him for.

"Ready to allow entry," he said.

Tal unlocked the entry seal, and Keylinn stepped aboard. She looked very calm.

"Is everything all right?" he asked.

"Everything's fine," she replied.

As instructed, the tech was already bringing them around for the Diamond. Keylinn took the third seat in the shortie, dropping into it in boneless exhaustion. We almost didn't need the tech, thought Tal; I'll have to learn match-and-link maneuvers on my own. He looked back at Keylinn and saw that she had her dagger out and had just drawn a score along her palm. She was regarding the blood that welled up with distant interest.

The tech followed Tal's fascinated glance, and his eyes widened. "What the hell—you're going to hurt yourself, cyr. Give me that." He left his seat and approached Keylinn.

Suddenly she was standing up, so swiftly it was hard to say when she'd done it. The dagger was pointing at the tech. "Stay away from me." She made a gesture-swipe at him. "Get back." The tech retreated. She followed. Within seconds he was pressed against the instrument panel.

"Keylinn," said Tal. When she didn't respond he said it louder. "Keylinn!"

She turned very, very slightly, not taking her eyes off the tech. "What?"

"Leave him alone, and give me that knife."

She blinked. Then she stepped back slowly. She handed Tal the dagger and returned to her seat.

The tech glared at Tal. "What the hell was that? Are your messengers all crazy?"

"The sanity of your fellow employees is none of your business. Do you want to continue in this line of work?"

The tech sat down again with a look that said he was far from satisfied. He readjusted the controls, and as he did so he cast a quick, nervous glance over his shoulder at Keylinn. She looked fast asleep.

It was about then that the *Kestrel* exploded, though they were far enough away that the tech had no idea it happened.

Tal thought: Asleep in the chair like that she looks like a child. One arm was flung over the armrest, and drops of blood fell on the floor from her cut.

Ideals can make people do horrible things, thought Iolanthe. This must be what they meant when they talked about the ends justifying—or not justifying—the means.

On the one hand it would be an enormous relief to tell someone, anyone, of the conversation she'd overheard between Adrian and Fischer.

And yet, regardless of what the Lord Cardinal had told her, now that she was here it felt very wrong to spy on one's husband and report back. Adrian had been very kind to her since her arrival. He wasn't a tenth as good-looking as Will Stockton, and she could never love him, but his courtesy deserved more than this.

She sat in the crimson armchair in the confessional room of St. Thomas the Doubter. Her chair and the empty one beside her stood on a raised oval in one part of the chamber; just below was the angel-shaped block of white marble where penitents major prostrated themselves to claim the mercy of the Church. The block was carved across a shallow pit, also of white marble, and reached by one of the angel's drooping sleeves, where steps cleverly cut into the folds of stone cloth. The pit, about man-high, was empty now. When a penitent major was there, it would be filled with heirophants and deacons armed with needles, ready to provide the penitent with either the grace of forgiveness or death. A rare spectacle, all highly dramatic, charged with music and color, she imagined vaguely; she'd never seen it, herself.

Iolanthe's confessions had always been made on the assembly line during the ladies' hour at her local church at home, surrounded by veiled women, quiet whispers, giggles. This was quite different. What an odd choice of furniture for such a place, too; surely the point should be to make a penitent feel uncomfortable? But this chair was big and soft, like a set of enveloping arms—so big that you almost felt like a child in it, and you had to lean back to rest your spine. And the air was so heavy and warm. In spite of the dread she felt of the Lord Cardinal's arrival, it was hard to hold onto that edge of alertness. She looked longingly at the cold marble, imagining how it would feel to nap there. Another ten minutes and she wouldn't be able to keep her eyes open.

Her gaze fell on the angel above the pit. She thought, I wonder how my mother would look stretched out there. She straightened her back; unfilial though this thought was, it somehow made it easier to face the interview.

Iolanthe rose when he came in. "Thank you for coming, Father."

"My daughter." He held out his hands and advanced over the marble floor. "I see you still bear the marks of your tumble in the pit. Disgraceful. I don't know what Adrian was thinking, and I wonder where your bodyguard could have been."

The fading marks reddened deeply as blood rushed to

her face. "It wasn't their fault, really, Lord Car—" she cut herself off. "Father." She paused. "I thought they were fading. They are fading, aren't they?"

"Of *course* they are," he assured her heartily, and cursed himself as she flinched. He took the confessor's chair, motioning for her to sit. "I think you've found the City is not the chamber of horrors you may have imagined back home."

"No, Father," she agreed. She waited.

After a moment, he said, "Hartley Quince tells me you're suffering a spiritual crisis . . . ?"

"Yes, Father."

"I trust you'll let me help you, Iolanthe. It is my job, you know." He made certain his voice was concerned, rational, even slightly amused; altogether reassuring.

Her eyes had been modestly down. Suddenly she raised them; the violet eyes that odes had been written to on the Opal, odes that her parents had never allowed her to read, but which the Lord Cardinal had read and filed. Violet eyes like an aesthetic blow. "Surely it can't be right, Father, to report on my husband to other people. Doesn't the Book say that husband and wife are one flesh, and the husband is the head?"

"My dear, troubled girl." He took her hand, holding it until she unclenched her fist. "First, the marriage ceremony has not yet taken place, has it? Second, isn't the hierarchy of husband and wife but a mirror of the hierarchy of priest and laity? Which itself is but a mirror of God's marriage with His people? And surely you can see, Iolanthe—I know you're an intelligent girl—that these three things themselves are ranked, and the husband/wife relationship is the lowest? And ought not the lower give way to the higher?"

She sighed. "I cannot argue with you, Father."

"I should hope you cannot," he said, a trifle surprised. "What has argument to do with Confession, or with any young girl's place?"

"I'm sorry, I don't express myself well."

He patted her hand. "Take your time, my dear. No hurry in the world."

The Lord Cardinal bore Iolanthe no ill will, and he could sympathize with the pressure the child was under.

She had her duty, and that could not be softened; but where he could give relief he would.

At last she said in a low voice, "I'm really not sure at all that you should have been called, Father. My silly ideas . . ."

"Not at all. No matter is trivial if it touches your duty, or your salvation. And as an old friend, I hope you believe me when I say that I would wish to know anything that disturbed you."

"I didn't really want to come *here*," said Io, looking around at the furnishings of the confessional room. "It's really not important. Hartley Quince insisted—"

"And rightly. We're assured of privacy here, child, and I think that that should be as reassuring to you as it is to me. Now, please, won't you tell me what's bothering you? I want to help." The Lord Cardinal was perfectly sincere, and perhaps this was his greatest weapon.

"It's about the Sawyer Crown."

Arno sat back. "I beg your pardon?"

The magnificent eyes, troubled, were raised to his again. "Father, Adrian believes the Sawyer Crown is on Baret Two, and he intends to get it for himself."

The silence in the confessional chamber was heavy. Then, slowly, the Lord Cardinal smiled. "My dear," he said, and his genuine affection showed in his voice, "the Protector was very likely joking with you. You're very young, and you take things so seriously, and young men do like to joke with their sweethearts. And boast, too." His smile broadened—not a cruel smile, for love mixed with amused condescension.

She said dully, looking down, "He didn't tell it to me. He didn't even know I was listening. He told it to his adviser of the sixteenth rank, Brandon Fischer."

Arno's smile faded. "Where did you hear this?" he asked, after a moment.

She told him, undramatically, reporting in dry tones her own indignity of listening in doorways. He was silent again. Then he said, "My dear, I absolve you from the sin of eavesdropping, and your doubts, and any other related matters. May I open my heart to you?"

The look on her face said she wished he wouldn't. "Of course, Lord Father."

He slid his large hands away from hers and stood. He tilted her chin up gently. "Iolanthe, my dear, this may not be serious at all. But what I would like you to do is keep very aware and alert around Adrian. Watch and listen, and let me know anything else you may learn that you think—or you even suspect—might bear on the matter. Would you do that for me, Iolanthe?"

"Yes, Lord Father." It would be difficult to sound less enthusiastic.

"Was that the only thing disturbing you?"

"Yes, Lord Father."

Arno presented her with his hand, which she kissed, signifying the sacramental part of the session was over. "I must return to the Opal immediately, I'm afraid. But I'm very glad you spoke to me. Don't hesitate at all, whenever you'd like to see me in the future, just speak to Hartley Quince."

She stood beside him, as tall as he was. "But, Lord Cardinal—" for now that the confession was over, she could address him by rank rather than spiritual relationship, and she was quick to do so, "—I thought you were going to stay on the Diamond until a new hierophant was assigned to us."

The Lord Cardinal looked surprised. "Who said that?"

"Hartley Quince."

"Ah. Yes, well, that was true, but some affairs have arisen at home that require my supervision." That much was perfectly honest. Seven sinners had been questioned by the EC Inquisitor, and five of them had asked for grace. The administrative details alone for such a purge could take untold man-hours. Nor had Arno given up on any of their souls, regardless of the shortness of the time or the amount of his other work. Nothing was worth the loss of a soul; a life was another matter.

He bid Iolanthe farewell at the door, and told her to trust in God, the friendship of the Lord Cardinal, and in Hartley Quince.

Who was waiting outside the confessional chamber, with Iolanthe's bodyguard. Arno commended her to his keeping and turned to Hartley.

"I must speak to you about this. Meet me in the *Wrathful Fire,* in Docking Bay Green."

Hartley nodded. "Serious?"

"It's possible."

They parted ways, the Cardinal much troubled in mind. One of the greatest sins a priest could commit was to reveal what was spoken in the confessional. But surely God could not mean for Adrian Mercati to have the Sawyer Crown, and steps would need to be taken. And besides, neither he nor Iolanthe had said the ritual words for a true confession.

This was a technicality, his heart said. He sighed. On my head be it, he thought; and in unconscious imitation of Iolanthe, he added mentally: Ideals can make people do terrible things.

Iolanthe was relieved on the following day when Will Stockton returned to the Diamond. He brought a new hierophant with him, and that pleased her, too. Iolanthe was under no illusions as to what Arno wanted of her. At one time she'd hoped to be valued for something beside an accident of beauty, but that no longer seemed to be a comfortable option.

She smiled when she found the sergeant standing outside her door like a familiar friend. Did people ever value him for his beauty, she wondered? "Hartley Quince told me you'd gone home to visit; I was afraid you would stay."

"I hardly have that choice, my lady."

He said it pleasantly enough, and as though they were friends; but he seemed to have no understanding of when he was supposed to lie gallantly.

Chapter 22

Keylinn:

I sat alone on a chair in an empty office on C deck, listening to the door unlock from outside. The room was sparsely furnished; there was a cot, a few print books that had been brought in from my personal supplies, and an entrance to a small recycler outlet. The lock on the inside had been removed.

"They tell me you won't eat," said Tal.

I looked up at him briefly, then off into the distance. No answer was called for.

He said, "I hope you've had time to recall that suicide would be a violation of contract. I have two hundred and eighty-five days left—"

"Two hundred and eighty." It was my first response.

"I think you're mistaken. Two hundred—"

"No."

"Well, we'll argue another time. I've brought you a bowl of bran-meal. It's foul-looking stuff, but they assure me it has all the nutrients."

I met his gaze, finally, but made no attempt to take the bowl. "When are you letting me out of here?"

"When I think it's a good idea. Let's say ... when you've eaten six meals in a row."

"What'll my supervisor in Transport say? I'll be thrown out."

"He's been notified you're on special assignment. Your assignment right now is to eat. Take the bowl."

I took it.

"Now put the spoon in, and start eating."

I swallowed one mouthful and took another. Through full cheeks I said, "I hate you. I hate you and me both."

Tal knelt down in front of the chair. "Then it's a good thing that that's not relevant to our contract." His voice was unfairly gentle.

I chewed and swallowed what felt like lumps of rubber.

"We'll chat again later," said Tal. He got up and went to the door. He unlocked it, stepped over the threshold, then stepped back in again. "I want you to keep on eating after I leave," he said specifically. "Keep eating until there's nothing left in the bowl."

I didn't reply, but then that wasn't necessary. Tal went away. I finished the bowl, noting in a detached way that my eyes continued to be bone-dry, as though I'd lost the knack of crying.

And as for this sociopathic Outsider, he was learning far too much about how to live with a Graykey.

* * *

I was released from captivity a few pounds lighter and
resumed shift-work on the Transport deck. The next few
weeks of the Three Cities calendar proceeded without incident. I acknowledged that I'd acted within contract and
honorably by Graykey standards; anything else was
buried in a shallow grave and I determined not to disturb
it. In time I went so far as to apologize to Tal "for any
difficulty," without specifying what that difficulty might
be or showing any inclination to discuss it.

But I was delighted when one day I found Ennis
Severeth Gilleys asking for me in Transport. "I'm released from contract, sister," he said, after we'd hugged
spectacularly, knocking over three mugs of coffee, "and
looking for honest work. Or any other kind. Could you
put me up here, do you think? It'd be nice to see a face
from home, you know."

"I don't have any pull with the supervisors here," I
warned.

"Ah, but you could try. I have great faith in you,
Keylinn O'Malley Murtagh. You know someone who
knows someone—who must know someone. And we're
practically comrades of the road, you know."

I laughed. "I know nothing of the kind." "Comrades of
the road" is a Graykey phrase referring to legendary he-
roes who shared adventures together. I hardly thought we
qualified.

But I went to see Tal in his secret office up in the high
decks. He looked up when I entered and raised an eyebrow, for it was unusual in those days for me to come
without being called.

"I want you to get a posting," I said, "for the other
Graykey from Baret Station. His name is Ennis Severeth
Gilleys, and he's waiting down in Transport now."

I realized somewhat belatedly that this was the first
personal desire he had ever heard me express. He put
down his papers and regarded me.

"I don't like to use my influence with Adrian. It calls
too much attention to me."

"But you do use it when it suits you."

"Yes." He ran a finger along a pen thoughtfully.
Thoughtfully how? I dipped briefly into *tarethi* water, try-

ing to extrapolate. He'd wanted me back up to speed, and
now here I was, not only talking to him but asking him
for a favor; which made him one point up in the Graykey
game. Nevertheless, he would be cautious. "This is the
Graykey you told me about who helped you get into the
Kestrel." He did not hesitate to say the name of the ship,
apparently unafraid that I might blanch or refuse food
again.

I said, "Yes, this is the one. He helped get you out, too."

"Does he have any reason to believe I'm an Aphean?"

I thought back to my checking of Tal's lenses while he
was unconscious. Ennis hadn't seen. "No. To the best of
my knowledge."

"But he may well hear things while he's here. And apparently Graykey have heard of Apheans, unlike most of
the rest of the universe. What happens when he leaves,
and mentions it to people?"

"He won't, if he takes an oath. I'll make him take it."

An oath from a Graykey is better than a raftload of
locks in the outside world; but Tal might not see it so. Although it would no doubt occur to him how easily Ennis
Severeth Gilleys might be gotten rid of in a Transport accident, if he seemed at all unreliable.

"This would be a favor, for you personally." It was not
a clarification, but a warning.

"I suppose it would."

The idea depressed me, and with reason. Tal smiled. I
wondered whether he was beginning to *like* me; there was
a frightening thought.

He said, "I'll see what I can do."

Section Three:
The False Knight On the Road

Chapter 23

The rat is the concisest tenant.
He pays no rent,—
Repudiates the obligation,
On schemes intent.

Balking our wit
To sound or circumvent,
Hate cannot harm
A foe so reticent.

Neither decree
Prohibits him,
Lawful as
Equilibrium.

EMILY DICKINSON

The last remains of winter turned to spring on the Diamond, at a daily median temperature of sixty-four degrees Fahrenheit as provided for by the Ministry of Climate Control. The internal heaters for individual residences were cut off on schedule on April 30. The temperature in homes and shops tended to remain a few degrees warmer even without the help, based on the size of the room and the number of people occupying it. Indoor capes came back into fashion on the upper levels, and jackets on the lower ones.

Techs taking a year or two's work on the Diamond were usually not happy with the slavish adherence to Earth cycles—most Cities techs were station-born, and had they wished to experience temperature variations they could have shipped out to a planet. Moreover, the use of a 24-hour day was particularly idiotic. Study after study had shown that the vast majority of humans had internal clocks that ran closer to 25 hours, and that in a long-term situation they adapted well to a 36-hour day with 10 hours of sleep. Baret Station used a 30-hour day, but at least they had the excuse of trying to match the natural cycle of Baret Two. The Diamond had nothing but tradition behind its calendar.

For the Diamond that was quite enough. From time to time troublemakers tried to explain that their seasons mirrored only a narrow bandwidth of old Earth's latitude (no one cared). There had been an alarming movement three centuries previously that attempted to establish a 25-hour day. But the Ecclesiastical Council had fought a successful holding action, pointing out that a currently reckoned lifetime of 80 years came to 29,220 24-hour days, but only 28,002.5 25-hour days. That reduction in one's allotted span stemmed from a fifteen-day loss each standard year, and massive rallies were held in Helium Park on the Diamond and Sawyer Square on Opal, protesting the loss of life. And so throughout the Cities people rose for their shifts, splashed water on their faces, and looked at the deep circles under their eyes as their ancestors had throughout Earth's history. They would have fought any other way.

Had they been consulted, there was one group that might have disagreed with these cycles, or at least the seasonal side of them. The ghosts, as always, had had a hard winter.

Eight of them gathered now in a makeshift room of sheetrock and plastic, on a ghost road that ran from H deck to G. The ghost roads were abandoned and forgotten corridors, maintenance runs, and freight tunnels, many of them not used since the original colonization of the Diamond; employed then for the setup of Curosa technology and for bringing cargo onboard, and now deserted.

They had not dared to build a fire all winter long, for fear that an automatic would respond somewhere and bring this road to the attention of the authorities. The purpose of the homemade hut was to conserve body heat. Nicolet, their leader, sat on a box eating from a container of rice and beans one of his followers had brought. Nicolet was in his early thirties, with a brown beard and brown eyes. He dressed in the same shabby stolen clothing the other ghosts did. But he was not as skinny as the others, for his tithe as ghost king was a choice of one-fourth of all food brought in each day. He was "king" only of his group of twenty, a number that changed as his subjects died or were captured or found new recruits.

They treasured him. Nicolet's number had come up for the recycler long ago, almost in prehistory; not the radiation levels, but a straight black card in the felons' lottery, a body sent to balance the food production with the population of that year. He was the longest-lived ghost on the Diamond, so far as anyone knew; the most expensive, with the biggest price on his head; and he knew every road and every trick that would get them through another day. Nicolet had been a ghost for eight years.

Tealeaf, a beautiful black-haired, almond-eyed woman of about twenty, sat with her head on his knees. They were not lovers. It was only that the boundaries of physical distance became different for ghosts than it was for the rest of the Diamond. After they had slept against each other and held each other through the heaves from bad food and fought with each other, physically, again and again, the formalities became alien.

The rice and beans belonged to Tealeaf. When he reached the one-quarter mark, he would hand it back to her. Nicolet was scrupulous about that—he never took a free spoonful. A man with the highest price a ghost ever bore could not afford to open himself to criticism.

"Here," he said now, and shook his knee slightly. She looked up and took the container from him, and also the spoon. There were three spoons among them, and every now and then they actually managed to get them washed. Water was scarce. Nicolet (historian of ghosts) said that for a while two years ago they'd thought they'd found a treasure in the form of a water-tank on J, but they noticed that the ghosts who swam there got sick and often died. More often than usual. It was another place-to-be-avoided.

All eight people in the hut were excommunicated by the Church, and considered themselves damned.

Fox and the Salamander sat nearby, sharing a stew that had been reconstructed from the garbage of The Green Man, that Nicolet had chosen to pass up. They ate with their hands, not willing to wait. The Salamander was in many ways the craziest of the ghosts. He provoked fights with citizens, stole food and clothing with a boldness bordering on insanity, and was in general a sign of the existence of God by his very survival, which was inexplicable any other way. He often told them the legend of the Salamander, that it was a creature so poisonous the very ground it had walked on was lethal. He gloried in that. The Salamander had never pulled a king of spades in the lottery, and never been in line for the radiation levels; he was simply wanted for murder. "Go to hell with the best," said the Salamander to his fellow damned souls, and by the best he clearly meant himself.

Now he looked up at Nicolet, stew smeared on his swarthy face and hands. "Saw Spider today," he commented.

Nicolet became very still. Tealeaf moved away from him.

Nicolet said, "I guess you mean you were above G level today, Salamander. Taking risks as usual. Because if you saw that fucking traitor below G, and didn't kill him or bring him to me, I'm going to bash your fucking head in."

"Saw him on the train," said the Salamander. "Don't know where he was going."

"He looked well-fed, I'm sure," said Nicolet.

The Salamander grunted.

"We aren't trying hard enough to get that son of a bitch," said Nicolet. "There are twenty of us. He has to come through the underdecks now and then. If I find out you let him escape—"

"It's the truth," said Tealeaf. "He was on the train." She gazed into the distance, her eyes wide and empty. Tealeaf was a rare ghost—she was here to escape charges of witchcraft. But she was no witch, thought Nicolet for the thousandth bitter time. She knew nothing of healing and forbidden medicine. She was a truthsayer, and should have been chosen as an Oracle long ago and taken to Pearl. But the upper deck searchers made no great effort to find Oracles below G. Now it was too late, and if she were captured she'd be executed as a ghost—by witchfire, if some of the priests had their way.

"All right," he said more gently. "He was on the train.
But he won't always be, and I don't want anybody to
miss him."

Fox, who should have known better, said, "I don't get
it, Nicolet. How could Spider have betrayed us? He knew
lots of the ghost roads—he knew the one we're in right
now, and nobody's ever come to get us. Why do you
always—"

His question was cut off by a blow to the head that sent
him sprawling and spilled the last of the stew.

"Nobody gets out of the recycler line except by betrayal," said Nicolet, breathing hard with anger. "Nobody
but a riff gets a cushy job in admin and their name taken
off the lottery list. You ever known it to be different? You
dumb son of a . . . but then, you two were friends, weren't
you?"

"Not really. We went on some runs together, is all."

"No?"

"No."

Nicolet walked around him, still clearly smoldering.
Nobody else spoke. Nicolet said, "It'd be nice for those
riffs to have an insider here. Maybe they'd like to wait
and get us all in one big sweep. Maybe one night when
we're all here, you're planning to creep away and get a
job and a uniform yourself. . . ."

"I'm not! It's not true!"

Fox started to rise with fear and indignation. Nicolet
put out one shabbily booted foot and pushed him down
again, not roughly. "Your highness," he said.

"It's not true, your highness," said Fox immediately.
Fox was well aware that Nicolet could order him to be
held down and have his skin pulled off in strips. The natural pain and poverty of the ghosts' lives had made them
reach some for punishments. He'd often heard Nicolet
hoping aloud that Spider could be brought in alive.

"I haven't seen him, I barely knew him, I never liked
him," wailed Fox.

Nicolet looked disgusted. "Oh, get up." He sat down
on his box and pulled his ragged quilted jacket tighter
around his shoulders. By the will of the Providence that
damned them, there were far fewer heating outlets on the

ghost roads. It was going to be another cold and shivery
night.

Fox quietly crept to the edge of the circle. Cold and
hungry he might be, but he would rather be Fox than Spider.

Chapter 24

A noticeboard on Mercati Boulevard, at F deck:

$8,000 $8,000 $8,000
EIGHT THOUSAND DOLLARS!
For information leading to the arrest of
NICOLET FOULARD
the Notorious Ghost
Murderer
and Thief
Report to your nearest Citycop Station.

The Starhall Theater presents
BECKET
A historical drama of Old Earth
taken from the personal library
of the Protector
May 12 through 24

The Hall of the Kennorite Brotherhood
of Strict Constructionists presents,
for the edification of the faithful,
a display of the recent burning of Opal
heretics. A talk will be given by Opal
guest Hierophant Tennyson under the
sponsorship of The League for Religious
Tolerance on the Diamond.
Kennorism is not a heresy but the true
path of light as originally laid down by
Adrian Sawyer. Don't be misled.
(Thanks to our brothers on Opal for

permission to show these. Free still-
pictures will be distributed afterward.
Tea and cake will be served.)

INTERESTED IN JOINING THE LUCRATIVE IMPORT-EXPORT BUSINESS?
Send a note with short background descrip., interests
to linkbox #4523988-00094.

Keylinn:

I stopped short several footsteps from the noticeboard.
Then I went back and checked that last linkbox number
again.

It was one of the numbers Spider had given me for getting in touch with him during an emergency.

Well. I continued on my way, pondering whether Spider might simply be constitutionally unable to stay out of
trouble. Could that sort of thing be genetic? And for a
person of natural sloth, Spider could be remarkably energetic when money was involved.

I reached the Starhall Theater and showed the admittance card Howard Talmadge had given me. Rehearsal
sounds were coming from the stage, so I entered by the
front door and slouched down in one of the seats till they
were finished. Spider didn't seem to be anywhere around,
but possibly he was backstage.

I let my mind wander, from Spider to Tal to the time
remaining in my contract, when suddenly my attention
was caught by the action on stage. This was interesting.
A mistake? I sat up straight, listening. I paid close attention for another quarter-hour, until they broke, and until I
eventually became aware that someone had sat down in
the seat next to me.

"I thought I saw you come in," said Howard Talmadge.

"Hello, Howard."

"What do you think of the play?"

"Interesting," I told him with sincerity. "But I thought
your historicals were mostly Shakespeare and Ayscough
and Gleisner."

"Usually they are. Jason—our manager—thought we

should have a change, and that if we picked something from Adrian's personal library it'd add a bit of cachet to the proceedings."

"It was his idea?"

"Pretty much. Anyway, Jason likes any excuse for funny clothes—he says it brings in the paying customers."

I said, "Is Spider hiding somewhere backstage? He said he would meet me here."

"He told me the same thing, and I've not seen him. I thought maybe he'd sent you in his place. He didn't give you anything for me, did he?"

"I'm afraid not."

"Ah," said Howard, disappointed but obviously wishing to be polite. "Well, Spider can be less than punctual at times."

I debated saying anything, then asked, "You don't think he might be in some kind of trouble, do you? I have the impression he has enemies."

For a moment Howard looked genuinely alarmed, then he laughed. "Spider was born slippery. Trouble can't hold him. And I wouldn't worry about his being late—not until he's more than three days late. Until then, this is all perfectly normal ... for our Spider. Give him my regards when you see him."

I stood up, and Howard walked me to the door. "You'll be coming to the performance, I hope," he said.

"I wouldn't miss it. You know, it's odd, because I have absolutely no ambitions in the area myself—but I find that good dialogue, well-spoken by fine actors, is one of the chief pleasures of life."

"The other pleasures of your life must be wretched indeed," said Howard with sympathy, as he held open the door for me to pass.

Perhaps it was Howard's parting remark rankling in my shirt pocket, but I decided to take Ennis up on his invitation to the Traveler's Bar. The Traveler's was an Outsider tech place, just off the working area of the Transport deck, and within the radius of Ennis's very limited pass. Tal had refused to even consider giving him a free-range.

Which led to some guilt on my part. Transport Deck

and Outsider Territory were a sort of prison to Ennis, and I knew from personal experience that spatial limits could be a continual torment for people like us. I really ought to spend more time with him . . . but I was so busy, dammit.

I sent a link-message ahead, and by the time I reached the Traveler's he was waiting.

"Hello, big sister," he said, bending over to kiss me on the cheek.

"Little troublesome brother," I said, taking a seat in the booth.

Ennis stretched his legs under the table. "I've just come from a double shift, sis, because one of the regulars on the third had the bad grace to die."

There was not a great deal of camaraderie among the Outsiders. They barely knew each other, and one and all believed that this was a temporary assignment, taken for the cash, no matter how many years they'd thrown into this hellhole.

"And the supervisor chose you? For your heavy technical experience?"

Ennis grinned. He'd required a certain amount of coaching to qualify for his position. "For the charm of my speech," he said. "I made an unfortunate reference to her appearance one day when she criticized my speed."

I sighed. "Oh, cuz. It's just a short-term assignment for you, isn't it? You've said you're going back to the Station once you put away a little more money. Can't you just hang on till then? Without annoying people, I mean?" I took a sip of the drink he'd snagged for me. "You're far too much like my own family—always in trouble." I looked up. "This isn't soda."

"No, I think it's whiskey."

I pushed it away. "Troublemaker. You know I don't drink."

"Then you're the only Graykey I ever met who doesn't."

"Not on assignment, I mean." I heard my voice drop and I must have looked embarrassed. I didn't like to speak of the contract.

"And how is your honorable *tarethi-din?*"

"Well, thanks."

He pushed the drink back toward me. "One sip won't put you over the edge."

I ignored it. "Ennis, are you happy here?"

"What do you mean?" He looked startled.

"Well, your last contract didn't turn out so well—that's just my impression, I'm not going to ask you about it if you don't want to talk—and then you show up on the Diamond hoping for a little time with somebody from home. And I haven't had much of that for you. I'm sorry."

Ennis looked down at the table. Was he blushing? I probably shouldn't have brought up his contract. "I didn't mean—" I began.

"I'm fine," he said. "I'm fine. But my days are of surpassing tedium. And since you're here now, O daughter of the O'Malleys and Murtaghs, maybe you could entertain me."

"I don't sing or dance."

He drained his own drink. "Tell me about the Diamond," he said.

I'd wanted to talk of home. "It's a big city. Do you want to hear about the language, the fashions, or the decor?"

"The legends."

"Ah. You want to hear about Deirdre of the Twelve? Or dive way back to the Curosa, and the animals going in two by two?"

"The Curosa . . . I was reading something about them just last night. About the Curosa leaving sacred objects behind for their converts, stuff for them to stumble over in a thousand years or so. You sure a beer would be too much, little sister?"

"No, thanks. . . . A thousand years or so? The only Curosa legacy I heard of that hasn't already been found would be the Sawyer Crown. I had no idea you were a scholar."

He smiled modestly.

I left early and decided, for no well-defined reason, to see whether Tal was in his office. Being with Ennis was not as much fun as I'd hoped when he came onboard.

Chapter 25

Spider had been delayed from visiting the Starhall Theater by the power of his own curiosity—usually an indolent force, but once roused, implacable in its effects on him. He had a stronger stash than ever before, thanks to his successes in siphoning inventory products, and it had occurred to him for the first time in his life that he could afford to buy an Oracle.

He was loath to spend any money on something that wasn't tangible, yet the thought kept teasing him. He was sitting in Tal's office, in Tal's chair, looking at Tal's link. It was a remarkably well-set-up link, with all sorts of access and communications capabilities. He couldn't get into most of it, but all it took for an Oracle was a connection to the City of Pearl and the transfer of money; and that he could do. And consider the privacy! If there were anyplace on the Diamond he would swear wasn't wired, it had to be Tal's office. Tal would've jammed any bugs long ago—he had no hesitation about using Outsider technology.

No, it was a silly idea. But— No.

Well— He activated the communications for a voice link, dropping a twenty-dollar piece into the link's maw.

"City of Pearl, please. I'd like an Oracle."

There was a pause, and then a voice said, "Of what standard?"

"What do you mean, of what standard?"

The voice rattled off, "Prophetic, Inspired, High Professional, Middle Professional, Low Professional, Journeyman, Retired."

"Good heavens." He cleared his throat. "I want the best."

"Prophetic," said the voice. "Please deposit ten thousand dollars. We will await receipt."

"Wait! Ah, how much is 'Inspired'?"

There was another pause. The voice said, with some
disdain, "How much do you have?"

Spider would have liked to wipe that tone out of the
voice, but he refused to be snubbed into letting go of
good hard cash. "What's your cheapest?"

"*Least expensive.* And it's 'Retired.' At a rate of one
hundred dollars per hour."

"I'll take that, then."

It warned, "You'll be charged for an hour even if you
take five minutes."

Spider counted out two fifty pieces. "Hear that? That's
your money coming through."

There was brief static. He wondered if they'd taken his
hundred dollars and cut him off. Then a querulous old-
lady's voice, a little like his mother's but much, much
older, stated: "This had better be good. I believe I was
working on a royal flush when you called."

"Good Lord," said Spider involuntarily.

"There's no need for profanity. Do you know what a
royal flush is?"

"Yes," said Spider, who knew very well. "I beg your
pardon—"

"And so you should."

"No—I mean—I beg your pardon, but are you really
an Oracle?"

There was silence at the other end. "Ho-hum, so be it,"
said the crone at last. Her tone swelled in intensity.
"Gather, powers that bless and curse—" The com's
speaker started to shake gently with the reverberation.
"Terror of night, terror of darkness, terror of the lost
way—"

"Wait a minute—" he choked out.

"Terror of the plucking of the eyes—"

"I'm sorry, I'm sorry, I'm sorry!"

There was a pause, and the voice said, like a shopkeeper, "What is it you want, then?"

He swallowed. "I have a question. Do—ah—do I have
to tell you what it is, or can you answer without knowing."

"I'm a tool of the Most High. Of course I can answer
without knowing. I won't, though. I'm nosy."

"Well . . . and I'd prefer you didn't answer this in blank

verse or anything ... will the business venture I'm planning be successful?"

"Yes."

He blinked. "Just yes?"

"You said you didn't want a confusing answer. Was
that all you wanted to know?"

"Well, ah—"

"No. She doesn't."

"Oh," he said humbly.

"She respects and esteems you as a friend."

"Oh. All right, then—"

"And she's not going to change her mind in a million
years."

"*I said all right!*" He took a deep breath. "I don't have
any more questions."

"Sure you do, and I'll be happy to answer them. But
tell me, first, is it true? My thumbs tell me that you're a
friend of ghosts and demons."

"Uh, what makes you say that?" There was a rather
disturbing silence at the other end. Spider said hastily,
"Just one demon, so far as I know."

"Thought so. I see him in my hand; his heart's an in-
land sea, it touches no other continents."

"That would be him," Spider agreed.

"Well, you're the first I've ever met to have such popularity," said the old-lady voice, "and I've been around a
long time. You must have good stories to tell."

Spider thought of the uncountable nights he'd woken
up and had to change his sheets. "To somebody else, they
might be good stories."

"Good enough, I'll bet, little bug. If ever you come to
the Pearl, ask to see Granny Tate. I'll show you around."

"All right." Spider was raised to be polite. Nobody
ever went to the Pearl to visit, and he had no intention of
starting a trend.

"You have our blessing."

"I do? Does this mean—"

"And as long as we're talking, no, your mother's not
going to die anytime soon. And she always knew about
that escapade when you were fourteen." Spider blanched
and reached up to deactivate the link. "Don't be so hasty!
Don't you want to hear about Nicol—"

It broke on the name. He grabbed frantically for the button to reactivate, but she was gone.

He started counting out money, pushing his coins out over the surface of the desk with a desperate air—maybe he could get her back—and the door slid open. He jumped.

"Where the hell have you been?" asked Keylinn.

"Oh, it's you." He took a deep breath, then frowned. "Must you say 'hell'?" He began scooping up money pieces and putting them back in his catchbag.

"Everybody else says it."

"But not ladies, sweetheart."

"You know, I had noticed that. One of the things I love about the Three Cities is the archaic speech patterns—of course, profanity and proverbs hang on longest all over the universe, but the Cities are special." She threw herself onto the couch. "And they won't let me participate! All this colorful talk, and I can only press my nose against the window."

This was a saying that made no sense to Spider. "Press your *nose?*"

"The thing I don't grasp is, there's an emotional effect in actually using the words that goes beyond the knowledge of their use. You see? I mean, I can refer obliquely to certain terms, or say that somebody else—or even myself—'swore like a soldier.' And people are amused. But when I open my mouth and say 'fuck' or 'shit' or 'cocks—' "

"Keylinn!" Spider put his hands over his ears. She saw that he was genuinely upset.

"I'm sorry, Spider, I'll try not to say it again. But we curse at home all the time, in the Old Tongue, and it really seems most unfair that I can't curse here."

"You're a *lady,*" said Spider.

"If you ask me, the female contingent of the Diamond has more need of tension release than anybody."

"That's not the point."

"What *is* the point?"

Spider put a hand to his forehead. At this moment he didn't know the point. He felt around on the desktop and his hand touched an envelope. "Here," he said with relief. "This is for you."

It was a stiff, square envelope, with *Keylinn Gray* in beautiful gold script on the outside. She opened it. A large buff-colored card proclaimed,

Adrian Mercati
The Diamond Protector

requests the honor
of the presence of

Keylinn Gray

for a hunt in Helium Park
Sunday, May 5
9:00 am
Refreshments to be served afterward.

A smaller, ivory-colored card dropped out. Spider picked it up and read aloud from a large, slanting hand: "The honor of your presence is also requested for a walk through the kennels beforehand, at 8:30."

They looked at each other. Why her? That blank space below her name seemed to call out for a title she did not possess. Clearly she was not the usual class of recipient for this sort of thing.

She said, "*This* came *here?*"

"A messenger brought it."

"Wearing court livery?"

"Wearing a messenger's uniform."

Her eyes grew distant, running through the possibilities. "Tomorrow's Sunday the fifth. If we assume the invitation is genuine, it could be Adrian's little message to Tal that he keeps close tabs on us all ... but then maybe Tal arranged it for me on his own ... but why, what does he want me to do? And Tal would send it to my quarters."

She was too preoccupied to notice Spider jump again.

A voice had just spoken to him, a little too loudly for comfort given the setting of his riccardi.

It said, *Spider, I won't be coming down there tonight, but I need some papers. They're the ones marked "Official Schedule for Opal Visitors." I'll send a messenger, so have them gathered together to hand him when he ar-*

rives. They're in the pile by the door—you'll need to look through it to find the right ones. Keylinn can help you if she's around.

"Hasn't he ever heard of a link-message?" inquired Spider of his God. When Keylinn looked at him he said, "I just heard from Tal—"

"I know. 'Official Schedule for Opal Visitors.' "

He stared at her. "You, too?" Then he shook his head and walked over to the pile, squatted down, and began pulling off the top papers. "Next thing you know he'll chain us up when we're not on duty."

Keylinn joined him. "We're always on duty, Spider."

"Speak for yourself."

"I do," she said.

Chapter 26

The essence of Graykey ambition derives from the following logical steps. One: The purpose of life is to gather knowledge. Two: The only real knowledge is bone-knowledge. The aim, therefore, is to gain as much bone-knowledge as possible. There is a Graykey saying: The gathering of tarethi is a selfish act.

Graykey rarely admit to any personal leanings, so it is difficult for the observer to tell how serious they are in their references to reincarnation. The idea behind it seems to be that, given the ridiculously finite human lifespan, sufficient tarethi simply cannot be accumulated. It is only by experiencing innumerable lives, subject to all sorts of influences, that true bone-knowledge may be gained.

The contract, when fully entered into, is a way for a Graykey to experience another life without having to die and be reborn.

> *Thus the term* "tarethi-din," *often mistranslated as* "contract-holder." *In fact, the word can apply to both contract-holder and Graykey equally, and literally means* "sharer(s) in bone-knowledge."

from CAUDLANDER'S
A Tourist Guide to the Graykey

Keylinn:

I found the kennels in a far corner of Helium Park. The stables were next door—wood and brick glowing mellow in the faux-morning-sunlight, horses being brought in and out by boys in old shirts and rolled trousers. Evidently the fastidiousness of the court dress code did not extend to those who cared for their animals. The smells here were overwhelmingly organic, disorganized, and openly disagreeable—so much, in fact, *what they were,* that I couldn't help breathing in deeply, letting the pleasure of it tease my Graykey roots.

There were more boys and men, and an occasional casually dressed woman, inside the kennels. It was very easy to spot Adrian. He stood midway down the aisle, barkings and yappings coming from all sides, straw falling out onto the cleared boards of the floor. He wore a dark blue shirt, a cape of the same shade, and black breeches with high boots. You had no sense of his being alien, however, to this environment; on the contrary, he looked almost annoyingly at home. It couldn't be the identity-shifting of a Graykey, so it must be the confidence of a strong ego. He squatted down as I watched and began unself-consciously addressing a small black and white dog.

"And how are you coming along, Davy? I see that nasty cut is clearing up." By now Davy had pushed his head and snout into Adrian's hand and began buffeting it until Adrian patted back. "No, I didn't bring any treats. You know that Thomas gets mad at me when I do that." The dog went on buffeting him, apparently sure of an easy mark. Adrian chuckled and stroked him, head to back, so that the tail started thumping like a piston. "You can't be so obvious, Davy, it's bad manners—"

He glanced up, caught sight of me and rose, giving the dog a final pat to show it was nothing personal. Davy ignored this change in behavior and tried to twine himself around the Protector's ankles. "Miss Gray," said Adrian. "I'm very glad you could come."

I felt slightly embarrassed at having walked in on him in a private moment. "Thank you for your invitation." And what did someone of my rank call him, anyway? It was proper to refer to him by his given name when speaking in the third person. Now that I'd moved up to second person, did the rules change? "Forgive me, I have no wish to offend, but I'm not sure how to address you."

"Sir is always acceptable," he said, without a trace of embarrassment on his part. "And so is Adrian. If you weren't living on the Diamond, and a temporary subject, then it would be 'Protector.' "

I was on my guard at once. Was I a temporary subject? They hadn't made me take any oaths yet, except the oath to do no physical damage while here. "Well, then, Adrian — thank you for the invitation. It took me by surprise."

"I've been meaning to have a talk with you ever since that little incident at Baret Station."

All my shields went up. Just at that moment Tal emerged from the room at the far end of the kennel, and for once I could read his face. If Adrian's invitation had taken me by surprise, it was coming as an absolute shock to him.

Then his shields went up, too, and he moved quickly to join us. "Tech Gray, isn't it?" he inquired with distant politeness. "How nice to see you again. Are you sightseeing?"

"I invited her to the hunt," said Adrian, and the smugness in his voice was palpable to both of us. I forced myself *not* to see how Tal was dealing with it.

"When was this?" asked Tal.

"Last evening," said Adrian. "We were so busy going over the records, I must have forgotten to mention it."

"I see."

Adrian began walking the length of the kennel, and we followed. He said, "Miss Gray, perhaps I should mention that we have riding habits available here should you wish to change."

I looked down at my sweater and trousers in surprise. "Isn't this all right for riding?"

"Perfectly. But I think you'll find none of the other ladies will be wearing similar clothes. I only mention it if you *wish* to change; I find that many people take a comment from the Protector as an order. It was not meant to be so."

I was beginning to feel out-mannered and out-classed on all sides. And there was only one of him! "Uh, thank you, sir. I'd be more comfortable in this outfit."

He nodded serenely. Tal said, "We seem to be being followed."

I turned, and Adrian laughed. Davy was trailing him down the aisle, narrowly missing his boots. He bent over and scooped up the little dog, deposited him in the crook of his arm, and walked back to the place he'd found him. There he kissed Davy on the top of his head, getting a pink, wet lick in the process, and set him down on the inside of the gate.

Tal looked at me. I started to whisper, but he shook his head. Adrian returned to us.

"An old friend," he explained. "Shall we go?"

"By all means," muttered Tal. We walked. I stole looks at my two companions, who were examining the floor with identical expressions of innocence.

At last Adrian turned to me. "Miss Gray," he began.

He was interrupted by a shout: "Goddammit!" said a man's voice. "Can't you do anything right?"

"Thomas?" called Adrian. "Is there a problem?"

There was a moment of startled silence, then Thomas's voice replied: "No, sir! Not at all, sir! Please stay where you are!"

Well. As though *that* line ever worked on any human born. We all peered around the bend at the end of the stalls to see what was happening.

An ugly little brown dog—so different from the trim, well-proportioned, dappled harriers we'd seen so far—was dancing nervously at the far end, his teeth sunk into the arm-guard of a teenage boy in coveralls. A short, gray-haired man in boots (Thomas, I assumed) stood nearby looking disgusted.

As I watched, the dog dropped his hold on the arm-guard and backed away from his victim. Neither the dog nor the human seemed happy. Thomas said, "*Two* sorry examples of stupidity through overbreeding." The dog's head and tail drooped, mortification in every line; the boy protested, "It's not my *fault*, Uncle!"

"Whose fault is it? Didn't I tell you he wasn't for training?"

"I wasn't training him!"

"No, you were creeping up behind him with the water dish, and you know he's got nerves like paper strips. Brains! I told my sister we need brains, not relatives! God *damn* it!"

He caught sight of us and stopped dead. He ducked his head politely toward Adrian and at once said, "I beg your pardon! I didn't expect you'd have a lady with you, sir! Forgive me, madam!"

I nodded back as graciously as I could, wondering: For what?

Adrian said, "This is the troublemaker you mentioned?" I gathered he was referring to the dog, not the boy.

Thomas said, tiredly, "Sired off a Nevsky at last planet-call. I told them it was a mistake, but you know the committee—all for experimentation, since Grace Dugan took over. He's too nervous to train, he ignores the pack half the time and wanders off by himself—he lives in a world of his own. If you ask me, Adrian, he's barely aware he's a dog."

I found the thought amusing, but Adrian didn't smile. He said, "Are you giving up on him, Thomas?"

"An inch away from it, sir."

I said, "What happens if you give up on him? Does he become a pet?"

Thomas looked at me as though I'd lost my mind. Tal spoke up clearly, filling in the silence. "He lacks the aesthetic to be a lady's pet and the training to be a gentleman's. And he bites in moments of confusion."

"So do I," I said.

"In short, he has a glorious destiny as someone's dinner," finished Tal, in a voice which was not quite bored, although what it was, was hard to say.

I was taken by surprise. "You eat dogs here?"

Fortunately, the note of shock drowned most of the accusation in my voice. One does not enter into a partnership of allies with another species and then *eat* it. It was un-Graykey.

No one else seemed startled at the idea, though. Adrian said, "We certainly don't eat our pets, Miss Gray, but I see no reason why an untrainable animal should have more claim on our mercy than one brought up for slaughter. He's had a good life here; I can assure you that Thomas treats all the dogs most humanely."

Humane had always struck me as an interesting word. However—

"May I have a few minutes, sir? Five or ten?"

He was too well-bred himself to show great surprise. "If you like. To what purpose?"

"I want to meet the dog."

He confined himself to raising an eyebrow, then shrugged and gestured: Be my guest.

Thomas, who was looking at me with a more open lack of confidence, said, "His name's Champ, madam. Wishful thinking."

"Thank you, but I don't want to use his name. Would you mind standing over there where he can't see you? And ask your nephew to move as well?"

They did so, their dour expressions showing them to be exceptionally unthrilled with this invasion of amateurs in their domain. I approached slowly until I was about ten feet from the dog, then stopped and squatted down. I held out one hand, palm open and down, fingers relaxed. "Here, sweetheart," I called softly. "Over here, darling. Come on . . ."

Tal and Adrian watched. This could be quite embarrassing. Still, that wasn't the point.

After a moment I heard Adrian say quietly, "She's a Graykey, isn't she?"

He was addressing Tal, but it broke my concentration. I heard the faint note of surprise (false surprise?) in Tal's reply. "Why do you say that?"

"The mark below her wrist. It's a Graykey symbol."

Well, I'd heard that Adrian read voraciously, and unstoppably, about the Outside. And the next question was, *Do you have her contract?*

Adrian didn't ask it. He said, "You did know that she's a Graykey?"

"Yes."

I closed them out, bringing myself back to the neverending seeking of *tarethi,* the imperative to change and retain, the knowledge that nothing in the universe was alien to me.

By now I had left Three Cities and Standard behind, and was calling softly to the dog with every endearment of the Old Tongue. I tried not to move a muscle, though my legs were cramping. "Come my own one, come my fair one, the delight of my heart. Come now, most beautiful. Come. Everything will be all right if you come. I won't let anyone hurt you, I promise. Come here now, moon of the night . . ."

"We could be here all day," said Tal.

"Shh," said Adrian.

And the awkward, suspicious little being came very tentatively and sniffed my outstretched fingers. I kept still, and kept talking. He came in closer, and very slowly, letting him see my hand move, I touched a spot at the side of his chin and gently stroked it. Then I trailed the hand to the top of his head—not leaving the soft coat, for there must be no surprises—and behind his ears, and by now he'd moved in closer and my other hand was working symmetrically. A minute later I was hugging him, and his tail was pounding the floor like a drumbeat. "There you are, sweetheart. There you are."

"You've made a conquest," said Adrian.

I looked up to see him standing beside us. "I've made a friend, I hope." The dog seemed to shy away from this new presence, and I had to reassure him with my hands. "It's all right, sweetheart."

The dog's eyes looked at me wildly, and I smiled and touched my nose to his. "I said it's all right. Trust me."

"I see your point," said Adrian, "but if all his training takes this long, he'll be a loss as a hunter or a pet."

"I'd like to buy him," I said.

"None of the dogs here are for sale; they're held in public trust. Besides, you could never afford to cover what we paid to bring the sire uphill."

"A minute ago you were going to make a dinner of him, sir."

"An expensive dinner, Miss Gray. Funds to go to the Treasury. I'm sorry, but we sell no living thing of the Diamond to Outsiders. Policy."

The tail was still lashing. Two paws planted themselves against my thigh and a rough tongue reached for my face. "I'd like to pay for his upkeep, then, out of my salary. There's no harm in keeping him as long as I can pay his way, is there?"

"I suppose not," said Adrian, with a touch of annoyance he seemed to regret at once. What an irritating Outsider I must be; hardly the best of guests. He bit his lip, bowed, and said, "Of course you can. We'll consider him unofficially yours. And if you'd like, I can get you a pass to visit the kennels as often as you wish. Generally the public isn't allowed in—they only get to see the occasional show."

"I see. Yes, thank you, Adrian, I'd be very grateful."

I couldn't help beaming at him. Finally he shook his head and smiled back.

The mounts had been brought out, and most of the party were gathered by the hill just beyond the stables. Adrian introduced "Miss Gray" all around. Iolanthe Pelagia was there, resplendent in a gold-and-black riding habit . . . so this was Adrian's betrothed. A Sergeant Stockton sat uncomfortably beside her, looking out of place on a horse. He had the unhappy expression I tended to associate with bodyguards at open social functions; I hoped that I didn't give off a similar aura.

This Hartley Quince, however, seemed very much at home. His seat was graceful, and he smiled at me, stroking the neck of his mount with an air of open, athletic pleasure in the day. He was a figure out of a painting, with Renaissance curls and a courtier's face, gently featured and sensitive to nuance. I distrusted him at once. Then I questioned my own reaction; I'd been spending ten minutes of every day in subjectivity sessions focused on Tal's *tarethi,* and I was beginning to suspect that Tal was not fully sane by human standards.

Adrian said, "You have a very gentle mount, Miss

Gray. We weren't sure of your experience. Brandon will be nearby if you get into any difficulty." Brandon Fischer bowed slightly from his perch on a massive chestnut.

"Thank you, Adrian. I've ridden at home. The saddles, I admit, are new to me." And the horses' manes looked strange, trimmed and braided.

There were a half-dozen other riders; mostly knights, I gathered, from the devices on their capes, piloting animals now instead of battle-capsules. They gawked at me to greater or lesser degree, and I began to suspect I was the only orphan of admin here among the glitter. Perhaps I should have taken Adrian up on his hint and changed clothes. Too late now. I felt like something between a zoo animal and a hired acrobat.

I was offered a swarm of names by the Protector, polite host that he was. Well, I could always surprise him later by repeating them all back to him while juggling oranges.

There was a mounting block at the end. As I stepped up on it, Hartley Quince maneuvered closer to me. With an open smile he said, "Would you consider tagging along with me, Miss Gray? I can promise you I'm more conversible than Fischer, and I have the advantage of pre-conquest. I've been longing to meet you."

That startled me so badly I nearly lost my balance climbing up on the mare the stableboy held for me. (A ladies' mare, too, gold and white stripes, the sign of an engineered temperament; what a humiliation *that* would have been.)

"Jewel," said the stable boy, giving me her name a bit distrustfully. Quince grinned, the wicked glint in his eyes clashing nicely with his bland smile.

He'd poked that stick at me purposely. There was something in Quince's style that reminded me of Adrian; perhaps they were some sort of distant cousins? I needed to do more research on the kinship networks around here.

A man came out of another set of buildings on the opposite side of the stables, bearing a hooded bird on his arm. I'd heard about this sort of thing, but never seen it. Surely the falcon would simply fly away once it was released . . . on the other hand, where could it go? I watched as the bird was transferred to Adrian. Apparently nobody else was getting one.

I risked a glance at Tal, who was watching Iolanthe—
Adrian's betrothed was in the process of putting as many
riders as possible between herself and Adrian's demon. I
felt myself smile and looked down, forcing it back. My
sense of humor had gotten me into trouble before. Tal, I
saw, did not find it funny; but then Tal would let vultures
tear out his liver before he let an honest expression cross
his face, at least in the presence of enemies.

Hartley Quince moved near Adrian, placed a hand on
his bridle and said, "Tell me, is this the place where the
Royal Hunt is held? I hate to put my faith in gossip."
Several of the knights shot him hateful looks. He went
on, "Of course, I've never seen one, but I understand the
entire Park is closed off. It must be a massive undertaking."

If he'd hoped to disconcert Adrian by a reference to his
own death, he was disappointed. From what I'd read, the
Mercati had not been born who was socially uncomfortable. Adrian smiled and added, "You must come by after
I do attend one. I'll let you know what it was like."

And then the dogs were released.

The pace was not quick at first. The dogs snuffled
happily around, glad to be out and stretching their legs.
None of the riders seemed to be in a great hurry to follow either; I saw drinks passed from a flask and people
laughing.

I maneuvered my way past Quince and Fischer to Adrian's side and, avoiding any nearness to the formidable-
looking bird of prey, said, "Sir, I wonder if I might speak
with you."

He matched his speed to mine. "Of course, Miss Gray."

"I was at the Starhall Theater yesterday."

"Oh?" For a second he seemed disconcerted.

"Are you familiar with the Starhall Theater, sir?"

"Yes. I've attended any number of performances
there." His face plainly said, *You have a strange way of
dipping into social chat.*

"Well, they're doing a performance of *Becket.* Their
notices say it's from a book in your personal library."

He smiled. "So it is. I let their manager—I forget the
gentleman's name—wander through and choose what he
liked. I'm afraid I haven't read it, myself. I will get to

Earth history one day, but there are so many other subjects to run through first."

I described the quarter-hour of rehearsal I'd observed
while waiting in vain for Spider. His smile vanished, and
when I got to the line, *Who will rid me of this insolent
priest?* he interrupted.

"This was passed by the Censor?" he asked.

"I would assume so," I replied, "or they wouldn't be in
rehearsals."

We rode on silently. I noticed that Quince was trying to
ride up a bit nearer, and Fischer kept blocking him.
Adrian said, "I see. Thank you for bringing it up."

"One of the actors told me it was their manager's
idea."

"Yes. Thank you." He looked down into my face,
seeming to regret something. "I won't forget it," he said.

For some reason I felt myself color. "I just thought it
was something you should know."

A hare was brought out of cover shortly, and the dogs
outdistanced the horses in their eagerness. I was glad to
leave court speech behind and let Jewel gallop, which she
did, unsurprisingly, in a thorough ladylike way. We don't
have engineered temperaments at home; we prefer to take
creatures as they come—it's cheating at Solitaire,
otherwise—but that meant taking Jewel, too, and I rather
liked her.

We left the majority of the party behind. Apparently
they'd come for social reasons, as I should have guessed
from the silk clothing. I didn't bother to scan for Tal.

We reached the top of a slope, overlooking a broad
green meadow where a brown stripe zigzagged with
drunken speed. "Better unhood him," called Brandon
Fischer, "or the dogs will get there first." Adrian freed
the falcon.

Its wingspan took me by surprise. It flew straight up
into a broad semicircle, then dropped like a stone. I'd lost
sight of the hare by then, but the falcon had no such trouble. The brown shape was pulled out of the long grass,
and a scream, piercing and eerie, like a baby's cry, rent
the false spring air.

The falcon knew it had first due; it grasped the haunch

and then tore out the liver with its beak. The dogs arrived a few seconds later for what was left.

I glanced around at the others as we descended the slope. Some of the later party had caught up to us, including Iolanthe and Hartley Quince. On various faces I saw interest, distraction, the excitement of hard riding, and actual boredom. But Will Stockton looked repelled. Another non-aristo, I thought.

Adrian appeared beside me. "Is this new to you, Miss Gray?"

"I've stalked prey before," I told him. "Once to pass a test, and after that for food . . . or other reasons. But never for sport—though I acknowledge that sport may be in it."

Hartley Quince came up on the other side. "No doubt you could skin this hare for us and cook it right here in the Park."

"If there were any left, no doubt I could."

Iolanthe, who had ridden closer in time to hear this, looked superior.

In fact, there would have been little left to cook. The whole process had taken about forty minutes, hardly worth the preparation, and I strongly suspected the hare's deck had been stacked genetically, as well. Barely a hunt; barely even a parlor game.

The consensus seemed to be that it was time for the refreshments to be served.

I dropped behind the rest on the way back to the stables, and Tal joined me. Adrian, noticer that he was, peered about and ambled over to us before Tal could say anything to me.

"So, Miss Gray, an excellent bit of exercise."

With emphasis on the "bit." I'd read up on hunting traditions; four out of five hares escape their coursers . . . but not on the Diamond, maybe, where people wore silk to the hunt. I found myself feeling judgmental. Breeding for slowness in prey destroys the point, from a Graykey perspective. "Yes, thank you, Adrian."

"Tell me, are you under contract to anybody here?"

I blinked.

Adrian said, "Tal's told me that you're a Graykey."

How much else did he tell? Adrian and Tal had been

out of earshot several times since the kennels. I wished I could look at Tal's face for direction, but was held back first by the knowledge that Adrian would pick up on it, and second by the fact that I knew it would tell me absolutely nothing.

I spoke with the boldness I had been taught. "As regards contract, sir, I'll speak plainly. I'm no man's Graykey. Except in the sense that while on the Diamond I'm subject to the Protector and the Council."

Adrian inclined his head at this polite reference. "Or woman's either?" he pursued.

"Or woman's either." Man: A human male. Technical squirms are allowed when they're all you've got.

Adrian grinned. "I hope I'll be seeing more of you, Miss Gray. As for your association with my demon here, you have my blessings. I suppose there's no accounting for taste." And he spurred his horse on to join the others.

So, Adrian thought our relationship was romantic rather than functional. My *tarethi-din* and I rode in silence for a while. I was damned if I was going to say anything first.

"That wasn't bad," said Tal finally.

"A few hints would not have been amiss."

"Short of holding up signs, I really don't know what you humans expect of me," he said with some annoyance.

"Well, never mind." I dutifully told him about *Becket,* a play wherein a ruler opposes his church and has a priest killed.

"That must have gone over well with Adrian. Especially considering the pressure he's under now from Opal. He has to be very, very careful these days."

"But why?"

Tal didn't answer at once. He looked around at the trees, the hills, the sky, and the group in the distance ahead. We dropped back further. I wondered whether he was going to answer at all, but finally he said, "Adrian has given me the impression that he intends, in some small ways, to lift these people out of the dark ages. To be tolerant of differences in thought. To use Outsider knowledge to relieve their suffering."

"But that should make him more popular, not less."

"You don't know a lot about humans, do you, Keylinn? There'll be a mob rush to get their chains on again."

"You sound positive."

"I've seen it before." He did not expand on this, and I filed the information away in my contract-holder file.

When the stables came into view far ahead, he said, "Don't the leaders of your own people have these problems?"

"Actually we've always been a democracy. The stresses are different."

"Democracies are unstable," he said in a voice of flat contradiction. "None of them lasts more than three centuries, and your people began over five hundred years ago, as I understand it."

I smiled and shrugged.

He thought a moment. "There must be a relatively small population on your planet."

"Possibly," I said.

"You could give me marks if I come close."

"No, I couldn't." I looked measuringly down the path to the stables and found myself taken by one of those reckless impulses, the kind that got me into trouble at the Academy. "I'll make you a wager, Tal."

"I'm not a betting man."

"I'll race you to the stable doors. The winner gets to ask one question, and the loser has to answer truthfully."

He regarded me speculatively. Then he smiled. "But Keylinn, I'm no Graykey. How would you know if I answered truthfully?"

"Do we have a bet?" I said.

"All ri—" I took off before he was finished. I'd never said that I would wait.

He spurred after me.

I weighed less and had ridden more. And Jewel trusted me. I beat Tal with ease, and felt myself grinning ear to ear as he reached the stable doors behind me.

"One question, *tarethi-din*."

"Ask it." He was breathing hard.

I'd thought about this. His name might be less than useless, since many places didn't register them; and if his name *was* registered, but a common one, that would be useless too. "Where were you born?" I asked.

"Arco Station," he said.

Which sounded very like a lie. Arco Station was two sector-gates away, a Republic research facility. The birth of someone with his genetic background could hardly have been kept secret on a station—especially considering his parents would have needed sophisticated medical help just to bring him to term. And considering how nosy the Republic was in the lives of its citizens . . . it seemed an impossibility.

I didn't press the point. But I wondered.

Chapter 27

The stables were cool and dark. Tal liked darkness. He took hold of Keylinn's wrist as she tried to walk by, and pulled her back.

"Keylinn . . . couldn't you let the dog go?"

She stared up into his face, genuinely shocked. "But I promised I wouldn't let anybody hurt him."

"You know, I doubt if he even speaks your language."

That was hardly the point, the sea-colored eyes told him. But she suddenly dimpled and said, "Why, Tal— they understand every word you say."

And she went off happily to hand her horse over to the master groom. Adrian, who had already finished doing so, strolled over to Tal. "A remarkable Outsider." Although Adrian was far too well-bred to remark on it, Tal noticed that his gaze dwelled with approval on the sway of Graykey buttocks in trousers as she walked away. "Such exotic coloring, too, don't you think?"

"I suppose." Tal's voice was curt.

"I wonder how she'd do in a gown. Do you think she'd like to attend the banquet tonight?"

"It might be awkward," said Tal. "She's a vegetarian."

Adrian looked at him in disbelief. "I had heard that some Outsiders . . ." he began, then stopped. "Well. I suppose I didn't really grasp it. Is this for ethical reasons, or some bizarre nutritional plan?"

"The former, I think. She told me that she simply didn't want the responsibility."

"And yet she told *me* she's hunted before, and for food."

Tal said, "Don't ask me to untangle the ethical labyrinth of a Graykey."

"Hmm. I hope I didn't offend her by asking her to the hunt. I suppose she'll be one of the stories of my rule, just like Deirdre was for Michael Veritie. One has to be so careful with legends." He glanced around; Iolanthe was watching expectantly from beyond the stable door, standing next to Prudence, yellow gown beside yellow hair, both of them golden in the sunlight. Adrian said thoughtfully, "They say Deirdre left because she was offended, but the books don't tell you why." He gave Tal an unreadable glance. "Well, I approve, in any case. A personal relationship will do you good."

He moved to join Iolanthe, and Tal watched him go, jaw clenched. Personal relationship? Sometimes the Protector presumed overmuch on his rank.

Personal relationship, indeed. Tal found that the hunt had left him with more energy than he needed, and he looked for a place to discharge it.

There was a spot that had served him well enough before. Requiem Row was the colloquial name for a section of deck between admin and residential territory, so-called for the number of sexually transmitted diseases contracted there. For which the Church prohibited any medical alleviation; if a man didn't want such a painful and early death, it pointed out, he should refrain from going there. As for the girls, they should turn penitent and volunteer for the recycler. Adrian had been a popular figure on the Row once, but then he could afford Outsider medicine and had no scruples about purchasing it. For the other customers the witches could provide, at a price.

Tal had only ever visited one establishment, a mid-sized house called The Cherry Branch. Adrian had brought him there one half-drunken night—incognito, as he so touchingly believed . . . sometimes Adrian had too much faith in his own charisma.

The house was moderately priced, moderately clean,

and had ten suites with two shifts of girls. The majority
of them were in their teens, and only one was over the
age of twenty-five. He presented himself there now to
the manager, a woman named Lena.

"Oh, it's you," she said, with more surprise than he
thought was necessary. "Well, you're just in time. Blossom was going to be leaving next week." Lena was in her
forties, slightly plump, and very respectably dressed. Not
for her the outlandish costumes other managers wore; she
wore a dress that looked more like an admin uniform. Tal
approved; he liked to be businesslike, and he liked not
having to talk.

She held out her podgy hand, and Tal put three twenty-
dollar pieces into it. "You want a full night, I see. Well,
you won't be disturbed. Blossom's in suite six."

They'd only ever sent him the same girl, but he had no
objection to that. Her real name was Beth-Ann. She hated
"Blossom."

Almost as much as he hated coming to this place. Not
morally, of course; and not the physical experience. But it
was distasteful to be forced into human society by an act
of biology; to lack, at least in part, the element of choice
in his companions. And to acknowledge that he couldn't
master the intricate dance of social cues that would allow
him to find solace elsewhere. *Keylinn indeed.* To hell
with Adrian.

He followed the turns in the corridor to suite six. The
walls along the way were covered with pictures that he
supposed were considered erotic. Bulging cheeks, rolling
eyes, expressions of acute discomfort ... the humans in
them looked as though they were going to be ill. Anyway,
he wasn't sure some of those poses were possible.

He pressed the signal for admittance, and she opened
the door.

"Hello, Beth-Ann."

"Tal." She smiled. "It's been so long since you were
here." Beth-Ann was almost twenty, a venerable age in
this house. She was brown-haired with wide blue eyes
and a pleasant face. It was not visible at the moment, but
there was a small red diamond-shape burnt into her right
shoulder, testifying that she was a whore and should
never be married or employed in any other capacity. She

was slightly plump, which was considered an asset on the Diamond, and she pleased Tal by not kissing him immediately. He'd told her once that he disliked that.

He walked inside and started unbuttoning his jacket. "They tell me you're leaving next week." This was unusual; most of the people on the Row had nowhere to go. He sat down on the bed—the only furniture—and pulled off a boot.

"Maybe not, now," she said.

The other boot came off. Beth-Ann slipped out of her robe and sat beside him, now entirely naked. Her whore's brand was visible. Her breasts were full, with dark nipples. "I don't understand," said Tal.

"Lena was going to toss me out because it'd been so long since you came. I wasn't bringing in any money."

"But surely your other customers are sufficient." He pulled off his shirt. Down to skin now, Beth-Ann judged it safe to put her arms around his neck and give him one kiss.

As she drew back, she said, "There are no other customers. Not since the first time you came here with Adrian." He stood up to remove his pants. She moved behind him and said, "Raise your arms." She reached around to undo the belt. "They're all scared," she said.

"Scared of what?" The underwear came off in a rush now, and he pulled her down on the bed.

"Scared to—well, the saying is, 'put their seed where a demon has gone.' They're afraid their manhood will shrivel up."

He pushed her gently back for a moment and looked in her face. "You're not making this up, are you."

"Uh-uh." She moved forward again, but he held her away with an effortless grip. She lay back down obediently, but was unable to refrain from glancing first at his crotch with the expression of one who'd failed in her duty.

After a moment he turned his head to face her. "Where do you go when they toss you out?"

She was silent. The eventual answer, they both knew, was to the recycler. Her nervousness around him had always been evident, but—

"Nobody told me this was a death sentence when I first came," he said.

Beth-Ann bit her lips. "Forget it," she said. She put one hand on his chest. "I'll think of something." Of course she wanted him to forget it, to have his money's worth; experience had taught her that men who didn't have a good time didn't come back, and she needed this one to come back. Her fear of him was the only thing that made her constant kindness bearable.

He continued to stare toward the ceiling, oblivious to her efforts. "How much do the girls make here on an average night?" he asked.

"About a hundred, if they're lucky. Sometimes less."

"And on holidays?"

"Well, some girls tell me that they make five hundred, but I've never seen more than ten go to anybody's room in a night. And even that's rare."

He said, "Ten at twenty dollars apiece. That's an average of a hundred fifty for a given day, less if you factor in the ratio of holidays to normal days in a regular calendar year."

"I guess." She risked running her tongue around the shell of his ear. "We don't have to talk about money at this stage."

"I like discussing money. I wonder how much of that Lena keeps, and how much she has to pay the Board of Sin Control."

"Forty-five percent," said Beth-Ann at once.

Tal was surprised. "You know?"

"I listen," she said.

He said, in a pleased voice, "Beth-Ann." And kissed her.

She smiled. "If I knew you liked money, I would have lined all my twenty-dollar pieces along the bedsheet."

"Would you?"

She grinned and began doing a few things with her hand that would get him hard again, and this time he didn't stop her.

After his usual courteous good-bye he went to see Lena. She was pacing the sitting room below as though she were just waiting for him to leave. As though, he smiled, demons made her nervous.

"I'd like to put Beth-Ann on a retainer," he said.

"On a what?" she asked blankly.

"A retainer. Like an attorney. I'd like her to be available whenever I visit."

Lena sat down on the polished rocking chair she kept in the anteroom. Lena was big on homey touches, apparently. "That's not something we *do*," she said.

"I don't see why not," said Tal reasonably. "You do everything else."

At that she gave him a sharp glance. She said, "It's out of the question."

"Of course it's not. You don't want to keep her around; you don't want to toss her out and annoy the Protector's friend." Lena was starting to look murderous. He said, "I suppose you *could* toss her out. But then you'd have to come up with a new girl each time I visit, and they'd be no use afterward. Your house could get quite a reputation for, how was it so charmingly put, 'shriveling up' people's 'manhood'?"

"Sir," she said coldly, "I have tried to show you every courtesy—"

"One hundred and fifty dollars."

She paused. "Per day? That does seem very fair—"

"Per week."

"Are you joking, sir? Do you know what our girls make here?"

"I know what Beth-Ann makes. Nothing, except for my rare visits. Why not be reasonable? You were going to toss her out—all this is pure profit."

Lena was silent, apparently doing math in her head.

Tal added, "And the Board need never know. It's common knowledge she's been ruined for profit by a demon. You could be paying Beth-Ann's upkeep yourself, out of charity."

"No one would ever believe—" she began, and stopped, a flush coming over her face.

Tal waited. She cleared her throat and said, "Two hundred?"

"Sorry."

She bit her lip, tapped her heels, and said, "Done."

Chapter 28

*Man is the only animal that can remain on friendly
terms with the victims he intends to eat until he eats
them.*

SAMUEL BUTLER

In his capacity as Iolanthe's bodyguard, Will Stockton
heard all the gossip on the Diamond. What he didn't
eavesdrop on at parties and banquets his subordinates
brought to him proudly, like housecats with small furry
prey, depositing their bits of fact at his feet and taking his
approval as reinforcement. Will knew that Iolanthe had
locked herself in an inner room in the women's quarters,
crying, for two days last week, because Adrian had commented that it was time to set the wedding date. He knew
that the Governor of Baret Station had agreed to sponsor
a conference between Baret Two and the Three Cities, to
take place on the Station shortly. And he knew that
Adrian was annoyed that once this agreement had been
reached, Opal had begun to be coy about participating in
a joint trade negotiation.

No one ever asked Will what he knew. He had no brief.
He gathered information solely on the principle that a Sangaree among aristos had to be ready to protect himself, and
he wanted to know where the blows might come from. To
this end he had Hartley Quince followed nearly round the
clock, whether his subordinates thought it relevant or not. If
Hartley had noticed that he often looked up at parties to see
an Opal City Guard standing in a corner flirting with a ladies' maid, he had not shown any sign of it.

Which meant nothing where Hart was concerned. Still,
to lessen suspicion, Will would take a shift of watching
himself when he knew Hartley was due to be at some
function Io would attend. When they went their separate
ways afterward, one of his people would take over.

Just now he was doing his share of watching at one of the ten thousand engagement parties that Diamond social scramblers were throwing for Adrian and Iolanthe. It was understood by everyone that Adrian was too busy to actually attend these functions, and the burden fell on Iolanthe. This one was at the Muirs', and presided over by Lady Muir, whose husband was still trying to push their son Harry for a departmental position. Lord Muir had cornered Iolanthe at the other end of the room, his large gray mustaches working up and down as he declaimed nonstop to Io, and Prudence Taylor tried vainly to get him to the drinks table. Iolanthe's eyes were glazing over. Will smiled sympathetically, and noted (by craning his neck past the entrance) that Hartley Quince had just vanished into one of the rooms at the end of the hall.

Will checked the time so that he could tell how long Hart was away from the party. It was just something he would like to know. Will collected facts, and did not force them to mean anything prematurely.

His wrist-stinger went off. He made his way through the crowd to the link at the far end of the buffet. As he reached over to activate it, a servant appeared at his elbow. "I can do that for you, sir," said the man.

"Thank you, I'd prefer to do it myself."

The servant seemed confused by this response. He hesitated, then retired with a slight bow. Will leaned over the link, lowering his voice so that it sank under the surface conversation of the party, and asked for Diamond Special Security. "This is Sergeant William Stockton of the Opal delegation. You wanted me?"

A distant voice said, "Sergeant. We're dealing with an emergency on the Transport deck, and we'd appreciate it if you could keep all Opal personnel away from there."

"What sort of emergency?"

There was a brief hesitation, then the voice said, "We have a report there are three bombs in that area. It may not be true, but it would be awkward for you and me both if any of your people got blown up before we could take care of the matter."

So it would. "Anything I can do for you?" asked Will.

"Just keep 'em out of our way. And don't mention the

reason if you can avoid it. Not that it's a secret—we're evacuating the whole area."

"All right. Thanks for the warning." He cut the connection and looked up. Nobody seemed to have overheard anything. Io was still trapped by Lord Muir. Will considered his situation; he knew where all the people he was responsible for were, and none of them was anywhere near Transport. He wasn't responsible for the Opal Hierophant, but luckily the man was sitting in a corner at this very party, eating deviled eggs and drinking wine. There were a few Opal aristos running about, but Will would not be held accountable for them. Though Hart might know where they were.

Will went back to the other end of the room and glanced down the hallway, considering. Then he walked to the door through which Hart had disappeared. It was a door of light and dark colored inlaid wood, with mosaics of red, white, blue, and green in abstract patterns. A circular portion in the center of the door showed a green and white hillside and stream on old Earth, with a fish leaping and a boy sleeping. The door was hinged, and there was a crystal knob. All this gilt and icing, and there was no com to make oneself known to whomever was inside; Will was often amazed at the lack of privacy aristos lived with. How did you know when it was polite to knock?

He came closer to the door and heard things. Damn. From the sounds of it he had a girl in there, and was showing her a good time. As Will hesitated the gasps and moans increased to an almost desperate pitch—apparently he was showing her an *extremely* good time. Will balanced courtesy against urgency, and as soon as the first peak was passed he knocked.

"What is it?" Hart's voice, slightly thick and distracted, came from the room.

"It's Will. I have to talk to you."

There was a pause and a very faint sound of footsteps, interrupted by frantic whispering. Then the door was flung open. "You worry too much, sweetheart," said Hart over his shoulder. "My friend Will has no interest in how the upperdecks of the Diamond spend their spare time."

Will saw Roger Parmias, one of the group of young Diamond aristos he'd seen Hart with before, looking swiftly and in vain for another exit from the room. He very quickly pulled on his clothes, rolling his stockings up into a ball and tucking them in his wallet. Then he pushed past Will with a frightened glance and fled down the hall.

He was embarrassed, and more than embarrassed, and for that Will didn't blame him. Sodomy was still a death offense—even for aristos, if they weren't discreet and somebody wanted to press charges. Hart watched Roger Parmias's back disappear with a look of amusement. "Do come in," he said to Will. "You have a habit of overlooking private moments, don't you."

Will followed him inside. "Sit down," called Hart, as he began picking up his own clothes from various heaps around the room and pulling them on. The only place to sit was the bed. Will found a spot on the edge and smoothed back the covers, feeling heat in his face. Why should *he* be embarrassed?

"I just got a report about some bombs," he said, not looking at Hart.

"Oh?" Hart paused for a second, then pulled a shirt over his head. "Where?"

"Transport deck. Maybe three of them. We're not supposed to go near that section."

"I consider myself warned," said Hart. "And I don't think anybody else from our bunch is over there. I assume Diamond Security will chuck them out if they are. Was that all you wanted to interrupt me for?"

Will faced him, as he always faced his duty. "Three bombs on the Diamond, Hart. Is this anything I should know about?"

For once Hart actually looked startled. He tucked a silken shirttail into his breeches and said, "It's the first I've heard of them, Willie."

The Transport area was deserted save for two lone figures who performed a sort of ballet. Each held a long silver rod with a cone at one end. The person on the left swept the air, up and down, to a full hundred and eighty degrees, while the person on the right copied this in mirrored symmetry. Every few feet they exchanged places and did this silver dance on the territory their partner had just covered.

Keylinn's sweep would locate any bombs made of that favorite explosive substance, ambrite, while the sweep of Ennis Severeth Gilleys would find any made of that almost-as-popular material, fleshique. Either could be molded to fit in a one-centimeter area, so precision was necessary.

They worked in silence, muscles aching from the same continuous movements. Ennis finally said, "Probably just a scare."

"Probably," agreed Keylinn.

They waltzed on. At the border of Bay Orange Keylinn got a flash on her sweeper; she ran it past again, and got another. "Wait."

Ennis put down his sweeper, cone downward, carefully deactivating it first. They both examined the wall. It appeared to be a small panel, like any of a million power chargers scattered all over the Diamond. Just pull back the casing and recharge whatever needs it . . . Keylinn did not touch the panel. "What do you want to bet," she said, "that there was no charger here yesterday?"

"Ambrite," said Ennis. "You ever play with this stuff?"

"Of course. I got a nice mark for blowing up a target building back home with ambrite. I used the classical setup; the hard part was getting inside." She continued to look at the panel, not touching it. "Better let them know," she said, and looking around, saw a link-station at the Bay Orange passage desk. She walked over to it and called court deck. "Adrian Mercati, please. He's expecting my call." She checked the time. "Sir, we've found one. I'm at the border of Orange and Blue."

Adrian's voice said clearly, "Thank you, Tech Gray. Security's on its way; they should be there in five minutes. I've sent Tal as well—if they're Outsider-made, maybe he can advise us. I appreciate your being on the spot."

She said slowly, "Just how much experience do your Security people have with Outsider bombs?"

She heard a laugh, but it was not a happy sound. He said, "There've only been two bombs in the last sixty years—each time Security solved the problem by setting them off after the area was cleared."

"Setting them off? Deliberately?"

"Well, not really deliberately. But they knew what the odds were when they tried to disarm them."

She exchanged an involuntary glance with Ennis at that. "I have some experience in this, Adrian, and so does the Outsider I'm with. If you want us to proceed, we will."

There was a brief pause. "Actually, I was hoping you would volunteer."

On the edges of fatality, this nonetheless intrigued her. "You didn't wait for Tal to volunteer—he wouldn't. You must have ordered *him* down."

"Yes, but you're a lady."

She felt the edges of her lips turning up and squelched it. This was no time for her unfortunate sense-of-humor-problem-under-stress. "I see. Well, thank you, Adrian. I'll remember your courtesy. If at all possible."

She turned off the link. "I have some equipment in my quarters. Can you fetch it? I'll start with the tools here." Ennis hesitated, and she said, "Excuse me, I hope I haven't presumed, brother. Do you have much experience with ambrite?"

"Not a lot."

Whatever his problem, she dismissed it. This was not the time. "Then please hurry."

Four minutes later Tal found her. He stood silently, waiting until she placed a section of wall on the floor and wiped her face, then said, "I'm here."

"I heard you." She stepped back and looked at her handiwork. There were two holes, one above and one to the side of the panel.

"Care to bring me up to date?"

"I'm coming in from behind—Ennis has gone to get me some round-the-corner tools. ... I'm assuming the panel is set to go off if anyone fools with it."

"That sounds like a reasonable assumption. Do you need anything from me?"

"Can you use a sweeper? The one over there is set for

ambrite. Keep going in that direction, and when I need
you to hold something for me, I'll shout."

Tal spoke no further, but did as directed. He saw Ennis
return a little later. No flashes came from the sweeper.

Soon he looked back and saw an incredible amount of
things lying on the deck; apparently Keylinn was taking
out most of the wall. And a few minutes after that there
came the sounds of argument. He put down the sweeper
and joined them.

"What is it?"

Keylinn cast a resentful glance toward her companion.
"He's lost his mind."

Tal turned to him, eliciting further enlightenment. "I've
worked a little with ambrite bombs," Ennis said, "at
home."

"So have I!" said Keylinn.

"I don't think we should be approaching it this way.
She's deactivating the points in the wrong sequence."

"It's a textbook setup!" she said. "It doesn't need creative thought, it just needs following the rules. And that's
what I'm doing. It's the right sequence, Tal, it's child's
play. I couldn't possibly be wrong."

From a Graykey that was a strong statement. Bordering
on heresy, and Tal put it down to the stress of the moment. He said to her, "Come here."

They moved to the other side of the passage deck.

She said, "I know what I'm doing. You've got to trust
me—"

"You think Ennis is giving you bad advice?"

She paused. She frowned. "Yes. He is."

"Any chance that it's deliberate?" When she hesitated,
he said, "I know it would mean blowing himself up, but
Graykey have never struck me as being particularly sane
in that area."

"It's a textbook case," she said slowly. "He ought to
know it."

"Maybe he's under contract."

She remembered the proverbs she'd always hated:
Trusting a Graykey is like picking up an alleycat. When
a Graykey swears, cover your ears. She said, "But he
took an oath."

"Well?"

"But he didn't even try to avoid taking it. He didn't try to limit it, or set up a technicality, or use any of the techniques—"

"But his advice is wrong. And the setup is out of a Graykey textbook."

"It is." She paused. "The bastard." She looked straight at Tal and said suddenly in a new and strong voice, "He didn't expect to be asked to disarm them."

"No," agreed Tal thoughtfully. "He probably expected Security to do its usual thorough good job."

Keylinn found that her fingers were twitching in a strangle pattern, and forced herself to take a deep breath. There were more immediate concerns. "From his advice, we might assume he wants to take out you, me, and most of Transport. Yet he's standing right next to the thing now, and he hasn't touched it."

"You have a blind spot here, Keylinn. He doesn't really want to die. He's putting it off."

"Cowardly worm."

"No doubt. But good for us. Listen: We go back and pretend that I take Ennis's advice over yours. How many more points do you have to deactivate?"

"Three." She described the order.

"I'll have you step aside, and ask him to do it himself. I don't care how prepared he thinks he is, the idea of his own death will put him off-balance. When I say his name, we both jump him. But knock him well out of the way of the panel."

She only said, "I'm glad you don't have any ideas about letting off energy weapons around ambrite."

They returned to Ennis, who was standing, rather palely, by their bomb.

"We'll do it your way," said Tal. Keylinn looked resentful, which was not hard under the circumstances. "Your classroom experience was more recent. Keylinn, give Ennis your tools."

She did so, not meeting his eyes. He said slowly, "You want me to finish?"

"If you would, please," said Tal.

Ennis swallowed and turned to the bomb. He deactivated another point. Two left. Then he withdrew his hand from the wall, transferred the tool to his other hand, and wiped sweat off on his pants. "Are you sure you want me—"

"Ennis," said Tal gently, and Keylinn slammed into Ennis, bringing him down with her hands around his throat. Tal barely had a chance to touch him. He prudently placed himself between the fight and the bomb. As Ennis seemed to be in good hands, Tal picked up one of the instruments and deactivated the last two points as per Keylinn's instructions. When he turned around again, she was smashing Ennis's head against the floor. Tal said mildly, "Keylinn, stop that. We'll want to question him later."

She stopped, still astraddle his prone body. Ennis turned his head sideways, looking dazed, as she stood up. She removed his Keith pistol from his boot top, then bent to search him for other weapons. He turned over with difficulty, spitting out blood and a tooth, and sat up— holding another pistol.

"Damn," she said weakly.

Tal started to move away. "Stay where you are," said Ennis. His words were barely intelligible.

Keylinn backed away a few steps. "Stop there," he said, and he inched over to the passage desk and used the corner to pull himself to his feet. "They say the O'Malleys are crazy fighters," he commented. "I should've known, bitch."

She was not insulted by the word; it was a Redemptionist term that held no emotional affect for her. He'd learned it in the Three Cities, clearly. Keylinn wondered on some distant level if it said anything about his contract-holder. She wondered if Ennis had been drawn into *tathiss,* the first level of Greykey mistake, or even *tathani,* the second. It was a pity it wasn't likely to be the third, for that was invariably fatal. Although it would be preferable to kill Ennis oneself.

Now he activated the link, still watching them both. "Opal, personal, status six connect."

Keylinn did not recognize the voice that answered. It was hard to make out what it said from where she stood, but it did not sound pleased. Ennis requested a support team. "You don't understand," he said through a mouthful of blood, "it has to be here within the hour."

She looked at Tal. The time limit on the other bombs? Ennis's contract-holder, if that's who he was, argued and finally agreed. "Stay where you are," the voice said. She heard that, it was expressed quite forcefully.

"No shit," said Ennis. He turned off the link. "I can accept docking from this desk," he said to them. "My rescue team will be here in twenty minutes, so why don't we just relax."

He looked toward the bomb with a mournful expression. Craven worm, thought Keylinn; and adding the worst damnation she knew, she added: *Unreliable.*

Tal took out a white handkerchief and extended it toward Ennis, who was still dripping blood. Ennis glared back at him, and he shrugged.

Abruptly, Tal coughed, holding the hand with the handkerchief over his mouth. Keylinn looked at him with a sharp expressionlessness.

"And what if they're late?" he inquired politely, returning the handkerchief to his pocket. "Do you intend to hold us both prisoner until we all blow up?"

Spider, who was pursuing business of his own in warehouse territory, heard that sentence over his riccardi. He listened a little longer and then he dropped his export list and ran for the nearest link.

"I have to talk to Adrian," he insisted to the first administrator he reached. From anybody else a reference to explosives might be a joke; Tal didn't make jokes. He was obviously in the deep stuff, and if he was, then Spider would be, too—it was just a matter of time. "It's an emergency," he told the second and third functionaries who answered and expressed themselves more than willing to hear whatever the emergency might be. "I have to talk to *Adrian*," he repeated. "Just tell him it's Stratton Hastings, who met him with Tal Diamond."

Five valuable minutes later he gave up, cut the connection, and ran out into a main thoroughfare of F deck. He looked wildly up and down the street; it was a good half-hour run to court deck from here. The train was way over on Demeth, where it cut Mercati Boulevard.

He bit his lips. There was a ghost road behind a warehouse in the next walkway, that went like a straight arrow from H to court. There was no other exit between both ends. He could get there in ten minutes, maybe, if he took it.

But he'd be visible for ages. If anybody was in there—
He ran for the entrance, sweating already.

The Long Straight, they called it. It opened in a hill near St. Kit's Walk, and was singularly unuseful for much of anything but a hiding place. Forays onto court deck did no good for any ghosts; there were too many guards, and the ghosts were dressed too wrongly. Spider opened the shaft door and looked back as far as he could H-ward, then closed it carefully behind him. He started to run along the ramp. He could feel a prickle between his shoulder blades, and every few steps he twisted his neck and peered behind. He hadn't been in a ghost road since the night Tal gestured him out of the recycler line.

Ten lifetimes later, he walked out of a hill on court deck—like a creature from an old fairy tale, had anybody been watching. But the hill was screened by birch trees and by the lure of the stream at the bottom that tended to keep people from this part of the landscaping. Thank God he was still in uniform. He made his way to the entrance to the Cavern of Audience—Adrian was supposed to be creating two new ministers today, and though Spider had never been inside a court building, he knew this was where it happened.

But today there was a crowd of aristos and high admins around the entrance, all talking excitedly, the ladies rustling the first silk dresses of spring, tapping each other with fans, and turning to their escorts with sudden questions. "What's going on?" asked Spider of a couple standing near the edge of the crowd.

The lady looked him up and down disapprovingly, but said, "The session is canceled. There's a report of bombs on one of the decks."

Worse and worse. "Where's Adrian, then?"

They ignored him. Spider looked around for someone else to try, and his gaze passed over the glass security booth outside the Cavern. Adrian was standing inside, talking through a link.

Spider pushed his way through until he reached the booth. Then he started to hammer on the glass. Adrian looked up just as two City Guards started to haul him away.

The Protector slid open the door and called, "Wait! Corporal Hastings, isn't it? Let him go, please. Thank you, it's all right." The City Guards backed off reluctantly, and Adrian said, "We're a little busy right now, Corporal Hastings."

"Tal's in trouble," said Spider, the words tumbling out. "I don't know where he is, but somebody's holding a gun on him and he said something about getting blown up." He looked pleadingly at Adrian. He knew he must sound crazy, but this was the Protector, wasn't it? He could do something, if anybody could.

All expression had left Adrian's face. "If you don't know where he is, how can you know this?"

Spider ran a tongue over his lips. Did he have to admit to being bound in Outsider technology, too? There seemed no way out of it. "I have a riccardi," he said. It occurred to him that the Protector probably didn't know what that was. "It's a device—" he began.

"I've heard of them," said Adrian. He was silent for a moment, giving Spider the chance to consider the fact that he'd just admitted possession of proscribed technology to the person most responsible for enforcing the law on the Diamond. Spider decided he was just going to have to strip this uniform off the second he got home—if they let him go home—and try to soak the sweat out. His waking life was really coming to resemble his nightmares more and more. It was enough to make a man consider suicide unless, like Spider, he knew he was going straight to hell at the moment of death.

Adrian motioned him into the booth. "Tell me everything you heard."

Twenty-five minutes had passed in Bay Orange. Conversation languished. At last Ennis received docking signals from his Opal friends, and he carefully manipulated the passage desk board—with one eye on Tal and Keylinn—to give them entry to the Bay.

It was very small even for a shortie. Ennis guided them to the nearest free Diamond dock and waited while the ship made its connections. A ramp appeared, and three men, none in uniform, walked out carrying light-rifles. "Energy weapons," said Tal. "Another suicidal group. But I'm sure they haven't been told."

Ennis glared at him.

"Only three," added Keylinn. "You must be popular."

Just then the emergency exit door to Bay Orange opened. Tal watched, disbelieving, as a score of men poured in, wearing not the red or gray of Guards uniforms, but the gold necklaces of knights, and carrying, God help us, crossbows.

Which were lethal weapons, after all. One of the Opal group fell at once with a shaft protruding from his chest. Tal saluted Adrian's creativity even as he dived behind a stack of freight boxes.

One of the Opallines raised his light-rifle. He got off a shot toward the knights and everyone there who knew about the bombs braced for death.

It didn't happen; roulette luck. A second later an arrow sprouted from the thigh of the man with the rifle, and he staggered back up the ramp. The third man followed. Ennis grabbed hold of Keylinn, using her body as a shield, and backed toward the shortie. "Sorry not to take Tal," he said, breathing hard, "but you're more dangerous anyway."

Tal wondered, with a tightness in his chest, if the knights would fire their arrows. Did they even know who Keylinn was, or who was friend or foe? But Ennis treated her so clearly as a hostage, and she was a woman, and they were well-brought-up aristos. Nobody fired.

And Keylinn was taken up the ramp and disappeared, and the door slid closed. The ship shook free of its docking connections. Tal ran for the passage desk, but the bay-departure routine was already in motion; automatics opened and closed for the Opal ship, and it sailed smoothly out.

One of the knights had begun talking on the link to Adrian; as soon as Tal heard the Protector's voice, he pushed the knight aside. "There's a ship leaving now from this bay. Keylinn's on board. Track it, and I'll follow. Tell me where it docks on Opal."

"Tal, that wouldn't—"

"Just track it. I'll take a shortie from here and contact you on the way."

"Don't you move." A rare ferocity was in the tone. "You have a job to finish—there are two more bombs down there. Hundreds of people could be killed."

Tal's hands gripped the sides of the link. He said flatly, "Security can handle it the way they always do."

Adrian's voice was cold. "Any new shortie that I see coming off Transport is going to be fired on. Do you hear me?"

His fists unclenched slowly. "I hear you."

He cut the connection and picked up Keylinn's abandoned sweeper.

Tal returned from Transport to find that court deck treated him like a hero. He'd disarmed three bombs and nobody was hurt; that was unprecedented. Suddenly all the suspicion and cold looks he'd gotten in his time on the Diamond disappeared; ladies smiled at him, and when he entered the Cavern of Audience afterward, there was some applause.

It made him uncomfortable. He had no experience in this kind of treatment. He ignored it as he'd ignored the other, but nobody seemed to care. A knight, gray-bearded and middle-aged, came to him after Adrian's postponed ceremony for the new ministers—only two hours after the kidnapping—and bowed respectfully. From his necklace there dangled a tiny gold crossbow, a light-rifle, a capsule-cannon, and a fencing sword. A man of many accomplishments. He said, "I know we're not to talk about it, but I want you to know I would have gone after the lady."

"I beg your pardon?"

"On the Transport deck. I was there. Adrian pulled out all of us who were in the Crossbow Club—I didn't know what to make of it, I'll tell you frankly. But I'm honored we could be of service. I heard what you wanted to do, and well—we all would have gone after the lady, that's all. But there wasn't a battle-capsule in the bay! I looked, I guess everybody looked. They're all in Green and Blue, and they're the only ships we know about. I'm sorry. But I thought you should know."

"Thank you."

Tal waited while the knight blathered some more, then left him. Finally Adrian was finished with his ceremonial duties. Tal walked up to him and said without preamble, "What are you doing to get back Keylinn Gray?"

Adrian glanced around to see who was within earshot. He took off his ceremonial cap of thick gold velvet, wiped his forehead and said, "Saul Veritie once told me the first thing a Protector learns is that expediency and justice are frequently not even on speaking terms. This time I must serve the former."

"Meaning?"

"I can't officially recognize that the kidnapping took place. I can't officially recognize that those bombs were anything but third-party terrorist sabotage. I can't admit to having taken a Graykey on board—in most people's minds they're one step ahead of witches. 'Protector' is a fine title, but there are a lot of things *I just can't do.*"

Tal's voice was calm. "You intend to leave her with that shipload of fanatics."

"This is no time to give Opal an excuse to back out of the conference. I've taken risks for you before, Tal, if you'll remember. One of them got you on board. But this is not the time."

Tal was silent, and Adrian said, "There are drinks over by the Obsidian Door."

"No, thank you."

Adrian regarded him. If Tal made no polite commendation of Adrian's use of the Crossbow Club, as so many others had, Adrian made no mention of Tal's near-mutiny on the Transport deck. The Protector often considered discretion the better part of friendship. He said, "I don't pretend to have the least idea what goes on in your mind. But if there's anything you wish to do personally, I won't stop you. And if there's anything you need that I can supply, I will."

The false gray eyes were thoughtful. "I want another exit pass—" he began.

Adrian held up a hand. "Brandon!" he called. As the Chief Adviser made his way to them, Adrian said, "Tell Brandon everything you need. I want to be able to swear later that I knew nothing of what you were doing."

"Should it come to that."

"Should it come to that, yes. I do like to be prepared. . . .
Hello, Brandon. Please give Tal here everything he needs.
His list might be a little unusual, but just give it to him."

Brandon Fischer smoothed his beard and smiled impeccably. "Why should today be different?"

Chapter 29

*There are three levels of Graykey mistake and one
level of knowledge. The three are:* Tathiss, *becoming overly identified with your client.* Tathani, *losing sight of your client's interests in the rush of data
that accompanies subjectivity sickness. And*
taberani, *becoming contaminated by your client's
worldview. In the case of an outsider (a non-Graykey contract-holder) the last is inevitably fatal.
Or so the Graykey claim, though it may be only a
legend.*

*Find a group of Graykey together, in any world
known to humankind, and the odds are that you're in
a bar. Nor would it be easy for you to locate any
people more cheerfully ready to drink, sing, or fight,
without an apparent serious thought entering their
heads. True, their bar fights are often ignited by disagreements over obscure philosophical points . . .*

Selections from CAUDLANDER'S
A Tourist Guide to the Graykey

Spider was on the sicklist for his shift. A statement attached to his sign-in sheet explained that he was in the
Infirmary of Saint Angelique, on F deck. In fact he was
in a long-range cruiser with Tal, six days out from Baret
Station.

It was a Diamond cruiser, Curosa-made, and twice as

fast as anything available at the Station. Perhaps, Spider thought—although he had never given the matter much consideration before—humans had become too dependent on sector-gate technology. They were willing to lumber around within sectors in ships that had not essentially changed in centuries. Brandon Fischer's name was on the exit visa and the authorization for this ship, but Spider had a strong feeling that if anything went wrong, that name would disappear quickly from the records.

Not that they were zipping around all that fast, he thought. Not following a mailship from Green Pastures to Harrow, taking its own sweet time. "At least, we *hope* it's a mailship," he muttered.

He did not mean that to be shared, but Tal said, "We have very good evidence." Tal was sitting in the pilot's seat, scanning the instruments every quarter hour, and reading a hand-held book.

"That's another thing," said Spider. "I can't believe you had Keylinn followed."

"Is that a problem for you, Spider? Isn't it a good thing for us all that I did?" He did not look up from the book.

Spider muttered something less intelligible. One did not follow one's friends, even if the information turned out useful later. Keylinn's maildrop contact in the cafeteria on Baret Station had led to an art store on an upper level, which led to a freighter pilot with a cargo bound for Harrow and an unusual flight plan. "We should've questioned the pilot."

"I doubt if he knows much beyond where to jettison the mailbag. If I were a Graykey, I wouldn't give strangers more information than they need." He looked up, checked the instruments, verified the course of the mailship, and returned to his book.

Spider said, annoyed, "We're getting farther and farther from Baret System. And they could be torturing Keylinn right now. Or they could've sentenced her to be burnt—she's an unbeliever and a Graykey, they can justify doing anything they want."

Tal did not respond.

Spider said, "She could be burning right now!"

Tal closed the book, leaving a finger in the page. "Since there's nothing you personally can do about it, why don't you go down the hold and check our packs and weapons."

"I've checked them forty times."

Tal looked at him for a few counts, then opened the book again.

"What are you reading?" asked Spider.

"Why don't you check the damned packs!"

Spider's eyes widened. It was the first time he'd ever heard Tal raise his voice. "It was just a question."

Tal closed the book and put it down on the control panel. He said, more quietly, "I am reading an Old Earth book called *Pride and Prejudice*. It is a work of fiction that purports to describe the relationships between men and women of that particular era. Is this enough for you?"

"I never saw you read fiction before."

"With good reason. Very little of it makes any sense. I include this book in that statement."

"Then why are you reading it?"

Tal's fingers tapped the surface of the control panel. "It was recommended to me by our mutual friend Keylinn Gray who, as you point out, may be burning at this very moment."

"Oh," said Spider weakly.

"She felt it displayed a perceptivity in regard to human motivations that might help me in dealing with them. Thus far it has not."

"Oh." Spider got up to go below, then looked again at the scanners. "He's slowed."

Tal's hands were on the controls at once.

"He's dumping something," said Spider.

"I see it."

Their quarry had jettisoned a small container, oblong, shown to be about thirty-six centimeters in length. Tal cut the drives. Spider said, "What if we've made the wrong decision, and we should be following the ship instead of the package?"

They were silent. A few seconds later the container started to broadcast a pickup signal. Tal said with satisfaction, "It's doubtful, Spider. Very doubtful."

The next step in the Graykey postal service came nine hours later, when a sleek and relatively speedy cruiser in-

tercepted the jettisoned container. Tal dropped a little farther out of range; he had a higher opinion of Graykey intelligence than the regular human norm.

And eight and a half hours after *that,* they found themselves above a green and brown planet, considering their
options.

"It's down in the atlas as a mining world, belonging to
a company I've never heard of," said Tal. "But the company pays taxes to the Empire, so I suppose the Empire
doesn't really care how they list themselves."

"I hate to be pushy," said Spider. "But considering the
time factor, don't you think we should land?"

"Any world with no navy, no armed forces, and no
large population must put a lot into their automatic weaponry. Let's not alarm them."

Spider said, "How do you know it's not a large population?"

Their com panel lit up. "Attention," said a voice,
"attention. Foreign ship, please identify yourself and state
your business."

Tal said at once, "This is Tal Diamond, from the Diamond and the Three Cities. We want permission to
land—"

"Refused. Please withdraw. This is a privately owned
mining concern. Your continued presence will be regarded as unfriendly."

Tal spoke with firmness. "We know this is the current
home of the Graykey. I need to speak to someone in
authority—"

Spider was looking at the board. He said in a strangled
voice, "They seem to have fired something at us." He
looked longingly at the auto-execute, which was near his
elbow.

Tal spared the board a quick, contemptuous glance.
"It'll take three minutes to reach us. Hold position.
They're just trying to scare us off."

"Oh, really?"

Tal said, "I'm here on behalf of a member of your order. She calls herself Keylinn Gray. Does that push any
buttons with anybody down there?"

There was silence from below. Spider said, "It's still
coming."

"Hold position."

At two minutes and forty-five seconds Spider said, "It's getting a little cl—"

The missile swerved. The voice on the com said, "Please hold yourself in readiness. Landing coordinates will be given to you in a moment."

Tal had the feeling there was something he was supposed to do. Then he remembered. "Thank you," he said.

The landing port was a brown square of muddy field with a single building, about eight kilometers from a small town. "Not very impressive, is it?" asked Spider, as he came down the ramp.

Tal's eyes were on the three people approaching them in a groundcar. It drew nearer and he made out the figures of three men; a sexual coincidence? He had not had the impression from Keylinn that gender dominance was a Graykey practice.

At least they weren't soldiers sent out to secure the strangers: One was old, one middle-aged, and one young. The car stopped by the ramp and the old one got out and said companionably, "Hello. I'm Chief Judge O'Malley, of the Cerberus Mining Corporation legal department. This is my colleague, Aaron Akiba, and this is Sean Gilbreth." The young man nodded. The two older men had beards, one white and one blond. They wore similar clothes, plain and warm, and sat with a straightness of posture that hinted of training. The young one, Gilbreth, was clean-shaven and more flashily dressed in an emerald jacket and white boots that couldn't possibly be practical in all this dirt.

"I'm Tal Diamond, and this is Stratton Hastings."

"So you said, or part of it," said the old man. He smiled. "You seem confused as to this planet's inhabitants. We're an Empire mining concern—see those hills? Full of zelignite. And iron ore is plentiful on the other continent. It'll be centuries before the world is exhausted."

"And meanwhile, it's not a bad place to live." Tal walked him back to the car. Chief Judge O'Malley held the door for them both to enter.

"Very true," he said, "it's not. We have schools and li-

braries and even churches for those who enjoy that sort of
thing."

And they had a lot of taverns, thought Spider, who
counted three as they traversed the road to town. He was
glad he could understand their use of Standard; he'd spent
a lot of time lately talking to Baret Station people, arranging some illegal inventory disposal, and his experience
had apparently done him good. Tal said calmly, "Well, we
seem to have taken advantage of your hospitality under
false pretenses."

"Not at all, not at all." Akiba, the middle-aged man,
put a hand on O'Malley's arm, and O'Malley shook his
head slightly. He said, "Tell me, you mentioned the
Graykey when you asked for landing permission. And
someone's name. What in the world could you want with
the Graykey? They're a legend. And why here, of all
places?"

"We have a friend," said Tal. "She's working on the
Diamond under the name of Keylinn Gray. We followed
her maildrop connections—mistakenly, it seems—here.
As for what we want with the Graykey ... Keylinn is in
a great deal of trouble. She could be being tortured or
killed at this very moment. I don't know how the other
Graykey would feel about that, but I thought they might
want to do something."

Akiba turned to the old man. "Bram—" he said.

"Wait." O'Malley said to Tal, "Look at me." Tal did,
turning on him the same blank exterior he presented to
every other being in the world. The old man said, "You
called her a friend. Is that all?"

Tal hesitated. Then he said, "She's also my *tarethi-
din.*"

O'Malley nodded. "I thought so. Ever since you
landed." He said to Akiba, *"Etcar sab gathrid."* Akiba
gave Tal a measuring glance. O'Malley put an old and
weathered hand over Tal's for a moment. "Don't worry.
Something will be done."

They were invited to a party. It was a pregraduation
party in the great hall at the Nemeter Training School, an
elderly and rambling brick structure whose walls echoed
and whose wooden floor planks gave slightly when any-

one jumped on them. Just now the floor of the great hall was throbbing with the countless stamping feet of dancers whirling madly. They wore crimson, orange, royal blue, forest green. Yellow scarves flew as they twirled.

"This is Sefill," said Akiba, who turned out to be the Dean of the College. "He'll take care of you." And Spider and Tal were left in the hands of a tall, elegant man with gray hair, who bowed his head and said, "Delighted."

Akiba went off to make (he said) some sort of arrangements. Spider said, "What happened to the other fellow? The young one."

"Who would that be?" asked Sefill.

Spider described him. "Sean somebody," he concluded.

"Ah, the mayor." Sefill grabbed two tall glasses off a passing tray and offered them to his guests. Tal declined. "He wouldn't be following up with your problem. That's a Graykey matter."

"He's not a Graykey? I thought everybody here was a Graykey."

Sefill shook his head. "The majority are not. I, in fact, am not. I'm not even native-born; I'm from Glassere, and I teach Outsider literature here at the school."

Tal entered the conversation for the first time. "They let an Outsider live here and teach?"

Spider was confused by the term "outsider." He'd only heard it mean someone who wasn't a Redemptionist.

Sefill laughed. "I'm retired as far as Glassere thinks. But who better to teach Outsider literature than an Outsider-born? I had to take an oath never to leave, but I haven't regretted it. They treat me very well here."

"I see."

"I also have a class in Outsider systems of ethical thought, quite well-attended."

Tal scanned the room as though waiting for someone. "I should think they would consider that a contradiction in terms."

"They do." Sefill looked to the main door, where a man of about fifty was entering with a young girl. "Ah, Keylinn's father and sister. You'll want to meet them, no doubt."

He started to go and get them, but Tal put a hand on his arm. "No," he said.

"No?"

Tal made himself smile politely. "If you don't mind."

"As you wish," said Sefill, clearly puzzled.

"What's in these drinks?" asked Spider.

"Pure whiskey, most of them. . . . I suppose it's just as well," continued Sefill, apparently following his last thought. "Keylinn's father was upset when she left, and her sister is shy around strangers, like many of her people."

The Dean appeared at the far end of the hall and caught Tal's eye, motioning him to come forward. "Stay and enjoy yourself," said Tal to Spider. "I may be a while."

A moment later he vanished, with the Dean, through a doorway. Spider leaned on a railing and watched them disappear. He said to Sefill, "Do you know what 'gathrid' means?" The word had jumped out at him from the brief exchange in the car—he'd once heard Keylinn use it of Tal, in no flattering way.

"As a matter of fact I do—it's from the Old Tongue, a very rich language. It means 'angel.' "

Spider was nonplussed. Then he said, "I must have the wrong word."

"Maybe if you could tell me the context—" began Sefill, then he laughed. "Of course, the word also means 'demon.' In the old tongue, the two are the same."

No wonder some people thought the Graykey were one step above witches. "That's pretty odd, don't you think?"

"Well, you must understand the history it stems from. The gathrid is a favorite character in Old Tongue plays— the propellor of the action, often. Things happen around a gathrid. And after all, the important thing to a Graykey is not good or evil, but consistency of behavior."

Spider straightened up from the railing. "You're not joking with me, are you?"

"No, not at all! If you knew the trouble I had getting my classes to understand Outsider mindsets— Forget it. Just take my word for it, that the Graykey respect consistency over goodness. They like to know where they stand. The contract is everything; a man who keeps his contracts is honorable, and can be trusted. The man who never keeps them need not be trusted. But an *apparently* honorable man who suddenly breaks a contract is beneath contempt."

Spider watched as Keylinn's little sister abruptly pulled open a cluster of dancers and joined them. She stamped and whirled wildly, the glitter on her shoes catching the light. Her head was thrown back and she shrieked as they turned a sharp corner of the dance. He said to Sefill, "I thought you said she was shy."

"I said among strangers."

Spider saw with some alarm that Keylinn's father had left a knot of people and was making his way to them through the crowd. What was he supposed to say to the man? He said to Sefill, "He doesn't know, does he?"

"He's not supposed to. But you have no idea how quickly rumors can— Hello, Rory. I see Jannie is stamping up steam on the dance floor. She's becoming quite a little lady, I don't doubt she'll be entering single combats soon."

Up close, Keylinn's father was a sad-faced man with brown hair and thick brows. He wore a green and black cap. He said, "You hear all the Outsider news, Sefill. What's this about a ship landing with news of Keylinn?"

"You'd be better asking the Chief Judge than me, Rory."

"It's you I'm asking. And who's this with you? I hope you're not forgetting your manners."

Sefill gave in gracefully. "May I present Stratton Hastings—Rory Camberil Murtagh."

Rory Murtagh inclined his head. "Stratton Hastings, of . . . ?"

"Of the Diamond," said Spider, giving up. "Honored to meet you, sir."

"The Diamond." Rory Murtagh had the sort of eyes that seem to expect the worst. He turned those eyes on Spider in mute inspection. "But you're not the gathrid, are you?"

"No, sir, I'm not."

"Ah, well, we may not be fated to meet. It's only the young and fearless who walk openly with gathrids and send letters home saying not to worry. Do you know if my Keylinn is all right, Stratton Hastings?"

"She was all right when I last saw her," said Spider, taking refuge had he but known it in the deception of "Graykey truth." It was a good thing he'd never met Keylinn's father, he thought, and had had no time to prepare; rehearsal always killed his ability to lie.

"But you've come here for some purpose," said Rory Murtagh.

Actually, sir, we seem to have lost your daughter. "I'm just along for the ride," said Spider. "You'd have to talk to the gathrid."

"I will, should fate and the Dean allow us to meet." Keylinn's father stood a moment, then bowed and left them.

Spider let out his breath. "Why hasn't somebody else told him?"

Sefill said, "It's a matter for the school and the Society of Judges. A contact matter. And besides, Rory Murtagh is not the most stable of men. He has black depressions, they last for months sometimes." He reached for a passing tray. "Ah, wine at last. My insides were not fashioned for hard Graykey liquor." He sipped, and watched Rory return to his companions. "It's a small place here. Everybody knows everything about everybody else."

The dancing had reached frenzied proportions and then slipped somehow into a waltz. Spider saw two young women spot each other from opposite ends of the hall. Evidently they had not met in a long time. They yelled joyfully, ran to meet, and went into a private dance of false fighting—feinting, jabbing, ramming into each other gently, and other physical displays. He'd seen this kind of affectionate horseplay among young men, particularly the City Guard, but never among women. Surely they held back from this sort of indignity.

Sefill saw his glance and said, "I was a bit shocked myself, when I first came. My people are much more reserved. We don't go in for such casual behavior. But the Graykey training has a strong physical component, you know; all that energy has to go somewhere. They lose their natural reticence."

"I see," said Spider.

"Old habits die hard. I've seen sixty-year-olds tumbling over each other like puppies. Why, my housekeeper came to see me one morning with her back thrown out, and when I asked her how it happened she said, 'I was saying hello to Bertil.' I knew exactly what she meant."

Spider saw that one of the women wore an old quilted jacket like Keylinn's. It was hard for him to imagine Keylinn here, even so. It was hard to imagine her anywhere but the Diamond, but as they were all making very clear, she had had a life before she came to them.

Now a little boy came out of the doorway where Tal and the Dean had disappeared. He was light-haired, only about seven or eight years old, and he carried a hat that was too big for him. He went up to one of the waltzing couples, tugged at the man's sleeve, and the man bent to speak with him. Then the man bowed to his partner and walked out of the room. The boy went to another couple; this time both heads bent low, and the woman gathered her skirts and accompanied her partner from the room. The boy went on through the dancers. All in all he stopped about a dozen couples, and although men and women of all ages were in the throng Spider noted that all those the boy called on were quite young.

Those left without partners quickly hooked up with others in the same position, or went to find food and drink. In a few moments the laws of the dance saw to it that the hall looked no different than it had before. Spider leaned thoughtfully against the railing and sipped his drink.

"These are your choices," said Akiba. He motioned to the twelve young men and women sitting in the plain wooden chairs in this empty classroom. They wore their dancing clothes, flamboyant scarves and heavy gold and silver earrings. But they all sat with a straight primness that hinted at other things.

Tal examined them; there wasn't one who was over the age of twenty. All of them were human—that was something he paid attention to. "They're young for humans," he said to the Dean.

Akiba said, "They're all cadets, all within weeks of graduation. They're practically first-rank Graykey now; all they need is contract experience. Keylinn was no older when she left us."

"How many ranks do you have?" He paced around the semicircle of chairs.

"The highest is seventh-rank. Only three people on the planet have that. You've met one—Chief Judge O'Malley."

"Yet you're only offering me first-rank."

Aaron Akiba's voice was cold and empty of mercy as a northern tundra. "You must take what you can get, stranger. I'm the Dean of this school; I hold student-contracts on all these folk. I don't hold contracts on any other Graykey." He paused. "Nor could you afford what they would require from you."

Tal said, "I've brought a good supply of gems with me. And I have access to other forms of currency."

"Yes, I know."

Tal stopped by the chair of a young woman with a dark green fringed shawl. Her hair was close to the shade of Keylinn's. He said to the Dean, "How long would I have them?"

"You say your ship can bring you to the City of Opal in four days. You may have them for five days. They know how to return here on their own."

"If they can do that without a ship, they must be re-markable." Tal walked around the last of the chairs and returned to the Dean. "Only five days?"

The Dean met his eyes squarely. "I will leave them no longer in the hands of a gathrid. With all due respect."

The gray eyes dropped, then came up again. "Keylinn doesn't mind what I am."

"How do you know what Keylinn minds? And as you point out," said the Dean calmly, "she may be dead in your service even now."

Spider was dancing with a woman whose hair was the color of light coffee. She showed him the steps and laughed when he forgot. Spider, too, was shy around strangers; but she'd come up to him and spoken in some far-fetched but lilting jargon, and Sefill had told her to speak Standard.

"Beautiful stranger," she said to him when he apologized for the ninth time, "dancing experience is not nec-essary."

"You talk differently from Sefill," he said, executing a combination successfully—rather to his surprise. "Is it just because he's from off-planet?"

"I'm translating from the Old Tongue as I speak to you. It's the proper language for romance."

"Is it?" he said, pleased at the implication.

"And as we're in the mood for instruction," she said, "note how I knot my scarf, like so. That's how a lady tells her partner to meet her afterward outside."

"I'll bear that in mind," said Spider, straight-faced. "Maybe one of the other ladies will—" and he had to stop because she'd stumbled against him in the dance and knocked the wind out of him.

"Sorry," she said, not looking sorry at all. She grinned. "What were you saying?"

"Not a thing." And then the little light-haired boy came to him and tugged at his elbow. Spider looked down at him. "I think you've got the wrong person, sonny."

"Will you please go to the front door and wait there?" The voice was high and serious.

"Are you sure you want me? Who sent you?"

But the boy simply said, "Front door, please, and wait." And he turned and left.

Spider tried to take his partner's hands again, but she looked at him in surprise. "It's the Dean's messenger. You must go."

"Must I?"

She withdrew her hands. Spider sighed. "I'm not likely to be coming back, you know. Not ever."

Her wide green eyes were serious. "Fate can do that, sometimes."

On certain very rare occasions Spider felt the force of impulses that seemed to come from some very alien spot; certainly they had little to do with his normal life. He felt himself surrendering to one now. He took hold of his partner, whose name he never learned, and walked her backward a few steps until she was against the wall of the room. Then he put his hands on either end of the gold scarf, pulled her head gently forward, and kissed her. A full minute later he let go, and she leaned against the wall. She said something low in another language. He turned to leave. "Fate and I have never even been introduced," he said, and he went to find the front door.

Tal was there. This did not surprise him. Tal was placed in the universe specifically to make his life complicated. "We're going for a walk," said Tal.

"I guess we are," agreed Spider, and he followed his companion out.

It wasn't much of a town, out there. The buildings were of old brick and wood, and the sidewalks were made of wooden planks. The streets were muddy. Spider wasn't disturbed by the enormity of the sky; it was framed on both sides by the buildings fronting the street, and not very different from the illusion of sky over Mercati Boulevard. "Funny smells, here."

"Vegetation and mud. Unrecycled air." Tal strode ahead.

"Where are we going?"

"The Dean may lend us some help—they're deciding now," said Tal. "We'll hear within the hour. We have time to kill."

"I was killing it fine inside the hall." They passed a field with white stones in it, and Spider said, "That's an odd-looking place. What is it?"

"A cemetery."

"What's a cemetery?"

"For the burial of the dead. The stones mark the places."

Spider looked appalled. "You're joking. What, you mean right in the ground?" He shivered. "Dirt in your face and all?"

"More or less. A lot of other humans are disgusted by it, too. I think that's why they put them inside boxes first, as though that made any difference."

There was a marble slab by the entrance to the cemetery. Tal sat down on it. "We may as well wait here for a while."

Spider looked wistfully down the little street. There were three taverns on it, all with friendly yellow-lit windows. The sound of singing came, very far away, from one of them. "This isn't a bad place," he said. "The green stuff on the hills looks nice."

Twilight settled over the town. Streetlamps turned on farther up the road, but the cemetery remained unlit. Spider got up and went over to a large, white granite statue near the cemetery entrance; it was a man in odd historical clothing, with a square hat and a beard, about twice life size. There was no name on the pedestal; instead there was a line in Standard: "Nothing is forgotten or forgiven." Below it was a date, a single Standard year: 2239. The statue stared impassively out toward the street.

He returned to the marble slab. "It's almost time to go to the port," said Tal.

Spider shivered. "Why is it so cold?"

"It's not, really. You're not used to temperature variations outside a certain range. Even 'winter' on the Diamond doesn't go below 48 degrees."

Spider stamped his feet on the ground. "How cold is it now?"

"It's approximately seven degrees Celsius," Tal replied, without reference to any apparent instrumentality. "Which would make it 45 Fahrenheit."

"Faren who? How can it be two things at once? The temperature is the temperature."

"Two different systems, Spider. Think of it like money."

Spider's face registered suddenly enlightenment. "Like dollars and yen! I see what you mean."

A handful of townspeople had appeared and disappeared across the street while they sat. Now a young couple walked along the sidewalk arm in arm, flushed and well-dressed in scarves and jackets, looking as though they'd just come from the dance. As they passed by the entrance to the cemetery, they turned briefly to the white granite statue. Their faces changed. First the woman, and then the man, spat on the ground. The man said a brief word in another language, and they went on.

Sefill had given Spider a warning, back at the dance, and it was not the sort of thing Spider forgot. The teacher said, of his hosts, "They're the most informal people in the world, except when they're talking about their damned contracts. Then they get all stiff and proper. But when they start to call you by all your titles and your full name, and sir and lord and everything—then's the time to worry. Because then they're thinking about killing you. They're very formal with their enemies, Cyr Hastings." "Call me Spider," Spider had replied, and Sefill had laughed; but Spider didn't feel much like laughing now. These people were serious in their hatreds.

Tal got up and went over to the statue and inspected the pedestal. "He lived four hundred years ago, but they hate him as though they know him personally. He lived before the Graykey even settled here."

"I suppose he was inconsistent," said Spider.

"Pardon?"

"You know, Sefill told me that the word 'forgive' isn't even in the Graykey vocabulary. I bet that's why they had to use Standard for the inscription."

"It's not in my vocabulary either," said Tal, "but I didn't know their memories were so long."

Spider said, "Let's not do anything to irritate these people, Tal."

"No," agreed Tal, "we'll try not to."

A groundcar met them at the foot of the main street. The town dribbled off into nothingness here, the road disappearing in brown scrub and dirt, with tracks of heavier vehicles pointing toward the hills in the distance. A young man sat in the car, a red band tied around his forehead. He wore a gray, sturdy looking jacket and pants, and a leather pack was in the seat beside him.

He smiled politely at Spider and Tal as he opened the doors for them. "Please come in, sirs."

Tal said, as he seated himself, "You're one of the team, aren't you."

"Yes, sir, I am."

They turned off onto a side road and left the little town behind in the gathering darkness. Lights disappeared as they drove on. Tal said, "Are we going to the port?"

The young man grinned. "And where else would we be going, sir?"

"Let me be more specific in my inquiry. May I take it the voting was in our favor?"

Spider glanced at Tal suspiciously. Voting? Who was voting, and where would they be taken if this vote went against them?

The young man said, "You may take it that way, sir. In fact it was unanimous. You have no idea of how the idea of rescuing Keylinn O'Malley Murtagh would attract a group of cadets. The rest of them are waiting at the port now."

"Then I can assume—"

"At this moment, we are *tarethi-din*. That's correct." The young man smiled cheerfully and gunned the car over a pothole.

"I'd like to make a request, then," said Tal, as he fell against the side of the vehicle.

"More careful driving?"

"No. Yes, that, too. My request is that you let me know if I seem to be nearing any contract violation."

The young man glanced at him. "I'll bear your wish in mind, sir," he said, with the usual Graykey noncommittance where commitment was not mandatory.

Spider looked out at the darkness, unreassured.

Chapter 30

An army of elves walked from the woods
Fell and grim, of shadows made.

Earth: Traditional

Four days in a crowded ship with a dozen young and energetic Graykey is an experience unlike any other, Spider reflected. For one thing, they ate like large and growing dogs—and from the bones he found stuffed into the waste chute he concluded that vegetarianism was not a philosophical necessity. And for the first day they all drank cheerfully and enormously from flasks they'd brought in their leather packs.

"It takes seventy-two hours to detoxify," explained a girl named Skeeter with close-cropped hair and a tattoo of a day lily on her shoulder. "We'll stop drinking tomorrow, and then we'll be short-tempered for a while."

"Ah," said Spider, thinking that he looked forward to *that*.

They partitioned the hold into individual sleeping quarters—more or less individual, a number of them shared their bedrolls—and Spider could hear them talking incessantly through the day and night. When they weren't talking, they were singing, and when they weren't singing, they were arguing. There was a brief fight on the second day ("the de-tox," thought Spider) but it was broken up, and whenever Tal came down into the hold, everybody became as polite as well-behaved little children visiting the parents of a friend. They called Spider "sir," too, although they also invited him to drink with them, which they did not do with Tal.

"A gathrid," explained one of the boys on the first night, making a sort of "I don't know" motion with his hand. "One likes to tread carefully."

Spider wouldn't argue with him. Remembering Sefill's warning he said, "Call me Spider—there's no need for formality, is there? And can I ask you something, friend? Why do some of you wear red headbands and some of you blue?"

The boy touched his red band and smiled. "Sentimental value. It's our last training exercise together. The Blues are the Gulls, and the Reds are the Herons."

"Keylinn was a Gull," put in a girl sitting nearby.

"One of the best," said another, raising a pewter flask. "She broke the point record for her team in taking the power station at Moliere."

"Hear, hear!" And everybody drank solemnly.

"Did you hear what she did during Peace Week?" asked the first boy, and somebody yelled tipsily, "Keylinn stories!"

Tal descended the steps, a sheaf of papers tucked under one arm. It was though someone had thrown a bucket of cold water over the sprawling cadets; the sense of playfulness vanished at once.

Tal glanced at his unpredictable crew. "Keylinn stories? Tell me one."

"Please tell us," said Spider. He looked at the silver-coated flask he'd been handed; it was engraved with some sort of coat of arms with wild roses. He took a sip and coughed.

The cadet hesitated, looking to his friends. Then he smiled. "Right. It was Peace Week—this was a few years back—and the Black River Graykey and the Portsmouth Graykey were meeting to try and iron out their differences. They'd been getting a little overly violent, you know? So they were all in the Conference Auditorium at Nemeter, with everybody watching, and their negotiators up on stage. Keylinn was part of the college arbitration team. Well, they went on and on, and partway into it she pulled out a book and started reading. That irritated them enough. Then they had to agree on a day to finalize their treaty, and they couldn't seem to do it. The Black Rivers suggested one day, but the Portsmouth group couldn't make it—they offered the next day, but the Black Rivers said they had to attend passage ceremonies—maybe the day after. But that's our holiday, said the Portsmouth Graykey, are you trying to comment on our founder's birthday? And Keylinn looked up from her book suddenly and said in a loud voice: "Maybe you can stand on the roof and semaphore to each other.""

The boy grinned, took another long drink, and said, "She got into a lot of trouble, no surprise to anyone; but you know, the negotiators were so embarrassed by the public sarcasm that they agreed to meet the next morning."

The girl beside Spider said, "I heard about that, but I always thought she was put up to it by the Dean. Because of her reputation—everybody knew Keylinn was a prisoner of her sense of humor. So nothing she did reflected back on the administration, it was just Keylinn being Keylinn."

"When we do get her back, you can ask her," said the boy.

"What good will that do? If she *was* put up to it, she's hardly likely to say so, is she?"

Both of them fell silent and tugged at their drinks moodily. "It's just like the Dean," said the boy. "He'll never kill two birds with one stone if he can get three for the same price."

One of the nearby cadets said, "You think that's what it was when she left? That it wasn't just a punishment?"

"Shut up," said the first boy, and he glanced at Spider and Tal. Then he added something in Graykey, or maybe Old Tongue, Spider didn't know which. Then they were all quiet for about a minute, which was as long as it got when they weren't meditating, or doing whatever it was they did.

Tal said, "I don't understand the point of the story."

The cadets looked at him as though he'd spoken in a foreign tongue and they lacked a dictionary of translation.

He shrugged and began passing out papers.

"What's this?" asked Spider.

"Maps of various sections of the City of Opal. Start studying them. We're going for the ecclesiastical detention cells, or some of us are. Others will be creating havoc and diverting Security to other areas. I trust you've brought your explosives."

"Tommy's the person to ask," said a girl, motioning to an ugly, raw-boned cadet with red hair who'd been sitting silently through the talk.

He looked up. "Of course. My personal preference is for ambrite, if that's acceptable to you."

Tal examined the boy. He was not prepossessing, but so far as Spider could tell he was the only cadet who hadn't brought a liquor supply with him. "Ambrite is fine."

"Good," said Tommy, and he crossed his legs and took a set of maps. He was also the only cadet who tended not to say "sir." As he was a Graykey, Spider could not tell if this meant a lack of respect, lack of enmity, or lack of interest.

Tal returned to the flight deck, and when the singing started, Spider joined him. "They exercise, too, you know," he said. "For hours."

"You could stand to join them," said Tal.

"God bear me witness," said Spider. "Is it my fault I've got a human metabolism? I've never seen you exercise in your life."

"Maybe you should follow me for a few days. I've been known to use the gyms on the admin level." He picked up the copy of *Pride and Prejudice*. "Would you like me to arrange an admission for you there?"

"Thanks, but I've got enough calls on my time as it is. Anyway," he said mournfully, looking down at his stomach, "if you thought I was out of shape, you could have left me home."

"I wouldn't do that to you, Spider. I know you hate suspense."

Spider took a seat and pushed it back into a lounging position. Three days to Opal; and God only knew what happened then. He'd been up for over twenty hours, but he felt wide awake. The sound of unintelligible but enthusiastic lyrics rose up from below. He snapped the chair upright again.

"Do you have any other books with you?"

"No," said Tal, turning a page.

Keylinn:

I was given a very nice room on the City of Opal, as detention suites went. This one was obviously meant for high-ranking prisoners—it was well-carpeted, with tables and chairs and a bed with a carved headboard. None of that served to reassure me as to my ultimate fate.

I would have been pleased that they left me alone for several days, if it weren't a procedure I'd been taught was standard for softening prisoners before interrogation. The reasoning behind this bothered me. I had no information I was aware of that Opal could want; so what did that leave? Given the political situation here, what if they wanted me to confess to something? They burnt people here, didn't they? I would have to be careful not to say anything that resembled confession—it would reflect badly on the Diamond and my contract-holder.

To fight my uneasiness, I did subjectivity exercises for hours, followed by physical ones. The subjectivity exercises bolstered my confidence; eluding the trap of a single ego always made death less frightening. When at last a guard in black came to escort me from the suite, I felt ready to be courteous and relaxed with my captors. Imprisonment is no excuse for rudeness, after all.

There was only one man waiting for me; he wore civilian clothing, breeches and a white shirt with rolled sleeves. He sat alone at a deskchair, with another pulled nearby for me, although there was no desk or table to hide behind. He was a big man. I took the seat when he gestured and said, "Lord Cardinal Arno, isn't it? You were pointed out to me once on the Diamond."

He looked faintly surprised. I wondered if he hadn't planned on introducing himself.

"You did leave on your ring," I pointed out, inclining my head toward the heavy gold and onyx piece he wore on his right hand. I could see, from the elegant angle of his hand resting on the arms—an elegance that did not go with such a large man—that it was engraved.

"So I did. But it would be wrong to take it off." His voice was deep and authoritative; it would, I thought, stand him well with Howard Talmadge's repertory company.

"Yes," I agreed, and waited.

There was no table, no bright lights in the room; no subordinate to witness and no obvious machine to take notes. Just the two chairs and what looked like a dying potted plant in the corner.

He said, "It would please me to speak to you as a friend."

"Certainly you may speak as you wish, Lord Cardinal."

Arno placed his big, workmanlike hands on his lap, the ring making a gold and black lump. "I have no personal dislike for you, Miss Gray. You're very young, and you had not our advantages in your upbringing. There are people here who would damn you for that, but I am not one of them."

"Thank you, Lord Cardinal."

"But as long as you're here in our hands—and you are in our hands, there's no getting around that—I was hoping you could assist us with some general information."

I leaned back. Did he know how insulting such an offer was to a Graykey? Couldn't Ennis have briefed him on that much? The very act of refusal was undignified. I felt the distant tickle of my personal daimon and heard myself say, in a voice devoid of respect, "You know, I once had a teacher who used to say, 'Keylinn, that soft head of yours is going to get you in deep trouble someday.' And heavens, it looks as though—"

Arno's slap cut me off. My cheek stung. One slap, and he was back in his chair, breathing heavily. I said, "You wanted information."

He smiled suddenly. "And you're a Graykey, and I should have specified."

"Yes, if I may be allowed the observation, Lord Cardinal. You should have. But I don't imagine you've learned much about real Graykey from Ennis Severeth Gilleys."

An eyebrow raised. "Would you prefer to be questioned by Ennis? He might be less likely to offend you inadvertently. And you know, child, you needn't address me by my full title each time you speak to me. In fact, you could simply call me "Father," if you wished—it's perfectly acceptable."

"Thank you, Lord Cardinal, I'm more comfortable with this form of address."

He smiled. "I suppose I cannot really disapprove of a proper respect for rank. And Ennis?"

"No, thank you, I have no desire to see him. I prefer to deal with you, Lord Cardinal."

He was not displeased with this response either. He leaned back, relaxing. "I regret the slap, Miss Gray," he said, surprising me, for he actually seemed sincere.

"Surely it's only good sense to keep prisoners off-balance."

"It is, but there was a component of personal temper in my action that was inappropriate. May I ask your forgiveness? You're under no obligation to give it, and I promise it will not affect our future relationship."

I'd really hoped to minimize our future relationship. "I forgive you freely, Lord Cardinal."

He nodded. "Thank you. You're very kind. And now may I point out some facts you've no doubt noticed lately? You're not on the Diamond any more, and no one from that city has made any effort to contact you or ask any questions about you. The Mercati is hardly likely to jeopardize his plans by admitting he's taken a Graykey into his city, and even into his private hunting party."

He leaned closer suddenly, although I was unaware of making any response.

"We know already that your contract-holder is the Mercati's demon, so you do him no good by denying it." He pulled his chair closer suddenly, with an irritated look, as though the gap between us was no longer to be borne. He said—and do you know, I believe he spoke sincerely—"All I wish, child, is to establish a relationship of truth between us. We can work from there."

"Go on," I told him.

"Some details of your time on the Diamond, that's all we'd like. I doubt you were privy to any great affairs of state, so why be shy? Minor things, very *small* details, that's all. Bear in mind you've been deserted by *them*. I don't know all the ins and outs of Graykey lore, but in my world a contract work both ways."

I looked at him quietly.

He said, "Have you considered that you might be going too far in the performance of your duty?"

"One cannot go too far in the performance of one's duty," I said flatly. "One either performs it, or one does not."

Arno's eyes lit with recognition of a fellow spirit. "My thoughts exactly," he said. The delight of finding another obsessed performer in this wasteland of the halfhearted was in his voice. "If only some of the priests I supervise felt that way! Oh, child, it would be a pity if we couldn't come to an agreement. Look at your situation truthfully, now—there's no way out of it, is there? And brave though you may be, you're still a woman, without a man's heart or his physical strength. I value your loyalty, I truly do, and I promise I'll continue to value it—once it's properly placed."

"I beg your pardon?" Now I was thoroughly confused.

"On the Opal, my dear, on the Opal! Ennis has only contracted for a year. We can make a special place for you—we don't usually put females in any position of responsibility, but I have the power to do it. Have no fear that we'll dump you onto Baret Station without airspace money. I appreciate intelligence and honor, in whatever guise it appears—you can work as a direct report to the Ecclesiastical Council, and I assure you that will command respect anywhere in the Three Cities."

I felt momentarily horrified, then blank. "I appreciate

your kindness, Lord Cardinal, but I really hadn't been planning on staying in the Three Cities. Thanks all the same."

His face fell, like a child's, the enthusiasm rushing out like water from a bath. His eyes hardened and I could see him place the metaphorical plug on the bathtub shelf and dismiss the disappointment from his mind. He would rise above it. He stood up. "And my questions?"

"As you said, Lord Cardinal, I'm just a woman. I doubt if I have any answers for you."

"I see." He grew businesslike. "Well, Miss Gray, I assure you that we will not use drugs in your questioning. Anything that tampers with the mind is against our religion. You interrogation will be straightforward."

"Umm . . . I assume that means painful?"

"Yes," said the Lord Cardinal. He was not a man who avoided facts.

I interrupted him as he walked to the door. "Lord Cardinal!"

He turned. I said, "I feel for my own sake that I should warn you about something. A large part of Graykey training is physical—"

"Yes?"

"Well, if I'm ever in any perceived danger of surrendering to interrogation—drugs or otherwise—my body has been prepared to kill itself."

He smiled. It was, I saw, a disbelieving smile. "Well, we'll see, shall we, Miss Gray?" And he left.

He really doesn't know the Graykey, I thought sadly. I blame Ennis for that.

Chapter 31

Arno's council rank permitted him not only a special office not far from the detention cells, but a private chapel, and he made use of it. He wanted guidance, and he wanted comfort to make up for the less comfortable as-

pects of his duty. Hartley Quince found him there an hour
later, still kneeling.

Hartley coughed. He had no intention of waiting
around until the old man came back to join the world of
lesser mortals. The Cardinal looked up, startled, then
smiled when he saw Hartley. He rose and walked to the
head of the short aisle where Hartley waited.

Arno gestured to the front of the chapel, where the
massive stone Cup stood on a pedestal. "Even in a tiny
chapel like this," he said, "the Presence can be felt."

"Yes," said Hartley, with some impatience. After all, it
had taken him a good forty minutes just to find the old
man. He said, "I need your signature on some papers for
the disposal of heretic property. I'm due back on the Diamond almost immediately, so I'm afraid I'm in a bit of
hurry."

The Cardinal sat down in the front pew, taking his time
about it and managing to suggest not only his superior
rank but a trace of hurt at Hartley's peremptory tone.
Arno was a master in his own way, mused the younger
man. He took the papers from Hartley, signed them one
by one, rustling them about fussily, and then held onto
them. "You've been spending a lot of time on the Diamond," observed the Cardinal.

"Our agents there need attention," said Hartley in a
tone of reasonableness, as he gazed at the papers wistfully. "And I'm popular with the aristos—no past to live
down with them, I suppose." There; that should add a
touch of the guilt-squirms, he thought.

Arno dropped his eyes at once and handed Hartley's
papers back to him. "I've just come from the initial
meeting with the Graykey girl."

"Have you? I trust any small information I could provide was useful, Lord Father."

Arno put a hand on his. "It was, it was. Really, Hartley,
you must overlook any temper on my part today. These
questionings always put me in a foul mood." He lifted his
head, his blue eyes vulnerable. "I don't know what I'd do
without you."

"I appreciate—"

"I mean it. My boy, I'm not supposed to tell you this
yet—" He smiled. Here he was, the terror of the Ecclesi-

astical Council, unable to hold back his pleasure. "—but
your promotion to deacon has come through. It will be
announced next week. This isn't just a regular promotion,
you know; I've gotten you an entry-seat on the council.
You can't participate yet, but you can sit in ... and I
know it won't be long before you *will* participate."

Not a participatory seat? Hartley forced enthusiasm
into his voice. "Sir!" he said, and it was wonderful how
thrilled he sounded. Sometimes he even shocked himself.
"This is wonderful. I can't believe it."

Arno looked very smug, all trace of his troubles with
the Graykey smoothed over. "Now, now," he said. "I told
you it would come. There's no need to thank me; I know
what's in your heart."

Hartley dropped at once to his knees and put his lips to
the Cardinal's ring. "Thank you, Lord Father. Thank you."

God, but Arno loved hearing that word. You could see
that hatchet face light up from inside. "There, my boy."
He put a hand briefly on Hartley's head, then took it
away. "I know you have work to do, so run along."

Hartley rose and kissed the ring again before he left. "I
hope I can justify your faith in me, Lord Father."

And there was that glow again. Hartley turned on his
heel and left the chapel.

He made his way through the administrative corridors,
considering. What a sorry day. Forty minutes to locate
His Tediousness, another eternity humoring him, and
what was the result? Not even a participatory seat.

No, the Diamond was spoiling him. The mice over
there ran a hell of a lot better.

If Arno had chosen to indulge himself with raping a
prisoner twenty-five years ago, that was his affair. But it
was fortunate, Hartley thought, that in appearance he took
after his mother's side of the genepool; or his lord father
here would have had to regretfully put him to death.

This ended Hartley's practical view of the matter.

The Lord Cardinal watched him go. He wished that he
was free to make Hartley aware of the fact that he was his
son, but it was safer for them both this way. And at least
they were together, and he could smooth Hartley's way in

the world—making up, at least a little, for his childhood in the holding pens.

Every time he looked into that face he saw Fiona. Mercati charm, they called it; whatever it was, Fiona had it. The same still brown eyes as Hartley, the same clear, childlike brow, the same self-contained look. She was a prisoner of the Civil War, scooped up on her way to visit downhill when the declaration was made. She shouldn't have taken chances leaving the City of Diamond when tensions were so high; but she was careless of her own safety, as many Mercatis were. And so she ended her life in an Opal detention cell, waiting for a prisoner exchange that was never going to take place.

Arno had had the questioning of her; one of his first serious assignments as a deacon. It was clear early on that she knew nothing of importance, but her family connections made ransom a possibility. Even then the Mercatis were dwindling; she was one of the last. The War took the others, except for Adrian. That Adrian should live and Fiona should die was the one thing in Arno's life that made him doubt the justice of God.

They read books together and talked together and argued religion together. It saddened him that she practiced the Diamond heresy, and that after all the hours of argument she would only put a hand on his arm and say, "If anyone could ever convince me, Richard, it would be you." And she would say, "You're my one hold on sanity, my love." And she would say . . .

Deacons may marry; higher ranks may not. But deacons cannot get prisoners released. He would have left off his ambitions for the council, if he could have had Fiona. He did leave off his spotless relationship with God, for he slept with Fiona, not once but many times. She was his one fall from duty, the one moment of humanity that had overturned him.

Perhaps it was God's will that she sickened and died, before he could fall any further. But he'd made up for that weakness, hadn't he? Over three hundred heretics had been identified and brought to ordeal by him alone, and over two hundred of them had accepted the light before they died. And he'd risen as far as his most ambitious thoughts had ever strayed.

God had forgiven him this one transgression, he thought now as he stood in his chapel. He was certain of it. The fruit of that deviation from duty was Hartley, good coming from bad, light from darkness. How else could the boy have survived those first years in the pens but by God's help? And survived to return to his father, a support and comfort in these lonely years.

His very existence was the sign of God's grace.

Keylinn:

I didn't like the look of this place. Even if you ignored the cross, and the table with straps, and the wheel whose purpose was unclear (and I hoped it would remain so), the gleaming metallic machines in a row in the center didn't look like gym equipment. My heart started pounding, and I began breathing exercises to calm it.

The black-clad EPs left me by the table and turned to leave.

"A moment!" called a pure, clear tenor voice. I looked up to see a chair on a balcony that ran the length of the room. Sitting in the chair was a man in a deacon's collar, but without the overjacket. He looked very ordinary—brown-haired, just starting to bald in front, a forgettable face. There was a small brown dog sitting beside him. The dog yapped as he stood. "Hush up, Lizzie," he addressed her, and he came and put his hands on the wrought-iron railing of the balcony. He said, "What are the margins? Can I use the flagellum? Am I to notify the Lord Cardinal during, or after? Haven't you any written instructions?"

One of the EPs looked up and said, "No flagellum. Scutia only—she's not supposed to die here."

If only that were reassuring, I thought.

The EP went on, "Check your link for authorization. Your choices are open, except there's to be no permanent damage."

The man walked around the balcony and came down some iron steps, his dog following. He was shorter than he'd looked up there. "Time limits, sirs?"

"I wasn't told," said the EP, and he looked to his companion, who shrugged.

"Our usual thorough organization," said the man. He picked up his dog and put her in the arms of the first EP. "Could you take Lizzie out with you when you go? She gets upset if I let her stay."

The EP looked disgusted, but he carried the dog away. When they were gone, the man walked up to me and said, "The outer doors are locked and more police are stationed there, so if you have any quaint Outsider ideas about there just being one of me and one of you, dismiss them."

I made a noncommittal sound. He said, "Well, I'd best go check my link-message. Make yourself at home."

He went through a small door at the other end of the room. I walked slowly around a bank of machinery with what looked like pads for kneeling. I wondered what that rod over there was for, and found several ideas occurring to me. At that point I went immediately to the center of the room and started running through the opening ritual of my subjectivity exercises, very quickly at first and then slower . . . slower . . . and slower. I took my pulse. There, that was better.

The man returned. "Tech Gray, is it? Very pleased, I'm sure. That's the scutia over there, in case you were wondering."

I followed the glance to a whip hanging on the wall. The strands looked like twisted paper, not that impressive. Although not having felt it, I could be wrong.

"But we're going to skip over that," said the man. "By the way, I have some basic questions that I'd like to run through here, while you're still thinking clearly. I'm sorry, do you want to sit?"

I saw nothing here I would wish to sit on. "No, thank you."

"Fine." He took out a piece of paper and read aloud. "First, why a Graykey took service on the Diamond, including personal background. Second, Officer Tal Diamond. Information on his daily routine. Foods eaten and where prepared. Information on your contract with same. Information on said officer's plans, or as much as you know about them. His Outsider name. His history. Adrian Mercati, as much of his personal habits as you know.

Why you were present at the last hunt with him. His relationship with Officer Tal Diamond. Any references made by anyone to the Sawyer crown." The man looked up. "Feel free to interrupt at any point; we can take these in any order you like."

I found I was biting my lips in an undignified way and stopped. He sighed. "Well, those are enough to begin. Nothing at all to say? Very well, Tech Gray, please remove your shirt."

"My shirt?"

"Your shirt. The white thing with the buttons. If you would, Tech Gray."

I unbuttoned my shirt and pulled it off slowly.

He pulled a canary yellow glove onto his left hand and opened a large jar. A pungent smell came from it, something like menthol. "Please stand still," he said, and he dipped his gloved hand into the jar and came up with a light green gel. He raised the hand toward my upper arm and I took an involuntary step backward. He blinked and said, "If you would please stand still, Miss Gray."

I stood still and felt the stuff being slathered onto my arms, my chest, and my back. He was actually quite gentle about it. I ran through the subjectivity ritual again and said (amazing myself with my calmness), "I see you're left-handed."

"Yes. Very rare in the Three Cities. I'm something of a freak." He pursed his lips. "Could you raise your arm, there? Thank you." He rubbed in some more, then said, "No, that spot is too difficult to reach. Could you put a dab there for me?"

I didn't move. He said patiently, "There's a squad of EPs outside this room who could hold you down and put this on you themselves, so your hesitation doesn't really accomplish much, does it?"

I still didn't move. "What is it?"

"Let's let it be a surprise."

"I thought in cases like this it's standard to tell the prisoner everything that's going to be done to them."

"Oh, don't let's be hemmed in by rules. I always feel improvisation is important in a relationship like ours."

I said, "Anyway, I don't have a glove like you do."

"Considering it's already over half your body area—"

"But not my hands yet. Although I hate to put the idea in your head."

He smiled and said, "Oh, very well. We'll skip that bit of skin, it's not very large. Would you follow me, please?"

He walked over to a large vertical board with straps. "Just lean against that, facing outward."

I found I was starting the ritual a third time. "Uh, I feel I should mention that Graykey training will make my heart stop if the interrogation seems to be getting anywhere. Arno doesn't believe me, but I thought it was something you should know."

"I assure you I'll bear it in mind. Now, against the board, please."

The whole nightmarish scene was reminding me of the unhappier medical examinations of my life. I wondered if that said anything about this man's technique, or about the techniques of medical personnel.

I continued the ritual mentally. He raised my left arm and strapped it to the board at the wrist. "This is to prevent you from hurting yourself," he said.

"Is that likely?"

"Well, it's possible. And we wouldn't want that to happen."

He fastened the leg straps, and I cleared my throat. "Uh—"

"Yes?" He looked up as he put the final snap in place.

"Nothing. I was thinking about begging and pleading for mercy, but I guess that's sort of undignified."

He stood up. "Oh, that won't bother you in a while," he said cheerfully. "But you may as well not, since it would be pretty useless. I mean, it's not in my orders to let you off, and if it's not in my orders, it's pointless to even talk about it, isn't it?"

"I suppose that's true."

He walked toward the door. "Believe me, it is, so don't even confuse yourself by thinking about it. Now, I have to leave for a little while. Everything's in place so you can carry on without me, and when I get to the end of the poem I'm reading I'll be back."

"I hope it's an epic," I said.

"Not very soon you won't. In about ten minutes you'll

wish it were a haiku. You know, you're lucky you came during my shift. Six hours later and you would've gotten Garrett, and he's much more conservative than I am. Does all the proper things, not much of a conversational-ist."

"But then," I said, "I suppose it's only a job to him."

"Exactly. He doesn't know what he's missing." He turned again at the door. "You know, I appreciate your sense of humor."

After he left, I said, "You're one of the few."

It was several minutes before my skin started to prickle. "Just suggestion," I said to myself. "Ignore it." I took the subjectivity ritual further and entered the first stage of incorporation. I thought of being one of my teachers in school, but that seemed a very long time ago and a very long way from here; instead I decided to be Tal. He was easier to do at this point and I'd had a lot of practice.

It was good to feel physically stronger than I usually did. It was good to know that I could take on just about anybody around me, and that they weren't that bright in any case. It was unfortunate that their behavior was so ir-ritatingly opaque—

A sensation of being infested pulled me back into my own subjective body. It felt as though thousands of tiny legs were walking over me—up and down my back, over my breasts, down my arms, up my neck.

I began to itch.

Less than half a minute later I was screaming. Every inch of the top part of my body demanded relief, and it was impossible to provide. It was impossible to think. I would have torn out the straps if I could—I would have torn off strips of my skin if I could have, normal pain seemed like a blessing. I pushed myself back against the board and contorted my body every way I could. Nothing helped. I writhed in the straps.

This went on for several years. Eventually the itching sensation became less fierce, than faded very slowly to a slight glowing feeling in the skin. I looked out through blurry eyes and saw the brown-haired deacon.

"How long have you been there?"

"About ten minutes," he replied.

I said a Graykey curse, then asked, "How long did that last?"

"Forever, they tell me."

I expressed a wish in the Old Tongue that he'd find himself in hell one day with all the people he'd worked on. He said, "That sounded poetic. I'm sorry I don't speak your language."

"So am I."

"We haven't very long," he said. "Have you had a change of heart?"

"Why don't we have very long?"

"One question at a time, please."

"No."

"Ah. We haven't very long because the second phase of your unfortunate skin condition is about to kick in. This one is a bit more challenging. I've brought my book in with me, and if you want anything, just call me." He sat down on the side of a piece of equipment. "I'm very good at differentiating that from the normal run of screams and cries."

I didn't feel anything now, beyond that warm glow. I said, "What's the second phase?"

"Heat," he said. He opened his book. "It's the 'Legend of Beatrice and the First Star Voyage.' Should I read it to you? You're right, it's an epic. Some of the language is a little odd-sounding today."

The warm glow began to escalate. Very soon it felt as though I were standing too close to an oven. How far would the sensation go? If it went too far, I would die, here in this silly room on Opal, worlds away from everyone who mattered. Given what I'd just gone through, the thought of death was more ambiguous than usual, but—

I gasped. It felt like a torch being held to my chest.

A bonfire followed. Joan of Arc at the stake. They burn witches here, don't they? I was vaguely aware that I'd started screaming some time ago, and I sensed, distantly, that now the screams were dying out. My heart was slowing down. And about time, too.

I slumped in the straps.

* * *

"Do you hear me?" said the voice.

"Do you hear me? Keylinn? We've stopped the interrogation. *We've stopped the interrogation.* Keylinn Gray, do you hear me?"

"I don't know," said another voice. "I've done all I can—"

I woke up in the detention suite. I put a hand to my chest and felt a light, woven cloth there—they'd given me a nightgown. My shirt was on a chair by the bed. I felt gingerly under the nightgown, ready for the aftereffects of whatever had burnt my skin, but there was no pain. I checked myself in the mirror in the bath; the skin looked as it always did.

God, what was that stuff? Maybe it was just as well only torturers knew about it, or sadists around the universe would be slipping it into other people's suntan lotion.

Actually, that was the sort of thing I might do to certain people myself, in dilute quantity. Oh, it was a good thing the Society of Judges had taken me in hand. Someday I might have gone over the edge ... there were those who thought I already had.

I walked around the suite, checked the door, and went back to bed.

It felt as though several days had passed before they brought me out again. This time I was taken to the pleasant room with the chairs. Arno was sitting in one, this time in his clothes of rank, and Ennis was lounging against the wall.

"Feeling better?" inquired the Lord Cardinal. "I'm sincerely sorry for what you've gone through."

He sounded as though he meant it. An interesting fanatic, the Lord Cardinal: He would order tortures, but he wouldn't watch them. Was that a sign of weakness or of mental health? Perhaps watchers were only sadistic voyeurs. I did not feel, as someone whose sense of humor appealed to a vocational torturer, that I was in any position to throw stones.

I took the other chair. "Hello, Lord Cardinal. I'm well, thank you."

"I'd like to put this situation back on a friendly footing," said Arno. "After all, you're not really one of us, why should you involve yourself in our little squabbles? I suppose you'll be leaving eventually, and returning to . . . wherever it is you come from."

I glanced at Ennis, whose face showed nothing. Had he told the Lord Cardinal where we came from? I wouldn't put it past him. If he did, he was going to have every Graykey in the universe on his trail, and I could almost pity him.

"That may be," I said.

"Then let me tell you how you came here. Let me tell you something of my own designs, and judge them for yourself. When I sent Ennis to the Diamond, I gave him three priorities: Kill or capture Adrian's demon. Create confusion and distrust in general. And physically sabotage wherever possible. I did mention that I'd like to meet the second Graykey, but I didn't make it part of my list."

He paused as though expecting some response from me. I said, "He didn't do a very good job, did he?"

"You're harsh, Miss Gray. I don't think he did badly, considering his circumstances. Now, may I tell you why I made these requests? First, the Mercati's demon is an abomination, which is in itself sufficient reason to end its unnatural life. But besides this, Adrian's counsel from this creature is contaminating the Diamond with Outsider filth—"

"You mean Tal's advice might give him an advantage in dealing with Outsiders."

"I mean what I say, young lady." Arno stopped and took visible hold of his temper. I suspected he was never contradicted on the Opal, and certainly not by anyone of my age and sex. "Child, I don't mean to be sharp with you. Can't you see that I'm being as open with you as I can? I want to convince you to stay with us voluntarily. I believe I can do that, because I believe the justice of our cause will be irrefutable—if only you listen with an open mind."

"May I be open as well, Lord Cardinal?"

He sat forward. "Please. It's what I've been wishing for."

"Then I would prefer that you not call me a child. I'm

twenty-seven standard years old, and a Graykey. I have been many subjects. I've traveled a long way. I've served more than one contract. I have killed people I don't even know. I am not a child."

I stared into his eyes, hearing suddenly a line from a poem: *I've known rivers more ancient than the world and older than the flow of human blood in human veins.* I felt like it, at that moment. He pulled away, looking shocked. Don't turn away, Lord Cardinal. This is what Graykey are. Ennis hasn't told you the truth.

Then he turned back, his eyes gleaming. "How many people have you killed?" he asked with interest.

My mouth settled briefly in a line of contempt. It was a typical stranger's question. Why did they only see the Graykey as weapons? There was so much to learn, and to teach, *if only* . . .

"Well?" he said.

Nor was it a question I liked personally. Before the Diamond I had killed only two people, one by my own will and one to fulfill my commitment to Cyr Elizabeth Vesant. Since the *Kestrel,* though— "I'm not sure of the exact number," I admitted.

Arno's eyes brightened. "As I expected. Tell me—did you take care of these people one-on-one, as they say, close up so you could see them?"

"I prefer to do it that way," I answered, a literally true statement.

He sat back, satisfied. "You don't mind speaking with me, do you? You said before that you didn't want to be questioned by your fellow Graykey, here—"

"I did not say that."

He seemed taken aback for a moment, then said, "Forgive me. You said that you didn't want to be questioned by this gentleman here on my right, known as Ennis Gilleys."

Arno's moments of sharpness were not a comfort. It was clear that, like me, he had an exact understanding of the requirements of his philosophy and lived within them. His understanding was a burden to me. Did his way of living really make him a fanatic?

Did my way of living make me one?

I said, "I'm very tired."

He had the presumption to let sympathy show in his face. He started to speak—

And from behind my left ear, as though he were standing in the room beside me, I heard a voice I knew very well.

Keylinn, this is Tal.

For a moment I was thoroughly disoriented. Then I realized: The riccardi. I sat up, shocked.

If you're alive I'm just within perimeter of your riccardi. I sincerely hope you're in one of the ecclesiastical *detention cells, because that's where we're heading. I base this on the fact it was Arno's voice I heard talking to Ennis in Transport, and that Arno is a greedy bastard who won't let any prize out of his own sweaty hands . . . neither will I, actually.*

We're docking now. I'm turning this over to Spider. Follow his instructions.

A moment later: *Keylinn, sweetheart?* Spider's voice came with nervous gentleness. *We're in Bay Green of Opal Transport. We've come in with some private trading freighters from Baret Station. We replaced one, in fact— never mind about that, though. Listen. I'm staying with the ship and Tal is bringing some friends of yours to get you out.*

Friends of mine?

You may need to make some noise shortly to let them know what room you're in. And be ready to hit the floor, Key. There was a pause. *God, I hope you're in good shape. And if you can hear me, tell Lord Cardinal Asshole to go to hell.*

"Go to hell," I said obediently.

Arno, who had been looking at me strangely, now reared back as though I had lost my mind.

I turned my eyes narrowly to Ennis and said in Graykey, "Nothing is forgotten."

Chapter 32

The cadets, all in brown lower-ranking admin uniforms, fanned out across the deck. Three went slightly ahead to do advance work for Tal; two accompanied him; and seven—including Tommy, the monarch of explosives—split into two more groups to create problems for Opal. These problems would begin with Transport.

Tal left them to it. His two groups had about a quarter-hour to reach the EP's detention cells—just barely possible, by the map. A Transport supervisor ran up to him.

"Sir, where do you think you're going? Where is your pass, your papers?"

The Graykey beside Tal shot him. "We don't have any," she said, putting the silver gun back into a holster beneath her uniform jacket. Women were not allowed in admin under any circumstances on the Opal, so her hair was cropped short and her jacket oversized. She smiled briefly at Tal and went out the bay exit.

Tal had never seen a gun like that one. It was small, but definitely not a Keith. He considered whether he should ask whether it was lethal or only a stunner, but decided not to waste either of their times on minor points. He stepped over the Transport supervisor and followed his Graykey out, hearing a distant explosion and people shouting as he did so.

They passed three City Guards on the way to detention, all of them running as though in answer to an emergency summons. None of them spared a look for Tal's group. None of the Graykey spoke; they had never assumed that getting in would be the hard part. They strode grimly through the decks and took the civilian lift banks as though born to them.

The maps were good enough to get them to the detention places, at least. Tal looked up at a sculptured facade that rose five intradeck levels. An angel of repentance clung spread-eagled to the front, ten times the height of a man, the wings brushing either side of the roof. The prisoners in there must number in the hundreds. How was he ever going to find Keylinn in that place?

The cadets didn't even break stride. They passed through the front doors, always open in case any citizen wanted to report on another. Tal checked the time; they had about ten minutes to locate Keylinn if they wanted any margin of safety in getting out. They managed to pass the front desk as though they knew where they were going, but in fact it was guesswork from this point on. There were no maps for the inside of the detention center.

The advance party met them at the lift bank, and they crowded inside. At least the inner lifts here only went up from this level, not down—the first clue as to direction. The doors opened on the next level to show a corridor of cells with one-way glass. More corridors joined it in the distance. A Graykey boy said, "We can look for her—it's glass." He started to step out, but Tal grabbed hold of his sleeve.

"We don't have time to do it that way." He motioned for them to continue, and they tried the next level. It was the same.

But the third level up opened onto a large room with a big curving desk, people running back and forth, and a scattering of black-clad EPs with prisoners. "A processing center," said Tal. "They would know."

The girl cadet raised an eyebrow. "Should we just ask them?" Clearly she did not mean the question seriously. Tal stepped out of the lift, and his cadets emerged behind him. The girl said softly, "If you weren't a gathrid, I would have overruled you for your own good. I hope you know what you're doing."

Yes. One did hope that. He went to the desk, motioning with a slight inclination of the head for them to fan out inconspicuously through the room. They did so. He thought briefly that they did seem very good at picking up his instructions with almost no explanation; perhaps there was something to the apparent mysticism surrounding the *tarethi-din* relationship after all. He also noted that somehow each Graykey ended up rather near an EP. He approved.

He listened to the admins behind the desk as they

talked. They were being brought new prisoners and notified of the release of old ones. One prisoner was being reclassified with a higher security rating. The admins handling the processing checked link-screens behind the desk as they spoke, but from what they said it was clear that they were familiar with most prisoner movements already.

Good. They were efficient. He hadn't hoped for that. He glanced around for the female cadet, met her eyes, and motioned for her to come over. Then Tal approached an admin at the end of the desk who was writing on a long piece of paper; there was no line waiting to speak to him.

"Excuse me," said Tal.

The man looked up. He had circles under his eyes that looked as though they'd been there since birth. He said, "The lines are over there."

"This is a special matter. Confidential."

"The lines are still over th—"

"It concerns you personally."

He was surprised into giving Tal his full attention; Tal had the impression it was not something he regularly did for anybody.

"Yes?"

Tal pulled a sheaf of papers from his inside jacket pocket. "See these papers?"

"Yes . . ."

He lifted a corner of them. "See the Keith pistol inside here? It's pointing at your head."

The man froze. Tal said, "My companion here does not have his hands inside his jacket because they're cold. He's also armed."

The man said, "Listen to me. This is impossible. You can't get out of here. You're both very young—"

"Shut up. Don't babble and don't look upset, or we will have to shoot you. All right?"

"All right." The man was pale now, and one hand shook.

"And I'm glad to see you haven't set off any alarms yet, because if you make one move of any kind—"

"No! I mean, I'm not." His foot had, in fact, been moving, but it stopped.

"We want you to locate a prisoner for us. Keylinn Gray, an Outsider tech from the Diamond—entered within the last few days. Push any buttons with you?"

"I'd have to consult my records—"

He made a move toward the link, and the cadet said, "Wait." She'd lowered her voice, but it still sounded female. The admin didn't look surprised, though—no doubt he put it down to youth and nerves. "He's lying," said the cadet.

Tal glanced at her. She seemed very sure. He said to the man, "You don't need to consult your records, do you." It was a statement.

"I do! You don't know how many people come through here—"

"It's a lie." Her voice was firm. "He knows about this prisoner. May I shoot him, sir? We can try someone else."

"All right! She's been in the POW suite, but she's not there now. An order came through an hour ago to take her to a questioning room by the Lord Cardinal's offices."

Tal had no idea at all whether this was a lie. He looked at his cadet and she nodded, satisfied. "It's true."

Tal said to the admin, "Where are the Lord Cardinal's offices?"

"Level five. First left."

He seemed eager to see them go. "You'll show us," said Tal.

"I can't leave," he said.

"You'll have to," said Tal. "Look around the room. Do you see some young admins in brown whom you don't recognize? They're all armed, too. They won't hesitate about killing you, your friends, and anyone else in the room. Do you understand what I'm saying?"

He saw the man's eyes move as he looked around the room. Tal turned his head slightly and ran a glance over the other Graykey; all were looking this way. All had interested, funny smiles that could only be called feral. Like a circle of wolves moving in on their prey. He hadn't told them to do that, but they seemed to slide almost into a gestalt—a spooky lot, the Graykey. He looked back to see the effect on their admin.

The man's eyes grew larger and more despairing. He tried to talk, and stopped, knowing it was hopeless. The

lines of his face looked as though they might collapse at
any time into shapeless dough ... the fear reactions of
humans were so physically based. Tal very rarely felt
fear, certainly not as this ravening *thing* the humans did,
though his survival drive was imperative. Interesting.
Worth later thought. He said, "Now, please. Get up and
walk to the door as though you were on business. Remember that these weapons are still pointed at you, and
if anything goes wrong, you'll be the first to die."

Clearly he was in no danger of forgetting that. The cadet said, more gently, "Nothing will happen to you if you
cooperate. We're not interested in you at all; why should
we want to hurt you?"

This was pointless, thought Tal. Why try to reassure
him? Anything they said could be a lie. And yet the quiet
words seemed to help the man to rise and walk toward the
exit. The other four Graykey in the room glanced discreetly toward them; the girl motioned with her hand and
they made their way casually to the lift bank.

The seven of them crowded into the lift, and as it rose,
the girl hummed a short line of music which made the
others break into laughter. Tal didn't recognize it. They
got out at level five and took their guide with them to
the first door on the left.

"It's not locked," said the girl with contempt.

"Who would disturb the Lord Cardinal?" said the
admin, as though defending his honor. "And this is the
EP detention center. Nobody would dare—" He cut that
one short, and managed to look embarrassed as well as
afraid.

She opened the door.

There was a room with a desk, a link, and bookshelves.
Three doors led out of it. Tal prodded the admin with his
Keith pistol, but the man said, "I've never been here be-
fore."

Time was pressing. Tal let the pistol fall and yelled,
"Keylinn!"

"Here!" It came from the room on the left.

The cadets were inside almost before he could move,
and Tal had always been pleased with his reflexes. For
humans, they were far from human. He pulled the admin
with him into the other room.

Ennis Severeth Gilleys and Lord Cardinal Arno were
there with Keylinn. She looked unharmed. Arno stood up
and took a step back. "What do you think you're doing?
These are my rooms! Get out!"

The Graykey all had their weapons on display. Tal
stepped forward and said, "Don't you recognize me in
this uniform, Lord Cardinal?"

The eyes seemed to focus suddenly. "The Mercati's demon." Then he gave a nervous laugh. "Demon or not,
you'll never leave the Opal. This is excellent, sir—I
asked to have you brought here, and here you stand!"

"Be polite," advised Keylinn, "or they might shoot
you." She stood up and walked around the chair to join
the other Graykey.

The Lord Cardinal glared at Ennis. "You handle personal security. How could they get in here?"

Ennis looked sick. "Are you crazy?" he said to his
contract-holder, with no respect at all. "They're *Graykey
cadets.*"

"And I think they're upset with you," said Tal.

Ennis moaned very softly. One of the cadets said,
"Should we take the shaman as a hostage?" He gestured
to Arno.

"More of a burden, I think," said Tal. "We'll just
knock him out. Try not to kill him, it would probably
cause an incident."

"You think this *isn't* an incident?" asked Arno, backing
away from an advancing Graykey.

"This didn't even happen," said Tal. "any more than
Ennis's bombs happened. How could we rescue someone
who was never kidnapped? How could we take a Graykey
you'll never admit to having under contract?"

Ennis said, "Wait a minute. I can show you how to get
out of the center. There's a security station by the lifts—"

"Don't tell them!" said Arno.

"It controls all the floors," said Ennis.

Arno said to Tal, "Don't do this. I give you my word
as a man of God that I won't do anything to stop you."

Tal ignored him, and the Graykey boy hit him with his
silver gun. Arno collapsed to the floor.

"Out," said Tal, and they all headed for the lifts. Once

there, Ennis was pulled against the wall by two Graykey. "Well?" said Tal.

Ennis opened a panel near the lift doors. "Emergency backup for security. Cells can be opened and closed from here."

The Graykey girl inspected the switches. "Ha! They've lost their minds from too much religion." She pushed some buttons. "It's all controlled by sound. One coded signal, and all the cells will be open—it should keep the EPs occupied for a while. Of course, there'll still be Special Security and the City Guard to contend with." She looked at Ennis. "What's the code?"

He leaned over and punched it in. No one made any threats to Ennis; clearly they felt it was unnecessary. A high-pitched sound seemed to pass through their bones, and they heard shouting.

"Hurry. They'll close the lifts in a few minutes."

Two minutes later they were outside.

They hurried through the admin territory corridors, changing routes each time they found the way back blocked by squads of City Guards. They turned into half a dozen new maze-openings. Five minutes later Tal said, "This isn't on the maps. We're lost."

Keylinn dug an elbow into Ennis's ribs. He said, "I don't know this part of the City."

"Well, you did say the maps were old," said a cadet. "And that Opal lies anyway about where things are."

Another cadet said, "Sir, I feel I must point out that our contract only has eighty-five minutes to run."

"All right, you've pointed it out." They forged blindly ahead, reaching dead ends, taking shortcuts through suites of offices and passing startled admins at their tasks. "We don't have time for this," said Tal. "By the way, I don't suppose you'd consider staying on past the end of your contract, for sentimental reasons?"

"Actually we would," said the cadet. "But the Dean was very specific."

They opened another door and came to a large chamber with a dozen people in white slave uniforms. From the markings they belonged to the Ecclesiastical Council. They were artisans, working on a statue of— "Good god," said Keylinn, "that's Arno."

"For his death memorial, I hope," said Tal.

A supervisor in a beige suit looked belligerent for a second, then stood back, apparently thinking the better of it. Tal glanced at his little army, shrugged, and strode to the platform in the front of the room. He stepped up to the statue's pedestal and announced to the room, without preamble, "Excuse our imposition. We are Outsider terrorists, and we're on our way to Transport. Anyone here who knows the way to Transport and will guide us there, we'll take away with us. As you know, slavery is illegal in the Empire."

The artisans stared at them blankly. Seconds passed. Then one of them, a light-haired boy in his late teens, threw down his hammer and chisel. He said, "I'll take you."

A girl with curly hair and a pale face grabbed hold of his arm. She said, "Don't be crazy. The Guard will kill you. Gabriel!"

He shook her off. "I'm sorry, Terry, good-bye." He didn't even look at her; his eyes were on Tal, as though measuring him for honesty.

The other slaves still looked stunned. Tal descended the platform and met the boy's eyes, his own face as blank as ever. He said only, "Hurry."

The boy led them through the back halls of priest-country. They came to another set of lifts, and Gabriel said, "I don't know if we can all fit in one."

"Three of us will take the next one," said a cadet. "Two and Ennis, just in case we're late. We should leave the admin; he can't hurt us now."

Tal nodded. They'd come a long way through the corridors; how far did they have to travel now? The first lift came and they entered it. Tal heard Ennis say to his captors, "I told you how to open the cells."

"We didn't contract for that information," came the soft answer. "But I thank you for the gift."

The lift doors closed. Tal drew his pistol and rested it gently against Gabriel's skull.

The doors opened onto a Transport bay. Tal removed the pistol. He pushed Gabriel out into the bay. "Follow the others," he said. The Graykey were already running toward the ship.

Another lifted opened and the rest of their party joined in the run, dragging Ennis with them. The Transport area seemed deserted by Opal personnel; smoke arose from some of the equipment. Evidently the diversion group had been busy.

One of that group ran to him now, a boy with a short nose and freckles just like Keylinn's. He said, "We're missing Tommy."

"Everyone else here?"

"Yes," said the boy.

Tal visualized making his explanations to the Dean, then turned and went toward the exit. "We've just spiked the lifts," called the boy after him, "but they'll overrule it in a few minutes!"

He found Tommy only a short way down the hall, through the exit doors. Tal would have liked to kill him. The ugly, shuttered face looked toward him as he approached. "Wait," he said, and because Tal had dealt with Graykey he waited.

They were just before a corner at a junction of routes. The sound of pounding feet echoed through the hall. "Security," said Tommy.

Tal waited. He heard more footsteps, this time behind him, and he turned. It was Gabriel. "What the hell are you going here?"

The boy looked as confused about the answer as anyone. Tommy glanced at him. "Just keep quiet."

A few seconds later two City Guards appeared at the far end. Two more came behind them, and then two more. All carried light-rifles. They reached the middle of the hall and hesitated. One man was talking to the others; they heard him say, "There was an explosion on the Green side. Maybe we should take the other route."

Tommy took hold of Gabriel's arm and pulled him close. In his ear he said softly, "Call them."

Gabriel looked horrified. His lips moved, but the words were almost inaudible. "They'll kill me."

"You're wearing Opal slave colors," came Tommy's voice, his mouth against the boy's ear. "They don't see you as a threat. Scream and beg for help. Say you saw us pass, say we took you prisoner, just scream and point this way."

The boy still hesitated. Tal said softly, "Do you have the faintest hope of surviving if we don't get out of the City?" Gabriel wet his lips with his tongue. "Call them," whispered Tal.

Gabriel stepped out into the corridor. He waved his arms, looking every bit as pathetic as he felt. Shouts came from the City Guards. "Help!" yelled Gabriel. "Help me! Sirs! They're over there, they're over there!" And he pointed frantically toward the bay entrance.

The shouts brought more men. The corridor filled with uniforms and light-rifles. When as many were there as Tommy deemed necessary, he said, "Curtain up."

And the lower half of the corridor burst into flames and screams. "One battalion down," said Tommy. "It'll take them a little while to send out another unit."

"Shall we go now?" asked Tal.

Tommy grinned and spit out a piece of gum, and they ran through the doors. Gabriel came after, sparing a single look back with a faintly vicious smile.

Behind them came a smell of roasting flesh.

Tal and the Graykey ran into the ship and Tal took the pilot's seat at once to begin take-off procedures. Gabriel tried to follow them in, but Spider moved to block the end of the ramp. "Hold on there, friend, where do you think you're going?"

Gabriel said, "I'm coming with you."

"The hell you are. Get down off the ramp."

The boy paled. "I *have* to—" he began, and realized that Spider was holding a gun. He peered over Spider's shoulder into the dim interior, where he could just see the shape of the Outsider commander. He threw a glance at the wall behind him to check the lift levels, which were lighting nicely—the Graykey sabotage had been overruled, Security was on its way. Sweat broke out on his face.

Spider brought up the gun. "Look, friend, I've never shot an unarmed man before, but if you continue to be irritating—"

Gabriel burst out, "Sir! Commander! Sir Terrorist!"

Tal glanced up briefly from the controls. "Let him in, Spider, I told him he could come."

Spider shrugged and stepped out of the way.

The hatch was closed and Tal cut them from the dock. He connected the computer-pilot to the traffic net and told it to open the bay. They took off.

Spider came up beside Tal at the controls. "Can I start to relax now?" he asked.

"No. I assume they'll try to shoot us."

"Christ! What are we doing about that?"

"Do you mind?" asked Tal, pausing over the computer entry. "I'm doing it now."

Spider muttered and withdrew. A moment later Tal said, "There. Let's see how bright they are."

His tone suggested it was no contest. Spider came forward to check the traffic monitor, where he saw a dozen points representing ships in and about the Opal. "We're not close to anything," he remarked. "They've got a clear field to target us."

Tal did not reply. On the monitor there was a brief flare on one of the blips. When it died, that blip was gone. "What was that?" asked Spider.

"That was supposed to be us," said Tal, with more than a little smugness. "I managed to lie to the traffic net."

Spider relaxed a little, then said, "Do you think there were any people on board?"

"I wouldn't know," said Tal. "I chose it for location." He went back to the controls, attaching their new course for the Diamond military port, an area of docking that would be better able to protect them if anyone in Opal woke up. A few moments later he said, "No. It was a drone. Listed here as cargo." Suddenly he laughed. "Listen to this—it's on the manifest as carrying gold bathroom fixtures for Lord Cardinal Arno's residence."

"How about that?" said Spider. "They're wrong, you do have a sense of humor."

Tal blinked. "*Humor* is not one of the things I lack."

"Gold bath fixtures," said Spider, then he whistled. "Some poor fool in Weapons is going to be in trouble tomorrow."

"Would you rather us than him?"

"No, but I can sympathize."

Tal looked around. The only other person there was

Gabriel, who was sitting in the corner trying to be inconspicuous. "What's become of Ennis the Disliked?"

"He's down in the hold with the cadets. And Keylinn."

Tal looked faintly startled. "Find out if he's still alive.
I wanted to ask him some questions."

Spider glanced at Gabriel and vanished down the stairs.
A minute later he returned, looking pale.

"Well?" asked Tal.

"He's alive. I gave them your message."

"What's the matter with you?"

Spider swallowed. "He was unconscious when I went
down. They were arguing about what to do with him. Tal,
I don't think the Graykey are people we ever want to offend."

"So I understand."

"If you let them have him, I don't want to know about
it."

"All right."

Spider looked over at Gabriel. "Don't you have anything to do?"

"No," said Gabriel.

"And there's another thing," said Spider. "What do you
intend to do with this cargo? Toss him on the Station? We
don't have the money to support him. Take him to the Diamond? He doesn't have papers."

"Adrian owes me a favor," said Tal.

"Fine, fine, why worry."

There was a sound of footsteps on the stairs to the
hold, and Keylinn appeared. Tommy came up behind her,
and she put an arm around his waist. Tal turned in his
seat to watch.

"Tal," she said, "I'd like to formally present Tommy
O'Malley, my . . ." She hesitated in translating. "My
cousin three times removed on my mother's side. I think
that's how you say it. Tommy, my *tarethi-din*. May you
both be friends, for the sake of contract-sanity and by my
own wishes."

Tal stood. "What should I do?" he asked.

"Bow," said Keylinn.

They both bowed, and Tal said, "A relative, eh? I
should have recognized the marks."

Keylinn was puzzled. "We don't look alike, except for the hair."

"I meant the affinity for explosives. So far as I'm concerned, Tommy . . . we're friends."

Tommy's ugly face grinned. "On my part, too." He took out a silver flask and swallowed from it. Then he offered it to Tal. "Your enemies are my enemies," he said, adding, "insofar as it's practical."

Keylinn was glad to see that Tal recognized a ritual when he saw it, and accepted a drink from Tommy's flask. It would have been unfortunate otherwise. "We have to get Spider into this now," she said.

The head of another Graykey cadet appeared at the hatchway stairs and said, "Oh, that's not necessary, sister. Spider's been drinking from our flasks for days. He's blood-tied to practically everybody here."

Spider looked up at this statement and appeared horrified.

They disembarked in the military docking area on the Diamond. Keylinn, her arm again around Tommy's waist, said, "I guess this is where you guys flap your arms and fly home under your own power."

She exchanged kisses with the other cadets. A boy who'd said once that he was captain of the Herons wiped tears from his eyes and said to Tal, "Will you formally release us early, sir? We have twenty-three minutes left." He pulled out a lace handkerchief and blew his nose sentimentally.

"How *will* you be getting home?" asked Tal.

The cadet gave a smile of engaging shyness. "Well, we were hoping to trespass on your hospitality for a lift to Baret Station. We can hitch on any craft you have going that way."

"Easily done," said Tal. He added, "I release you."

Cheers came from some of the cadets. "A gathrid," Tal heard one say, "and we still made it out alive!" The captain of the Herons waved a hand in Gabriel's direction and said, "Would you like us to take him along? We can probably find something for him to do at home."

Gabriel looked alarmed. He circled behind Tal. "No! I'm staying with you, aren't I?"

"I'm staying on the Diamond," said Tal.

"Fine," said Gabriel.

The cadet shrugged. "So be it." He joined the other Graykey, who were consulting the Diamond traffic net for the next ship to Baret Station.

"Relax," said Keylinn to Gabriel. "No one will interfere with your fate."

He still looked wary. Tal called, "Spider! Take our new possession to the office and tuck him in on the sofa. He looks tired."

"He's not the only one," said Spider as he joined them.

"And you might want to give some thought to creating papers for him, just in case."

Spider glared briefly at Tal, then gave Keylinn a quick, shy kiss on the cheek. "Welcome back. Come along, you," he said to Gabriel, and he started walking away. Gabriel hesitated, then followed.

"We'll have to stop at my mother's," she heard Spider's voice as if faded in the distance. "She'll be worried that I missed my visit. Do you like cookies?"

"You've made a conquest," said Keylinn. She paused, looking uncomfortable, then said, "I wasn't sure you would come. I thought it might be politically embarrassing for Adrian."

Tal smiled, not nicely. "All of this happened off the books. When next we meet the Lord Cardinal, it will be business as usual. So much for human politics in action."

"Except that now he hates you on a personal level. I'm not sure you should have let him get cracked over the head—I think he would have kept his word."

Tal looked at her. She said defensively, "Odd though it may seem, I think he's a man of honor in his own way."

"Would he think it necessary to keep his word to a demon? Anyway, considering that he wanted to kill me before for solely philosophical reasons, I don't think his feelings can make much difference."

She said seriously, "Purified hatred always makes a difference." Then she laughed. "Here I am being critical. I don't mean to complain that you got me out. Thanks."

"Well, why shouldn't I? I still have two hundred and forty days left on your contract."

Her smile vanished. "Two hundred and twenty-seven days."

"We'll argue it later."

But she said, "Tal, you do understand that you don't need to protect yourself against the ending of the contract? I told you, the secrets of past contract-holders are privileged. I don't suddenly become unreliable."

He said nothing.

She spoke more loudly, "You believe that, don't you?"

"I understand it."

She looked at him sharply. Was Graykey truth catching?

Out of nowhere she said, "Tal, what's the Sawyer Crown?"

"The what?"

"Your pardon," interrupted Tommy O'Malley, coming over to them. "All's well, sister-cousin. There's a ship in three hours' time, and the *Fixed Star* is in port at the Station waiting for us." He said to Tal, "That's one of ours, kept on ice to return any prodigals. My sister-cousin could have taken it, in an emergency."

She grinned a twisted grin. "If I thought they'd let me set foot on Home before the seven years were up. Good journeying, my love."

They hugged. Tal said, "That's an unusual name for a ship."

"Ah, well," said Tommy. "It's a reference to our vision of what life is all about—namely, to discover the truth and live by it, no matter what the cost. It's meant to be funny."

"Oh? Graykey humor sometimes escapes me."

"It's from a very old song," explained Tommy, "before the Age of Exploration. 'Castles are sacked in war, chieftains are scattered far; truth is a fixed star, Eileen Aroon.'"

Tal still did not look enlightened. "But there *are* no fixed stars," he said reasonably.

"I know," said Tommy, and he smiled as though at the joke of it.

Chapter 33

Or from Browning some "Pomegranate," which, if
*   cut deep down the middle,*
Shows a heart within blood-tinctured of a veined
*   humanity.*

ELIZABETH BARRETT BROWNING

It was to be a June wedding. The date, the sixteenth, was chosen by an Oracle on Pearl for luck. Iolanthe's headaches increased as the joyful day approached.

Adrian was so hatefully good to her—she couldn't possibly hide from the knowledge that when she was angry at him, it was her own temper and not his fault. She occasionally thought that it would do wonders for their relationship if some things *would* be his fault.

She'd been prepared for living among enemies, but this half-and-half state was unendurable. He was a heretic . . . he seemed honorable enough. He was rumored to be the murderer of Saul Veritie . . . he was always gentle with her. He kept a pet demon . . . well, there was no way around that one. Iolanthe joined the private and lonely club of those who never got a good night's sleep—pity we can't wear badges to identify each other, she thought; we could commiserate, at least. She thought she spied occasional marks of membership in Will Stockton.

One morning she called Will in and asked him to sit with her at breakfast. You could do that, she thought defiantly, on the Diamond; so why not do it? Anyway, he was a bodyguard, he was supposed to be at her disposal. She gave him coffee and date-bread and they regarded each other through tired eyes.

She sighed. At last she said, "You know how to reach Hartley Quince."

"When I have to," said Will warily.

"I need to talk to you about some things. I need to make them clear so you can pass them on without any misunderstanding."

Will's glance passed over the room and returned to her. *Here?* it said.

"I don't care," she said, answering the gesture.

He pushed his plate away. "Talk," he said.

She smiled a wry smile. Will Stockton, ever the courtier. "I'm getting married in two days."

"Yes."

"It wasn't my idea, you know. I came here because other people wanted me to. But now that I'm here, I think I should live up to what's expected of me. As best I can."

"I'm not sure I-"

"Will, I'm going to be Adrian Mercati's wife. Do you think it's honorable for Adrian's wife to report back on him to the Lord Cardinal? Even if it was the Lord Cardinal's idea?"

Will blinked. This was not a question he was in any position to discuss truthfully. Not to mention the complication that Will's truths on this subject tended to veer from the official version. He said, "My lady . . ."

She put a hand on his. "Never mind 'my lady.' I shouldn't have asked you. But let me put it this way: *I'm* not sure that it's an honorable thing to do."

"I see." Very neutral.

"That's what I want you to tell Hartley Quince. Not to expect anything from me. I'm sorry, but that's how I feel. I've already—I've done enough. And I don't want him calling the Lord Cardinal over to talk to me. From now on I'm seeing the hierophant with our delegation—and if *he* gives me a hard time, I'll go to one of the Diamond heretics."

He couldn't keep the grin off his face. This was the little girl he'd thought might run back down the ramp when they left the Opal. "Well, my lady," he said, "you're a grown woman, and you have to do as you think best."

She looked at him suspiciously. "Are you laughing at me?"

"I would never do that." He picked up the hand that still covered his and kissed it as he'd done when they first met. "I'll pass your message along." He rose from the table, still grinning.

"You haven't touched your coffee."

"That's all right. I prefer tea anyway." He bowed and left her. There would be another Sangaree guard still outside, she knew, because that was the way Will was.

She sat there alone and stared thoughtfully at the door. Her hands were slowly and with a life of their own pulling apart a piece of the date-bread. A quarter-hour later she looked down at her plate in surprise and saw a mound of crumbs.

Well, who knew what would come of it?

"What do you think her problem is?" asked Hartley. "Do you think she's in love?"

Will said, "How do I know what's going on in her head?" He knelt silently for a moment in his pew at St. Tom's. Up in the front of the church people were hanging garlands and long white banners. "But, no, I don't think so. I think she just likes Adrian and believes what she's doing is wrong."

" 'Wrong,' eh? Interesting concept. Maybe she just needs a small jolt of reality."

Will turned to scan his face. Hart was looking straight ahead to the Symbol with a respectful expression. Will said, "She seems pretty firmly decided to me."

A small smile appeared and disappeared on Hart's face. "No cause for alarm, old chum. By the way, how was your sister's wedding? I never asked."

"It was fine. I was best man."

"Glad to hear it. Have you heard anything about where you're going after our Io's settled in as a Mercati?"

"Going?"

"Your next assignment, Willie. Once she's married, they can't have an Opal citycop running bodyguard duty for her. She'll get Diamond protection."

Will said, slowly, "No, I haven't heard anything yet."

"Well, let me know. I hate to have old friends drop out of sight."

Somewhere above them a harp and a durami clashed as the respective musicians tuned them.

* * *

Three large rooms in court territory had been turned over to Barraci and Sons, the tailors who had won the wedding rights. Last-minute alterations were being made in nearly everybody's clothing, and people who had accidentally gotten red sashes when they should have gotten blue (and vice versa) hurried in and out with boxes. Decorators were milling around as well, double-checking the colors of the wedding party for their match with the banners and flowers in the church and the ballroom.

"I thought all this was supposed to have been done weeks ago," said Iolanthe. She stood on a footstool in the midst of this chaos with a woman from Barraci's pinning the hem of her gown. Prudence Taylor was with her. Even Prudence looked a little done-in; she'd pulled over a small hassock and collapsed on it with an expression of relief.

"It's never done," said Prudence. "Even tomorrow morning people will be running around—right up to the last second. I don't really know why—it's the way human beings are." She sighed and fanned herself with the program for the wedding music.

Io caught sight of herself in the mirror across the room. The welts on her face were almost completely gone, and cosmetics could take care of the remainder. She was glad she'd spoken to Will yesterday morning, it was a weight off her mind in one sense ... and in another sense, another weight put on. She could just visualize the Lord Cardinal being told of her treachery. Or her cowardice ... however they would see it.

"Honey, do you have another headache coming on?" asked Prudence. "Your face has that look."

In fact, she did have another headache coming on. "I'll be all right," she said.

"Where's the aspirin I gave you?"

The tailor-woman showed no reaction to this reference to forbidden drugs; she was probably used to showing no reaction to anything the aristos said or did. Io said, "It's in my purse."

"Well, it won't do any good there, sweetheart."

Io had tried Prudence's aspirin before; it was about as effective against her crushing headaches as a good heart was against a Keith pistol. (She had once heard Will use that metaphor.) "Really, Pru—"

"I'll get it." Prudence rose and went over to a chair on the side of the room, where she found Iolanthe's purse under a pile of silk. The purse was small, of pink satin and ribbons, and perfectly in this season's style. She brought it back to Io, obeying the age-old law that one does not root around in another woman's purse, even if one already knows everything inside it.

Iolanthe opened the drawstrings and pulled out a small gold case, from which she removed two little white pills. Prudence brought her a cup of water from the refreshment table in the corner of the room. "Drink up," she said.

Io hesitated. "I wish you could have gotten more things from that lady," she said; meaning witchcraft herbs from the witch on Mercati Boulevard. Io was more discreet than Prudence in speaking in front of servants.

"Well, she's not in her shop lately; I don't know where she is, and we'll just have to do without her. Swallow 'em, now."

Io put one of the aspirin in her mouth. She often had difficulty swallowing pills, and she found herself hesitating . . . hesitating longer than was usual . . . the taste of the aspirin was foul, even more sour than normal. She felt an overpowering urge to spit the stuff out. Good heavens, not in front of everybody! But the urge swelled, so that between one second and the next she found herself frantically searching for a trash pail. There! She spied one, jumped off the stool, ran over to it, and spit. She couldn't have held back another moment.

She breathed hard with relief, still gagging. Oh, lord, and now she had to turn and face people.

Prudence rushed over to her. "Io, what's the matter? You jumped like you'd been set on fire. Are you all right?"

Behind Prudence Io could see the tailor-woman standing and staring at her, not troubling to hide her complete loss to explain the ways of spoiled aristo girls, and her contempt. "I . . . I'm okay, I just . . ." How could she possibly explain this? She had no idea what had come over her.

"What happened?" It was a new, male voice, and Iolanthe looked around in shock. Tal Diamond was standing beside her. He must have come over from the other side of the room.

"What are you doing here?" she said.

He set down a white oblong box on the table beside the trash pail. "They sent me the wrong color sash. What happened here?"

Prudence had an arm around her now. She looked up at the demon and said, "Iolanthe wasn't feeling well, that's all. Are you better now, honey?"

"Yes. Thank you. I just ... I felt strange, that's all—"

Tal reached out and gently opened her fist. Under ordinary conditions this would have been a shocking breach of courtesy, but Iolanthe was too drained to stop him.

He plucked the other aspirin from the palm of her hand. He said to Prudence, "Where are the rest?"

"See here, Officer Diamond—"

It was odd. Iolanthe had the definite impression that Tal had caused the pill to disappear into one of his pockets, but she couldn't swear as to which pocket it was. He said, "Were they in your possession, or Iolanthe's, since they were bought?"

Prudence's eyes widened. "You don't expect that someone here would—"

"I have no expectations at all. I do have access to a lab. Give me the rest of the pills."

His hand was out. Prudence picked up the gold case and gave it to him.

"Prudence," said Io.

"It's all right," said Prudence. "It's not as if this officer will complain about breaking church law."

"But it's all so ridiculous. I really don't know why I made such a fuss. And I surely don't know why it should be taken seriously."

"It's never pointless to investigate," said Tal. "And if you don't protect yourself, who will?" He bent and took hold of the trash pail. "I'll carry this along, too."

Prudence made a face at that, but Tal merely placed it under the curve of one arm and reached for his box. It must have been awkward to manage, for he opened the cover, tossed the box away, and slung the sash over one shoulder.

Io spoke up then, and her voice had changed. "You said you'd been given the wrong color sash."

"Yes."

Had she but known it, she was speaking in the same tone of voice Will Stockton sometimes used, and a gen-

eral suspicion of the universe was in it. "But you're a
member of the groom's party, and it's blue."

Tal's hand went to touch the softness of the royal blue
satin. "Very true," he said, "but it should be white. I'm
the best man, you know."

This rocked her. "No. I didn't know. Adrian didn't—
nobody told me."

"I see." He was silent, then addressed Prudence Taylor.
"I hope it will not be taken wrongly if I suggest greater
care in watching over the lady." He bowed, a bow to the
very centimeter of his rank, and went to the tailor's line.

"Well, my dear wife, you're fortunate in your reflexes.
I wish my own were as fine." Adrian had thought it best
to tell her himself that the aspirin was poisoned. "It's not
enough to kill you, not unless you took four or five. One
or two would just make you very ill."

"Are you telling me this to reassure me?" A fine, high
color had come into her cheeks with her anger; her husband admired it. They were alone in Io's chambers, at his
request—even Prudence had left and gone to pass the
time with Will Stockton out in the corridor.

"It *is* reassuring in a way. I'd heard there were animals
and aliens who could sense poison, but I didn't know
people could do it."

At that Iolanthe's temper was unleashed, and she
slapped Adrian's face, hard. He stepped back, more to
control himself than anything else, then took her hands at
the wrist. "I meant it as a compliment," he said. His eyes
were angry.

"Yes, I'd forgotten how much you like animals and
aliens." She wrenched her arms away.

He grinned suddenly. "I do like them. I like you, too."

It was her turn to step back. He was too good at this;
how could you fight with someone who threw down his
weapons anytime you asked?

I like you. Iolanthe could not remember anyone ever
having said that to her, not in her entire life. She turned
and paced away from him in the chamber, to give herself
time to recover her poise. She said, "Have you arrested
anyone yet?"

"No, and we're not likely to. Everybody in the universe

was in and out of that room all day, anyone could have tampered with your bag. Tal told me that he'd been there for ten minutes or so, and you didn't even notice him."

She faced Adrian. "He was quick to guess it was poison."

"He's quick to think anything is poison. He wouldn't have had it analyzed if he'd done it. I say that for your benefit; I already know that he didn't do it."

Aliens and animals; you could never sway Adrian on the subject of his hobbies. She forced anger back into her voice. "Twice now I've been almost killed while under your protection. No one's even been arrested yet for that trick at the vastule pit. When will that be? Somebody's walking around still pleased with themselves, somebody who ought to be punished. And now there's poison practically put into my hand, and beyond some sympathy, what do I get?"

Adrian's lips quirked in a wry smile. "You want satisfaction. You have no idea how often I want it, too, and know it won't be coming." He walked over to her. "Io, everything in life does not get tied up neatly, like a storybook. You'll have to face the fact that we may never know who did this." He put up a hand to forestall her protest. "I know, we'll try as hard as we can to find out, but the odds are low. There are too many candidates, for too many reasons, and too much opportunity all along the way. These things happen to me occasionally, too, you know; it's just another aspect of politics."

She was shocked out of her temper. "It happens to you?"

"Of course. Did you think it was something against you personally?" He smiled.

That made it easier to endure in one way—and harder in another. They had never warned of this on Opal, that marrying Adrian would put her in physical danger. Surely the Lord Cardinal had known?

And then, just yesterday she had sent word to the Lord Cardinal that she no longer wished to spy on her husband—and now this happened, a few hours later. No ... that was a disloyal thought. She could not imagine Arno initiating such a thing. She said, unhappily, "So this could happen again, at any time."

"True. It's something we must live with." Adrian made

no attempt to soften it; it was information she should know. "But look, sweetheart; here I am, quite healthy and alive. And Saul Veritie lived a long life and died of old age. If we're both careful and prudent, there's no reason we can't do the same. You have Will Stockton to look after you for the time being—would you like me to assign you a food-taster?"

"Do you have one?"

"No, but then I eat publicly and communally whenever possible. And when it's not possible, Brandon or Tal or someone else I trust supervises the preparation."

"I'll eat with you, then," said Io, and he smiled. She said, "After all, I'm your wife."

Well, it was a lovely thing to say, and she looked so lovely standing there . . . he kissed her. He meant it to be short and friendly, but it was starting to lengthen when he pulled himself away. "You're welcome to accompany me to dinner every night. Don't wait for an official invitation. But when you do eat alone, have Will see that the food is untampered with."

"I will."

He was silent for a moment, and when he spoke again it was with hesitation. "Did no one from Opal . . . explain this to you?"

"No, sir, they did not."

He left shortly thereafter to attend to business, of which there was a surfeit. Between the wedding and Baret Two, there was a great deal to be done these days.

It was quite within Adrian's prerogative as Protector to be called "sir" by his wife, but her relentless acceptance of marriage as her duty irritated him. He wished that Opal had not left this girl to twist in the wind. He wished she trusted him a little more.

Most of all, he wished the wedding night were over. It was beginning to assume unnatural proportions in his mind.

He spoke to Will Stockton before leaving the women's wing. "I suppose you're aware of what happened at the fitting."

"I was just told." He nodded after Prudence Taylor, who was disappearing into Io's room. "One of my subs was on duty, but he only reported that she seemed unwell.

He was keeping track of the people coming in and out—he saw that the lady Prudence and Special Officer Diamond were there, and they didn't seem unduly alarmed. Rather than force himself on their company—"

"I'm not bringing it up as a complaint against your man. I appreciate your presence here, Will. Io is here, she's well, she's alive—as far as I'm concerned, your assignment was a success."

Will noted the past tense. He was under no illusions; the only reason he wasn't being deservedly crucified for the incident was that his tenure on the Diamond was over anyway. It wasn't worth the trouble with Opal to change him. He waited.

Adrian said, "It's customary for the bride to spend the night before the wedding at the home of a relative, usually her parents. Under the circumstances, Iolanthe has expressed a wish to remain on the Diamond tonight. I've offered to move her into my aunt's quarters; she's the closest thing to a relative I have."

Will said, "Excuse me, sir, but I advise against it." This was the polite method of applying bodyguard veto. "We haven't done the work on your aunt's quarters, and there are three people working right now at the lady's parents'."

For Will, "doing the work" meant sending people through with sweeps, noting all entrances and exits, getting lists of authorized inhabitants, and giving maps and instructions to everyone involved. Circumstances, and plain aristo stubbornness, sometimes didn't let Will "do the work," and he was always upset when he didn't.

Adrian smiled as though he found Will's attention to minutiae charming. He said gently, "Will, understand my position—"

Will's eyes shifted. Adrian had a powerful smile that made you like him in spite of yourself. At times like this it was clearly sincere, that was where the power came from. He heard Adrian say, "You're going back to Opal in a day or two, at least I assume so; anyway, this particular assignment will be over. You're going to have to relinquish control to the Diamond in any case, so we're just both going to have to hope that we're competent, aren't we?"

"There's been no groundwork—"

"Will, the only people who know she's going to my

aunt's are Iolanthe, me, and now you. How much more security do we need?"

Will sighed. He said, "I want to see your aunt's quarters and make up a bed for myself there. I want to be able to move around to different rooms if I have to."

"Of course, Will," said the Protector, as though Will's preferences were to be taken for granted. "Anything you think is best."

Adrian's aunt was an eccentric. She lived by herself, but for a maid, in five rooms near the end of court territory by the entrance to the gardens. It was a horrifying waste of space, but nobody was going to tell the old lady to move out. She was a Mercati by marriage, not by blood, and once the rooms had been filled with family. That had passed, like everything else she'd known.

She was not, as everyone knew, "all there"; but Adrian thought he'd managed to make clear to her who Iolanthe was and why she was coming. He and Will escorted Io there after dinner, in a closed chair, and Adrian dismissed the porters before he rang for admittance.

It was his aunt who opened the door, which did not surprise him. He'd never known the maid's name, but she did little in the way of work and could usually be found lounging in one of the inner rooms. "Hello, Aunt Celeste." He put his arms around her and kissed a withered cheek. She was quite old, his aunt; the wife of his father's oldest brother, who was the first of nine children—all dead now, leaving just the two of them with no blood in common and minds in different worlds. She wore a dark green dressing gown, and had bare, pale feet.

"Hello, Adrian." He was one of the few people whose names she kept straight.

"This is Iolanthe; I told you about her." Aunt Celeste focused uncertainly on Iolanthe, but said nothing. Adrian suspected she had no idea why they'd come. Long experience with his aunt told him to just press on. "And Will here you've already met."

"Yes!" For a moment the old face lit up with the success of recognition. "The pretty boy. Yes, I know him."

Will flushed. People had occasionally called him good-looking before, but nobody had ever called him "pretty."

Particularly not little ancient women in dressing gowns whom he didn't even know. Io seemed to be smiling, which only made it worse.

But they all went inside and Adrian talked to his aunt for a while and listened solemnly to her chatter; and Will put his overnight bag down on the cot he'd set up in the common room earlier that day. As a guard he was neither fish nor fowl, a sometime social companion but still a hired body, not really expected to join in the conversation unless invited. This time he was glad of that. Old people made him nervous; you didn't see many of them in San-garee. He looked around the quarters at the embroidered pillows and the endless pictures on the shelves of people dressed in clothing popular decades ago. It was the sort of place he could never feel comfortable in.

Meanwhile, Iolanthe settled into a bedchamber farther in, dislodging the so-called maid, a girl with blonde hair who looked at her resentfully as she moved. But Will had designated this room for Io, and she wasn't going to make his job difficult. She picked up some old perfume bottles on a vanity nearby and unstoppered them. The stoppers still smelt faintly of former days, though the perfumes had all mostly evaporated.

"Io?" said a voice from the doorway. It was Adrian. "I have to go now. I guess . . . I'll see you at the wedding. I'll send a chair for you at eleven to take you back to your rooms. Is that all right?"

"That's fine, Adrian. Thank you."

There was an unexpected fondness in her tone and Adrian took a step toward her. She thought for a moment he was going to kiss her again, but then he turned a little uncertainly and left.

She put down the perfume bottle she was holding, a beautiful thing of frosted glass. She was impressed with the way Adrian dealt with his aunt, at how he stood and listened to anything she had to say and never revealed a trace of irritation or annoyance. There was something moving about the strong showing patience with the less strong.

She stopped suddenly and blinked. She hoped that *she* wasn't the less strong, too.

* * *

They ate cold meat and bread from Aunt Celeste's larder that night, and the maid sat silently with them at the table. Will ate by himself, but Iolanthe suspected it was more from a feeling of discomfort than from an effort to maintain social distinctions. Aunt Celeste talked of this and that, of dresses and dances long out of fashion, and of Adrian and Adrian's dead relatives, making it hard to tell whom she meant at any one time. When nobody else showed any inclination to clear the table, Io did it herself. The dirty dishes offended her sense of neatness, and her complete lack of experience made her find the job intriguing. Coming back to the dining table she spied a picture she hadn't noticed before: a wide, cloud-filled sky with shafts of light, some rocks by a sea, and a young girl. "Oh, where did you get that from?" she asked. "It's lovely."

Aunt Celeste peered up at it. "That's me, in my birthplace."

Iolanthe stared at her. "You're planet-born?"

"Of course I am. I married the ship, oh, let's see—it must be almost seventy years ago." She was doing arithmetic on her old pale fingers.

Io was still staring. Aunt Celeste smiled. She sat down on a peach-colored couch and patted the cushion beside her. "Sit down, child. Would you like to hear about it?"

Io suspected she used the word "child" because she couldn't remember names. She sat down beside Adrian's aunt and said, "Yes, please. Tell me the story, Aunt Celeste."

The aunt said, "I grew up on Lilyflower. My family were Redemptionists, of course, and we had quite a lot of money. We called ourselves 'comfortable.' My father was an architect, and we had three houses—oh, do you want coffee, child?"

"No thank you, Aunt Celeste."

"Well, it was quite a day when the Diamond came to trade. I was sixteen when they appeared in our system, and eighteen when they were preparing to leave. I was at the unveiling of 'The Long Call'—the painting the Diamond had brought us from Seville 3 as a hospitality gift. Magnificent. Afterward Adrian's uncle came up to me and asked if he might button my gloves. We had not then been introduced."

Io was tired, and she settled on Aunt Celeste's shoulder. "He called on me all that summer. Carriage rides through the lanes with my little sister in the back, and picnic parties to the cliffs ... concerts with our friends, when he would insist on sitting beside me. Of course he was tall and handsome, and a little exotic looking in his Cities cape and bars. Curly black hair, which I loved, and a black mustache, which I despised. They were in fashion then on the Diamond.... I have always disliked mustaches. Clean-shaven, yes, and beards, yes—but there has always been something grotesque and silly to me about mustaches. Neither one thing nor the other, you see. Half an idea, and in a ridiculous place. —Well. He came all that summer. He was a pleasant enough companion, and as demonstrative as he could be, considering I was a Redemptionist girl and always chaperoned. Often he would ask me to marry him, but I could never be certain that he wasn't joking. He had a way of saying things as though he were not quite serious ... my parents approved of him. And it was—and still is, I suppose—the custom for the Cities to pay a good brideprice when they took a Redemptionist woman off her native planet.

"They were due to leave. He came to see me the final afternoon. My parents left us alone in the parlor of our house outside the city, and kept the servants away from us.... The bars of light through the curtains were the last sunlight of summer." Her voice hung in the air, gentle and far away. "We lived in the north, you know; the light was like a halo at that time of year. It glowed on faces, poppies, long fields of meadow. It seemed to come from within the things themselves, not an outside source at all.... He asked me to marry him again."

Iolanthe was lying back on the couch, her eyes closed with weariness, half-dreaming of dappled alien sunlight on her body.

"I wasn't in love, you see, and love was very much the fashion in my city then—as my maid tells me it is now on the Diamond. But I knew from one or two bruises in the past that I wouldn't be able to live with a man who could make me laugh without falling in love with him eventually. So I told him I would marry him if he would shave off his mustache.

"He called for soap and water, and shaved it off right there in the parlor. When he left, I went with him."

She put a cold hand on Io's wrist, but it wasn't enough to bring her fully awake. "I really didn't think he would do it, you know. That was my escape route, to make it his refusal and not displease my family. I thought he had too much pride and wouldn't accept a condition from a lady. . . . And so here I am. I've been here for sixty-eight years.

"I fell in love with him, too. But he died in the Venn System Battle. We'd been married for eight years.

"That day he shaved for me was the last day I saw real sunlight.

"That's all I can tell you about love, child."

Chapter 34

It was ordained for the mutual society, help, and comfort, that the one ought to have of the other.
                                   Book of Common Prayer

What is wedlock forced but a hell,
An age of discord and continual strife?
                        SHAKESPEARE, Henry VI, Part One

On the late morning of June sixteenth, Tal looked over the collection of lenses on his desk. Aesthetically, the blue lenses would go best with the clothes of the groom's party, and it would be more proper to appear at Adrian's wedding in an eye color not associated with demons. Of course, one never knew Adrian's preferences for certain. Sometimes he was discreet, and sometimes he pushed things dangerously. It might even amuse him on some level if Tal appeared in the cathedral with no lenses at all.

Tal stared speculatively into the mirror on his wall. Naked golden eyes looked back quietly; it was a view he didn't often see, and others never saw. He didn't understand why humans found his eyes troubling, but they did. They had made that very clear to him in his younger days. He'd tried to analyze it, without success. Half his genes came from the Elaphites, and *they* were yellowed-eyed—and were notoriously appealing to humans. So much so that neither the Republic nor the Empire even tried to stop mixed human-Elaphite marriages, provided the couples submitted to irreversible sterilization first. The story they gave out was that childbirth was too dangerous under those conditions, which in a way it was. And then there were cats with yellowish eyes, and humans liked cats. So why did his own eyes bother them so?

No, it was possible that Adrian might not be amused after all. It was dead odds Iolanthe would not be. He lifted a set of lenses and held them to the light. Blue, then. He would be above reproach.

Meanwhile, Iolanthe had arrived at her own quarters and was quickly taken inside by Prudence Taylor and helped into her gown. Five other women, friends of Prudence, were waiting in Io's rooms with flowers, gloves, and the Mercati heirloom necklace Adrian had sent over. Io stood uncomfortably as Prudence applied cosmetics carefully to her face and the others bustled about; she had a large white bib tied around her neck, to keep the gown from harm, and felt silly. It was so unfair, she thought, as Prudence wiped her lips dry with a cloth—like a mother with a year-old baby—and tried the color again. *Why are the standards for women so ridiculous?* she thought resentfully. Men didn't have to go through this self-critical nonsense.

"Where's Tal?" asked Adrian for the sixth time. "Is he here yet?"

"They'll send him straight in when he gets here," said his valet. Lucius pulled the white sash over Adrian's shoulder and began attaching it to the sash at his waist. They were facing a three-way mirror, and Adrian groaned.

"I can't believe it," he said, touching his face.

"Stop looking," ordered Lucius.

"I can't *help* but see it—"

Tal appeared then in the doorway. "You wanted me?

By the way, I put on blue lenses. I thought it would be more appropriate—"

"Forget your eyes," said Adrian, jettisoning courtesy in the urgency of the moment. "Look at *this*." He pointed to a pink area on his nose.

Tal walked over and took a look. "It's a pimple."

"It's huge," said Adrian.

"It's not even visible," said Lucius, with a warning glance at Tal.

"It's the size of a fully grown planetoid," said Adrian, groaning again.

Tal walked over to a carved wooden bench nearby, sat down and crossed his legs. "And this is a man who controls the fate of four million people. I'm glad you're focused on what's really important."

"Doesn't anyone understand me?" cried Adrian. "Dammit, Tal, this is serious. I'm getting *married* today. And tonight we're ... what's she going to think? I've barely even kissed the girl. Do I have to shove this, this *eruption* into her innocent face?" He felt the end of his nose experimentally. "Tell me honestly, Tal, am I being paranoid?"

"Yes. You're being paranoid."

"I don't believe you."

Lucius, meanwhile, had exited from the room and returned almost at once with a small glazed pot of brown stuff, about an inch in diameter. He extended it toward Adrian. "Here you are, sir, try this. I got it from Lady Joanna, and she's close to your skin color."

Adrian looked down at the jar as though it were an alien artifact whose safety was not yet proven. "I can't wear that. It's for ladies."

From his chair Tal said, "Do you want to postpone the wedding? Or do you want to wear cosmetics? Or do you want to believe Lucius when he says it's not noticeable?"

Adrian considered the matter for a moment. Then he reached for the jar.

St. Tom's was filling up. Even by invitation only, there were far more people who thought they should be at the ceremony than actually had seats. Spider, to his delight and his mother's pride, had gotten an invitation, even if it was for a seat way off to the side with people who were probably afterthoughts. You could barely see the Symbol from here, and Adrian and Iolanthe would most likely be blocked by that big Corinthian pillar, but here he was.

His mother would probably have a better view. The whole thing was going to be shown live on the big screen at Nemiah Circus, and Mrs. Hastings had gone there last night with three of her cronies to stake out a place to sit. Spider had suggested coming along—his ticket to the wedding showed a number that hinted he wouldn't be anywhere near the couple—and his Ma had said, "Stratton Hastings, are you out of your mind? You're the only person in our neighborhood with an invitation. I told everybody about it. Don't you dare not go." So he'd kept any moral qualms to himself. This was the first church he'd set foot in since his excommunication order, back when he'd run off to find the ghosts. Technically, of course he'd been reinstated . . . but if anybody found out he'd been fraternizing with demons, taking orders for pay when he wasn't under any Diamond service obligation to do so . . . well, *he* knew, and it made him uncomfortable.

At least his concerns today were spiritual, he told himself. A wedding was no place for ghosts.

Saint Tom's, like the Cavern of Audience, was a huge space cut into the rock that made up the inner frame of the Diamond. It had been used as a cathedral for hundreds of years. Tunnels came into it from scores of places; utility tunnels, water tunnels, tunnels for access to the rectory nearby, tunnels for service people, and other tunnels. High above the congregation a railed ledge ran around two walls of the cathedral; partly it went through the rock and was invisible to the people below, and partly it appeared as the bottom of two frescoes cut into the wall. Even with the railing at the frescoes, it did not look like a passageway. Nobody knew it was there but one or two church historians, who, if asked, could have explained that once upon a time a watch of priests used to oversee the sanctuary from there on holy days. In less kind years monitors had been placed there to watch the congregation and report any who seemed inattentive. Nobody asked these historians, though, because nobody knew about them or much cared.

It was to the first of these frescoes that the Salamander

brought Tealeaf, to escort her to the wedding. Tealeaf usually avoided his company, as the Salamander was known far and wide to be crazy even for a ghost. But the gift of intuition that had taken her out of normal human society told her that he did not mean anything violent or sexual by this invitation, which made it pure sophisticated charm by Salamander standards. He said that he had a surprise, and there was an echo in the way he said it of her parents at Christmas. So she let him bring her through the ghost roads to court deck, through tunnels she'd never even heard of, until she stepped out on this ledge and saw an enormous space, banners, and a sea of people in fine clothes below. The murmur of the crowd as it settled in camp up to her like a single, swelling note.

"Thank you," she said, turning to him at once. Her delight was plain in her voice. "It's beautiful."

He looked shyly pleased. They sat down together on the cold stone ledge, their legs against the railing, and peered out over their betters.

The Salamander considered in passing that if he'd met any of these people in the underdecks, dressed like that, he'd have killed them at once and gone through their purses. For her part, Tealeaf wished she'd known she was coming; she would have made an effort to find some water for washing.

As she gazed, content in the spectacle, her eyes were drawn to a spot farther down the rows of pews by the wall. There was a scent, a taste, of familiarity about it . . . she couldn't quite place it, it was like a name you knew very well but couldn't quite . . .

"Spider," she said.

"What?" said the Salamander.

"Spider's here. He's sitting below."

The Salamander got up on his knees and peered over the railing. "Where?"

She pointed to the very place where Spider sat in his borrowed finery dutifully wishing he could have wangled his mother an invitation.

The Salamander said, "I don't see him. You can barely make out faces from here. How do you know it's Spider?"

She turned her almond eyes to him and said, "I know. You know I know."

He sat back down. Below them a train of priests started down the aisle. Another half hour of preparation followed before he leaned to her and said, in a low voice, "Best not tell Nicolet we came."

The higher ranks of Opal priesthood had been invited to the wedding, but nobody expected them to come. It would be interpreted as lending their countenance to Diamond heresy. Other ranking Opal personnel were invited, however, including almost everyone in the current delegation. Will Stockton, having delivered Iolanthe to the wedding party and surrendered her into the hands of eight Diamond priests for the pre-ceremony, climbed the steps outside St. Tom's to enter as a normal invitee. His duty was over. Barington Strife met him near the doors.

Will didn't mind wearing the shirt, which was silk, but he hated the stupid red sash. It kept coming undone, and he had to keep stuffing it back into place and hoping the aristos weren't looking at him. Will was a little on the tall and broad side, and the tailor had assured him the sash was extra-long. The tailor had lied.

Will bent a head toward Barington so they could talk privately, giving another poke to the sash as he did so. Maybe it would stay in place till he took his seat. "So where's Hartley sitting?" he inquired.

"He didn't come," said Barington.

"What do you mean, he didn't come?"

"He told the hierophant he wasn't feeling well. I left him in his rooms."

Will looked at Barington Strife; it was a tired, seen-it-all, Sangaree sort of look, and Barry knew what it meant. He protested, "The guy's sick at home! What can he do? It's not like he can cause any problems with anybody—everyone else in creation is at the wedding."

Will sighed. He pulled the cursed red sash off and gave it to the other man. "Hold onto this for me, will you?"

"Sarge, you're being a little paranoid, aren't you?"

He probably was. But you gave extra rope to Hartley Quince at the risk of being hanged yourself. "Let me know how it turns out," he said, as though the wedding were a sporting event.

"Yeah. I'll put down bets for you. Sarge, I don't know

what you have against this guy, but except for a little smoke he hasn't been in any trouble since day one of our arrival."

"See you later," waved Will, as he descended the steps. At the bottom there was a crowd of the uninvited who'd gathered to watch the upperdecks arrive in their wedding clothes and hired chairs. Somebody was selling pictures of the happy couple. Adrian's visage was clearly lifted off his posters, and Iolanthe's face a composite of every princess in a fairy tale. At least they got the hair color right. Will spied a thin-looking girl in a faded red dress, and said, "Here! Want to go to the wedding?" And he handed her his ticket. She looked at it uncertainly, and he grinned because her thoughts were stamped on her forehead: *This man is probably crazy, and this ticket is probably counterfeit.* "No charge," said Will, and because he left without looking back, he never knew what she decided.

The pre-ceremony was a bloodletting, and Io had always felt queasy at these events. Hierophant Cole placed the metal leech on her forearm. It felt cold. After three minutes he took it off again, and Io swayed slightly and was helped to sit. Luckily nobody hissed to her (as they had been known to in the past), "For heaven's sake, it's only a few ounces." The hierophant merely smiled sympathetically and continued his ritual, blessing the blood now inside the leech and handing it to a deacon for transfer to the cup.

Io gazed mutely around at the dome of the Church Office. It was only about forty feet in diameter, nothing at all compared to the grandeur of the cathedral itself, but at least one was close enough to see details and what one saw was reassuring. Sky-blue background with black bands partitioning the dome into sections; and at the base of each section, an illustration of one of the sacraments in the life of a Redemptionist. The fifth one, a quarter-way across the circle, was a wedding. Look, Io, she said to herself: It's not like the ceremony is lethal. There are plenty more things to follow—look at the christening, doesn't that look charming? I wish *this* were a christening, and all the fuss over with.

But, damn, if Adrian can stand it, *I* can stand it.

* * *

Bishop Kalend approached her as she was brought to the vestibule. He said in a low voice, "Iolanthe, Adrian tells me you had a bad reaction to your Confirmation."

This took her by surprise. "Yes. I was sick for weeks." How had Adrian heard, and how dare he discuss it with this stranger?

"A wedding should be happiest day in a young lady's life, and I don't want you to worry one bit about the ceremony. But you should know that people who have had bad reactions to their first exposure often have ... the same, with their second." Or worse, his voice seemed to imply. "I've brought you a little extra of the Sacred Breath. It should take care of any problems." He uncovered a small bowl and held it in front of her.

Making it through today in one piece was her very first aim, so Iolanthe bent and breathed in the fumes heavily. The bishop pulled the bowl away after a moment and covered it again, then steadied Io with one hand. "All right, child?"

"I think so."

"It'll make you a little light-headed. Nothing awful, it's just like being slightly drunk. You'll have to be careful where you step and what you say."

"Oh."

"It's better than collapsing at the altar and being sick for weeks."

Tell me that again, she thought, if I do anything to disgrace myself in front of the entire City.

"Lend me your arm, please, Father."

"Certainly, daughter."

"They're almost ready," said Tealeaf, excited. She peered down at the procession of brightly colored priests and aristos. Up at the approach to the altar stood the best man and several of the groom's wedding party; down by the vestibule entrance were a flock of women in trailing gowns. "Isn't it wonderful?"

The Salamander had a thoughtful crease in the center of his forehead. He said, "I think I should follow Spider when he leaves. Maybe I'll find his sleeping compartment. We could take him in the night."

She glared at him, annoyed that he would break the drama. "How will you find him in the crowd when the church empties?" she snapped. "You might as well try to find a flea turd on Mercati Boulevard."

"I can do whatever I want," said the Salamander quietly. He gave her a look from under his heavy-lidded eyes and she recalled that he was, after all, crazy as a loon, and decided to say no more.

Because it was an out-City marriage there was a symbolic capture-element to the ceremony; Adrian had to go down the aisle, take her from the vestibule, and escort her the neverending length of the cathedral to the front.

The priests' drugs had an unexpected benefit: She was too busy concentrating on her feet to pay attention to the rows of eyes all staring at her.

In Nemiah Circus, Mrs. Hastings turned to her friend Mrs. Cathcart and said, "Oh, doesn't she look like a proper bride! So modest, but that darling smile." Mrs. Cathcart agreed, and Mrs. Hastings added, "I'll have to ask my Stratton, when he comes, if he had a better view of her face."

Mrs. Cathcart sighed. It was the tenth time she'd mentioned Spider in an hour.

Braziers around the church had been filled with Sacred Breath, and now deacons went among the rows lighting them. The smoke from the drugs began rising into the enormous space of St. Tom's. Much of it reached the congregation in a highly diluted form, just enough to make acceptance of the pure Curosa sacrament more physically palatable. One larger brazier, however, was underneath the fresco of Archangel Michael Pointing the Way from Earth, a marvelous thing with the blue-and-white globe in the background, the City of Opal twinkling nearby in space, and the blue-and-white angel's wings brushing the length of the picture. Michael's form was the entire left third of the painting; he wore steely blue armor, had red-gold curls, and was pointing sternly into deep space. One foot was crushing a viper (how this was to be done against the vacuum of space was a thing generations of children had wondered) and the other touched the bottom of the frame, where Tealeaf and the Salamander sat on their ledge breathing in the priests' drugs at nearly full strength.

Adrian and Iolanthe were met by Bishop Kalend at the bottom step of the altar. He wore his orphrey now, bordered in roses and cups and thorns. "What is your wish, my children?" he declaimed, giving the question that was asked at the beginning of all Redemptionist sacraments.

"Happiness," they said together. That was the answer when the sacrament in question was marriage, and Iolanthe thought it was wishful thinking on the part of the Church.

Meanwhile Will Stockton had reached Hartley Quince's quarters and stationed himself where he could watch the door. It would be a shame, he thought, if Hart had already left and he missed the wedding for nothing; but Hart was a deliberate soul, the sort who—if he did plan on going anywhere—would most likely wait till he was sure everybody was safe in church.

And so it was. Hartley Quince emerged fifteen minutes later, minus his officer's jacket and his new deacon's pin, in a plain green aristo cape and white breeches and boots. He was carrying a small box.

At once several possibilities ran through Will's head, none of them credible to him. Drug-selling? Instructions or payment for agents? Hart did not take obvious risks.

Will followed, very, very carefully, as his quarry strolled, touristlike, through the residential corridors and the parkland and boarded the Mercati Boulevard-bound train at the edge of court territory. Will sat two cars behind and checked the windows at each stop.

It was a Sunday, as well as Adrian's wedding, and there were few people aboard. Hart left the train at D deck in St. Anne section and took a freight lift; that nearly did Will in, but he knew there was a connecting train stop on H and his guess proved right when he emerged from his own lift and saw Hart farther down the platform.

They ended up in Helium Park. Will just managed to keep sight of him through the trees. The huge park was nearly deserted; it was patronized mainly by the upperdecks, who were all either in St. Tom's or home where no one could see that they hadn't gotten an invitation. Practically every other citizen who didn't have a work-shift had made their way to Nemiah Circus or one of the other transmit screens that was showing the wedding.

Will heard the scrunch of a twig under his boot as the only human-made sound for miles. Alone in the universe with nobody but Hartley Quince. There was a thought to engender true paranoia.

Hart stopped at the edge of the stream that led to the central lake. Will waited under the maple trees until he saw a figure detach itself from a stand of birches on the bank and walk toward Hart. It was a girl in a white party dress. She put her arms around Hart's neck and he kissed her.

Will saw them in silhouette against the bright water of the stream; he saw Hart pull down her arms from his neck and motion for her to turn around. Then Hart opened his box and dropped the cover and bottom on the bank, and took out a necklace of some sort of heavy dangles and put it around the girl's neck.

Will sat down on the damp ground and prepared himself for a long wait.

Just a run-of-the-mill assignation. And for this he'd missed Iolanthe's wedding.

Iolanthe would have missed it, too, if she could. As it was, she accepted the cup from Bishop Kalend with only slightly unsteady hands and drank a mouthful of preserved Curosa blood. She remembered how shocked and disappointed she'd been at her Confirmation when she discovered the foul taste of it. Her lips puckered involuntarily and she handed the cup to Adrian, who drank with equanimity, as he did everything else.

Only halfway there. She watched as the bishop emptied the contents of her leech and Adrian's leech into the cup, and they passed it around again. Her face had gone rather pale by this time and she put aside all other fears—of marriage, of death, of the disapproval of Opal—and concentrated on not fainting.

Servitors were handing out tablets of quick-frozen Curosa blood serum to the congregation. This was timed to counteract some of the necessary side-effects of Sacred

Breath, which, while cushioning the human system against foreign invaders, had the unfortunate tendency to arouse people sexually. There was a time when weddings on the Diamond were not quite as staid as they were now, and it had been a mark of honor some centuries ago to have the consummation take place right in the cathedral. However, as far as the bishops were concerned, that time could not too soon be forgotten.

As usual Iolanthe's system was not quite like anybody else's, and as she revived slightly and listened to the bishop drone on about her new responsibilities, she considered the fact that Adrian was not half bad-looking, and a nice fellow to boot. She wondered how he'd look with that cape off; as she recalled, he had a nice little fanny.

It was a good thing, she thought, that she seemed to be in control of the situation. That Sacred Breath had worried her.

She wondered where Will was. Talk about fannies—

"My lady?" said the bishop.

"Yes?" she said, startled.

"Do you understand and accept these responsibilities?"

Adrian and the bishop were both looking at her funny. "Yes, I understand and accept them." Really, what was their problem?

"Adrian Mercati—" said the bishop, and off he went again.

Eventually Adrian slipped the ring on her finger, a nice circle of diamonds, of course; and he kissed her. Yes, he was a fine person. He'd been very nice to her, after all. She decided to open her mouth a bit the way her cousin Beverly had recommended, and she felt Adrian's start of surprise. He started to draw away a little, but she put an arm around him, knowing he wouldn't obviously refuse a lady in front of the entire City. The kiss went well beyond the usual length of a wedding kiss.

The cathedral was shocked to silence, but in Nemiah Circus the applause went on and on.

And so the wedding party filed out, and after an interval of singing, the rest of the church was allowed to follow. Although Spider had no acquaintance here, he overheard a lot, and he noted that conversation was limited to several topics: What the bride wore; what a little hussy she was, and what a climber—have you even *heard* of her people on Opal? Adrian's got himself a handful, hasn't he (said with some envy by a Diamond lord). And, finally, on everyone's lips: Are you going to the ball?

The wedding ball was at seven. Spider had not been invited.

He could go back to his compartment and maybe stop on the way for some cheap food.

He could back to his compartment and maybe stop at a bar on the way.

He could go visit his mother and let her glorify him to her friends.

He brightened at that. And Ma wasn't above slipping a little comfort into the teacup, especially on a day like this. He grinned and stepped out into the throng making its way down the side aisle.

As the cathedral gradually emptied, four deacons emerged from the alcoves and went to clean and empty the braziers. Two boys came out to take down the wedding objects from the altar.

One of the deacons wrestled with the huge brazier by the fresco of Saint Michael. The aroma of the Sacred Breath ashes was still pungent. High above him in their niche, Tealeaf and the Salamander had fallen asleep, naked, in each other's arms.

Chapter 35

If once a man indulges himself in murder, very soon he comes to think little of robbing; and from robbing he comes next to drinking and Sabbath-breaking, and from that to incivility and procrastination.

THOMAS DEQUINCEY

*The sole cause of man's unhappiness is that he does
not know how to stay quietly in his room.*

PASCAL

Will's pants had gotten damp from the grass and he was
nodding off. It was, after all, a pleasant Sunday afternoon,
and he had no official duties to speak of. And Hart and
the girl had gone swimming and were now lying on the
bank, talking lazily. Will wished he had had the fore-
thought to bring a girl himself.

The most interesting part of the afternoon had come
earlier, when Hart and this girl had stripped and Hart had
demonstrated that he was every bit as attentive to female
needs as male. Anyway, the girl had given that impression. Now was the boring aftermath, and Will didn't even
have the advantage of any personal tension release to
make his tedium the pleasant thing it no doubt was for
the couple on the bank.

Raised voices from the direction of the stream made
him open his eyes. The girl had gotten up; she was looking down at Hart, still spread on his back with his hands
under his head, and they were arguing. Or she was
arguing—Hart was just lying there, answering in a quiet
voice that was no more than a murmur from this distance.
Will could only make out a few words from her harangue;
no was chief among them, and *not enough*, repeated several times. *What about me?* she yelled at one point. And
finally, *Just wait, my friend, just you wait!* This last was
delivered with venom, and she scooped up her clothes
and turned to leave.

Hart was up in a second, his hand on her arm. He
talked for a solid minute, then bent over her shoulder and
addressed something to her ear, nibbling on her neck a little as he did so. She giggled. She let herself be coaxed
into surrendering her clothing, which Hart threw back on
the ground. Then he pulled her out into the stream and
they started making love in the water.

Lord, thought Will, I could've been back in my quarters by now. I wonder what Lysette is doing?

Hart and his girlfriend were thrashing about in the
current. A certain amount of horseplay was only to be ex-

pected from any couple that would make love in the middle of Helium Park, and it took Will quite a few irreplaceable seconds to realize that the girl was being drowned.

Hart was efficient; she hadn't even been given a chance to yell. Will broke from his hiding place and ran into the stream. He grabbed hold of an arm and shoulder and tried to pull her away from Hart. Her arms were still moving weakly. Hart jabbed Will viciously with one hand, using the other to keep her face well under the surface. He wasn't letting go; Will's only chance was to attack Hart directly, and he did so. Hart blocked the blows, still one-handed, refusing to let go even to fight back. Seconds passed. Finally, Hart, who was bleeding from the nose, pushed the girl's body away and dived at Will. They rolled over onto the shore. In a blaze of anger the like of which he had not known since childhood, Will threw a storm of blows at Hart. His lack of success brought with it a heartsick frustration that was reminiscent of other scenes, long ago; through the haze Will saw Hart's bleeding face and remembered abruptly who and where he was. And what an ass he was being. He pulled away from Hart and started to run downstream.

He was tackled from behind. Of course. Every second of delay was on Hart's side, that was what the fight was about; Will ignored the red-hot lava that threatened to explode in his brain and twisted coolly aside, kicking Hart on the side of the head to extricate himself. He managed to get to his feet.

And saw, very far downstream now, a naked body on the current. It seemed to hover by the curve of bright water by a stand of birch trees; then it was gone.

There was a very faint sound, almost like a whimper, and he realized that he'd made it. He turned around. Hart had gotten to his knees, and without a pause for thought Will aimed a vicious kick at his kidney.

Hart managed to catch Will's boot with his hand, not canceling the blow but softening it. He grunted, and when he'd caught his breath he said, "Willie. It was only a couple of seconds, and she was probably already dead."

He meant that it was only a couple of seconds that Will had wasted in pummeling Hart on the bank when he should have been running downstream. He meant, don't take this as a personal failure.

Will hated Hart for knowing what he'd been thinking. And he hated him for mentioning those seconds and making concrete the fact that Will had to share responsibility for her death.

He looked down at Hart, his lips twisted in a sour line, and said, "You're under arrest."

Hart said, "I beg your pardon?"

"I said, you're under arrest. Get up."

Hart got to his feet. He reached for his shirt, and Will jabbed him with a Keith pistol that had suddenly materialized in his hand. "I didn't think that kick had loosened your brains."

"Willie. I'm only reaching for an explanation. I have a card case in there. Do you mind?"

He slowly brought out a gold case from his shirt pocket and opened it. He rifled through the calling cards and then from the middle he pulled out a card embossed with the imprimatur of the Ecclesiastical Council. Will took it from him and read: "The bearer of this card is entrusted by the Council with the authority to do as he sees fit to maintain the security of the City. All Opal citizens will render him what assistance he requires."

Will had heard of these cards. He flipped it into the underbrush. "Too bad you lost it."

"Whose brains got loosened now?" said Hart. "Willie—"

"I know. You've got a hundred more at home. You should've remembered to bring one with you—it might have stopped me from turning you over to Diamond Security."

Hart froze. "*Diamond* Security? Jesus Chr—"

Will poked him with the Keith. "Come on."

Hart said, recovering, "Do you think you ought to leave that card where just anybody can pick it up?"

Will glared at him for a second. Then, still holding the pistol on him as Hart got dressed, Will squatted down and started feeling around on the grass for the card.

* * *

They took a long, silent ride on the train. Will didn't motion for him to get out until the end of the line, on court level, and Hart said, "What's the idea?"

"I'm going to file a report to Opal first from the link in my room. So nobody can say I didn't do my civic duty."

The pathways and corridors were filling up again; the wedding must be over. Will kept his Keith in his pocket. At the door to Will's room, Hart paused.

"You'll get a bad reputation, Willie, inviting men home to your quarters."

"Just get inside."

The door opened into the main room with its four cots. One of Will's men was there already—TJ, standing at a mirror, adjusting the laces on his dress shirt. He looked at them in surprise as they entered.

Will said, "What are you doing here?" Nobody off-duty spent their time in these cramped quarters when all the Diamond was available.

"I'm getting ready for the ball."

Of course. He'd forgotten. "The others already leave?"

"Uh-huh. I know it doesn't start till seven, but they're opening the hall at five."

Will nodded. "We're going to talk in the other room. Knock on the door when you leave." The link was in this room, but Will felt awkward about using it in front of TJ. TJ was already looking at him like he wasn't making sense. He motioned for Hart to precede him into the other room—it was a tiny space with a folding chair and wall pegs for capes, and Will thought it must have been a supply closet once. He thanked God it was there; otherwise they would've had to go into the spit, and heaven knew what TJ would have thought.

He closed the door. "Make yourself at home," he said, gesturing to the chair.

"Thanks." Hart seated himself negligently, leaning back and stretching his legs.

Will wished that he smoked. "Adrian likes to sit that way, too," he said.

"Does he?"

Will took the few paces the narrow space afforded him. He wished TJ would finish primping and get out.

"Willie?"

"Yeah?" He looked over at Hart and into a small silver handgun.

He cursed. Hart stood up, walked to the edge of the room, and said, "Put yours on the chair—slowly, and all that."

Will placed his Keith gently on the chair. Hart said, "I bought this off a Graykey on the Opal. How do you like it? It's half the size of a Keith, and lethal whenever it hits. I understand the Graykey are like that."

Will didn't respond to this.

"You have to be consistent, Willie. I can understand your choosing not to search me; every one-on-one search is taking a chance. But if you don't, you shouldn't take your eyes off me later."

Hart liked to give him little lectures on life back in school, too. Will said, "I could yell, and TJ would be in here in a second, ready to shoot you."

"Well, that's probably true. You'd be dead and all, but I guess you'd see it as your duty. So let me give you a few reasons why nobody here should get killed, if you don't mind."

Will folded his arms. "All right, try."

Just then there was a knock on the door, and a muffled voice said, "I'm leaving now, Sarge."

Without turning Will called, "Could you stick around a little longer, TJ?"

"Okay," said TJ's voice, puzzled.

Hart said, "Let's make a trade. Information for freedom."

Will frowned. "What kind of information?"

"I don't know, what kind would you like?"

"This isn't funny—"

"We could start with the girl. Would you like to know who she was? Ask me who she was."

"Wait," said Will, and he took out a pocket jammer, activated it, and set it on the floor. "Who was she?"

"Her name was Isabelle Saddler, but before we go on, do we have an understanding? You're not going to call your slobbering Doberman out there, and I'm not going to shoot you? And we're all going our separate ways?"

Between gritted teeth Will said, "What in your pointed little brain makes you think we're going our separate ways, when you've just killed somebody?"

"Well, she's dead, you know. Past fixing. And I have an explanation." Hart leaned back against the wall. "And you have a problem, Willie. You like to know things. We worked on your other problems back in Sangaree, but this is one we never got to."

Will had a quick and unpleasant flash of breaking into the teacher's residence because he wanted to know the truth about Miss Smith. He banished the memory. "Maybe I've overcome it on my own."

"If you're going to turn me over to the Diamond, why did you just take out a jammer?"

Will had no immediate answer for that. Hart said, "Well, we'll pass over that. Ask me about Isabelle Saddler."

"Who was she? Was she an informant?"

"Everybody's an informant, but Miss Saddler knew the market value enough to insist on actual cash. You know Brandon Fischer, the First Adviser? Isabelle knew how he was going to vote on anything before he even walked into the council chamber."

Will considered this. "Why? Was she his mistress? A friend, a relation?"

"Not exactly. She lived in his house. She was his daughter's maid."

Will started to chuckle. "We're scraping the bottom of the barrel here, aren't we? Brandon Fischer's daughter's maid."

Hart said, "It's not necessary that a connection be direct, only that it be accurate."

"Well, hooray. Why did you kill her? Just don't like girls?"

"Really, Will," said Hart with some disappointment. "Just because you're under the confused impression I'm homosexual—"

"I don't think you're homosexual. I don't think you're heterosexual either. I think you're an omnivore. I think you'd do it with a turnip, actually, if you thought it would get the turnip into trouble."

"I forgot. It would be a matter of Sangaree honor, wouldn't it, to be just a little rude to a person holding a gun on you."

Will said nothing for a moment, then: "Do you have other informants on the Diamond?"

"Naturally."

"Why *did* you kill her?"

There was a sound of voices from outside. One of the others had come back, probably to hurry TJ along; so much the better, two more armed people against Hart's one.

Hart moved closer to the door to listen. As Will backed away, he brushed accidentally against the tiny chair, tipping it over. It bumped against the wall, wood on metal, then thudded on the floor, his guard pistol with it. At once there was silence in the other room. TJ rapped on the door. "Sarge, are you all right in there?"

"Yeah, I'm fine," said Will.

"Are you sure? Do you want me to—"

"I said I was fine! I tripped over a chair, don't make it into a case for the Inquisition."

"Sorry." The sound of footsteps retreated.

"How will you explain that?" murmured Hart rhetorically. He came over to Will and placed the silver gun against his temple. "I killed her," he said, "because she was unreliable. I knew that she was going to tell Fischer about me, no matter what she said; the truth was in her voice when she was angry. I would've been expelled permanently from the Diamond. I need access to the Diamond, Willie—that story's a little too long to go into right now. Take my word for it."

"Are you going to tell the Ecclesiastical Council what you did?"

"They would give me a medal for preserving our cover. Do you think they care about someone they'd call a Diamond whore? I'll mention it to Arno if the mood strikes."

"What about your other informants?"

Hart pressed the barrel a trifle more firmly against Will's skin. "Willie, you have it bad. A cold little metal circle is making indentations in your forehead, and you're still asking me questions."

Will's face felt damp. He said, "So? What do you want from me, an apology?"

Hart said, "Sangaree honor again. You might have had

a slight chance earlier, if you'd called in your friends. Was it worth it, for a few answers?"

"I don't know."

"You don't know?"

Will swallowed. "I haven't been dead yet."

He felt Hart chuckle. Hart put the elbow of his other arm around Will's neck and pulled an inch or so, like a twelve-year-old in friendly horseplay. "Willie. I'm sorry I even *thought* about killing you." And even as he said it he'd flicked something on the gun, turned it around, and applied the other end to Will's neck.

Will felt a sting. Then he seemed to be kneeling on the floor, looking dazed, and then the overturned chair was in front of him—sideways. His head was pressed against the cool of the floor tiles. He had the feeling someone had helped him down. He closed his eyes.

"Don't ever change," said Hart, putting away his gun. He went into the outer room and saw that TJ was still there, waiting patiently, though the other Sangaree had left. Hart said, "Don't bother him. He said he wanted to think."

TJ accepted this order, though he managed to look resentful and suspicious as he did so.

Ten minutes later Hart was on a train bound for Transport. When he disembarked, he showed the deck supervisor his diplomatic pass and settled back in a seat on the next Opal shuttle. He noted that there were very few ranking Diamond or Opal people aboard, and none who knew him. In any case, there was a strong chance Willie would keep his problems to himself.

He thought ahead to Arno, and how he would have to present these events, should it become necessary; but his mind kept drifting back to Will. He contemplated Will with the patient pleasure of a gourmet planning a future meal. What a straight arrow he was! And he tried so hard. He hadn't changed at all since school, thank God.

Hart sighed happily as the shuttle closed. It was good to have a hobby.

Spider stopped off at Tal's office on the way to his mother's. He kept a bottle there, which would be useful to bring along in case his mother's supply ran dry.

He found the ex-slave Gabriel sitting on the sofa, and

quickly controlled a reflex to reach for his pistol. "What are you doing here?"

"I've been reading. From the history books off the link. The Lord Demon said it would be all ri—"

"Don't call him the Lord Demon. People are antsy enough about him as it is. Anyway, he didn't tell me you could come here."

Gabriel blinked. "He brought me here himself, and gave me the books and told me not to bother him."

That sounded probable. He hadn't given Gabriel the code to get in, then, and the link was secure enough. They'd gotten the boy a job as a messenger, but he'd been following Tal around whenever he had free time. Being shadowed, even by a fifteen-year-old boy, seemed to get on Tal's nerves amazingly.

"Spider's a funny name," said the boy.

Apparently he was trying to be friendly, though Spider found his topic ill-chosen. "Gabriel's not a regular name either. We don't give angels' names for christening on the Diamond; the priests say it's disrespectful."

"They gave all us boys in the slaveyards angelic names," said Gabriel, with a touch of hard sarcasm that surprised Spider. "To teach us to be good. The girls got saint's names. Working saints, like Therese. The type who scrubbed floors and got off on it."

"Whoa! You're a cynical little bastard, aren't you?" Spider found himself warming to the kid.

"Your demon doesn't seem to mind. He's great, isn't he? He got those papers from the Mercati, and—"

"*Don't* call him my demon. If he's anybody's demon, he's Adrian's, and sometimes I wonder. Call him Special Officer Diamond."

"I'm sorry. Special Officer Diamond."

Spider got his bottle out of a drawer and checked the level of the contents. Not that he distrusted this kid, exactly, but it was good to check. "While we're doing names, try to remember you're a good Diamond subject now. Adrian is Adrian, not 'the Mercati.' Okay?"

"Okay."

Well, he wasn't a bad sort, really. And Spider disapproved of slavery on moral grounds. He said, "Reading anything good?"

A look of animation came over Gabriel for the first time. "*The History of the Three Cities,* by Corfu, and *The Battle for the Venn,* by Tyler. There's a Baret System section from the Encyclopedia, but I haven't gotten to it yet. The demon—Special Officer Diamond says not to believe everything that's in the Encyclopedia."

"You should never believe everything anywhere," said Spider.

"He said that, too," agreed Gabriel.

The sound of the door opening made Spider turn. It was Keylinn, in, of all things, a dress.

Spider stood up. Without thinking, he blurted in anguish: "You're going to the ball!"

"Yes," she said distractedly. "I came to see if I left my packet of hairpins here—hello, Gabriel."

Gabriel had already been coached in this. He rose and said, "Hello, Miss Gray."

She grinned as though catching him out. "I thought you were told 'Tech Gray'?"

"But you're wearing a dress," pointed out Gabriel. "I can't call you 'Tech' if you're wearing a dress."

"There is some logic in this," she said to Spider. "He's trying to make the distinction between the roles of duty and social participation. Not bad for his age, true?"

Spider merely repeated, "You're going to the ball!"

"Why, aren't you going?" She seemed to focus on his reaction for the first time. "Oh, Spider. I am sorry. I think Adrian only invited me out of guilt for not intervening when I was kidnapped."

"I suppose Tal is escorting you."

"It's a wedding ball—an escort isn't required."

Spider turned away, looking like a child whose Christmas presents have just been taken away and given to another little boy whose parents love him. Keylinn came over and put a hand on his shoulder. "Spider—"

"You should wear gloves with a dress like that. You're supposed to."

"They're in my quarters. Turn around, please?"

He turned. Her dress was a soft, satiny gray that looked deep enough to fall into. There were highlights when she moved. A band of dark green beads was around her neck and another was on her wrist. She hadn't fastened the clasp properly, and it was starting to fall off. "My dear Spider," she said.

"Wait a minute," said Spider. He lifted her wrist into a better position and began refastening the clasp.

As he worked it shut, she said, "I missed the New Year's Ball at home again this year. I wish so badly sometimes that I was home."

"I know that feeling. I wish it myself sometimes. And I *am* home."

"That's the saddest thing I've heard in years. What a pair we are, Spider. I suppose we could both shoot ourselves, as our celebration of choice on Adrian's wedding day."

Gabriel's voice said, "Adrian got married?"

They both looked at him. "Is that a joke?" asked Keylinn.

"Where have you been?" asked Spider. "For the last few weeks, I mean."

He returned their looks blankly, then said, "Nobody invited me either."

Keylinn smiled suddenly. "Can you get music out of that thing?" She gestured to the link.

"Sure," said Gabriel. He got up. Spider started to go to the link, too, but she put a hand on his arm.

"Let Gabriel do it."

"What kind do you want?" asked Gabriel. "I can only get into the public access paths. Special Officer Diamond hasn't given me any link-privileges."

"Find me a waltz," said Keylinn.

Within seconds the air was full of violins. She put out her arms. "Dance with me, Spider."

"What? I can't dance." He ducked his head uncomfortably.

"I don't believe you." She pulled him into the center of the office, and they swirled into a waltz, from the door, past the sofa, behind the desk, around the edge of the wall, back to the door.

He was very good. "Another lie," she said breathlessly into his ear, when they finally broke by the door and she leaned back to rest.

"Not only that," he said. "You're not the first Graykey I've danced with."

She started to laugh. Depression, elation, and sudden

physical exertion took their toll, and they both became
hysterical, there by the door. They ended up sitting on the
floor, still laughing, Keylinn's legs sticking out awkwardly from the pile of gray dress stuff.

Gabriel was facing them from the link, and he was
laughing, too.

"Why are *you* laughing?" said Keylinn.

"I don't know," he said, and they all broke up again.

A minute later Keylinn started to rise. Spider pulled
himself up at once and helped her to her feet. "Oh, dear,"
she said, still quivering. "It's been a long, hard winter for
us all, boys."

"Have a good time at the ball," said Spider.

"Aye, I'll work on it. Should I stop by and see you afterward?"

"Don't bother. I'll be at my mother's, and with any
luck I'll be passed out."

"Good night, sweetie, acushla." She kissed him on the
cheek. She waved to the boy at the link. "Good night, Gabriel."

"Good night, Miss Gray."

When the door had closed behind her Gabriel said,
"Corporal Hastings? Spider? Things are very different
here."

Keylinn had missed the wedding because she was on
duty, but she appeared at the ball a fashionable twenty
minutes late (she had done social research). This put her
in the same category as the Opal clerics who trooped in
a body through the Obsidian Door—they also had missed
the wedding, but had no intention of passing by the food
and drink.

The ballroom was just off the Cavern of Audience, and
if there had been any more guests, they would have had
to relocate to that vast space. As it was, the hall was
packed with Diamond admins, knights, and lords, with
occasional Opallines, and with ladies in shimmering
gowns with llong white gloves. The styles of the Three
Cities, Keylinn decided, were not always flattering to the
old and out-of-shape; she passed three gray-haired
women at a sideboard with jewels in their coiffures and
ruffles framing the loose skin of their upper arms. The

enormous hanging earrings lent no elegance at all to their faces, only calling attention to the age spots and the jowls. She found herself looking down at her gloves and imagining her own hands gnarled and wrinkled, and wondered if Cities people were just plain uglier than the ones at home. No, that couldn't be true; she'd known some wondrous specimens of ugliness at home—but they seemed to wear it better.

Actually, Spider's mother was older and fatter, but she seemed fine. Maybe it was just that the wealthy didn't know how to dress. Keylinn took up some cheese and bread on a plate and walked past the three dowagers, who were laughing and chattering happily. Aware of the jewels and not themselves, she thought; I hope I'm as blind if I ever need to be.

The marriageable girls were all either dancing or trying to look occupied. *They* looked delightful in the ruffles and silks, and perhaps here was the answer: The fashions were designed to sell a commodity, and this was the particular commodity in mind. Keylinn balanced her plate in one hand and looked around to see if there was anyone she knew. In fact, there was. Lord Cardinal Arno had just come in with several Opal hangers-on.

She faded back into the crowd.

This was not auspicious. Even at his wedding ball people tried to pull Adrian off and talk to him about things they wanted. Iolanthe found herself deserted several times, though always with an apologetic smile, and always when Prudence or Brandon Fischer was there to entertain her.

Not that Fischer's stiff remarks did much in that area. She sent him off to get her another glass of wine and sat for a moment beside Prudence.

"That was quite a wedding kiss," said Prudence, whose predictably sky-blue gown was predictably magnificent.

Io blushed. Her head had cleared somewhat since the afternoon, though she was wondering now if the wine was a good idea. Still, two glasses wasn't much, and she was bored . . . when she wasn't worried about tonight. "It seemed a good idea at the time," she said.

"Oh, it would seem like a fine idea anytime to me,"

said Prudence. "I wasn't criticizing. I always thought
Adrian was cute as a new puppy."

"Really?" said Io, and hearing the surprise in her voice
she hastened to cancel it. "I didn't think anybody—else
felt that way."

Prudence had had five glasses, but then she knew she
could handle it. "Oh, definitely. I always thought he had
the most charming little butt-end—"

"You, too?" said Io. They both started to laugh. Io stole
an abandoned wineglass from a nearby table and emptied
it. "Speaking of which, do you know who else is good in
that area?"

"The Opal delegate? Quince?"

Io shook her head. "Too pretty. Will Stockton."

"Oh, *yes!*" They both went off into peals of merriment
again. Brandon Fischer approached them with Iolanthe's
wineglass.

"Something amusing, my ladies?" he inquired.

"Nothing. Really." Io made an effort to compose her
lips to seriousness. Fischer shrugged and handed her her
glass. Then he sat down in a chair beside them, pausing
to straighten the creases in his dress trousers as he did so.
For some reason this threatened to break Io down into
laughter again; she caught Prudence's eye watching
Fischer and knew the same thought was going through
her mind. A soft giggle exploded from her throat, and she
quickly coughed to cover it.

"Not feeling well?" said Fischer.

"Just a tickle in my throat." She changed the subject
hastily. "Isn't that your sister, Prudence? The one you
pointed out earlier?"

Prudence peered out over the crowd. "By heaven, I
think you're right. She's dancing with Harry Muir. Good
for her."

Prudence's sister was on the plain side, and had had a
tiff with the gentleman everyone was working to get her
engaged to. "Carmichael's one of Harry's buddies; maybe
the competition will wake him up." She sipped her wine
thoughtfully. "Not that I really want her involved with
Harry's crowd; they're a little wild."

"It's just a dance, Pru."

"Yes, I sound like somebody's mother, don't I? I'll have them married before the set is through."

Io grinned, then said, "Look, it's Will! I thought he wasn't coming."

Will Stockton had just spotted them down the length of the room. He was wearing a silk shirt with his uniform breeches and his best dress jacket; the stupid red sash, thank God, was optional for the ball. His only other set of good clothes had gotten somewhat rumpled earlier that day in Helium Park.

He approached Iolanthe at once and bowed. "Congratulations." He looked around then, and said, "I hope you're in good hands."

She knew he meant bodyguard hands, not Adrian's. She smiled and tilted her head toward the wall. "That over-large gentleman standing under the garlands."

"He might be a little closer. Not that I mean to criticize."

"No offense taken. I'll have to decide whether to forgive you, though, for being late."

He put his head down, and she said at once, "I'm only teasing you, Will. And you're not the only one. Pru just pointed out to me a few minutes ago that nobody's seen Hartley Quince, either."

"I don't think he's coming," said Will. "He wasn't feeling well earlier today."

Prudence said, "That's a shame. That he'll miss the ball, I mean."

"You're not looking too well yourself, Will. Would you like a glass of wine?"

"Thanks, but I'm just tired. Wine would put me to sleep."

"Coffee, then." She gestured to an urn nearby with cups set out beside it.

"No, thank you. I'll take tea if there is any."

"If it's in the hall," said Io, "we'll find it for you. Brandon? Do you know if there's tea about?"

Brandon Fischer sighed and got up. First Adviser of the Diamond, and it had come to this so soon—running minor errands for a seventeen-year-old girl, for the ultimate benefit of a young man with rank so low Fischer didn't even know what level it was. Still, one couldn't refuse a bride on her wedding day.

"Allow me to search," he said with disciplined gallantry, and he bowed.

Tal had found Keylinn in the crowd and they stood now watching the swirl of dancers.

"You're wearing blue lenses today," said Keylinn. "Did you think it was more aesthetically proper?"

"As a matter of fact, I did."

"Well, for you that's quite a concession to friendship."

"It was a concession to social propriety."

"Which would rebound to Adrian's benefit. Iolanthe looks like she's having a good time, doesn't she? She looks happier in Adrian's absence than his presence."

"Whereas Adrian looks the opposite." Tal turned to where Adrian was surrounded by three elderly Diamond aristos, among them Lord Muir. "Pushing to get his son Harry a post again. He'll have a coronary if anybody else gets the security chief position."

"Where is this fabled Harry?" She turned to scan the crowd and found herself face-to-face with Lord Cardinal Arno.

"Miss Gray," said the Lord Cardinal. "It's good to see you again. May I present Hierophant Bell, of our delegation?"

Keylinn's face had gone utterly blank. "I'm honored, Hierophant."

"Miss Gray," murmured Bell, who looked pleasant but confused.

"And Officer Diamond I believe I have already met," said the Lord Cardinal.

"Yes," said Tal, "at the ceremonies marking the end of Separation. I do recall it." He bowed, the proper bow for a high-rank to a higher.

Arno's face was courteous, but the hands clenching the front of his robe gave Keylinn to think that murder was not far from his thoughts even now. Tal might really have made a mistake in letting his cadet strike Arno down; but it was history now, and they'd have to deal with it.

"May I get you a drink, Miss Gray?" Arno inquired.

Keylinn gestured to the glass in her hand. "Thank you anyway."

"Water, I see. How unusual."

"I had to ask for it."

"Then, may I have the honor of this next dance with you?"

Good heavens! Did Lord Cardinals dance? Apparently they did. For one unprofessional moment her head swirled with panic. Then she put one hand out blindly, found Tal's arm, and said, "I'm flattered, my lord, but Officer Diamond has already requested this dance."

Tal's ability to pick up social cues was unpredictable, at least to humans. But this time he simply smiled and said, "If you will forgive us, Lord Cardinal, Hierophant," and led her out onto the floor.

"I hope you can dance," she whispered.

"I hope you can teach me quickly," he replied.

They finished more or less in one piece, near the musicians' stand where Adrian was still trapped by the three lords.

"Was that all right?" asked Tal.

"I think we passed, from a distance." Actually he had learned the steps as soon as she'd explained them, and performed them without error. It was a far cry, however, from her earlier dance in Tal's office. "Your reflexes and memory can't be criticized, but if you ever want to really learn, you might ask Spider to teach you. He knows how to let go."

"I thought I was supposed to hold on to you in this particular dance."

"That's not what I—never mind, it's not important." Adrian had caught sight of them, she saw, and was approaching with a desperate look in his eye.

"Tal! —You must excuse me, gentlemen, I promised Officer Diamond I would speak with him earlier. So good of you to wait, Tal."

For the second time that evening Tal patiently accepted his role in the general deceit of humans. Lord Muir and his companions broke with reluctance and disappeared in the crowd.

"Thank God," said Adrian. "Hello, Miss Gray. Thank you for coming."

"Congratulations," said Keylinn.

"Thank you. Are they gone? Don't look over my shoulder too obviously."

"They're gone," she said.

"Blessings on you both. I suppose Iolanthe is fuming—no, she seems cheerful, she's laughing with Prudence Taylor."

Tal said, "Maybe she's hiding it well."

Adrian focused a sharp look at him, but with Tal it was hard to tell the difference between a dig and simple factual reporting. Possibly he didn't even make that discrimination. Adrian said, "I hope you're enjoying the ball, Miss Gray, and that there are no . . . hard feelings?"

She smiled. "You acted as your position required. I had no expectations or claims on you. Tal has told me, however, that you provided background support, and for that I thank you."

She seemed sincere, and Adrian relaxed. She reminded him of his panthers a little; apparently tame, but one knew quite well they were not. He said, "Tal seems to have pulled off a miracle there. I don't know quite where he dug up the mercenaries he used—he hasn't been very forthcoming on that subject, except to say they weren't station personnel."

Keylinn chose some words rapidly. "I spoke with them myself on the way back." She played with her green bracelet. "They seemed a mixed lot, in their way. I believe they're from out-system."

"It wouldn't surprise me," he agreed. "Tal did say that you dispatched Ennis yourself." There was no condemnation in his tone, only respect. He turned to Tal. "I'm glad she's on our side."

Keylinn glowed at the compliment. Tal saw the look on her face and pondered it; it was so easy for Adrian.

A young Diamond bravo approached them and asked for Keylinn to honor him with a dance. Her glow intensified. "I don't think—"

"Go ahead," said Adrian. "Please don't let me stop you."

She was drawn away, and Adrian turned to Tal. "Three things," he said. "First, a combined trade team has been officially invited downhill to the Baret Two capital. Second, you will accompany our team members as an adviser. Third—"

It was like Adrian to wait and then drop a series of facts like a series of heavy books on one's feet. "Hold on a minute," said Tal. "Nobody is going to want to take advice from a demon. Especially not in a combined team—the Opal members will throw a fit."

"Doesn't it make sense that an Outsider should have the best advice for dealing with Outsiders?"

"When was Opal ever rational in its decisions? For that matter, when was the Diamond?"

Adrian just grinned. "Tal, notice that I've gotten everything I wanted. I have a combined team instead of two rival groups, and I've gotten an actual invitation from the Duke to come. That will give us points before we even go in. The final thing I want is for you to go down with the team and keep them out of trouble. Trust me, I can put this one through just like the others."

"Is there enough time in your lifespan to put this one through?" inquired Tal rhetorically.

Keylinn and her partner whirled past. "Clever of that bravo to choose to ask her for a couples-dance," noted Adrian. "Most of the others for tonight are pattern-dances. So . . . she doesn't know your mercenaries either."

Tal smiled. "Keylinn is a Graykey. You must always listen very carefully to everything she says."

The Protector blinked. "Third," he said. He pulled a piece of paper from a pocket and handed it to Tal. It was a printed list.

The first item on it read:

One (1) arctite painting by Timelo Vangelis, titled "Young Woman in Starlight."

Tal looked up. Adrian said, "I want to give it to Iolanthe as a wedding present. I understand the Duke has it in his private collection. I really want it, Tal. At the same time, I don't want to mortgage the Diamond for it. Bid as carefully as you can."

Tal read further.

One (1) oil painting, pre-Starflight, in preserved glass. Title: "Young Woman Reading a Letter."

Eight (8) boxes handmade Everun lace.
Sixteen (16) boxes Vairanan coffee.

"You can send the coffee and the lace up in my private
yacht," said Adrian. "The lace is for Iolanthe too, but the
other painting is for me. Have you ever seen it? The quality of light is extraordinary."

Tal considered that possibly Adrian just liked pictures
of young women, but decided not to mention it. He read:

Twelve (12) pictures, minimum, holo, of Everun and sur-
rounding area. Purchase or create.
One hundred (100), minimum, books. Preference given to
books only available on Baret Two. Subject preference:
Alien species, history, Empire fiction, in that order.
One (1) set clothing in current planetary style.
One (1) Sawyer Crown.

He looked up. "One Sawyer Crown? What is this, your
laundry list?"

Adrian seemed to be thinking of something far away.
"Do you know what I could do with the Sawyer Crown?
Do you know what I could do if the commons accepted
me as the heir to Adrian the First?" He spoke softly, and
Tal had to turn to see his lips in order to make it out. The
music from the orchestra played around them.

"A lot, I suppose."

Adrian met his glance. "A lot," he agreed. "I would
prefer that the things on this list be negotiated for privately," he said. "You're to be the only Diamond person
involved—especially when it comes to the crown."

"Is this crown also in the possession of the Duke?"

"I don't know where it is. Only that it's on Baret Two."

"I see," said Tal. "How lucky for me. Is this a test?"

Adrian said, "I have every faith in you." He said it sincerely.

Tal folded the list and put it in his pocket.

Adrian said, "Let me clarify. In comparison with the
rest of the list, the crown is the only thing that matters. In
comparison with our team's trade agreement, the crown is
the only thing that matters. You will be the only person
with a correct agenda; everyone else will be confused."

Keylinn's dance was ending. Tal said, "The last will be
nothing new." His voice was noncommittal.

"Do this for me," said Adrian, "and I'll do something
nice for you."

"How high am I empowered to negotiate for the
crown?"

Keylinn made her way through the crowd toward them,
her eyes bright from the dancing.

Adrian said, "As high as necessary to acquire it."

"And nonnegotiated methods?"

"Do whatever you have to do," said Adrian.

A second later he remembered that he had just said this
to an Aphean, and wondered if he'd made an error. But
Keylinn had joined them by then and was pulling Tal out
onto the floor again.

She smiled joyfully at Adrian and blew him a kiss before she turned to show Tal the steps. Adrian grinned and
shook his head, trying to reconcile this with the story
of Ennis.

He joined Iolanthe, but turned again to watch the
Graykey and the demon as they danced at his wedding.
"And what she sees in *Tal*—" he murmured.

"I beg your pardon?" said Iolanthe.

"They make an interesting couple," said her husband,
nodding toward them.

Iolanthe watched with disapproval. She had seen
Keylinn Gray before. No woman as plain as that had the
right to carry herself the way Keylinn Gray did. She
seemed completely unaware of her own looks, or lack of
them. That was bad enough, but she seemed to confuse
other people into being unaware of it, too—which made
all reason flee from the universe. What was the point of
being beautiful if women like that were going to act as
though it weren't necessary? It was like working all your
life to put money in the bank, only to be told the currency
had changed when you tried to withdraw it.

"You know," said Adrian, "so far we haven't even
danced at our own wedding. May I have the honor?"

Iolanthe saw the way he was looking at her, and
smiled. There were still some funds in this particular in-
stitution. She put out her hand, knowing he would take it
up, knowing he would lead her to the floor with style and

dance impeccably and—whatever else he'd done—he would never disgrace her socially.

That was her seventeen-year-old romantic story-filled conclusion: She could have done at lot worse.

Later that night, Iolanthe waited in the Protector's bedchamber, in his great four-poster bed. She was alone in a strange room, wearing the nightdress that Prudence and the other ladies had dressed her in, ready to endure whatever else other people wanted her to do. *Choice* was not something Iolanthe looked forward to becoming acquainted with; her expectations of life had never been great, and they were contracting by the minute, despite her husband's apparent good humor.

The laughter and singing outside the room died down. The leftmost of the two great walnut doors swung open a few inches, and Adrian slipped inside, still carrying a bottle of wine.

"Put your shoulders to the door, gentlemen!" called a voice behind him. "We may catch a glimpse of the fair one Adrian seeks so modestly to hide!"

The fair one's paralysis lifted enough for her to look around for heavy objects. Iolanthe came from a temperamental family and the image of connecting something hard and metallic with any presumptuous fingers that reached around that door's edge gave her courage.

But Adrian shut the door and hit the lock before it became necessary. He offered her a smile she knew was meant to be reassuring.

It chilled her. *Io, darling, have I warned you about what he'll expect of you?*

He placed the bottle carefully on the floor and walked over to the bed. "You look lovely. I'm sorry about the silliness outside; it's the custom here. They don't mean to offend."

She was silent. He reached out a hand and touched her shoulder tentatively. "Have I said you look lovely?"

She tried to endure it, but she could feel herself clenching like a fist. He stepped back thoughtfully. "It's been a long day, I guess." He retrieved the bottle of wine and plucked a glass from the sideboard. "Here."

She took it. Maybe he was right; sometimes doctors got their patients drunk before painful operations, didn't they?

He knelt beside the bed, so they were at eye level. "Io . . ." His expression startled her; it was the look of a man screwing his courage up to do something awful. She clutched her gown involuntarily. "Io . . . I've, uh, been wondering . . . have you . . . did, uh, they talk to you about . . . well, sex?"

His skin, she noted, had flushed with embarrassment. She let go the grasp of her gown. "Of course they did, Adrian."

"They did?" Relief suffused his face. "Thank god! So I don't have to . . . discuss it with you?"

"I'm not a child, sir."

"No, of course not."

"And I'm fully ready to perform my duty, however disagreeable."

He froze. From the look on his face, this didn't reassure him as she'd thought it would. He lifted the winebottle and took a swallow directly from the mouth, licking his lips uncomfortably. "Io . . . sweetheart, do you know, many people actually enjoy the act itself."

"I know," she said. "Men."

"Armed with wit," he said ruefully, sipping again from the bottle. Io, who had meant no witticism, was startled.

"Forgive me," she said at once, for that sort of thing was not encouraged at home. "I only wanted to assure you that I've been prepared. My cousins and my mother told me everything. Although I would feel better, I confess, if I knew which sort you were."

"Which sort?"

She felt her own face get hot, and said nothing. Adrian took her empty glass away—she had no memory of drinking it—and poured her another. "Beloved wife," he said, "I give you my most sacred word of honor, that all my experience tells me that ladies take as much pleasure from this act as gentlemen."

"Perhaps in some spiritual, or philosophical sense . . . suffering can ennoble—"

"Dammit, in the physical, here-and-now sense! I tell you, every woman I've bedded has expressed this sentiment to me!"

"Perhaps they were being polite."

He stood and began to pace in frustration. "They were *not* being polite."

Io, who had thought they were discussing a philosophical point, was surprised at his tone. She fell silent again.

He approached the bed and knelt once more. "Dear heart, I really believe I could convince you of my argument if you would let me."

She examined his face, the sincerity of his expression. "Will you strip?"

"I beg your pardon?"

"Will you remove your clothes, sir?"

He stared at her. Finally he said, "With a dedicated heart, madam." He stood and methodically unbuttoned his shirt. He unwrapped the satin sash from his waist and dropped it, then peeled off his breeches and underclothes. He straighted up, facing her. "Well?"

She looked him up and down as though determining his species. Then she said, unsteadily, "I believe I've been misled, sir."

"Misled?" He glanced down at his anatomy.

She began to snort, to chuckle, and to blush fiery pink, simultaneously. Misery and humor warred for supremacy. There was a touch of hysteria in the laughter, but she couldn't hold it back. "They told me . . ."

"What?" He looked down at himself again, worry in his tone.

". . . that there was . . . a corkscrew . . . oh, I'm such a fool—"

Tears and laughter mingled. She was horrified at her own honesty and wondered whether he would mock her or be offended. He sat on the bed and put his arms around her.

She said against his neck, "Never tell anyone. Never, never—"

"I never will."

A little later, when Adrian slipped into bed beside her, she asked, "What were you just doing?"

"Turning on the recorders," he said.

She sat up. "I beg your pardon?"

"Turning on the recorders. For the archives."

She threw back the spread, covered with white lace roses. "Our wedding night is going on the record? Sight-and-sound?"

Adrian pursed his lips like a man wondering how to get out of this one. "I guess . . . this is another thing Opal didn't tell you."

"Well, I'm telling you right now, Adrian Mercati, that if you want a record of this, you can record yourself. I'll be in the chair over there."

"Sweetheart—" He reached out.

"Don't you dare touch me while that thing is on!"

He folded his hands. "Darling, nobody is ever going to see it. It's just for legal purposes—to protect you, in fact, if I ever tried to annul the wedding. It goes into the archives, locked, and when we die, it's destroyed. It might as well never have existed."

"If it might as well never exist, why make it?"

"Sweetheart, Opal would never acknowledge the marriage without it. They insisted on it, it's in our contract—I told you, it's for *your* benefit."

She sat miserably on the edge of the bed.

"Nobody will ever see it," he said again.

Eventually she said, "Promise."

"I promise. The only reason it would ever be taken out would be if I tried to annul the marriage, and why would I even try since I know the proof is there? That's why these records are never used, Io."

She still sat there, looking unhappy.

"Can I touch you now?"

She shrugged, and he put an arm around her shoulder. "You know, we're actually pretty lucky. There was a time a few centuries ago when they insisted on having live witnesses to the consummation."

She gave what was almost a laugh. "I'll bet they begged for invitations to that even more than to the wedding."

"I don't doubt it." He kissed her forehead and started unbuttoning her gown. "And imagine the pictures the streetvendors sold."

She surprised herself by chuckling as he let her back down on the bed. My, he was good at instilling courage, she thought; an excellent companion for battle. Perhaps there would be survivors of this sortie after all. And he was certainly very generous with wine. In the back of her mind she heard Prudence Taylor's voice say, ". . . the most charming little butt-end."

Adrian, who was kissing his way down her breasts, took her shaking laughter for newfound passion and was more than pleased with himself.

Section Four:
The Sawyer Crown

Chapter 36

Baret Two. Settled by discontented Empire subjects in 2390, the Baret System has been mainly self-sufficient ever since. A chain of physical disasters in 2410 led to a request for Imperial governorship, which was answered by the installment of the Arbrith family on both planets in 2413. Prior to this a series of local warlords had taken power on Baret Two, each one hanging his predecessor in chains from the top of the capital fort. The Arbrith family rode its understandable popularity with competence, instituting judicial reform and reapportioning land slowly and with caution.

Elysia Arbrith was converted to Redemptionism in 2449, changed her name to Edith, and insisted on the immediate conversion of the rest of the Arbrith family. All survivors had converted by 2453. Since then the Arbriths have traditionally been Redemptionist, as have some of their court. The great majority of Baret System are Cantists and agnostics. With the exception of two civil wars, the religious preferences of their leaders are regarded by the people of Baret System as a tolerable eccentricity.

Baret System has been a largely peaceful place for centuries. Aside from some rare gourmet foodstuffs, the chief export of Baret Two is handmade lace in the so-called "Everun Pattern."

Sum total of Baret Two information in the
Imperial Encyclopedia.

"As usual, much of what is here is out of date."
Marginal note in the hand of ADRIAN MERCATI

Jane Emerson

"I've never been downhill before," said Brandon Fischer to Tal. They seemed to be standing on a silver beach under a blue and white sky, while breakers rolled against the sand. In fact, they were standing in the audience chamber of Baret Two's ruling family. The rest of the trade team, as well as a gaggle of Baret Two hangers-on and other people waiting for introduction to the Duke stood around them. If you squinted your eyes a certain way the dimensions of the actual audience chamber took precedence over the beach scene; otherwise it was a ghostly double image, apparent only enough to keep people from falling down steps and banging into the furniture.

Mechs offered drinks to those waiting, and Brandon Fischer winced as he took one. All this non-Redemptionist technology bothered him. "I understood the ruling family were of our faith," he said.

Tal shrugged. "Maybe not all Redemptionists are as orthodox as those in the Three Cities." Fischer was taking it relatively well, he thought; Hierophant Gomez, head of the Opal contingent, allowed open discomfort to show on his face.

The Arbriths employed a herald, as every worthwhile planetary authority did; an educated liaison knowledgeable in the customs of greeting of other societies and species, not likely to offend. The Arbriths' herald was a plump middle-aged woman with a weather-lined face. A member of her staff stood beside her—the Three Cities specialist? Whatever that young man knew, it was out of date, more out of date than the Cities' own information, which at least came from the Encyclopedia. The Three Cities hadn't traded in this part of civilization for centuries.

Tal noted with distant amusement the change in shading in the face of Hierophant Gomez. The drinks-mech had been replaced by a human servant offering him a choice of finger foods. Like most of the humans on Baret Two, she had skin of rich, dark brown, and wore golden earrings; this particular servant was also young and one of her breasts was bared. What's more, a golden hoop matching her earrings had been placed around the chocolate nipple, and the hierophant's gaze kept returning to it in a shocked and involuntary way.

And now the herald was striding forward. Like all the civilians of the capital she wore a long pleated skirt that stopped just above her ankles; the Barets considered legs an object of modesty to be revealed only to lovers. "We give welcome to our brothers from the Hollow Hills," she announced in a clear alto tone. "The Hollow Hills" was an old phrase from Redemptionist poetry that meant the Three Cities. "Will they come forward and meet their siblings, long separated and now well-met?"

Brandon Fischer motioned for the rest of the team to come together. In a low voice Tal said, "Do you think they'll want to do the knife ceremony?"

Fischer glanced at the gold-hooped woman, who was walking past them with a tray. "I wouldn't even attempt to predict what these people will do."

The team gathered before the dais, Tal well to the back of the group. Because it had been clear weather in Everun that dawn, Brandon Fischer spoke for them; had it been a misty morning, the hierophant would have done so. That piece of advice had come by a hideously expensive Oracle of Pearl. Fischer bowed. "We were honored by your invitation," he said.

Duke Peter sat on a cushioned chair on the dais, his prerogative as a nobly born member of a ruling Empire family. At least, it would be his prerogative till Baret One brought the revolution, and Duke Peter and all his kin came to an abrupt end. How long? Five years at most, was Tal's best guess; Baret One had gone Republican some time ago, and mixed planetary systems never lasted. Of course, it could happen tomorrow.

As long as it didn't happen while they were there.

The doomed Duke Peter was a thickset man of about fifty standard years, black-haired like everyone here, with noncommittal dark eyes. He wore the long pleated skirt and a green vest edged in gold, but with no shirt underneath. Tal wondered if the Opal hierophant was getting tired of looking shocked. The Duke's sister, Elizabeth Mard Arbrith, sat with her husband beside him. She was younger, very fashionably dressed in dangling bracelets and anklets, and very sharp-eyed. She had a bright smile

that Fischer said later "had false written all over it." She
wore a vest like her brother's. There was a white target
drawn on one side of it, where her breast would have
shown. A regular trendsetter, thought Tal.

Her husband looked innocuous enough in his own fashion choices. From what Tal had heard, it was possible he
didn't want to compound the error he had made in marrying Elizabeth Mard.

She said now, "Of course, we all understand that you
asked for the invitation." Her smile remained wide and
fixed as she spoke.

Fischer and the Duke both looked annoyed. She
smoothed her skirt and let her bracelet jingle pleasantly.

Duke Peter said, "And we're pleased that you honor us
by accepting." He spared a brief glare for his sister,
whose zombie-smile did not waver.

While the Duke and Fischer exchanged the required
pleasantries, Tal scanned the assembly. Far down the false
beach, long past the true ending of the room, a black stallion played in the surf. From the Arbrith coat-of-arms, he
remembered. No doubt there were state security people
on hand in the group here; no doubt, too, Republican
agents were present. Perhaps that plump herald was
one—there was something off about her accent when she
spoke. Still, for all he knew, nine-tenths of the people attending were on the Baret One payroll, and as long as he
was careful, what was it to him?

Empire nobility and servants, mainly . . . some prosperous looking traders . . . his gaze stopped suddenly. The
sector-gate must have opened recently. What were
Elaphites doing here? He stared at the golden couple
across the room, sharers of half his biological heritage.
Without warning the male met his eyes, and Tal resisted
a sudden urge to turn and face the wall.

Elaphites. He had never liked them, never gotten along
with them. Humans fell all over themselves catering to
the golden people, rhapsodizing about their appearance,
their manners, their good nature. Their eyes.

Their stupid yellow eyes that were supposed to be so
gentle, so compassionate, so *insightful*—

They were a waste of evolution. Never had he met a

species more pointless and ineffectual—he forced himself to move his gaze onward.

Consider the crowd. Think. What do they tell you about the pattern of things here? More aliens, over near the dais. A family of Tamatri, continually spraying each other with water. Well, they didn't look much like Republican agents, anyway. Besides, while the Republic claimed to welcome all species, it was pretty well known they only trusted fellow humans. And not even them, really.

The sector-gate open. What factors did that bring in? The connections from Baret Station were Tubol, Bakan-adanaraka—no point in even thinking about them, they had nothing to say to humanoids—Limis Three and Four, and Carthenat, a hub with twenty-three routine connection points. Tubol and Limis, being in the same sector as a hub, would be prosperous, industrialized places; being one gate away from a hub was enough to make Baret System a relative backwater. Being two gates away would mean a frontier world, overlooked or even forgotten by the mainstream of Empire/Republic life. Adrian claimed the Three Cities picked up a fair amount of trade from the forgotten worlds; it was the advantage, perhaps the only one, of bypassing the gates.

What were Elaphites doing on Baret Two? Possibly they were from Carthenat; hubs often had a diversity of population. Anyway, there was no reason to think they had anything to do with him. No reason to think of them at all.

He brought his attention back to the dais, where Fischer was winding things up with the Duke. Peter and Elizabeth, good Redemptionist names. Did the masses not really care that their rulers were "Blood-Christians?" Not that they let it stand in their way, apparently. The tiny blue box attached to Duke Peter's chest showed that he was under a medical monitor, a technology forbidden in the Cities.

Fischer bowed and withdrew from the dais, followed by the rest of the trade team. Everyone seemed to be breaking up and heading for the food spread out on tables around the edge of the room . . . or knee-deep in the surf, depending on how you looked at it. Tal noticed that the Elaphites seemed happy to stay on their side of the room;

good. The male picked up a small silver fish and fed it to the female. Everyone around them seemed to find it a charming thing to do.

He found himself near the chief herald. At this range, the lines in her face were even more pronounced. Her hair was in a little bun on top of her head. She had filled a great goblet with the local wine they called "tiko" and at this particular moment she was gazing intently at the smoked fish, as though the table held the mystery of the universe. Tal walked closer and said, "Herald? Excuse me, herald, but I'm a commoner of the Cities."

Knowing now the way to address him, she turned at once with a smile. "Thank you, cyr, for your consideration. May I recommend this fish to you? It's native-derived, and excellent with hard bread and a bit of cheese."

"Thank you, but I'm going out for dinner later. In fact, it's about that that I'd like to consult you."

"Ah! You'll find no better tour advice, I assure you. I know the pleasures better than a native, for I came here myself from Tubol not five standard years ago, and I've tried all the places one should try."

"Yes, I thought you might not be native-born."

She seemed briefly surprised. "I was physically matched by my agency on Tubol. The Arbriths requested it."

Her accent and grammar declared her origins, though that would be impolite to say to a herald. "Your hairstyle is unlike that of any other person in the room. Also, I note that many of the women here leave one breast bare." He nodded to a young noblewoman who passed, with a veil wrapped around one breast and shoulder, and a circlet of gems on the other.

"Ah, well, I have not her architectural support," replied the herald.

"Surely not so," said Tal. Keylinn had taught him that this was the proper response to make whenever a woman employed self-criticism about her physical characteristics.

"Alas, cyr, yes," she said. She gazed down at her plump chest mournfully. "It would take a flying buttress built under each to accomplish what that youngster does by youth and size alone."

"The universe is large—"

"And standards of beauty differ. I know. But I learned my standards on Tubol, where—tall and thin people being genetically rare—tallness and thinness were most prized. As were young, flat, boyish figures. These cultural traps we set ourselves, but what are we to do? Not until we are too old to change our ways do we see them for what they are."

Never having entered into his culture's imperatives, this meant little to Tal. He said, "But you were going to advise me on the pleasures of Everun."

"Yes, here we may shelter under my expertise." She smiled happily, crinkling her clear brown eyes. "For what sort of thing are we searching? Food, sex, drugs? Places of dignity and elegance, with high prices?"

"I would be interested in hearing about all three, actually. But what I'd really like is a more informal atmosphere. Somewhere loud and talkative. Perhaps even on the edge of legality, if that doesn't offend you, herald."

"Ha! The young always want to fly across the take-off routes. Does your family know what you're doing down here?" She grinned and wiped her mouth with the edge of a sleeve. "Well, you're not the first to ask a herald for that sort of information, cyr—indeed you must avoid becoming a cliché."

Tal waited. She said, "It would be hard to miss the sort of place you seek if you go to the Lankio Quarter. Dens of iniquity on every corner. Be sure and check that they have a state license, or you might get in over your head."

He extended a hand and they shook, Empire style. "Thank you for your hospitality."

She picked up another goblet of tiko and buried her face in it briefly. "Five kilometers from here, seaward and north. Do you have a car, cyr?"

"Yes, thank you, I do."

He did have a car, and a driver as well, and he left them both at the reception. He could move more easily alone.

The ducal grounds were on a hill, hedged with sculpted bushes and gardens, and the sea air blew a salt smell over the roses and honeysuckles. Leaving them and entering the city proper, he could perceive why Everun was called "a city on slopes." The flat strip of land that held the main street of the capital and the few blocks on either side ran up the coast like a very long snake; behind it rose the Morning Mountains, green and tall and misty. The city climbed the first slopes for several kilometers before the incline steepened and the convenience of humans gave up the effort. Looking up the mountainsides one saw only the occasional flash of white in the constant green: A waterfall or a noble's villa, it was impossible to tell from down here.

Night was falling swiftly, and birds were wheeling in from the sea. Tal headed north to begin his constant work, to make the first connections that would let him inquire in time about Belleraphon.

Behind him on the hill the display lights for the garden turned on. Silhouetted against them stood a man in the trousers and jacket of Baret state security, talking into his wrist. A thorny rose was embroidered on his pocket.

He watched Tal disappear into the dusk, then he turned and went in to the party.

For Iolanthe the week since the wedding had passed swiftly. Aside from being moved into the Protector's suite, her life had not undergone any radical change. There was still Prudence to talk to, and new court ladies to become acquainted with, and clothing to select—the last item being as political as all items were now; she realized that everything she did could be twisted to reflect badly on Adrian, if she were not very, very careful. As for Adrian himself, she hardly saw any more of him than she did before the wedding. He was always busy. First he was closeted with the Diamond half of the trade team for three days, and now that they were downhill he seemed to have no difficulty in finding ten thousand more things to do.

It was therefore a surprise when he appeared in their suite in the middle of the day, striding in and pulling off his shirt at the same time, then rolling it into a ball and throwing it into a corner with far more force than was required.

"What are you doing here?" she asked, without think-

ing. She'd come to think of the suite as hers in the daytime.

"I came to wash," he said shortly. He disappeared into
the spit, where she heard him cursing the absence of soap
a minute later. "Lucius! Where the hell is Lucius?"

"He went to get your shirts." She'd never seen Adrian
angry before.

"Why isn't he ever here when I want him? When I
don't want him, he's underfoot all the time."

There was no good answer to that, so she was silent.
He slammed out of the spit in his underwear and went to
the link. She heard him say, "Paul? Tell Chin to clear out
the hall, and bring up the cats. . . . Ten minutes. . . . All
right, fifteen. I'm not waiting more than fifteen. . . . Well,
they can do it somewhere else. Good-bye."

He glanced up and saw her looking at him. He took
three deep, shaky breaths and said, "I beg your pardon. I
must go out for a while."

"Is something wrong?" Very clearly yes.

"No. Well, yes, but it's nothing that can't be handled in
time. I just had a very disagreeable interview with the
Lord Cardinal of Opal."

She waited nervously.

"He's talking about breaking the team. After we signed
a goddamned, spelled-out, every-fucking-thing-taken-
into-account contract. After I have shown, as God is my
witness, the patience of Job—" He halted suddenly and
took another deep breath. "I ask your pardon again. I am
no fit company for a lady. I suggest . . . I suggest we stay
in our separate chambers tonight. Perhaps by morning I'll
be more worthy of your presence."

He got up, looked around blankly, and then retrieved
his crumpled shirt. He put it back on and strode out of the
room, the front of the shirt still unlaced.

Iolanthe stared at the door. Suddenly the suite had
taken on that quality of quiet that follows a disaster. She
stood there frozen for a few seconds, then she tapped
open the door and stepped out into the corridor. There
was no sign of her husband. Her first-shift bodyguard,
however, was lounging against the wall across the way.
He snapped to attention when she came out.

"Please come with me," she said firmly.

"But madam, you're not scheduled to go out this afternoon."

"Something has come up. Are you going to accompany me, or should I travel on my own?"

This was horribly unfair to the poor man, and he chose the lesser of two evils. As he fell in beside her, he said, "May I ask where we're going, my lady?"

"To the Cavern of Audience."

The halls outside the Cavern were choked with disgruntled people moving in the opposite direction. Whatever had been going on inside that day had been summarily interrupted.

She found Adrian at the entrance. Their eyes met, and he said, "What are you doing here?" It was an unconscious imitation of her own question to him.

Before she could think of a sensible answer, a man in a black silk shirt and breeches came up, leading two marble panthers on leashes. Io took a few steps back. The panthers wore black hoods, and though the man with the leash seemed to be in control, this was really closer than she had ever planned on coming to these creatures.

She could see the grace of their muscles as they moved. Guided by their keeper, they padded silently to the entrance, where, as they stood waiting, she could clearly hear the tap of an impatient claw against the floor.

Adrian pulled on a pair of thick, dark gloves. He said, "How much did you give them, Paul?"

"About seven cc's," said the man in black silk.

"Good," said Adrian. "I'm restless, I want everybody else to be restless."

He seemed to have forgotten her. She felt a sudden stirring of anger herself, and it was this more than anything else that made her say, "May I come in, too, sir?"

He turned to her in surprise. Not half as surprised as I am, she thought distantly. "This is serious," said Adrian shortly. "These animals are dangerous. They've been fed and they've been a little tranked, but their instincts are not friendly to humans. Understand? I'll see you tonight."

"Of course I understand, I'm not a child. I want to come in with you."

He seemed about to lose patience. *"Why?"*

"Because I'm your wife."

He had the look of a man who'd suddenly gone down a step he didn't see. In other circumstances she would have been tempted to laugh.

When he spoke, the sharpness was gone from his voice. "I can't. Io, if anything happened to you in there, Opal would hold me responsible. Reasons of state."

"Do we have to do everything for the sake of Opal? Can't we do anything just for us?"

"No."

She pointed to the cats. "This is for you alone, not for the City. If you died, life would be chaos here, but you risk it anyway. Tell me how prudent that is."

He stared and then gave a strained laugh. "Outreasoned by a seventeen-year-old girl. It's true, my love, but you're unkind to point it out. Very well, take my gloves." He stripped them off and handed them to her. "They tend to go for hands and wrists first, I'm not sure why."

"What about you?"

"I can't wait for another pair. They want to get in."

He gestured to the panthers, but it was clear to Io that he wanted to get in, too.

"All right, open the door," she said.

The huge carved entrance called the Obsidian Door swung open. She followed Adrian inside. The cavern looked strange empty; all that space—you never saw it without hordes of people. It was like the end of the world. When they were far enough in, Adrian turned and said, "Now, Paul."

Two black-green shapes flowed past them. The Obsidian Door was closed.

How clever of her. She was alone with Adrian Mercati, reputed murderer of the last Protector, and two lethal panthers.

She turned to him. "Well, my husband, what is it you do now?"

Chapter 37

In the Sangaree section of Opal, Will Stockton was waking up late. He breathed in rose perfume and became aware of a backbone curved against his. Lysette was beside him, as she had been since his return from the Diamond, and he was happy.

She'd finally agreed that since the date was set for their wedding, they might follow the custom of assuming retroactive marriage. By the laws of the Cities a couple once wed was wed forever, and always had been. Hallalujah, thought Will, and he lost no time in moving into her room in Duclos Avenue.

It was enough to wash out the memory of Hart and the dead girl. And to soften the knowledge that reporting Hart would lead nowhere but to the radiation levels for Will himself. Hart was a superior officer, and that was the way the system worked.

Will rolled off the bed carefully so as not to disturb her. He liked to make love to Lysette first thing upon waking, whereas Lysette liked to remain fully unconsciousness until the afternoon was well underway. This had been an area of compromise.

The compromise was that he would go and get a cup of strong tea and drink it by the link while he checked to see if his new assignment orders had come through. And then he would take a walk through Sangaree, drop in on Johnny, maybe take the train to visit Bernadette at her new address, and eventually come back to the compartment to find his betrothed gone out for rehearsal. This was the way most of his compromises with her went.

Anyway, she was usually eager enough after the show. One couldn't have everything. He dropped a spoonful of blackleaf into a large cup and poured boiling water over it, then sat down at the link and presented his Guard code.

PLEASE HOLD YOURSELF IN READINESS, said the link-screen. That was unusual; was somebody trying to call him? Why wouldn't they leave a message with someone on the public link in Brissard Street, or with Bernadette, for him to call back? And he knew that they couldn't have traced him through any such call on the local links because no Sangaree, especially not Bernie, would ever have given his location to anybody. They just didn't operate that way.

A minute later a new message appeared. REPORT TO ROOM EIGHT, ECCLESIASTICAL COUNCIL, 16:00. YOUR ASSIGNMENT WILL BE GIVEN AT THAT TIME.

The message stayed a moment, then was washed away and replaced by the screen-filling imprimatur of the Council.

Good lord, what was this about? He wasn't told to report to the duty sergeant at Guard headquarters. He wasn't even sent a proper link-message in writing. Just a screen that came and went and left no evidence.

God . . . had Hart filed some kind of negative report on him? Did they just want to bring him in easily so they could terminate him?

No. There wasn't any need for paranoia. He'd been on the Opal for six days. Surely they would have killed him before, if they were going to. Well, unless it got held up in Administration. . . .

No. Thinking this way was pointless. What was he going to do, run off and join the ghosts just because he was jumpy? And it seemed to come down to either that or reporting to Room Eight.

He took a few deep gulps of tea. At least his hands were steady. He put the empty cup down, wiped his palms on his trousers, and saw that he'd drunk half the bitter tea leaves without noticing.

"Room Eight?" he asked the secretary, a young deacon. "Through there."

Will was always nervous at being this close to the center of ecclesiastical power. The halls were filled with EPs in their crisp black uniforms, and like all Sangarees he considered the EPs to be little more than stormtroopers. Joining the Guard had led to a few bar fights, but had he been ill-advised enough to enlist in the Ecclesiastical Police, his body would long ago have been stuffing a ventilation tube in Sangaree. He still occasionally had quick and painful spurts of memory of the day the men in black came to school and took Tommy away. Five or six times a year the playback would hit without warning, knock him in the gut, and then pass by without leaving a ripple.

He pressed for permission to enter Room Eight. The green light came on and the door slid open. Will stepped into a high cleric's office, well-appointed, with dutiful pictures on the walls from the sacred books, an expensive carpet, and a tapestry hanging behind the desk.

Hart sat there, writing on a pad. He glanced up for a millisecond and said distractedly, "Just give me a minute, Willie, I'll be right with you."

Will closed his mouth. He found himself checking the exit and stopped.

Hart looked up and grinned. "Like the office? I've been promoted. Thirteenth rank."

Will focused on him. "Why am I here?"

"With rank comes responsibility. We must never forget that. I've just been handed a dandy little project involving some negotiation with Baret Two as well as some information-gathering on the Diamond." His smile was wide and sunny. "I enjoy travel."

"I didn't know you were on the trade team."

"I'm not. Officially. I won't be looking for salt and coffee. How has your time off been? Pleasant, I hope—what was the name of your fiancée? Lisa, Leslie—?"

He knew better than to lie. "Lysette."

"Lovely girl. I've seen pictures."

"Why am I here, Hart?" He hadn't turned in any reports about the girl in Helium Park, and Hart must know it. Nor should it surprise him—it would take an idiot to try something as futile as that. What did they have to discuss?

"Why are any of us here?" inquired Hart, and as Will opened his mouth again, he added, "But you as an individual are here because you're now on my personal staff."

The phrase seemed to echo. The enormity of this vision of hell hung before Will's sight, momentarily obscuring his view. Hart was polite enough to give him a few seconds to digest the news. Then he said, "Willie? Are you still with us?"

There seemed to be a ringing in Will's ears. Then he stepped back from the precipice and in a completely logical tone of voice he said, "Someday one of us is going to have to kill the other."

"Willie, you smooth talker," said Hart. He was scribbling on a piece of paper, which he handed the sergeant. "This is the address of my tailor. He does a lot of uniforms for the higher admin ranks. Please patronize him. I couldn't bear to have to look at you all day in that standard-issue stuff."

Will took the paper mechanically. Hart gave him a diagnostic look and said, "You ought to take the rest of the day off. Oh, and don't worry. You can still keep your little Sangaree personal set of guards."

Will's eyes widened in alarm. "You didn't transfer them, too!" They would kill him.

"No, no. Why add the stress to their already depressing and pointless lives? They don't have the mental stability you and I enjoy." Will felt a muscle in his face start to twitch. Hart continued, "No, I just had them assigned temporary cross-departmental duty, reporting to you. They know the Diamond now, it seemed best."

And so Will joined the Men in Black.

Chapter 38

"Actually," said Adrian, with a sheepish look on his face, "I usually just sit and think. I'm not used to having somebody else in here with me."

"Couldn't you sit and think by the cages in the zoo?"

"There's a difference between that and being in the same room with them."

There certainly was. Io was aware every second of the black-green shapes padding up and down the Cavern, where each was and in what direction it was moving.

"Besides," said Adrian, "I like to pace next to them."

Heavens above, thought Io.

He added, "It helps me concentrate."

"Couldn't a few cups of coffee give you the same effect?"

"No, no—this makes me *less* nervous, not more."

She pressed herself against a marble slab as one of the panthers stalked past. It seemed to take no notice of her.

Adrian *did* appear more calm than he'd been outside. "They're lovely, aren't they?" he asked, gesturing to the cat padding away from Io.

Of course, she thought, taking a deep breath. They're beautiful, they're alien, and they're dangerous. What more could he ask for? "I suppose I can't complain," she murmured. "My reactions to things never seem to be normal either. So I'm told."

"Is this bothering you?" he asked.

"Oh, no. I'm fine. Just a little, a little . . . I didn't expect to be here today. That's all."

He smiled. "Why did you come?" He took her hand and helped her up onto one of the high marble slabs, then climbed up and sat beside her. The surface was cold under her gown. Below them one of the cats looked up with an impersonal curiosity. Its eyes were gleaming onyx stones.

"I wanted to be with you."

This was apparently the right thing to say. He put an arm around her. "I seem to be losing all that frustration," he said. "Maybe I should just have stayed with you in our suite—it would have saved everybody here the trouble of clearing out."

She sat there both scared and content, enjoying the warmth of his body and the cool of the marble. She still did not share his enthusiasm for their marriage bed, but in considering the matter she had to conclude that sex had brought them closer. Perhaps all people who were comrades in necessary, disagreeable experiences felt that way—like maintenance teams who cleaned out recyclers.

Luckily she did not share this point of view with Adrian, who might never have recovered from it.

Instead she put her head on his shoulder. "I wish I had someplace like this to go. Something to do."

"I'm sorry, sweetheart, haven't we been figuring a

good schedule for you? I told them to leave a certain amount of free time, but maybe that was a mistake."

"Oh, no, there's plenty to do—I just mean, I'd like something to *do*. Something besides going to dinners and being fitted for dresses."

"Well, why don't you go through the link-library and see if there's anything that strikes your fancy?"

She abruptly pulled herself straight. "You let women use the links here?"

"Of course."

"I mean, to *read?* I could read anything I wanted?"

"If it's in the public access paths. Uh, you know how to read, don't you?" He would think that an aristo girl would have been taught, but with Opal one never knew.

"Of course I know how! Are you saying I could just call up whatever I wanted?"

"More or less." He looked puzzled.

Io moved restlessly, as though she were about to take off then and there. At that second she caught sight of a graceful furred shape beneath the slab, and backed closer to Adrian. "I'll wait so we can both leave together."

He laughed and put his arm back on her shoulder. After a minute she relaxed. He said, "But you do think they're beautiful, don't you?"

She looked down at the feline shape still below; lethal or not, one longed to run a hand through the deep fur. "I do. I wish I could touch them."

"I slept with them one night."

"No!"

He nodded. "It's true. It was very late and they'd been given a little too much trank, and we'd been in here for hours." He grinned. "I was asking their advice on how to handle the Uprising. Anyway, we finally all fell asleep on my cape. It gets a little cold in here, you know, and when I woke up, we were back-to-back."

"Good heavens!"

"Don't tell Brandon. It would only upset him."

I don't believe he killed Saul Veritie, she thought. The thought came out of nowhere. Her forehead touched the nape of his neck; another thought occurred, and she spoke it. "Your hair reminds me of their fur." She ran a finger through the dark, soft mass.

"Does it?" His voice sounded strained.

"Yes," she said softly, and then he was kissing her in a way that even six days had taught her he only used when he meant business.

Her silken shawl was dropped below, where it fell featherlike to the marble and caught the attention of both cats. Io glanced around as though suddenly in need of an escape route. She caught a glimpse of black, dangerous eyes shining up at them, sharp and interested. "Let's go back to the suite," she said.

"No, here." His face was buried in her neck.

She pushed him gently back. "The suite."

"Please, Io. I really want to stay here."

"We'll upset the panthers."

"They're a couple themselves," he said. "They'll understand." He pulled off his shirt and placed it as a pillow for her head.

Well, it was her duty to put up with a husband's conjugal desires. And she did ask to come. "I suppose it'll be all right. . . ." A little patience, and then they could leave.

Adrian's face lit up. "Thank you." He pulled off her high laced shoes and they went over the side, too. Then he lifted up her gown and her two petticoats, and his head disappeared.

"What are you *doing?*" she asked.

The brush with danger was having a strange effect on him, she thought worriedly; it had disordered his wits. She felt his mouth on the inside of her thigh and gasped. It was warm and barbaric, simultaneously. The movement of his tongue called up confused images of being made love to by a giant, dark panther.

She ought to climb down, call in the counselors for help . . . the poor man.

Although, *she* seemed to be the one feeling lightheaded. . . .

Keylinn and Spider sat at ease in the main room of Howard and Dominick's compartment, contentedly replete with butterscotch cake. Why Howard and Dominick never gained an ounce was a mystery to Keylinn.

She held out her cup of hot chocolate. "To Dominick. Congratulations."

He smiled and wheeled his chair a few inches in mild embarrassment.

"To Dominick," said Spider and Howard. Howard added, "And to *An Answer to the Dead.*"

An Answer to the Dead was Dominick's new play. Word had just come from the company that morning that it would be in this year's repertory. Dominick had not had a play accepted in some time, and Howard had taken to the news like a tonic, inviting them both to a private party and telling Spider to "feel free to bring a gift."

Spider's gift, whatever it was, had been passed to Dominick in private and cheered him up considerably.

Then Spider recited the gossip from G level and the court both, some of which he had to have learned from Tal, and Howard contributed some scandals from the player's company that had to be of interest to any breathing humans, regardless of whether they knew the people involved or not.

Now Spider sighed happily and sipped a third cup of chocolate. "And Tal is downhill, far out of range. I never hear from him."

"I wonder how he's doing on the trade team," said Keylinn.

"Endearing himself, no doubt. Explaining to everyone in exquisite detail how wrong they are."

She smiled. "Adrian wouldn't have sent him if he thought Tal couldn't keep his ego in check."

"Huh!" said Spider, seeming to feel that was all that need be said.

Dominick said, "Do I understand Adrian's demon has a slight problem with discretion?"

"Not discretion exactly—" began Keylinn.

"It's his bloody sense of superiority," said Spider.

"We all feel superior," said Dominick. "The point of socialization is to learn to conceal it."

"No, no—" said Spider, but Keylinn interrupted.

"He's right. Three Cities people feel superior to Outsiders; Outsiders think Cities people are hicks. Graykey feel superior to non-Graykey. Apheans feel superior to humans. Maybe it's just something tied in with our genes, that we can't get rid of."

"I don't feel superior to anybody," protested Spider.

"That's because you're the most mature person I've met here."

Spider glanced at her face, but she did not appear to be joking. Howard said, "I know. Spider is wise where the rest of us are merely clever."

"What's a Graykey?" asked Dominick.

"An Outsider philosophic school," said Keylinn. "It's rather dying out now, I believe."

"And how is the 'favored couple' doing?" asked Howard, returning the subject to its proper nature, gossip. "Has anyone heard? Millicent Greeve told me the other day that *she* was told that Adrian's been seen on Requiem Row."

"I don't believe it," said Dominick.

"You're a romantic," replied Howard.

"No, I just believe Adrian would have better sense. It's too close to the wedding."

"What about you, Keylinn, what do you think?" Howard appealed to her.

Even over gossip and butterscotch cake, a Graykey tried to be accurate. "I suppose it's possible. But I agree with Dominick that he's probably too sensible of how people would take it." She considered her few encounters with Adrian and what rumors she'd heard. People seemed to like him; she liked him herself. Adrian was a Mercati, and expected to be eccentric, though he compensated well; Iolanthe was given to migraines and black depressions. What would the children of that union be like? They were both bright enough, but back home two highly strung thoroughbreds would not be encouraged to mate.

Not that there was much to choose from on the Diamond; the centuries had taken their toll in mental health. Was it any different on Opal? The representatives she'd met—like Stockton and Hartley Quince—seemed normal enough. Arno she dismissed as a statistical factor; fanatics popped up everywhere.

She was unaware of how far her thoughts had taken her from the issue at hand, and found herself grinning. It seemed that Spider and Tal were the sanest people she'd found, so far—what a telling statement about the Three Cities. Tal was at least normal for an Aphean—as well as anybody could tell—and Spider was—well—

"Spider's all right," she said.

"This we have already established," said Dominick.

She smiled. "I was thinking about the nature of people on the Diamond."

"Only a single nature?" inquired Dominick. "People are like poems, you know, each unique."

"I can't say it's a comparison I ever thought of."

"Oh, yes. And you may not always know what a poem *says*, but you can generally tell the form. Take you, for instance."

"Take me, then." A haiku? She'd been brought up on them, and foreigners generally found the Graykey subtle to the point of opacity.

"A sonnet, definitely a sonnet. A strict and classical form. By the rulebook, A-B-B-A, or you'll know the reason why. I think you'd die before you broke meter."

She froze, and then laughed, a little uncomfortably, and Spider laughed with her although he'd never heard of a sonnet. They taught grammar and spelling where he'd gone to school, not poetry. She put a hand on his shoulder. "Don't forget Spider," she said.

Dominick fixed him with a measuring look. "A limerick."

He put down his cup with a thud. "Now that I *have* heard of," he began to protest.

Dominick bowed from his chair. "An underappreciated form," he said, "with a surprise in the last line."

Spider subsided. "I suppose I don't mind that."

Keylinn said, "What about Adrian?"

"An epic."

"Tal?"

He hesitated, apparently at a loss for the first time. "Ask me another day," he said finally.

"A Zen koen?" she suggested, but met blank looks.

"Give me some time," said Dominick. "At the moment he's the only member of your little triumvirate I can't get a handle on. Perhaps it's because I hear about him secondhand."

"I think he's just a verb," said Spider, waving his cup.

"A verb?"

"It's the only word that can stand alone and still make a sentence." He grinned. "Usually imperative, too."

* * *

On the way to the boulevard she said to him, "I've been thinking about the poem for Tal."

"Oh?"

"Yes, I'd been trying on this form for me, but now I think I was wrong. It's far more Talish."

Spider's mind was on Dominick's face before he'd given him the medicine. His friend didn't have a lot longer. "Oh?"

"A haiku."

"Pardon? Did you sneeze?"

"Haiku—another underrated form, with a *resonance* in the last line."

He said, "What's a resonance?"

"It's a quality that sounds good and has to be there, to make it right and give the whole thing meaning. And it can't be said in any other words."

Spider blinked. He was tired, and sometimes Keylinn's Graykey stuff seemed to be coming from another galaxy.

"I've never seen any resonance," he said.

"Give it time."

It was two hours past midnight when Adrian entered his bedchamber, his eyes shadowed, his shirt half-buttoned. He stopped short.

Iolanthe was lying across the bed with a stack of books. She'd angled the light to illuminate the pages open before her; a rich illustration in blues and reds covered the righthand side. She glanced up and jumped guiltily.

He said, "I thought you'd be in your own room tonight."

"I'm sorry—I forgot the time."

"Don't apologize. I only meant that since I was working late, I didn't think you'd want to be disturbed when I came in." He smiled. "Although I seem to have disturbed you anyway."

She was busily clearing the books off the bedcovers. "You said that I might read things from the public access paths."

"Of course—look, you don't have to—" But she was stacking the volumes beneath the bed, as though she didn't want to intrude on his attention. Probably some love stories or something she felt embarrassed about his seeing; he was careful not to look closely. Even Fischer had given up the spy idea. "Do you want to go back to your room?" he asked diffidently.

She looked up from where she knelt beside the books, her face breaking into a smile like a twelve-year-old angel. "Why would I want to do that?"

"Ah," he said, suddenly at a loss for words. And tried to beat down the smile he felt taking over his own face.

The shaded balcony overlooked half a mountainside as well as half the administrative quarter of the city. A long way down, the red, white, and black roofs of governmental buildings spread along the main streets of "the Flat." Slightly nearer, residences and private clubs nibbled at the slopes, finally to be swallowed up entirely by green as the eye moved closer to home.

Tal sat at a white metal table on the balcony. An untouched glass of tiko was in front of him, and across from him sat Elizabeth Mard and her husband. Hyram Det Arbrith was dark-haired, like most Barets, with a quiet face, a neat mustache, and a pair of data-intaker's spectacles still hooked over his ears. He was clearly absentminded.

Elizabeth Mard Arbrith had pulled the hair on one side of her head back and placed a white flower in it. Her skirt and vest were flowered also, in a colorful pattern, and two side slits showed just enough calf when she sat to get the attention of a native Baret. She smiled at Tal and continued to look at the papers he'd brought.

Tal did not always grasp the finer points of Adrian's policies for dealing with people, but he could learn from them. He had made his aims known to Duke Peter and his daughter, and then dropped the matter and waited for this invitation to Elizabeth Mard's villa.

His patience with human games was still not the best, however. The Arbriths had had plenty of time to go over his list earlier. He got up—returning Elizabeth Mard's questioning look with a meaningless smile of his own— and walked to the railing.

A few droplets of rain fell past the striped awning. The balcony was carefully shaded from the sun; since most

Barets were dark-skinned, lighter shades were considered more beautiful—as the chief herald had pointed out, it was the usual perverse system of human aesthetics.

"Are we boring you, Officer Diamond?"

He turned back to face her. She had asked the question a half-touch playfully, another half-touch reminding him of his place. She seemed to feel that anything she said could be forgiven her if she smiled brightly when she said it.

Tal smiled back. "Yes, I'm afraid so."

Her face went blank. He found he preferred it that way.

"I beg your pardon?"

He said, "I'm not a negotiator, you know. I'm only with the trade team as a cultural adviser. I'm afraid the subtle ins and outs of these things go over my head."

She continued to stare. He went on easily, "I can't even tell whether you're interested in selling any of these items or not. If you're not, please don't feel compelled to show interest out of politeness." When the Duke's sister acted from pure courtesy, the birds would fall from the sky. "Just let me know, and we'll pick up similar items at our next trade stop. As you can see, none of what's listed is essential to us. It won't affect our regular negotiations, I assure you."

"I wouldn't say we're not interested," she said, back-pedaling swiftly. She'd certainly implied that earlier. In fact, she'd all but danced it out in code.

He could only assume she'd been waiting for him to crawl and beg, but his schedule was limited and time did not permit it. He had three nibbles in Lankio Quarter on the subject of Belleraphon, and there was still the Sawyer Crown to think of. Taking Elizabeth Mard to dinner and bribing and flattering her, letting pass all her digs—and for all he knew walking her dogs—would eat into his other plans, aside from boring him to tedium.

He said, "Duke Peter led me to understand that he was interested in selling the arctite painting in his home. We can make do with that and the coffee and lace, and skip the—what did you call it, the *Vermeer*—in your lovely villa here."

In fact, Duke Peter owned both paintings, and had assigned his sister to handle the sales. He would probably not be happy to learn they'd fallen through.

She said, "Cyr, you misunderstand me. We invited you here to do business. I don't know why you would think we're not interested."

"I beg your pardon," he said. "Perhaps I misunderstood." He sat down again.

She said, "We feel eighty-six thousand e. u. for the Vermeer would be a fair price."

At last she was speaking a rational language, though the numbers were inflated. The fact that she preferred empire units to yen suggested a basic distrust in the stability of her own government that would be impolite to point out. No doubt she was lining her own pockets to better finance a getaway before the revolution; he would be, in her place.

He said only, "I noted a certain amount of damage in the left corner—" and the dealing was underway. Hyram did not join in the bargaining; aside from showing the painting earlier and describing the plants in their garden, he had not spoken a word.

When they had agreed on a price and discussed export arrangements for the coffee and lace, Tal pushed back his chair. "Before we conclude, I'd like to mention something you may or may not find of interest."

"Oh?" said Elizabeth Mard. A small terrier scampered from the villa proper, then glanced around uncertainly; Hyram picked it up and put it in his lap.

"As you may gather from the list, my lord is something of a collector. Any rare books you might have, I'd be happy to look over ... and in addition, the Protector would be interested in any things of religious, historical value."

She frowned. "You mean gold crucifixes, jeweled Symbols, that sort of thing? I think we have a few items in the State chapel you might want to look at, but they may be registered as Historical Treasures."

"My lord is most interested in items sometimes referred to as 'Curosa legacies.' "

Hyram let the terrier fall from his lap, and shrill barking ensued. His wife said, "Curosa legacies? I thought that—stop that, Linnet. Linnet, shut up! Hyram, could you—"

Just then a child of about six or seven ran out onto the balcony. She had long brown hair, startling blue eyes, a snub nose, and a harelip. She ran to Hyram and announced, "I want Linnet."

"Take her, please," said Elizabeth Mard. "Hyram, give her the animal."

The child disappeared under the table. Tal felt a confusion of legs down there and then she scrambled up on the other side, Linnet in her arms. She ran off without a good-bye.

Elizabeth Mard said, "My husband's adopted daughter."

Why not "*our* adopted daughter?"

Tal said, "I couldn't help but notice her disfigurement." Or was this one of those things humans didn't like remarked upon? They did tend to remark on such disadvantages, though, when the possessors were not in the room.

Fortunately Elizabeth Mard was too insensitive herself to fully appreciate insensitivity in others. She merely said irritably, "We're going to get to it. We're busy people. We haven't had time to schedule her for a resculpt."

Tal shrugged. "We were speaking of Curosa legacies."

"Yes, and I thought all the Curosa legacies had been left to Adrian the First, and were on the Three Cities. Isn't it we who should be approaching you about legacies?"

"Well, one never knows." He turned the glass of tiko around thoughtfully. It was inscribed with the flowers he'd seen in Hyram's garden. "The Curosa went to other places before Earth; some stories say they even came to this section of the galaxy *after* Earth. And other stories say they left guardians to accompany and watch over the Redemptionists."

"There are all sorts of stories, Officer Diamond. I can't be held responsible for them."

"Of course there are. That's my point. It's possible there are Curosa legacies in other places beside the Cities; and if you come across any, we'd be interested in seeing them. For instance, the Cloak of Grace, say, or the Sawyer Crown."

She laughed. "I've lived here all my life, cyr, and I can assure you that if the Cloak or the Crown were here, I would have heard of them. They're just dreams from the Book of Prophecies—I don't think they're meant to be taken literally." She seemed amused at the fancies of Three Cities backwater farmboys. Even their fellow Redemptionists felt superior to the Cities.

"Well, it was just something to mention." He stood up. He had an appointment in Lankio Quarter in two hours, and something to do back at the Visitor's Residence first.

Elizabeth Mard had been put in a good humor by his last request, and she showed no irritation at his ending the interview instead of leaving that option to her. She stood also, and extended a hand.

"We've both done pretty well today, cyr. You have what you wanted, I trust, and I have a fair price for them." She smiled, and this time her smile was different, though Tal could not isolate what factor made it so. The falseness was missing from it, but surely "falseness" was not a tangible physical attribute. She said, 'I never liked that painting."

"In that case," he said, "you've done *very* well."

"Yes, I have." Hyram gave over a hand to shake as well, and then his wife said, "May I have my driver take you back to the Residence?"

"Thank you, that would be most considerate. Lady Arbrith, Mister Arbrith." "Mister" was a title of nobility in the Empire, the lowest rank, one step above "cyr." Hyram *looked* like a mister.

Tal left the little shaded balcony, considering that he'd come in well below Adrian's estimated figures. Good, he thought, and then he put the matter out of his mind permanently. There were more important things to think about than the "Young Girl Reading a Letter."

The Visitor's Residence was a large whitewashed building in the shadow of the Duke's Hill. Right where state security could keep an eye on everyone, thought Tal, as Elizabeth Mard's driver pulled up to the front steps. He wondered if he should tip the driver, but he wasn't certain of custom in this case, and in moments of doubt he always preferred to retain money.

He got out in silence and went up the steps. Keylinn had been training him to expand his use of the phrase "thank you," but surely that wasn't necessary if he was never going to see the man again. Tal entered and climbed more steps, and then more steps. The Residence was six stories high, with two wings, five sets of stairs, and no lifts at all. It was one of the first buildings constructed in Everun. It was also full of human servants, no doubt all in the pay of state security.

He opened the door of his room on the top floor and found Spider and Keylinn sitting on the bed playing cards.

"Hard day?" said Spider.

Tal grunted. "I see you both made it down. Let's go for a walk."

He turned and went out again, and they followed. On the stairs he said to Keylinn, "I was afraid they wouldn't let you come. Adrian and his friends have odd ideas about women, and a planetary leave has to have his seal."

"I think Outsider techs come under another mental category."

"But now he knows you. I've heard him refer to you as a 'lady.' "

She grinned. "A desire to have all the fun is nine-tenths of the law of chivalry."

She'd spoken it like someone else's words. "Who said that?"

"I don't know, but we quote it at home when the men give us trouble."

They had reached the outside by now and Tal took them down the front road toward the turn that led out of the administrative quarter. He said, "We may as well talk here. I suppose it's marginally safer than the Residence."

"Adrian said you might want assistance off-the-record."

"I do, but probably not for the reasons he thinks. I've been asking about Belleraphon."

Spider and Keylinn exchanged glanced.

They met later that night in a Lankio bar. It was a place on the slopes, where the neighborhood was full of wooden houses with bedrooms on top and gambling parlors, noodle shops, and dancehalls on bottom. Establishments rarely mixed their pleasures; when Barets gambled, they were serious, and resented distraction. When they ate, even the lowest of rank turned into finicky gourmets. Their dancing was barely dancing at all from a Graykey point of view—no jumping or twirling, just a slow and steady arm-in-arm to the accompaniment of atonal music. But they seemed oblivious to the world when they did it.

Their drinking was serious, too, Keylinn decided, looking around the bar. The patrons of Fortune River House had gone through enough liquor per capita to put an off-duty Graykey to shame.

"I don't know," said Spider, looking into his tiko glass. "It's not beer, it's not exactly wine, and it's not whiskey. What is it?"

"They claim it's wine."

"Well, they did something to it after the grape let it go. Here, taste."

She sipped Spider's drink. "I dunno, acushla. You think there's a market for the recipe on the Diamond?"

He looked surprised. "It didn't occur to me."

"A never-sleeping entrepreneur like you, and it didn't occur?"

"Hmmm. Maybe with reason. A man likes something familiar when he drinks. I don't know if—"

Tal appeared, seemingly from nowhere, and sat down at the third chair. "All right, report in."

Keylinn looked at Spider, who said, "Ladies first."

She said, "One possible, a fortune-teller on the Avenue of Willow. Claims to have had dealings with a man named Belleraphon about six years ago. Says he set her up in business, and that's as far as she wants to talk on three hundred yen."

"A fortune-teller?" said Tal.

She shrugged. "A very fashionable fortune-teller about six years ago; Elizabeth Mard Arbrith used to go to her. Make of that what you will."

Tal considered, then said, "Spider."

"Not a nibble, not a bite, not a dinnerpail in sight. And I went up and down these damned hills all day."

"Well, there's always tomorrow."

"Oh, hell, Tal. This is my first time off the Diamond. Practically. Can't I look around for awhile?"

"No." A woman with a long dark ponytail and short blue skirt came over and asked Tal what he wanted to drink. She bent over to take Spider's empty glass and Keylinn realized belatedly that the blue skirt must be shocking to Baret eyes. Or more particularly, the long brown legs ringed with gold chains must be shocking.

"I'll have another pummet-juice," she said. The woman nodded, then paused.

"Any of your party require company? We have males, females, any size, any combination."

Well, apparently there was one pleasure they didn't mind mixing. Maybe they didn't take sex seriously. "Not me," said Keylinn. She looked at her companions. "Boys?"

Spider flushed, and Tal said, "I don't think it will be necessary." Since Keylinn was present, he added, "Thank you."

When the woman had left, Keylinn fixed him with the uncomfortably alert gaze of a *tarethi-din.* "You don't seem to have trouble adjusting to Empire mores. Why don't you stay on Empire territory? You'd be an illegal person, but the penalty for ... your problem ... isn't death, here. I'll bet they'd be pleased to see you, in fact, especially closer to Imperial Center. Your birth mix has a reputation for brains, and they're afraid of a Republic drain."

"Under house arrest, with my every move observed? I've got more liberty on the Diamond, even with their bizarre ideas." He accepted a tiko from the server and added, "Unfortunately, brains aren't the only thing we have a reputation for. If I accepted the Empire's hospitality, I'd never sector-travel again. With Adrian, I can go as far as a Curosa drive will take me."

"And sector-travel is important."

"Yes, it is." He took a sip of the tiko, which was unusual for him.

"Because of this Belleraphon."

"Because of a number of reasons."

"Name one."

He put down his glass. "Didn't anyone tell you," he asked, "that travel broadens the mind?"

Chapter 39

"Well, if you leave out his personal life, he was a happy man."

> neighbor's comment at the funeral
> of a successful poet

Tal walked back to the Visitor's Residence alone. A slight feeling of disorientation slurred his footsteps, the product of just a few sips of tiko. He knew better than to touch alcohol; what had come over him? Maybe he was beginning not to care . . . he'd done the same thing for so long, asked the same questions, and whether the answers came in a thousand different accents or forgotten dialects or sullen silences, it always ended in the same futility. Although this was the first time he'd had help. It felt odd to put a section of the search into the hands of Keylinn and Spider. Very odd.

The texture of the ground beneath his boots told him when he reached the driveway of the Residence, because his footsteps made no sound. It was dark down here at the bottom of the hill, perhaps to discourage visitors from leaving at night. A salt smell blew in from the sea.

"Special Officer Diamond?"

It was a woman's voice; he turned at once in the direction of the source, wishing Adrian had not decreed that hand weapons would be offensive to the Duke. Nevertheless he did not answer, but waited. His night-sight was better than a human's—let them locate him, if they wanted to try.

She stepped out from the feathery jocasta trees. She carried no light, and had clearly been waiting long enough for her own sight to adjust. She was dark-skinned and wore the long pleated skirt, like everyone else, and she walked gracefully from the bushes that lined the drive to where he stood.

"I do have the right person? Tal Diamond?"

"Can I help you?" he asked. This close, he could see by the starlight and the faint spillover of the floodlights on the residence that she was young; barely twenty standard, if that. She wore one earring, where most Barets wore two: A small gold stud sculpted in the shape of a rose. She was also one of the most beautiful women he had ever seen in his life.

"Yes, I recognize you by description." Her accent was soft but cool. "I'm here to help *you*, Officer Diamond. And in several areas."

Again, he waited. If this was some kind of sex-trap by Baret Two state security, it was terribly coarse and obvious—but then, many governments were like that. She seemed to follow his thoughts, for a faint smile appeared on her face. She was nothing if not poised. "I understand you're seeking information about Belleraphon."

He almost reached out to take her wrists, and the reaction shocked him. Any number of people along the way had claimed knowledge of Belleraphon; why should he take this one seriously? He said, "I infer, then, you're claiming to have such information?" He kept his voice disinterested.

"At any rate," she said, "I believe I know more about the man than you do. You may have heard rumors that he was active in this city a few years ago. I was here at the same time—it was when I first came to Everun."

"You must have been all of fourteen."

"Yes. Opportunities were more extensive here than they were in my home town."

There was a thriving market in Lankio Quarter for boys and girls of that age. Still, it was none of his business. "You're saying you had some contact with Belleraphon then?"

"I'm saying nothing, cyr, at the moment. I prefer trade."

Tal had run through much of his bribe money in the course of the day's inquiries. "I'll have to withdraw from our team's treasury. I can't get at it till tomorrow."

She shrugged. "We can meet tomorrow evening. Shall we say, at the Fortune River Bar at the fourth hour?"

He looked at her. She smiled again and said, "I prefer to keep track of the people I do business with. As a sign of my good faith, let me assist you in another matter. The Sawyer Crown."

This time he did take her wrists. He backed her into the stand of jocasta trees and said, *"Who are you?"*

She made no resistance. "If you would calm yourself, cyr. You're not the first person to have made discreet inquiries. Well, yes, yours were the first that were actually discreet. Other members of your team have been asking any number of people about the Crown—most notably the Opal hierophant. I hesitate to call him *stupid,* being a Redemptionist myself, but—"

He let her go. This put his assignment in a new and more difficult light.

She said, "I believe the Arbriths know more about the matter than they've been willing to share. If I may make a suggestion ... there's an old definition of winning a war that says, 'Get there first, with the most men.' In this case I would say, 'Get there first, with the most money.' "

"Why should you care?" he asked her.

"First, if a Curosa legacy exists, it should belong to the Hollow Hills. I told you I was a Redemptionist. Second ... no Curosa legacy will be safe if the Republic takes over our world."

"Do you think that's likely?"

"Don't you?" When he was silent, she said, "Already a number of the aristocracy have found reasons for supervising their estates off-planet, or visiting long-disliked relations. Only those of us without the titles and money to leave are trapped here. And the Arbriths, who won't admit the truth until they go down with the ship."

She had put one cool hand on his arm as she spoke. It made him feel strange, or maybe it was the tiko. He said the first thing he thought of: "You seem far too rational for a Redemptionist."

She removed the hand. "There's no need to mock your own faith, cyr."

"I beg your pardon. Tomorrow evening, then, at the bar."

Her smile returned. "Do bring a lot of money, officer."
She turned and walked into the black Everun night.

Tal didn't like enigmas, particularly of the female kind,
and in a fit of irritation he hoped she would stumble in
the dark. Small chance of that, though. Long after her figure had merged into darkness he remembered how gracefully she'd walked. . . .

He made some withdrawals from the Diamond team's
treasury not long after sunrise. Brandon Fischer was not
pleased, that much was obvious, but Adrian had warned
him beforehand to let Tal do what he chose without inter-
ference.

If that business about the Opal hierophant were true,
time was of the essence. He requested and received ten
minutes' conversation with the Duke that very morning,
and found himself ushered into the aftermath of a huge
breakfast—a great table littered with dishes and cups and
fine silverware, napkins thrown down every which way
and chairs pushed back. The place was empty but for
Duke Peter, who sat at the head in a blue silk robe, with
a half-cup of coffee and a book. A terrier was at his feet,
and he reached down every few seconds with a table
scrap.

The Duke appeared a thinner, older man here at home,
and out of state clothes. He looked up at Tal in a perfectly
friendly way. "Do forgive the informality," he said, without any embarrassment, "but you said it was important,
and this is my only free ten minutes all day."

He put down the book, and even Tal understood
enough to say, "I'm sorry to interrupt your leisure, my
lord. It *is* an important matter to me, though you may not
see it as such."

"Well, a courteous beginning deserves courteous listening. Have you breakfasted? There are some sausages left,
I don't believe Tanya here has eaten them all."

"Thank you, I'm not hungry."

"Coffee?"

"Thank you, no." Caffeine was worse than alcohol to
his system.

"Well then, how may I help you?" Duke Peter leaned
back in his chair, and the top of his robe fell open enough

to show the blue medical monitor on his chest. We can assume, thought Tal, that the first thing the Republicans will do will be to turn *that* off.

He said, "I'm more than satisfied with the outcome of my negotiations with your sister, my lord. I hope you feel the same. But collectors are hard to satisfy, and Adrian Mercati is a collector."

"He objects to our agreement? Yet he empowered you to close the deal. It would seem a bit late to complain now."

"No, no—he's made no objection to me. I was speaking of further items he would be interested in purchasing."

Duke Peter smiled pleasantly, but with a touch of superior amusement. "My sister mentioned your interest in the Cloak and the Crown. Forgive me, but your lord has been misled by a fantasy. The Hollow Hills are perhaps a bit removed from the flow of life out here in the Empire."

Tal smiled back. As usual, it did not reach his false gray eyes. He said, "I would not want to tell my lord that something referred to in the Sacred Books is a 'fantasy.' The Protector is very pious."

"Of course! As I hope we all are. Are you sure you won't have sausages, young man? No, I meant merely to suggest that you Three Cities folk interpret Scripture a bit too *literally*. It's long been accepted here that the Cloak of Grace refers to the absolution of blood in the penitential rite. A *symbolic* cloak, cyr."

"I see. Your lordship phrases it very plainly. That would be a new way of looking at the situation, certainly."

"And the Crown would be the crown of immortality that comes from embracing the true faith. Thus, each of us becomes a victor in his or her own right."

"I'd never thought of it that way before, my lord." This was certainly true. He'd never wasted a second thinking of it at all. "But—would your lordship see the difficulty I'm in? I've already reported to the Protector about certain rumors I've heard in the city, that the Sawyer Crown is here on Baret Two. Now nothing will do but that he purchase it and put it in a place of honor on the Diamond.

In fact, he's sent me an almost embarrassing amount of money to buy it."

"Oh?" The terrier yapped unlistened to at the Duke's feet.

Tal reached into a pocket and removed a lady's comb. It was shaped like a peacock, cast in pure gold with a tail of diamonds, rubies, emeralds, and sapphires. The workmanship of the peacock was exquisite, and the gems were set in patterns that displayed their different cuts. He cast it carelessly down by the Duke's breakfast plate.

Where it was taken up in a second. "My God, it's worth a fortune."

"I suppose. I wonder if your lordship would mind accepting it as a gift? Then I could tell the Protector that I've presented it to you in gratitude for your offering to keep an eye out for the Sawyer Crown. After all, you know the capital better than anyone. And it would make a lovely present for your charming sister."

Duke Peter was still staring. Shrill barks came from the terrier, until the Duke said, "Oh, hush, Tanya!" and picked up a sausage and threw it against the wall. It hit with a soft splatter and the dog went after it. The Duke turned to Tal and looked at him sharply. "This is offered with no strings attached?"

"As I said, it's a gift."

"Gifts can be more expensive than contracts." But the Duke put it in the pocket of his robe and contemplated the air at the end of the table. Then he turned back to Tal. "Yes, I've heard these rumors about the Crown myself, from time to time. I wouldn't like to put a lot of stock in them. I'll poke around, young man. Can I reach you at the Visitor's Residence if anything . . . turns up?"

Tal inclined his head. Duke Peter stood and tightened the sash of his silk robe. The terrier was back at his feet again. "I'm afraid Tanya and I have a lot of work to do, cyr. Good morning."

With a liberal use of yen, Tal was able to persuade his driver to stay behind in the Residence garage and amuse himself. Baret Two used Wender Corporation groundcars, with only minor differences between these and those he'd grown up with on a world a long way from here. He had several appointments in Everun that day, and no wish to risk missing the final one in the Fortune River Bar.

He met with Keylinn's fortune-teller, and found that someone named Belleraphon had set up a number of small businesses in the capital about six years previously. A fortune-teller, a brothel, a manufacturer of technical components, a boat-builder—there seemed no common thread. Whether it was his own Belleraphon or someone using the name was impossible to tell. It came as no surprise to Tal that there were no witnesses, no one who claimed direct physical contact with the man.

Why would anyone use the name Belleraphon, including the person he was searching for? Except possibly out of ego. Tal had small hopes of turning up his quarry this way; the more likely outcome, if he was ever successful, would be that Belleraphon would hear that someone was asking for him, and make himself known.

Or not. It was a long and disheartening day. He parked on the outskirts of Lankio Quarter; the wilderness of buildings on the slopes of that neighborhood had no pattern of streets to speak of and no room to maneuver anything larger than a handcart. He passed a gambling hall on the way to the Fortune River Bar, and saw there was a fight going on outside. He glanced with little interest through the shoulders of the crowd.

Spider was getting the crap beaten out of him.

As far as Tal was concerned, there was a lot in Spider that could use beating out, but should it be necessary Tal would do it himself. He pushed through the crowd, lifted the man who was smacking Spider's bloody face, and threw him a good five meters. A sigh of disappointment came from the bystanders—Spider and Tal were foreigners, after all. The man showed an inclination to get up again, so Tal kicked him on the chin and he lay still. Then Tal picked up Spider and started walking him away. He seemed to require a fair amount of support.

When they reached the car, Tal let him down in the dirt and went to open the door. He pulled a canteen from inside, walked over to Spider and poured it in his face.

Spider's arms started moving in a phantom parody of a fight, his fists clenched. He snarled. Tal poured more water down.

Spider became aware that he was horizontal, and someone was standing over him. Tal.

"Forget our tranquilizers today? Get in the car." Tal made no move to help him up.

He pulled himself into a sitting position, not without pain. Tal walked back to the car, opened the door, and slid into the front seat. "Seven-four-one-two," he said. Spider got slowly and shakily to his feet and tottered over to the other door. He tried the handle, screwing up the lock combination. He hit the buttons again and fumbled with the handle. Nothing happened. He looked expectantly toward Tal, who sat unmoving in his seat. "Like Patience on a bloody monument," muttered Spider. On the third try he got it. He let his body down carefully onto the cushion and turned to Tal. "You could make an effort, you know."

"I'm making an effort now not to take you up to the Diamond and leave you on H deck with your hands and feet tied. You can avoid this by telling me just what you were doing all day. Start with when you got up."

"Well," said Spider after a moment, "I wasn't actually on official business all the time."

"Really."

"You see, it's like this—"

"Spider, I've seen you lie valiantly when unexpected trouble hit. I've also seen you make a mess of it when you've had time to think. You have a really extraordinary talent for deceit—"

"Thank you."

"—but it only seems operational when you're with strangers, or under the pressure of improvisation. In this regard, I'd like you to bear in mind that any question I ask you now I will also ask you tomorrow. In the cold, rational light of preparedness. Do you follow me?"

"Ah."

"Feel free to take a few minutes to get your thoughts together."

Taking a few minutes to get his thoughts together was fatal to Spider's cause. He gave up. "It's not like I've been doing anything terrible."

"It's only terrible if it affects me."

"Yes, I know, that's what I meant. I have a friend—"

"Whose name is—"

"Whose name is Eustace O'Connell. You know how we get a lot of overstocked items sometimes in Inventory. Well, it seems a shame to just store them when there are people who can use those items."

"So you and your friend help balance this inequity."

"I sell to G and F decks and he sells below G and to the ghosts. Anyway, that's what we've been doing. Lately I expanded a little bit to bring in some people on Baret Station—"

Tal sighed. Spider said, as though in answer to a protest, "We have things they really want!"

"I'm sure. May I take it that this fight had something to do with your trying to expand your territory a little further? Like, opening up a planetside end?"

Spider looked repentant. "Now that the sector-gate's open, they're already running a similar operation. I guess they don't believe in a free market."

"Where are you keeping your profits?"

Spider hesitated. Then he said, "I sent it all to the branch of the Commons Bank on Baret Station. They tapped it into the Empire Credit Net. I used my own name so I wouldn't have trouble getting it out—it's not like they'd notify the citycops, they don't care where money comes from."

For the first time since Spider entered the car, Tal turned and looked him full in the face. "You opened an account at a Commons Bank and gave the Three Cities as your address?"

"I don't see what's wrong with that."

"Spider, they will tax you within an inch of your life—" He stopped himself. "I'm not here to give you financial advice."

Spider smiled to himself. He'd noticed before that discussions of money could divert Tal's attention.

Tal checked his timepiece and powered up the car. "I'm going to drop you off at the Residence's medtech. Can you make it up the steps yourself? I have an appointment."

"Sure."

They drove down the slopes to the Street of Dreams that ran through the Flat. Awnings hung with colored lanterns bloomed in the darkness. Tal said, "Has it just been thievery and smuggling, or are you dealing in anything illegal in itself?"

"By whose standards?" asked Spider, wincing as he tried to sit more comfortably.

"Anybody's."

"Well, yes. I've been buying drugs on-Station—I was hoping to sell some of them down here, they're very portable."

"What sort?"

"The usual—heroin, aspirin, opium, bonz."

"I see. No taxmal?"

"What's that?"

"Nothing. Well, you've been saved a lot of trouble, Spider, you never would have made a profit. Drugs of all kinds are legal in the Empire proper. They'll even let you have vigilis, which turns humans into raving murderous lunatics—but you have to take that under supervision at a government drug center, and they keep you there till it's out of your system."

Spider shifted position again, with the same painful result. "Why would anyone want to be a murderous lunatic?"

"I'm not clear on that. But it seems to be highly addictive, and quite popular as these things go. The only drug illegal in the Empire is the telepathy drug, because it invades the privacy of others."

"What's the name of that one?" asked Spider. Wrecked though he was, he seemed ready to pull out a notebook and write it down.

"I don't recall." They reached the end of the Residence drive and Tal brought them to a halt. "All right, go."

Spider got out of the car, took a step, and collapsed to his knees. Tal muttered something briefly and left the car. He pulled Spider up by the collar, took an arm, and helped him up the steps. The medtech was on the second floor. Three steps into that flight of stairs Tal gave up on this method and picked Spider up and carried him bodily. He deposited him by the medical notification bell. He pressed the button, then turned. Spider was still lying on the floor.

"I really have to go now," said Tal.

"Fine," said Spider into the floor.

Tal descended the stairs and went out to the car. He drove as quickly as he could get away with to the border of Lankio Quarter.

At the Fortune River Bar he approached the hostess. Tonight her skirt was short and red with yellow fringe. Her breasts were covered up to the neck. "Has anyone been looking for me?"

"Not to my knowledge, cyr. Are you expecting someone?"

"Possibly. Has there been a young woman in here, without any escort, just sitting and waiting?"

The hostess smiled. "No young woman would wait here alone for long. But no, I haven't seen anyone like that in the last hour."

"All right, thanks. I'll take that table there, if you don't mind. And bring me a glass of tiko and a glass of water."

He sat at a small table near the bar that gave a complete view of the patrons, particularly around the entrance. A small window on the right showed the passersby outside. He was only five minutes late, and no rational person would give up a chance of profit for five minute's wait. Especially if they were an Empire subject and a Redemptionist, looking to cushion the fall when the Republic came. Cushioning took money.

An hour later he asked for another tiko. The hostess said, "But you haven't touched this one, cyr."

"Please enjoy it with my compliments." She shrugged and went away, and returned with two new glasses.

And another hour later she brought two more glasses. "I see the water at least meets with your approval."

"Yes, it's excellent quality."

"Artesian wells," she said, and retrieved the tiko. Her hips swayed as she walked away.

Later, when she set down another glass, she said, "Since you're not drinking them, we're watering them down by three-quarters. I mention this in case you decide to take a sip."

"I appreciate the warning."

He stayed at the Fortune River Bar all through the night. Eventually the white light of sunrise came in the window on his right, and two girls moved tiredly among the empty tables, cleaning. The hostess came over and pulled out the other chair of his table and sat down, crossing her long legs. She said, "We generally close for a few hours around now, and get some sleep."

"Yes." He put his palms on the table, shifting his weight to rise.

"Cyr, I hesitate to intrude on your privacy. But is there anything you need that I can get you?"

He looked at her face, lined and pure in the dawn light. "I wish you could help me, but you can't."

He rose. As he walked away she called, "If it's love, it will pass. Believe me."

He went out into the morning, the quiet morning of a pleasure district. He walked to the car and drove back to the Visitor's Residence. The administrative quarter was filling up with government employees and people on the way to their businesses. He surrendered the car to his official driver, who shook his head, and went in to sleep.

A message was waiting for him from the Diamond: Adrian wanted his immediate return. He turned, went back out again and found a ride to the port; and as the full day of Everun got underway, he lifted off on a shuttle, spent and exhausted.

A transmitted bill was waiting for him when he arrived in Diamond Transport. It was a cleaning bill from the Residence. Spider had gotten blood in the car.

"You wanted to see me?"

Adrian looked up, tossing away a thick sheaf of color-coded reports. "Things have gotten a bit hot up here. Rumors are going up and downhill faster than shuttles." He pulled Tal out into the hall and started walking swiftly. "I want you to attend a council meeting with me."

Tal stopped. *"Now?"*

"Yes, now. We've been waiting for your arrival, Brandon's already here. They couldn't reach you down at the Visitor's Residence. Where were you, by the way?"

"Taking care of business. Adrian, if things are really heating up, then this is hardly the time to spring me on them in a council meeting."

"On the contrary, they'll accept it during an emergency if they ever do." The Protector pulled him along. "It's amazing, because I haven't said anything, I don't think Brandon's said anything, and you as we know practice the silence of the grave when it suits you—but everybody seems to have heard about the Sawyer Crown."

Tal considered this as they reached the nearest lift station. "Where are we going?"

"The Flux Chamber. I'd prefer security on this . . . for all the good it's going to do me. I suppose if you'd had any little success in locating the Crown, you would have mentioned it? Yes, I thought so. Well, Opal's in the act now and the council wants to know what to do about it, which means what am *I* going to do about it, and why weren't they informed, and don't I trust them, which of course I don't.—Zero level, please.—So as the agent-in-place, I thought it would be good to present you to them."

"Is that what I am?" The glass lift dropped through the levels like a coin in a pool.

"It is now. The attitude we're going to present is, everything is going according to plan. Whatever's happened, we anticipated happening. The object is basically to keep the representatives out of our way so we can function efficiently."

"A limited democracy in action. Very well. How much success should I report?"

"How much have you had?"

"None."

"We won't phrase it that way. We'll say that your questioning of informants and searching of local museums and churches is proceeding according to schedule."

"I doubt if it's in a museum."

"Not the point.—Lock, please," he said, holding the lift for the return journey. They stepped out and strode down the shining corridor that led to the Flux Chamber.

"Interesting," said Tal, as he examined the shifting patterns of color on the walls. "I suppose we're only inches from the drive."

"Really?" said Adrian, with a jaded lack of interest. "Here we are." He coded open the Chamber door.

A tableful of Diamond lords and the highest admins stared at him in polite shock. Only Brandon Fischer was not surprised; he merely looked tired and morose. *Not used to shifting circadian rhythms,* thought Tal. "Here he is," called Adrian cheerfully. "I thought it would be more informative to just bring him along. Tal, you've met everybody, haven't you?"

"I believe so."

"Lord Salter, were you saying something as I came in? Don't let me interrupt your point."

Lord Salter, a veteran of council meetings since Saul Veritie's day, inclined his head. "Merely passing the time, Adrian. Now that you're—both—here, I'm ready to turn to the issue at hand."

"Excellent. I thought, before we have any questions, that Officer Diamond would report on his findings thus far." Several representatives who'd looked tensed and ready to spring now looked cheated. Tal was off-balance himself; he'd hoped for a few minutes to get his cover story together.

He said, "There's little to report at the moment. Events are running according to schedule. Our people—" *People, indeed.* "—are looking into various historical archives, questioning informants, following procedure."

"And thus far they haven't found the Crown?" The question was from Lord Salter. Adrian did not reprimand him. The Protector had found it expedient not to follow any rules of order but those that served him best at the moment.

Tal said, "Even negative information is of benefit in a search."

"What about Duke Peter? What about the Arbriths?"

"They claim not to know about the Crown, although the Duke has promised to make an effort to locate it for us."

"Did we have to pay him for that promise?" The question came from one of the admins.

Tal looked at Adrian, who was politely attentive. Tal said, "Yes."

"To be expected," said Lord Salter. "I don't see that that gets us anywhere. So much the better if the Duke is indebted to Diamond money." He turned back to Tal. "What are they like, the Arbriths? Can we trust them?"

"Beyond the fact that they like to associate with dogs who make irritating noises, I know little about them."

"But even negative information," Lord Salter smiled, "is of benefit in a search."

Adrian still did not seem disposed to intervene. Tal said, "Very true. In this case I would point out that the Duke's loyalties are far from predictable. If he takes money from us, I see no reason why he shouldn't take money from Opal. He hasn't promised to actually hand the Crown over to anybody, you will note."

This caused general muttering at the table. Apparently the obvious had not occurred to them, but then they'd been given little time to think the matter through.

Lord Salter—the leader of the loyal opposition?—said, "We can sweeten the pot."

"I intend to," said Tal. "I was going to make another withdrawal from the team treasury today. Of course, that plan also has negative aspects, but if our primary aim is the Crown—"

"So, gentlemen," said Adrian at last. "You see where we stand."

"What negative aspects?" asked the admin who'd spoken earlier.

Lord Salter looked down at the pen he was playing with. Whatever they were, Adrian clearly did not want them mentioned. The Protector could make life difficult at times, and Salter chose his moments of protest carefully. This was not one of them.

There was a silence at the table. Adrian said at last, "Go ahead, Tal, explain your 'negative aspects.' "

Tal said, "From the point of view of obtaining the Crown, there are none."

"From any other point of view?" asked the admin.

"It depends on the importance you place on it. As we know, Baret Two is ripe for revolution."

"Indeed," said Lord Salter grimly, "if only we had had more current information before we agreed to come here."

Adrian returned his gaze innocently. "The universe is wide. We're lucky if our information is only thirty years out of date."

Lord Salter harumphed.

"You were saying, Officer Diamond?" said Adrian.

Tal's voice remained emotionless. "Baret Two is under

great pressure from Republican agents. Just the knowledge that Baret One has gone Republican must be enormously stressful to the inhabitants. I understand that those who can are leaving while the option is open to them."

"Your point?" The admin reminded him of the Arbriths' terriers.

"I beg your pardon, I thought it was clear. The Diamond has now entered into the politics of Baret Two as a destabilizing factor. Our just being here for trade would add to the general confusion, but now we're trying to outdo Opal in administering bribes to Duke Peter. Perhaps they go into his treasury to expand the army and weaponry. Perhaps they go into his private account to finance a quick escape. Either way, we're doing more than our part to push your brother and sister Redemptionists into a bloody war. Which, as we know, they cannot win. Which we are not going to volunteer to assist them with. Not that our assistance would count for much in any case. And which at the first sign of trouble we will leave them to fight, and remove a good distance away to enjoy our profits."

Adrian's elbow was on the table, his chin on one hand. "Does that answer your question, Rodney?"

Tal said, "Of course, as a demon, it's not relevant to me. But I thought it was something you might want to take into account in your own decision making."

The council members looked at each other, and you could see resentment on some faces: *Why is it he can get away with saying things like that? What gives him the right to muddle Diamond policy and point out all the reasons why our plans may be wrong?*

Adrian hid his smile. *Because,* he thought, *it's his job.*

"You were magnificent," said Adrian.

They sat in loungers in the parlor of Adrian's suite. Iolanthe was in the bedroom with a headache.

"Was I?" Tal looked pleased, but cautious. "I thought I'd veered from your recommended path back there."

"It was bound to come up, and as you can see, they still voted to go ahead."

"Yes, I did notice that. Greed, or fear of Opal?"

"Perhaps it was patriotism and civic duty."

"No doubt you're right."

Adrian grinned. "You impressed them. You had a complete grasp of what you were saying."

"Rare in humans. I can see why it made an impression."

"Oh, don't be such a snob. Just say thank you. Your first council meeting. They'll be far more ready to accept you now when it comes to my future plans." Adrian strained to pull off one of his boots.

Tal was silent, and Adrian said, "Aren't you going to ask?"

"I'm just going to say thank you."

The boot wasn't budging; Tal shook his head and tapped two fingers against an ottoman. Adrian obediently placed his foot there and Tal pulled one-handed from the heel. The boot flew against the wall. The Protector gazed sadly at it where it lay. "You're being cooperative simply to thwart me, aren't you?"

Tal said, "You'd be disappointed otherwise."

Chapter 40

Plots, true or false, are necessary things
To raise up commonwealths and ruin kings.

                              JOHN DRYDEN

Will Stockton was on his way to meet Hartley Quince in Transport, and he had timed it so he would reach there at the last possible minute and still be able to get into uniform.

He carried a gray bag with that uniform inside, as well as a change of underwear, some toilet articles, and a blue satin hair ribbon belonging to Lysette. On the border of Sangaree he entered Proclamation Square, a public space designed for sermons, state speeches, and the notification of local political events. A statue of Adrian Sawyer's first Curosa friend was at one end. It was the only alien statue in all the Three Cities, but Will was too familiar with it

to be very impressed by it. He cut diagonally through the
Square, intending to take the lifts on the following street
to C, and catch a train there for Transport.

Between the cleaner's and the restaurant at the Square's
end was an alley. Will saw a man hurrying down that alley toward him, clutching a little girl's hand in his own.
The man was in his thirties, respectably but rumpledly
dressed, and for some reason he reminded Will of his
Sangaree neighbor, Mr. Teksa. Maybe it was the strained
expression on his face. The little girl wore a blue dress
and looked unhappy and confused.

The man's glance darted all around the Square. He
dragged the girl with him as he hurried onward. When he
reached Will, he looked quickly back toward the alley
and spoke in a low voice. "Please, sir. The EPs are coming for me. I've been complained against."

The voice was intense, demanding. Will took an unconscious step backward.

"Please, sir," said the man. "My daughter, you know
what will happen to her. We need a place to go, just for
a while."

The desperation of begging a stranger in the street for
what you know he will not give. "I *have* no place," said
Will, and it was the truth. Send this trouble to Bernadette
or Lysette? Come back from his assignment and find one
of the women he loved in the pens, or tortured and dead?
He had no place of his own to offer.

"*Please,* you *must,* there's no one who will help me!"

The little girl squinted up at Will. She couldn't know
what was going on, but she looked miserable.

Christ, for all he knew these were plants sent by the
EPs to test the loyalty of their newest member. He stood
there like a fool, and the man's head whipped around
again toward the alley and he started dragging the girl
away.

Will had the nagging sense of having missed an opportunity. *At crucial moments of choice,* he remembered
reading somewhere, *most of the business of choosing is
already over.* The two were moving away from him then,
and as he was just touching his failure, getting accustomed to it, his paralysis suddenly lifted. "Wait!" He ran
over to the man and said quickly, "There's a utility tunnel

off Tanamonde Street in Sangaree. Behind the medical offices. Ghosts still go there sometimes, you might be able
to make a connection." The man stared at him, his expression strained and unchanging. "But citycops go there,
too, they know about it, so ... I don't know. Take your
chances." Shit, why didn't the man move? "That's all I
can do, I can't do anything else."

He turned on his heel and walked very quickly away.
Behind him a girl's voice said, questioningly, "Daddy?"
and a scared reply: "Shut up." Hurried footsteps followed.

Near the lift station he passed three EPs going the way
he'd come. He stepped inside and stood there alone,
thankful there were clean clothes to come, for his shirt
was cold and wet under his armpits. Then the lift doors
opened and he went out, clutching the bag with the EP
uniform until his fingers turned white.

"You're late," said Hart, as Will buckled into the shuttle seat.

"Thanks for waiting."

"Any problem? You don't look terrific."

"No problem, I just had to change into uniform."

Hart raised one classic eyebrow. "Wearing civilian
clothing off-duty can be a court-martial offense."

"Court-martial me, then." Will leaned back in the seat
and stretched his legs as far as the space allowed. "If you
think I'm wearing this thing in Sangaree, you're out of
your mind."

Hart did not reply. He leaned his head back on the seat-
rest and closed his eyes. He liked to savor the sensation
of lift-off without visual stimuli to interfere.

A few days of Everun faded the memory of the man
and the little girl quite thoroughly. It was literally another
world, with a flood of stimuli, and in an incredibly short
span of time, Opal began to seem distant and irrelevant.
Will walked the slopes joyously, delighting in the *downhill* of downhill. He passed roasting nuts in little stalls
outside of restaurants, he listened to strangers on the
street talk in their fantastic accents. He watched girls display their chests shamelessly. The day after he arrived, he

went to the *ocean* and walked on the *sand*. He was flushed with a thousand sensations. That night at dinner in the Residence, Hart said, "You're not having any difficulty?"

"Difficulty?"

Hart poured a glass of the stuff they called tiko. He said, "A certain minority of nonplanetborn never adjust to downhill. Not very many rave and run hysterical, but a fair number are unhappy and nervous."

"Really?" Will took it in blankly. "I don't see why. We've all seen pictures of other worlds. Why should it come as a shock?"

"You're one of the lucky majority, then. I have heard that stationers have a harder time than Cities people. I don't know why."

Will thought about this a few days later when he gathered his clothes and left the sex-bar in the highest reaches of Lankio Quarter, where the six Baret guards he'd been drinking with the previous night still lay snoring on the floor. He went out to the porch and looked down at the city. The usual morning mist of Everun had gathered from the mountains, and lay like a fairy tale over the shuttered roofs. The sun was far behind it somewhere, friendly and known. Will put on his shoes and wished he had some tea, but he didn't want to wake anybody.

Imagine being upset by *this*. He shook his head and, slinging his shirt over one shoulder, descended the steps. The sex-bar was on stilts, being in the favorite pathway (they told him) of a spring run-off from the mountain that Lankio Quarter sat on. He threaded his way through the gambling halls and restaurants and houses until he reached the Flat and the Street of Dreams.

It was about an hour's walk to the Residence from here. Will stopped in a store with a particularly colorful awning and let the woman inside show him a red silk scarf. Unfolded, it was a good five feet square—Bernie could wrap herself in it, if she wanted. The color was superb, and it felt like a cloud. The woman told him the price, and he whistled. Still, how often was he downhill? He was ready to pay when he remembered that Bernie thought she didn't look good in red. And he really shouldn't spend the money anyway. . . .

In the end he got two, red for Lysette and green for Bernadette. He was lighter for the equivalent of two weeks' pay, but he kept whistling as he walked the streets. He imagined their faces when he gave them the scarves—separately, of course; Bernie and Lysette had never gotten along.

When he reached the Residence, he folded the scarves carefully into his bag and went downstairs to meet Hart and report on what he'd heard from his drinking partners.

Hart took him to the second floor of a brothel in the administrative district. It was also the top floor, and Hart paid for the entire use of it themselves. The manager gave Will an odd look as he followed Hart up the stairs.

Now what was that for, thought Will? They must be used to all kinds of goings-on in here. Although ... although, I hope that Hart is really interested in business, and not in just making me nervous.

Hart closed the window and put a jammer on the floor, two reassuring actions as far as Will was concerned. The morning was warming up, and Hart pulled off his red headband and used it to mop his forehead. Then he grinned and let himself fall on the huge bed, and turned to Will and said, "So—what did your newest drinking buddies have to tell you?"

There was a teapot on a stand by the bed, with a little flame underneath. Will poured a cup. "I'm hungry."

"They don't have food here. We can send down for coffee."

"Thanks, I prefer tea."

Hart folded his hands on his chest and looked at the low ceiling. "Of course, they can probably provide things like nuts, whipped cream, honey. Skin foods, so to speak."

Will set the cup down firmly on a stool. "I didn't find out much. The Duke's popular enough with the army and the local guard. They're not looking forward to a clash with the Republic, but they can scent it in the wind."

"And the rest of the family?"

"They call Elizabeth Mard the 'Smiling Bitch.' They don't call her husband anything. Either way, though, I don't think they really care."

"Ah, well, neither do we, really. What's this about their daughter? She's deformed or something?"

"The kid's name is Sara Jean Arbrith. That's her Redemptionist name—her real name is Casamara Tonnelly."

Hart sat up straight and looked at him. The expression he reserved for nonserious pastimes, like torturing Will, was gone. Will said, "Yeah. Her father was Lord Kermis Tonnelly. You remember there were rumors of some kind of purge going on at Imperial Center a few years back? Kermis's wife died after giving birth—under shadowy circumstances, they claim, but who knows—and his lordship wrote out a document removing the baby from the line of succession. Then he shot himself. But just before that, he sent the kid off to the custody of his old school friend, Hyram Det Arbrith. Hyram had her baptized Redemptionist right off and he's brought her up as his daughter. The deformity is a harelip. Officially her title is still 'Princess.'"

Hart was silent for a minute. Then he said, "They don't seem exactly strict about enforcing the canons around here. Why haven't they corrected her lip, do you think?"

Will shrugged. "Maybe it's true that they just haven't gotten around to it. She's only six years old. And it's not like anybody would make fun of her for it—they wouldn't dare. And her parents really are busy—they're active government participants, not figureheads." He paused. "On the other hand I don't really know, because it's the first thing *I* would have done."

"Of course a few of the Imperial family have been born with harelips. Maybe they don't want people to forget she's a Tonnelly."

"Dangerous reminder for them." Meaning the Arbriths.

"Umm. Well, never mind for now. I don't suppose anybody came out and said, 'Willie, old pal, I hear you're looking for the Sawyer Crown, it's in my basement'?"

"It was more like, 'I hear you're looking for the Sawyer Crown, you Cities Redemptionists must be the most naive saps we've met in a long time.'"

"Huh." Hart sat cross-legged on the bed, staring at the dirty windowpane. After a few minutes he spoke in a quite different voice. "Willie, attend."

"I'm listening."

Hart reached into a pocket, pulled out a small plastic rectangle and tossed it to Will. It had red and white stripes and a blue corner square with little five-pointed symbolic star-shapes. Hart said, "You know what this is?"

"Sure I do," said Will. "I've seen it on half the walls in Sangaree."

"But what is it?"

"It's just a symbol. It means we're the land of the free and the home of the brave."

"I've been reading the early chronicles of the Cities, Willie, and it means more than that. Do you know Sangaree was settled by descendants of some of the first families of Opal?"

"Yeah? I wish they'd brought their money with them."

"Pay attention. Sangaree was settled by families descended mostly from Americans and French. Even more specifically, the eastern seaboard of America, and the city of Paris."

Hart seemed to expect something from him. "I can't tell you how little those words mean to me."

"They were geographical locations on Earth. You've heard of Earth?" Irritation crept into his tone.

"I've heard of Earth. We're from Earth. Everybody's from Earth."

"Oh, a chink of light." Hart glared at him. "Adrian Sawyer was from Earth, and more importantly from our point of view, he was from the United States of America."

He was saying all this like it should mean something. "All right," said Will.

"Don't you get it? The highest concentration of American descendants by far is on Opal—*not* on the Diamond—and Adrian Sawyer was an American."

Will said, hesitatingly, "I guess that's quite a coincidence."

Hart raised his arms for heaven to witness his frustration. "Willie, I know there's a brain in there, I built it myself. Don't you see that Adrian Sawyer obviously meant for leadership of the Three Cities—and therefore the Crown—to go to Opal?"

"For the sake of your blood pressure I wish I could say I saw the connection."

"He was an American! He would want Americans to be the leaders!"

Will shook his head. "Hart, I know you're very bright. But isn't this far-fetched? How could anyone possibly care one way or another about which planetary subdivision they get born into? It's just not reasonable."

"Willie, you have no idea. From the records I've gone through, they thought about nothing else. They had wars about it all the time."

Was Hart just making this up to play with his sense of reality? "It's hard to believe."

"Willie, twenty-five years ago we had a war with the Diamond based on two different interpretations of the penitential rite."

"But that was *important*."

Hart sighed. "Never mind. We will not discuss it from a theoretical point of view. Let me put it this way: We deserve the Sawyer Crown. If it's to go to the true spiritual descendants of Adrian Sawyer, it's to go to the Opal. We can all agree on that, can't we?"

"I guess so."

"And if it's to go to a Mercati," said Hart, "it's to go to me."

Will leaned forward and stared at him. Hart said, "You want to add something?"

Will quickly went through a dozen responses, and said, "No."

"Good. Now, here's the interesting part. I hope you won't think me eccentric."

God!

"But I've taken the liberty of notifying the City of Pearl of our mutual intentions. Adrian's and mine, I mean."

"Ummm." Will was losing the ability to comment intelligently on this conversation. He hoped that it only reflected Hart's insanity and not his own.

"They claim they can identify the true Crown when it's located, and they're interested in doing so. Very interested.—Oracles don't make you nervous, do they? They do some people."

Will shook his head.

"Good, because you may have to meet one when he or

she comes to the Opal to identify the Crown, assuming, of course, we find it." He turned toward Will's cup. "You're not drinking your tea."

Will picked up the cup mechanically and drank from it. Hart said, "Logically, our purposes are two: First, to locate the Crown, and second, to confuse and embarrass Adrian Mercati. Doing the second will give us a more clear field for the first."

"I like Adrian," said Will, and he heard himself to his own horror. He'd drunk too much last night, and dealing with Hart was taking its toll.

Hart glared again. "I know, Willie, he's a likable person. Can we not drag in irrelevancies?"

"Sorry."

The brothel they were sitting in was an old wooden structure, and the top floor had been used for assignations for two hundred years. A floorboard outside the door had been left warped and creaky, Will had been told, to warn any lovers of the approach of a jealous mate. It was meant more as a joke than a real warning.

The floorboard creaked now. Their eyes met, and Will was out the door in a second. He pulled in a short balding man with a blue cap slouched over one eye—pulled him hard onto the floor, where the cap rolled off and he banged an elbow and cried, "Yow!" This didn't stop him from scrambling for the door again, kicking and biting on his way.

Will was forced to give him a good blow to the chin to slow him down, and the man responded with an immediate faint onto the floorboards. "Clay jaw," said Will. He looked for something to tie the hands with, but nothing presented itself. Trying to tear the Baret skirt the eavesdropper was wearing proved futile. "Well, it's not like he's dangerous. I guess they'll send someone up here to find out what the racket was. Maybe we should push him under the bed."

"If it's between consenting species I doubt if they care," said Hart. He nodded toward the man on the floor. "What do you think?"

Will examined him. "He's not wearing state security clothing. And if he's working out of uniform, he's not very good. Also, we were relatively careful about people following us on the way here. Also, even if they did, they would probably assume we came here for the obvious reasons. I think he's an independent, just looking for some kind of edge. Saw two foreigners with money come up and decided to see what he could find out."

The man groaned. He shifted his head left and right, his eyes still closed. Hart spun the dial of his accent a few degrees closer to Sangaree, assuring unintelligibility to a native Baret.

Hart said, "You think he's somebody's riff?"

"I doubt it. Just a nathy who got in over his head."

"Let's make him *our* riff, then."

Will looked at him.

Hart said, "We need to make contact with the less respectable folk down here. Besides, it's proper procedure, isn't it? For the Guard and the EPs both."

"Have I had a chance to thank you yet for getting me transferred?"

Hart allowed some impatience to show. "We're working on a time limit, old pal. The Diamond is breathing down our necks. As far as I'm concerned, if this person knows anything we can use, it belongs to us by eminent domain. Or right of force. Or finders keepers. I don't care." He stood up. "Do your job, sergeant."

Will bent over the intruder, put one hand on his chin, and began waking up their new riff.

His name was Maltin. He didn't seem to bother much with a second name. He was a thief and blackmailer, and regarded himself as generally harmless—beneath the notice of your lordships, if he could be permitted to say.

But he did understand something of the flow of money in Lankio Quarter, and the direction that most of the bribes went in when they vanished in the administrative district. "Everybody knows they're collected by the minister's people."

"Which minister?" asked Hart.

"The Minister of Truth."

Will said, "They have a department for that here?"

"He means the propaganda arm of the government," said Hart. He stood up and paced across the room. "There's a party at the Duke's tonight, the minister will probably attend." He came back to himself for a moment and noticed Will and Maltin were both looking at him. He laughed, took out a wallet of hand-worked leather fat with notes and threw it to Will.

"Pay our riff, Willie. And ask him to keep in touch."

Ten days later Will was invited to the villa of the Minister of Truth, halfway up a mountain at the far northern edge of Everun. There was no question of walking that distance, and in fact he was flown in the minister's private aircar.

The villa was by a mountain river. On the trip up they rose over a long, long waterfall and pierced through the curtain of mist steaming from its foot. Will kept his head turned to look out the window all along the way.

Hart was already there when he arrived, sitting on the balcony over the river, but he seemed unimpressed by the view. His gaze was on the interior of the house, with the look of one whose judgment is in some manner suspended. Will was shown onto the balcony by a small boy in an embroidered red vest, who said, like an adult, that he would be happy to bring refreshment should the cyrs wish it. The cyrs declined, and when the boy left Will said, "Maybe someday I'll be that self-possessed."

"Umm," said Hart, still looking toward the house. "Did you have any trouble over the last couple of days?"

"No, why should I have trouble?"

Hart didn't answer that. A moment later two men and a woman came out to join them. One was the Minister of Truth, a man on the edge of old age, wearing the jewels and colors of his rank as though they were a slightly tedious set of business clothes. He sat down at once at the antique wooden table beside Hart's chair. "Complete," he said briefly to Hart, and squinted up at Will. "This your man?"

"More or less," said Hart. "Can I see?"

The man and woman who'd remained standing wore the trousers and jacket of Baret noncivilians; the thorny rose on their jacket pockets showed them to be members of state security. The woman, Will noticed, was one of the most beautiful he'd ever seen, with a face that could come from one of the frescoes in church. She was young, and she wore a gold earring in one ear in the shape of a rose.

She carried a malachite box, which she placed on the table before Hart. He opened it.

"God," said Will, and he moved closer for a better view. Hart lifted the object gently from the box and held it in the sun. It was a crown of gold, worked in a complex pattern that rose in three places to the Symbol of eternal life. Bending closer, he saw that occasional bits of the pattern formed actual representations—here was a small open book, The Book of Sawyer, and there was a cross, and further on an ancient syringe. Will crossed himself. "Is it—Hart, is this it?"

"It looks like it, doesn't it?"

He became aware that Hart was watching him. They all were, in fact.

Hart placed the crown back in the box and closed the lid. "Very believable," he said, and Will felt a lump of disappointment. Nothing so beautiful should be false.

The minister crossed his legs and leaned back. "You were going to discuss possible approaches with me."

"Yes," said Hart. "The agent who's Adrian's main negotiator for the Crown has been called uphill for a few days; so much the better. He's left a couple of assistants here, and it will be more credible if we approach through them. Also, I suggest that Miranda make the first contact—let them do the work of bringing it up to your level."

The minister turned to the Madonna-like beauty in the security uniform. She said, "I see no difficulty."

Her voice was cool and sweet, like running a string of pearls over your skin. Will pulled himself together. "I'll take that drink now," he said. The minister touched a bell to summon his boy again, and Hart pulled out the chair beside his in invitation. Will sat down.

Hart leaned over. "You have a young lady at home," he said softly.

"I know," Will replied, irritated. "What did I do?"

Hart raised his voice. "Forgive me for verging on the vulgarity, Lord Minister, but my time is short. Would you mind terribly much if we discussed money?"

"Cyr," said the minister, "I bow always to the energies

of the young. — I believe we mentioned a lower figure of
four hundred thousand? — Miranda, could you bring me
my scarf? It grows chilly."

Hours later, when the sun had passed to the other side
of the mountains, Will accompanied Hart to the aircar on
the upper terrace. Hart put up a hand when he reached for
the door.

"You're staying here for a while, Willie," he said.

"What do you mean, *here?*"

"At the villa. As a guest. I have to go uphill myself for
a few days, and I want somebody on the spot to watch
over the operation."

"I don't think the minister wants anybody watching
what he does. And it's his operation, not mine."

Hart said briefly, "He invited you." And he opened the
door and got inside.

"As a hostage? To guarantee payment, or secrecy about
the crown?"

"Stop worrying, Willie, it kills you when you're still
young. Enjoy the company of Miranda—she can end a
man's life in eight different ways, and only four of them
are taught in state security."

Will looked at the driver, who waited impassively. He
lowered his voice. "Are you really going to have the minister give that thing to Adrian as the Crown?"

"Of course not, Willie, I'm going to have him *sell* it to
Adrian. It wouldn't be believable if we *gave* it to him."

Will saw the lights of Everun far below, the strip of the
Flat as it curved north and south. "I'd rather stay at the
Residence."

"Look, I don't have time to go over everything with
you, I'm going straight to the port. You'll be perfectly
safe here, probably safer than if you were down there."
Hart closed the door with finality. Faintly, Will heard him
shout, "Don't worry, if Lysette asks for you, I'll say you
were delayed."

The terrace vibrated gently as the car powered up. Bastard. Still, that parting shot *was* reassuring in a way. Hart
would never leave him here to die when there were so
many awful things he could still do to him.

The stars were blotted out for a moment by the car

shape. Then they winked on again, as though from a universal power surge. There was a silence on the mountain, a silence made of quiet sounds—the river, the wind in the trees, insects and other night creatures. He stood there, not even turning back toward the house.

Eventually he became aware of a change in the silence. Behind him, a voice like pearls on skin said, "Sergeant? Are you coming back in or not?"

Chapter 41

*Presentiment is that long shadow on the lawn
Indicative that suns go down;
The notice to the startled grass
That darkness is about to pass.*

EMILY DICKINSON

Keylinn didn't think she liked this Miranda. There was a quality that Graykey society recognized called *sabi*, a thing that accumulated with age and grace and wisdom. If a jeweled sword from the ancient craftswoman Tirial were laid side by side with a perfect reproduction, the original would possess *sabi*. The copy would not. It felt as though this Miranda had no *sabi* at all, as though she were entirely self-created, unmarked by anything she'd gone through.

But if they could really get the Sawyer Crown through her, an antipathy was not important.

Still—"Tell me you didn't like her either," she ordered Spider, as they walked from their latest meeting in Lankio Quarter back to the Visitor's Residence.

"I didn't like her. She made me nervous." Although he wouldn't have minded having a *picture* of her—

"And I still don't like her jacking up the price last time. We agreed on four hundred thousand."

"She said it was her principal who wanted the price jacked."

"She said."

Spider pursed his lips. "You think Tal got our message about wanting more bribe money?"

"I suppose. Unless something went wrong. Don't worry, Spider, I phrased it very discreetly."

Spider looked mournful. "Let's stop at a tiko bar."

"We have to meet Miranda again in four hours, and we may need to reach Tal."

"That's what I'm hoping to avoid. There's probably a message waiting for us that'll blister our hands to pick up. We're two hundred thousand over budget, Keylinn, he'll skin us and roll us in salt."

Keylinn breathed deeply, unfazed. "Speaking of salt, isn't that a lovely breeze? You miss that sort of thing on the Diamond, don't you?"

"Oh, hell," said Spider. They trudged on through the dark.

A message light was in fact blinking for them when they came through the lobby. Keylinn entered their code and was presented with a box of blue steel, about the size of two palm-widths and just as high. A note with it read, "Your request was received. Tal."

They looked at each other. "Let's take it outside for some privacy," said Keylinn.

"*Hell,*" said Spider very softly.

They walked out to the back garden.

Spider said, "Let's ditch it and pretend it didn't arrive."

"Whatever has come over you?"

He scuffed around in the pebbles uncomfortably. "We asked for a ton of money." He regarded the box sourly. "He didn't believe us. It's probably a bomb."

"Spider," she said. She reached into the inner pocket of her jacket and removed a thin silver key.

"I mean it," he said. "He probably thinks we wanted the money for a stake, and we're going to disappear. The sector-gate is open, there are a lot of ships in port...." His tone was wistful.

Keylinn pushed the key into the lock and took it out. The box opened.

Spider unclenched his eyes and saw twelve neat piles

of exchange notes. She was removing them methodically. He started to laugh.

He said. "I always wondered who was training who." He picked up a pile and flipped through it. Keylinn took it out of his hands and put it with the others. "As a matter of fact," he said, although not too seriously, "there really are a lot of ships in port."

"What would your mother say?" she smiled.

"I know," he said.

Tal came downhill himself a few days later and took over the closing of the deal. By then the principal at the other end had deigned to involve himself, and a man came with an aircar and flew Tal to the leisure villa of the Minister of Truth.

He returned with a malachite box and a golden crown.

"A lot of fuss over headgear," he said to Keylinn the next morning. They stood in his room in the Residence, as she held the crown up in the light slanting from the window.

"It's very beautiful," she said. "And I suppose it possesses great *sabi*."

"Can't you tell?"

"I'm afraid I'm not as perceptive as most, that way. It must be my problem, interfering with *tarethi* judgment." By problem she meant her sense of humor. Tal wondered what she could have done seven years ago that still loomed so large in everyone's mind. "Why, I'm holding this in my hands right now, but I don't sense any more *sabi* in it than in something made last week."

"Antiquity holds no charms for me. Why revere something for its age? If that thing *had* been made last week, it would look the same."

A soft chime announced the arrival of the maid. She was a dark-haired girl who carried in fresh sheets and flowers every day, and never spoke to anybody. She went straight to work now, pouring out the water from the old vase and replacing it with new, setting out a bowl of potpourri, changing the programming selection on the room's music, and then vanishing into the bathroom.

Tal said, "You're due to leave for the port this afternoon. You have time to be a tourist, if you want. Take Spider, I don't need him today."

"He's still asleep. I hate to wake him, he has trouble getting a full night's rest."

A long, low booming sound came from somewhere in the distance. There was a pause, and then another booming sound. Keylinn opened the window. To the north and west smoke was billowing skyward. Somebody in front of the Residence yelled. The maid appeared behind them, looked briefly over Keylinn's shoulder, and then returned to her work in the bathroom. It was a clear, sunny day, and Keylinn couldn't smell the smoke yet on the wind, just the salt from the sea. But she could smell trouble and pain. She shut the window.

They looked at each other. "Do you think this is it?" she asked.

He didn't answer immediately. "Fires and explosions and emergencies in general happen all the time. We think of Baret Two as unstable—and it is—but it's been in trouble for years. There's no reason to think it'll topple just while we're visiting."

"I know." But they both turned to look again out the window, identical suspicion on their faces.

Keylinn said, "Besides, any trouble would be likely to start gradually, and we haven't heard anything. It's been pretty much business as usual."

"We're probably letting our nerves affect us."

"Probably."

Nevertheless, Tal went into the bathroom to ask the maid if she knew of any faster transport to Baret Port. Keylinn heard him say, "What are you doing?" and she hurried in.

The sink was full of water. The girl was on her knees by the tub, the taps on full-force. She looked up at Tal and spoke for the first time, pitching her voice above the sound of the tub filling. "The water supply," she said, "will be the first to go."

Keylinn noted a brief pause while the universe rearranged itself. Then Tal said, "Wake Spider and pack whatever you need to keep. You bring the Crown. I'll get a car and be out front in ten minutes."

"Right."

* * *

Getting a car was not as easy as it sounded. By the Duke's policy there were no aircars kept in the Residence garage. It made sense for Baret Two: It kept visitors more or less confined to a certain radius of the capital, where they could be better watched and controlled. But an aircar would have gotten them to the port in fifteen minutes. As for the groundcars, they were swiftly disappearing, as employees took them to go wherever they felt it necessary to go in an emergency.

Fortunately Tal knew the code for the car he'd been assigned, and a blow to the head cut short the protests of his driver, who'd been trying to climb in when Tal interrupted.

People were running in and out of the garage, shouting at each other. Apparently tempers were not easy. Tal felt a touch on his arm as he reached to close the door and he prepared to strike.

He pulled himself short at the last second. The man was familiar—young, blond, wearing a Baret vest but Diamond breeches. One of Adrian's knights, wasn't he?

"Excuse me—you're Adrian's demon, aren't you?" the young man asked.

"Yes, I am," said Tal. "May I give you a lift?"

"Thanks." He climbed in.

Tal powered up. "Do you know about the rest of the team?"

"Well, I *was* going to mention . . . Lord Canniff and Sir Thomas Netherall are waiting for me in the drive. I think most of the others were out in the city, sightseeing. I'm Sir Valentine Sondheim-Lubel, by the way."

"We will be a crowded bunch." Tal took the curve out of the garage at top speed, not braking at all for the man waving his arms in the tunnel exit. That person finally gasped the obvious and leaped to one side, hitting himself hard against the wall.

They burst into daylight. Tal didn't see any likely looking candidates for knighthood standing in front of the Residence, and he didn't intend to wait. "Where are they?"

"Not sure, friend Demon. I left them hiding in the shrubbery."

Keylinn and Spider were on the steps. Tal opened the door and Sir Valentine Sondheim-Lubel stood up, hanging onto the side of the car, and yelled, "Tom! Ricky! Hurry up!"

Two men in Diamond clothing ran out from the bushes—young and strong-looking, Tal noted, like his first passenger. They might need to impress somebody with that along the way. "Sondy?" asked one of the knights. Sir Valentine Et Cetera grinned and said, "Look who I found, it's Adrian's demon. Get in, the forces of darkness are on our side."

There were muttered apologies as their four new passengers piled into a car not designed for six. Keylinn found herself on the lap of the one they called "Sondy." Not becoming the dignity of a Graykey—it would have been all right if he were on *her* lap.

Tal said pointedly, "Do we have everything?"

"Yes," said Keylinn. Spider had the Crown in his pack.

The force of acceleration threw them all back.

Some of the streets had already been closed by state security. Whenever Tal saw barriers and guards, he turned and drove down other routes. "It's no good," he said finally, "we're going to have to go through one of the bad areas."

The bad areas could easily be identified by noise and smoke, and the occasional fleeing family.

"It's the only way to get to the port," he said.

Sondy asked, "What if we get there and there are no shuttles?"

"Is that a rhetorical question?" asked Tal.

They drove toward the smoke. Tal said, "May I ask how many of us are armed?"

One of the knights said, "We weren't supposed to have weapons."

"I've got a knife," said Sondy.

"I've got a Wender-three pistol," said Keylinn brightly. She felt Sondy's start of surprise. "It's accurate over fifty meters, and then it dissipates."

"I knew we could count on you," muttered Spider.

Sondy said, "My lady, but what if the Duke's people had discovered it?"

"They wouldn't have."

Inspiration struck Spider. He said, "These cars are only supposed to be driven by government employees. And I bet half of them are really state security."

"So?" asked a knight.

"So maybe the *car* is armed. I mean, times haven't been good around here, have they?"

Tal said, "Very good, Spider, I've been looking. So far I haven't found any likely buttons."

As one, they all peered over at the controls. "How about that blue thing?" asked a knight.

Getting technical advice from a Redemptionist knight was really too much. Tal halted the car. "If one of you would like to take over—"

"No offense," said the knight. "It's just that, in a battle-capsule, that's where the cannon controls are. It's convenient for someone who doesn't have a lot of room to move. I beg your pardon if I seemed importunate."

Tal started up the car again and his passengers resumed their postures. He flipped open the "blue thing" and saw a set of controls that *might* be weapons-related. The middle thing looked like a targeting device.

He decided it was not relevant to mention.

They were crossing Schuyler Plaza, a huge cobblestone expanse, when a spray of something hit the front window. Tal steered them immediately behind one of the fountains. "Damn," he muttered.

"What is it?" asked Spider.

"Our front window is melting. Does anybody see anything?"

The nearest buildings were thirty meters away. The plaza was littered with abandoned vehicles, though, and there was a makeshift platform where somebody had recently been giving a speech.

"There—the paisley car on its side," said Keylinn briefly.

Tal's attention locked onto it. "How many?"

"I don't know, I just saw a movement."

"I can't shoot them from where we are. Even if I was sure I knew what I was doing."

Nothing happened for a minute. "We can't sit here forever," said Sondy. "And the longer we wait, the less likely we are to get a shuttle."

"Does that mean you have an idea?" asked Tal.

Sondy lapsed into silence.

Another few minutes passed. Then two men came out from behind the paisley car. Their Baret skirts had been ripped short to make fighting easier, and they wore white bands tied to their arms.

"Rebels," said Sondy unnecessarily.

They each carried a light-rifle. Two more men and a woman appeared from behind a fountain to the far left. "Everyone is armed but us," said Spider. His voice was higher than normal.

"I think we should try to look harmless," offered Keylinn, "but if you want, I can lean over these gentlemen and get a few shots out the window."

"We're supposed to be neutral," observed one of the knights. No one commented on this.

The rebels reached the car. They trained their rifles on the occupants. Tal ran down his window and said, "Is there something we can do for you?" He let a Cities accent fill his speech.

"Who are you?" said one man.

"We're citizens of the Diamond. Just trying to get to the port."

"Redemptionists," said the rebel woman, a sneer in her voice.

"Neutral Redemptionists," said Tal. "The Cities have agreements with the Republic and the Empire both, not to interfere in any . . . private problems."

"We're not Republicans," said another rebel. "We're freedom fighters."

"Well," said Tal, "that's good. We'd just like to get to the port—

The rebel woman screamed suddenly. A white halo surrounded her and her flesh crisped. What was left of her collapsed to the cobblestones. The other rebels scattered at once.

"Shit," said Spider. "Half a dozen of state security, behind us."

"And we're in the middle." Tal powered up hopelessly.

Driving out wouldn't work, but neither would anything else.

More spray hit them. The entire left side of the car started to melt.

"Everybody out!" Keylinn kicked out the opposite door, startling the knight she lay across to do it.

They scattered behind the fountain and the nearest vehicles. Light-rifles and pellet-guns were firing all over the place. Keylinn found herself behind an abandoned truck filled with pastry; where was her *tarethi-din?* It wouldn't be polite to ask him to yell and give away his location, but she was worried.

"Tal!" she yelled. "If you're alive, shoot that light over the cupid fountain." Could anyone even hear her? It was fifty-fifty, she figured, that he had a weapon.

The light over the cupid fountain exploded.

Well, that relieved some stress. A figure ran over to her, and she saw it was Sondy. "Are you all right?" he asked.

Here to protect a lady, with his trusty knife. "I'm fine, Sondy."

A dozen men and women in state security uniforms were pouring into the plaza. Other people, probably rebels, were firing from nearby buildings. Keylinn looked down, and saw that Sondy was dead.

It was about then that she lost track of what was happening.

Tal saw that people were hand-fighting in the plaza; state security was probably desperate to take prisoners for questioning. It was less important at this stage to kill people than it was to pinpoint leaders and locations before things got out of hand.

Then he saw Keylinn out there. She had what he assumed was the Wender pistol in one hand, and a large knife in the other, and she was moving like the indiscriminate wrath of God through the fighters. She'd already killed three rebels, which was bad enough for a neutral, but wasn't that a state security person she'd just dropped? How were they ever going to explain that?

Her eyes were blank, and she was smiling steadily.

* * *

Keylinn didn't feel blank, she felt occupied. Busy. It was too bad the knife and pistol were so slow.

In front of her she saw a rebel knock a light-rifle out of a security man's hand, and crack him on the knees in the next second, bringing him down. She was vaguely aware that it *was* the rebels they needed to get through, so she shot that particular rebel and picked up the discarded rifle.

She tested the trigger and the releases. A state security rifle was keyed to the retinal pattern of the person it was issued to that day, and for the next ten hours would function only in their hands. Unless they were unlocked by the issuee speaking that day's codeword.

Around her was dust and blood. She sought out the rifle's owner on the ground and met his eyes.

"Release it!" she yelled over the din. "Release your weapon to me! It'll be all right. I swear!"

The private lay there, all of seventeen, maybe, looking at her with calm despair. In a sudden, time-slowing pocket of silence Keylinn could hear the old sayings:

When a Graykey swears, cover your ears.

Trusting a Graykey is like picking up an alleycat.

Graykey truth has a new color every day.

He couldn't possibly know what she was. Graykey and dirt soldier, paired statues, part of a fountain grouping of their own. She came out of it to the realization that the release light was already blinking. She pulled down the bolt and looked through the sight, getting a rebel near Sondy's body in target and allowing the weapon to read her retinal pattern. It would respond only to her for the next ten hours.

She let the Fire take her again.

The battle moved on, as guerrilla battles do, off toward the Hill of Landing with its monuments just to the west, and the office buildings beyond it. Nothing much was left behind but broken cars and weapons and no longer valuable bodies.

Tal walked carefully over to where Keylinn was sitting on the edge of a fountain of grouped stone eagles, her chest still panting with hard, rasping breaths. "Are you all right?" he asked. She still clasped the light-rifle in one hand and he removed it very slowly and put it on the ground. Lord Canniff and Sir Thomas Netherall emerged from their hiding places, dirty but safe. "Where's Spider?"

Spider pulled himself out from under the paisley car. His shirt was ripped. He looked at what was left of their transportation and winced.

Lord Canniff called, "Sondy?"

"Don't bother," said Keylinn.

Tal turned back to her. "That was crazy."

"Yeah. It happens to my clan sometimes."

"It's only random luck you weren't killed."

She shook her head as though he were being irrational. "They never hit when the Fire is on you."

Her face glowed with quiet rapture, and he felt a stab of fear. Maybe she'd be all right when they got back uphill. She stood up and walked over to the car. "This one is out of the question. Let's go see if the pastry truck is operational."

She walked stiffly. This return to practicality was reassuring, and Tal fell in beside her as they reached the truck.

A smell of fresh apple pie came from the back. "Are you sure you're all right?" asked Tal. She turned to him. Her braid had come down and her hair hung around her face in tufts. At another time she might have looked foolish, but her eyes were still shining with exaltation.

"Did we miss anybody?" asked Tal. It would be a pity to get shot in front of a load of pies. His voice seemed muffled to his own ears, as though it were coming from a long way off.

She turned to scan the area, and he saw for the first time that a streak of blood, somebody else's blood, was splattered on the other side of her nose, across her cheek to the corner of her left eye. It was the final straw. He pulled her over to him and put his mouth against hers.

There was a second, not of surprise, but of faint startlement. Then she put her arms around him and things seemed to recede even further.

Somebody was calling him. Had *been* calling him. He pulled himself away and said, "What?" just as Spider came around the corner of the truck.

Tal's hands were on Keylinn's shoulders. Spider said, "Are you okay, Key?"

"She's fine," said Tal. "What is it?"

"One of the uniforms left a hand-com on the ground. I've been talking to their officer. There's a squad transport with a bunch of state security coming and they say they'll escort us to the port."

"Good," he said. He put his hands down and followed Spider out into the plaza.

Keylinn walked behind them both, as though she'd get lost if she didn't, still feeling oddly disoriented. Still feeling Tal's hands on her shoulders. They rejoined the two knights, who had brought Sondy's body out beside the fountain. One said, "We want to take him back. To recycle him into the Diamond." He said it defiantly, as though expecting Tal to argue, but Tal only shrugged.

"If there's room in the transport, it's not my affair."

A groan came from a state security man—more of a boy—on the ground. Keylinn walked over to him. It was the private whose rifle she had taken.

"This one is still alive," said Tal. "Kill him."

His eyes were open. Very wide, they were. She knew he could hear, but fear had taken away his voice.

Tal said, "We're supposed to be neutral and you just took out any number of rebels—not to mention anybody else. This is the only witness."

"See here—" began Lord Canniff.

"Sir, Adrian will explain this to you when we return," said Tal. "Meanwhile, shut up."

When a Graykey swears, cover your ears. Trusting a Graykey—

"I don't believe he'll say anything," she said. "And if he does, we'll just say he was hallucinating."

"Why should he hallucinate?"

She reversed the rifle abruptly and brought it down against the side of the soldier's head, knocking him unconscious. "Because," she said viciously, "he's got a head wound."

She threw the rifle on the ground and walked away. Then she said, "Unless, of course, you insist."

"No. I don't insist." He felt at a total loss.

They sat down the edge of the fountain to await their escort. One of the knights said, "But her marks are on the rifle."

"This isn't a murder trial," she said tiredly. "It's a war. Nobody's going to check."

The other knight—Tom, she'd heard him called—held onto Sondy's body. Eventually there came the vibration of the squad transport.

Chapter 42

It would be superfluous in me to point out to your lordship that this is war.

CHARLES FRANCIS ADAMS

In contrast to most of the sections of the city they'd just traveled through, the port was busy. A gray shuttle with the huge red circle stamp of Baret Station lifted off on one grid while an out-system ship blinked impatiently on another. The state security escort passed their party through the arrivals and departures building, almost empty when they'd first arrived downhill and now crammed with middle-class Baret Two families who had reason—or believed they had reason—to fear the coming of the Republic. They had blankets spread on the floor, and what they would do when the food ran out was anybody's guess.

The escort brought them to a man behind a counter at the end of the room. A line of people stood stoically before the counter, holding bags stuffed with their possessions; they watched with hostile eyes as the Diamonders were herded to the front of the line.

The man looked up. He was young, harried, and had a stationer's tattoo. "We're interviewing for acceptable occupations in the other room. Unless they can pay—can they?"

He spoke to the security officer, ignoring them. Tal

said, "Thank you, officer, I'll take it from here. We appreciate your assistance."

The stationer focused on Tal. The security officer shrugged and motioned his men to leave—there was plenty to do elsewhere. The stationer said, "Cyr?"

The very form of address was an inquiry about money. Tal's lips curved briefly and he said, "We have transport of our own, thanks. Could you pass word to them we'd like a pickup? The Diamond will pay all port communications fees."

"I see," said the man, relaxing somewhat. "There should be no difficulty with that. There's a lounge behind me, if you don't want to stay out here."

Keylinn, Spider, and the two knights waited no further, but passed into the next room. Tal said, "Do you have any word as to what's gong on?"

"Troops from Baret One landed on Western Continent this morning—or rather, last night, our time. They claim they were invited by the local subgovernor."

"The local subgovernor has no power to invite outplanet troops."

The man shrugged. "Who said he did?" His gaze passed over the line of Baret Two natives in their rumpled clothes, all with the same desperate look on their faces. "The dirtsiders are premature," he stated calmly. "A few rebels rose in Everun, but it was based mostly on rumor. State security is cleaning them up now. Whatever happens on Western Content, it'll take a while to reach us here."

"Have you announced that to them?" asked Tal.

"I'm not a newscaster."

"Especially not when they're lined up to sign their lives away to Baret Station Authority."

The man blinked his light blue eyes. "Is that a criticism?"

"No. Just an observation. The lounge is through there, is it?" Tal took hold of his pack and followed the bedraggled remnants of the Diamond trade team.

They had dropped their packs and were sprawled on the thick carpet. At the far end of the room a glass wall showed the turmoil of workers around the grids outside. They almost had the lounge to themselves; a small group of aristocrats huddled in the corner by the glass wall, talking in low voices. One woman looked as though she were taking all her jewelry out on her body.

Tal said, "The rest of the team might be all right if they keep their heads. State security will probably have the rebels here rounded up in a few days, and our people can start trickling back to the port. It'll be safer if they don't try to go back to the Residence, though—you never know how popular outsiders are at a time like this. And it *is* part of the Duke's grounds."

"You mean this is temporary?" asked Lord Canniff. "It'll all blow over in a few days?"

"No. The revolution has definitely begun. It's just a matter of time until it grinds over Everun—a few days, weeks, a year. But it looks like there'll be time to get the others off."

Keylinn was stretched on the floor with her head on her pack. She said, "The pleasant gentleman from the front counter is coming up behind you, Tal. On your left."

Tal stood. "Is there a problem?"

The stationer shook his head and held out a piece of paper. "This is for you. A message. I forgot about it in all the excitement."

"For me?" Tal did not take the paper.

"You were described very specifically."

"What do you mean, you forgot? When were you given this?"

"Yesterday. Do you want the message, or not? I don't care, I've already been paid."

Tal's group were looking at each other. Yesterday?

He took the paper, unfolded it, and read, in graceful script, what looked like a poem:

Belleraphon.
On the sixteenth of the Month of Changes,
At the fourth hour,
Alone.
I stood on the Street of Dreams,
At the mouth of Ocean Avenue.
The wind was cold.

He folded it again and sat down. The month of changes . . .

"Tal?" said Keylinn.

"What?" His voice was distracted.

"What's going on? Is it something I should know?"

"No." He was staring out through the glass wall. "Just a personal message."

He realized after a few minutes that the stationer had gone and that his companions were looking at him oddly. The two knights shrugged; he was a demon, after all. But Keylinn and Spider seemed disturbed.

He said, "Excuse me," and he left the lounge. Ten minutes later he returned and said, "Keylinn, I'd like to speak with you for a moment."

She followed him to the far side of the room. He said, "I'm not going uphill with you."

"Tal, the situation down here is serious, whatever that idiot out front thinks. People were shooting at us a short time ago, if you'll recall."

"Things should quiet down somewhat over the next day. I'll stay here at the port until tomorrow."

"It's this Belleraphon, isn't it?"

He said, irritated, "It's none of your business what it is."

"It's exactly my business."

"Enough. I'm not going to discuss it with you." He paused and said, "Not now, anyway. I'm telling you this because I want you to pass the Crown along to Adrian. Tell him the safest place on the Diamond is the vault in my office. It's got an Empire-style time lock tied into the computer links, he can set it for when he needs to remove the crown. Nobody will get it out before then. Show him how to use it if he needs to know."

She glared at him silently.

He said, "I'm not unaware of the danger. I'm also not unaware that as soon as word of this filters through the brains of the Diamond and Opal councils, they'll be all for pulling out of this system as soon as they can. Adrian will want to fold up his tents and leave—that's why I can't go back now—I might not be able to get another exit pass." He paused, then asked, "Are you following me so far?"

"You're doing the talking."

"Look. I just bought this, illegally, from a security officer in the port. He'll say he lost it." He brought out a hand-com from one pocket, shielding it so no one else could see. "I've arranged with the helpful gentleman at the counter to patch any communications over this through the synapse at Baret Station. I'll give you the protocol, and you can link with them from the Diamond."

"Not as efficient as a riccardi, I suppose." Her voice was cold.

"It will have to do. I need to know when things get close. I need to know if it looks like the Cities are ready to pull out. It should take a while—they should need time to close out their deals with the Station, pull in their workers, all the things they need to do before Blackout. But they might panic and go too fast, so I'll need to know."

"You could just come uphill."

"But since I'm not going to do that, you're going to keep me informed on this little communications chain."

She put one firm hand on his arm, as though somehow to stop him from falling through this hole, and he was suddenly back behind a truck full of fresh apple pies in an entirely separate net of confusion. She said, "Whatever this note is, I don't think it means you any good."

"Very likely," he agreed.

"Then why go against the percentages? It isn't like you."

"It's too late now," he said simply, as though it were an explanation, and maybe it was. Somewhere in that sentence were a score of star systems and an endless assembly line of worlds full of hostile and unknowable humans, and a goal that might or might not be reached. If *the sixteenth, the fourth hour, alone,* were the answer, how could he not look?

She dropped her hand and turned back to the group. He pulled her back. "Am I in violation of Graykey contract?" he demanded.

"Do you think you took advantage of me? You've been on the Diamond too long."

"Answer my question. Don't give me 'Graykey truth.'"

She shook off his grip. "It was a tense moment. We were both running on nerves. We'll let it pass, this once. Don't try it again, or I'll have to act." Her hair was falling down again, and she pushed it back angrily. "I've stated my judgment. So be it."

She sat down beside Spider and began braiding her copper hair with tense, white fingers. Tal walked to the glass wall, where he saw the out-system ship had finally received clearance to leave. It lifted off from its grid, away from the mess this planet had become, toward home and freedom.

Chapter 43

> *"Yes," I answered you last night;*
> *"No," this morning, sir, I say:*
> *Colors seen by candlelight*
> *Will not look the same by day.*
>
> ELIZABETH BARRETT BROWNING

Keylinn:

"Why does he do these things?" asked Adrian. He closed the malachite box and placed it in Tal's vault.

"I don't know, sir," I answered. "I'm a Graykey, not a telepath." My voice was as devoid of emotion as I felt. I was losing track of where that weary barrenness came from, whether exhaustion or pride or good sense; I would have been able to produce it from my exercises, but there had been no need to try. Perhaps it came from simple self-preservation.

Two members of the Diamond council stood against the wall, witnesses to the receipt of the crown and its delivery to the vault.

Adrian hesitated over the lock. "I don't want to do anything wrong," he told me. "Perhaps you'd better watch. I want to set it for Thursday at two; that's when the City of Pearl said their Oracle would be here."

"You're doing it properly. Hit the blue and then the red when you're done; that'll seal it to Tal's program."

Adrian did so. He pushed the button to close the vault door; it was as thick as his hand and made of durasteel, and when it shut, there was no line between it and the wall. He smiled. "All as it should be, Miss Gray?"

"At least according to my instructions, sir."

He motioned for the councillors to precede them from the room. In a low voice he said to me, "Please let me thank you again. I don't think you'll be displeased to hear that the Lord Cardinal and his friends sounded terribly put out when I announced the Crown's arrival."

It was a charming image. I felt a grin breaking the surface of my empty lake; he caught it, answered with one of his own, and went on, "I thought Arno would have a str—"

His voice cut off as he saw Lord Muir and his son Harry waiting in the corridor outside.

"Adrian!" said Lord Muir. "They thought you might be here. Never been in this part of town, myself."

"Sightseeing?"

"Ha! Sightseeing! Isn't that rich, Harry boy?"

Harry boy, I thought. That child has a lot to put up with.

"No, no," went on Lord Muir jovially. "We're here to congratulate you on winning the Sawyer Crown. Word's all over the ship."

The councillors looked somewhat alarmed at that, but Adrian appeared not to care. He said, "Thank you. That was very thoughtful."

"It was Harry's idea, actually. He suggested it as soon as we heard."

Harry was the picture of a son dragged unwillingly along in the fulfillment of parental obsession.

"Thank you, Harry, how kind of you."

"You're welcome," said Harry, in a kind of despairing tonelessness.

So this, I thought, was the famous Harry Muir. He looked his age of eighteen, no more nor less, and just at the moment he did not appear to be the picture of a potential security minister. He seemed more like a young man at a large party who's drunk too much and is wondering abstractedly if he's about to throw up on a potted plant.

Adrian smiled. "Perhaps we could walk together to court level and you could tell me your ideas for ship's security."

I thought: *Adrian, you're too cruel.* The elder' Muir looked ecstatic. Harry looked close to physical illness. I would have liked to do something, but it was not my place to interfere with Adrian's personal pleasure. No doubt he had few enough.

But Adrian relented. "I'd forgotten, though, I have another appointment. I'm rather late, so if you two gentlemen will excuse me—?" He accepted their bows and said, "But thank you again for your congratulations. The Muirs have always been the most loyal of families on the Diamond, always contributing to our success in one ministry or another. Clearly Harry is following in your footsteps, Lord Muir. I'll see you, I hope." And he walked very quickly down the corridor, having dispensed enough honey to salve the disappointment of Harry's father.

"Did you hear that?" Lord Muir asked his son.

"Can I go now?" asked his son in return.

I rounded the corner of the corridor and heard Lord Muir's voice as he raised it into a full critique of his youngest child—his understanding of politics, his choice of companions, and his lack of appreciation for all his father was trying to do. I quickened my pace until the voice had faded. It was a living incitement to murder.

Chapter 44

Will was awakened in the grayness just before dawn by a hand on his chest. He grabbed hold of the arm it was attached to and was starting to try a maneuver when he realized it was a woman's hand. Miranda. He stopped, and it was just as well, for the arm hadn't budged. The woman must be made of stone.

She lifted her hand. "Are you awake, Sergeant?"

"I guess so. More or less. Is anything wrong?" His room was on the third floor of the villa, and the glass

doors near his bed led out to a tiny balcony overlooking
the mountainside. The sound of birdsong came into his
room, adding to his disorientation. Planet birds must get
up early, he thought.

"It would depend on your viewpoint," said Miranda.
"Troops from Baret One have landed on Western Continent. There's no official word from the city, but we can
assume there'll be trouble there today."

"Shit," said Will, in Sangaree. He felt around on the
floor for his socks.

"The rest of the household has been up for two hours,"
she said. "We almost forgot about you."

"Oh." He started pulling on his pants. Ordinarily he
would have been uncomfortable dressing before a lady,
but this gloriously beautiful Miranda had all the warmth
and humanity of an android.

He froze. No, that was a crazy idea, and born of his
own neurosis. He buckled his belt.

"I'll see you downstairs," she said in her troubling
voice, and she left him.

No, the odds on having to deal with two simulacra-
passing-for-human in his life were too much. So why did
Miranda remind him so much of Miss Smith?

His footsteps echoed in the halls as he went down the
stairs. He found Miranda in the kitchen setting out a plate
of bread and fruit. She wore her uniform, and on her the
trousers clung snugly. It was a cold morning on the
mountain, but she wasn't wearing her uniform jacket; it
hung over one of the chairs. "Where is everybody?" he
asked.

She turned her wide, dark eyes to him. "The minister
has been called to make a tour of inspection of Eastern
Continent troops, to assess morale. He left half an hour
ago. Those of the household staff he didn't bring have
been let go for the duration of the emergency."

That made sense, the man was in charge of propaganda, after all. He'd want to check out the troops and
see what was likely to go over with them and what
wasn't.

Why did it sound like a lie?

"Will you eat before we leave?" She gestured to the
bread and fruit.

A final meal? "Where are we going?"

"I was asked to drive you to the port. Your presence is no longer needed, and you'll be in danger here. The minister's address may be known to various malcontents."

"I see." He bit into one of the local fruits. He'd seen it on scores of fruitstands along the Street of Dreams; it was red and soft and he didn't know its name. "What about you?" he asked.

"State security will assign me to a new project."

"The idea of the Republic taking over doesn't bother you? I'd think they wouldn't be kind to Empire security people."

"I'll survive." She didn't say *What do you mean, take over?* the way a good Baret Two security officer should.

He took a swallow of the bread. It was crispy and fresh and had been kept warm for him. A sudden fantasy scenario flashed through Will's head; he saw himself opening doors along the corridor upstairs, finding evidence of things broken and stolen, dead bodies of servants who'd not yet run away. And then opening one of the closet doors with their pleasant shutter design on the outside, and finding the minister with a red line around his throat, among the brooms and jackets.

Paranoia. Paranoia had come into his life, and he could trace it to the moment he'd found Hartley Quince in Iolanthe's sitting room on the Opal.

Or maybe dealing with Hart had strengthened his sensitivity to the way things really were. Did he want to go open any doors upstairs?

"You're not eating," said Miranda. She pushed a silver pot toward him.

"I'm not very hungry. —Thanks, no, I don't drink coffee."

"Then we shall leave." She put on her jacket and buttoned it methodically.

Will got up and followed her out to the front terrace. "A groundcar?" he asked.

"The minister took the aircar when he left on his inspection tour."

"Oh." Will debated getting in. But if she were truthful, there was no reason not to; and if she weren't, she could probably run faster. And he ought to stop this psychotic fit right now.

Miranda took the driver's seat and powered up. They started down the long, snaky, dangerous mountain road. Her gloved hands were light on the controls—she drove like an angel, in fact, which didn't surprise him.

Will realized that his own hands were trembling and he put them on his knees. He tried to stretch unobtrusively. Whatever his problem was, it was getting worse. They came to a fork and she took the left-hand side. True, that was the direction that Will's senses told him was *away* from the port side of Everun, but there were lots of possible reasons for that. The road twisted and turned every which way, it might switch back further on; the right-hand road might lead to a thoroughfare at the bottom of the mountain that could be in a dangerous neighborhood for a day like this; she might just want to take an alternate route to the port. Maybe she knew where there was an aircar in this direction.

He could keep coming up with reasons all day. They drove further, and his directional sense kept telling him this was *wrong*.

Christ, Willie, be sensible. If you think she's a murderer, why didn't she kill you back at the villa? What could she possibly want with a Sangaree sergeant?—I don't know, he responded mentally. *But I don't think it's in my best interests. I just don't feel a long life line in this direction.*

Then he did something that he hadn't known he was going to do, but that was just as well or he wouldn't have done it. He reached over and put an arm around Miranda's shoulder. After all, a woman as beautiful as that must be used to men behaving obnoxiously.

"I need to concentrate on my driving, sergeant," said the voice like pearls.

"Sorry." He removed his arm.

Her neck and cheek had been cold. But machine-cold? Or just chilly? His own hands weren't very warm.

The mountainside dropped off to his right in a forest of green trees and undergrowth, bushes and wildflowers.

He opened the door and rolled out in one motion. And kept rolling, over sharp stems that whipped up to cut him, and stones, and tree roots. The slope was too steep to stop himself. When he finally fetched up against the hollow of a grandfather tree, he'd come much further than he'd planned.

And the wind was knocked out of him, and he couldn't move.

Way up above, the car had stopped. She'd powered it down to hear better. "Sergeant?" he heard her call. "Will?"

He couldn't have answered if he'd wanted to. He felt his heartbeat as though it belonged to someone else. Could she hear him? Could she see the heat of his body here in the dirt and stones? Nothing would surprise him.

You've just lost a free ride to the port, Willie. Now she'll tip-tap over to the car in those cute little boots and drive away and leave the crazy Diamonder to fend for himself.

A bolt of white light hit a tree a few yards to his left. The tree crisped and began smoking. Where the hell had she gotten a light-rifle? He hadn't seen one in the car.

He had his wind back. Will sighed sympathetically for the cuts and bruises his body already had garnered, and dived down the slope again. Gravity took him, and the undergrowth covered him in a tomblike highway.

On the Diamond, Keylinn was admitted to Adrian's suite. Iolanthe was perched on a lounge chair in the sitting room, reading a book. She glanced up at Keylinn and back down again without commenting. Adrian said, "What is it?"

Keylinn handed him the paper that the Transport deck link-boy had given her half an hour ago. She knew the contents by heart.

>17:06<
>RETRANSMIT FROM BARET STATION<
>TO KEYLINN GRAY, TECH<
>THE CITY OF DIAMOND<

You have lately had in your possession a crown of 28-karat gold, weighing 5 kilos, with an abstract design of twisted rope, bearing three main Redemptionist eter-

nal life Symbols, and a number of minor representations
worked into the design.

This crown was lately constructed in Everun, at the
instigation of two agents from the City of Opal.

Should you wish the genuine Sawyer Crown, seek for
it in the possession of Hyram Det Arbrith.

Adrian looked up. "There's no signature?"

"And Baret Station denies any knowledge of the
sender. It came along a regular communications path, and
was sent with normal port messages. Credit to pay for the
retransmission accompanied the original message."

The Protector started to pace. Iolanthe put down her
book and watched. He said, "Of course, it could be a
hoax."

"Yes," said Keylinn. "Although—"

"Although they know what the crown looks like so aw-
fully well."

Iolanthe said, "Adrian?"

He put up a hand. "Wait." He paced some more, then
said, "We'll go take another look at Tal's vault. The Oracle from Pearl will be here tomorrow at two. Damn! If
only I could reach him! He *would* stay behind on a world-
ful of revolutionary crazies—"

"I can reach him," said Keylinn. It was a gray area, but
she felt Tal would want her to tell Adrian in these circumstances. He looked at her sharply and she corrected,
"Theoretically, I can reach him. I've got a protocol to
Baret Station that Tal's matched his hand-com to."

"What's he doing with a Baret hand-com? Never mind.
Do it, do it."

"With your permission," said Keylinn. She sat down at
the link in his sitting room and addressed a greeting
through the Baret connection. There was no response. She
tried again. A message appeared: VOLUNTARY FAIL-
URE.

Adrian was beside her. "Who fails voluntarily?"

"They mean Tal has his com turned off. He knows that
at the very earliest we couldn't pull out of Baret System
for hours yet. And he doesn't want to be disturbed."

Adrian looked at her—a heavy look, a veil of
sheetmetal, and it occurred to her that perhaps her discus-

sion of Tal's motivations should not appear so effortlessly certain.

"The hell with him," said Adrian. "We'll break into his damned vault without him."

Iolanthe had stood up pointedly and was waiting for some attention to be cast in her direction. "Sir, are you going to tell me what's going on?"

He seemed to wince very slightly at the "sir." He said, "Yes, of course. We'll all go. Come on, Io, we're going to talk to a security lock."

"I'm very sorree," sang the lock. "I cannot open until 14:00 hours on July 21. This command cannot be overridden. Thank you!"

The lock itself appeared to be physically no more than a small red light on the smooth surface of the door. Its voice came from the link speakers by Tal's desk. Adrian found himself turning to the speakers when he talked, which irritated him. He turned to them again now. "Are there *any* circumstances under which it can be overridden?"

"I'm very sorree! I am only a minor technical device," said the lock. "Questions may be addressed to my governing security program, named Center."

"Center!" called Adrian.

"May I assist you?" said a deeper, more confident voice. "My framework is Empire-designed, by Katroe Venderhof of Deal. My subprograms are completely flexible, and may be redesigned and customized by any intelligent user skilled up to Level 23 in security technicals."

"Thank you," said Adrian politely. "Perhaps we'll create something at a later time. Right now, we'd like to do something about the lock on the vault in this room. Can we reset the time for it to open?"

"Allow me to investigate. —No. My subprogram, named 'Morgue,' informs me that it is not authorized to allow any such thing, and will resist it most severely."

Adrian had started pacing again. "Mmm. Well, I suppose there's no reason we can't bypass the lock and go in with brute force and metal cutters."

Keylinn said, ". . . Maybe."

Jane Emerson

He pursed his lips. "Center, could you rephrase my last remark as a question and give a reply?"

"A scenario as you describe would have a point oh-oh-oh-one chance of success. Highest probability would result in three explosive devices going off, killing all life outside the vault within a fifty-meter area."

Adrian rubbed his forehead with the heel of one hand, closing his eyes. "He always has to be so bloody efficient," she heard him mutter.

Iolanthe had been sitting in Tal's desk chair. She got up now and put her hand on her husband's. "Perhaps," she said forcefully, "it's time that we found a little help."

"Yes," agreed Adrian. He turned to Keylinn. "Tech Gray, this is your project: Call Baret Station and have them send over an expert in technical security."

"Yes, sir."

Adrian headed for the door. "My reputation will be in ragged strips if Pearl declares my crown a forgery. Let me point out that if my hopes and dreams go down the recycler, so do the lives of those less comfortably placed on the Diamond. Like Outsider techs and nonhumans."

"Yes, sir, I had already made the connection."

He paused and said more gently, "Yes, of course you had. Please continue, Miss Gray, and any ideas you may have on this subject, I'll be happy to listen to." He turned at the door to let Iolanthe precede him. "And keep trying to get through to Tal. When you do, tell our demon that he'd better retrieve this fiasco, or I'll send him straight back to hell."

Chapter 45

In the interests of "containment," it was Spider and Keylinn who met the security freelancer coming over from Baret Station. Adrian didn't want any more people involved in this than could possibly be helped.

"Jesus," said Spider, when he saw their expert.

She was perhaps sixteen years old, with very long

blonde hair tied back in a knot and a pony tail. She didn't just have a station tattoo, she had dozens of them—all over her body. Which you could see. Because, as Spider noted, she wasn't wearing anything. She stepped across the Transport deck with the grace of an athlete. That was an augmented body, or Keylinn was a two-headed bonz dancer.

"Freelancers," muttered Keylinn. Augmented body, tattoos of rank and achievement—clearly their expert had every intention of trailing her skin, like a professional calling card, past all potential customers.

"Urp," said Spider, staring. Then he pulled himself together and said, "We can't take her through the city like that."

Keylinn stepped forward. "Cirrus?" she asked.

The girl turned and walked toward them. "Cyr Gray, Cyr Hastings?"

Keylinn was peeling off her jacket. "Here, they won't let you into the city otherwise." She handed it to Cirrus, who looked at it unhappily.

"I don't like clothes."

"I hope you don't like money either, because the clothes go with the job."

Cirrus made a face and put the jacket on awkwardly. It just covered her torso, but left her legs almost totally visible.

"They'll have a stroke," said Spider. "We'll all get arrested."

"Wait," said Keylinn. She found an off-duty worker who was wearing a cape and brought it back to Cirrus. "Put it around like a skirt and I'll pin it."

Cirrus said, "Are you people joking with me?"

"You knew you were coming to a strange place when you took the commission."

Their expert grumbled, "I thought I'd be working with the relatively normal part of the population." She draped the cape over her hips and Keylinn pulled it straight and pinned it closed.

Keylinn said, "This is the Diamond. There *is* no normal part of the population."

* * *

They brought her to Tal's office and stood her in front of the vault. She looked at it blankly. "What's this?"

"It's the door you're supposed to open," said Spider, who was getting the hang of her accent now.

She stared another minute, then started to laugh. "Children, children," she said. "Take me to your computer. It's the program I have to talk to, not the door."

Freelancers, thought Keylinn.

Obnoxious twit, thought Spider.

They sat her down at Tal's link. "Is this one okay," asked Keylinn, "or do you need another one? This is the access point the program was probably customized through."

"Ummm. I may want a different one later. We'll stay here for now. What's my time limit?"

"Nine hours. We can stretch it to twelve, but we'll all feel better with nine." Keylinn sat on the couch.

Cirrus scratched her nose unhappily. "Uh, you're not going to stay here, are you? I can't work with other people in the room."

Keylinn sighed. She said, "Come on, Spider," and they went into the back office.

Three hours and twenty-seven minutes later Cirrus came in to see them. She'd shed her clothing, and Keylinn did not protest. She merely said, "How's it going?"

"Too soon to tell. Just getting the hang of it. Got any stimulants?"

"Just caffeine." Cirrus looked far too stimulated already. Her pupils were dilated. Keylinn said, "There's coffee and tea in the other room, and a pot."

"I finished it already. I'll need plain water, too," said Cirrus. "My throat's getting sore."

Spider had already gotten up, and Cirrus followed him out. When he came in again, he brought a cup for Keylinn. "Think she's all right?" he asked.

Keylinn shrugged.

Two hours later Cirrus entered again. "Just stretching my legs," she said. She was sweating as though she'd been exercising and her expression was distant but radiant. She resembled nothing more than a woman who'd just tumbled from the bed of a gifted lover. "Excellent job. Very stiff. I keep punching, and it doesn't give. Truly rigid, truly."

"Really," said Keylinn.

"Oh, yeah. The program has a forced neurosis, one of the sickest things I've ever seen." She paused. "Did I say sick? I meant slick. Although that, too."

She disappeared again. Spider looked at Keylinn.

"Don't ask me," said Keylinn.

At ten hundred hours Cities time Cirrus came in and said hoarsely, "Cracked, jobbers. Finished, complit, blown into bonz dust."

Keylinn called Adrian. Then she said to Cirrus, "You're sure?"

"I wouldn't say it if I weren't sure." She stretched, her breasts rising and falling as she lifted her arms. Spider stared, fascinated. "Lovely subprogram, not squishy at all. There's always fat, always softness somewhere, always dead-ends and things not well-considered. Not this. Every piece interlocks. Privilege to destroy. Know the creator?"

"Somewhat," said Keylinn.

"Still living? The Center personality was only copyrighted two years ago."

"So far as I know."

"When you see him or her, tell them I'd sleep with them if I were younger and stupider."

"Ah," said Keylinn, who wasn't sure if that was a compliment or not.

Spider said, "He'll be coming back to the Diamond pretty soon. You could hang around for a day or two and meet him, if you don't have another assignment."

"Thanks," she yawned and did another stretch, "but I've already met him. A customization job is better than a psych-profile." She reached for her jacket.

Keylinn said, "You'd better wait for Adrian. He has to authorize your pay, in any case."

They followed her back into the main office. Spider said, "What do you mean, you've already met him?"

"Intelligent, cautious, doesn't talk about himself much? Not exactly an optimist? Wouldn't trust his mother?"

"That's amazing," said Spider.

"Elementary," she beamed, "if you've been poking around in his head for the last few hours. Look: Most security programs have booby traps. You expect it, they don't want people to tamper with them, right?"

"All right," said Spider.

The door slid open and Adrian came in. He paused for a moment, taken aback by the girl without any clothes. Keylinn noted that his eyes went straight where Spider's had.

Cirrus paid no attention, she was in the heart of her obsession. "Well, your friend—maybe I should say your acquaintance—did a tight job. I mean, occasionally the extra-careful will put in two booby traps. How many do you think your friend had?" She paused. "Six. And in order of ascending difficulty. It'd take a sharp person even to *spot* the fifth one. And, of course, by the time you find it, you're so demoralized you could spend the rest of your life looking for the sixth. Which of course is the trap."

"How do you mean?" asked Adrian.

She turned her attention to him. "There *is* no sixth. The door is open now. Just push the damned button."

Adrian glanced over at the vault. "How do you know?"

"It's my judgment, cyr. I just think that the irony of someone's having the key and being too afraid to use it would appeal to the mind that created this program."

"Then all we have to go on is your feeling," said Adrian slowly.

"That's all you ever had to go on, I'm afraid."

"I don't suppose," said Adrian, "that you'd like to open it yourself?"

"Not in my job description, your highness." She put on Keylinn's jacket and picked up the cape. "In fact, maybe you could wait till I reach the Transport area before you do anything rash."

Adrian smiled back at her, but it was not the type of smile, thought Keylinn, that she herself would like to receive. "You've got a lot of faith in your own abilities, for someone who's running out in the middle of a job."

"The job's over, cobby, I just said—"

"It's not over if it's not disarmed," said Adrian.

"Then open it," said Cirrus coldly. And she waited.

Adrian went over to the door and pushed the button. The door swung open, and you could hear four breaths being let out.

"There you are," said Cirrus, a trifle shakily. "No problem. As I said."

Adrian laughed. "As you said," he agreed. "You'll find eight thousand Empire units in the Commons Bank waiting for you."

"We only agreed on five thousand," she said.

"A bonus," said Adrian, "for having the guts to stay. Corporal Hastings, escort our visitor to the Transport area."

He removed the malachite box.

"Well," said Spider, "it was nice meeting you."

"You, too," said Cirrus. "You're nice people, for religious freaks."

"Thank you," said Spider.

They waited for the shortie's grid to go on-line.

Cirrus said, "And I'm glad to see your friend has one flaw, anyway."

"What's that?" asked Spider.

"Ego. He's not used to having people who can follow his tracks. He didn't expect anybody to get past the fifth trap."

"I see," said Spider. "So you could pick it out so quickly, because it's your weak point, too."

She turned and looked at him, wide-eyed. He said, "You didn't leave the room when you had the chance. And you might have been wrong, you know."

She stared, and then laughed. It was involuntary laughter, straight from her soul, and it passed quickly. She said, "Thank you, Corporal. It's never the things we know about ourselves that bring us down, is it?"

Chapter 46

Bell, book and candle shall not drive me back
When gold and silver beck me to come on.

SHAKESPEARE, *King John*

Finding a car at Everun Port was not as difficult as it had been at the Residence. Any travelers at the port on this particular day wanted to leave by shuttle, not by car, and in a vertical direction. Tal was able to get hold of a vehicle easily, but it was still ground transport—those with aircars had taken them to try for other ports.

He drove down the Street of Dreams. There was no traffic, and he only passed three pedestrians in the entire long length of the Street. Shops were dark. The famous striped awnings of the Street hung over empty stands, and here and there were shards of broken glass from the colored lights.

And it had only been a day. Ocean Avenue was north up the coast from the port, about three-quarters length of the Flat. It took him half an hour to reach it. He parked in the shadow of a snack-food bar and took out the handcom.

He sent the greeting and got a transmit response. Then he said, "Keylinn?"

"Tal?" Her voice was clear and strong over the little transmitter, and it somehow depressed him. "Where are you?"

"I'm in Everun, of course. Where else would I be?"

"I wouldn't know. You often don't see fit to share the little details of these things with me."

He paused. No adequate reply presented itself, so he said, "Is there anything I should know?"

"Yes. No more Diamond ships are going to be risked at the port, so if you want to come uphill again you'll have to do it through Baret Station."

"All right."

"And Adrian wants to kill you."

He paused again. "Metaphorically?"

"Yes." He heard a trace of laughter in her voice. "But it's serious, Tal. We got a message up here that the crown you brought back is a fake. Before you ask, we don't know who sent it. We don't know it's true. But they addressed it to me, and they described the crown in exact detail."

He took that in, "I suppose he's upset because I'm not there to open the vault."

"He was, just a trifle. Meanwhile, it's good that we still have someone on the scene. The message also said that Hyram Det Arbrith had the real Sawyer Crown."

Tal looked at the Street of Dreams, empty as far as he could see in both directions. It was ten minutes before the fourth hour. "How long do I have?"

"Adrian's appointment with the Oracle is in three hours, City time. He said he would try to stall. I don't know enough about this, Tal. Apparently the authority on Pearl claims that they have some way of testing whether the crown is the right one or not. And Adrian seems to feel if they say they can do it, they can do it. You've had more experience with these people that I have. Do you believe he's right?"

"Ask me something I can answer. I don't even know if Adrian really believes in Redemptionism or if he's just going along with it to keep the Protectorship. Humans claim all sorts of things, Keylinn, am I supposed to judge? My personal policy is to believe nothing any of them say without evidence."

This time the silence was on the other end. A quiet voice said, "You speak in the third person, Tal. I'm human, too."

"Yes. I keep forgetting." He opened the car door. "I'll be in touch. You can tell Adrian you spoke to me. —Oh, Keylinn? Don't try to force open the vault."

"*I know.*"

He smiled. "Out."

He turned off the hand-com. The salt wind blew from the east, over the dunes at the edge of Ocean Avenue. Grains of sand had spilled into the street, and no one was here to sweep them up.

He walked around the car, his hand on his pistol. The edges of the striped awnings flapped in the breeze. No walkers, no cars, no air traffic. No one in any of the windows nearby. He got into the car again.

Thirty minutes later he powered up and drove away. He headed south and west this time, toward the villa of Hyram Det Arbrith and Elizabeth Mard.

The sun was on the shoulder of the mountain when he reached the edge of the grounds. There was a high wall and a gate, and sparklers atop the wall. Defenses to go through, an entire villa to search—almost a lost cause before it was begun—and then there was the time it would take to get to the port. Whatever happened, he wasn't going to make the Oracle's deadline. He hoped Adrian's talents extended to a very long stalling effort.

He sat in the car and waited for full dark.

It was twilight on Will Stockton's mountain when a voice said, "Well, stranger, where are we going?"

He froze. He'd been wandering through the woods for an entire day and night, he was hungry, he was faint, his arm pulsed like a bitch where he'd skidded on it, and he kept getting turned around. Every now and then he'd see part of Everun below, but when he tried to locate a path he found himself doubling back miles out of his way. He was painfully aware of time passing. The Cities were going to pull out of this place, he knew that; whatever was happening was violent and bad for business. He'd felt the Panic of the true Cities-born cut through him twice: The Fear of Being Left Behind. He'd read about it and seen it in plays and now he knew it was real. He'd run blindly through the woods, tripping over roots, falling down slides of pebbles, beating his hands in the dirt. Even now he could feel the Panic holding off, somewhere beyond where normal thought took place.

And he hadn't heard anybody near him.

"You want to answer my question, friend?" Two shapes filtered out of the trees, both armed with light-rifles. He saw they wore camouflage pants and jackets, but the thorny rose of state security was embroidered in miniature on their pockets and this did not reassure him.

Miranda had been state security. Miranda had carried a light-rifle.

"I'm a Three Cities citizen," said Will, and was stopped by a fit of coughing. He tried to talk again, and was stopped again. One of the state security men handed him a canteen, warily, and he drank a good part of it. "I'm a Three Cities citizen," he finally managed. "I've been aiming to reach Everun Port, but I don't seem to be," a final spate of coughing, "getting very far."

"You wouldn't, in the direction you were going," said one of them. They looked at each other and lowered their weapons. "Where are you coming from?"

He wasn't sure why he didn't tell them about the Minister of Truth, except that Miranda was involved in that story and the whole concept of Miranda made him very nervous. Besides, why lead up to a moment when he'd have to tell security personnel that an officer of their organization shot at him? They might figure she had a reason.

"I was sightseeing in the mountains. Hiking. You don't see many mountains where I come from ... I guess I got lost."

They looked at each other again. "So you haven't heard? You don't know any of the news?"

"What news?" He tried to look dumb. It probably wasn't hard, he thought, under the circumstances.

One of the guards spit. "We've got a slight problem," he said, "with a revolution."

"Shut up, Tev. Listen, friend, these hills are more dangerous than you know right now. We'd better take you back to our camp. They'll know what to do with you."

He motioned for Will to hang onto the canteen. Will followed his new friends—or whatever they were—farther up the mountain.

"So you're a Three Cities citizen." The camp commander was middle-aged, bearded, and wore the same camouflage outfit his people did. He looked Will up and down. "You're not used to this sort of terrain."

"No, sir."

"Well, neither are most of the boys and girls here. We're mostly city people, from Everun. But those of us who aren't shooting rebels down there have to shoot rebels up here. It's the luck of the draw. The medtech handle your arm all right?"

"Yes, sir." The pulsing pain had cut down considerably.

"I'm not a cyr," he said, misunderstanding Will's pronunciation, "I'm a commander."

"Yes, si— Commander."

The commander stood up and walked around Will. "There's something military about you, Diamonder. I've been in state security for fifteen years, it's not something I would miss. Were you in the army up there in your City?"

"I'm a City Guard, commander. Internal security. We don't have an army as such."

"I didn't think I was mistaken. Good, you'll be useful."

"Sir? Commander?"

"Face it, son, you're not going to reach Everun Port any time soon. Things have gone a lot further a lot faster than anybody thought, even yesterday. You heard about troop landings on Western Continent? It's no secret anymore."

"The guards who brought me in mentioned something about it," he agreed.

"We thought this was a simple roundup here in the capital. A good two-thirds of the rebels were cleaned out yesterday, mostly down in the city itself. The rest of 'em are up here, or that's my opinion. So why aren't we happy?"

This was a rhetorical question. Will waited.

"Because, Diamonder, I'll tell you why. Because yesterday morning five of the chief government ministers were assassinated. Throats slit in their beds. Just like that."

Will remembered the empty halls in the villa of the Minister of Truth.

The commander said, "Things are in chaos. Everyone who could get out of Everun got out. More troops are landing on Western Continent. And why am I telling *you* this?" He paused. "Because I want you to understand my position. We need manpower. Welcome to state security, son."

"What? I'm a citizen of the Diamond."

"Got any ID?"

"Well," said Will, "not on me—"

"Welcome to state security. Tev will show you where to sleep and see what you know about weapons."

Suddenly Will felt faint again. He swayed. The commander got up, took hold of him, and walked him out to the firelight. "Tev! Jenny! Get this boy some food."

He let Will gently onto the ground. Will must have fallen asleep, because when he opened his eyes, he found the guard Tev standing over him with a bowl of something hot. He had a wild memory of running along a grid at Everun port, pounding after a ship that was already lifting—obviously a dream. He wrenched his mind back to the reality of Tev and supper, and took the bowl.

"We're low on spoons," said Tev. "But there's water to clean your hands later." He was staring at Will curiously. "You're one crazy outworlder, friend. Did you know you were flailing around in your sleep, beating on the ground and yelling? You tried to hit Jenny."

"What was I saying?"

Tev shrugged. "Couldn't make it out—real funny accent, not like what you're talking now."

"Maybe I wouldn't make a reliable soldier."

Will pulled out two finger of stew and put them in his mouth. Tev grinned. "The commander did say to make sure you were entirely awake before we gave you a rifle."

Tal inched around the ledge on the second floor of the Arbriths' villa. How did he let Adrian get him into these positions? Below him a floodlight showed on one of the Arbriths' personal guards walking the perimeter of the house. Tal glanced back toward the utility run he'd climbed over to pass the wall. Barely accessible, if none of the guards was looking when he came out. If he came out.

Most of the rooms he'd passed were bedrooms and sitting rooms. There was one large hall suitable for parties. Not promising; humans tended to keep their vaults in better-protected locations, usually in the basement—some ancient digging instinct, perhaps. Unfortunately the bottom floor was too well defended. He'd have to go in here and make his way down.

The lock on the bedroom window was pitiful. In any case, it they were serious about not wanting guests, why use glass? He opened the sash and swung into the empty room. He moved soundlessly to the door, not needing a light, and listened.

Maybe the family had already made a run off-planet. Maybe the guards were just left behind to guard the property.... Maybe anything, it hardly mattered. Time was passing. He opened the door to an empty hallway.

The backstairs were at the end. He took them down as far as they went, not exiting at the first floor, and opened an old hinged door slowly at the bottom. It was a large, cold room. No lights were on. There was one window, high on the other side, with an open curtain; dangerous if anybody walked by and saw him. But from the other side, in this darkness, a human would be unlikely to make him out. There was a long table in the middle of the room, covered with papers, books, and general flotsam; a smaller table near the corner, with a chair; a cot by the wall, not made up; and, he would bet his life, a vault on the blank wall to his left. In matters like this humans fell into a statistical predestiny.

He moved across the room toward the wall. A light snapped on.

He blinked and turned, his pupils adjusting rapidly. Through the brightness he saw the bundle of blankets on the cot move. It wasn't empty after all.

Sarah Jean Arbrith, Princess Casamara Tonnelly, sat up and swung her six-year-old feet to the floor. "Who are you?" she asked, eyes wide.

He went at once to the window and closed the curtain. If she had screamed, he would have stopped her. However, she didn't seem about to scream. He stared at her for a full ten seconds, then turned and surveyed the walls of the room.

"Are you going to hurt me?" she asked at last.

"I hadn't planned on it," said Tal, as he knocked on the left-hand wall.

She appeared a little nettled by his lack of interest. "Then why shouldn't I scream?"

"Because if you do, twelve ferocious bears will follow me into this room and tear you limb from limb."

She rocked for a moment, then recovered. "They will *not*. How can you tell such lies?"

There was no answer.

"What are you looking for?"

No answer.

"I'll bet I know," she said. "I'm not stupid. In fact I'm a genius."

"Really? So am I." He ran a hand along the floorboards. There might be a control there.

"I'm not making it up!"

"I didn't think you were. Ah!" He lifted a trapdoor, looked inside, pursed his lips delicately, and closed the door. He moved farther down the room and squatted again. He tapped the floor with his knuckles.

"It's the Sawyer Crown, isn't it?"

He looked up, suddenly giving her his full attention. It was as though a row of spotlights had hit her face, and she stepped back. He said, "Where is it?"

Now that she had control of the conversation, she deliberately waited a minute before answering. "You could look all night and not find it."

He straightened up. She said quickly, "And I could yell at the top of my lungs and have a dozen people in here in a second."

"But you're having too good a time to do that, I hope." He walked toward her, and she backed up a few steps.

She touched the edge of the table as she moved away. Her hand ran over one of the gamepieces and her fingers picked it up without any conscious command. "Have you ever played Hotem?"

He glanced at the glass box on the table. There were marbles set in various places on the top side of the square. "I've heard about it. I've never actually played it."

"I can teach you the rules."

"I forgot to mention that I'm in a hurry. Perhaps some other time, Princess."

"You know who I am! I knew you knew who I was. They sent you here to kill me, like the others, didn't they! Hyram told me it might happen—"

He said, "Shut up!" and she did, to both their surprise. "I'm here for the Sawyer Crown, madam, as you so clev-

erly realized. I don't give a damn about you personally.
So please be quiet, so I don't have to kill you, all right?"

"I see." She sat back down on the cot, looking distressed.

He said, "You implied you knew—" But the Princess
was crying. She pushed her stuffed animals off her cot
with a fine disregard, and sobbed into the pillow.

Tal stood there, wondering what he was supposed to
do. She raised a reddened, swollen, harelipped face, and
said through tears, "Nobody cares. I'm here all alone, and
nobody ever comes. Nobody even comes to *kill* me!"

He sat down next to her. "I'm sure you're exaggerating," he said. "I'm sure an assassin will be along any
time now. In fact, if you don't mind some advice, I would
get off-planet if I were you. The Tonnellys are unpopular
with the Republic, you know."

"Hyram told me to wait," she said into the pillow. "But
he hasn't come back, and neither has that bitch."

Tal sensed she was not referring to her terrier with that
last remark. He said, "Hyram told you to wait in here, because he thought this room would be safer."

"Yes. I can go out through the little window if I have
to. But it's been two days—and he never came to see me
before, anyway. They didn't let me have any friends,
and—"

"All right, all right." Would Adrian pat her head? Tal
patted her head. "You know, he might be busy. He's one
of the chiefs of government, after all."

"He just does what the Duke tells him." Her pillow
was getting damp.

Tal said, "You mentioned the Sawyer Crown—

She sat up abruptly. Tears and mucus were on her
cheeks. She wiped them with the sleeves of her nightgown and walked over to the table. She raised one of the
Hotem pieces and waved it. "You could play with me!"

"As I said, I'm in a hurry."

The Princess was suddenly cold. "You could be here all
night otherwise. Do you want this stupid Crown or not?"

Tal walked over and picked up one of the marbles,
rolling it between his fingers thoughtfully. It was made of
carnelian. "If I win—"

"I'll show you where the Crown is."

"What if you win?"

She considered. "I should get something. Empty your pockets." He did so. "Is that a real state-security handcom? I'll take it!"

"I'll have a hard time getting home without it," he pointed out.

"You haven't got anything else worth taking," said the Princess. She pulled over the chair from the desk, and motioned for him to take the stool. He sat on it awkwardly. "The red-and-black balls are mine. The green-and-black ones are yours. I go first."

"I sense that going first is a good thing," he said mildly. "Shouldn't we draw lots?"

"Never mind about that," said the Princess. "And, oh, listen. I know I'm just a kid, but I beat Hyram all the time, and he was planetary champion for eight years. I mean, in case you were worried about being fair."

Tal bent over the square. "I wasn't," he said.

Keylinn and Spider were waiting in Tal's office when Gabriel came in. "Hello," he said, and he went straight to the pile of books he'd left behind the couch and began putting them in the sack he'd brought.

"What are you doing?" asked Spider.

Gabriel beamed. "The Lady Iolanthe advertised among the link-boys for someone who knew how to read and would be interested in helping her put together a tutorial library for herself. She wants to go through every history book we've got access to—anyway, she wants someone to scan them with her and figure out which ones to concentrate on." He kept putting in books. "Isn't it wonderful? I can spend all the time I want to in the records now. *It's part of my job.*"

Keylinn said, "Does she know your history? Where you're from?"

Gabriel's smile went out. "I don't think so. Why? Was I supposed to tell her?"

"No," they said at once. Spider said, "Does Tal know about this?"

"I mentioned it to him when she was interviewing. Just before he went downhill. He seemed to think it was a good idea."

"He would," said Spider.

"Is something wrong?" asked Gabriel.

"No, no. Not a thing."

Keylinn said, "He means that we congratulate you on your new job, and we're sorry we won't be seeing as much of you here. Isn't that what you meant, Spider?"

"Yeah, that's what I meant. Good luck in your new post."

"Thank you," he said uncertainly. He swung the pack over his back and staggered under the load. "I'll be back for the others."

He left and the door slid shut behind him.

"Poor little thing," said Spider sadly. "So young to be a spy."

"Let's hope he has a career to go to," said Keylinn pointedly. The vault door hung open, a mute reminder of their problems.

"If anything happens to Tal," said Spider, "I'll be on line in Transport, finagling a ride to the closest station."

"You'll be second on line behind me," said Keylinn. "And I'm sure nothing would please him more than to hear us admit it."

"Good thing he's not here." Spider cast her a quick look, then looked away and said, "Key?"

"Yes?"

"How long do you have to go on your contract?"

Silence.

"Well, what are you going to do when your time's up? What's *Tal* going to do?"

A longer silence.

"You know, maybe we should call him on that handcom. It's been hours since you gave him the word. We're just lucky nobody's shown up from Pearl."

"I don't know. He might be busy." Keylinn stretched her legs in the desk chair.

"He might be having trouble."

"In which case a chat with us will be of dubious benefit."

"You've been hanging around him too long."

She stopped swinging in the chair, placed her fingertips on the desk and stared at them as though they were alien.

"Sorry. I was trying to extrapolate. It's hard to break in and out of pattern."

Spider said, "You know, a couple of times in the last few weeks I've thought you were getting a little close to *taberani*. Isn't that the word for it, the third level of Graykey mist—"

"Why, Spider, you can read after all," she said coldly. He couldn't know what a wounding thing that was to say to a Graykey.

He flushed. "That's exactly what I mean."

After a moment she said, "I beg your pardon, Spider. There may be some truth in what you say. I've done my best to walk the line, but the danger is always there. The circumstances here are not what they are at home." She inspected her hands, flexing them as though they belonged to someone else. "Let's leave the topic alone, if you don't mind. I would prefer it that way."

He started to pace. "Well, I still think we should call him."

Keylinn sighed. She activated the desk link and put through the greeting sequence to Baret Station's communications path. In a moment she heard Tal's voice.

"Yes?"

"Are you all right?" she asked.

"I'm fine."

Spider moved over to join her. "Are you having any problems?"

"Yes."

"What?"

"My so-called allies are interrupting me."

"Oh," said Spider. He switched off.

Keylinn leaned back in the chair and closed her eyes. "Spider? The other day in Schuyler Plaza? I'm surprised you hid under the car. What if the whole thing got sprayed?"

"Don't think that wasn't going through my mind."

She pulled the chair up straight and let her feet down with a thump. "He's been down there for hours. What can he be doing?"

"Your move," said the Princess.

"Don't rush me." Tal studied the board. He'd already

lost two sides' worth of stones. This side he was taking his time between moves. Suddenly he smiled, reached over, and moved two green stones. "My set," he said, and tilted the cube to the next side.

The Princess looked at him angrily.

"Not a bad sort of game," said Tal, three sides later, as he took the Princess's final defense stone. "I win."

She got up quickly, scattering pieces on the floor. "Nobody beats me at Hotem! Nobody!"

"Maybe the loss will be good for your character."

"Ha! Were *you* ever beaten? Was it good for *your* character?"

For a moment he seemed to be actually casting about for a response. Then he said, "You were going to show me the Crown."

She stalked coldly out of the room. Tal waited. He stationed himself near the window, not that that would do a lot of good if a dozen guards started pouring in.

In a moment she was back. She was carrying another stuffed toy—a teddy bear. She handed it to Tal.

It was ice-cold. He said, "Thanks, but I'd prefer the Crown."

She put a finger on the bear's stomach. "It's in there."

"The space isn't big enough."

"You don't know anything about it," she stated, and there was truth in that. "It's in his tummy. Hyram put it there."

"*Why* would Hyram put the Sawyer Crown in a teddy bear?"

She looked disgusted with his stupidity, rolled her eyes and stamped a foot. "*Listen.* I said for him to put my bear Totie in the freeze. And he said he would, because that could do two things at once. Nobody'd ever believe there was anything valuable in it."

This story seemed to be veering off into unreality. "Why would you want to put your bear into a freezer?"

"Because he'd get old and messed up, of course, if I didn't. Everything does."

Yes. Of course it does. She said, "I saw other dolls get all dirty and old, and Hyram said it was because of entropy. And I told him entropy wouldn't get Totie for a long, long time if we put him in the freezer. So I gave him all my best animals—the giraffe and the dragon and the pouncer—and my other two bears—and he put them in the freeze for me. See?"

"But you can't play with them anymore if they're in the freezer."

She stated, "You have to make sacrifices in this world."

Yes, a six-year-old was explaining this to him. "I see," he said.

She looked around at the pile of animals she'd pushed onto the floor earlier. "I only keep the ones out here I don't like." She made a face at them. "For the rest of my life, I'll know that my bears and things are safe in the freeze. Except for him," she pointed at Totie. "He'll get old and die now, but I promised if you won."

Tal examined the stuffed toy in his arms. "Actually, he won't get old."

"That's right, I forgot. You'll have to rip him up."

There was a note of relish in her voice. She seemed to be dealing with the idea without any difficulty, so he said, "Would it bother you if I cut him open here?"

"You don't believe me!"

"Well, I'd like to open him here."

"Huh! Go ahead. But it hurts the Crown if you get it warm, that's why it was in the freeze."

He considered that. The bear would continue to provide cool insulation, providing he didn't disembowel it here and now. He took out his knife, made a rift along the belly, and stuck in one finger.

He touched something hard, cold, and metallic. Whatever it was, it didn't belong in a toy. It would be interesting if this were a bomb, set to go off when the temperature had risen sufficiently—say when he was a certain distance from the house. He imagined a succession of bears, given to presumptuous thieves. He peered through the rift in the bear's fur and made out a kind of prong. He drew it out slightly. It was marked with a Curosa symbol. He pushed it back into the bear's belly and pulled the skin closed.

"Very well, Princess, I'll accept your bear."

He went to the window and drew the curtain aside slightly. Three guards had met beside a tree nearby for a smoke and a talk. Very lax, these people were. "You might get your Crown back after all, Princess. It looks relatively crowded out there."

She said, "It wouldn't be fair to take it away from you. You won the game."

"I don't think they'll care about that."

"It's true," she said, "they're not very understanding." Then she smiled. "How about this? It's been ages since I've thrown a tantrum. I'll go out on the balcony upstairs and start screaming. You have no idea the attention it gets. People come running from all around."

"I think a balcony on the other side of the house would be even better."

"Oh. Yes, I guess it would. All right." She moved for the door, then stopped short. "I forgot," she said contritely. "I'm Princess Casamara Tonnelly." She held out her hand in the correct Imperial manner for a formal introduction.

Tal took it, and hesitated. "Tayel Shuan," he said, and kissed it.

She flew through the door. He heard running footsteps, and very shortly thereafter, the sound of screams rising on the night air. You would think she was being murdered.

He waited another moment, then let himself out the window.

Chapter 47

I hate extremes; yet I had rather stay
With tombs than cradles, to wear out a day.

JOHN DONNE

Tal had recommended to Adrian that he keep the Sawyer Crown (and Tal said there was a seventy percent probability it *was* the Sawyer Crown) in a below-freezing temperature. So Adrian took the chilly, charcoal-colored links of the rather bizarre chain his demon presented him with, and placed it in a small cold-box. Then he waited for the Oracle from Pearl to come and declare its authenticity.

And waited. He couldn't say that he wasn't *glad* the Oracle was seven hours late; but now that he had the Crown (possibly), the suspense was unbearable.

He walked up and down in one of the anterooms off the Cavern of Audience. He wished he could loose the marble panthers, but today was not a day to indulge himself. Brandon Fischer, Iolanthe, and a handful of advisers and other witnesses huddled uncomfortably in the room, murmuring to each other from time to time and looking as nervous as Adrian.

At last Adrian went to a link and activated it with his fist. Brandon Fischer pursed his lips; he had often reminded Adrian that it was inappropriate for the Protector to send his own link-messages. Nevertheless he was not going to bring the matter up at this time.

"Reverend Father?" asked Adrian with controlled politeness, when he'd gotten through to the City of Pearl.

"What?" asked the voice on the other end.

"A prophetic-level Oracle was supposed to arrive on the Diamond several hours ago. We're still waiting for them."

"Well, what of it? They'll get there eventually."

The advisers glanced at each other. Typical behavior from the City of Pearl.

Adrian said, "We were hoping to accelerate the process."

"Patience ought to be cultivated by lay persons." The voice was superior.

"A fee was paid for a prophetic-level Oracle," said Adrian. "Maybe we should arrange for its return." And he dropped the use of the plural subject and said, "I'm not standing in this room waiting all day and night. I've got a life to live."

The witnesses looked shocked, but the voice from the City of Pearl merely said, "Oh, very well. You don't need someone there in person anyway. Just leave the Crown at room temperature for a while; then you'll know if it's genuine or not."

"Why?" Adrian frowned. "What will that do?"

But the connection had been cut at the other end.

Adrian stared at nothing for a minute. Then he got up, opened the cold-box, took out the chain, and laid it on the back of a chair. "Make sure the recorders are going," he said to Fischer.

"They are," replied the First Adviser. He walked over to Adrian. "I only hope we're not making fools of ourselves for permanent record."

Adrian set down a wooden chair backward and planted himself in it, a hands-breadth from the chain at eye-level. He didn't take his eyes off it. He said to Fischer, "Tal won this by playing Hotem with an Imperial Princess."

"Do you believe every story a demon tells you?" Fischer's voice was worried.

"He's never lied to me that I know of." Adrian's gaze remained on the chain. Fischer sighed and went back to stand with the others.

Iolanthe was beside him. He said to her, with a trace of bitterness, "*Tal* says an Imperial Princess gave it to him."

She turned to him. "Are we off the recorders over here?"

"Supposedly."

"What do you know about Tal?"

Fischer looked faintly surprised, and shrugged. "What can I know? I assume Tal is short for Taliesin. That's a fairly common Empire name, especially in the area where Adrian picked him up."

"I thought Tal was from the Republic."

Fischer looked surprised again. "He doesn't have the air of a Republican. Although I suppose, with a demon, how can one tell? It was an independent planet . . . I just assumed he was Empire-born. Now that I think of it, I don't believe Adrian ever told me."

"What planet was it where Adrian found him?"

"Brevity. A real scum-hole. On top of a sector-gate, useful for us because we needed some general trading. Half the undesirables from that corner of the Empire were there; apparently the local government was not strong on ID, as long as one could pay. Just the sort of place you'd expect to find a demon, in short."

"Brevity," she repeated, as though impressing it on her memory.

"It was our second stopover since he'd become Protector," said Fischer. "At the first one he brought back a new kind of dog for the kennels. At the second one he brought back Tal."

"Tell me, Brandon—" But she stopped short, for Adrian had moved.

The Protector reached for the chain, lifted it, and put it on his head. It fit well, the links lying about an inch above his brows like a charcoal-colored wreath of flowers.

Brandon Fischer walked back to him and bent over to whisper. "This isn't the coronation, you know."

"I know. I only wanted to see what if felt like. It was just an impulse, Brandon; we'll present the public record as starting at a later point."

"You want me to turn off the recorders?"

"God, no, we need an unbroken master in case anybody challenges us." He smiled. "Relax, my friend. Save your worry for whether the thing's genuine."

"I've got plenty of worry to go around." He returned to his place beside Iolanthe. "I don't like this," he told her. "I wish he would take it off."

"He has made the point to me more than once that the Sawyer Crown is his, deeded by Saul Veritie—"

"—whose right to deed it is disputable—" muttered Fischer.

"—and I guess he's making that point again now. What can we do?"

"About as much as we usually can do." Fischer suddenly realized that he was treating this Opal-born girl as an ally. When had that happened? Somewhere along the way she'd convinced him of her regard for Adrian.

Her violet eyes narrowed now. "Brandon, am I crazy, or is the Crown *moving?*"

His gaze snapped back to Adrian. What was she talking about? It was just a chain . . . a chain whose links now heaved, like a ripple passing over water. Fischer was there in a second, pulling at it. Adrian's hand went to his head. "What are you. . ."

The chain gave way abruptly, as though it had been unfastened in back, and closed itself around Adrian's wrist.

"It's *alive*," breathed Io. It wrapped itself like a charcoal snake around the wrist, one end moving against the flesh of his arm as if seeking something. Fischer tried to pull it again, but it was plastered onto the flesh and too slippery to get hold of.

The dark bracelet twirled off Adrian's wrist and disappeared below the cuff of his white shirt. A sluglike shape could be seen moving speedily up the arm. He groped for his diamond buttons, ripped them open, and pulled down the shirt. By now some of the braver witnesses had gathered around his chair. One of them reached for the thing as it appeared at Adrian's throat.

"No!" said Adrian, in a voice that made the man jump. "Get away." He added grimly, "Keep the recorder going."

"What?" asked one of the witnesses, confused.

"You're blocking the view for the recorders," said Iolanthe in a choked voice. "Stand back."

She didn't want them to stand back, she wanted them to rip that alien thing off Adrian's neck, but she couldn't stop herself from explaining to them. He'd so clearly wanted it done.

The thing inched back along the skin to his forehead, where it fastened, this time immovable. One end of it trailed down like the ties left from a knot; it trailed to the back of his neck where the two tendons stood out, and plugged itself happily into the soft pocket of flesh between them.

Adrian screamed. It came without any warning and they were all shocked. People moved back and forth helplessly, and a keening sound rose in the chamber. Fischer had thrown out Adrian's orders and was trying to pry the thing out with his nails.

Coronation Day: On G level, Mrs. Hastings lost hold of her precious teapot and collapsed on the flowered carpet, having forgotten how to stand. Mrs. Cathcart, on her way to visit her old friend, stopped short in the middle of Mercati Boulevard. She would have been run down by a man with a recycling cart, but he'd halted his pedaling and his feet dangled in the air. In the home of Howard Talmadge and Dominick Potiyevsky, Dominick had pushed his wheelchair next to Howard's tattered armchair and was shaking him desperately. "Howard! What's wrong! Howard! Jesus, Howard, answer me!"

On the City of Diamond, over nine-tenths of the population found themselves a lot more intimate with the Protector than they'd ever planned on being. Not telepathically, not even in a clear enough way to know what was happening or who was involved. But emotionally, emphatically—it was a shift in viewpoint, a shift that came like an earthquake.

It lasted all of four seconds. Nobody who'd been through it was ever able to explain it satisfactorily to anybody who hadn't. Mrs. Cathcart became aware of her presence on the Boulevard and the proximity of the recycling cart. She dived to the pedestrian walk with a reflex she'd never learned. The cart handler, who was paid by the mile and never stopped if he could help it, halted and jumped down. "Are you all right?" A call went out for a doctor, but Mrs. Cathcart stood up, smoothed her dress, and assured the crowd, in a rather distracted voice, that it wasn't necessary. Howard Talmadge came to himself and touched Dominick's cheek. "You're crying, Dom. I'm okay. I just had the strangest— I don't know what it was."

Brandon Fischer's eyes were wet, too. He'd failed to pull this awful thing off Adrian, and then he'd been thoroughly shook up by—this whatever it was. He looked to the Protector now and saw that the Crown had come off; it was lying in Adrian's lap. Fischer reached over.

"Don't touch it," said Adrian. "I don't think it's safe." He nodded to one of the others and said, "Bring me the cold-box."

"Adrian—I just—" The man he'd addressed stuttered.

"I know," said Adrian. "But get the box."

The man brought it over. Adrian put it open-side-down on his lap and tilted his legs to let the Crown spill into it. Then he closed the box, leaned back in the chair, and let out a long breath.

"You're bleeding from the back," said Iolanthe. She'd come up next to him and now she took out a handkerchief and applied it to the back of his neck.

He craned up at her and took the hand on his shoulder. "Sweetheart, did you—"

"Yes. It was interesting, but let's not do it again very soon, all right?" Her voice was unsteady.

Brandon Fischer stumbled as he walked across the chamber. Adrian noticed that nobody commented or thought it odd; they all walked the same way. What happened hadn't been painful or horrifying in itself, but they all were reacting physically like people who'd just been through some great disaster.

"Doctors are going to be busy," said Adrian. "I think there'll be some people in trouble over this."

Fischer turned slowly. "You don't think," he began, and then went on, "you don't think it reached out of this room!"

"Yes," said Adrian. "I think it reached out of this room."

And they began the calls and the reports and the analyzing that would lead them to the figuring of just what *had* happened.

On a hill half a day's walk south of Everun lay the ruins of a house belonging to the Hansard family, the oldest human family on Baret Two. They had been war chiefs during the time before the Empire, and before the general settlement of the planet they had been farmers. Several of the later Hansards had dragged their enemies in chains through the city that preceded Everun before hanging them from the fort tower by the sea for birds to dispose of. That was all very long ago, though, by human standards. In the year the Three Cities came to Baret, the only living Hansard was a man called Hyram, who had changed his surname so as to be allowed to marry into the governor's family. He had not even visited the ruins of their old great house, except once on a childhood picnic.

An overgrown door on the side of the hill led to the Hansard tomb. There the mightiest of the Hansard dead were stacked in stone drawers, laid out in a more peaceful aspect than many of them had assumed while alive. Carved faces on the outsides of the drawers glared down at any observers. *Rob this tomb, if you dare.* In the farthest interior reaches of this large mausoleum the hillside came down again, as though pushed by a fist, and a human would have to bend very far to see into the end. There they would find a drawer by itself, of green and black swirling marble, with a Curosa symbol on the front.

Underneath, in English, letters read: "This was placed by Adrian Sawyer, in his ninety-fifth year. Rest well, good and faithful servant."

No humans did come to the tomb, and if any had, they would not be ones who could read English or recognize a Curosa symbol.

The drawer was open now. A creature lay in it, man-like, shivering, and despite its deviations from human facial expression, clearly unhappy. It raised a hand and stared at four grayish fingers, tinged faintly with blue. It put its arms around itself and shivered more violently still.

The Crown was activated. He should be there to supervise its use, that was his task. Why was no one here to help him? If the human brothers had reached sufficient grace to use the Crown, why were they not considerate enough to send people here to assist him in his waking?

His body spasmed suddenly, and he clasped himself, whimpering, and then let go. The Crown was becoming quiescent again. There was no question of lapsing back asleep, though, not now; he must try to rise. He put his hands on the side of the sarcophagus and tried to pull himself up. He was too stiff. He lay down again and rolled from side to side, trying to loosen muscles that seemed to be in another body, somewhere else. He reached again. Eventually he would succeed, eventually he would get up, for that was his duty.

It took an hour. In the end it was anger born of frustration that forced him out of his coffin and got him standing—his weight on his hands clutching the tomb, mostly, but standing—in the dark hillside. Now he must search for the opening.

Brother? he asked mentally. There was no answer. He was aware suddenly of the weight of the hillside, the limits and the darkness of his resting place. *Brother!*

There was only silence. For a moment he wanted to scream, and that was a shocking thing for one of his breed to do, but he fought down the panic. Perhaps his brother was still asleep. It had been a long time, after all. No doubt he would awaken soon and tell this unworthy one what needed to be done.

He was not alone. No, he wasn't.

* * *

"Pearl says they felt it," said Fischer a few hours later. "They don't need the record, they're ready to declare the Crown authentic."

"Shed any light on what happened?" asked Adrian.

"Useful knowledge from an Oracle? Don't hold your breath."

The second security minister said, "Whatever happened on the Opal, it wasn't like here. The council denies everything and asks what we're talking about, but my sources there tell me something did take place. Not of an intensity like ours."

"Not everyone from here felt it," said Fischer. "We're trying to get a partial list of those unaffected, and try to figure out why."

Another minister protested, "We don't even know why anyone *was* affected!"

Fischer shrugged.

The minister went on, "And should we be asking people these leading questions? Should we admit something took place when we don't even know what it is?"

"If you think you can do the job better," began Fischer.

Adrian said, "Gentlemen, please." He needed some rational counsel. He looked around irritably. "Where's Tal?"

Three of the unaffecteds were in Tal's office, blissfully unaware of the general turmoil around the City.

Tal put his head into the vault and drew it out again. "She opened it just like that?" he said.

Keylinn replied, "Well, not just like that. It took several hours."

"*Hours.*"

"You would think you'd been doomed to death. There are a lot of bright people in the world who share some of your technical knowledge, you know."

Spider said, "She said a number of things about you."

"Really."

"She said that you wouldn't trust your own mother."

"If you knew my mother, you wouldn't trust her either." He put his head into the vault again and inspected the connections.

"She also said that you have a fatal weakness."

Tal was running his hand over the doorway, checking. He paused. "Did she, now. And did she say what it was?"

"Yes." Spider smiled. "But I think my life will be more enjoyable if you don't know it."

Tal glanced casually at Keylinn, who shrugged and remarked, "She didn't say it to me."

He closed the vault and took the seat by the desk link. He sat there for several minutes. He didn't say what he was doing, but Spider would have bet his life that Tal was reviewing the security subprogram.

Keylinn had gone back to her reading. Spider said, "Tal, is it true that you won the Sawyer Crown by playing some kind of marble game with a six-year-old?"

"Yes."

"So tell me," said Spider, after a minute. "Did you cheat?"

Chapter 48

I feel like one
Who treads alone
Some banquet hall deserted
Whose lights are fled,
Whose garlands dead
And all but he departed.

THOMAS MOORE

Will Stockton sat in the crook of a tree near the bottom of the mountain they called Butter Hill. A multitude of stars gave him just enough light to see movement down the road that led to Everun—when there *was* movement. Just now there wasn't, and that pleased him.

It had been eight days since he was forcibly welcomed into state security's little army. Ironically, he was a sergeant again. His unit had merged with another six days ago, and their own commander had taken charge of the whole force. Will had found himself promoted, along with most of his comrades, no doubt for political reasons. The other unit had *not* had a wave of promotions.

It wasn't that bad. They'd had to explain to him the difference between yards and meters, but on the whole he'd picked things up quickly enough to surprise himself. Some of the city kids in the unit were still disoriented, especially at night when the constantly illuminated streets of Everun were far away and the mountainside seemed full of things to stumble over. But Will had been trained by the Opal City Guard, whose idea of antisabotage practice consisted (among other things) of letting their cadets loose in a totally blacked-out tunnel three miles long, full of booby traps and assigned enemies. Exposure to darkness had no fears for Will. As for the rumors of rebel snipers lining the road beyond—the only access to Everun from this part of the mountain, called "the Alley"—it made him properly nervous, but that was all. The rebels didn't even have heat-IDs on their rifles. If they did, they would've been shooting every stray night-hunting animal in the hills.

Including Will. But as it was, there was more than an even chance of keeping one's skin. And the others in the unit were all right; he could get used to having women on patrol, and even more used to having them in camp afterward. Even the language was like the Guard back home in more ways than he'd anticipated. He'd been shocked to find that some of the profanity he'd thought native to Sangaree, and of modern origin at that, were in common use on Baret Two and apparently had been for generations.

The only problem came when he started to think about time. He tried not to do that, the way he tried not to look up into the sky, because either action tended to bring on an attack of the Panic. Bad enough to endure when he had the luxury of doing so safely, but when he was on watch, like tonight, it could be fatal.

Eight days. The Cities would have pulled back most of their shorties and their shuttles, accelerated their business contracts with Baret Station . . . they could be preparing for Blackout even now.

Will forced nine or ten deep breaths and made his mind

turn to the hypothetical snipers down in the Alley, a less alarming concept.

Forty minutes later he found himself watching a shape make its way down the mountain. Was it going to find Will's tree in the darkness, or keep going all the way to the Alley? This could be interesting.

No, he or she stopped by the blueoak and hissed. Will slid down silently. This could become even more interesting, because while the rebels had no heat-IDs, there was no guarantee they didn't have some advance people close enough to spot moving human shapes. Will stayed by the trunk of the tree and waited.

It was one of Will's new superior officers, a captain from the unit his group had merged with. They were about the same age. Will didn't know his name.

In a low voice the captain said, "Aren't you supposed to salute a superior officer?"

"I give up," said Will. "Am I?"

"Yes, Sergeant, you are."

Will shrugged. "Well, if you want me to, I will."

"What the hell is that supposed to mean?"

Will said, "There are supposed to be snipers all through the Alley, Captain. For all we know there's one out there looking up our asses at this very minute. If you want me to let him know which of us is the superior officer, I will."

The captain glowered. Then he said, "Your boots are filthy."

Will blinked. He was silent.

"Did you hear me, Sergeant?"

"Yes, Captain."

"Do you have anything to say about that?"

Where do they find them? Will thought. He said, "This afternoon these boots were so clean you could see them shine halfway down the mountain. After supper I was told to take the advance watch, and the first thing I did was to put some mud on them. Now, I don't have a nice uniform like yours, Captain, but I'm sure you've noticed that a lot of officers have taken off that white collar-stripe. I'd suggest you do the same."

The captain turned and left. Another half-hour passed, with dawn still five hours away. The captain returned, and handed Will a penlight. "You're to move down toward the Alley in fifty-meter intervals. If you see any rebels, take note of their positions and stop. If they look like easy pickings, you can do some sniper practice of your own. Go as far as you can toward Everun Tunnel, then make your way back."

Christ, did I offend you that much about the boots? thought Will. He said, "What's the light for?"

"For your way in again—when you're inside the advance perimeter, you can flash it, and I'll know where you are."

Will stared at him. This was going too far. He said, as clearly as possible, "If I flash it, *everybody* will know where I am."

"I can't challenge you until you flash it."

"Then don't challenge me. Please."

"I can't let somebody back into the camp perimeter without challenging them, Sergeant, that's basic regulation procedure. Now take this—"

"Sir, I'm telling you right now. I'm not flashing this stupid thing, and if you come within a hundred meters of me while I'm scouting, I'll blow your fucking head off."

The captain's neck flushed a deeper shadow in the darkness, and the shade began creeping up his face. He turned sharply and left. Fifteen minutes later he was back again, accompanied by the commander. "Tell the commander what you told me, Sergeant."

Will turned to him. "I said that if he came within a hundred meters of me while I was scouting I'd blow his fucking head off."

The commander looked at the captain in disgust. "This is a direct order, Sergeant: If he comes within *two* hundred meters of you, blow his fucking head off."

The commander went on his way, leaving the captain to follow. Will checked the road down to the Alley as far as he thought prudent, then returned and spent a quiet night in his tree.

At dawn he was relieved and he went to grab a few hour's sleep at camp. He was awakened, far too soon, by his new friend Tev.

"Commander wants us to hear what he has to say," said Tev. So Will got up, rolled up his blanket, and splashed water on his eyes. They'd been aching from lack of proper sleep for the past eight days.

The commander had the fifteen people in camp at that time gathered in a circle outside his tent. He nodded when Will arrived, and said, "Good. We're all here. When the others come in, bring 'em to me, and I'll update them myself—you do it, Tev, you had a full sleep last night."

Tev looked as though he could dispute the point, but nodded.

The commander said, "We've finally gotten some word from on high, and I'll tell you the way it is: Just about all the government has pulled out of Everun. It's a dead city, strategically, and we're to leave it to the snipers to pop at each other in. We've been ordered to join the regular army, which is ninety kilometers north of here near Sham Waterfall. That's where Duke Peter is."

Murmurs at this: "Duke Peter's alive?"

"So I'm told," said the commander.

One of the women protested, "But the city? We're supposed to abandon the city? Our families are still down there! Our friends!"

The commander said, "Those are our orders."

Tev spoke up. "They can't be serious. Commander, there aren't that many rebels *left* in Everun. If we just clean up the ones here in the hills, we can march down to the city as nice as you please. But if we leave, they'll just go back and we'll never get them out—not without firepower."

Will saw looks exchanged around the circle, as the people there considered the picture of bringing destruction down on the city they'd grown up in.

The commander said tartly, "You seem to be explaining this to me as though I had some say in the matter. I don't. Chain of command has been reestablished."

"But, Commander, can't you—"

"No, Tev, I didn't make the slightest attempt to clarify our situation to Command. No, I'm a complete idiot. No, I didn't talk to them for as long as I was allowed to."

Tev swallowed. The commander said, "This is irrelevant. We have our orders. Boy and girls . . . my friends, we start north as soon as our scouts are back." He turned and started back toward his tent. He pressed his hands against his back, as though stiffness and pain had settled there unexpectedly. And maybe age, too, for Will saw he was walking like an old man.

North. Will went to pick up his blanket and the remainder of his rations. *North. North.* It was starting to pound into his head like an icepick. Everun Port was south. *North.*

He hoped he wasn't going to have some kind of fit right here in front of everybody. The rations were gotten into his pack with great difficulty; his fingers seemed numb and hard to control. *North.*

He took a ragged breath and slipped out of camp, past the commander's tent, heading down the slope toward Sniper Alley and the road to Everun.

The One Newly Awakened stood on a hill just south of the city called Everun. He shivered in the night air. His awareness of the Crown had moved over the past few days; sometimes it seemed deep under the earth, other times high in the heavens. Clearly it was aboard some type of craft.

He pulled his stolen clothing more tightly around his shoulders. The human shirt fit him badly, hanging over his bony frame. He'd stolen these from a house he'd passed, a dwelling with no one in it, and he'd taken a cloak from there, too. A dog had been there—he recognized the species, a subworker class used by humans—and he'd fed it from a jar of meaty stuff he'd found in the kitchen. It was no more than his duty, for it looked as though no one else was coming to feed it, and the need of the dog had been palpable, its aura sickly grayish-white.

He had taken food from the kitchen himself, ingesting the rotting fruit and stale bread he'd discovered. He considered the dog a long time, but he did not feed on any sacred food; under the circumstances, it seemed not only unlawful but cruel. The creature seemed far from its own kind of sanity as it was.

He was relieved now to see that a city stood where a city had been planned. A fenced area to the southeast marked out a landing field, gridded for short-range craft.

Excellent. He almost called for his brother again, before remembering he had promised himself not to do that. There was still a fair margin of time for his brother to awaken, and no need to make himself nervous by calling vainly in the dark. Meanwhile, there was a city, a port, and a Crown, and much do to do if his brother was to be proud of him when he did rise.

He hoped that all was well here, and he could declare himself as soon as possible. He was very hungry.

On the City of Diamond, Tal was becoming a familiar figure in the council meetings. "Purely as a consultant," Adrian kept saying—but he said it in a way that did not allow for debate.

It was Tal who now finished the report on what he so tersely called "the Crown effect." Adrian had put the assignment in his lap at the meeting two days previously, adding that "Officer Diamond is excellent at isolating variables."

"The pattern seems clear enough," Tal said. "Any human who participated in a 'sharing' ceremony within the last two years experienced the effect to some degree. Since Curosa blood elements are involved in a sharing, even though of minute quantity, it seems reasonable to suppose that these elements are somehow involved in the process. I would advise bringing a medtech into the City to begin analysis of some of the blood used in sharing, as well as physical analyses of a sample of those affected. I would also strongly advise that Adrian have a complete check-over by this medtech."

Adrian glanced at him, an eyebrow raised. Tal had not mentioned this part of his report earlier.

Tal folded his hands, and disagreement broke out at once.

"An Outsider? A *medtech!* Are you mad? Even for a demon—"

"I really don't think we can see our way—"

"Even if we assume this report is factual, I don't see—"

"Gentlemen!" said Adrian. "Brandon, I think you were first."

Brandon Fischer pushed the paper before him irritably

around the table. He invariably brought a blank sheet of paper with him to these meetings, and invariably never wrote on it. He said, "Even if we assume this link between a sharing and—what happened—is accurate, and even if we assume that there are no other significant links, which I by no means stipulate—"

"Yes, Brandon?"

He scowled. "Well, why should we decide it's the blood elements that are responsible? Can't we say that people who have participated in more sharings have reached a higher degree of spiritual awareness than those who haven't? Why can't that be the relevant factor?"

Tal opened his mouth and Adrian jabbed him with a pen under the table. This was not the time to display to the council his demon's sarcasm on the subject of certain tenets of Redemptionism. Nor would it be polite to Brandon.

Adrian said, "That's certainly a point to consider. And I'm very interested in any other factors you may perceive here—over time, we're going to have to look carefully at all the possibilities. But my suggestion for the present is, let's keep Tal's report quiet for now and concentrate on our other problems. Heaven knows we have enough to do, with closing out our agreements with Baret Station and readying for Blackout. Does that sound reasonable?"

Fischer did not look happy. He said, "May I assume from that, Adrian, that you have no intention of taking out the Crown again until we've had time to study this further?"

"You may assume that," said Adrian blandly. "After all, we've gotten all the political mileage out of it we could want, and isn't that why we searched for the Crown in the first place? Opal will have a hard time claiming spiritual superiority over us now, gentlemen."

There were some smiles at that, although not from Brandon Fischer. What Adrian did not say was that any potential rivals for the Protectorship would have an even harder time now; which was all to the good, they didn't want another Uprising—but using a Curosa legacy for that purpose disturbed him.

Lord Salter spoke up. "Is it absolutely definite, then,

that we're abandoning our trade with Baret Two? Is the situation that difficult?"

Fischer said, "We expect the entire Western Continent to declare for the Republic any day now."

"Well, so much the better, isn't it?" said Lord Salter. "Things will quiet down, and we can deal with whoever's in charge."

"Things are not quieting down on the Eastern Continent," said Adrian. "They're getting worse. Were we gunrunners, we might find a profit here. But we're not. And Baret Two has become too volatile a trading partner."

He saw an ironic expression pass over Tal's face, and he could almost read the thought: *Not that we had anything to do with this.* Don't say anything, said Adrian mentally. Please. They're doing what I want, don't distract them.

Lord Salter said, "Some of our vastule-produced components can be used in Empire weaponry; so I understand."

"It's too dangerous."

"I don't see why."

Adrian said, "Tal?"

Tal looked at Lord Salter. "Worthy though your aims are, it would destroy our agreements with the Republic and the Empire. In order to remain neutral we would have to supply both sides, and the Republic already has all the weapons it needs. We would end up supporting the losing side, and we don't know how soon that side is going to lose. It seems more prudent to leave now, while we're in control of our goods and our timing, than to race out pursued by Republican cannon." He paused. "Or so it seems to me. Perhaps your lordship has a different view of the matter."

Brandon Fischer pretended to a great interest in his blank sheet of paper while Lord Salter reddened. It was amazing how insulting Tal could be when there was nothing in his actual words you could object to.

"Well," said Adrian pleasantly, "I think we all have the general picture. Is there any disagreement with the Blackout plan as I presented it earlier? Brandon, will you pass out copies?"

* * *

Afterward, Adrian took Tal aside. "I'd prefer not to be surprised in the middle of a meeting."

"You like to surprise *me*. Continually."

The Protector looked sour. "That's very true. But I have few enough pastimes, don't I?"

"You didn't answer my point. About being checked over by a medtech. You don't know what damage that creature might have done, Adrian."

Adrian's hand moved involuntarily to the back of his neck. There was a bandage there, under the collar. He said, annoyed, "When I want a doctor, a witch, or a medtech, I'll send for them myself. And I don't need demonic advice about my own bodily functions."

He left Tal alone in the council room.

Text of a memo from the Lord Armorer to Inventory Distribution:

To: Raoul Simponella, Chief of Distribution
From: Benjamin Lawless, Lord Armorer
Re: Clarification of Rules Regarding Hand Weapons
Date: The Feast of Saint Kimberley, City Year 536

My most esteemed colleague:

As you point out, numerous citizens are traveling back and forth to Baret Station, under a time limit which makes control difficult. We would not want to interfere with the right of our citizens to defend themselves under the dangerous circumstances under which these Outsiders live. It is for this very reason that a weapons outlet was put on the Transport deck several years ago, so that citizens exiting our City could defend themselves and return safely. Our policy is that they then deposit the rented weapon in our outlet.

I have consulted my fellows, and we do not consider it relevant that the workers are stopped at the Station docks and their weapons confiscated by Station Security. They have paid our office for the right to carry them, and they may carry them where they will, practical or no.

Nor do we consider it necessary to issue a warning with each rental request, explaining this confiscation procedure to them. This has never been our policy before and the paperwork it would entail would force us to raise our rental fee.

As these weapons are generally returned to our citizens by Station Security upon their leaving, I see no great harm in this practice. I am sure that the stress our workers feel on leaving the protection of the City is much alleviated by their being allowed to carry a hand weapon. Your suggestion that this confiscation-and-return procedure slows down our Blackout preparation effort is, it I may say, mistaken.

Your remarks on any matters relevant to this department are always valuable. Your advisers may have misled you slightly on this one matter. May I say that I congratulate you on the fine organizational job you are doing in Inventory Distribution—your reputation has reached me—and add that I look forward to seeing you at the Kimberley Ball.

Text of Reply:

To: Benjamin Lawless, Lord Armorer
From: Raoul Simponella, Chief of Distribution
Re: Your Memo on Clarification of Rules Regarding
   Hand Weapons
Date: The Feast of Saint Jeremy, City Year 536

My most esteemed colleague:

I was honored to receive clarification from you personally on this matter. I fear that in my original message to you, I failed to express myself well. The protests I listed against the rental of hand weapons on the Transport deck were indeed made to me by a number of our workers, but the real problem is that I believe such rental is illegal by Diamond law. Actually there are other problems—there are those who feel that having weapons floating around in the presence of so many Outsider techs is not a good policy—but again, it was the *legality* of the question that I meant to bring up.

I regret that I was unclear.

Text of reply:

To: Raoul Simponella, Chief of Distribution
From: Benjamin Lawless, Lord Armorer
Re: Further Clarification of Rules Regarding Hand Weapons
Date: The Feast of Saint Ethan, City Year 536

My most esteemed colleague:

I am always delighted to hear from you. I trust those long days and nights of dealing with Outsiders has not affected your thinking! (A joke, sir.)

I know not to what you refer with your reference to legality. Nor do my advisers in the Armory. I'm sure you will see, when you consider the matter, that a custom of such long standing as the rental of hand weapons in Transport cannot possibly be against the law.

Perhaps you are referring to some Outsider law about the carrying of hand weapons onto a Station? I believe my previous memo answered that concern.

Please feel free to consult me if you have further questions.

Text of a memo from the Chief of Inventory Distribution to Geoffrey Farnham, Chief Minister of Security

To: Geoffrey Farnham, Chief of Security
From: Raoul Simponella, Chief of Distribution
Re: Clarification of Rules Regarding Hand Weapons
Date: The Feast of Saint Tolliver, City Year 536

My most esteemed colleague:

I regret disturbing you when you are so ill, but I seem to have reached an impasse. As you will see from the enclosed memos, I am having difficulty getting a ruling on the legality of hand weapons on the Transport deck. As Chief Minister of Security, I know this issue will be as important to you as it is to me. Could you send me a copy of the relevant regulations, initialed by your office, so I may send them on to the Lord Armorer? I would hesitate to continue approaching one of his exalted position without the knowledge of your support on this matter.

This memo was never answered.

Will came through the Street of Dreams tired almost to the point of hallucination. He stole food and water from abandoned shops, and he would have stolen a car if he could find one operational; but he couldn't, so he trudged on.

He couldn't stop. When he tried to sleep, the Panic kept moving him forward. He would put his head down on anything looking vaguely soft, and a voice would say, *Ten days. This could be the last day, the last shuttle could be lifting now.* And sleep became out of the question.

Sniper Alley. It was misnamed; there hadn't been many snipers in Sniper Alley. Will had only killed two.

He was glad neither of them had been a woman, because whatever they thought here, that would have made a difference.

The city was like a new corpse—damaged, but still recognizable. Too near life not to make you nervous. He threw an empty canteen into the open door of a shop where insects were gathering, but didn't stop to check what was inside. Most likely it was just abandoned food, but it could be anything. There had been occasional signs of life in Lankio Quarter; shutters slamming shut abruptly as he passed, once a sound of fierce whispers behind a door. People waiting for scales to tip one way or another. But here in the government district it was as though the entombment had already taken place—not a movement, not a human sound; there weren't even abandoned cars here—anything that could move had already been claimed.

All the birds had flown and the cage was rusting. He cut through the outskirts of the Duke's grounds and came down the back of the hill. Nobody in the Visitor's Residence either, or not that he could see. Will didn't stop; if anybody *was* hanging around here, he preferred not to call attention to himself.

He made his way through the hills of the south district, past shops and warehouses. He was physically exhausted, but on another level he was less tired, more stimulated than ever. He was so near his objective. His heart was pounding as though he'd just had eight cups of strong tea; the rhythm was unfamiliar, like someone else's body. He found he kept walking faster and had to stop himself because he knew he couldn't take it.

At the base of south district he came over the ridge and looked down the hill: Everun Port.

He stood there, breathing deeply, and bent to put his hands on his knees to relieve his back. His eyes didn't leave the port. The rows of grids were all empty and powered down. The administration building was dark.

He straightened slowly. Then he was running down the hill, his feet pounding on the street. He ran until he came up against the port fence—he put his hands on it, knowing it was powered down, too, and stared in at the deserted space.

Too late.

Chapter 49

Hartley Quince had been trying to avoid this interview for several days. Theoretically he could just keep telling the secretaries not to admit these two petitioners, but they were insistent and eventually, somewhere, he'd have to deal with them. Better to do it now and retain some control of the situation.

He checked over his office, having swept some stray

papers and files into a drawer, and saw that everything looked wealthy, official and authoritative. Good enough certainly for two young Sangaree women.

Then he went to the door himself, to retain the advantage of bestowing courtesy, and opened it and bowed to the two young women. "Mrs. Freylinger? Miss Verdigris? Won't you come in?"

Will's sister and fiancée entered. He'd seen pictures of them both; Bernadette Freylinger was small, plump, and ruddy-haired; her eyes were sharp and hostile, and she perched herself in the pink plush chair by the desk with the air of one who is ready to leap up and do physical battle at any time. She wore her most ultrarespectable middle-class outfit, a long skirt of dark blue and a flowered shawl with a pin. Lysette Verdigris was taller, with a calm face but wary eyes. A skirt pulled over her hips softened but did not hide the fact that she was wearing her bar-singer's costume beneath. She took the seat just beyond Bernadette's and settled back, crossing her legs, and putting her own arms squarely on those of the chair. Everything about her said that she was here for the long haul, for whatever amount of time it took, and Hartley sensed that she was perhaps the more dangerous of the two.

He resumed his seat behind the desk, under the picture of Adrian Sawyer, and smiled impersonally. "Now, how may I help you two ladies?"

"We want to know," said Bernadette at once, "what you're doing to get back my brother."

"I beg your pardon, madam?" said Hartley. "You're Sergeant Stockton's sister, aren't you? Is he missing?"

"You know damned well he's missing," began Bernadette, her Sangaree accent getting thicker.

Lysette interrupted. "He hasn't been home for days. In fact, he hasn't been home since he went downhill. Now, as all three of us know, he never came back from Baret Two. Could you fill us in on what you're doing to retrieve him?" Her voice was clipped, precise, and certain.

Hartley smiled politely. "As you must be aware, Sergeant Stockton has long-term assignments from time to time. He can't always be with you two ladies, can he? I'm sure if you'll just be patient—"

"He can send link-messages!" yelled Bernadette.

"He could if he were in the Three Cities," said Lysette.

Two pairs of eyes glinted at Hartley like adamantine steel. He sighed inwardly. In his way, Willie seemed as good at getting loyalty as Adrian Mercati.

"Really," he said, "I'm not sure what you think I—"

"We checked at Guard Headquarters," said Lysette in her firm voice. "Will's been removed from the rolls there. They say that now he's one of your direct-reports."

Hartley was well aware that they should have said nothing of the kind. But both women were attractive, and there were Sangaree connections among some of the Guard. "May I ask who led you to believe that?"

"His name slips my mind," said Lysette.

"Who cares about his name?" demanded Bernadette. "We're getting ready for Blackout! We're leaving Baret System and Willie is still downhill!"

"Mrs. Freylinger," began Hartley. "May I inquire why your husband is not here today to assist you in this matter?" He already knew why: Because Jack Freylinger's company was frantically trying to close up its business with Baret Station before the Transport area was cut off for Blackout.

"Why should he be? Willie's my brother. And Jack knows I can take care of myself."

"If you were familiar with regulations, Mrs. Freylinger, you would know that inquiries regarding the whereabout of Opal citizens on official business must be made by the closest male relative; in this case, by your husband. We have many secretaries available outside who would be happy to assist him in filling out the necessary forms. As for you, Miss Verdigris," he turned to face Lysette, "I must confess I'm not sure of the reason for your presence at all. Is it to provide support for Mrs. Freylinger?"

"I'm engaged to Sergeant Stockton."

"Ah. Is that engagement registered with your parish?" She hesitated. "No."

"I see. I'm afraid that does not put you in a privileged position in terms of obtaining information." He paused as though waiting for something further, then said, "I'm afraid there's little I can do for you at this time. I suggest you have Mr. Freylinger initiate this inquiry, if it's what you really want—"

Bernadette stood, her fists balled up. "I want to know where my brother is!"

"We don't intend to leave, Deacon Quince," stated Lysette. "We don't have a lot of time to spare."

He could, of course, have them thrown out. He reached a decision. "Miss Verdigris? Mrs. Freylinger, would you sit down? I'd like to speak to you off the record."

Bernadette glanced a her ally and sat down, uncertainly.

Hartley said, "Sergeant Stockton is, in fact, on Baret Two."

"I knew it." Bernadette said this very softly, as though she'd been hit in the stomach. Her eyes were wide and scared.

"He's been out of communication with us since the trouble began down there."

"Trouble?" asked Lysette. The question didn't surprise Hartley. The news aboard the Three Cities was parochial in the extreme; a system-wide war in the offing had not even made the gossip circuit on the Opal. That a Blackout was coming, people knew; the reasons behind it, they were not informed of, nor did they much care.

"Fighting in the streets. The start of a revolution."

"Lord," said Lysette, and she was silent, too.

"We've done what we can to locate him," *which came to absolutely nothing,* "and we're still doing what we can. But it doesn't look hopeful."

Bernadette had clasped her flowered shawl so tightly around her shoulders that the pin had broken and was hanging loose. She was not aware of it.

"The best thing you can do now," said Hartley, "is not to interrupt me in my task. Understand?"

"But . . . but what are you doing?" asked Lysette, whose mind had an unfortunate tendency to go to the root of a problem. "What *can* you do? Haven't all shuttles been forbidden to leave for downhill?"

"Miss Verdigris, at the risk of being rude, I would remind you that you have no actual right to be here. I've already told you more than I should. In return, I would ask that you leave now and let me work."

The two women looked at each other. They didn't move from their chairs.

Hartley said quietly, "Do you really want me to call the EPs to take you out? They wouldn't be pleasant."

They looked at each other again, and finally Lysette nodded. She stood up. Bernadette walked slowly toward the door, still clutching her shawl. Lysette turned and said, "I can't promise we won't be back, Deacon Quince."

"Actually it's Officer Quince," he said mildly. "My other rank is higher and takes precedence."

She followed Will's sister out.

Hartley saw to it that his door was locked, then went to his desk and sat back in his chair to try to relax. He'd been far more upset by this than he cared to show, mostly because he was powerless in this situation and he knew it. He tried to manage all situations so that he was *never* powerless, under any circumstances—it was absolutely necessary that the options always be his—but in this case, there was nothing he could do. He *wanted* to get Willie back, but the bar-singer was right; the shuttles were off-limit, and that restriction was not going to be lifted because Hartley Quince wanted to find a Sangaree sergeant. Whatever he could talk Arno into, he couldn't talk him into that, not yet, and he himself didn't have the power—not yet.

Nor would the Ecclesiastical Council look kindly on any request from the person whose assignment it had been to find the Sawyer Crown before the Diamond got it. Opal could and would deny that the Crown was there, but everyone knew perfectly well that it was. And that Adrian Mercati had it.

A double screwup. Hart tapped his fingers on his desk, feeling that sense, that thing he hadn't felt in years, crawling through him; that thing that said they could do what they wanted to him and there was nothing he could do about it.

He put up a mental wall. It wouldn't hold forever, but it would hold until he could take action on it. There were drugs from Baret Station that he kept in a floor-box under the expensive carpet beneath his feet, although he preferred not to take them unless no other idea presented it-

self. A better move would be to call in one of his
direct-reports and convince him that he'd done a rotten
job on something he hadn't done a rotten job on. Maybe
later, when his need was more sharp.

He walked over to one of the pictures on his wall, a
picture of Old Earth. *Willie, where are you now?* Hartley
was aware that one of the more mercenary members of
the ecclesiastical police might have been a better choice
as his agent; but it was so much more fun to have Willie,
who tried so hard. You put a wall here and one there and
watched him skitter around. Besides, you could never be
sure of people who operated only on the money
principle—there were always others around to offer them
more, and they might not stay bought. Whereas Willie's
efforts to do the right thing were absolutely reliable.

Besides, he was the only person Hartley'd known well
when he was young who was still alive.

"Shit," he said softly in Sangaree.

A line of new tech-applicants spilled out of the ship at
Diamond Transport. They were herded into a bunch by
the side of the bay and left to mingle while the interviewing process began. None of the Diamond supervisors
wanted to interview job seekers at Baret Station any
more—this close to Blackout, leaving the City made a lot
of people nervous, brought on a touch of the Panic. They
shipped all the applicants over to the Diamond now, and
shipped back the ones who didn't measure up. A fair
number were Baret Two refugees, and their qualifications
were carefully examined, for the Station was charging a
transport fee for every accepted candidate who'd been
lifted from the planet.

Bay Green's supervisor walked over to the milling
group and reached in his hand and pulled out a tech-
applicant in a blue shirt that hung awkwardly on bony
shoulders. "What's this?" he yelled out. "We don't hire
aliens."

The One Newly Awakened stood nervously, feeling the
human's tight grip on his upper arm. The man's accent
was less troubling than that of the stationers who had
picked him up, but it was still unfamiliar; nevertheless,
his thoughts were clear. His aura was one of annoyance

and his current ruling mental configuration was that of
Disrupted Procedure, one of the three hundred and six
ruling configurations shared by humans, Curosa, and
Curosa-derived.

It would be best not to annoy him further. The One
waited, hoping that the human in authority who brought
him here would intervene.

The human did so, no doubt moved by self-
justification. His ruling configuration was in turmoil. "He
says he knows all about Transport programming, and Empire and Republic models. If it's true, he's invaluable."

The One had studied his interviewer's configuration,
and given answers that molded it into the necessary
shape.

"He doesn't look like he knows a talmic switch from a
grid socket. Here, you—" and he stared at the One,
"show me how you would activate Grid Six in this bay to
accommodate a Station ship like the one you arrived in."

The configuration of Disrupted Procedure had been replaced by Satisfaction in the Vanity of Earthly Effort. He
expected the One to fail. The One looked to the other human, whose configurations were so amorphous and
changeable, but whose mind projected such sharp visual-
izations.

The One saw the control board for this Bay, with the
appropriate panels lit in a glowing red outline. He went to
the board and touched the first switch.

"Hey!" said the supervisor. "I didn't say to *do* it. Just
point."

The One pointed here, and there, and there. He stood
away from the panel.

The supervisor looked disgusted. "It's not our policy to
hire aliens," he said again.

The other human said, "We're almost at Blackout, and
we're low on techs. If he doesn't work out, we can let
him off on the other side."

"Sectors away from where he started? Well, if he
doesn't care, I don't. You hear me, alien?" The supervisor
raised his voice, and spoke slowly. He was used to Outsiders who had trouble with Diamond speech. "You don't
care if we let you out in some other sector? We got places
to go, here, right?"

"Fine, good," said the One. He did not risk further words now, for a misunderstanding would be catastrophic. This phrase had served him well at the port and on the Station.

"Fine, good," repeated the supervisor. "Well, put Fine and Good in the group that's staying, okay, Davey? And tell him to keep out of the way, he makes me nervous."

The One found himself led to a place farther along the deck, where applicants were waiting to be given identification. He was very pleased. The Crown was definitely near, closer than it had been any time since he woke up.

He waited patiently, and the First God smiled on him. Two humans were walking along the docks—one was plump and older, the other was thinner and younger. The other, whoever he was, bore the marks of the Crown in his aura. It was a strange aura of pearllike translucency, such as he had never seen before on any human, but clearly marked by the Crown. As they walked closer, the One revised his opinion—the second was thinner, but not younger; physically he resembled the younger humans, but the background support for his configuration showed the complex overlayering that accumulated with the passage of years.

The One did not wait (it would not please the First God to show hesitation before his gift.) but went at once to the human who was marked and took his arm. "Sir and brother," the words spilled out, "I see you have touched the Crown. Joy between us! And to your friend, too! Joy between us!" He shook the human's hand enthusiastically, as he had been trained to do long before.

They were clearly startled. Startled and—oh, dear—annoyed. They didn't comprehend, he was at fault, he'd not made clear the truth—if only his brother were here—

"What's this fellow saying?" asked the plump one. A *man*, not a *woman*, the One was nearly certain, although bundled in this clothing they would be hard to distinguish.

"I can't make it out," replied the other.

"He's crazy. Ignore him, and let's get on."

But the other was staring. "How did they take an alien on board? Look, Spider—look at his face."

The plump one shivered. "Argh. He gives me the creeps. Let's just go, Tal."

"No, wait" He still stared at the One. "I don't recognize the species. You! Do you understand what I'm saying?"

The One understood perfectly, and only wished he could *be* understood as well. His own thoughtless exhilaration was to blame. This human's configuration was the clearest he had ever seen or expected to see—it was amazing how the species had developed. It should be child's play to make his words mold a configuration like that.

He aimed his words at the pattern, with the sureness that only one who speaks the truth can bring. "I said, sir and brother, that I see you are one who has touched the Crown. I am joyed by our meeting. Are you not expecting me? I am the One Newly Awakened—the Guardian of the Crown. I was Left Behind."

The human called Spider said, "Can't make head nor tail of it."

But the other said slowly, "I'm not sure if I was expecting you or not. Could you wait here a moment?"

The One smiled; his human brother's pattern was overlaid with wariness. His configuration had changed to Surprising Reappraisal. It was beautiful how clear it was, it could bring tears to one's sacs. He said, "Please. I am only here to serve and help."

Tal was looking around the deck. "Where's the nearest link?"

"What's going on?" asked Spider.

"I think Adrian had better talk to this one."

"How can Adrian talk to him? You can't understand a word he says."

Tal lowered his voice and said, "I think it's possible he's a Curosa."

Spider stared at the One in shock. "He doesn't *look* like a Curosa. Not like the ones in the pictures."

"Curosa-derived, then. He says the people who left us the Crown left him here as a guardian."

"When did he say that?"

But Tal, not spotting a link within acceptable reach, went back to the One. "Do you have a name?"

The One lowered his head. "Not as yet. If you wish to name me, I would be honored."

"Thanks, no, we'll skip it for now. Tell me—how did you know I had anything to do with the Crown? Did somebody tells you?"

"Its mark is in your aura." The One gestured toward Tal's head. "It's very clear. Has no one remarked on the change in it to you?"

Tal hesitated. "It must have slipped their minds. Listen: I'd like to take you to our person in charge here. I know he'll be very interested in meeting you, is that all right?"

"Of course, sir and brother."

Tal paused again. "I'm not a Redemptionist, you know."

The One was puzzled by this term. Nothing in this Tal's configuration clarified it, so at last he said, "We are both marked by the truth."

"Umm." Tal motioned toward the Bay exit. "This way, please."

Spider said, "Is this a good idea? Since when do you believe what some alien tells you—especially *this* story?"

"I don't . . . but it sounds like the truth." Tal's voice was troubled.

"Maybe he's an assassin," said Spider gloomily. "Maybe he just wants to be introduced to the Protector so he can kill him. He's got wonderful long fingers for strangling, did you notice?"

The One was fluttering his hands in indecision. "I was told to wait here as part of your City's procedure."

"Don't worry," said Tal. "I'll take care of it."

"I don't worry," agreed the One at once.

He followed Tal and Spider out of the Transport area. On the train his two human brothers seemed to wish to keep him away from the other travelers; he cooperated with their desires. It was a pity the plump one was so difficult to read, for he seemed to wish to communicate. The One spoke very slowly and carefully to him.

"They left you behind, did they?" asked Spider, as the streets of the Diamond flew past their windows.

"Yes."

"Well, what've you been doing all this time? Any hobbies?"

The One understood this question, as much as he could, more from Tal's mind than Spider's. "I was dead," he explained.

This caused a silence on Spider's part. The One hoped he had not been unclear again. "This is a state of nonparticipation," he begun, but Spider looked at Tal and said, *"Dead?"*

"I think he means dead in the eyes of his people," said Tal, although he was by no means sure of that interpretation.

"Oh!" said Spider, and he smiled with relief. He clapped the One on the shoulder, a sign of affection which pleased the One. "Is that all? I've been dead myself. It could happen to anybody."

They led the One from the train to a shining corridor, whose texture and shape gave him great pleasure. From the corridor he was taken to a room with desks and people working and other people sitting in chairs as though they were waiting for something. "Stay here for just one minute," said Tal. "I'm going to warn Adrian I'm bringing you in. Spider, stay next to him."

"Right."

Tal went into the next room, which depressed the One. It was too hard to communicate with this other, and Tal's aura had an exoticism which pleased the One to watch—the more so since the mark of the Crown was on it.

He stood with Spider, surrounded by this roomful of humans, some of whom were staring at him openly. Their configurations were chaotic. It made him nervous, so he closed his eyes, pretending solitude.

—Well? Is the Awakened One awake?

His eyes flew open. But the words had come, as he knew in his heart, not from one of the humans here but from the other place.

—Brother? he asked.

—Who else?

Joy and relief overcame him, and he began to do a little dance of happiness, there in front of everybody.

—Blessed am I, he sang, for you did not desert me. In the blackness of the tomb, we were together. In the turning of the years, we were together—

—Yes, said his brother. But where are we now?

—What?

—Where are we now? This looks like no tomb that I was shown.

—We are aboard the City of Diamond, my brother. One of the Cities our people built for the humans to aid them in spreading the truth. We are waiting now to speak to their highest person. Is it not wonderful?

—Idiot.

His feet stopped dancing.

Tal came out then and said, "Well, let's go in and confuse someone else. Are you all right, uh . . ." When no form of address sprang readily he said, "You look a little unwell."

The One's head was down, and he felt miserable. Already he had done something wrong.

"He was dancing a minute ago," said Spider.

Tal shrugged. "We'll drop it in Adrian's lap for now. We've got enough to do before Blackout."

They escorted him inside.

The One sat in the polished wooden chair in Adrian's office. The surface of the chair spoke to him of life that was once free, of the long unchanging configurations of trees, now a corpse in the service of comfort. It was the way of things; the One noted it but was not disturbed by it.

Adrian Mercati had hold of the arms of the chair and was staring down into his face.

Adrian's aura, whatever it had been was totally subsumed by the violet flickering of the Crown. It was obvious that he had used It recently. He bore the pressure well, though—indeed, he seemed unaware of it.

"He doesn't match the pictures," said Adrian. "What do you think?"

The three of them stared at the One, who shifted his feet nervously. The chair was high for him, and his toes just reached the floor if he stretched. His eyes were ridged, but without brows; his skin was tinged with bluish gray, but that was temporary; his lips were the same color. "For one thing, he's smaller," said Adrian. "And his skin's too blue. And he looks—I don't know, he looks more *human* than the Curosa did."

Well, of course, that was true. Like his brothers, his features came together in a very humanoid gestalt. And the way his mouth quirked and his eyes moved were all expressive, in the human way of things. That was the way it should be.

"He's got hair, too," pointed out Tal, and so he did—sparse, but present.

"Sir and brother," said the One to Adrian, "it's you whom I've come to help. I'm so proud, so admiring, that you've grown up to use the Crown. Although—" He wondered if it were polite to say so, but from the chaotic mental configurations he'd passed on the way here, he was not entirely sure that using the Crown was a good idea.

He paused, and Adrian turned to Tal. "I can get every couple of words."

Tal said, "I'm not too sure of that speech myself. He was talking more clearly before."

"No, he wasn't," said Spider. They looked at him, and he stood his ground. "He wasn't. Tal's been translating."

Adrian bent over the One again, his configuration stabilizing into Controlled Curiosity. "Talk to *him*," he said, pointing to Tal. "Explain to him why you're here."

The One turned at once to Tal's beautifully clear configuration. "I was left here by the masters to guide you in using the Crown. I see from his aura that this one in charge of you has used it recently. I wish to express my pride and admiration of his strength, but with all respect, I have doubts about the readiness of your people to handle the full sharing. I hope, I beg, that we may talk further before he uses it again." He aimed his words straight for the heart of the configuration and watched them disappear into the target.

Tal blinked. Adrian said, "You understood that?"

Tal said slowly, "He wants you to put off using the Crown again until he's had a chance to look things over."

"He says the Curosa left him here to help us with this?"

"That's what he says."

"Well," said Adrian, standing up straight, "I can't say that that's unreasonable. Especially since we hadn't been planning on using it at all. I didn't know you had this rapport with Redemptionist aliens, Tal."

Tal regarded him seriously. "It's not a talent I feel comfortable with."

"He has some oddball talents himself, doesn't he," mused Adrian. "You weren't even involved in the Crown effect. He picked you out just by knowing you'd physically touched it."

Tal glanced warily at the One, then back to Adrian. "I have a lot to finish before Blackout, Adrian. What do you want done with him?"

"Let's think things through before we make anything public. Put him in some rooms out of the way somewhere, give him whatever he needs. Blackout's getting closer, it's true—let's face one complication at a time."

"Good," said Tal, with some relief.

They left Adrian's office. Tal said, "Spider, take him to C and put him up there until I can clear some rooms."

"Me? What are you going to be doing? You want me to walk a dangerous alien through the City by myself?"

"I'll be cleaning up the mess you left in smuggling to Baret Station." He said to the One, "Go with Spider here, he'll take care of you. Tell him what you need."

"I'll go with Spider," agreed the One.

"See how cooperative he is?" asked Tal.

Spider still looked put out. "It's not my fault the smuggling operation got interrupted. I didn't start the war."

"Was I blaming you?"

Hartley Quince was alone in his office when he was informed of a live link-message from Baret Station.

"Accepted," he said, "This is Officer Quince."

"I'm the Coordinator of Refugee Determinations for Baret Station," said the speaker on his desk link. "I was given your name by one of our clients."

"Oh?" said Hartley.

"We've picked up someone claiming to be an Opal citizen. We made three planetary descents in the past week to clean out any Station personnel who might still be on-surface—or any other customers—and we evacked this one from Everun Port. He says his name is William Stockton."

There was a pause from the speaker, then it went on: "He says you'll pay his transport fees."

"He does, does he?" said Hart. He could imagine the scene: Will at the port, maybe with a handful of refugees, being offered evacuation at a price. How many people took the Station up on it? He wouldn't be surprised if Will were the only one that day.

Willie could have had a life on Baret Two. He'd have to start over, but he was bright and trained and he could always join one of the armies—the Republic's, if he had any brains. They'd look out for their own after they won. But if he took the Station's offer and then couldn't pay for passage and upkeep, not to mention all the other ransom items they'd add to the bill, they certainly wouldn't bother to return him downhill. Willie had just effectively limited his options to the Opal or death.

And his life would be personally expensive. "He does, does he?" said Hart. "Egotistical bastard." But he was smiling.

Chapter 50

He had been he said, an unconscionable time dying; he hoped they would excuse it.
　　　　MACAULEY, OF CHARLES II OF ENGLAND

Geoffrey Farnham was dead. The old Chief Minister of Security had been lingering more or less on his deathbed these past ten years, and people had gotten into the habit of thinking he would lie there immortally, when his widow sent the notification to Bishop Kalend and the black banner was let down in front of Saint Tom's.

Barely were the funeral rites over when Lord Muir trotted out his son Harry before Adrian, humbly suggesting his fitness for the post. Brandon Fischer preferred Virgil Au-Yeung, an admin with twenty years of experience in internal administration. He wasn't quite noble, but they could shove him up a rank or two; nobody would object to seeing him on the lowest aristo rung. "It fits in with your policy," he pointed out to Adrian. "Promoting people who can actually work the department, instead of figureheads."

Adrian nodded at this, as he did at every suggestion, and on the following Sunday he called a special meeting of all ministry chiefs and their first admins in the Cavern of Audience. It had to be after service, of course, and St. Tom's was packed that day with people who considered themselves on the cutting edge of information, craning their necks to see if Adrian was with anybody, or looking at anybody.

He wasn't with anybody but Iolanthe, and she could hardly be the candidate. He sang "I Believe" in a good, strong, enthusiastic voice, as though he hadn't a care in the world. "I believe for every drop of rain that falls, a flower grows. I believe that somewhere in the darkest night, a candle glows." One of the oldest admins leaned over to a colleague beside him in the pew and whispered, "He doesn't believe anything of the kind."

The colleague looked over at Adrian, looked down at his music, and did not reply.

Nobody requested an absence from the meeting in the Cavern. At the appointed time Adrian took his seat and glanced over the turnout with satisfaction.

"I won't keep you long today, my friends," he announced. "It being the Sabbath, I know you'll want to be home with your families."

Nobody looked interested in leaving, however. He continued more solemnly, "As you know, we've lost a good comrade and valued contributor to our City in the death of Geoffrey Farnham."

Sympathetic murmurs followed this statement.

"But our duty requires that we do not stop for mourning, but at once designate someone to pick up the burden he carried all these years. The post of Chief Minister of Security is empty. I've given a great deal of thought to the matter, and I want to thank those of you who gave me your assistance."

Harry Muir was standing in the front row of the crowd. His father stood just behind him, his hands on Harry's shoulders.

Adrian said, "I would now like to inform you I am giving the position of Security Chief to Special Officer Tal Diamond."

A complete and disbelieving silence ensued. Tal, who had been asked to be present as part of his usual routine, took a step forward, looking as shocked as everybody else.

"Officer Diamond has performed his duty admirably by our City, and for me personally. I know you will give him your support in his new tasks."

Lord Muir's hands had fallen from Harry's shoulders. A dissatisfied rumbling began among those present.

Adrian smiled. "Please feel free to adjourn and return to your homes. Thank you for your kind attention."

He rose and headed speedily for the door. He estimated that about half those present would try to interrupt him when they'd pulled themselves together. As it was, Brandon Fischer and Tal were both on his trail.

"We have to talk," puffed Fischer, as he jogged to catch Adrian.

But Tal reached him first. "Have you lost your mind?" he said.

Adrian smiled. "Promotion hasn't made you forget your graciousness." He looked back and saw stirrings of life in the crowd. "Not here, Tal, I'll never get out. —Brandon, I know, but not here."

"Where?" They both said.

"I'll call you." He ducked out the door.

"Don't think I don't know what you're trying to do!" called Fischer irritably.

Tal first, he decided. He gave his demon a few hours to consider the situation, then summoned him to one of the administration offices, the one he used least often. It was less likely they'd be looking for him there.

"The thing is already announced," Adrian began. "So let's take if from there."

Tal held his chair with the immobility of a statue. Finally the marble lips moved. "Adrian. First, nobody wants me to hold a ministry; second, *I* don't want to hold a ministry; third, I'd like to think I can leave the City at any stop we make."

"And so you can. If you do, I'll just give it over to Harry Muir."

There was a suspicious silence from Tal. Then he said, "This appointment covers only Special Security, doesn't it? Not the Guard, not the EPs."

"Yes. You've grasped the situation admirably."

"Well, there you are. I don't know anything about Special Security."

Adrian grinned. "In case you asked, I had my link call up some books for you—they're printed and in your office. The *Internal Security Manual, A History of Security Crises in the Three Cities,* an organizational chart ... there are bundles of stuff for you."

Tal got up from his chair in what for him was almost a burst of impatience. He walked as far as the wall, turned, and said, "Just what is it you want from me in this, Adrian? Just what plan am I supposed to follow?"

Adrian leaned back and folded his hands. "Your inclinations."

Tal took that in. He returned to his seat and smiled. "Well. I will, then."

"Good."

"I mean it."

"I know you do."

Tal thought some more. "What if somebody gives me trouble over anything I want to do?"

"If it's legal, hit them with your title, and refer them to me if they get uppity."

Text of a memo from Tal Diamond to the Lord Armorer.

To: Benjamin Lawless, Lord Armorer
From: Tal Diamond, Chief of Security
Re: The Closing of the Weapons Rental on Transport
   Deck
Date: August 10

This is to inform you that the weapons rental office on the Transport deck, presently run by your department, will be closed tomorrow, August 11. This closure will be permanent.

The closure is in compliance with Regulation 36, Para 12 of Internal Security, which states that the distribution

of hand weapons to civilians is at the discretion of the
department of Special Security.

I realize that the above conflicts with your understanding of the situation. Nevertheless I believe it to be true.

Upon finishing the dictation, the secretary program on
Tal's link inquired, "Do you wish me to rephrase this
memo so it is consonant with the general style of memos
between department heads? Some softening of tone will
be necessary."

"Touch it," said Tal, "and your personality will be dis-
mantled by morning."

"Yes, sir," said the secretary program. "Sending now."

It took Hartley Quince forever to get live communications access to the Station medical complex. He brought
one of Willie's Sangaree henchmen, one Barington Strife,
to his office in case he proved useful in getting Will's attention; but as things stood the hard part was getting
through to Willie at all. He was bounced to thirteen separate administrators, some of them refugee handlers,
some medical supervisors, and some just there to slow the
advance of progress.

Finally he reached a hospital administrator who listened long enough to accept a money transfer, and a few
minutes later he heard: "Hart, is that you?"

"It's me."

"Get me out of here!"

"Willie, I am working on it. They tell me you're dehy-
drated, underfed, and suffering from exhaustion. The nice
people helping you are afraid they won't get paid if they
let you go in this condition."

"How close are we to Blackout?" Yes, Will's voice was
definitely tense.

"Several days at least," said Hartley. "Stop worrying.
You're practically here now."

"They won't let me go at all if you don't pay them
first," said Will.

"Didn't I just say to stop worrying?"

"I can recover at home! There's nothing wrong with
me!"

Hartley sighed. Will's voice came again, plaintively: "Get me out of here, Hart."

"I'll call you later," said Hartley, and he cut the link. He looked over at Barington Strife. "I want you to go to Baret Station."

Strife looked startled, and more than startled.

Hartley said with some impatience, "Wipe that look off your face—we've got plenty of time till Blackout, so if you have a Panic attack, it's your own damned neurotic fault. I want you to go and tell Sergeant Stockton that I'm working on getting him released."

"You just told him. Sir."

"I want you to tell him what you've seen me do— calling the admins here, the Station people, the hospital. Be specific."

"Why go all the way over there? He knows what you just said!"

"But from you," said Hartley, "he might believe it."

"I gave it to Tal," said Adrian simply. They were sitting together on the edge of their bed. His boots were half-off, and her hair was unbound for the night, falling past her shoulders in a straight, dark river.

"You must be joking," said Iolanthe, who had heard enough criticisms of their demon from Fischer to doubt Adrian's sanity. "Tal believes that self-interest and blackmail are what bring the human race together in happy fellowship."

"And Harry believes for every drop of rain that falls, a flower grows. Not a useful attitude in a security officer."

She fell back on the bed with a thump. "I'm not sure I *like* Tal."

Adrian's lips curved. "That leaves you in solitary company, doesn't it?" he said.

"Maybe the rest of us realize something you don't," she said, and as Adrian reached for the top button of her robe she said, "No, wait. It's true, isn't it?" She stared into his face. "You *do* like him." It came out as an accusation.

"All right, I do," said Adrian. "But more importantly in a post that involves weaponry, I can count on him."

"He has no soul," pointed out Iolanthe. She raised herself on one elbow.

"I can't argue theology," he said, reaching again for the button. "But I know that I'm the only supporter he has in the Administration."

"It seems," she said, "that blackmail *is* what brings the human race together."

"In happy fellowship," agreed her husband, pressing her back down on the bed.

When he woke later, it was in darkness and to an empty bed. He rose and put on a robe and walked out to the sitting room of their suite.

Iolanthe was stretched out on the sofa, a pile of books on the floor beside her. The top one, he saw, was labeled *Legends of the Three Cities: A Sociological Perspective.* The one in her hands was *The Politics of Empire Colonies.* The reading light from the wall just above her cast a halo on her face.

She looked up. "I'm sorry, I didn't mean to wake you."

"You didn't. I guess I just missed you."

She sat up and swung her feet to the floor. Her white nightgown had slipped off one shoulder, and Adrian began thinking that it was just as well they were both awake. She said, "Sweetheart, I have to talk to you."

He found himself grinning. *Sweetheart* didn't happen often.

"Seriously," she said.

"All right." He wiped the grin away, at least on the outside.

"How could you be so blind as to make Tal your security chief? Do you realize that gives him override privileges on all the City's weapons?"

"Darling, I think I know what the position entails a little better than you d—"

"No, Adrian, listen to me! Don't think I don't know what you're doing," she said, in an unconscious imitation of Brandon Fischer's words earlier that day. "You're slipping him onto the Council, where he can be a lightning rod for all the unpopular things that have to be done but you don't want to be seen as the one doing. Everybody can resent him for bringing them up instead of you. And then, Security is the customary focus for anybody who wants to take over the Protectorship. But you think, how high can this Security Chief go? There's a natural ceiling on the career of a demon."

Adrian blinked. "This can hardly be such a brilliant move, if everybody sees through it."

"Oh, it'll work anyway. Seeing through it won't help anybody . . . as you already know, my love."

Adrian sat there for a few minutes, then said, "When you asked about the links, I thought you meant to read books of romances."

"I'm sorry," she said, with her first trace of uncertainty. "Have I offended? You said I could read anything in the public access paths."

"Yes. I mean, yes I did. No, you haven't offended. I'm just surprised. I didn't expect my seventeen-year-old bride to give me an analysis of our latest organizational change."

"I was eighteen six weeks ago."

"So you were," he recalled. "We had a party."

She stood up. "My last headache gave me time to think," she said. "And I went through the library catalogue again when I got up. I know why we've never downloaded the last edition of the Imperial Encyclopedia, Adrian. We're still on the first edition even though in some places it's centuries out of date. I know, it costs money, and I know, *all* the editions are out of date, but the fact is that the last editions were censored before they were released."

Adrian was staring at her. "Well, well," he said. He got up and went over to the table beside the door and turned on the reading lamp there. Then he sat down again.

Io said, "They're supposed to be updated, but they've been cut. The last edition doesn't mention Apheans at all."

"You have been checking on Apheans, have you?"

"Yes, I have. You see, I didn't call him a demon, did I? Even though you do sometimes yourself." She knelt beside Adrian's chair and took his hands. "I'm not saying he doesn't like you. He probably does, in so far as he's capable. But he can't help what he is, Adrian. 'Incapable of learning proper socialization.' Do you know what that means? It means that when it's more profitable for him to destroy you than to preserve your life, he will. And he'll probably be a little surprised that you didn't expect it."

"Io, sweetheart, I've read these pages, too." He clasped her hands.

"Have you? Did you read what some of these children did, before the government realized what was happening and outlawed that birth-mix? It's no accident that every Aphean on record was killed before his fortieth birthday."

"Tal hasn't killed anybody lately."

"That we know about. You're anthropomorphizing, Adrian."

Well, *well.*

She went on, "He looks like a human, walks like a human, talks like a human . . . more or less. So you start to expect him to be one all the way through. But he isn't, Adrian. This is a *careless mistake.* Forgive me for saying so, but I'm your wife and I don't want to see you hurt. He's your little piece of the Outside you've taken up just for yourself—all right, that much you could get away with. But now you've grown jaded and you're bringing your panthers into the room without tranquilizers."

"I would never do that."

Her eyes had teared up in her passion, and now she sniffled. "I was speaking metaphorically."

"So was I." He kissed her. "What a package of surprises you are. I suppose Prudence was right when she said she'd see herself revenged one day."

"You haven't been *listening!*" She hit his thigh with her fist, still sniffling.

"I heard every word. Listen, darling, you see that light over there that I turned on? By the table?"

"Yes."

"I turn it on whenever I come home, and now I want you to do it, too." She looked up at him, puzzled. "It's a jammer, love—in case anybody is trying to listen in."

"Do you think somebody *is?*" Her voice was shocked.

"I have no reason to think so. And we guard against it. But there's no harm in being safe, so if there's any possibility I'm going to be discussing policy, I turn it on."

She frowned, considering. "And now you're telling me to. Why now?"

"Because, my beautiful counselor, you seem to be metamorphosing into an adviser on a par with Brandon Fischer. But without the beard, of course." He kissed her again.

Was he humoring her? She said, "Does this mean you'll take back the security ministry?"

"No," he said, "But it means you can give me a hard time about it as often as you like. And any other opinions you may have in stock."

She hauled herself into his lap and threw one arm around his shoulder. "Adrian—"

"No. I don't let Brandon Fischer shoot me down more than so many times a day, and I won't let you either. Save it for tomorrow, adviser." He put his lips to her neck. "Oh, the benefits of a physical relationship with one's cabinet. The options expand before me like a land of dreams."

"Do you think that they've been listening to us make love?" she asked thoughtfully.

"Maybe." He pushed back her hair. "At least it will bring some joy to their barren, chalklike existences."

"How do you know they're barren and chalklike?" She opened his robe with conscious boldness, pulling the silk sash very slowly out of its loops and dropping it over one of his shoulders. He laughed gently.

"Compared with ours? How could they not be?"

Chapter 51

Angels are bright still, though the brightest fell.
                              SHAKESPEARE, *Macbeth*

Macbeth: What is the night?
Lady Macbeth: Almost at odds with morning, which
is which.
                              SHAKESPEARE, *Macbeth*

Hartley Quince was waiting for him in Transport. Will walked down the ramp of the shortie feeling very self-conscious; aware that Hart had paid a lot to get him back, aware that he was out of uniform, and aware before all else that this was Transport, Opal, where he'd half-expected to never be again.

Hart raised an eyebrow as he approached. "Well? All over our little Panic attack?"

"That wasn't the Panic," said Will. "That was annoyance and worry. You haven't seen the Panic, believe me."

"I guess I'll have to." He motioned for Will to fall in beside him. They were heading, Will guessed, for the ecclesiastical administration section. "A little update for you: We've lost that excellent and valuable forgery of a crown to the Diamond: and we've lost the original in that direction, too."

"Oh," said Will, awkwardly. What does one say?

"Yes. Things were a little difficult for me at one point, but never mind. That was then and this is now. By the way, you are not to officially admit anything of the kind."

"I see."

"There was also a rather odd mental burp we all took a few days ago; no doubt some one will mention it to you. You felt nothing on the planet, I take it?"

"I don't even know what you're talking about."

"Just checking. Good to have you back, Willie."

"Yeah." Will had some items on his own agenda to bring up. "Listen, Hart, I was in that Station hospital for a while. I heard a lot of the things they did—to other people, I mean." They entered the lift for the administrative levels. "And they drugged me up a lot of the time, even when I told them not to."

"Well? What of it?"

Will gazed at him directly. "You didn't tell them to fit me up with anything while I was over there? Throw in one of their little Empire gadgets while they had me on hand?"

Hart looked back coldly. "Try not to be any more paranoid than you can help, Willie."

"Something to keep track of me, or keep me in line?"

"Willie, I will say this once more only. I did not tell the hospital staff to fit you up with anything. Do you want me to write it in stone?"

Will looked dissatisfied, and continued to look so as they exited the lift and walked to the entrance of council administration. They climbed the front steps, and Hart said, "Oh, by the way. You don't have to come all the way up to my office—there are people waiting for you just inside."

Will froze. "What people?" The man and the little girl who'd begged for his help flashed into his mind; the man had been a plant after all, and the EPs were waiting for him. The men in black, the same ones who'd taken Tommy away.

Hart was watching impatiently as he stood there. "I have a busy day."

Will's legs started moving again. He passed through the doors on autopilot, and just inside he saw two people: Bernadette and Lysette.

"I'll leave you for now," said Hart, and he walked on.

His sister and his lover were staring at him, crying. Bernie took a step toward him, and then they were both running, both gathering him up in a double hug. The three of them stayed together for quite some time.

Finally they broke a little apart, still touching, and Will wiped his nose. He was impressed as well as surprised; Bernie and Lysette had never gotten along for any purpose, not even for Departure Day dinner. He started to talk and had to clear his throat. Then he said, "I got you both presents. But I lost them."

Lysette shook her head. Bernie grabbed his neck in the crook of her arm and pulled his head down and kissed him again. She muttered something to herself in a voice heavy with love and relief; he thought it sounded like "asshole."

And still touching, the three of them turned and walked outside and started down the steps.

In the little room on C level, the One Newly Awakened sat on the edge of the cot—they called it "his" cot, as though in some manner it partook of the One's nature— and held out his skinny grayish arms to accept his dinner.

The kitchen private gave him the bowl. He wore an Inventory uniform and was here on Spider's recommendation as to his discretion. Two Special Security men were stationed outside, having no idea what they guarded; they were unnecessary, for the One understood that he was not to roam the City should he become bored. However, it made his friends feel better to have them there.

The dinner bowl contained beans, rice, and corn. This time the One used a spoon; he didn't always. But scooping in his long fingers would have meant touching the inside of the bowl, which was plastic, a material he hated to feel. "Thank you, brother," he said to the kitchen private.

The private's configuration was more stable with each visit, becoming accustomed to his new charge. "You're welcome," he replied. His aura was strained, like a dog on a leash; it was clear that he badly wanted to ask questions of the One, but something prevented him.

"The Masters' blessings on us both," said the One, trying to set him at ease.

"Right," said the private. He waited till the One was finished, and retrieved the bowl. "Am I bringin' these fast enough for you?"

"I have sufficient calories at present," said the One. "May I inform you if I need more?"

"Sure. That's why I asked. I'm supposed to give you whatever you need."

"My thanks, brother." The One leaned back on the cot, feeling sleepy. He heard the footsteps of the private leaving; he saw the configurations of the two guards outside change as he passed.

Food was good. Even sleep was good, in its place. He felt warmly content.

—What a great slug you are.

—My brother, how can you say that? I have dared the night sky, all alone. Without even you. I made my way here—

—To sleep and eat. My congratulations.

The One twisted uncomfortably on his cot. —What would you have me do? These people are busy with their own lives. They say they'll give me time as soon as they change sectors.

—*Give* you time? Why are you not using the time you have? Do you even know where the Crown is, *Guardian?* And what do you know about these descendants of our old students, except what you've seen in passing in a handful of configurations?

The One was shamed. —I am not as strong or alert as I was. . . .

—Whose fault is that? I'm made weak myself by your dawdling. When did you last feed?

—I haven't fed since I woke up, brother.

—Not at all? What's wrong with you? Why not?

Here he felt on firm ground. —Because you were not here to tell this unworthy one if it was lawful.

—I'm here now.

There was a shivery feeling, like the touch of a night breeze. Then his brother said,

—Hear me. I have reviewed your situation. This human who brings us our food looks healthy and well-configured; when next he returns, feed on *him*.

The One considered this. His brother would not—could not, in fact—tell him to do anything that was wrong. But . . . —Who will bring me my food if I take him?

—They will find another, this City is full of humans. Did not this one say he was to give us whatever we needed?

—Very well, my brother. I will take this human, since you tell me it is lawful.

—It *is* lawful, said his brother,—if we don't get caught.

Text of the final letter from Keylinn Gray to her home, before leaving sector.

For delivery to Rory Murtagh, Harp Valley.

Dear Father,

Forgive me for not writing sooner. The truth is that I would not be writing now if I were not leaving our sector. Courage rises with distance, as the saying goes.

I've never spoken of my expulsion to you because I knew you would expect me to ask your forgiveness for the disgrace to our family. And because I wouldn't ask for forgiveness I wouldn't speak to you. But I'm leaving now, and this childishness seems like a luxury.

I wish you could see this place, Father. Right now the

City is humming, figuratively, with activity on every level and in every street and corridor; ships are being called in and communications cut off for the Blackout. Soon, they tell me, we'll be humming literally. This letter goes out on one of the last ships to Baret Station, and when it'll reach the other end of its flight, Fate knows. Or even if. I don't trust that spooner-of-potatoes in the Station cafeteria, Father; tell them to keep an eye on him.

These people are not bad, Father. Of course they are notoriously inbred, and delight in their ignorance; but I've often thought the same of our own folk. [The second half of this sentence was removed by Keylinn upon re-reading.] Now, since I've begun by being wholeheartedly honest, I must tell you that since arriving here I have had several brushes with subjectivity sickness. My contract-holder has a very powerful undertow in his *tarethi*—probably you are not surprised by that, since he is a gathrid, after all. But *please* do not be concerned on my account. I'm taking every possible precaution. Naturally some blurring is necessary if I'm to anticipate his requirements, which are of course pretty alien to me. But I'm doing core meditation twice a day, and any other time I think I need it. Think of the *tarethi* I'll acquire from this contract! It may rival the Twelve. [This last sentence was also deleted by Keylinn, as smacking of hubris.] I know it's a dangerous road, but I did have the very best teachers. For which I have you to thank, as for so much else.

The other thing that bothers me most is—I don't know any way of putting this that doesn't sound ridiculous— wondering if I'm meant to be one of the latest Twelve. It doesn't seem probable on the surface, given my record, and yet ... here I am, off-planet on orders of the Judges, reporting back. It does *sound* like a Twelve assignment. Am I crazy for even considering it? And what if it's true? I never wanted that kind of responsibility. How can I say whether the Outside is ready for us to come back or not? How can anyone judge through me? I don't even know what signs to look for. The Judges can't, they *can't* have such expectations about me; I

won't support them. Surely they aren't so confused
about my abilities. Oh, I wish I knew what you thought.
I wish I could talk to you and Sean.

Keylinn deleted the entire paragraph above.

As for when you'll see me again—nobody knows how
time works during a Blackout, but it would be extremely
rare for it to occupy more than a few years of planetary
chronology, and probably a lot less. I'll make my way
back when I can.

My love to Uncle Bram, Sean, and Janny. I wish I could
see Janny, all grown up. Tell her if she wants to wear
my sapphire pantaloon dress with the weapons-cache,
she may. But I don't want anybody borrowing the red
slashed-back one. When I return, I plan on wearing it to
the Academy Ball. I'll dance with you there, if you've forgiven me by then.

> Your loving prodigal,
>
> Keylinn O'Malley Murtagh
> daughter of the Harp Valley clan

"It's called the War Room," said Tal. He motioned for
Spider and Keylinn to precede him on the walkway surrounding the holomap. Around them were communications stations; one comm operator for every dozen or so
battle-capsules. Three of the stations were taken at the
moment, by two young men and a woman directing Diamond knights out on a series of practice maneuvers. Inside, in the map, glowing points represented Diamond
capsules and other ships, while a changing strip overhead
gave the mathematical coordinates for each point.

"It's busy for a place that hasn't been used since their
war with Opal," said Keylinn.

"It's always good to be ready," said Tal. He pointed to
a metal and glass booth up on the top walkway. "I'm
making that my office."

"I thought the Security Chief's office was up on the administration levels," said Spider.

"Not any more." Tal took a report that had just printed out from a link by the map and handed it to Keylinn.

She glanced at it, then at Tal. "Well? I don't even know what this means."

"Start studying. I'm transferring you to Security."

She accepted the news calmly. "Is that a good idea? I see one or two women here, but none in Security uniforms. Outsiders are accepted in Transport, but how popular would they be in such a sensitive area as this?"

Tal's smile was not without irony. "See if you can come up with a point for debate that I haven't already used myself. As for you, Spider—"

Spider had been hanging on the railing over the holomap, staring at the changing colors that would mean life and death in a real encounter. Now he looked up. "Me? You're not getting me into this place, Tal. I'd lose half my income if I left Inventory."

"Well, not immediately. But after all, Keylinn only has a hundred eighty days left—"

"One fifty-two," said Keylinn.

"And I'll need someone to take over from her then. Don't worry about money, Spider; from what I've been able to determine, this whole department is riddled with graft. People pay for the arrest of others, to escape arrest themselves, for protection form overzealous City Guards. They pay for just about everything."

Spider made a face. "That's immoral." He looked around at the expression in Keylinn's eyes. "No, I mean it. At least when somebody pays me now, it's because I've delivered actual goods to them. It's not because I've promised not to hurt them in future."

"Of course, these goods are stolen to begin with," pointed out Keylinn.

Spider shrugged helplessly. "What do you want? Perfection?"

"In any case," said Tal, "Adrian wants the whole thing cleaned up, so expect any profits we make to diminish as time goes by. Ah, and here are two people who didn't believe me—when I try so hard to be clear."

Keylinn and Spider turned. Three armed Special Security guards were escorting two men. The men were middle-aged, and one wore SS trousers and a civilian shirt, not entirely tucked in. They looked as though they'd been routed out suddenly and not given time to pull themselves together.

"Officer Tulloch," said Tal in greeting. "And Officer Brognara."

The men's faces were sullen, and just a little worried.

"I asked these gentlemen to escort you here because I understand you haven't been following my new guidelines. I thought they were more than generous. And more than clear."

"Sir, I don't think—" began Tulloch, a skinny red-faced man. He was the one in uniform trousers.

"Shut up, Tulloch." Tal spoke without heat. "I'm not trying to change the habits of a lifetime overnight. All I require is that bribes be limited to protection cases, and not actual arrests. And that the fee schedule for protection money be reduced by ten percent each year. Is that asking too much? Doesn't that give you all plenty of time to make other financial arrangements?"

Officer Brognara said sulkily, "We don't take bribes."

"I see this is a waste of time," said Tal. "Still, though you're both losses to my area, you can serve a useful function as warnings to others. All the arrests you made in the last ten days are being reviewed, by me personally. If even one is overturned for either of you, whichever man is responsible is going to the recycler line. We don't dally with a trial; this is Special Security, after all."

They both looked horrified. "You can't do that!" cried Tulloch. "Do you know who my family is?"

"Yes. They're a minor bunch of functionaries who live mostly on D level. Maybe this will motivate them to pull their snouts out of the public trough. Wake up, Tulloch—nobody reviews Special Security. You know that, you've counted on that fact for years."

Brognara said, "Wait a minute. I might have made a couple of mistakes—"

Tal withdrew his attention from them. To the guards, he said: "Please keep them in solitary holding cells until I notify you of the execution schedules."

"Yes, sir." The two prisoners looked as though they would have liked to say more, but the tip of a pistol was put to Tulloch's shoulder and they both subsided.

Tal was glad that he'd remembered to say "please" to a subordinate in Keylinn's presence. "Well," he said. "So much for that. Let me show you the office."

They followed him up the walkway. "I don't think Adrian knows what he's started," stated Keylinn.

Tal didn't pretend not to understand her. "He knows. He has his panthers, too. He likes to push things to the edge; it's the only flaw I've been able to find in him."

Her voice was disapproving. "Do you always search your friends for flaws?"

"Well," he said mildly, "you never know when you may find a flaw useful."

Adrian checked his responses from all City departments. Transport had shut down, Communications had notified the Station and Baret Two (if anybody down there was listening) that they were readying to leave and would accept only emergency messages from now on. Inventory had taken on all the items they could manage in the allotted time. One man hadn't come back from the Opal trade team, apparently; Adrian hoped for his sake that he was dead and not trapped forever on Baret Two.

Opal, Pearl, and Diamond had put their drives into coordination. It was time to send the word out to all citizens that Blackout was set for five hours from now.

His link blinked red. Adrian said, "Yes, what is it?"

"Communications, sir. You said to accept only emergency messages—"

"Yes, yes, what's the problem?"

"There's a small craft in our vicinity, and they say they have a message for Special Officer Diamond."

"Have you warned them that they'd better not be close to us in five hours?"

"Yes, sir."

"All right. Put them through to me here."

A moment later a woman's voice said, "Special Officer Diamond?"

"This is Adrian Mercati, Protector of the City of Diamond. We're preparing for Blackout, madam. What is your emergency?"

The woman's voice was soft and cool. "I beg your pardon, sir." She said sir, not *cyr;* she knew Cities protocol, he noted. "My shipmates and I are Redemptionists, nobility from Baret Two. We had to leave rather hurriedly, as I'm sure you understand."

Irritation was replaced by guilt. "Yes, madam, how may we help you? I must warn you that our time is limited."

"This won't take long, sir. I understand from Duke Peter that gentleman named Officer Diamond was bargaining for pieces of art from some private collections. We have a few rare pieces with us and would very much like to see if he is interested in them—"

"I'm sorry," began Adrian. "But you must see that in the circumstances we really don't have the time—"

"Please, sir. I don't need to tell you that any money we could raise would mean a lot to us under these conditions. All our wealth was on Baret Two. It would take less than an hour to dock with you and make an exchange."

Adrian bit his lip. Then he said, "Wait." He touched a button. "Adrian here. Is Security Chief Diamond in the War Room? Put him on." Right first guess; he would've tried C deck next. "Tal? I'm talking to a woman who says she's a refugee from Baret Two. She claims to have some artwork on board that she'd like to sell us before we disappear. Take a look at it and strike some kind of deal, would you? I'm going to be busy for the next few hours."

"What about money?" asked Tal's voice.

"I'll pay. Be a little generous—even if the stuff doesn't look very good, buy it anyway and add on some extra notes."

"If that's what you want."

Adrian let him go and said to the woman, "Madam, I'm going to put you through to Security Chief Diamond. He'll negotiate with you."

"Thank you sir, I'm most grateful."

"Not at all."

He cut the connection and returned to his list of Blackout preparations. It was several minutes later that he was called again.

"Communications, sir."

"What *now?*" he asked, and reprimanded himself mentally. "Yes, what is it?" he said, with a touch more mildness.

"Sir, I put through that transmission to the War Room

. . . but it's changed protocol standards. We can't monitor it."

"You don't need to monitor it, son, it's hardly urgent."

"But I ought to be *able* to, and I can't."

Adrian froze. Then he said, "Link, prime command. Patch through the communication now taking place between the War Room and outside craft."

The link said, "I cannot comply with that request. A seal has been put on the sight-and-sound access."

"Where was the seal applied?"

"The War Room."

He cursed softly. "Wait a minute. Link, prime command. Can you give me a printed readout of all words exchanged in this transmission?"

"Yes."

"Do it now." A minor mistake, but then they hadn't had much time. Paper began rolling from the other side of his link. He picked up and started to read, his fingers tightening on the page.

"I'm told you have pieces of art you want to dispose of."

Tal stood by the link in the War Room. Keylinn was flipping idly though a report while Spider had gone over to peer into the holomap again.

"Officer Diamond?" The woman's voice was clear and young.

"Yes."

"Have you a visual circuit at your end?"

Most links didn't, but this was the War Room, where exact communication was important. "Yes. I don't know if it can translate your protocol, though."

"Switch it on."

He did so. A screen on the wall above the communications operators sprang to life. He saw a woman there; in fact, he saw the same young woman who'd approached him outside the Residence that night.

She was no longer in Baret Two-style clothes; she wore a green jersey and her dark hair was pulled to the top of her head, where it fell in a mass down her back. Her skin tone was lighter than it had been. He stared warily.

Keylinn had somehow appeared beside him, and she said, "It's Miranda."

Spider's interest had been caught as well. He dropped down from the edge of the holomap, winced as the force of his weight hit his feet, and limped to join them. "It's her," he said. "She was working for the Minister of Truth."

Tal continued to stare. Presently he said, "And for a number of other people, I surmise."

Miranda smiled. Her teeth were as perfect as the rest of her. "How good of you not to make me explain."

"You're one of the Republic's agent provocateurs. That's why you encouraged me to add to Duke Peter's treasury."

"Very true." She was certainly unembarrassed by the fact.

"Do you realize," said Tal conversationally, "that with only the firepower within twenty meters of me, I could blow your ship away?"

"I want *you* to realize it. Perhaps then you'll be willing to listen to me."

He tapped one finger, once, against the link-top. Then he said, "I'm listening."

"Can you restrict access to our conversation? I can scramble from here and give you the key, but it would be easier—"

"Security override," said Tal to the link. "Seal this communication from third party access, audio and visual both."

"Accomplished."

"Well?" he said to her.

"Don't you see?" she asked. "We come from the same place you do, don't you understand yet? We're the *others.*"

The angle of view widened to show four young men standing behind her. Hair shades varied but they were all light-skinned and beardless. One nodded politely. They gazed out from the screen with detached interest.

Grouped this way, there was a similarity of feature that suggested a closer relationship than simply one of species. A similarity that Tal shared.

His face had lost color. "Prove it," he said. "Show me your eyes."

"Show you . . . ? Ah, I see," said Miranda. "You're wearing colored lenses. Ours are transplants. We operated on each other; we can operate on you, too, if you like."

Tal was silent. She went on. "We spoke once before of Belleraphon. Of course you were interested, being the only one and the youngest. We at least had each other for company, brother—"

"Don't call me that. I don't know you."

She was unoffended. "We can remedy that. All of us here have met Belleraphon; in fact, it was he who sent us."

"Crap, you're from Belleraphon. Shit, you're from Belleraphon." Keylinn was standing beside Tal and she saw his fingers move slightly toward the "Activate Live Weapons" switch; this alarmed her almost as much as the unaccustomed profanity. She actually took hold of his arm.

"Adrian said to negotiate."

"Adrian doesn't know what he's dealing with!"

Miranda said coolly, "We won't discuss family if it upsets you."

"I'm not upset." He glared at the screen. "Why are you here?"

"We've been searching for you for years now, Tal. Not as actively as we might—we do have tasks of our own to do. But we travel a great deal. We came on your tracks once or twice in other sectors—the Aphean universe is a small one, it seems."

"Congratulations. You've found me."

"Yes, so we have." She leaned back and inspected him, with interest if without affection. "And now we'd like to offer you a place with us. As an equal partner. All profits to be shared six ways."

He froze in place, like an animal that hears a twig break somewhere in the woods. "Why?"

"Why not?" She shrugged. "Another set of abilities is always useful. And I think you'll find life with us . . . more easy than with humans."

He stood there, thinking. Spider watched him closely. Then Tal said, "What else?"

"Yes." Miranda smiled again. "There *is* an entrance fee. Make yourself valuable to us, Tal. Did I hear you referred to as a Security Chief earlier?"

"You may have. That is my post."

"How delightful. Does it give you override privileges on the City's weapons?"

"By the rules it ought to. I haven't tested it."

"Well, then." Miranda looked as pleased as a child given a new toy. "I had another idea before, but this is better. I suggest the following scenario: Use your override to cripple the Diamond's external weaponry. Sabotage their transport. And take what you can in the way of negotiable wealth and come and join us. You know what's available to you more than I, of course, but if you have access to the Sawyer Crown, I suggest you bring it. We can probably sell it to another group of Redemptionists."

He took this in. Spider and Keylinn looked appalled, they seemed to be waiting for him to spurn this attempt to disrupt his loyalty. At this moment they felt more alien than ever, and several universes away. He said, "What do you know about the Crown?"

She looked smug. "A sign of our good faith, brother. It was I who sent the message telling where it was."

"I see," he said wearily.

"We could have taken it ourselves, but we wanted it and you both."

"And anything else I can bring."

"Yes."

She pulled no punches here, and it was her greatest selling point. He looked at Miranda, fresh and young on the screen, his older sister; and he looked at his brothers who waited so carefully to see how this negotiation would turn out.

Miranda: Her expression would not greatly change, he knew, whether he refused or accepted; and by that, he could see what she was offering. Consistency. Comprehension. The blessed relief of not forever having to explain oneself. No more sidelong glances when he gave some incorrect response in the human give-and-take. And no more of being blamed for doing what was sensible, and no more trying to unpick the convoluted motives of these people, no more trying to read their damned *cues* about hatred and the expectations of duty and the availability of sex. When Miranda had something to say to him, she would say it.

He was very aware of Keylinn and Spider standing close by, and even of Adrian somewhere up on court deck. They were nervous and vital, like campfires burning on a dark night, their life force showing in his peripheral vision as though on an infrared strip. Easy to destroy. And behind Miranda's image, the cold impersonality of the stars. If he went with her, he would live in a world of clarity.

And, he thought, he might never be warm again.

He considered sabotaging the Diamond, and the thought did not greatly bother him. Could it even be done? How much control had he been allowed over the external weaponry? He activated the live-weapons switch, and Spider stepped forward, shocked.

"Hey!" said Spider.

The control spoke through the link. "These switches can only be activated in the event of war. The signature of the Protector is necessary."

Tal turned to Spider. "Lie to it," he said, pointing at the link. "Tell it we're at war."

Keylinn said, "If we're at war, it'll use live rounds."

"Look," said Spider, "I try to be obliging. But there are limits, you know? I may have been a ghost, but I'm still a Diamond citi—" He cut himself off, staring at Tal's Keith pistol. "I'm not really authorized to declare war, you know," he finished in an entirely different voice.

"Use Adrian's key signature. I've seen you duplicate it hundreds of times."

"That was as an intellectual exercise!"

Tal said mildly, "Get some exercise. You look sickly." He touched the pistol to Spider's neck, and Spider shivered.

"I'm too nervous," he said.

"You're at your best under pressure," replied Tal. He addressed the link. "Official notice from Chief Minister of Security, check my voice: a state of war has been declared. The signature of Adrian Mercati to follow."

Spider sat down and took up the pen. The link-screen dissolved to a soft gray, waiting.

"One chance only," said Tal.

Spider intoned the word "Hell" in a voice of doom. "I knew I was going there." And he signed it quickly, with the flourish Adrian always put in.

"Accepted," said the link.

Tal threw the live-weapons switch.

Miranda still watched with interest from the screen. "I take it this means yes," she said. "If you wish to bring the forger, you may; we can sell him, too."

"I always knew—" Spider muttered.

Tal glanced at the holomap, where the glowing numbers froze for reading every five seconds and then continued their constant shuffle.

"—straight to hell," said Spider.

Several communications operators were looking toward them curiously; they sensed something was happening, but they had heard none of the audio transmission. Tal went to the Security Chief's console; his hands moved quickly over the board. "Can you track that?" he asked the link.

"I have it now," the link replied.

"Keylinn, take the shooter's seat." He pointed to a seat at a nearby console.

Keylinn took it, but said, "I'm not familiar with these controls."

"It's not necessary. They were designed for our own fighters, fine Christian knights of limited intelligence. When the circle turns black, you hit the activate button."

She nodded. Tal said, "Cannon fire. Five point nine."

"Performed."

As the link spoke, Keylinn's circle turned black. She hit the button.

Her head swung up to look at the comm-screen. It had gone blank.

"Target?" inquired Tal.

The link replied, "Target has sustained minor damage, and is leaving periphery of the Diamond at a rate of twenty-six point eight over three."

"In other words," said Keylinn, "it took off like a scalded cat." Her voice was shaking very slightly, and she wiped the palms of her hands on her breeches.

"Is that good?" asked Spider. He turned to Keylinn and

pulled up a cocky grin. "I take it this means *no,* lady," he said, addressing the absent Miranda. Then he frowned. "You scared the hell out of me!" he yelled at Tal. "Why didn't you tell me what you were doing?"

"I hadn't made up my mind," said Tal simply.

"Christ!" yelled Spider. If anything, the reply brought more color to his face. He turned and stomped out of the War Room.

Tal put the switch back into practice mode. Keylinn said, "Why the forgery?"

"Adrian wouldn't have wanted me to shoot at them. But I wanted to."

"For a rational being, you're a pretty twisted individual sometimes." She handed his report back to him.

"I was brought up with humans," he said. "Frankly, I don't think it was good for me."

"Am I to understand your siblings there were *not* brought up with humans?"

Tal was silent. He looked tired.

The all-citizens-notice bell went off. A voice said, "Ready for a message from the Protector. All citizens, ready for a message from the Protector."

"And what will Adrian's response be?" said Tal, in the same exhausted tone. "Damn. I don't want him told about this."

The bell sounded again. "This is Adrian Mercati speaking, giving first notice that Blackout will take place in five hours. That's five hours, my friends. I want to say that you've all done a splendid job of preparation in the time we had to work with. All drive-sensitive individuals, report to your parish facility. All facility directors, start checking your lists. Notify Special Security to pick up anybody not checked in within the next ninety minutes." There was a pause, then, "Report any emergency situations to Security Chief Tal Diamond." Sound of a throat clearing. "This is the last you'll hear from me until just before Blackout. Good luck to everybody; remember, if your neighbor needs a hand, offer it to him. We're all on the same side in this. Adrian Mercati, signing off." The bell sounded a third time, even longer.

Tal sat in the console chair, not moving. Then he said, "You'd better check on Spider. He's drive-sensitive."

He got up and moved to the walkway stairs. Keylinn went with him. She said, "So why did you refuse?"

He smiled wistfully. "It was a lie from the beginning. They would have taken the Crown, and whatever else I brought, and dumped me."

"You can't be sure of that," said Keylinn.

"They're my relatives," said Tal. "I should know."

"You'd be an asset. They might have kept you, just as Miranda said."

"Well, we'll never find out now, will we?" He turned and climbed the stairs to the glass and metal booth, and walked inside, alone.

She went to look for Spider.

Chapter 52

Men's judgments are a parcel of their fortunes.
        SHAKESPEARE, *Antony and Cleopatra*

The citizens of the Three Cities prepared themselves with that combination of routine and nerves that their ancestors had brought to meet hurricanes, blizzards, floods, and other natural disasters. Nonessential personnel were dismissed from stations. Families locked themselves in their quarters with extra food supplies—technology, like human biology, functioned intermittently during a Blackout. A small percentage of people, less than one percent, would die before they returned to normal space; they preferred to do it with their loved ones.

On the Opal, Will accepted his new brother-in-law's invitation and found himself in close quarters with both Lysette and Bernadette, wondering about his wisdom in not staying in the City Guard dormitories. Hartley Quince, being unburdened with loved ones, retired to his well-appointed suite with several stacks of paper data he wished to consult and a small container of illicit substances to beguile the tedium of the danger.

Spider had a bed in the parish infirmary, where he

could be better looked after in case his system went into
shock. There he was surrounded by emergency cots and
the families of other drive-sensitives. Spider had been
through twelve Blackouts in his lifetime and the controlled chaos was familiar to him. Kids ran up and down
the aisles, until they were herded off by their parents or
by the neverending procession of deacons, nurses, and
volunteers pushing carts of water from bed to bed. At one
hour to Blackout, his mother swept in, puffing, with her
own emergency food supply: a basket of iced cakes and
shortbread, followed by gin chasers. "My own," she said,
kissing him and swinging the basket onto the bed in one
practiced movement, "my back won't let me do this much
longer." She took a folding chair from the stack by the
wall and set it beside the bed.

Spider manfully stayed out of the bottle at such times;
he considered himself his mother's champion in the
world, and *one* of them ought to be sober, in case of
emergency.

Like Hartley Quince, Tal preferred to be alone.

He was surprised, therefore, when the door to his office
over the War Room opened, and Adrian walked in.

"Where's your entourage?" Tal inquired, when the first
startlement passed.

"Strolling about down below." Adrian shut the door. "I
see your stations are all locked down."

"Not much call for weaponry when you're separated
from the universe at large."

"Which raises the question of what you're doing still
here."

"Working," said Tal, shortly, in the manner of one trying his best to end a conversation.

"Working," Adrian repeated, as though the word were
new. "Your link will only function intermittently."

"Then I suppose I shall have to use it intermittently."
Tal looked at him. "Is there some reason I'm not permitted to remain on duty?"

"Of course not." Adrian seated himself on the cushioned bench against the front window, adjusting his cloak.
"It's just that this is a time when most people prefer to be
with others. It's almost ostentatious, this gap you insist on
putting between yourself and humans."

After a moment, Tal said, "It's less than an hour till Blackout. If you're experiencing some psychogenetic pull to huddle with your fellow primates at this time, I suggest you seek out your wife."

Adrian smiled, his charming Mercati smile. "That's very good. You usually don't share with me the treasure of your disregard. Is it because Fischer's not here as a target, or do you just want me to leave?"

"Now why would I want that?"

"Where's Keylinn?" Adrian asked idly.

"In Transport, with the rest of the techs. What does that—"

"And how did that little matter with the Baret refugees go? Did they have anything worth buying?"

Tal hesitated. Adrian looked boyishly expectant, which worried him. "I hope you didn't have your heart set on more artistic loot, because they backed out of the deal."

"You surprise me. They seemed quite desperate."

Tal shrugged. "I can't always fathom the motivations of others, especially aliens."

"I know what you mean."

Adrian continued, disconcertingly, to gaze at him. And it occurred to Tal suddenly that Adrian wanted something from him, the way he wanted something from his panthers, from his bride, from every citizen whose regard he won so effortlessly. Something whose nature was obscure to Tal, but which he was fairly confident he did not possess.

Faith? Could princes afford faith, or did they only collect it from others?

Adrian said, "I don't think you should stay here alone. I considered inviting you to spend Blackout with Iolanthe and me—" He broke off and laughed. "If you could see the look of horror on your face. It was only a passing thought, I assure you." He stood. "But you'll go to your quarters, Tal. That's an order."

The uneasiness Tal felt deepened. "Will you have me escorted?"

Adrian's eyes were still on his. The Protector smiled slowly. "Why on earth would I do that?" His voice was soft, and made Tal feel no better.

"I don't know."

"Well, you're the Security Chief. Perhaps you think I'm feeling insecure."

Tal's voice revealed his tiredness. "I wouldn't presume to know what any of you are thinking." A second later he realized his voice had revealed something else: bitterness. If he had gone with the others—

He'd be dead.

Adrian opened the door. "Don't concern yourself about it. I have every faith in your ability to understand it all in time. Like a game of Hotem."

He walked out, closing the door. Tal stood at the window and watched him descend the steps, watched him collect his escort and take them all away with him, every one. Leaving him here to follow orders quite of his own accord.

He made sure the entire section was locked down before he left. If there was one thing he was good at, he considered, it was keeping people out.

Keylinn played Solitaire on her bed in the temporary Transport dormitory; she turned up the joker just before the lights cut out. In the parish infirmary, Spider took his mother's hand—she was always quite passed out by this point and never knew, but he didn't like to think of her going into Blackout alone. Will and Bernadette were arguing at the dinner table, while Lysette and Jack kept a discreet silence, exchanging the glances of people who loved but wondered about the sanity of their chosen objects. When the hum beneath their feet increased, Will and his sister faltered—then continued arguing. Hartley was unconscious. Iolanthe looked up from a book to share something with her husband, then fell silent. In his cot in a guarded room on the Diamond, the One and his Other felt the vibration climb, familiarly, toward an exit from this reality, and both of them smiled with a single mouth.

Faith, Tal thought, in his quarters. The word had an alien, faintly sour taste.

And together, they leaped into the darkness.